When Gol[...] the ground by shock, King Harold himself lifted the limp young woman in his arms and turned towards the house. Aileth gained her feet. 'It's all my fault,' she said shakily to Goldwin. 'We had a quarrel in the street – over nothing, but her Norman accent was recognised!'

'I knew something like this was bound to happen,' Goldwin growled. 'From now on it might be a good idea to stay away from Felice altogether until this trouble has passed.'

Aileth glared at him. 'Felice is innocent, alone, and in need of help. I never thought that you were the kind of man to be nought but a fair-weather friend.' Turning her back on him, she followed the King into her house.

'She's Norman!' The harsh condemnation was snarled by Aileth's brother Aldred. 'Small wonder that you were attacked in the street!'

'She has done nothing wrong!' Aileth retorted with equal heat. 'Yes, she's a Norman, but can you see her coming at you with a shield and sword? What kind of threat is she to your manhood?'

Aldred's fair skin burned red. 'By the Rood, if you were in my discipline, I'd take a belt to your hide! Our father was always too soft with you! And Goldwin's no better. Where is he? I've got some advice for him!'

'Peace, Aldred,' commanded Harold sharply. 'Master Goldwin is the best judge of how to rule his own household. As your sister says, the woman lying here is no threat to us, even if she is Norman.'

'But . . .' Aldred began, then swallowed powerfully and tightened his lips.

THE
CONQUEST

Elizabeth Chadwick

WARNER BOOKS

A *Warner* Book

First published in Great Britain
in 1996 by Little, Brown and Company
This edition published by Warner Books in 1997

A CIP catalogue record for this book
is available from the British Library.

ISBN 0 7515 1177 3

Typeset in Bembo by M Rules
Printed and bound in Great Britain by
Clays Ltd, St Ives plc

Warner Books
A Division of
Little, Brown and Company (UK)
Brettenham House
Lancaster Place
London WC2E 7EN

ACKNOWLEDGEMENTS

There are several people I would like to thank for their help 'backstage' while I was writing this novel. First of all my husband, Roger, who copes amiably with the domestic chaos engendered by my absence in my study, and brings me cups of tea at frequent intervals. Secondly, my parents, Robert and Joan Chadwick, for their support, child-care services, and baking of home-made cakes when there have been more chores in the day than I have had hands. I would also like to thank my agent Carole Blake and all the staff at Blake Friedmann for their support, enthusiasm and encouragement. I am grateful to Barbara Boote at Little, Brown and Warner, for giving *The Conquest* the chance to see the light of day.

A special thanks goes out to Kim Siddorn of Regia Anglorum, with whom I had several illuminating discussions concerning the Battle of Hastings and the Conquest period in general. I am indebted to him for his comments and suggestions. I must also thank Mark Knight of Ledecestrescise for the Norman battle commands, and members of Deoraby, Abbandum, and the Conroi du Burm for a general broadening of my knowledge.

PART I

AILITH

CHAPTER 1

LONDON,
DECEMBER 1065

Ailith, wife of Goldwin the Armourer, swept her gaze around her long hall, inhaled deeply of the rich, forest scent, and sighed out with pleasure. Great swags of Yuletide evergreen garlanded the roof beams and the timbered walls. At spontaneous intervals she had hung kissing bunches of the sacred white mistletoe and blood-berried holly. Above the place of honour near the hearth, a magnificent pair of stag's antlers had been nailed, and the reflected firelight stained the broad edges and polished tips of horn a glossy crimson.

Tomorrow night her brothers had promised to find time from their duties as bodyguards of the great Harold Godwinson, Earl of Wessex, to bring her the traditional Yule log and stay to dine. She was greatly looking forward to the meal, for apart from Goldwin, Aldred and Lyulph were the only family she possessed, and their visits were precious.

A sudden commotion at the door heralded the return of her two serving women from the markets in the heart of the city. Braying in protest at the weight in his laden panniers, the pack ass was led round the side of the house by the younger maid, Sigrid. Wulfhild, puffing and plump, staggered into the long hall, her arms weighted down by two net bags of provisions.

'God save us, Mistress Ailith, I've never seen such crowds!' She dumped the bags on the new, thick floor rushes and pressed her hands into the small of her back. 'An' all the stall holders charging what they like. We got the best bargains we could, but if it weren't Yuletide, you'd say the prices was shameless robbery!'

Ailith's generous lips twitched at her maid's indignation. 'I am sure I would,' she commiserated gravely as Wulfhild handed her a small drawstring pouch. It was considerably lighter than it had been at the outset of the excursion.

'There would be less in it still if Brand the Fishmonger hadn't got a soft spot for Sigrid,' Wulfhild continued to grumble. 'He let us have the pike and salmon you asked for at only half the price he was charging everyone else. And when we got to the onions, you'd ha' thought they was made out o' gold the way . . .'

'Wulfhild, I believe you!' Ailith said a trifle impatiently. Over the maid's shoulder she saw Goldwin enter the hall. Even in the raw December cold his sleeves were pushed up to his elbows, exposing his brawny forearms. He was wearing a stained leather apron over his old tunic and his face was smutty from the forge. His right fist was closed around the nasal bar of an iron helmet.

'Take those bags to the store and unpack them,' Ailith commanded. 'I'll inspect everything later. And before you do that, bring out some bread and ale for Master Goldwin.'

Wulfhild half-turned, saw Goldwin, and in consternation, picked up the bags and hurried from the hall, dipping the master an awkward curtsey as she passed him.

Goldwin paused to watch her, then looked enquiringly at Ailith. His eyes were a warm reddish-brown set under prominent black brows. Beneath his scrutiny, Ailith felt herself grow warm and begin to melt.

'The markets are expensive today with Yule so close and the King and Court in residence,' she told him. 'The bargains were few and Wulfhild has taken it to heart. You know how she loves to haggle.'

Goldwin took the purse she held up for his inspection. 'I was warned that becoming a married man was expensive,' he observed with mock dismay.

'Would you rather have remained in your bread-and-water

bachelor state and amassed a solitary fortune then?' Ailith challenged, jutting her chin at him and setting her hands to her hips. She had large, regular features moulded upon a sturdy bone structure. A healthy mare was the way her father had described her during the marriage negotiations before his death last year; a good worker, strong and buxom. Ailith knew that her father's words stemmed from his pride at how well she had coped with the burden of household duties in the eight years since her mother had died, but it had not blunted the pain of the wounds he had so unintentionally inflicted. If she had not loved Goldwin for anything else, she would have loved him for saying on their wedding night that her statuesque figure and wealth of corn-blonde hair put him not in mind of a mare, but of a wild, fierce Valkyrie.

Goldwin rubbed his jaw and pretended to consider. 'Would I rather have remained in my bread-and-water state?' Without warning he pounced on her and drew her beneath one of the mistletoe kissing bunches. 'What do you think?' he breathed. His lips pressed down on hers. She felt the silkiness of his beard, the forge heat still upon his skin, and tasted salty sweat. Running her hands over his naked forearms and across his broad, blacksmith's shoulders, she buried her fingers in his hair and returned his kiss with enthusiasm. Against her hip she felt the clumsy bump of the helmet he was still holding.

Wulfhild returned from the stores with a pitcher of ale and a loaf of new bread which she placed on the trestle near the hearth. Ailith and Goldwin broke their embrace and looked at each other, making a silent promise for later. Lightly slapping her rump, Goldwin sat down at the trestle and Ailith ladled out two steaming bowls of onion pottage from the cauldron suspended over the hearth.

'You're in a fine good humour.' She put the soup in front of him and sat down at his side. 'Is it because you've finished this?' She lifted the helm off the board and turned it delicately over in her hands. It was a beautiful piece of work, its austere lines tempered by the details of bronze brow ridges and decorated strengthening bands.

Goldwin grunted and spooned pottage into his mouth. 'I'll be in a better humour still when the mail shirt to go with it is done. Earl Harold wants it for the New Year and it's not but two thirds completed yet.'

Ailith was not deceived by his complaint. Goldwin's work was going very well indeed. If he had not been extremely pleased with the helm, he would never have brought it from the forge to show her, feigning nonchalance, but seeking her approval. Looking at his hands as he broke bread and ate soup, she marvelled anew that their rugged ugliness could create a thing of such simple, but intricate beauty. And then she thought of their gentle touch on her body and a little shiver ran through her. She tried the helmet on.

'Do I look like a Valkyrie now?' she asked mischievously, and was amazed at the loudness of her own voice in her ears.

Goldwin chuckled. 'Not unless such women are cross-eyed and wear old homespun kirtles.'

Ailith stuck out her tongue at him and removed the helm. Immediately her focus restored itself to normal. She wondered how men managed to keep a clear vision in battle with a nasal bar between their eyes. She looked at the helm and imagined it gleaming on the leonine head of Harold of Wessex, and again she shivered.

'I'm not really complaining,' Goldwin said as the hot soup and fragrant fresh bread mellowed him. 'I owe your brothers a great debt for putting Earl Harold's custom my way. Without their recommendations I might still be struggling in that poky little workshop at Ethelredshithe.' He gazed with pride at the thick timber walls of the spacious hall, clothed in their festive evergreen.

So did Ailith. It was not every bride could boast a brand-new house, light and roomy by the standards of the wattle and daub dwelling in which she had grown up, and situated within sight of St Peter's and the new palace and abbey on Thorney Island.

Three years ago Goldwin had repaired a dented helm belonging to her brother Aldred. Aldred had been so impressed by the work that he had recommended Goldwin to all his soldier acquaintances and custom had flourished. So had the friendship between the two young men. It had seemed only natural that Goldwin should offer for Ailith when his reputation and fortune had grown to the point where he felt secure enough to support a wife. The match had been made to mutual satisfaction all round. Ailith had always known that she would have no say in the choosing of a husband and had been mightily relieved when her father and brothers had mooted Goldwin.

He was short of stature and slightly bow-legged, his hands permanently darkened from working the steel, but his warm smile and his diligent, amiable nature, made him the most handsome of men in her eyes.

'Aldred and Lyulph are bringing the Yule log tomorrow eve.' Ailith returned her attention to Goldwin, taking pleasure in seeing him enjoy the food. 'I'll have to neck those chickens before dark, I suppose.' She pulled a face. Although she was competent at all domestic tasks, killing the yard fowl was the one she disliked the most. It seemed such a betrayal of trust. You offered the birds corn from your hand day in, day out, talking to them, caring for them. Then you stole their eggs and wrung their necks at the whim of the cooking pot. She could have bought freshly killed poultry from the booths in West Chepe, but to her housewife's conditioning, that was a shocking price to pay for squeamishness.

Goldwin wiped his lips on a napkin, poured himself a mug of ale from the pitcher, and stood up. 'It'll be good to see Aldred and Lyulph again,' he commented. 'Now Earl Harold's almost sitting on the throne, they're in attendance of him all the time.' He took a long drink, topped up his mug, and stifling a replete belch, walked to the door. On the threshold he turned round.

'Aili, I forgot to tell you; old Sitric's house next door, it's going to be occupied. I saw the abbey steward this morning and he told me.'

Filled with curiosity, Ailith raised her brows. Their elderly neighbour Sitric had retired to St Peter's at Martinmas, bestowing all his worldly goods upon the monks in return for board and lodging until he should die. His house had stood empty these past four weeks, checked over now and then by the abbey's lay steward, but otherwise forlorn. 'Did he say by whom?'

'Apparently it has been rented until next hogtide by a wine merchant.' Goldwin looked down into his wine. 'A Norman wine merchant, from Rouen.'

'Oh.' Ailith did not quite know how to respond. There were plenty of Normans in London. King Edward had spent his youth across the narrow sea and his preferences were for all things French. Rumour said that he even desired to bequeath his childless crown to Duke William of Normandy, when every decent-thinking Saxon knew that it ought to go to Harold of Wessex. She grimaced. To speak of Normans in front of her brothers was to invite a tirade of abuse. But it did not follow that a person was to be spat upon just because they were foreign. Harold of Wessex himself was half-Danish.

'Don't mention it to Aldred and Lyulph,' she said. 'Leastways not tomorrow. I don't want the feast to be spoiled.'

'Why should I tell them when it is none of their business?' Goldwin answered bluntly. 'I only told you because you keep saying what a disgrace it is to have that house standing empty and unused.' He shrugged and looked uncomfortable. 'I would lief as not have Normans for neighbours myself, but I trust I can keep a civil tongue in my head. And while Aldred and Lyulph are under my roof, I will expect them to do the same.'

Ailith nodded, but looked uncertain, knowing how hot-tempered and impetuous her brothers could be. 'Is this merchant alone or does he bring a family?' she asked.

'A wife, I think the steward said, and the usual household clutter of servants.' His tone bore mingled amusement and irritation. 'You'll see when they arrive.' He left the hall. Moments later Ailith heard the clang of his hammer in the forge. Her optimistic mood somewhat dampened, she cleared the trestle and went to inspect the fruits of the shopping expedition.

When everything had been put away on the storeroom shelves, she set the women to making a bacon and pease pudding for the evening meal, together with fried fig pastries for the morrow's Yule feast. Then she took herself down the garth to the chicken run, intending to neck three victims to honour the pot.

Immediately outside the door, within easy picking distance, were Ailith's herb garden and vegetable plot. She lingered among her plants, twitching stray late weeds out of the soil, admiring the fat, white stems of her leeks, and frowning over a slug-chewed cabbage. But she could not procrastinate forever. Reluctantly she walked among the slender trunks of the young apple orchard, paused at the pig pen to scratch the sow behind her floppy grey ears, and came at last to the killing ground of the chicken run where she had intentionally kept her hens this morning. Not a bird was to be seen. Even Alaric, the indolent rooster who never did anything but eat corn and make love in a bored, absent-minded fashion with his wives, had taken advantage of the freedom offered by the latch which Ailith had failed to secure in her haste to be about other tasks.

'Bollocks!' Ailith swore, and, hands on hips, stared round the empty garden. Soon it would be dusk, and they were close enough to the countryside for foxes and stoats to be a real threat. 'Chook, chook, chook,' she called, then held her breath to listen. A light drizzle drifted down, grey and cobweb-fine. Shivering, rubbing her arms, Ailith called again.

A single, speckled biddy came running from the direction of Sitric's empty garth and began pecking hopefully in the grass around Ailith's feet. She stooped, grabbed the indignant hen, and tossed it into the fowl run, this time making sure that the door was properly latched behind it. Then she heard Alaric's unmistakable harsh crow from Sitric's side of the wattle fence. Swearing again, Ailith hitched her gown through her belt for ease of movement, marched down her own garth, round the back alley, and entered Sitric's property.

Some of her hens were pecking in the long grass of his orchard. One actually sat in the branches of a gnarled pear tree and watched her with a beadily cocked eye. The others had ranged as far as the stable buildings adjoining the house and were scratching with great gusto in the heap of old dung and straw beside the stable door.

Ailith sighed heavily and smothering the urge to scream, said instead, 'Chook, chook, chook,' in a soft, encouraging voice. The greedier, less canny ones fell for it, but the others kept their distance, revelling in their illicit freedom. Abandoning the gentle approach, Ailith waded in with grim determination. Amidst a squawking flurry of bright eyes and beaks, scaly legs and a snowstorm of detached feathers, she managed to grab two hens by their feet and toss them across into her own garth. Shouting for Wulfhild and Sigrid to come out and catch them, she made a grab for two more. Alaric, in an unaccustomed display of temper, pecked her hand and flapped to the top of the midden. Ailith looped another swatch of her kirtle through her belt and began scrambling up the damp straw after him. If she could catch Alaric and throw him over the wattle boundary, she reasoned that his wives would probably follow.

She had reached the top of the heap and was about to throw herself upon the rooster when the first rider guided his mount around the side of the building and, reining to a halt, stared at her, his mouth gaping in astonishment. Horrified, Ailith scrambled down from the dung heap, frantically tugging her gown out of her belt and shaking it down to conceal her smeared white legs.

'I beg pardon,' she stammered, gesturing at Alaric who was belligerently fluffing out his feathers at the top of the midden. 'The hens have escaped and I'm trying to catch them!' Even through her panic she assumed that the rider was a representative of the abbey, for he was dressed in the sober, good-quality garments typical of an administrator. Her notion was disabused even before he spoke by the appearance of a second rider who certainly had no connection with the church. It was a young woman, her oval face possessed of symmetrical, delicate features, her eyes soft and dark beneath plucked, Romanesque brows. Slim, beringed hands competently checked her high-stepping chestnut mare. Her cloak and overgown were richly embroidered.

The man addressed the woman in rapid French and her elegant eyebrows rose to meet the fluted edges of her immaculate wimple. She answered him briefly, but with a bubble of laughter in her voice. Ailith wished that it were possible just to vanish from sight. She was painfully aware of every stalk of straw, every smear of dung on her working kirtle and tattered apron. These people were quite obviously the new Norman neighbours, and what must they think?

The young woman addressed Ailith in English, heavily accented but understandable. 'I see you have a problem. My hens also have strayed before. Let my husband's men catch them for you.' Turning in her saddle, she issued a command in Norman to two youths who had just jumped down from a laden baggage wain to stretch their legs.

'Thank you,' Ailith muttered with chagrin as the young men set about the pursuit and capture of the wayward birds, succeeding with insulting ease. Alaric was fetched in high dudgeon from the top of the dung heap and presented to her with a cheeky flourish by the younger of the two youths. Ailith tucked the rooster under her arm, her broad freckled face as red as fire.

The man leaned over his saddle to address her. He too spoke English. 'Perhaps you will ask your master and mistress to call on us?' he said with a warm, wide smile. 'We would like to meet and be friends with our neighbours.'

Ailith swallowed. Her shame was so deep that she knew she would never be able to hold her head above it again. 'I am the mistress,' she said stiffly.

The Norman stared her up and down, nonplussed. Then his mouth twitched and he quickly raised his hand to cough.

His wife stepped courageously into the breach. 'We should not have jumped so swiftly to conclusions,' she soothed. 'It is only natural to go about household tasks in old clothes if you are not expecting to meet anyone.'

Ailith only felt worse. The man's face was dusky with suppressed laughter.

Please, you will still come?' Anxiously the woman extended her hand.

'I will speak to my husband,' Ailith replied, raising her chin a notch, but refusing to look at either of them. 'Thank you for your help.' And then she fled, certain that she could hear the sound of their laughter in pursuit.

Goldwin did nothing to soothe her mortification by guffawing loudly when later she told him what had happened.

Ailith ceased combing out her thick, slightly coarse hair and glared at him. He was reclining on their bed in the sleeping loft, a cup of mead in his hand. 'It is not funny,' she snapped. 'They want us to call on them!'

'Yes, I know.' Goldwin's voice was husky with laughter. 'You were still shutting up the hens when the Norman came to the forge to introduce himself. He said that you had been very embarrassed and he was sorry if he had offended you. He was also insistent that we dine with them soon.' His eyes sparkled.

'Goldwin, I can't!'

'Nor can you skulk indoors for the rest of your life in the hopes of avoiding them.' Laughing, he refilled his mead cup. 'They seem decent enough people, for Normans. His name's Aubert de Remy and he's hoping to make a fortune selling wine to the English court being as King Edward's so fond.'

As Goldwin spoke, Ailith's initial panic faded into dismay. She resumed combing her hair, tuning her mind to the orderliness of the strokes. Goldwin was right. She could not hide from her neighbours indefinitely. It would be best to make a jest of the whole incident. Laughter was supposed to break down barriers of reserve and suspicion – but she would rather that the laughter was not at her expense. 'Did you meet his wife?' she asked casually.

'No, she was busy with her maids, but he told me that her name was Felice and that her old nurse was English, so she speaks the tongue quite well.'

'She is very beautiful.' Ailith put down her comb and removed her grey woollen gown. Conscientiously she folded the garment over the end of her clothing pole. What she really wanted to do was throw it on the floor and burst into tears. Her expression screened from Goldwin by her unruly hair, she plucked at the stray stalks of straw still embedded in the dress.

Goldwin set his mead cup on the floor and left the bed. She felt his rough hands upon her shoulders, his breath animal-warm at her throat. 'I have all the beauty I need here,' he murmured, turning her in his arms until she was facing him. 'Come to bed; take me on the white lightning to Valhalla.'

Despite herself, Ailith smiled at his blandishments. He obviously desired her – if the growl of playful lust in his voice was not evidence enough, then the hard bulge in his braies certainly was. Even above her need to love and be loved, was Ailith's compulsion to be needed. Garlanding her arms around his neck, she pressed herself against him, and felt the power surge in her loins as he softly groaned her name.

As their passion mounted, she discarded the thought of the Norman neighbours in the same way she had discarded her clothes. Tomorrow she would clad herself again with both, but for the moment they had no place in her world. She was a Valkyrie riding the storm.

CHAPTER 2

Ailith's brother Aldred took a hearty bite out of a roasted chicken thigh and complimented his sister on the excellent flavour of the meat. 'Better than anything we get served at court, eh, Lyulph?'

A younger man, less broad in the shoulder, brushed crumbs from his luxuriant corn-coloured beard and nodded vigorously, his mouth bulging with bread and meat.

Ailith laughed with pleasure at their praise and their vast appetites. To watch them eating now made keeping hens worthwhile, whatever her earlier thoughts on the matter. It was wonderful to see her great, blond brothers in their finery. Her hall seemed almost too small to contain them. Aldred's red wool tunic was banded with silk braid, and around Lyulph's throat was a heavy silver cross and a necklace of amber and garnet beads. Their strong, axe-wielders' hands were bare of rings which might foul a blow in a moment of crisis, but both men's wrists were adorned with gold and silver bracelets, gifts from Harold Godwinson, the man they served.

'What do you get at court then?' asked Goldwin, and stretched his legs in contentment towards the enormous Yule log burning upon two iron props in the firepit. His mead cup rested lightly on his gilded belt buckle and his own tunic was fine tonight, bordered with Ailith's skilful embroidery.

Aldred snorted rudely. 'Custards and curds for King Edward's ailing belly. Chicken blancmange and sops in wine.'

'Oh come now, I don't believe that!'

'Well, not all the time,' Aldred grudgingly conceded. 'But most of the food is mashed up and smothered in fancy sauces.'

'It's the Norman fashion, a murrain on the bastard,' Lyulph sneered, his brilliant blue eyes full of contempt. 'When Earl Harold's on his own estates, we get to eat decent, English fare.'

Ailith exchanged a wry, pleading glance with Goldwin. Responding, he valiantly sought to close the crack before it could become a chasm. 'So the King still sickens?' he enquired.

Aldred wiped his lips and smoothed down his moustaches between forefinger and thumb. 'Daily,' he said to Goldwin. 'He's not attending the consecration of his precious abbey tomorrow because he's too weak. Our lord Earl will wear the crown before Candlemas, mark what I say.'

Goldwin tactfully guided Aldred and Lyulph into talking about Earl Harold, and then conducted them from the table to the forge to show them the armour he was making for the lord of Wessex. They were much impressed by the helm and the almost completed hauberk.

'The Normans often use archers,' Lyulph said, fingering the triple-linked rivets. 'Will this stop an arrow?'

'Not at close range, but at medium- and long-distance, yes, depending on angle, of course.' Goldwin looked sharply at the two young men. 'Are you expecting to be fighting Normans then?' He added wryly, 'Other than the usual?'

Aldred plucked a hunting knife from Goldwin's workbench and examined the blade. 'Oh yes,' he said, his voice soft and bitter. 'Normans, Flemings, Brabants, the dross of all Europe.'

Goldwin frowned a question.

'Is it not obvious?' Aldred tossed the knife end over end and caught it deftly by the wooden haft. 'Even if Earl Harold is named king on Edward's death, he will have to fight for the right to sit on the throne.'

Goldwin began to feel queasy and wished he had a clearer head. As well as the gift of the Yule log, Ailith's brothers had brought a keg of sweet, strong mead. The honey brew was Goldwin's particular weakness and he had consumed more than was wise. But then wisdom was not usually a prerequisite of Yuletide feasting. He tried with limited success to focus his mind. 'Duke William of Normandy, you mean?'

Aldred's face reddened and he stabbed the point of the dagger viciously into Goldwin's workbench. 'The whoreson says that Edward promised him the crown fifteen years ago . . . but it was never Edward's to promise. The High Witan decide who shall be king!'

'What if the High Witan decide upon Duke William?' It was a facetious question, but Goldwin was annoyed at Aldred's cavalier treatment of a very fine langseax, not to mention his bench. Carefully he eased the weapon out of the wood.

'The counsellors back Harold,' Aldred said shortly. 'They don't want a Norman backside on our throne.'

Lyulph, ever Aldred's shadow, growled assent. At only twenty years old he was the youngest member of Earl Harold's bodyguard, but his fighting abilities were as precocious as his luxuriant tawny beard.

Goldwin shook his head. 'Surely invading England will be too great an undertaking for the Norman Duke?'

Aldred jutted his fierce jaw. He was big-boned, with a fighting man's loose-knit grace. Like Ailith's, his eyes were a clear, deep blue, but more closely set with downward corner creases. 'Perhaps it will be so, but if not, I'll be waiting on the shoreline to kiss him welcome with my axe!' Aldred had been sitting on Goldwin's bench, but now he rose, and fishing in the pouch at his belt, brought out a fistful of silver pennies.

'I want you to fashion me a new axe,' he said intensely, 'and I want you to inscribe Duke William's name on the blade.' He banged the silver down on the bench in punctuation. Several coins rolled to the edge and spilled over, landing hard and gleaming on the beaten earth floor.

Goldwin stared at the coins, his queasiness becoming the cold squeeze of fear. 'God save us, Aldred, you truly want me to do this?'

'I do. Is there enough silver here to pay for your work, or do you want more?'

'Nay, I don't want any at all!' Goldwin fanned his hands back and forth in denial.

'I want to pay.' Aldred narrowed his eyes. 'I must pay. It will make the charm more binding.'

Lyulph jerked open his own pouch and spilled yet more silver onto Goldwin's bench. 'Make me one too, the same!'

Goldwin could not refuse his own wife's kin, but he had a real feeling of dread as he scooped up the coins, still warm from their touch, and put them in his pouch. He had made Aldred and Lyulph weapons before. Their mail shirts were of his fabrication, and the superb swords they wore at their hips. He was no stranger to fashioning the terrible Danish war axe, both two- and one-handed varieties. And frequently he had set inscriptions into the steel, or along the polished wood of the haft. Names, talismans, they were all familiar to him. But in some way he did not yet understand, this was different and made him afraid. Never before had he felt the winter cold in his own forge.

When they returned to the hall, by unspoken agreement none of them said anything to Ailith about what had happened in the workshop, but there was a constraint to their feasting now, an undercurrent of tension that she could not fail to miss. She did not ask any outright questions, because conversations that took place in the forge were always men's business, but nevertheless she was concerned and curious.

It was beyond dusk, but still early when Aldred and Lyulph took their leave, declining Ailith's plea that they stay the night.

'We're on duty at dawn,' Aldred said, hugging her close.

She felt the taut power of muscle beneath his Yuletide finery. There was a hardness in his face that she had never noticed before. Perhaps all warriors became that way, tough and unyielding like the rawhide bands rimming their shields. It was a disquieting thought to take into the New Year and as she embraced her brothers, she felt as if she were bidding farewell to more than just the old season.

She watched them ride away in the direction of the royal palace, watched until the last gleam of harness and horsehide had disappeared into the night, and the sound of hoof and voice could no longer be heard. Over her head a distant pin-point of light blazed an arc across the sky. 'Look, Goldwin!' she cried, pointing.

He stared sombrely upwards, his eyes quenched of light. 'I have a premonition,' he said softly, 'that tonight I have grasped the tail of a falling star.'

Ailith was frightened by his tone and the strange look on his face. 'Goldwin?' She touched his sleeve for reassurance.

A shiver rippled through him, as if he was trying to shake off the fey mood that seemed to have gripped the night. Laying his hand upon hers, he turned to look at her, a half-smile curving his moustache. 'Too much mead,' he said ruefully. 'You know it always makes me weep. Did you make a wish?'

Ailith nodded and followed him back into the house. 'For both of us,' she said as he barred the door, his motion a little too forceful as he shut out the world. And Ailith, her hand upon her flat belly, wondered if she had wished for the right thing.

CHAPTER 3

In the sleeping loft of the rented London house, Felice de Remy spoke to her maid. 'The amber beads and brooch,' she instructed the woman. 'They go best with this gown.'

'Yes, Madame.'

Felice smoothed her palms down her overtunic of blue-green wool, seeking reassurance from the rich, heavy cloth. It fell in pleated folds to shin-level and was hemmed by a border of gold braid. Her undergown was of tawny linen, its edges skimming the toggle fastenings of her soft leather shoes.

The maid returned with a string of polished amber beads and a round brooch also set with lumps of amber. The jewellery had been a wedding gift from Aubert and he liked her to wear them whenever they had guests.

Her maid arranged the beads and secured Felice's yellow silk wimple with the brooch. It was a colour that few women could wear well, but Felice, with her warm complexion and glowing brown eyes, was one of the fortunate.

'You look lovely, Madame, fit to dine with King Edward himself!'

'Why thank you, Bertile!' Felice laughed, while wondering dubiously if she ought to have dressed less elaborately. Fit to dine with the King was perhaps not fit to receive their Saxon neighbours, especially after that first, impromptu meeting across a midden heap. Would the wife think that she was being mocked?

Felice had glimpsed the husband on several occasions. He was square and stocky with brown hair and a darker beard, his garments filthy from the forge. Aubert said that he was a master armourer and had crafted weapons for the great Earl of Wessex himself. Many times during the past three days Felice had stood at her doorway hoping to catch a glimpse of the armourer's wife and perhaps speak to her, but the young woman seemed to have gone to ground.

Descending from the sleeping loft, Felice gazed around the hall with a critical eye. The new rushes on the floor had been scattered with dried herbs – lavender, rosemary and marjoram – that yielded up their scent as they were trodden upon. She had dressed the bare walls with embroideries in bright colours on pale linen backgrounds, and the room was illuminated by expensive beeswax candles. Her best napery was laid upon the dining trestle, and instead of the usual eating bowls of polished wood, she had brought out her precious set of glazed earthenware dishes. An appetising smell wafted from the cooking pot suspended over the firepit, which was being assiduously tended by an elderly serving woman.

Outside, she heard the thud of hooves in the yard and her husband's voice chivvying one of the serving lads. Moments later, Aubert flung into the house, his stride choppy and energetic, his mobile, ugly features pulled into a deep frown.

Felice took his heavy winter cloak and woven Phrygian cap. Aubert kissed her briefly on the cheek, then pushing his stubby fingers through his frizzy grey curls, strode to the flagon which had been filled in anticipation of their guests. Pouring himself a full measure of wine, he took a long drink.

Felice hung his cloak and hat on a wall peg, her movements fluid and calm, although her stomach was churning with anxiety. 'Does your business not go well?'

Aubert de Remy raised and lowered his bushy, prolific brows. 'Well enough,' he said gruffly. 'I've an order of wine from Leofwin Godwinson, Earl Harold's brother. It is just that the negotiating went hard.'

Felice nodded and smiled. She knew that he was lying, that

the source of his frown was something else, but she had no intention of pressing him. That his concerns extended into clandestine regions beyond the mere selling of wine she had long since realised, but for her own well-being, she had never sought to know too much.

'Something smells good.' Aubert hung his nose over the cauldron.

'It's coney ragout.'

His eyes narrowed with gluttonous joy. 'I shall soon be as fat as Martinmas hog!' He laid a rueful hand upon his belt where the merest suggestion of a paunch was confined by the gilded leather.

Laughing, Felice tortured him further by telling him the other courses she had organised.

'Stop it, stop it!' Aubert groaned. 'You will be the death of me!'

She started to ask him if she should take his remark as an insult or a compliment, but was forestalled by the arrival of their guests – the armourer Goldwin, and Ailith his wife.

The young woman stood proudly on the threshold beside her husband, her head carried high, her manner almost defiant. She was easily as tall as Aubert, and of generous proportions. From beneath a veil of blue silk, two fat, corn-blonde plaits snaked the length of her short, rose wool overtunic. The undertunic was the same blue as the veil and enhanced the colour of her eyes. She wore a beautiful necklace of polished glass beads and a silver cross upon a cord. A set of housewife's keys jangled importantly from the tooled belt at her waist. Suddenly Felice was very glad that she had gone to the trouble of dressing elaborately herself.

'Enter and be welcome,' Aubert said formally, and extended his hand in an ushering gesture.

The armourer stepped forward, ill at ease, but dogged. 'Peace be on this house,' he responded with equal formality. His wife followed, her eyes modestly downcast.

With a pleasant smile and welcoming words, Felice set about being a good hostess.

Mistress Ailith remained aloof throughout the courses of the meal which Felice had so carefully planned. While the husband began to relax and genially respond to Aubert's conversation, devouring with relish the chicken broth with saffron dumplings, the coney ragout, tiny pickerel in ginger sauce, and apple comfits, his wife pushed her food around on her trencher as though it had come from one of the dubious cookshops attached to the city shambles. And yet, judging by her ample proportions, she must have a good appetite on other occasions.

'I hope your hens are none the worse for their escape the other day?' Felice was driven to enquire by her exasperation.

Her guest turned a deep shade of pink. 'My hens, no,' she said and looked down at her trencher. 'I'm sorry I cannot do your food justice. I know you have gone to a great deal of trouble.'

Felice murmured a disclaimer. 'It does not matter; the men have enjoyed more than their fair share, and what is left can be used tomorrow.'

'You must think me very rude and ungrateful.'

Seeing the defensive colour in Ailith's cheeks and the rigid set of the full lips which should have held a natural, soft curve, Felice was moved to compassion. Having found an opening, she took full advantage. 'I think nothing of the sort,' she said untruthfully.

Ailith sighed. 'If Goldwin had not dragged me to your door, I would not have come tonight. I still feel so embarrassed.'

'Oh, but you mustn't!' Felice touched Ailith's arm. 'It could have happened to anyone. I think you managed the situation very bravely. I was going to come and tell you so earlier, but I was unsure of my welcome.'

Ailith reddened again. 'Probably I would have run and hidden, I'm not brave at all,' she admitted and pushed her mauled trencher to one side. A spark of reluctant humour kindled in her eyes. 'Still, I found it easier than usual to neck three chickens for the pot.'

Felice laughed. 'Then you are more accomplished than I. Last time I killed a chicken, it ran one way with its head on one side, and I ran the other, screaming, in front of my maids. You are not the only one to bear a cross of embarrassment!'

Ailith smiled and Felice realised how attractive she actually was. Perhaps they could be friends after all. Admiring Ailith's garments, she asked her about the particular sewing techniques she had used.

Ailith's response was hesitant at first, but she rapidly warmed to her theme, and soon the women were deeply involved in needle sizes and fabric weaves, stem stitch and couch work.

Goldwin heard the warmth and confidence begin to flow back into his wife's voice, saw her hand raised in animated description of an embroidery style, and relaxed a notch. He found Aubert's company stimulating, and the food excellent beyond compare. It would have been a great pity to leave early because Ailith and Felice were not compatible. Part of the problem he knew was the incident with those dratted hens. Ailith's chagrin was still raw and she was very much on her dignity. At least now she appeared to be thawing into the true Ailith he knew and loved. He heard her laugh and saw the gleam of her teeth between the fresh, warm pink of her lips. His loins twisted pleasantly and he had to ask Aubert to repeat what he had just said.

'I wondered how well you knew the Earl of Wessex?' Aubert refilled Goldwin's cup almost to the brim and poured considerably less into his own.

'Not very. Ailith's brothers are members of his bodyguard and it's through them that I got the commission to make the armour.'

'But you have met him?'

'Of course. I had to take his measurements and check the fit.' Goldwin took a swallow of the wine. At first he had drunk it to be polite, much preferring ale, but the taste was insidious. No matter that its tang on his palate caused him to shudder, he found himself compelled to repeat the experience.

'What is he like?'

'Why?' Goldwin regarded Aubert curiously. 'Are you hoping to sell him some wine? He drinks it when he's around

King Edward, but he drinks ale when he is with his own men.'

'A man of expedience then,' Aubert said lightly, his mouth smiling, his eyes cool and watchful.

'He inspires great loyalty. Ailith's brothers worship the ground he treads. All his men would die for him. And I doubt any man would stand up and die for King Edward.' Goldwin was aware through a growing haze of wine fumes that perhaps his tongue was running ahead of his mind.

'So you think he will make a good king in the future?'

'Better than anyone else.'

'And he desires that for himself?'

'Of course he does.' Goldwin narrowed his eyes. 'Why are you asking all these questions?'

Aubert laughed and rubbed the side of his short, bulbous nose. 'I am seeking the lie of the land – finding the best place in the market from which to shout my wares. If I pushed you, I'm sorry. Once a merchant with an eye to a profit, always a merchant.'

Goldwin grunted, somewhat mollified, and took another sip of the wine, rolling it round in his mouth, trying to pin down the fruity, acid taste. 'Your Norman Duke wants England's crown,' he said, deciding to turn the tables upon Aubert. 'Have you ever met or seen him?'

Aubert looked slightly taken aback, but then he shrugged. 'Only the once. I have a good friend who breeds horses. I was visiting his stud when Duke William arrived to choose a war stallion.' The wine merchant nodded to himself at the memory. 'A huge fire-chestnut caught his eye. Late autumn it was, the blood-month, and I would have sworn that it was not breath but smoke that came from the beast's nostrils. It threw the Duke three times, but in the end he mastered it. Anything that defies him is either tamed or broken.'

Goldwin thought about the axes which Aldred and Lyulph had asked him to carve. 'Breaking Earl Harold will not be the same as breaking a horse,' he said.

Aubert inclined his head. 'Oh indeed not,' he acknowledged. 'I pray it will never come to such a conflict.' Tactfully he changed the subject. He told Goldwin more about his friend Rolf and the stud that had been built up from a small nucleus herd two generations ago, to a breeding stock of three stallions and sixty mares of the highest quality. 'My wife's chestnut is one of Rolf's – a gift before we left Normandy. I gave Rolf a tun of wine in thank you, but I would like to send him something else, something personal perhaps.'

Before he knew it, before he could refuse, Goldwin had been inveigled into making a hunting knife for Aubert's friend. It was on the tip of his tongue to ask what name he should carve on it, but the quantity of wine he had consumed was making speech difficult. And he could only manage slurred yeses and nos to Aubert's overtures.

Indeed, after that, he had only the vaguest recollections of being aided to his feet; of Ailith's half-anxious, half-amused attentions as he was helped outside and to his own door; of fond farewells; then the blessed comfort of a goosedown mattress and sheepskin coverlet and the weight of Ailith settling beside him, the scent of her hair, her lips on his cheek.

He woke late in the morning, not of his own volition, but because Ailith was shaking him vigorously and shouting in his ear. Head pounding, he parted gummy lids and fended her off with a growl of protest.

'At last,' Ailith declared impatiently. 'I thought you'd never wake up!'

The hammer beats of pain in Goldwin's skull sent spears of nausea jabbing into his gut. He started to sit up, then changed his mind and fell back against the pillows, his forearm bent across his eyes. 'Leave me alone,' he groaned.

There was a brief silence, but he knew she had not gone away. He could feel her exasperated gaze hard upon him. 'Has the drink affected your ears too?' she asked. 'Don't you hear the bells?'

Goldwin listened. Beyond the miasma in his head, the pounding continued, clear and relentless; toll, toll, toll. He lowered his arm and looked at her.

'King Edward is dead.' Ailith went to his clothing pole and found him a shirt, chausses and warm tunic. 'Earl Harold has been chosen as his successor and they are crowning him tomorrow.'

'How do you know?'

'Aldred told me. He's come to collect the hauberk and helm. I've given him bread and ale while he waits, but he's in a hurry.'

Goldwin swallowed. His mouth tasted foul and his throat was parched. He began to dress, half-fearing and half-hoping that his head would fall off. Against the shutters he heard the spatter of rain.

Ailith's eyes sparkled as she helped him with the laces and leather toggle fastenings that his fingers could not manage this morning. 'You are now the King's personal armourer, Goldwin, just think!'

Goldwin managed a wan smile in response. Thinking, however, was beyond him for the moment. His skull was like the hollow cave of a bell with an enormous clapper striking from side to side. Or perhaps it was just the abbey bell in his ears, tolling the soul of King Edward to heaven, and hammering his own into the ground.

CHAPTER 4

BRIZE-SUR-RISLE,
NORMANDY,
JANUARY 1066

Stinging sleet borne on a vicious cross wind hit Rolf de Brize as he stumbled down the wooden steps between the motte and bailey, and crossed the lower courtyard. The torch he carried did nothing to alleviate the pitch darkness of the January night for the flame guttered this way and that on the whim of the wind, sending acrid streamers of smoke into his face. He skirted the midden and the snapping lunge of the gatekeeper's mastiffs as they surged on their chains, and entered the stone stable block.

A blood bay mare threshed on the floor of the first stall, and uttered small grunts of pain. Her hide was dark with sweat, her nostrils distended, and her eyes showed a white ring of fear.

Tancred de Fauville, his overseer, was kneeling in the straw at the mare's head. 'I thought it best to summon you, my lord. She's having a bad time of it – been labouring four candle notches now and no sign of her delivering. I'd say there's a foot stuck.'

Rolf extinguished his torch in a puddle outside the door, and as it spluttered out, crouched beside the horse. She had Arab blood in her veins and had cost him a small fortune at a horse fair in Paris two summers ago. Her first foal was now a leggy yearling and showing promise of excellence, but to recoup her value, he needed at least four out of her. That was why Tancred had sent for him. It was too great a responsibility to rest on his overseer's shoulders.

Rolf laid his hands upon the mare, stroking her cheeks,

whispering in her ears. Beneath his soothing touch, she calmed a little and the white ring diminished around her liquid, dark eye. She had the heart and courage that would breed greatness into her offspring. Rolf knew that he could not afford to lose her.

Still patting and soothing, he coaxed the mare to her feet. Her tail swished; a hind leg jerked up, hoof pointed, to strike at her distended belly.

'Easy, lady, easy,' Rolf murmured, rubbing her soft, black muzzle. To Tancred he said, 'Has the water bag broken?'

'Aye, my lord, just after midnight. She's been working hard ever since.'

'Right, get a groom to help you hold her, and I'll take a look.'

Rolf tethered the mare to a ring in the stable wall, and kindled another covered horn lantern to add to the one shining down from a ledge above the manger. The light flickered on his hair, revealing it to be as dark a red as the mare's hide and bearing a ripple of unruliness, a characteristic that frequently spilled over into his temperament.

The mare stamped again and uttered a long groan as another fruitless contraction tightened her abdomen. Rolf watched her effort and decided that Tancred's prognosis was probably correct. The foal was lying in the wrong position and could not be born unless it was turned.

Petting the horse, he persuaded her to stay on her feet, and when he was sure of her, he stripped off his tunic and shirt, revealing a wiry, muscular body.

Tancred returned with the groom who bore a jar of grease and a rope.

'Hold her,' Rolf instructed. 'Keep her as still as you can.' He slathered his left hand and arm in a thick coating of goose fat, then, muttering a prayer between his teeth, drew aside the mare's bandaged tail and eased his hand into her vulva. He probed gently in search of the obstruction. Compared to the winter cold of the stable, the mare's flesh was like a furnace. He hoped that the rope would not be necessary. If the foal had to be pulled from her body by force, rather than being naturally pushed out, there was the dangerous risk of its ribs being fractured by the pressure.

His questing fingers encountered a small bump. Careful investigation revealed a slippery little leg folded under at the knee, and the other leg caught beneath it at an awkward angle, effectively forming a barrier. The foal could not be born without his intervention, but the problem was relatively simple to correct. He waited until the next contraction had shuddered away, and then quickly pushing and manipulating, straightened out the bent leg, taking great care that the tiny hoof did not scrape the side of the birth passage. With the next squeezing contraction, he drew the freed leg forward. The mare grunted and tossed her head, obviously in great discomfort. Tancred and the groom struggled to hold her. Rolf murmured soothing words, patting her rump with his free hand. When the contraction eased, he grasped the second leg and tugged it into position.

'All right, let her go,' he commanded, and retreated, his arm slick with bloody grease and birth fluid.

Free of restraint, the mare folded onto her side and within moments had pushed out the foal's forelegs and head. Rolf dropped to his knees and helped her deliver the rest of her baby. Working quickly, he stripped the birth membrane from the foal's face and body, and cleaned out its mouth and nostrils so that it could breathe.

'A colt,' he announced with pleasure to Tancred and the groom.

'There's no mistaking old Orage's blood,' Tancred grinned, as relieved and delighted as his lord. 'Look, he's even got the same star marking between his eyes.'

Orage, the foal's sire, was Rolf's prize stud, a striking golden-chestnut stallion of stamina, mettle and intelligence. Almost every foal born to his siring was chestnut, and this trait had become an identifying mark of the stud at Brize-sur-Risle.

Already, despite the difficult birth, the foal was struggling to coordinate his spindly legs and rise. His mother swung her head towards him and uttered a low, encouraging nicker. Rolf gathered the damp baby in his arms and placed him under the mare. She snuffled at her foal, drinking in his scent, and then began to lick him vigorously with a muscular pink tongue.

Rolf swilled his arm, donned his shirt and tunic, and stayed to watch the foal take his first drink from the mare's dripping udders. Satisfied that all was well, he left mother and son to Tancred, and returned to the keep.

At the top of the wooden stairs bridging the slope between the castle mound and the lower courtyard, he paused to watch the dawn break over the lands of Brize-sur-Risle. Veiled in sleety rain, they yielded a vista of dull greenery to his eyes. He could see the thatched roofs of the village and the grey stone curves of the church where his father was entombed. Full of sluggish power, the iron ribbon of the river Risle flowed away from him towards the port of Honfleur. Staring at the water, he felt a sudden stab of poignant longing that possessed neither rhyme nor reason. This was his home, his inheritance. Why was it not enough? Or perhaps the pull of the river was stronger than the pull of the land to the fierce Viking blood in his veins. The icy air was cauterising his lungs. He stared for a moment longer, then, shaking his head like a man shaking off a dream, went inside his keep.

Berthe, the wet nurse, was suckling his infant daughter before the fire in the great hall. As Rolf came to warm himself, the woman lifted the baby off her breast, shrugged up one shoulder of her gown, and yanked down the other side. Rolf stared, mesmerised by the enormous blue-veined globe, the wide areola and fat brown nipple. His daughter bobbed her head frantically from side to side, found what she sought, and attached herself with a single, voracious gulp.

Berthe looked up at Rolf with sly, knowing eyes. He remembered her heaving, hot body beneath his in the straw, her enormous breasts slippery with leaked milk and sweat, the tight sucking of her lower mouth. His loins coagulated and his stomach jerked. It was too early in the morning to be contemplating such images.

Avoiding her avid gaze, he prowled to his chair at the high table and directed a servant to bring him bread and wine to break his fast. His steward approached with a query, and then the priest, Father Hoel, wanted to ask a favour. Rolf dealt summarily with both, impatience crawling through his bones. The servant returned with a dish of hot, new bread, a crock of honey, and a jug of watered red wine.

'How's the mare?'

Rolf sucked honey off his thumb and glanced at his wife as she took her place beside him. She was as pale as a moth, as elegant and insipid. Two long, thin braids of silver-brown hair fell over her flat bosom to her narrow hips. Her face was smooth, her features pretty, falling just short of beauty. Her eyes were a striking clear grey with a darker, smoky rim between iris and white.

'Well enough. The foal's forelegs were stuck, but once they were free, she delivered without a problem – a fine colt; should fetch a good price if I decide to sell him.'

She broke a morsel from the loaf in front of Rolf and nibbled at it. 'You might keep him, you mean?'

'One day I will need to replace Orage. I have to look at every colt born and assess whether this is the one.' He watched her toy with the food. Their suckling daughter was almost five months old now, but it had taken Arlette all that time to recover from the birth. She never carried well. Before Gisele, there had been three miscarriages and one stillbirth. In Rolf's opinion, she did not take enough care of herself, scarcely eating enough to sustain a sparrow. Small wonder that she had been unable to feed the infant and they had had to employ a wet nurse. He often entertained the disloyal thought that if she were a brood mare, he would have disposed of her long since despite her illustrious bloodline. But she was a superb chatelaine, possessed of formidable domestic skills. Tidiness and industry were the codes by which Arlette ruled her world. The hall was well ordered, food was never burned or undercooked; his clothes were kept clean and in a good state of repair. If she had been more fruitful and of a less prim nature, he would have had no complaints. As it was, he tolerated his lot, but without any gut-sparking surges of love or joy.

Arlette continued to nibble at her crust, moistening her mouth with dainty little sips of wine. It was like sitting next to a mouse, Rolf thought with irritation. Deliberately wolfing his own food, he pushed himself to his feet.

Arlette gazed up at him, her grey eyes wide and startled. 'Where are you going?'

'To look over the yearlings. William FitzOsbern asked me to search out some likely ones for training up.'

'In this weather?'

'It is better than being cooped up in here.' Brushing perfunctorily at the crumbs on his tunic, which was already stained from the stable, he left the hall.

Berthe had tucked her breast back inside her gown and was winding the baby. Her eyes followed Rolf hungrily. So did Arlette's.

Free of the smoky atmosphere and the constraints of the hall, Rolf breathed a sigh of relief and went to check upon the mare and foal again. The colt had folded up in the straw to sleep, his small belly as tight as a drum. The mare dozed on one hip, standing protectively over him. Smiling, Rolf left them and ordered a groom to saddle up the old black gelding he used when working among his herds.

While he was waiting, he heard a commotion down at the bailey gates, and emerging from the stables to look, saw the riders entering the yard two by two, liquid mud spraying from the shod hooves. The leading man carried a brilliant yellow and black gonfalon, the dagged edges snapping out in the vicious, sleety wind. Behind him, astride a prancing chestnut stallion, came William FitzOsbern, one of his regular customers. He was a close relative and trusted advisor of Duke William's, and very powerful. With this borne in mind, Rolf put a smile on his face and went to greet him.

FitzOsbern grimaced as his horse was led away to a warm stall. He stamped his feet briskly on the ground to restore feeling and beat his hands upon his thick woollen cloak. He was between forty and fifty years old with fine spider lines creasing the gaze of shrewd hazel eyes and deepening into seams between nostrils and thin-lipped mouth.

'Hirondelle looks fit,' Rolf said, as with resignation he retraced his steps towards the confines of the hall. He doubted that William FitzOsbern would appreciate viewing any stock until he had been warmed by fire and wine.

'Full of himself,' said FitzOsbern expressionlessly. 'Tried to buck me off twice this morning. If I had known how frisky he was going to be, I'd have thought twice about buying him off you.'

Rolf glanced sidelong and saw the glint of amusement in FitzOsbern's eyes. When Rolf had first started dealing with him two years ago, he had found FitzOsbern's expressionless delivery extremely disconcerting. Was the man speaking in earnest or in jest? Rolf had since learned to read the signs, but they were hardly obvious – a slight turn of the lips, a deepening of the eye creases, if you were fortunate.

'You'll thank me for the fire in his feet when you take him on a battlefield,' Rolf retorted.

'Interesting you should say that.' FitzOsbern preceded Rolf into the hall and looked around with the keen eye of a connoisseur. His gaze lit on Arlette, who was supervising the clearing away of the breakfast repast, her hands busy with a drop spindle and fluff of carded fleece.

Noticing the men, she hurried over, her pale complexion suffusing with pink.

'My lord, what a pleasure,' she said to FitzOsbern.

Rolf could tell that she meant entirely the opposite. He could see her mind flurrying to the kitchens to check if they had enough food, could see her wondering where they were going to accommodate FitzOsbern and his entourage if he decided to stay the night. She would manage, she always did, but not without a deal of anguish and hand-wringing in private.

'The pleasure is mine,' FitzOsbern returned as a matter of form, inclining his head.

'Bring us hot wine to the solar,' Rolf said, then added to FitzOsbern, 'Will you stay to eat with us?'

'Thank you, but no. I have to press on to Rouen, and if this sleet becomes snow, the roads will be difficult.'

Rolf could almost hear Arlette's sigh of relief as she hurried away to mull a pitcher of wine. He took their guest to the long room on the floor above the hall. It had been divided up into living and sleeping quarters by the artful use of woollen curtains and embroideries. Near the window a woman was busy weaving at a tall loom. Rolf dismissed her and directed FitzOsbern to a cushioned box chair positioned close to a glowing brazier. He fetched himself the stool on which the maid had been sitting.

FitzOsbern sighed and extended his feet towards the warmth. Rolf watched his face, hunting for nuances of expression. 'You said that it was interesting that I should mention taking Hirondelle onto a battlefield?'

FitzOsbern returned Rolf's stare and the suggestion of a smile curved his narrow lips. 'I am here with the offer of a commission from the Duke himself. He needs warhorses, and you are the man to supply them.'

Rolf gently caressed the palm of his right hand with the fingertips of his left while he absorbed this information. 'How many and for what purpose?' he asked after a moment.

The thin lips twitched further into a smile and then straightened. 'The number has yet to be judged; several hundred, I would imagine.'

Rolf was stunned. 'There are not several hundred horses in the entire stud, let alone for sale.'

'I know, and those you do have, I want to purchase now for my own use.'

Rolf was totally baffled and FitzOsbern's smile developed substance. Rolf opened his mouth to demand a coherent answer, but subsided as the door swung open and Arlette came in bearing a pitcher of gently steaming dark wine and two of their best cups. The fragrance of cinnamon perfumed the air as she poured for the men and set a bowl of warm, fresh honey

cakes at the guest's right hand. FitzOsbern exchanged pleas-
antries with her, enquiring after her health and that of the infant
to whom he had sent a birth gift of an exquisitely carved ivory
cross. Arlette murmured the proper responses, her grey eyes
modestly downcast. Rolf fiddled impatiently with his cup, fully
aware that FitzOsbern was drawing out the tedious chit-chat
just to tease him.

He tap-tapped his finger ring against the side of the cup.
Arlette looked at him, made her excuses and left.

'Well trained,' commented FitzOsbern, his eyes on the
door. 'Robert Strongarm's daughter, isn't she? Some useful
connections.'

Rolf said nothing. He had little contact with Arlette's family. Since Strongarm's death, they were mainly a network of
nuns and widowed aunts, albeit with bloodlines allied to the
Ducal house. He had as little to do with them as possible.

'Very well, I'll stop teasing you,' said his visitor. 'The Duke
desires to take King Edward's crown from the usurper
Godwinson. As you are doubtless aware, the throne was
promised to William more than fifteen years ago, and
Godwinson swore an oath that when the time came he would
help him sit there.'

Rolf raised an eyebrow. 'No-one ever expected Godwinson
to keep that oath.'

'No, but it still makes people look on him as a perjurer.
There is to be a council held at Lillebonne to discuss the possibility of taking an army across the narrow sea. Will you come?'

Rolf spread his hands. 'I am only a small landholder compared to great men such as you – what difference will my word
make?'

FitzOsbern began to smile again. 'What difference does anyone's word make when our Duke is set on his purpose? No, we
need men of practicality there for when the decision is agreed –
shipwrights and armourers, chandlers, sailmakers and the like.
Numbers and quantities will have to be estimated and the work
set in motion. Your task, as I see it, will be to find the extra
horses that the Duke will require for remounts and such. You

have contacts and you know a sound beast when you see one.'

'Do you need my answer now?'

'It would be useful.'

Feeling dazed, Rolf looked into the brazier cupped in its wrought iron stand. While he did not want to neglect the stud, the thought of buying horses at the Duke's expense, with little risk to himself, was very appealing. He could almost smell the freedom on his skin like a warm, salt wind.

He raised gleaming eyes to FitzOsbern. 'Yes,' he said. 'I will come.'

That night, lying beside Arlette in the great bed, he stared up at the ceiling, his mind ploughing one thought after another like the bows of a galley surging through a brisk sea. How much fodder would an army's horse rank need? How long did Duke William intend keeping them in one place before he embarked? The quantities of urine and dung would be phenomenal. Transporting horses on ships was never easy even in calm weather. If a storm blew up, the only resort was prayer, and Rolf was all too aware that while God was good, he was also very fickle.

Beside him Arlette raised herself on one elbow and peered down at him. 'Can you not sleep, my lord?'

In the dim light of the single night candle her body was all gold and shadows. The way she was leaning had squashed together and lifted her small breasts, giving them the hint of a cleavage they did not possess.

'I was thinking.'

'I know, I could almost hear you.' Her hand stole out to stroke his arm. 'Is it because of FitzOsbern's visit today?'

The touch of her smooth fingertips upon his bicep provoked a lazy interest lower down. Nothing drastically vigorous, for the moment FitzOsbern had departed, he had quenched his nervous excitement within Berthe's copious, greedy body. In the stables, fully clothed; five minutes of blinding oblivion.

'He wants me to buy some horses for the Duke,' he said neutrally. 'I've to go to Lillebonne to discuss the details.'

Her fingers ceased to move and her body stiffened. 'When?'
'Tomorrow.'

'So soon!'

'I've to get there and find lodgings. Besides, if I'm on the road, I might as well do some buying and selling on the way.' He reached out to cup her dismayed, delicate face in his palm. 'You know that I always come back,' he said softly. 'You know that Brize-sur-Risle is my harbour and you are my anchor. I'll bring you a bolt of silk to make a gown and thread-of-gold to trim it.'

'How long will you be gone?' Her immense eyes were troubled and he felt a pang of guilty irritation. Harbours and anchors were all very well, but he longed with all his heart for the wildness of the open sea.

'I do not know, perhaps a month.' He drew her head down to his and kissed her. 'Think of the prestige for Brize. And it will mean more money for Gisele's dowry when the time comes. Perhaps we will be able to secure her a great husband.'

Arlette was silent, but he could sense her thoughts. She was proud of her status and would like nothing better than to improve it and then show off to their neighbours. Mollified, she relaxed against him.

'You should have a son to inherit,' she murmured. 'I know I do not carry well, and I am sorry that Gisele was a girl, but if we try again, mayhap we'll be more fortunate.'

Rolf smiled wryly in the dark as she parted her thighs for him. He knew what was expected. Arlette was a firm believer in the Church's view that the carnal act between husband and wife was for the sole purpose of begetting children. Pleasure was a devil's wile and to be shunned. If it was experienced, it was to be confessed, and penance done to cleanse the sin.

He serviced her as swiftly and impersonally as Orage servicing one of the brood mares, his body brought to release as much by his inner vision of new horizons as by his wife's passive flesh.

CHAPTER 5

Ailith had wished upon a shooting star at the Yuletide feast. Now another star, trailing a line of fire, had blazed in the April sky for almost a week and she knew for a certainty that her wish had been granted.

'I believe I am with child,' she confided in Felice as she pinned her cloak and prepared to go to market with her neighbour.

Felice widened her eyes. 'Ailith, I am pleased for you! How soon, tell me when!'

'Between November's end and Yule, I think.' Complexion pink and radiant, she told Felice about making her wish. 'Goldwin said that the strange star bodes us ill, but I know he is wrong,' she added, laying her hand upon her belly which was flat, revealing nothing of the new life it contained.

'Have you told him yet?'

'No, but I'm going to roast a hare tonight and ply him with our best mead – make it a proper occasion to celebrate.' Ailith spoke brightly, but anxiety lurked beneath her sparkle. Goldwin had been dour and taciturn of late. He spent far too much time at his forge. Every day he was up before dawn, working until well after dusk, squinting by candlelight to complete death-bladed axe-heads, seax's and swords. He no longer saw beauty in the world, only the killing brightness of edged steel.

'I too have had a gift from the star.' Felice leaned close to

Ailith lest the accompanying maids should hear. 'Four years Aubert and I have been married. I thought I must surely be barren, but this week I have missed my second flux.'

'Truly?' Ailith's face kindled with delight and she gave Felice a hug. 'Then we'll be outgrowing our girdles together, and neither will be able to bore the other with talk of breeding and babies. Do you know what I did this morning?'

Felice shook her head.

Ailith giggled. 'I stuffed an unwoven fleece beneath my robe to see how I will look in six months' time. You should try it too!'

Felice smiled, but Ailith received the impression that it was a trifle forced.

'How long will Aubert be away?'

Felice's expression became wary and the lustre left her eyes. 'He never knows with these wine-buying forays. Sometimes he is home within two weeks, sometimes it can be as long as two months.'

Ailith pulled a face. Despite Goldwin's current sour humour, he was always there, solid and steady, his bulk warm and comforting in the bed beside her at night. 'I would hate that.'

Felice gave a little shrug. 'You become accustomed . . . only sometimes it is harder than others.'

'Do you miss Normandy?'

'A little. I loved our house in Rouen, and I was safe there. Here, if I open my mouth, people hear my accent and look at me with hatred because of our Duke and your King. I think that when Aubert returns, he will take me back to Normandy until peace is made.'

Ailith nodded and agreed that it was the most sensible course to take, but knew that if Felice did leave, she would miss her dreadfully. After the inauspicious beginning to their relationship, she and Felice had rapidly become good friends. And now, the fact that they were both pregnant only served to draw them closer. She did not want to see it sundered by the politics of power-hungry men.

Despite, or perhaps because of the portentous star in the sky, the market stalls of the Chepe were louder and busier than ever. Ailith purchased plump silver sardines and a cheese wrapped in cabbage leaves. She laughed with Felice at the sight of a small dog fleeing from a butcher's stall, its jaws strained by a beef rib fully half its size.

Together the women bought lengths of linen to stitch swaddling bands, and visited the apothecary's booth to pore over childbirth remedies.

'An eaglestone, that's what you need,' Felice declared, holding up an egg-shaped brown stone threaded on a ribbon while the apothecary looked on, contemplating his profit. 'It will ease the pain of travail, or so I've been told.'

Ailith eyed the stone dubiously, and wondered how. The price the apothecary had suggested was extortionate. She knew that she could walk down by the river's strand and pick up stones that looked suspiciously similar. 'Later perhaps.' She shook her head. 'There is time aplenty to think of such trinkets.'

Felice, however, was not to be dissuaded, and purchased the eaglestone for a price that horrified Ailith. Her friend went on to buy nearly every remedy that the gleeful apothecary suggested. Ailith watched the packages mount on the counter and seeing the hectic colour in Felice's cheeks, the unnatural sparkle in her dark eyes, began to feel disconcerted.

'Have you gone mad?' she demanded as they returned to the bustle of the streets. 'What do you want all those for?'

'Security,' Felice said and gave a brittle laugh. 'I can bear anything but pain.'

Before Felice looked away, Ailith saw the terror in her wide stare. 'It will be all right,' she tried to comfort, taking her friend's stiff arm. 'The pain doesn't last for ever, and you'll 'forget it the moment you have your new baby in your arms.'

'My mother died in childbirth,' Felice said woodenly, 'bearing me, her first. I am told by my family that I am very like her.'

'But not exactly the same.'

'Oh, it's all right for you!' Felice snapped, shaking her arm free. 'You're built like a barn. All you have to do is open your doors and the child will just walk out!'

Ailith recoiled as if Felice had slapped her across the face. Although she knew that Felice was striking out from the depth of her fear, it did not make the words hurt any less. She tightened her lips and quickened her pace, feeling a small, desolate spurt of gratification as Felice had to run to keep up.

'Ailith, wait, slow down. Oh curse me for a shrew, I didn't mean it!' Felice panted, clutching at Ailith's cloak. 'It's just that I'm so envious of you!'

Ailith stopped. 'Of my size, you mean? You would like to be built like a barn too?'

'I wish I had your hips,' Felice admitted, 'but it's more than that. I wish I had your honest joy, a taste for the simple pleasures.'

'So I am a peasant too?' Ailith arched her brows.

'No, no, I implied no such thing . . . you know I didn't!'

'I am not so sure,' Ailith retorted. 'After all, our first meeting was between lady and servant, wasn't it? Me sitting on the dung heap and you on your dainty mare. Is that how you see us, Norman and Saxon?' She began to walk again, her heart thumping painfully against her ribs. Whatever had made her say that? Jesu, she had not realised how deeply the resentment had bitten. Felice was her friend, but a few more exchanges like that and the relationship would be totally destroyed.

Ailith turned round, intending in her own turn to apologise, and saw to her horror that two rough-looking men from a nearby rag-and-bone booth had approached Felice and were haranguing her. Obviously they had both heard enough of the argument to deduce that the slim, dark-eyed woman was Norman.

'Why don't you go home?' One of them pushed Felice's shoulder with the heel of his hand so that she staggered and almost fell. 'We don't want Normans on English soil, not unless they're sewn up in shrouds.'

Felice's warm complexion was as sallow as vellum. She

clutched her cloak to her throat and licked her lips. 'Let me go about my business,' she said unsteadily. 'You have no right to block my path.'

'No right, hah! Do you hear that, Edwin! The Norman bitch says we have no right!' The trader looked at his fellow in mock-astonishment. 'There's no end to their insolence, is there? What do you reckon we should do with her?'

The other man leered at Felice and tugged his earlobe. 'By rights we ought to take her down to the docks and throw her off English soil,' he said, 'but I reckon as she ought to be given a message to take back to the Norman Duke.' Advancing on her, he seized her roughly round the waist and tried to kiss her. Felice struggled, jerking her head from side to side, her eyes wide with terror and revulsion.

'Leave her alone!' Ailith waded in. 'Do you truly think Harold Godwinson would be proud to call you supporters of his cause?'

'Know him personally, do you?' enquired the first trader, looking her insultingly up and down.

'Yes, my husband is commissioned to him,' Ailith answered coldly. Inside she was seething with terror, but she faced down the traders with an outward display of calm. 'And the Godwinson family are acquainted with the husband of this lady you have laid hands upon.' She was conscious that a a crowd was gathering to watch the spectacle, and knew that if sides were taken, she and Felice would fare badly. 'Let her be.' Reaching out, she plucked Felice away from the trader. His eyes narrowed; his whole face was pinched and puckered with anger, but she had sown enough doubt to make him hesitate.

'Quickly!' Ailith drew Felice away towards the broader thoroughfares of Chepeside. 'They may yet change their minds.' Even as she spoke, a cabbage struck Felice in the back, causing her to stagger against Ailith with a frightened cry.

'Norman whore!' came the bellow. 'Norman bitch, go home!' A clod of filth from the gutter followed the cabbage, flattening in a starburst of hostility upon Felice's lovely soft cloak, spattering her wimple and cheek.

Felice uttered one short scream of terror, then bit it off behind compressed lips.

'Hurry!' Ailith drew her urgently onwards. 'They won't start a riot among the mercers' booths.'

Hampered by their skirts, the women ran, Ailith dragging the daintier Felice with ungentle haste. She did not stop until they reached the safety of the cloth sellers' quarter, where many of the stalls were owned by Flemings who had certain alliances with Normandy. Duke William's own wife Matilda was Flemish. Surrounded by opulent bolts of richly dyed wool, linen and silk, listening to the foreign accents conducting their mundane business, Ailith felt secure enough to pause for breath, Felice clinging to her side like a wilting flower to a rock.

A mercer who knew Ailith gave them the shelter of his booth and offered to lend them his senior apprentice to see them home.

'It isn't safe to go about the streets unescorted these days,' he advised Felice as he sat her upon a stool inside the house that adjoined the shop, and gave her a small wooden cup of sweet, strong mead. 'Best thing to do if you are Norman is go home until the trouble is over one way or another.' He had a kindly face and was genuinely concerned, but there was a hint of irritation in his tone that let Ailith and Felice know that he thought them out of their wits for venturing abroad in the first instant.

'We did not realise that the ill-feeling was so strong,' Ailith said in a small voice. She felt cold and shaky now that the danger was past. 'They just pounced on us out of nowhere.' She turned to Felice, whose lower lip was chattering against the rim of the mead cup. 'I did not mean those words I said; I'm sorry they brought that mob down on us.'

Felice shook her head. Her complexion was the unhealthy hue of raw dough. 'My fault too,' she whispered, and began to cry. 'I wish Aubert was here.'

In the months she had known Felice, Ailith had come to admire the Norman woman and feel more than a little envious of her sylph-like figure, her graceful bearing and poise. This bright April morning, however, Ailith realised what a slim façade her friend's sophistication was. Her own plain, robust strength of character was a far better protection against the slights of the world.

It became obvious to Ailith that whether they had protection or not, Felice was incapable of walking home. The merchant, with an eye to future profit, lent them his pack pony. Perched on its back, Felice clung miserably to the rope bridle as the mercer's apprentice guided them through London's streets towards the suburbs beyond the old Roman wall.

'Ailith, I don't feel well,' Felice whimpered as the pony clopped up the dirt track. 'My stomach . . .' She clutched at her belly, her face screwed up in pain.

Dear Jesu, she's miscarrying, Ailith thought with a rush of panic that did not show on her face. 'A moment longer and we'll be home – just round this corner.'

Felice swayed on the pony's back, her eyelids fluttering.

'If you fall off you will kill yourself and the child for a certainty!' Ailith snapped. 'You must hold on!' She pinched Felice's thigh as hard as she could.

Felice gasped. Her fingers clutched convulsively at the reins.

Ailith grabbed the pony's rein from the apprentice. 'Here,' she said with authority. 'I'll lead the beast, you catch her if she slips.'

They rounded the corner and in the curve of the next bend, Ailith greeted the sight of the thatches of home with a thankful prayer. Her initial relief died when she saw that several horses were tied up outside the forge. The harness and trappings were expensive and in the next moment she recognised Aldred's sturdy brown cob and Lyulph's roan gelding. An extremely handsome iron-grey stallion was drinking from the rain butt against the forge wall, and a mail-clad huscarl was patting his neck. Goldwin emerged from the forge, in conversation with a broad, fair-haired man who dwarfed him. Links of rivet-mail glistened on the man's arms and torso. Beneath the mail and the quilted coat he wore under it, a tunic of gold-embroidered scarlet dazzled Ailith's eyes. He was swinging his arms to test the fit of the mail.

'God and all his angels, it is the King!' Her hand went to her mouth.

Goldwin looked up in mid-comment and she saw him lose the thread of the conversation as his eyes met hers. Making an apology to Harold, he started towards her. Felice began to slip from the pony. The apprentice managed to catch her after a fashion and lowered her to the moist grass at the verge of the muddy track. Ailith knelt at her side, feeling sick with fright.

'Ailith, what in Jesu's name has happened?' Goldwin demanded. There was a breathless quality of fear to his voice and because of it, an underlying roughness of anger.

'We were attacked by some ruffians in Chepeside. Oh Goldwin, I think she is miscarrying!' Ailith's voice broke. Her chin puckered as she fought not to cry. 'Help me take her into the house so that she can lie down . . . hurry!' she added as he stared at her blankly. 'Do you want her to die out here on the road?'

'Do as your wife says, man.'

Ailith looked up at Harold Godwinson and saw a lion personified. His eyes were the same tawny colour as his hair, which fell in a heavy mane to his collarbones. A torc of twisted gold wire gleamed at his throat, and beneath it, thrusting out of the embroidered opening of his tunic, were wiry glints of body hair.

When Goldwin did not move, still rooted to the ground by shock, Harold himself lifted the limp young woman in his arms and turned towards the house. Ailith gained her feet. There were two cold, muddy patches on her gown where she had been kneeling. 'It's all my fault,' she said shakily to Goldwin. 'We had a quarrel in the street – over nothing, but her Norman accent was recognised!'

'I knew something like this was bound to happen,' Goldwin growled. 'From now on you can send the maids for whatever you need. And it might be a good idea to stay away from Felice altogether until this trouble has passed.'

Ailith glared at him. 'Felice is innocent, alone, and in need of help. I never thought that you were the kind of man to be nought but a fair-weather friend.' Turning her back on him, she followed the King into her house.

A bracken mattress had been pulled out of a recess and Felice lay on it before the fire. She stirred, licked her lips, and murmured several rapid words.

'She's Norman!' The harsh condemnation was snarled by Ailith's brother Aldred who had been helping himself to a pot of soup from the hearth cauldron. His blue gaze flew accusingly to his sister. 'Small wonder that you were attacked in the street!'

'She has done nothing wrong!' Ailith retorted with equal heat. 'Yes, she's a Norman, but can you see her coming at you with a shield and sword? What kind of threat is she to your manhood?'

Aldred's fair skin burned red. 'By the Rood, if you were in my discipline, I'd take a belt to your hide! Our father was always too soft with you! And Goldwin's no better. Where is he? I've some advice for him!'

'Peace, Aldred,' commanded Harold sharply. Leaving Felice, he removed the pot of soup from his huscarl and tasted it himself. 'Master Goldwin is the best judge of how to rule his own household. As your sister says, the woman lying here is no threat to us, even if she is Norman.'

'But . . .' Aldred began, then swallowed powerfully and tightened his lips.

'She is your neighbour?' Harold turned to Ailith.

'Yes, Sire.' Ailith's heart was pounding so hard from the confrontation with Aldred that she felt sick. 'Her husband is a Rouen wine merchant. They came here at Yuletide, just before King Edward died.'

Harold nodded thoughtfully. 'His name?'

'Aubert de Remy. He told us that your brother Earl Leofwin had bought some wine from him.'

'Yes, I remember.' Harold's eyes narrowed. 'It was good wine too,' he murmured. 'Where is he now? Surely he should not leave his wife so ill-attended in times like these.'

Although Harold's voice was reasonable, Ailith's spine prickled with a sense of danger. 'He is away buying wine, I do not know where, but Felice expects him home soon, I think. Aubert did not realise that she was with child when he left.'

The King drank off the bowl of soup and wiped the drops from his moustache between forefinger and thumb. 'It seems that we must care for his lady until his return,' he said. 'And whenever that should be, I want to see him. I think that I too would like to buy some of his wine.'

Aldred made a spluttering sound and Harold sharply ordered him to wait outside. Glaring, the young man strode out of the door. Harold waited until he had gone, then bent a frowning gaze upon Ailith. 'Your husband is a loyal, hard-working man and I know that you have the same integrity. As you say, it is not this poor lady's fault that she is a Norman, and she is of no danger to us, but it would be in the interests of her own safety to keep her confined. When she is well enough to be moved without danger to her health, I will have her placed in the convent of St Aethelburga to be cared for by the nuns until her husband should return. I will make it known that she is under my protection and that if harm is done to her, matters will go ill with the culprit.' He smiled bleakly. 'Whatever Duke William thinks, I am a man of my word.'

Ailith bowed her head, torn between a deep relief that the matter had been lifted out of her hands, and anxiety at the deeper implications. Felice was virtually a prisoner, and if Aubert returned, he would likely face arrest.

'You keep the best soup cauldron this side of the river,' Harold said as a parting compliment, dazzled her with a smile, and ducked outside to his men.

A sound from the pallet caused her to spin round and discover that Felice was awake. The young woman's brown eyes were hazy with pain, but fully aware. 'I'm sorry.' Her whisper was weak. 'I have caused you so much trouble.'

'You would do the same for me,' Ailith said stoutly, concealing her misgivings. 'I'll send Sigrid to fetch her aunt Hulda.

She has skill in midwifery and matters of the womb. Lie still, everything is going to be all right.'

'Felice has not lost the child, but she might yet do so, and very easily,' Ailith told Goldwin when she brought him bread and meat to the forge at dusk. Her tone was frosty for she had not forgiven him for his lack of support earlier. 'Hulda says that the bleeding has stopped, but that she must rest abed for at least a sevenday . . . and that means here with us.'

Goldwin scowled. He banged another rivet into a link of the mail shirt he was making. Ailith watched him. She knew that he wanted her to go away, but she refused to yield. Their life together had been very sweet until recently and she had no intention of allowing it to sour any further than it had already done.

'I am with child too,' she said during a silence between the tapping of his hammer. 'I have been looking for a favourable opportunity to tell you, but you always seem to be frowning and short-tempered.'

Goldwin carefully set down his small hammer and his handful of rivets and links. 'You are with child?' he repeated, and instead of looking at her, he turned his back to fiddle with a stone jar of nails on a shelf. 'When will it be born?' His voice was gruff.

'At Yuletide, or just before. Are you not pleased?'

His hand slipped and the jar smashed on the hard earth floor, scattering the nails far and wide. He swore and she saw that he was shaking.

'Goldwin, what's wrong?' Worried now, Ailith hurried round his workbench and grasped her husband's sleeve.

'Oh, Aili, Aili!' His voice and control broke. Dragging her clumsily against him, he buried his face in her wimple and shoulder, his body shuddering. 'I have had such dreams of late – of battlefields and piles of bleeding corpses. I cannot think straight any more.'

She held him, rocking and soothing him like a child, a lump in her own throat.

'There is talk of war with the Norwegians,' he groaned into her neck, 'and William of Normandy is gathering a huge army across the narrow sea. I feel as if we are nought but a bone in the midst of a starving wolf pack.'

Ailith stroked his hair, then brought her palm tenderly down his face, over scratchy stubble and curl of beard. 'It is small wonder that you suffer nightmares the amount of time you spend in the forge. You cannot equip the entire English fyrd single-handed. You must cease toiling and fretting like this, or you will lose your wits.'

Goldwin inhaled shakily and kissed her palm. He squeezed her waist which was still trim, without sign of her impending motherhood. 'I could not be more proud that you are to bear our child, but I fear for our future, Aili.' Disengaging himself, he sat down on his bench and ran a distracted hand through his hair.

'It will be all right,' she said softly, and after considering him for a moment, picked up the trencher of food she had brought him. 'Come, we'll take this to bed with us and you can eat it there.' *And fall asleep with your head on my breasts*, she thought. *It is what you need.*

He looked at his bench and the beckoning pile of hauberk rivets and rings. Then he looked at the shards of pottery on the floor and the bright scattering of nails. Slowly he stood up. A weary, tentative smile curved his lips.

'If it is a boy,' he said, 'we shall name him Harold after the King.' Taking her free hand, he led her out of the forge into the starry April night, its darkness scored by the curve of the strange Dragon Star.

CHAPTER 6

NORMANDY,
JULY 1066

Eyes narrowed against the dazzle of the sun on the sea, his chest bare, Rolf rode the dun gelding fetlock-deep through the gentle cat-lap of the waves. Behind him, on leading ropes, trotted two more acquisitions for Duke William's supply of Norman warhorses, and further behind still rode three grooms with the rest of the mounts – a dozen in total from his most recent expedition. He was required to deliver them to the main muster point at Dives-sur-Mer within the next fortnight.

Rolf had been busy since the early spring, scouring the countryside and the market places of Norman and Flemish towns and villages for likely beasts. In doing so he had reached the satisfying conclusion that his stud at Brize had few rivals this side of the Pyrenees, and that only the stallions of Spain and Nicaea could better his own.

He urged the dun to a trot, his body rising and falling smoothly to accommodate the change of gait. Silver fans of spray skimmed away from the dun's hooves, and returned to the sea in a mesh of spangled droplets. The other horses quickened pace.

Higher up the beach, close to a small harbour and the huts of a fishing village, a gang of shipwrights toiled upon one of the vessels that were to transport the anticipated two thousand warhorses across the narrow sea to England. Three had already been completed and rolled at anchor in the bay, awaiting the command to tack up the coast to the muster at Dives.

A group of sailmakers sat in the lee of the dunes, stitching heavy linen canvases to equip the vessel under construction. Rolf looked at the dark red stripes woven through the buff-coloured linen and imagined the sail bulging in a stiff breeze. For a moment the movement of the horse beneath him became the pitch and roll of a ship's deck, and he fancied that he could hear the creak of the hemp ropes and clinker-built timbers. The strain of Norse blood in the line of Brize-sur-Risle might be in its fifth generation now, but it still exerted a powerful tug on Rolf's soulstrings.

His gaze left the sailmakers and crossed the open sea until it encountered the blue smudge of the horizon. He had met a merchant once who claimed to have sailed off the edge of the world and discovered a land inhabited by strange, copper-skinned men and even stranger beasts. Rolf was not sure if he believed him. The merchant had stayed for several nights at Brize-sur-Risle and when he departed, had made Rolf the gift of a red toadstone which he said would cure lameness in horses. Rolf wore it around his neck beside his cross and a small, battered silver hammer of Thor which had been handed down father to son since the time of his pagan great, great grandfather.

It might be interesting to sail off the edge of the world, but for now what lay beyond the immediate horizon would do. England. He savoured the word, and a shiver of anticipation ran through him. Perhaps on a similar shoreline, unseen across the glint of water, a Saxon warrior was staring out to sea and honing his axe in readiness. The thought filled Rolf with so much restless energy that he wanted to burst. The dun broke into a canter beneath the tension in his master's thin fingers, and the sea water splashed higher, soaking Rolf's linen chausses and tossing cold spray over his midriff and shoulders.

At the edge of the waves near the village, a man was sitting on the beach close to the shoreline. His hands were bound around his raised knees and he was staring out to sea as hungrily as Rolf had been a moment since. Now and then he picked up a stone from the tidemark and flung it at the water.

Rolf slowed the dun. Then he reined to a halt and dismounted in the sandy shallows with a splash.

'By God's beard, do my eyes deceive me, or is it Aubert de Remy sitting on a beach in the middle of nowhere with naught to do but throw stones at the sea?' Laughing, Rolf gave his horses into the care of the following grooms and sat down in the sand beside the merchant.

'I'm waiting for the night's tide.' Aubert clasped Rolf's tough, blistered palm, then lightly punched the hard bicep.

'The night's tide to where?' Rolf eyed his friend speculatively. Aubert had a thriving, legitimate vintner's trade, but Rolf had known him for long enough to be aware that he dealt in more than just barrels of wine.

Aubert smiled and tossed another stone at the sea. 'England, where else?'

'At night, from a small port like this?' Rolf looked at him sidelong.

'I'm making contact with a wine galley from Bordeaux in mid-channel. We'll sail into London without harm. Harold of Wessex is not at war with the peoples south of Normandy.'

Rolf licked his forefinger and held it up to the snags of salty breeze. 'You'll need good oarsmen, there'll not be a wind tonight.'

'There's an eight-man crew, nine including myself.'

'And when you get to England, what then?'

'That long nose of yours hasn't got any shorter with age, has it?' There was amused exasperation in Aubert's voice. 'How is Arlette these days, and the baby?'

Rolf grunted. 'They were both well when last I saw them.' His tone was perfunctory. 'What about Felice?'

Aubert's mobile features creased into a frown. 'I am concerned about her,' he admitted. 'I should never have left her in London, but events moved so swiftly that I had no choice but to do so at the time. I was hoping to return for her in May or early June and bring her home to Rouen, but there hasn't been an opportunity. Duke William is a hard taskmaster, as well you know.'

'So what will you do?' Rolf dug a shell out of the sand and cast it towards the gentle shush of the waves.

Aubert sighed. 'Fetch her when I can. She has never said anything to me, but she knows that my trade has certain irregularities.'

'How long do you have . . . before the invasion, I mean?'

Aubert narrowed his muddy hazel eyes and looked Rolf over very carefully, as if by assessing his companion's physical form, he could see into his mind. 'I do not know which is more dangerous,' he said, 'your curiosity, or your thick-skinned refusal to leave a subject alone.'

Rolf grinned. He knew that the only way to win Aubert's approval was to persist. Sometimes, if the merchant was in the right frame of mind, Rolf learned things. If not, then the repartee still helped to sharpen his mind and stave off boredom. 'Tell me what I want to know and I'll buy you a haunch of mutton and a wheaten loaf in yonder hostelry.' He indicated one of the dwellings clustered beyond the dunes.

Aubert's mouth curled in a sardonic smile. 'Now I see the value you set upon my word.'

'Very well, I'll throw in a dish of buttered worts and a flagon of cider too!' Rolf added flippantly.

Aubert snorted, and with a shake of his head, stood up. 'Your generosity overwhelms me into acceptance!' He dusted golden grit and scraps of mussel shell from his short tunic.

Rolf gestured to one of the grooms, and the youth tossed him a crumpled shirt and tunic from a saddlebag.

Donning the garments as they toiled up the soft sand of the beach towards the houses, Rolf said, 'We are summoned to muster in two weeks at Dives-sur-Mer, but I suppose you know that.'

'I had heard it was so.' Aubert pursed his lips. 'But do not expect to sail before harvest time.'

Rolf frowned. 'Most of the Duke's men are hired warriors; they don't need to take time away to cut the corn.'

'But Harold's do,' Aubert said smugly. 'His army has only a small core of permanent soldiers. The rest have estates and farms to tend. He cannot keep them stood to arms indefinitely.'

'So William is going to wait until the Saxon coast is unguarded and strike then?' Rolf made a face. 'Sooner rather than later, I hope, or else the provisioning of our army will kill us before we set out.'

'It will be a difficult task, I grant you, but easier than for Harold. And our Duke has the edge on him when it comes to being ruthless. Harold has a heart, he's courageous and impulsive. Those are the chinks in his armour and William knows it.'

The two men entered the hostelry. Rolf ducked just in time to avoid being brained by the top of the door. At a little above two yards in height, he dwelt in permanent danger of injury from apertures made for smaller men. 'You have met Harold then?' he asked as they seated themselves at a trestle bench and the proprietor hastened to bring them a jug of the locally brewed potent cider.

The walls gleamed with new whitewash. A wooden statue of the Virgin and Child beamed down on the men from a recess.

Aubert glanced at it and piously crossed himself. 'Briefly at court when King Edward was alive, but I know all about him from my neighbour where I rent my house in London. Goldwin's an armourer and he does much work for the Godwinsons. His wife's brothers are huscarls of Harold's. The information I have gleaned from that quarter has been invaluable. Speaking of which . . .' Unlatching his belt, he slid a knife sheath off the decorated strap end. 'This is a gift for you – a thank you for the chestnut mare you gave to Felice. I commissioned it from Goldwin at Yuletide.'

Rolf took the weapon from Aubert and examined it with pleasure. The length of the tapered blade spanned his hand from fingertip to wrist and a haft of polished antler fitted his grip perfectly. The craftsmanship was superb. He tested his gift on the haunch of mutton that the hostelry keeper set down on the table before them.

'Slices keener than your wit,' Rolf pronounced to Aubert as he speared an oozing pink morsel and draped it on his tongue.

'You had better warn the Duke if this man is making armour for Godwinson.'

Aubert smiled, but the humour did not reach his eyes as he refastened his belt and drew his own knife so that he could eat. 'He has become a friend,' he said, 'and in my trade that is less than wise.'

CHAPTER 7

The August night was so sultry that the air itself felt like a hot, oppressive blanket lying on Ailith's chest. She stretched her legs, trying without success to find a cool spot in the bed. Beside her, Goldwin snored, and stale mead fumes wafted her way each time he breathed out. She was worried about the amount he had been drinking of late, but had said nothing to him in the hope that once the uncertainty of imminent war had passed from their lives, he would become his usual, amiable self.

Ailith turned restlessly and as she tried to settle, felt the tiniest fluttering throb in her belly. Laying her hand over the place, she was rewarded again, and smiled. Felice's baby had been kicking and churning vigorously for over a month now and her belly looked huge. Ailith, on the other hand, was scarcely aware of being pregnant. Her breasts had swollen and were tender to the touch, but her waist had scarcely thickened, and the mound of her belly was no bigger than a small cloth pudding. Nor had she suffered any of Felice's debilitating sickness or spotting of blood. Hulda, the midwife, said cheerfully that she expected Ailith to deliver her baby as easily as shelling a pea from a pod. Asked about Felice, Hulda had admitted that the fit was going to be tight, but being as the husband was not a man of large proportions, with the blessing of God, and the excellent care of the nuns at St Aethelburga's, the Norman woman would be all right.

Indeed, she would be all right if that ne'er-do-well husband of hers would return, Ailith thought angrily. He had been absent since late April and it was August now. How could he abandon his wife in a hostile land for nigh on four months?

The baby did not kick again. Ailith sighed and rolled onto her back, her mind somersaulting like a butter churn, her body sticky with sweat. Two days ago Aldred and Lyulph had set out with the English fyrd to defend the south coast against a possible attack from Normandy. They had come to the forge to collect the weapons that Goldwin had made for them, and they had said their farewells in stiff and formal fashion. When Ailith had offered them ale and honey cakes in the house, they had declined.

'The only Normans I will love,' Aldred had said, 'are the ones who die on the blade of this axe.' He had run his fingertips over the edge of the steel. 'And before you tell me that the bitch in yonder convent is innocent, it might interest you to know that her husband is a Norman spy.'

Ailith's stomach had contracted. As so often in childhood, she stood up to her brother, jutting her chin at him in bravado. 'I do not believe you.'

'The King himself told me.' Aldred's eyes were filled with scorn. 'The little arsewipe wasn't selling wine at court in January, he was buying information. 'Why do you think he hasn't been back?'

'I don't know, I . . .' Ailith had found herself floundering.

Aldred had nodded with triumph and again stroked his axe. 'So I tell you that the only Normans I will love are those whom I kill.'

'But Felice is innocent, she doesn't know!'

Aldred had just looked at her and stalked off. Lyulph had hesitated, staring between his older brother and Ailith. Then he had put his arms around her in a brief, but powerful bear hug. 'Your heart is too soft,' he said, 'and Aldred's is too fierce, but I love you both.' Then he too had turned and left, the steel tip of his spear sparkling at the sky, his stride long and proud.

Ailith tossed and turned. She was sure that Felice was not

involved in any of Aubert's more questionable activities, although as his wife for more than four years, surely she must have some suspicions. More and more Ailith found herself pitying the young Norman woman, and despite Goldwin's dark looks, she continued to visit her regularly at the convent.

She fell into a restless doze and dreamed that a flock of ravens flew over London and settled in such numbers on the roof of her house that the thatch collapsed and buried her beneath it. She awoke with a gasp, her heart thundering in her breast. Grey fingers of light were prying through the cracks in the shutters and she could hear Alaric's relentless crowing. Goldwin still snored. Quietly, so as not to disturb him, Ailith left the bed and donned her shift and undertunic.

Below stairs, Wulfhild was scratching herself and yawning as she coaxed last night's banked fire to life and prepared the soup cauldron. Sigrid was clattering about in the storeroom behind the screen. Ailith joined her and collected a shallow, wooden bowl of chopped up scraps from the previous evening's meal, then went outside to feed the hens. The birds were able to find most of their own food in the summer months, but a small supplement ensured a reliable supply of eggs. Frequently there was a surplus and Ailith would trade these with a neighbour for cheese or butter.

Entering the garth, she let the hens out of confinement and scattered the scraps for them to peck at while she set about collecting the eggs, warm and damp from their straw. She gathered eight in her wooden bowl, and was deliberating whether to serve them scrambled and piled in a buttered, scooped-out loaf, or hard-boiled, when she caught sight of a man sidling cautiously into her garth from the house that she still thought of as Sitric's.

Alarm winged through her and roosted in her stomach as she recognised him. 'Aubert!' she cried, and almost dropped the eggs.

'What's happened? Where is everyone, why is our house empty?' Less than cautious now that he had been seen, Aubert strode up to her. His face was as brown as a sailor's, with paler creases fanning from his hazel eyes. He had lost weight and there was a tired drag to his mouth corners. 'Where's Felice?'

'If you had taken her with you four months ago you would not have to ask!' Ailith snapped. 'I do not know how you have the audacity or foolishness to return here now!'

'In Jesu's name, Ailith, what has happened to her?'

There was a note of panic in his voice that almost caused her to relent and pity him. 'She is safe, with thanks due to the people whose hospitality you have so lightly abused,' she said stiffly. 'Do not look to receive a welcome in my house, and do not insult me by pretending you do not know what I mean.'

Aubert stared at her, a look of shocked astonishment on his face. Then he rallied. 'Whatever you think you know of me, I still love my wife and it was never my intention to harm you or your family.'

Ailith eyed him in return. His manner seemed sincere, but then he had always appeared affable and genuine when he was winkling information out of Goldwin about the Godwinsons. She shook her head. 'I cannot give you my trust again. Felice is safe in the convent of St Aethelburga, but if you try to see her you will be arrested on King Harold's order. He knows you for what you are.' Her lip curled. 'Take ship for Normandy, Aubert, and do not come back.'

'But I need to see her. I want to take her home to Rouen!'

'That is impossible. You will have to return as empty-handed as you arrived. If Felice travels any distance it will be the death of her. She is with child, Aubert, and there have been some difficulties.'

He looked stunned and the lines of exhaustion on his face deepened further. Against her will, Ailith began to feel sympathy for him, but she hardened herself against the impulse to invite him inside to eat and drink. He was their enemy and he had abused their trust.

'What kind of difficulties?' Aubert rubbed his forehead.

'She came close to losing the child in her second month – she bled for three days. If you value her life, leave her alone.' Ailith gestured brusquely. 'Now go. If Goldwin should come out and discover you, he will kill you with his own two hands, and I would not blame him.'

He chewed his lip and hesitated. 'Ailith, I . . .'

She did not want to hear what he was going to say, whether it be an apology, a justification, or a stumbling plea for her aid. 'Aubert, go!' she cried. 'Must I drive you off by screaming for help?'

Numbly he shook his head and turned away. Clutching her wooden bowl before her like a shield, Ailith watched him limp dispiritedly down the garth and compressed her lips so that she would not call him back.

CHAPTER 8

In the September dusk, Rolf stood on the bridge between the courtyard and the keep at Brize-sur-Risle, and gazed out upon a small army of footsoldiers and grooms, knights and equerries, the caretakers of a herd of warhorses more than two thousand strong. The last glimmerings of sunlight flashed across glossy hides, burnishing chestnut into fire-red, gilding dun to gold, and polishing black with a rich patina of bronze. A feeling of awe joined Rolf's elation as he watched the gleaming, equine bodies which were going to bear Duke William's endeavour to victory or doom within the next few weeks.

The holding camp was in the act of being transferred from Dives-sur-Mer to St Valery-sur-Somme which was closer to the English shore and in a better position to receive winds favourable to a crossing. Most of the supplies for the invasion had travelled up the coast in William's huge war fleet, but Rolf had deemed it less stressful to bring the horses in his care overland. Soon enough the destriers would have to be led on board ship and securely tied and hobbled for the sea crossing. Their role was vital and they had to arrive in England healthy and undamaged.

Rolf had practised loading and unloading the horses in Dives, starting initially with his own docile dun and progressing through the various levels to the Duke's highly strung black Spanish stallion. Once a rhythm had been established, the task had not been too difficult. Horses that baulked were blindfolded. Others were sweetly coaxed. Rolf discovered the troublesome ones

and practised with them, not only practised, but learned, building upon his expertise. The Duke's horse was given a placid old
sumpter pony as a companion in his stall and immediately
became more manageable. Not that Rolf had to load every single one of the two thousand. His responsibility lay with those
of the most value, those of the Duke's personal stable, and
those belonging to William FitzOsbern, Rolf's mentor.

The sun sank behind a banner of solid grey cloud, although
the sky was still underlit with burning rose, and the river was as
bright as a honed sword pointing towards the sea. The neigh of
a horse floated up to him and the loud laughter of a soldier at
one of the camp fires. Small midges hovered in the twilight. It
occurred to Rolf that he might be looking out over the lands of
Brize-sur-Risle for the last time, that a month from now his
bones might be lying at the bottom of the narrow sea, or
bleaching on an English headland. It was a sobering thought,
but he was not depressed by it. Rather it served to add a certain
piquancy to his determination. Without a little uncertainty,
life was apt to become as dull as unsalted bread in Lent.

Above the fading rose colour on the skyline, the first star
twinkled out, bright and tiny. He watched its winking pinpoint
and savoured the strange pang of pleasure-pain in his soul.

'My lord, will you not come within?' Arlette joined him,
laying her hand upon his tunic sleeve. He saw her glance wander over the huge horse herd which had become a single shape
in the dusk. He knew that she was afraid he was going to spend
the evening hours at the camp fires with his comrades, rather
than with her. She had dressed to please him. Her gown of blue
wool was moulded to her figure, accentuating her small waist
and clinging across her breasts. A scent of herbs and dried rose
petals rose from her garments. His hunger sharpened. He had
not been home very often these past few months.

There had been women available in Duke William's camp at
Dives; a whole industry had been built up around servicing the
needs of the large contingent of mercenary soldiers and keeping
them happy in the field. Sometimes Rolf had availed himself of
their sweaty charms – there had been a particularly athletic, if

pungent fisher-girl at Dives, but for the most part he had practised abstinence. While Rolf had a weakness for women, it
seldom extended to the sluts and harlots in the army's tail.

He smiled and kissed her because that was what she
expected, and followed her into the keep. A portion of his
brain kept up a sensible conversation with Arlette while the rest
busied itself itemising all the things that had to be done before
the morning when the destrier herd would continue its journey
to St Valery-sur-Somme.

Arlette had prepared a farewell feast. He could see her hand
at work in all the little fripperies and garnishes adorning the
fare. There were a lot of small, dainty morsels and very little
that could be heartily attacked. Concealing his irritation, Rolf
sat down in his carved chair. His chaplain blessed the food,
although Rolf doubted the ritual would make the fare any
more substantial, and having muttered their 'amens' everyone
began to eat.

Rolf engaged himself in conversation with Tancred, his
overseer, who was to have sole charge of the herds at Brize for
the next two months at least. Tancred was a cheerful, able man
in early middle age. He was also one of Rolf's vassals, and had
a hall and lands of his own six miles away at Fauville-sur-Risle.
He had risen to his status of senior overseer by dint of hard
work and a natural talent with horses, which was rewarded by
a ten per cent share in the price of each horse that Rolf sold.
He was a widower with a ten-year-old son whom he intended
to inherit this lucrative post in the fullness of time.

'Where's young Mauger tonight?' Rolf looked around for
Tancred's sturdy, blond-haired shadow. His overseer took the
boy everywhere with him, showing him how things were
done, teaching and explaining relentlessly.

'He's gone with one of the grooms to see the horse herd and
look at the camp fires. I'm joining them later, but I knew
you'd want to see me first.' Tancred smiled. 'The lad was that
excited when you all arrived. It's not something he'll see twice
in a lifetime.'

'No,' Rolf agreed with a slightly more rueful smile of his

own, and settled down to discuss the mundane but necessary details which would ensure the smooth running of the stud during the coming months. Arlette might have preferred more delicate conversation on this last night than covering mares and selling yearlings, but Rolf was bound by the limits of diminishing time, not by his sensibilities, or more to the point, by hers.

In the private chamber above the hall, Rolf eased his sword from its scabbard and held it up to the candlelight. Fingers wrapped around the leather grip, he swung the weapon and felt the power leave his arm and enter the steel. What would it be like to strike out at an enemy in battle? To know it was kill or be killed? He had been involved in minor skirmishes when called upon by the Duke to perform his obligatory forty days of military service, but he had never gone further than perfunctory blows and vigorous spear waving. During the month at Dives-sur-Mer there had been plenty of opportunity to train and he had taken full advantage, setting out to learn as much as he could about the Danish war axes he would be facing across the narrow sea. He had even bought one from a mercenary who claimed to have killed its former owner. The curving blade, mounted upon a haft of ash wood five feet long, gleamed viciously at him from a corner of the room.

Rolf sheathed his sword, propped it against his long kite shield and hefted the axe instead. It was much heavier than the sword, far less easy to control and more tiring to wield, but once a rhythm was established, the increasing speed of the whirling axe, up and round and down, meant certain death for anyone who stood in its path. Mail was no protection. The only defence was agility and a fast spear. Spreading his legs, Rolf swung the axe and imagined himself on a battlefield.

Arlette entered the chamber and screamed. Abruptly she stifled the sound against the back of her hand, but it was too late, and their baby daughter awoke in her cradle and started to howl as if giving vent to her own battle cry.

Feeling guilty and irritated, Rolf lowered the axe, and then set it down with his other weapons.

'Can't you keep those things in the armoury?' Arlette demanded as she stooped over the cradle and lifted Gisele out.

'Everything has to be checked. I have to make sure that nothing is weak or damaged.'

Arlette sniffed. 'Let a servant do it.' She rocked the baby in her arms. 'It's all right, *poupelet*, Mama's here, Mama's here.'

'Would you trust a servant with my life?'

She said nothing, but he saw the pain grow in her large, grey eyes.

'I always check my weapons myself, you know that.'

'Yes, Rolf, I'm sorry. I just don't like to see them in our chamber on the eve before you go to war.'

'I've finished now anyway.' He took his winter cloak from its peg on the wall and threw it over the weaponry. He wished that she had not seen him with the axe.

'Thank you,' she said with a shaky sigh of relief.

He shrugged and came to look over her shoulder while she tucked the baby back in her cradle. The child was already Arlette's replica in both looks and mannerisms: the same martyr's grey eyes, the same silver-brown hair. Of himself he could detect nothing. The infant's eyelids drooped. 'Mama,' she said softly as her eyelids closed.

Rolf stared at his wife. She returned his bold look with a darting glance, and blushed. His scrutiny descended to the rapid rise and fall of her small breasts beneath the blue robe. He cupped one in his hand, seeking the tender peak of her nipple, and lowered his lips to the rapid pulse in her soft, white throat. His other hand caught her by the haunches and pulled her against the urgent warmth of his crotch.

Arlette gasped and pushed at him. 'Rolf, not here, Gisele might wake up again!'

'Damn Gisele!' he muttered through his teeth. Arlette went rigid in his arms. For a single moment Rolf contemplated throwing her on the floor beside the cradle and taking her whether she willed it or not. Not once in their seven-year marriage had he succeeded in winning a spontaneous response from his wife. Her mother had told her that men were beasts in their lust for copulation, and Arlette had embraced that belief so early in her life that now it was an irrevocable facet of her character. The occasions that she did respond to his lovemaking were always marked by a visit to the confessional on the following day.

The moment's threat of violence passed. Resisting the temptation to prove her beliefs right by ravishing her where she stood, he led her by the hand to their bed.

In the morning, Rolf attended mass in the village church of Brize-sur-Risle and then departed to break his fast at one of the camp fires in the fields by the river meadow.

'Do you not wish to eat in the hall?' Arlette asked, the disappointment huge in her eyes.

Rolf shook his head. 'Much as I would enjoy your company, I have too much to do in the field.' He sugared the lie with a kiss, which ended prematurely as he saw a young knight walk past, his hand on his sword hilt. 'Ho, Richard, wait a minute, I want a word about that new horse of yours!'

The touch of Rolf's lips still tingling on hers, Arlette watched her husband run to catch up with Richard FitzScrob, one of the knights helping to escort the destrier herd to St Valery. Rolf's hair shone a bright, autumn-red against the grey of the September sky. She heard him laugh and saw him slap FitzScrob's shoulder with a slender, energetic hand. His stride was long and arrogant, his blue cloak swirled, revealing a flash of yellow lining as the two men mounted up and rode away together in the direction of the river.

Ever since Duke William had fixed his mind upon taking the English crown away from Harold Godwinson, Rolf had been acting as if there was a demon in his brain. For weeks on end he had been absent, inspecting and purchasing horseflesh, making plans to transport the animals across the narrow sea, his expertise avidly sought. There was no room in his life for anything else.

Arlette was miserably aware that the more she tried to hold onto him, the further he slipped from her grasp. He said that she was his place of safe anchor, but it was difficult to watch him yearning to be gone from her harbour and to know that he might never return.

She thought of the urgency of his lovemaking last night, of the weak pleasure that had flooded her limbs as he moved within her. Sometimes, despite what the priests and her mother had taught her about such feelings being the work of the devil, her body would respond unbidden and she would have to stifle her cries against her hand, or compress her lips. Last night had been such an occasion. Even to think of it now softened her loins. Arlette tightened her jaw and quickened her pace.

As she made to enter the hall, two squires emerged bearing some items of Rolf's baggage. The second youth wore Rolf's shield on his back, slung from its long strap. In one hand he carried a spear; in the other he gripped the Danish war axe.

Brought face to face with the weapon once more, Arlette knew that it was a portent. She stared with revulsion at the gleaming, curved blade. The squire stood aside to let her pass, and as she did so, it seemed that she felt the cold touch of the axe across the back of her neck.

In the hall by the fire, Berthe, the wet nurse, was suckling Gisele. Keeping them company was Berthe's great-grandmother Ragnild. No-one knew how old Ragnild was, but by general reckoning, she had seen at least fourscore winters. She had once been the village midwife, but swollen joints and the general debility of advancing years had put an end to that occupation more than five years ago. Her mind, however, was still as sharp as the knife she had once used to sever umbilical cords, and the villagers continued to seek her out for advice, for herbal remedies, and because she could read the runes.

Normally Arlette would not have dreamed of consulting Ragnild about anything, for it went against all the teachings of the Church, but today she was in sore need, and her state of grace was already smirched by last night's abandon.

Walking directly to the fire, she stood before the old woman. 'I want you to read the rune stones for me,' she demanded without preamble.

Ragnild sucked her gums. Her skin was as wrinkled as oak

bark and her eyes were so deeply set that they looked like small caverns sunk in weathered stone. 'And what would you be wanting with the pagan old ways, mistress?' she asked. Her voice was cracked, but its depths held the remains of a once alluring huskiness.

'Please, I will pay you well.' Ill at ease, Arlette unpinned her silver cloak brooch and put it in the old woman's misshapen claw. 'There is something I have to know.'

'And praying on your knees will not give you the answer, hmmm?' Ragnild gave a wheezy chuckle in which there was more than a hint of malice. Berthe joined in until the old woman rounded on her. 'Go and suckle the child elsewhere, you useless slut. Me and my lady has business together.' She stowed the brooch in her pouch, and brought forth a small drawstring bag. Glowering, Berthe left the fire and went to sit at a trestle table on the other side of the fire.

Arlette looked round the hall and shifted from foot to foot. Already she was beginning to regret the impulse that had made her speak to Ragnild.

'Rest easy, my lady, no-one's looking, they're all too busy this morning. It won't take but a moment.' Ragnild blinked up at Arlette through the twirling hearth smoke. 'What's your question?'

Arlette licked her lips and clutched her cloak together at the throat where the clasp had held it. 'Lord Rolf, will he be safe?'

Ragnild smiled contemptuously and shook a score of bleached white stones onto the hard earth floor at the side of the hearth. Each stone bore an angular rune and she leaned over the pattern in which they had fallen, squinting short-sightedly, the edges of her dirty linen wimple concealing her face from Arlette's view.

'Well?' said Arlette nervously as the silence stretched out.

'Pick up the stones for me, daughter, my hands are none too nimble,' Ragnild commanded in a softer voice than she had thus far used. Its lack of vinegar filled Arlette with foreboding and she hastened to do Ragnild's bidding.

'What is it, tell me!'

Ragnild shook her head. 'Peace, wait a moment. You have the stones in your hand? Now, throw them again, yourself.'

Arlette tossed them, and watched them land, their pattern more scattered this time. Ragnild hung over them, her breath hissing between her lips. 'You ask me if your husband will be safe,' she crooned. 'The runes say that Odin's ravens will glut themselves on many battlefields in the months to come, but that they shall not feed on the flesh of Brize-sur-Risle.'

Arlette was flooded with relief and actually found herself smiling at the revolting old woman. 'Then he will come back to me?'

Ragnild's leathery face was impassive. 'He will come back to you, mistress.'

Arlette gathered up the runes and hastily returned them to their grubby linen bag. Now that Ragnild had given her reassurance, she wanted desperately to escape from her.

'They say our Duke has moved harbours to be closer to English soil,' Ragnild muttered as Arlette turned away. 'Beware lest others do the same. The axe will chop the mooring rope clean in twain.'

But Arlette did not hear, for the priest had entered the hall, seeking to break his fast, and she was already hurrying towards him as if towards a haven.

Rolf was dining on bread, cold sausage and watered wine at one of the camp fires when he saw a dishevelled, exhausted-looking Aubert de Remy join the host and gratefully take a cup and a portion of food from the soldier in charge of the provisions. Excusing himself from present company, Rolf hurried over to the travel-weary merchant.

'You are haunting me.' Beneath his smile, Rolf's curiosity was as sharp as a knife.

Aubert returned the smile in a preoccupied fashion and took a gulp of the wine. 'I wish I had the time,' he groaned wearily. 'It was long after dark when I rode in last night, and I plan to be well ahead of your horse convoy by dusk. One of your grooms is saddling me a remount even now.' He rubbed his buttocks. 'God, my arse has more callouses than a leather-worker's palm!'

'You are bound for St Valery then?'

Aubert nodded and looked at Rolf from beneath his frizzy grey brows. 'I sailed into Dives last night on a Flemish trader. The narrow sea is empty; Harold has disbanded his fleet and sent his southern troops home. He hasn't been able to keep them provisioned in the field.'

'It was anticipated.' Rolf felt slightly cheated. Although it was good news, it was expected, and the tension in Aubert's manner had led him to believe that something more spectacular was afoot. 'So now we pray for a southerly wind.'

'There is more.' Aubert glanced round and lowered his voice. 'Harold might have disbanded one army, but he's gathering a fresh one on the march even as we speak. I have heard that the Norwegians have landed in the north of England. King Harald Hardraada has put forward his own claim to the English crown, and Harold's rebel brother Tostig is with him.'

The Scandinavian element in itself was no surprise. In Normandy it had long been known that the King of Norway also desired to be the King of England, but that he should attack now, aided by Tostig Godwinson, put a new twist on the thread. Thoughtfully Rolf drained his wine. 'So when we land on England's shore, we may not have the English to face, but the Norwegians.'

'Yes.'

Rolf's spirits lightened. The odds against Norman success were considerably diminished by Aubert's news. 'Whatever happens can only be to our advantage,' he said. 'Our army will be coming fresh to the fight, and whoever wins, Harold or Hardraada, he will have taken a softening punishment from the other side.'

Aubert nodded. 'And the winner will also have to march south to meet our army – providing that the winds allow us to sail and we don't all founder in mid-channel.'

A groom led a chestnut courser up to the camp fire and tugged his forelock to Aubert. Aubert acknowledged him and groaned once more. 'I never want to see a saddle or the sea again after these last few days,' he complained as he finished his food in two swift bites. Wiping his hands on his chausses, he reached for the bridle.

Rolf chuckled. 'God speed you on your way, and may it not be too rough on your backside!'

Grimacing, Aubert gingerly lifted himself into the saddle. Adjusting his stirrups, he suddenly paused and looked at Rolf. 'Felice is still in England,' he said sombrely.

'Could you not get her away?'

'She is with child, Rolf, and not carrying well. I did think about it, but if she had made the journey home with me, she would likely have miscarried and perhaps died. You know how dangerous these matters can be.'

Rolf knew that Aubert had resigned himself to the fact that Felice was barren. To have it proven otherwise, to know that she was at such risk must be devastating. Aubert adored his vivacious, dark-eyed wife. She was his pride and joy. 'I am sorry to hear it,' he said gravely. 'So she is still in London?'

Aubert fiddled with the leather stirrup strap. 'I am afraid that she is, and I am known for a spy there. My Saxon neighbour, the armourer – he and his wife have taken Felice to the convent of St Aethelburga for refuge, but I know that Harold has set a watch on the place lest I should go there seeking my wife. I would go to her if I could, but what use would I be to Felice and the child as a corpse?' He sighed heavily and, straightening in the saddle, drew on the rein to turn his horse around. 'I tell you, after this campaign, I am never going to be other than a simple wine merchant ever again!' Saluting Rolf, he guided the chestnut around the camp fire, and urged him into a trot.

Rolf rubbed the back of his neck and watched him leave, glad that he had no such burdens of his own to bear. River mist smoked around the horse's forelegs with ghostly effect. A blood-red sun pierced the dampness of the autumn morning and splashed mount and rider with ruddy gold. When they were out of sight, he turned back to the camp fire, and gave the command to begin moving out.

CHAPTER 9

'Sister Edith says that I still have at least another two months until the birth, but I know I shall burst before then,' groaned Felice, her hand upon the mountain of her belly. 'I'm as big as one of Aubert's wine barrels now!'

Ailith, who was visiting Felice at St Aethelburga's, contrasted Felice's impressive mound with her own which was no more than a gentle hillock. She too had another two months until her confinement.

'I asked Sister Edith if it could be twins, but she just laughed and said that there was a lot of water around him.'

'Him?' Ailith smiled.

'From the way he kicks me night and day, I know I am carrying a boy. Only a male could be so inconsiderate. Oh! Feel him now!' Taking Ailith's hand, she placed it over her swollen stomach. Ailith felt the vigorous thrust and surge against the palm of her hand and was both surprised and a little disconcerted.

'If what you say is true, then mine must surely be a girl,' she said. 'I have felt nothing like this – tickles and flutterings that is all. Dame Hulda says that I will suddenly swell up, perhaps in the last month.' Dame Hulda had not said a great deal, although she visited Ailith frequently to keep an eye on her wellbeing.

Felice's condition had improved tremendously since her arrival at the convent. There were two Norman nuns and a Fleming among the thirty-strong community. The Abbess herself, although English by birth, had a sister who was married to a Norman merchant, and these connections made Felice feel less of a foreigner.

The outside world intruded little upon the daily routine of the nuns. Their time was spent in prayer, contemplation and hard work. Felice, as a boarder, was not required to go to prayer at all hours of the day and night. Indeed, being in a delicate condition, she was positively cosseted by the holy women. Her security restored, Felice had recovered much of her confidence and poise. She was still terrified of the ordeal of childbirth, but for the nonce she was able to control her fear. 'He will be named Benedict,' she told Ailith dreamily. 'That was the name of Aubert's father.'

Ailith curbed herself from uttering a sarcasm concerning Aubert's loyalties. No cause would be served by making hostile remarks to Felice about her absent husband.

'Have you decided on a name for yours?' Felice asked when Ailith said nothing.

'Goldwin says Harold for a boy, Elfled for a girl.' Ailith had been sitting on the edge of Felice's bed, but now she rose and paced to the window. It was a square opening in the wall of about shoulder height, and with the shutters thrown back for fresh air and daylight, yielded a view of a swept yard containing animal pens and a well housing. Sleeves pushed back, overskirt pulled through her belt, a nun was winding the bucket. 'My brothers are home from the shore watch,' she said into the natural silence which had fallen. 'Harold could not keep the army together any longer. There has been no sign that your Duke will make a crossing yet.'

'He is not *my* Duke.' Felice petulantly plumped up the bolsters at her back. 'I wish he had never laid claim to England.'

'So do I,' Ailith said with a heavy heart. She watched the nun cross the courtyard with her full bucket of water. The weather was still and grey, a waiting day. Abruptly Ailith turned from the window. 'I have to go, Goldwin doesn't like me to be away for too long.' Leaning over Felice, she kissed her on the cheek.

'Come again soon,' Felice entreated.

'If I can.' Ailith forced a smile. 'God willing, this dispute between Harold and William will soon be over.' In her own ears her voice sounded false and overbright, as if she stood at the bedside of a terminally ill patient, reassuring them that they would soon be on their feet.

When she arrived home, her brothers' mounts were tethered outside the forge, and she saw that the horses were laden for a journey. Hauberks and quilted tunics were rolled up and strapped behind the saddles together with bundles of provisions. More ominously, held by a twist of leather at the horses' flanks, the heads of their great Danish war axes gave off dull gleams of light. Propped against the forge wall were two round shields and two ash-hafted spears. A third saddled horse dozed on one hip, and beside it stood her own irascible pack ass. Ailith poked her head around the forge door, but there was no-one inside and the fire was low. Goldwin's workbench was devoid of the usual clutter of tools. A feeling of dread came upon Ailith. Running to the house, she flung open the door.

Seated at the table near the hearth, Aldred, Lyulph and Goldwin broke off their conversation and looked at her, their expressions a mingling of surprise and guilt. The board was littered with the crumbs of a hasty meal. In a corner Wulfhild was sniffing and wiping her eyes on her apron.

'What has happened?' Ailith demanded. Her gaze flew to Goldwin and she saw with rising panic that he was wearing a quilted gambeson and had strapped a langseax to his belt. 'Why have you taken your tools from the forge?' On the trestle she noticed his own lightweight hauberk rolled into a bundle and secured with a leather strap. She met his eyes. 'You are going to war,' she managed to say hoarsely before her throat closed.

'Aili, I must. The King will need an armourer in the field.' Jerking to his feet, Goldwin hastened around the table and took her in his arms. 'If I stay here and brood any longer, I will explode like a barrel of overheated pitch.' His embrace tightened.

Never before had he smelled so strongly of the forge and

acrid masculine sweat. Ailith saw with painful clarity the way his hair curled on his brow, the squirrel-brown of his eyes and the density of his lashes.

'I cannot bear it,' she whispered, her fingers tightening in the quilting of his tunic.

'Sweetheart, I know how you feel, but I have to go.'

'To prove your manhood?' she snapped. 'Surely there is proof enough of it here!' She pressed his hand against her belly. 'It is this you need to stay and protect, or are you going to do like Aubert de Remy and leave me to fend for myself!'

Goldwin whitened beneath the lash of her tongue. 'It is for the very reason of my unborn child that I am doing this,' he answered huskily. 'So that it may have a future. Aili, please!'

She bit her lip and laid her head against the erratic thud of his heart, her own heart leaden with terror. 'So William has landed?' she asked after a moment, when she had swallowed enough of her bitterness to be able to speak without screaming.

'No.' It was Aldred who spoke as he and Lyulph rose from their hasty meal. 'The King's brother Tostig and Harald Hardraada of Norway are ravaging the north country. York has fallen and the armies of the northern English lords have taken a severe battering. If you want to save your child, pray as never before that the winds continue to keep William of Normandy from our shores and that we can hold back the might of the Norwegians.' His mouth a tight, grim line, Aldred went to the door. 'We have no time to tarry if we are to march out before noon.'

Ailith tightened her grip on Goldwin. There was so much she wanted to say, but all of it was locked inside her, and intertwined with it was a tide of helpless rage. 'Oh, Goldwin, have a care!' she choked out.

Her lips were smothered by his kiss, hard and long. 'And you too.' His own voice was strangled with emotion.

It was impossible; she could not let him go, and finally he had to pluck her arms from around his neck. Striding to the trestle, he took up his bundle, and swiftly walked out of the door.

Ailith followed him outside and watched him mount up. Her brothers embraced her, first Aldred, then Lyulph, and then they too were in the saddle and turning their mounts for the ride to the muster point.

A numb disbelief settling over her, Ailith stood in the middle of the dirt road and watched her menfolk ride away to war.

CHAPTER 10

The dappled stallion's coat was dark silver with sweat and his eyes were wild, displaying a dangerous rim of white as Rolf and two grooms fought to hold him.

'Richard, in the name of Christ and Thor, whatever possessed you to buy this brute?' Rolf demanded of his anxiously watching friend. 'The state he's in, he'll kick out the side of the ship for sure!'

Richard FitzScrob scratched the back of his shaven head and pulled a face. 'He's all right saddled up with a rider on his back. He doesn't like ramps, that's all.'

Rolf swore beneath his breath at the understatement. Not even Duke William's Spanish black had been this difficult to load, and Rolf was horribly aware of how short of time they were. All of the horses had to be on board the transports and out of St Valery before sunset in order to take advantage of the outflowing tidal currents. The Duke's fleet had been held up for long enough already, and there would never be a better occasion to embark.

A stiffening easterly wind ruffled Rolf's dark auburn hair and spun the weather vane on the roof of the church of St Valery. Duke William had wanted to sail two weeks ago, but the wind had refused to change until the aid of St Valery himself had been invoked and his relics paraded through the town, escorted by the entire Norman cavalry to the accompaniment of drums, trumpets and horns. Their entreaties must have reached the saint on his heavenly couch, for this very morning the wind had changed direction, banking to the east, and the scramble to embark had begun.

The grey lashed out and a shod hind hoof narrowly missed one of the grooms. The horse waiting behind sidled restively as it caught the scent of the grey's fear.

'Fetch a blindfold,' Rolf snapped at one of his men. 'Richard, take Hamo's place.'

The groom ran off and FitzScrob grasped the stallion's cheekstrap and hung on grimly while the grey sawed up and down. Rolf beckoned the equerry waiting behind to lead his horse up the steep ramp onto the vessel. She was a deep merchant galley with higher sides than the Duke's spearhead of fast, dragon-prowed warships whose sleek lines strongly resembled the raiding vessels of the first Viking Normans. The Duke's own ship, the *Mora*, was already provisioned and rode at anchor in the bay, separated from the chaos on the beach. The Duke himself was to be rowed out later. For the moment he was stalking up and down the shoreline, supervising the preparations to embark with his customary vigour. Rolf hoped that he would not choose to inspect this particular vessel just now.

'I ought to make you travel with the beast!' he panted to Richard, his arms burning with the effort of holding the grey. The groom returned with the blindfold and the fight began to tie it around the stallion's eyes. 'Where in the name of God did you get him?'

'Not in the name of God, but of Allah the Merciful,' Richard replied between gasps. 'My father bought him off a Moorish trader and found him a little too light compared to the Brabancon stallions he usually rides, so he gave Sleipnir to me.'

'Are you sure there was no other reason?'

'I told you, he's superb to ride,' Richard said defensively. 'He just hates ramps. Stop scowling. Wouldn't you like a Moorish stallion to service your mares?'

'Not if he's going to impart qualities like this!' Rolf snapped. 'First thing I'd do if he were mine is geld him!'

Richard grinned. 'You wouldn't, I promise.'

The blindfold in place, the grey calmed enough to be led onto the ramp. His damp silver shoulders and quarters twitched and trembled. Sweating with the expectation that at any moment the horse would run amok and charge them both off the edge into the freezing sea, Rolf coaxed the destrier on board the ship and after a brief deliberation, tethered him at the end of the line of warhorses in the open hold.

'It will be easier to reach him and cut his throat if he panics once we're at sea,' Rolf said darkly to his friend. 'I mean it, Richard.' He patted his belt. Beside his short meat dagger hung the longer bladed English scramaseax. 'If one runs wild, then the rest will follow and the ship will go in short order to the bottom of the sea.' He gave the quivering grey a jaundiced glance. 'For now, the blindfold remains.'

Accepting Rolf's decision, but looking none too happy, Richard left the ship.

The first vessels sailed out of St Valery in the hour before sunset. Rolf's command was one of the last to leave, since embarking the horses had been left until late to avoid stressing the animals too much. Ships containing men and supplies followed the *Mora* in ragged procession out of the Somme estuary and into the cold green waters of the Channel. The east wind ruffled their striped sails. Here and there oars were broken out and scuds of white water curled on the surface of the waves. The setting sun was a low slash of orange on the skyline, the tide flowing out fast as Rolf's galley cast off her moorings and to the escort of a dozen wheeling, screaming gulls, set her sails to the wind.

Rolf watched the port of St Valery slowly diminish across the water until it became tiny and unreal. The reality was the creaking deck beneath his boots, the muscular thrust of the sea beneath the caulked timbers, the salt tang of spray exploding against the sheer-strake, and the chill wind searing his ears and face. He fetched a hood and shoulder cape from his baggage and as the sun sank beyond the horizon and Norman soil vanished from sight, he ordered the ship's master to light the lantern on the mast.

In the middle of the night, the invasion fleet hove to so that England would be reached at first light rather than in the pitch-darkness of the hours after midnight. The channel was as smooth as molten jet, with only the gentlest of swells to rock the ships. The crescent moon had set several hours since. In the deep of the night, Rolf watched the twinkles of lantern light which marked the position of the other vessels. Isolated but not alone, he was aware of a feeling of utter tranquillity. A tiny voice warned him that this was literally the calm before the storm, but he paid it no heed except to cast it overboard and commit it to the deep.

On board one of the ships, someone was singing a melancholy tune in the Breton tongue. The sound drifted across the water and filled Rolf's soul with yearning. The moment was as beautiful and eerily mournful as the last drawn-out note of the song. It was with a feeling of deep regret that he left his position on the prow of the transport and stepped down to the open hold to check up on the horses.

CHAPTER 11

Ailith was standing over a cauldron in the garth, poking hanks of homespun wool in a steaming brew of stewed bracken leaves and rusty nails in the hopes of dyeing the wool to soft green, when Aldred and Lyulph brought Goldwin home.

The breeze drove acrid smoke into her face from the fire beneath the cauldron and she was wiping her streaming eyes on her apron when she saw her brothers coming towards her, their arms linked basket-fashion to carry Goldwin. His arms were around their stalwart necks and she saw that his teeth were gritted with pain, the tendons standing out like cords in his throat as they bore him. His left leg was heavily bandaged from ankle to knee, and a naal-knitted sock covered his shoe-less foot. Ailith dropped her dyeing stick and ran to meet them.

'Jesu, Jesu!' she cried. 'What has happened?'

Goldwin tried to smile at her. 'Not as bad as it looks,' he gasped. 'I'll be all right by and by.'

'With rest and God's fortune you will,' said Aldred shortly. 'He's a lucky man, Ailith. A fraction deeper and he'd have been gutted by a Norwegian spear.' Aldred bore a long cut on his face that ended in a deep gouge at his helmet line. His blue eyes were red-rimmed with weariness. 'The ankle's nothing, he turned it when he insisted he was fit to mount his horse without aid and promptly fell down.' His tone was slightly patronising, but it also bore approving pride for Goldwin's courage.

'There was a rut in the road,' Goldwin said through his teeth.

Ailith thought that he looked terrible. All the colour had drained from his normally ruddy face and she did not like the way he was trembling. For certain he had a fever.

'Bring him within,' she said brusquely to her brothers, and as they carried him, she ran on ahead, shouting for Wulfhild and Sigrid.

While Ailith attended to Goldwin in their bed in the sleeping loft, she learned from her brothers about the bloody battle that had been fought and won against the Norwegians at a place called Stamford Bridge, about King Harold's rebel brother Tostig being killed by the royal huscarls, and about the grim news that had arrived during Harold's victory feast in York.

'William of Normandy has landed troops in the south,' Aldred said, his lip curling. 'Thousands of them – infantry, archers and cavalry. We are to muster for a few days in London while King Harold gathers fresh troops, and then we are to march out and put an end to the Norman bastard.'

'I'll be all right by then,' Goldwin said from the bed. He strove to sit up, then desisted with a groan.

'Not with a gut wound like yours you won't,' Aldred snorted.

Ailith lifted her husband's tunic and looked with dismay at the dirty bandages wound around his midriff and half-concealing a thicker wad of linen. Her stomach turned over and over as in her mind's eye she saw him upon a battlefield facing a berserker.

'Lie still,' she said as he started to protest again that there was very little wrong with him. 'Let me have a look at your injury. Certainly it needs clean bandages, these rags are disgusting. Aldred, Lyulph, why don't you go below and let Wulfhild give you something to eat?'

Aldred was all for staying at the bedside, but Lyulph, possessing slightly more tact, managed to drag him away.

'So you rode all the way from York with this wound?' Ailith asked as she unwrapped the bandages.

'It was important . . . if you had seen the King's face when the messenger interrupted the feasting with the news that the Normans had landed . . . ah!' He stiffened as she began to peel the linen wadding away from the site of the injury.

'So you were well enough to sit and feast?' she asked neutrally, her tone displaying none of her fear and anger. Goldwin had a mulish streak in his nature. Probably in the presence of her brothers he had been determined to show no weakness, to prove that he was as tough a warrior as they.

'There were others in far worse case than I. Some of them had to be borne into the hall on litters. I walked.'

The note of pride in Goldwin's voice caused Ailith to tighten her lips.

'In truth, the wound did not pain me at first,' he added. 'I rode the first three days from York without it troubling me. All I need is a short rest.'

Ailith gently lifted away the last of the wadding and looked at the wound with which Goldwin had walked and ridden for the better part of two weeks. A nasty red gash had opened him up from navel to hip-bone, slicing through layers of fat and muscle. The gash had been stitched in a rough and ready manner. Pus oozed between the threads, some of which had broken apart, and the entire area was puffy and inflamed.

'God have mercy!' Her hand went to her mouth; her belly heaved. 'Goldwin, you cannot think of marching anywhere with this!'

'Harold needs every man. He lost too many in the north,' Goldwin gasped.

Ailith opened her mouth to remonstrate with him, but closed it again, the words unsaid. It was obvious from his condition that no matter how he pushed his will, his body would be incapable. All she had to do was keep him lulled and quiet, giving his flesh the chance to knit.

'So be it,' she murmured, 'but tonight you must sleep. May I ask Sigrid's aunt Hulda to look at your wound and give you a potion to help the healing?'

Goldwin nodded and closed his eyes with a sigh. 'Indeed I am very tired,' he mumbled. 'I've hardly slept since the battle. It is the ravens pecking at the corpses. They won't leave me alone.'

Rolf slid wearily from Alezan's back to stand in the ankle-deep sludge of the wooden fort that one of Duke William's adjutants had pretentiously dared to call Hastings Castle. A bitter wind drove his sodden cloak against his back and whipped the stallion's tail between his mired hocks. The rain which had held off briefly as they rode through the marshy, deserted countryside began to whisper down again, fine in the wind as wet mist, a rain to penetrate the bones until they would never be warm again. Rolf removed his helm and absently touched a sore patch at his temple where the leather lining had chaffed.

Across the bailey the stable quarters were frantic with activity as patrols returned from a day of foraging the hinterland for provender. An outlying scouting party had galloped into the camp with the news that the English army had been sighted in the great forest known as the Andredeswealde not seven miles' distance. Riders had been sent out forthwith to summon in all the outlying Norman troops, and the command had gone out to stand to arms.

Rolf led Alezan to the stables and dismissed the harassed groom who came to take the bridle. 'Go to,' Rolf said, stroking the chestnut's whiskery soft muzzle. 'Attend elsewhere before the Duke has a battle right here among his own knights.'

The man hurried gratefully away towards a swearing Breton count whose stallion had just stepped on his toe.

Alezan snuffed Rolf's hair and face, his breath moistly warm as the man rubbed him down with a wisp of balled up hay. 'Give over, you brute,' Rolf muttered as the horse lovingly nipped the back of his neck. The chestnut's coat was thickening up for winter, the golden blaze of his hide muting to red. Rolf lifted each one of the stallion's hooves in turn to check that the shoes were still securely nailed and that the frogs were clean. As he straightened from his examination, his eye was caught by Richard's grey destrier in the horse line opposite, and he paused to admire the animal.

To look at him now, it was impossible to believe how difficult he had proved on the beach at St Valery, and again at Hastings. It was as Richard said; the stallion hated ramps, but in every other way was a beast of exceptional quality. He did not have the bulk of some of the north Norman destriers with their strong influx of Flemish blood, but he was fast, could turn on a penny, and his endurance was phenomenal. Even now, after Richard had been out on him all day, he still looked fresh, his ears pricked, his liquid eyes curious. Rolf admitted ruefully that he would have to eat his pride and go cap in hand to Richard to beg him for the use of the horse at stud. In his mind's eye he saw his friend's smug grin and winced.

By the time he left the stables, the daylight was almost quenched. Torches glimmered in the wooden huts and tents of the vast Norman encampment of seven thousand men. Rolf went to one of the ramshackle cooking sheds that had been set up within the bailey. A bulky Fleming with forearms the size of hams was tending a huge iron cooking pot suspended over the flames. He stirred the contents with a large, shallow ladle, wiped his forehead on his rolled-back sleeve, and looked at Rolf.

'What you brung this time?' he demanded in heavily accented French.

Rolf held out his hands to the warmth of the fire. The smell of the bubbling, rich stew teased his nostrils and his stomach growled. 'Enough to keep your cauldron simmering for another day at least,' he said as he handed the man his wooden eating bowl, and sat down on the crude bench at the side of the cooking pot. Unbidden there came to his mind's eye a vision of the angry, bewildered peasants from whom the supplies to feed the Norman army had been reaved. He saw their village burning orange beneath the grey October sky, inhaled the dark coils of smoke, heard the wails of the women and children, the furious despair of the men.

The ravaging had been a deliberate ploy of the Duke's, an attempt to lure Harold onto the Hastings peninsula and there force him to do battle. William wisely did not want to move too far from his own precarious supply lines. He reasoned that when Harold heard of the destruction of estates whose earl he had once been, he would take it as a personal insult and his impetuous nature would bring him roaring down to the south coast, intent on throwing the Normans back into the sea. It was William's plan to persuade Harold to give battle before his troops were rested and back up to full strength after their hard battle in the north. Tonight it seemed as if that plan had worked.

The Fleming leaned over the stew to ladle a generous portion into Rolf's bowl and hand it back to him. There were greasy chunks of mutton floating in it, and a mish-mash of vegetables. Rolf cupped his hands around the bowl, savouring the heat, and sipped. A comforting warmth reached his vitals and began to thaw his limbs.

Outside the shelter the rain started to thud down hard, filling the hollows in the churned mud of the bailey floor. A boy ran across the courtyard with a torch in his hand, and disappeared into the wooden keep. Another foraging party rode in with a milch cow and bellowing calf, and a packhorse laden with sacks of flour and strings of onions. The men were swearing roughly in Flemish, cursing the foul English weather, but their manner was jovial. They had also raided a barrel of mead which Rolf knew would never find its way to the quartermaster.

Another man trudged across the courtyard towards the cauldron, his hood drawn up around his face and his body protected against the rain by a cloak of double thickness fashioned of the hairy wool preferred by the Danes.

'Stinking weather,' commented Aubert de Remy by way of greeting and accepted a bowl of the scalding mutton broth.

Rolf murmured assent and shifted along the bench to make room for the merchant. Two reconnaissance scouts on dark bay horses entered the fort at a rapid trot. Torchlight and rain gleamed on helms, harness and mail.

'Are you on duty tonight?'

Rolf shook his head. 'No, I've been on forage detail all day, but I doubt I'll sleep for all that. Do you think Harold will attack?'

Aubert pursed his lips. 'I doubt it. I believe he is planning to keep us penned up on the peninsula while he waits for more troops to arrive and strengthen his force. It is what I would do if I were him. Mind you, if I were him, I would have stayed in London and made William come to me.' He sleeved a drip from his nose and hunched his shoulders. 'Time is on Harold's side, not ours. He could have afforded to wait.'

'Not necessarily. The Pope has given his blessing to our cause. God is on our side. When word of that gets spread abroad, some of the English might not be quite so willing to fight.'

'Perhaps,' Aubert conceded with a shrug, 'but he could well have taken the risk for the sake of a few more days – could have waited until we had to move out in search of supplies.' He drank his broth and looked sidelong at Rolf. 'Tonight the priests and chaplains will be taking confessions and shriving those who desire it. It is more than possible that we'll march on Harold at dawn, providing that he does not march first. And as I have said, I think he intends to remain where he is.'

Rolf thought of the battle axe in his tent. He slept with it naked at his side like a mistress. It had become a talisman, his defiance of fear. Tomorrow he would be brought face to face with thousands like it, and if one even so much as caressed him in passing, he knew that he would die. Without conscious thought, his fingers curled around the comforts of the Cross of Christ and the hammer of Thor that hung upon his breast.

CHAPTER 12

'*Ut, Ut, Ut!*' howled more than seven thousand English throats. Spears hammered on shield rims in a pounding, relentless rhythm. '*Ut, Ut, Ut!*'

Rolf stared at the seething host of warriors on the ridge, packed together twenty men deep; the bristle of spears, the metallic flash of sharp iron points and the death-smile curve of axe blades. His throat was as dry as chaff; to try and swallow was to choke. Cold sweat clammed his armpits and made his hands slippery upon Alezan's bridle. Norman battle cries retorted to the Saxon invective '*Dex aie! Thor aie!*' But it was like hurling peas at a sheet of beaten iron. The slope of the ridge was littered with the corpses of the Norman infantry who had rushed the Saxons in the wake of volleys of arrows from the Norman archers. No visible softening of the Saxon defences had occurred and now the cavalry was to go in against the great Danish axes.

'Christ on the Cross,' muttered Richard FitzScrob, his eyes on the Saxon line and the Norman dead littering the ground in front of it.

'Your ventail's undone,' Rolf said huskily.

'What?' Richard released his grip on the grey's reins and raised his hands to fumble with the loose mail flap which would protect his lower face from injury. It also made it considerably more difficult to breathe. Free of control the grey sidled, pressing up hard against Alezan. Rolf cursed as his leg was crushed, and the chestnut lashed out. A ripple shuddered down the line, as each horse and rider was forced to adjust. Richard snatched the grey's reins and brought him back under control, dragging the stallion's head down until its muzzle almost touched the tassels on the decorated breast band. 'I need four hands,' Richard gasped apologetically, and then, 'Jesu, I'm going to be sick.'

'Not now you've fastened your ventail, you'll choke! Pull yourself together, man!' Rolf's own voice cracked with strain. Grimly he adjusted his shield, which appeared to have a mind and mobility of its own, and shifted his wet grip on the shaft of his spear.

Richard gagged, glanced sidelong at Rolf, and clenched his jaw.

William FitzOsbern, commander of Rolf's section, rode his sweating stallion along their line, his standard bearer following on his heels, gold silk pennon snapping in the breeze. On their flank, Alain Fergant's Breton cavalry set their destriers at the ridge. Hooves thundered, the earth shook.

'God is with us!' roared FitzOsbern. Raising his mace on high, he faced the Saxon line and his lips contorted in a snarl. *'Laissez Corre!'*

Rolf spurred Alezan. The Norman line surged up the hill, the knights thigh to thigh, keeping pace. Breath and hide steamed like hell-smoke. The ground was soft and he could feel Alezan's shoulders and quarters straining, the stallion's hooves gouging out great clods of earth. The vibration of the charge thundered up through Rolf's saddle and into his straining body. Beyond Alezan's pricked ears, he saw the packed rows of painted shields, some long and triangular like his own, others circular with half-globe iron bosses. And within the shield wall, the axe-wielding, mail-clad huscarls who dealt death to anyone who came within range of the sweeping arcs of their weapons.

Spear tips spiked the sky; a hail of stones, wooden staves and steel caltrops assaulted the charging horsemen. Rolf kept his shield high, his head down, and hoarsely called upon Christ and Thor to protect him. The stink of blood, excrement and sheer human terror fouled his nostrils; the battle din roared in his ears until he was deaf.

He clutched his spear, and prepared to hurl it as Alezan strained within range. To his left an axe flashed as a Saxon warrior struck. The dark brown horse of the knight next to Rolf pitched to its knees. Blood sprayed; a warm wetness spattered Rolf's face and he saw the man hit the ground, defenceless against the Saxon huscarl who, in one massive blow, spliced the knight as if he were a bacon pig. Rolf twisted hard on the bridle, and before the axe could rise and whirl again, rose in the stirrups and cast his spear at the huscarl with all the strength in his arm. The Saxon screamed and staggered, clutching at the shaft embedded through mail and gambeson in his side. Rolf yanked the reins, squeezed with his thighs, and hauled the chestnut away. They half-galloped, half-skidded down the slope, mud churning beneath the destrier's hooves, missiles singing after them, and turned once safe, to recoup. On Rolf's other side, Richard tore off his ventail with frantic fingers and leaned over Sleipnir's withers to vomit.

'They're not men, they're devils!' he gulped.

The yellow banner of FitzOsbern rippled and the commands roared out for the cavalry to close ranks and advance again. '*Estroitez I droit! Mettez en bandon!*' Rolf snatched a spear from a convenient stack, fretted the chestnut on his hocks, and rejoined the assault.

This time, an axe man actually ran to meet Rolf as he rose in the stirrups to cast his spear. Rolf saw the deadly iron arc sweeping towards him and tried to stab the Saxon with the lance. The axe took off the spear head clean through the haft and continued to describe its deadly half-circle. In desperation Rolf tried to cover himself and the chestnut with his shield. The curved blade smashed through the linden planking and sank into the destrier's neck. The horse reared, and the Saxon's face beneath the nasal of his helm was suddenly a mass of red, shattered bone. Howling, a second axe man darted forwards. Rolf sawed on the reins, and spurred his wounded horse out of the melee.

Alezan carried him halfway down the hill and then the chestnut's legs buckled and Rolf was pitched headlong into the muddy grass. He lay bruised and winded. The thunder of the

Norman charge and retreat surged in his ears. He could hear the triumphant Saxon roar of '*Ut, Ut, Ut!*' Three knights galloped past him, their mounts flinging clods of soil. Someone was screaming in terror for a priest. Alezan kicked, shuddered, and died.

Rolf looked numbly at the blood-streaked golden-red hide. He had bred the stallion up from a foal, had exerted much time, effort and pride in his training. Now he was nothing but carrion for the ravens; a heap of meat among a thousand such heaps on this gory battlefield.

The screaming had stopped. Rolf pushed himself to his feet and guarding himself against the barrage of sling-stones with his broken shield, limped towards the Norman baggage station on Telham Hill to saddle up a remount. After five paces he stopped in mid-stride and stared, his blood freezing. A riderless grey destrier stood trembling beside a body. The stallion's withers and neck were saturated in blood, but Rolf could tell that the horse was not injured.

'God's sweet life!' he muttered through his teeth and ran to catch the bridle. Another knight had the same idea, but Rolf arrived first, and snarled him off. Then he knelt beside the fallen man.

'Richard? Richard, Christ, man, get up!' He shook his friend's shoulder.

Richard FitzScrob's reply was silent. His head lolled beneath the vigorous demand of Rolf's hand, revealing the shattered throat where his unfastened ventail had exposed him to a blow from a nail-studded club.

Fury pierced Rolf's numbness. He had a savage desire to leap astride the grey, hurl himself at the Saxon line and kill every last warrior. Pushing himself to his feet, he exchanged Richard's undamaged shield for his own, jammed his foot into the stirrup and mounted up. '*Aliez!*' he urged the stallion and dug in his spurs.

It was about noon when the Breton left flank, unable to take any more punishment from the English battle axes, broke and fled, leaving the remainder of the Norman army dangerously exposed. The centre drew back and the right flank wavered. The Bretons were heatedly pursued by triumphant English fyrdmen, and the two forces joined battle again in the marshy ground at the foot of the ridge. The Saxons had the advantage. Panicking, floundering, all the Bretons desired was to escape with their lives.

Rolf felt the infection of fear pierce his own exhaustion, but he held his place in the line. Where was there to go? Back to the ships in disordered confusion to be killed ignominiously on the shore? Even as these thoughts bolted through his mind, the impetus of the Norman assault wavered. A knight cried to him that Duke William was nowhere to be found, that he was down, that he was dead. Rolf found himself facing the line of shields and axes with no-one to either side of him. Wrenching Sleipnir's bridle, he turned back.

'Stand firm!' roared William FitzOsbern to the men of his command. He rose in his stirrups, his usually impassive features brimming with rage. 'Are you no better than the Bretons that you run like cowards?' He levelled his mace at a young knight. 'Do your duty to your sworn liege lord, or by God I'll kill you myself! Until you hear the command to retreat given from my own lips, you will assault that shield wall. Now get back up there and win this damned battle for Normandy!'

'Yes, my lord.' The young man's face was bone-white beneath his helm.

And then the Duke himself strode into their midst, his helm thumbed back and his ventail unfastened to show himself to his frightened men. Apart from a thin stone-cut down one cheek, he was unharmed. He was also horseless. 'You, de Brize, give me that grey,' he demanded.

Inwardly cursing, but leaping from the saddle with alacrity, Rolf presented William with Sleipnir.

'You won't go unrewarded,' said the Duke as he gained the saddle. 'I always honour my debts.' And then he was gone, smacking Sleipnir's rump with his sword blade, plunging through the mêlée and rallying his troops. Rolf wondered gloomily if he would ever see the grey again.

The battle continued, each foothold bitterly contested in blood. Harold's brothers Gyrth and Leofwin were killed. The English who had charged down the hill in pursuit of the Bretons were cut to pieces by William's cavalry, and the Normans were able to gain the ridge and begin eating their way to the core of the English defences. Gaps appeared in the shield wall and the less well armoured men in the ranks behind had to step forward and bear the brunt of the Norman assault. As the light began to fade towards dusk, the Duke employed his archers again, instructing them to fire high and aim for the rear of the Saxon lines where Harold's standards flew: the bold red dragon of Wessex, and the equally impressive silks of his Fighting Man banner.

Rolf, astride a third horse now, was one of the first Normans onto the ridge. His sword arm was aching, his borrowed shield was battered almost to pieces, his mind was made of wool. They were close to victory, so close, and yet it still lurked just out of their grasp, and if they had not managed to seize it by the time that dusk fell, it would never be theirs. Empty-handed except for their dead, they might as well return to their ships.

An anguished howl swelled from the rear of the Saxon line. Moments later, the determination of the shield wall wavered and contracted. The less well armed English began to flee the field. FitzOsbern's yellow banner ploughed a path through the Saxons. Rolf followed, hacking with his sword, defending with his shield. The peasants were easy meat for they wore no armour and were inexperienced with their weapons. Rolf lost count of the number he cut down. His horse stumbled on bodies, and sometimes they screamed.

Then the fighting changed and grew hard again. The peasants were gone, and in their place were heavily mailed huscarls wielding swords and axes. These were the professional backbone of Harold's army, the men who fought for a living and were fiercely loyal to the house of Godwinson.

An enormous huscarl planted himself across Rolf's path. The warrior was standing over the cloven body of one of his companions, and tears were streaming down his face. He howled words that Rolf did not understand and swung his axe in a glittering arc. For the third time that day Rolf lost a horse. The force of the fall knocked the sword from his hand and the helm from his head. He tasted mud, and the salt of his mount's blood. A spear leaned half-upright in the trampled ground beside him. Rolf rolled over, wrenched it free, and thrust it with the last of his strength into the body of the warrior swinging the axe.

He felt the point of the spear tip grinding through mail to reach the vulnerable, soft core. Above him the huscarl screamed, staggered, and toppled, the spear shaft snapping off as he crashed forwards. The deadly axe carved a long gouge in the trampled ground beside Rolf's head. Shuddering, clawing at the buried shaft, the Saxon rolled over. Utterly spent, Rolf stared into still lucid, but dying blue eyes. The huscarl had a luxuriant beard and moustache, the colour of ripe barley, but close up Rolf could see that he was scarcely out of adolescence. A boy, younger than Richard by several years. The eyes held his like a curse while death rattled in the young warrior's throat. The stare fixed upon Rolf and dried. Rolf crawled away from the corpse.

A Norman warhorse leaped over him, its rider spurring hard towards the core of the melêê. Rolf covered his head with his hands, but his reactions were slow with exhaustion and pain. The tip of a hind hoof struck the side of his head, and like Thor's great hammer, the darkness smashed him down.

When he came to his senses, it was full dark and nearby someone was grunting with effort. Beside him the dead Saxon was as cold as stone. The warrior's axe head and hauberk gleamed with a dull, blue light, and his mouth was frozen open in its final death snarl. The grunting came from a figure who was bending over the corpse of another soldier next to the young huscarl. Rolf almost cried out for help, thinking it was a priest, but then he heard the tug of a knife severing a leather cord, heard the jingle of money in a pouch and realised that he was watching a looter at work. And if the looter was English and discovered a living Norman during his search, that knife would be employed to more deadly intent than simply cutting purse strings.

Pain hammered through Rolf's head and the accompanying feeling of nausea threatened to overwhelm him. Hampered by concussion, his mind floundered. The scavenger abandoned the corpse and moved on to stand over the Saxon at Rolf's side. The looter muttered to himself as he worked, his breath an intermittent cloud of white vapour in the dank air.

Rolf wondered if he should lie very still and permit himself to be robbed, but almost immediately abandoned the thought. His body would be too warm, and it would be all too quick and easy for the looter to slit his throat. A silver cross flashed as it was ripped from around the Saxon's neck. Decorated arm bracelets were tugged off the wrists. A finger was hacked to obtain a ring. That final act finished any thoughts Rolf had still harboured about lying passive. In one movement he rolled over, grabbed the axe halfway down the haft, and swayed to his feet. His vision kept blurring, the pain in his skull was vicious, but he clung grimly to consciousness. The looter, a scrawny, pale specimen, leaped away from the huscarl, his knife brandished to defend himself, his left hand clutching the corpse's jewellery.

'Get you gone!' Rolf snarled, lifting the axe.

The looter sidled, and Rolf had to turn to keep him in sight. He could feel the strength draining from his legs, and knew that in a moment he was going to fall. Like a buzzard, the looter backed off, waiting his moment.

Over to his right, Rolf thought that he saw the glimmer of torches and heard the sound of voices speaking in French. 'Ho!' he bellowed, putting all of his failing strength into his voice. 'Help me!' He keeled to his knees. The looter darted at him. Rolf struck out, the axe held short in his hand. His adversary easily avoided the weapon, but instead of making a kill, leaped over Rolf and melted rapidly away into the night.

Breathing harshly, Rolf hung his head. The torchlight wavered nearer and soon he felt a gentle touch on his shoulder.

'My son, you are wounded,' said an anxious man in priest's robes. The light shone on his tonsure. Rolf recognised Herfast, the Duke's own chaplain. 'Can you stand?'

Groggily Rolf tried, but his legs seemed to be made of wet rope. 'No,' he said.

A litter was fetched, and as he was being laid upon it, he realised that the Duke himself was standing over him. 'You are the luckiest of men, Rolf de Brize,' William said. He had changed his mail for an embroidered tunic and rich cloak, but in the torchlight, Rolf could see the dried blood caked beneath the spatulate fingernails.

Rolf was not sure that he agreed with his liege lord. He was lucky not to be dead, he supposed, but he would not count a broken wrist and split skull as good fortune, nor the loss of his horses.

'Did we conquer?' he asked faintly. 'The last I remember is striking the wall of Harold's bodyguard.'

'The oath-breaker is dead.' William's mouth tightened into its familiar harsh line. 'He took an arrow in the face during the final assault and was ridden over and cut down in the last charge. Now we have to find his body from among all the others who died with him.' There was a hint of weariness, of distaste in William's voice.

Rolf noticed that his Duke was accompanied not only by his senior officers and priests, but by two women in Saxon dress. One of them had pure, strong features and copper-red hair that fringed her brow before being covered by her wimple. From the tales Rolf had heard, she could only be Edith Swan-neck, King Harold's handfasted wife, the woman of his heart, although for political purposes he had been married to Edith, King Edward's sister. If they needed Harold's mate to identify her lover, then God alone knew what she was going to find.

'I have tied that grey stallion of yours at FitzOsbern's horse lines,' William recalled Rolf's concussed attention as two priests made to bear him away from the battlefield. 'Never have I ridden such a fine animal.'

Dizzy although he was, Rolf was not about to admit to the

Duke that Sleipnir did not belong to Brize-sur-Risle, and he held to a prudent silence.

William's narrow lips curved the merest fraction. 'Breed from him for me, Rolf. I will give you English lands to sow a crop of destriers to be the envy of all the world. My pledge on it.' Tugging a ring from his finger, he placed it in Rolf's good left hand.

Through his pain and exhaustion, Rolf felt a spark of exultation, and it showed in the gleam of his eyes, even if the words of gratitude he spoke to the Duke were somewhat garbled.

William's eyebrows lifted as he saw the battle axe which lay at Rolf's side on the deerhide litter. 'What's this,' he mused, 'a souvenir?'

'A talisman, my lord,' Rolf answered. His eyes began to close, and his voice sank to an incoherent mumble. 'A reminder of how this day was won.'

CHAPTER 13

LONDON,
DECEMBER 1066

'Ailith, Ailith, where are you?'

Goldwin's voice reached Ailith in the garth where she was feeding scraps to the hens. A bitter frost the night before had silvered everything with rime. The sun had risen, but it wore a misty halo and was much too weak to pierce the December cold.

'Aili, where's my cloak?'

She scattered the last handful of corn and chopped pork fat and sighing heavily returned to the house. There was a dragging ache in the small of her back. It had started last night just as she retired, and this morning it was worse. She tried to ignore it. If it was the baby coming, she would know soon enough. The pain which Goldwin still endured made her feel guilty for her own minor twinges.

'Are you going out?' Taking his cloak from the mending pile, she handed it to him.

'I thought I would go into the city and see if I could glean any news.'

'Can you walk so far?' Ailith eyed him with concern. He was still very thin, and his health was precarious. Although his injured ankle had healed rapidly, the main wound was still troublesome. Along the line of the scar, swellings would develop, becoming hard, red, and extremely painful before they burst in a welter of pus and blood. A low fever accompanied these bouts and left Goldwin querulous and weak. The last attack had been only eight days ago and Ailith knew he was not yet fully recovered.

'Alfhelm's taking his cart that way; I'll ride with him.' Goldwin set the cloak around his shoulders, wincing as the movement aggravated his wound.

Ailith winced with him, but did not offer to help. She knew how touchy he was on the matter of his independence. 'Be careful,' was all she said with anxious eyes.

'How can I be any other with this damned hole in my side?' he answered testily. 'Would to God that Norwegian axe had cleft me in twain!'

'You do not mean that!'

He sighed and walked slowly to the door. 'I wish I did not,' he said wearily.

When he had gone, Ailith sat down before the fire to spin a pile of carded fleece into yarn for making winter socks. She twirled her spindle and drew out the fleece to make an evenly textured greyish-white thread. Her back continued to ache and now and then she shifted position, trying to ease herself. Spinning wool did not require much mental effort, it was a knowledge of the hands, and once learned was very much an unconscious process. Her mind was free to probe the misery of the last two months, like a knife searching a wound for splinters.

On the day of the great battle between King Harold and the Norman Duke, Goldwin had been so sick with the wound fever that Ailith had despaired of his life. Father Leofric had been sent for, and Goldwin had been shriven – although the good father had been somewhat disapproving of the way Goldwin kept muttering about Odin's ravens. For three days his life had hung in the balance and Ailith had known nothing but her own fight to save him. When she remembered, she prayed for the safety of her brothers and an English victory, but these moments were perforce snatched from chaos.

At first, when she heard the church bells ringing out in the city, she thought that they were celebrating a victory, but her ears had quickly become attuned to the single, dolorous notes of the death knell, and soon after that, she had learned of the disaster that had befallen them on Hastings field. When she heard that King Harold had been killed, she knew that her brothers would not be among the defeated, demoralised warriors trickling into London. Aldred and Lyulph had been members of the élite royal bodyguard and fiercely loyal. Harold's lifeblood was their lifeblood, and she had no doubt that it mingled with his in the battlefield soil.

Somehow she had managed to keep the news from Goldwin for an entire week while he grew stronger. When the urge to cry became too great, she would go out into the garth, to the privy, or down the path to the cold forge. Once, she and Wulfhild and Sigrid had all stood there, among the equipment for fashioning weapons, weeping together in mutual grief and fear.

Ailith felt tears prickling behind her lids now and had to cease twirling the spindle to wipe her eyes. It had been horrible telling Goldwin the news, seeing his thin, fever-wasted face slacken with despair and his eyes dull to the colour of mud. She had cried in front of him then, long and hard, the tears hot and empty of healing.

Since that time their future had been filled with uncertainty and fear. Rumours abounded – King Harold's sons by Edith Swan-neck were planning to avenge their father. Edgar Atheling of the old West Saxon royal house was going to be declared king and take up arms against the Norman Duke. And at dawn this morning they had heard that the Norman army, having ravaged the villages and countryside surrounding the city, was within striking distance of London itself. The gossip was that Edgar Atheling, the Mercian earls Edwin and Morcar and Archbishop Aldred had ridden to intercept William to tender their submission and offer him England's crown. It was this that Goldwin had gone to investigate.

Felice had told her that Duke William was a harsh master to serve, that he expected implicit obedience from his men, and that he was scornful of anyone without the stamina, endurance or ambition to match up to his own. He would destroy anything that stood in the path of his desire.

'But once you accept his yoke, he is fair,' Felice added judiciously. 'Aubert says that he has known him execute one of his own soldiers for looting a house after peace had been agreed, and the same for rape. He has a strong regard for keeping his word, and he demands the same from others.'

That particular discussion with Felice had taken place while Goldwin was in the north, and it had been their final one. Since her husband's return, Ailith had found neither the time nor the inclination to visit St Aethelburga's. Now her thoughts strayed to Felice. Her time would be close too. What was she thinking and feeling at the news of the Norman approach? Ailith wound a length of spun wool around her spindle and pondered. Aubert de Remy was the Duke's man, and it seemed ever more likely that the Duke was to become England's next king. It was only common sense to keep the friendship with Felice alive, a reason to persist through the emotions of hatred and resentment. Felice could not help being a Norman any more than Ailith could help being English. For the sake of the future, the bond between them had to hold.

The decision made, Ailith's dark mood lifted. Setting aside her distaff, she rose to tell Sigrid to bring some more wood to the fire. There was a strange sensation deep within her belly, followed by a drenching gush of hot liquid between her thighs. For a moment she was rooted to the spot by mortification, believing that she had lost control of her bladder, but then she remembered what Dame Hulda had told her, about the bag of water surrounding the baby, which often burst at the onset of labour.

Instead of fetching logs, Sigrid was sent running for her aunt Hulda, while Wulfhild helped Ailith to climb the stairs to the sleeping loft, and then set about preparing for the coming ordeal.

''Tis a boy, Mistress Ailith, you and master Goldwin have a son!' Dame Hulda placed the squeaking scrap of life upon Ailith's belly. Streaked with blood, slick with birthing fluid, he moved his limbs feebly and bobbed his head.

His hair was dark, so were his eyes, which were open as he entered the world. Ailith was amazed at how tiny he was, and also a little frightened. If she touched him, surely he would break. Hulda cut the pulsating cord and tied it off with a piece of twine. Then she took a linen towel from a craning Sigrid and wrapped the baby in it.

'You done well, Mistress Ailith,' she nodded. ''Tis only noon now, and the mite's small enough not to have caused you any damage down below.' She presented Ailith with her son. 'You and he introduce yourselves while I sees how the afterbirth is coming along.'

Ailith gathered her son in her arms. She could feel his limbs moving within the towel. His face puckered and he mewled at her, the noise high-pitched and feeble. Her labour had been swift and she had felt more discomfort than actual pain. *You're built like a barn. All you have to do is open your doors and the child will just walk out.* Felice's words returned to her now. First she smiled, and then, unaccountably, tears filled her eyes and overflowed.

'Here now, lass,' admonished Dame Hulda, raising her head at the sound of Ailith's loud sniff. 'There's no cause for that. You put your boy to suckle and thank God you be safely delivered.'

Ailith swallowed and placed the baby inexpertly to her breast. His head rooted back and forth, snuffling and seeking. Finally he latched onto her nipple, but once he had it in his mouth, he took two weak sucks and then pulled away with a feeble wail. 'He's not hungry,' Ailith said anxiously.

'Some bairns are like that at first,' Hulda said comfortingly. 'Besides, he popped out of you so fast that like as not he's got a mortal sore head. Ah, here comes the afterbirth. Push when I tell you, mistress.'

Later when the baby had been bathed and his gums rubbed with honey and salt in the age-old tradition, Hulda wrapped him in linen swaddling and laid him in the bed beside his mother. Although she said nothing to Ailith, the midwife was concerned. The child was very small – no bigger than one born a full moon early, although she knew that Ailith had gone to her full time. His extremities had a bluish tinge and the rest of his body was unhealthily pale. Ailith had tried to suckle him again, and Hulda had observed that although the infant was interested in the sustenance, he did not have the strength to suck for long.

'How do you intend naming him?' she asked, thinking that the sooner the babe was christened, the better.

'Goldwin desires him to be Harold, but I am not so sure. It doesn't seem to be a name that carries good fortune with it.' Ailith sighed. 'Edward perhaps. It is a good English name, but with Norman connections.'

Hulda snorted and folded her arms vigorously beneath her breasts, making it quite clear what she thought of that notion. 'And if King Edward hadn't been so fond of all things Norman, our King Harold need never ha' died.'

Ailith chewed her lip. 'Hulda, I know what you think about the Normans. God knows, the ambition of their Duke has caused much grief in this household, but I want you to do something for me.' Hulda raised her brows, and Ailith plunged on before her nerve failed her. 'Will you take a message to Felice de Remy at the convent of St Aethelburga, and tell her that I send my greetings and the news that I have been safely delivered of a son?'

Hulda eyed her darkly. 'I don't know as I should,' she muttered.

'Please, I would not ask unless it was important. It may be that we will need her goodwill in the months to come, and I want to keep our friendship fresh in her memory. I promised I would send word as soon as I was delivered, and she did the same.'

'Very well, mistress,' Hulda capitulated, still looking none too impressed. 'But it will have to wait until I'm up that way. I'll not make a special journey.'

And with that Ailith had to be content.

Goldwin came home at dusk. His face was grey with fatigue and Ailith could see from a single glance that he had pushed himself too far. But there was a sparkle in his eyes that had been absent for a long, long time. He sat down heavily beside her on the bed and she presented him with the son born in his absence.

Goldwin cradled the sleeping baby gingerly in his arms and gazed into the puckered little face. 'God save us, Aili, I've never seen anything so small in all my life,' he said in a voice of wonder.

'Hulda says he'll grow.' Ailith's voice was a trifle defensive, but then she smiled. 'His eyes are going to be dark like yours, and his hair too, I think. And he has all the proper equipment to make him a fine man.'

Goldwin kissed her clumsily and she saw that there were tears in his eyes. 'My son,' he said, his throat working. 'Perhaps I can think about rebuilding our lives now.' He returned the baby to Ailith and left the bed to sit down stiffly on the stool beside it. Wulfhild approached to remove his boots, for he was unable to bend over and manage for himself. Sigrid brought him bread and ale.

'Did you hear any news?' Ailith asked as Goldwin began to eat. At first he just nibbled, but as his appetite took hold, his bites became larger and more appreciative.

'The Norman Duke is to be offered the crown and London will officially surrender to him on the morrow or the day after,' he said between rotations of his jaw. 'There is no-one of Harold's status to hold us together any more, and our best warriors are gone . . . as well this household knows.'

'So the Norman army is to enter London?' Ailith asked apprehensively.

Goldwin nodded. 'Resistance would be foolish, and I have heard from all quarters that the Norman Duke is a man of his word. If we surrender to him now, he promises to be lenient.' Goldwin rested his gaze on the sleeping baby in her arms. 'At least we have certainty now,' he said in a voice full of weary relief. 'It was the not knowing that was killing me.'

Two days later the Normans rode into London to claim it as the greatest spoil of the English conquest thus far.

In the convent of St Aethelburga, Felice flung her arms around Aubert's neck and greeted him with floods of tears and passionate kisses. 'Oh, Aubert, I thought I would never see you again!' she sobbed. 'Every day has been like a siege!'

'I know, I know,' he soothed, his hands stroking. 'I have lived through torments myself, wondering if you were all right and unable to reach you.'

'Just look at the gift you left me,' she sniffed, patting the enormous swell of her belly. 'I almost miscarried in the early days, and now he doesn't want to come out!'

Smiling, Aubert let her guide his hand to her belly and was rewarded by a vigorous kick. His smile broadened.

'Ailith bore a son two days ago,' she told him. 'Their mid-wife came to tell me this morning – and a grumpy old besom she was too.' Her expression grew pensive. 'I wish that I was Ailith and that it was all over.' A note of fear entered her voice and she checked herself, knowing that if she dwelt on thoughts of her labour, her qualms would only intensify in the direction of terror. 'Goldwin was badly wounded in the battle against the Norwegians, and Ailith lost both her brothers at Hastings. I haven't seen her for almost three months.'

'I'll make sure that Ailith and Goldwin suffer no hardship under William's rule,' Aubert promised, and then grimaced ruefully. 'I do not suppose that the sight of my face will be welcome at their door, but I'll do my best to heal the breach.'

'I'll be glad if you can.' She looked tentatively at her husband. 'I don't want to return to the house yet. I'll feel much safer here until our son is born. The nuns know healing and midwifery.'

'Of course, I would expect you to do no other. Besides, the house is likely to be bursting at the seams with billeted knights for a few weeks at least. Do you remember Rolf de Brize?'

Felice laughed with something of her old humour. 'How can any woman not remember Rolf? I have never met a man so beautiful, or so dangerous!'

'A good thing I am a trusting, unjealous husband!' Aubert chuckled. 'He's going to stable his horses at the house and live there awhile. William is going to grant him the lands of a dead thegn on England's south coast, but he cannot take them up until the Duke has been anointed and officially pronounced rightful king. Rolf almost fell prey to looters on Hastings field, but he's recovering well.'

'Were you involved in the battle?'

The humour in Aubert's face abruptly died, and Felice realised that she had made a bad mistake in asking him. 'No,' he said after a moment. 'But I saw it from the baggage lines on Telham Hill, and it will stay with me until my dying day. I have never seen such waste, so many good men. I watched the English shield wall smash our cavalry in the first hours, and in turn I watched our cavalry smash their shield wall.' He drew his hand down over his face. 'Do you know, when we left Hastings, there were piles of bodies rotting where they lay, and the looters were so fat with plunder that they ceased combing the battlefield. Flocks of carrion birds arrived every morning at dawn and stayed feeding until dusk. Even the Duke was moved to pity by the sight of so many dead men.'

Felice's stomach churned. She compressed her lips, her colour fading. 'Aubert, no more,' she begged.

His gaze refocused, and he quickly sat her down on the spartan convent bed. 'I won't speak of it again,' he promised. 'Indeed, I did not mean to say as much. Are you all right?'

Felice swallowed and managed a valiant nod. She did not think that she was going to be sick, but her stomach was still queasy when she thought of Aubert being involved in such an undertaking.

'Now then,' he said, changing the subject somewhat jerkily, but with firmness of purpose. 'Have you thought of a name for our offspring while you've been waiting for me?'

CHAPTER 14

Ailith looked down at her son in exasperation. He had fallen asleep at her breast scarcely before he had drawn any sustenance, and now both of her nipples were dripping with milk of which she seemed to possess an over-abundance. Hulda had shown her how to express the surplus, and frequently she had to, feeling like a prize milch cow.

Little Harold, as Goldwin had insisted he be christened, was almost two weeks old. Ailith had recovered magnificently from the birth, and despite being scolded by Wulfhild, who was of the opinion that no woman should rise from childbed for at least a month, she was picking up the threads of her household activities. If she had stayed abed any longer, Ailith knew that she would have died of boredom. Harold was such a quiet baby and spent so much of his time asleep that she was scarcely aware of his existence. Sometimes she worried about his lack of response, about how tiny and frail he was. Even the act of feeding at her breast exhausted him. Hulda had been taciturn in her responses to Ailith's anxious queries, merely saying that it took some infants longer than others to recover from the ordeal of being born.

Goldwin adored his son and would sit by the cradle, a doting look on his face as Harold closed a tiny fist around his scarred blacksmith's forefinger. During the brief occasions when Harold was wide awake, Goldwin would carry him down to the forge and show him everything that would one day be his.

Sighing deeply, Ailith checked the baby's swaddling. It was still clean and she put him down while she bound up her heavy breasts with a linen band and shrugged up her chemise and undergown.

Below the sleeping loft, the hall was silent. Sigrid had gone to visit her old mother in the town with instructions to buy a bundle of kindling on her way home, and Goldwin was absent purchasing supplies for the forge. Harold's birth had jolted him out of his depression. Now that the Londoners had accepted William of Normandy for their king – he was to be crowned at Yule – Goldwin anticipated a return to stability. Even his battle wound seemed to be healing at last.

Ailith left Harold with Wulfhild, who was sewing in a corner by the light of two horn lanterns, and went outside to visit the privy. Ten paces later she stopped and stared, her eyes widening.

A large, dappled-grey horse was trampling her carefully tended winter cabbages. Now and then it lowered its head and snatched at an outer leaf with powerful yellow teeth. Where on earth had it come from? It was wearing a leather headstall from which trailed a frayed length of rope, and there were faint saddle marks on its back. Iron shoes glinted as it pawed the soil, deliberately trying to uproot one of her cabbages. Then it paused from its endeavours to urinate. Ailith's stare was drawn in reluctant fascination to its elongated penis, and the equipment behind. It was a stallion, entire in every way. In her knowledge, the only male horses that kept their testicles were either for breeding or for war. None of her neighbours owned such a beast, therefore it must belong to a stranger, and the only strangers in the city were Normans.

The grey ripped one of her plants out of the ground and tossed it up and down in its mouth. Ailith's temper sparked, replacing astonishment. Norman-owned or not, she was not about to stand here like a ninny and watch the beast destroy her winter vegetables. Marching into the storeroom, she grabbed Sigrid's birch besom from the corner and stalked back outside to do battle.

'Shoo, go away!' Waving the broom, she advanced on the stallion. It regarded her with pricked ears and its jaws circled, loudly crunching her cabbage leaves.

'Shoo!' Ailith waved the broom more vigorously. The horse skittered sideways and trampled two of her young leeks. Its hind hooves sank into the soft earth and clods of soil flew everywhere as it gouged itself free and friskily bucked.

Ailith was on the verge of abandoning the besom in favour of a Dane axe from Goldwin's forge when a piercing whistle and a masculine shout caused the horse to abandon its frolics. Nickering joyfully, it trotted away down the garth, its crest arched and its tail foaming high.

Ailith stared at the ruin of her garden, at a full year's work gone to waste. She felt like crying, but when her eyes did fill, the tears were of blazing fury. Tightening her grasp on the broom, she marched down the garth, determined that she would have reparation even if the culprit was the Norman Duke himself.

In her orchard, a man had caught the stallion's rope and while tethering him to a pear tree, was remonstrating with the animal in French. Ailith had learned a smattering of the language from Felice, but the Norman was speaking too quickly for her to understand most of what he said. He was long-limbed and auburn-haired with clean, strong bones. There was a sword at his hip and a knife in his belt. He wore a quilted gambeson over his tunic, but that was probably as much for warmth as military protection. Blue trousers, grey leg-bindings and ankle-high boots fastened with a strap and leather toggle kept his lower limbs warm.

As if sensing her scrutiny, he suddenly raised his head and she in her turn was rapidly appraised by a pair of shrewd eyes the striated green of moss-agates.

'Your horse,' Ailith said in laborious French. 'He has destroyed my garden.' She gestured over her shoulder. His reply was too rapid and she shook her head. 'Speak more slowly, I do not understand.'

'I am sorry. He has learned how to untie his rope.' He spread his hands in a disarming gesture. There was an apologetic half-smile on his lips, but she was determined not to let it sway her unless it was accompanied by hard proof.

'And he likes cabbages,' she said, returning his stare unflinchingly.

'Cabbages?' The man's eyebrows rose in alarm. 'He has been eating cabbages? How many?' His glance flickered to the horse with concern and he set one hand on its flank. The stallion swung his head and gave his master a loving nudge.

Ailith shrugged. It was beyond her French to say that the horse seemed to have sampled indiscriminately without recourse to any one plant. 'Come and see for yourself,' she invited.

He followed her through the garth to her desecrated vegetable plot. His left hand rested lightly on the semi-circle of his sword hilt, and although she knew it must surely be from habit, she still felt uneasy. He was so tall, so fluid of movement. Her brothers were tall too, but their tread was bear-like, and this Norman walked as lightly as a cat.

'See,' she spread her arm to encompass the devastation. 'My leeks too.'

He folded his arms and stood with his legs apart, a frown knitting his brows. 'Sleipnir adores cabbages.' He paused, seeking for easy words to help her understand. 'Horses, they should not eat such things, but he does not care. He had very bad colic in Winchester when he raided a market stall. I was worried that he would die – if he did I would be unable to replace him.'

Ailith had picked up enough of the gist to be further angered. 'I lost my brothers to your butchery at Hastings!' she snapped. 'They were irreplaceable too. Do you think I care about your stupid horse?'

He unfolded his arms. She saw him inhale to speak and then suddenly think the better of it. Instead he rummaged in the pouch at his belt, and withdrew a handful of small silver coins. 'Will this pay for the damage?'

She wanted to dash them to the ground at his feet and

screech that she would not touch money that had been dipped in blood. Quivering, she fought off the impulse. It was what she wanted, wasn't it? Compensation? 'For the damage to my garden, yes,' she muttered gracelessly and took the silver from him. All fingers and thumbs, she struggled to place it in her own small pouch.

He watched her in silence. After a time he said gently, 'I too suffered losses at the great battle. Many good friends I will not see again in this life . . . including his former owner.' He looked over his shoulder at the horse.

Ailith made to return to the house.

'No, wait, please.'

Against her better judgement, the urgency in his voice made her turn round.

He grimaced and pinched the end of his fine, straight nose.' I am not the most tactful of men,' he said. 'I offer you a full apology for the damage my horse has caused.'

Ailith nodded stiffly. 'It is accepted,' she replied, her tone cold and far from gracious.

'My name is Rolf de Brize-sur-Risle,' he continued. 'Aubert de Remy is my friend and I am billeted with him for the moment. From what he has told me, you must be Ailith, and your husband is a master armourer?'

Ailith did not understand all that he had said, but she understood enough to be much taken aback that he should know who she and Goldwin were. It was an uncomfortable thought that a Norman stranger should own such knowledge. Mutely she nodded.

The Norman drew the knife from his belt and showed it to her. 'Aubert asked your husband to make this for me. It is the best work I have ever seen. Aubert says that he made armour for Harold Godwinson himself.' His attention suddenly cut towards the house.' And this is your husband coming now?'

Ailith turned and saw Goldwin moving stiffly towards them.

'Yes,' she said, 'this is my husband. He speaks no French at all.'

Goldwin reached them and Ailith saw his gaze travel grimly

over the ruined vegetable garden before coming to rest on the powerful grey horse tied to the pear tree. 'He has made recompense,' she said quickly. 'His name is Rolf de Brize-sur-Risle, and he's a friend of Aubert's.' Hastily she explained the rest of the situation and finished by saying that the Norman had praised Goldwin's craftsmanship. 'You made his knife apparently.'

Goldwin looked the handsome stranger up and down, then fixed his eyes on the scramaseax in the man's hand. 'And where is Aubert now?'

Ailith translated, and the Norman shrugged. 'He should be here soon. I think he is visiting his wife. She is great with child.' He sheathed the knife. 'Duke William has need of craftsmen. It may well be that Aubert and I could put some useful business your way.'

Goldwin drew himself up as Ailith explained what she believed Rolf had said. 'Norman business?' he growled.

'Tell him that a man has to eat.'

'I will tell him nothing. He will come to his own decision,' Ailith said stiffly.

Rolf de Brize chewed his lip for a moment, then nodded. 'I will visit another time,' he said. 'I have to treat my horse for the colic.' A grimace crossed his face. Inclining his head to both Ailith and Goldwin, he turned away.

He was untying the grey from the tree when Aubert came walking up the garth, his mobile features pensive. Obviously, Ailith thought, he had heard voices and decided to investigate. Aubert paused to speak briefly to the other Norman. De Brize replied, shrugged, and with a salute, led his horse away.

Goldwin permitted Aubert to continue up the garth, waiting until there were only feet between them.

The Norman cleared his throat and attempted a smile. 'It is good to see you, Goldwin,' he said, and extended his right hand in friendship. 'I heard you were wounded at the battle for the north.'

Goldwin ignored the gesture. 'You are *nithing*,' he said in a soft, contemptuous voice. It was the worst insult that an

Englishman could use to another, and such was its power, that it was known and used in Normandy too.

Aubert blenched. 'Listen, I want to tell you that I never intended . . .'

His words fell on deaf ears. Goldwin looked straight through him, then turned his back and walked away. 'Come, Ailith,' he commanded.

She dared not defy him. With a single, frightened glance at Aubert's shocked face, she followed Goldwin into the house, leaving Aubert standing alone amid the ruins of her vegetable plot.

'I'll find custom without his help,' Goldwin muttered through his teeth as Wulfhild served them with bacon pottage and Ailith unlaced her bodice to feed the baby. 'He lied to us, betrayed our trust. God's eyes, I'd rather do business with that red-haired horse-warrior than I would with Aubert de Remy. Wine-merchant, hah! To think of all the occasions he sat at our board listening to our conversation, and all the time he was gleaning information for William of Normandy. And then he has the gall to expect me to remain his friend!'

'I believe he is sorry,' Ailith murmured, trying to be fair. 'Perhaps he had no choice.' Harold did not want to wake up. She blew gently on his face. He grimaced, half-opened his eyes, took one attempt at her nipple, enough to make her milk drip, then returned to sleep. He had scarcely fed all day, indeed had scarcely woken up. She laid the palm of her hand against his little body, but he did not appear to have a fever. Perhaps in the morning she would ask Hulda to have a look at him.

'He can be as sorry as he likes,' Goldwin grunted. 'I have called him *nithing* and *nithing* he will remain. And from now on, you will have no more ado with that wife of his either.'

Ailith bit her lip in dismay. 'Aubert used you once,' she said. 'Now it is your turn to use him. He can find clients for you, rich Normans. Surely it is foolish to turn your back on what he can offer.'

'No!' Goldwin snapped. 'I will hear no more on the subject. Let that be an end to it!'

Ailith bowed her head over the baby and swallowed her exasperation. She knew Goldwin could be a stubborn ass when the mood was upon him, and trying to make him change his mind would only cause him to dig in his heels as hard as he could to the detriment of all common sense. She would hold her tongue today in the interests of using it tomorrow.

'I did not expect to find him so altered.' Aubert hunched over the desultory fire burning in the central hearth and rubbed his hands together. 'So bitter and angry when before he was so good-humoured and steady.'

'There have been a few changes since then,' Rolf observed wryly, glancing up from the piece of harness he was repairing. 'And he must have his pride. Don't worry about it, I'll bring him round.'

Aubert threw a kindling twig at him. 'How, by letting your destrier trample his garden?' he said acidly.

'The garden is his wife's domain, and her temper calmed when I spoke her fair and sweetened my words with a recompense of silver.' Rolf chuckled. 'If you thought her husband was angry, you should have seen her when I arrived in their garth. Dear Jesu, she was chasing Sleipnir with a besom, and she looked magnificent! I thought for a moment she was going to set about me as well. I half-wish she had,' he added wistfully.

Aubert glanced at him sharply. 'Duke William says that he will hang any soldier caught molesting the Londoners' women, and he will make no exception for rank.'

'Peace, Aubert, I did but jest,' Rolf said with amused irritation. 'I thought she was handsome, but I was admiring her the way I would admire a horse.'

'You mean you wondered what she was like to ride?' Aubert said archly.

Rolf shrugged. 'It went no further than a mild curiosity. I've no desire to fetch up a gelding. There are mares aplenty to

mount in London without me chasing one that is not for sale.'
Finished with the harness, he set it to one side. Not that he
intended scouring London for a woman. He would happen on
one soon enough, as he had happened on Gifu in Dover and
Milburga in Winchester. He poured wine from the nearby
pitcher into his cup. Although his face betrayed nothing to
Aubert, the thought of Ailith was still on his mind. He was
remembering her assaulting Sleipnir with the besom. The way
her eyes had flashed, the gleam of her blond braids, the thrust of
her jaw. Thinking back now, she reminded him of the huscarl
who had died beside him on Senlac field. The warrior's axe lay
among his baggage. Rolf had slicked it with oil and wrapped it
in waxed linen to prevent the head from rusting. When the time
came to claim his lands, he would hang the weapon on the wall
of his new home as a trophy and a talisman.

Outside the door, a dog barked loudly in warning, and as
Rolf and Aubert reached instinctively for their weapons, Rolf's
watchman entered the house, followed by a young man dressed
in a plain tunic and cloak. He proved to be a lay worker from
St Aethelburga's whom the abbess had sent with a message for
Aubert.

'Your lady wife has begun her labour. The Abbess asks that
you come with all haste.'

'Is there something wrong?' Aubert sheathed his knife and
reached for his cloak.

'I do not know, sir. The Abbess just said I was to fetch
you.' The young man sniffed, sniffed again, and drew his cuff
across his nose. His hands were red with cold.

'God grant you a healthy wife and child,' Rolf said as
Aubert took his sword and went to the door which showed a
narrow rectangle of late afternoon dusk. 'It would be auspi-
cious if Felice were to be delivered on the day of our Duke's
crowning.'

Aubert smiled, but the gesture was no more than a mean-
ingless expansion of his lips as he ducked out into the cold.

Rolf thought that he had never seen the merchant look so
worried. He tried to recall if he had been similarly distressed

over Arlette when she had borne their first child, a stillborn son. He thought not, but then he had been able to immerse himself in the stud. He realised guiltily that since leaving Normandy, Arlette and Gisele had scarcely crossed his mind. Sometimes when he had been cold and wet and hungry on the circuitous six-week march from Hastings to London, he had remembered the roaring fire in the hearth at Brize-sur-Risle, the dainty glazed cups full of mulled cider, Arlette's little curd cakes that were gone in one bite and tasted like heaven, the minstrel plucking his crwth and singing of glory. On those occasions, he had been seized by nostalgia, but never home-sickness, and his feelings were for Brize-sur-Risle in its entirety, not his slender, silver-haired wife.

When he returned to Normandy, he would take her an English tapestry for their chamber wall and some new table-ware for the dais. That was sure to please her. Having dealt with his guilt to his own satisfaction, Rolf put Arlette from his thoughts.

CHAPTER 15

For nine months, sleeping and waking, Felice had lived with fear. Sometimes it affected her but mildly, a nagging anxiety she could almost forget. On other occasions it became pure terror that winkled her out from every crevice in which she tried to hide. Now, with each contraction it pounced on her, mauled her until she screamed with terror and pain, then let her go. But she knew that in the end, she would be devoured.

'Make it go away!' she wept to the nuns and frantically clutched her eaglestone. 'Oh please make it go away! Holy Mary, Blessed Virgin, help me!'

The nuns did their utmost to soothe her. They rubbed her swollen belly with herbal oils, they loosened her hair so that no knots would bind the babe in her womb. They gave her a calming tisane to drink, but she was so tense that it had no visible effect. The Abbess, a woman who was as pragmatic as she was compassionate, sent for Aubert and took Felice to task.

'You must calm yourself,' she said sternly. 'The bag of water has not yet broken, and when it does, you will need your strength to push.'

'*Ave Maria, gratia plenia,*' Felice whispered. Her brown gaze sought the aumbry and pleaded with the plaster statue of the Virgin presiding over her ordeal. Beneath her thighs the thick layer of bedstraw chafed her skin. The nuns had put it there the previous night when she had complained of low back ache. They said that it was to absorb the blood and fluids which would leak from her body as labour progressed. Ever since then, a vision of her life drip-dripping away had whetted the teeth of the predatory fear. She was going to die, she knew it. And when she was dead, one of the nuns would take a knife and rip open her belly to see if they could save her child.

Aubert arrived and was ushered into the birthing chamber. Usually men were allowed nowhere near such a sanctum, but the nuns were becoming desperate. Felice's screams had been heard throughout the convent until she had lost her voice.

'Aubert!' Felice pushed herself up on the mound of pillows. 'Aubert, I'm dying, aren't I? That's why they've sent for you!'

Removing his cloak and cap, Aubert sat on the bed and took her in his arms. 'If you were dying, they would have sent for a priest first,' he reassured. 'They summoned me because the Abbess thought it was the only way to calm you down.'

'But it hurts so! I don't like it, and it's getting worse!' Felice quivered in his embrace. The fierceness of another contraction tore through her loins and she gripped him, digging her nails into the soft wool of his tunic. 'I'm so frightened!' she gasped.

Aubert pulled a face. 'So am I when I see you like this. Felice, beloved, you cannot go into a battle believing that you will lose it. How would we have fared if Duke William had given up at Hastings? You must fight. Do as the nuns tell you, they are wise. I'll be here, I promise – if not beside you, then right outside the door.' He kissed her temple and her cheek, the trembling corner of her mouth.

As if from a great distance Felice heard his words. The strength of his arms around her gave them emphasis and a little of the darkness cleared from her mind. 'Help me, Aubert,' she whispered. 'Dear Jesu, help me.'

With Harold cradled in one arm, a pitcher of mead in the other, Ailith went down to the forge. She was worried about the baby. Although his eyes were open, they were dull, and every time he expelled air from his lungs, it was with a wheezy little grunt. Nor had he fed that morning and her breasts were bulging with the discomfort of excess milk. Hulda had promised to come and look at him, but not until later in the day because she was attending a birth.

Ailith heard the sound of Goldwin's gruff laughter. She pushed open the forge door with her shoulder and her husband turned his head when he saw her enter. So did the tall, red-haired Norman Rolf de Brize. Ailith felt a stab of irritation, and a queasy sensation only just short of fear turned within her stomach. De Brize inclined his head. He was leaning against Goldwin's workbench, watching Goldwin fashion mail rivets from coils of iron wire.

'Look, Aili, I've acquired a new apprentice,' Goldwin jerked his head at Rolf.

She wondered how the Norman had succeeded in worming his way into Goldwin's good auspices so rapidly. The man did not even speak English, and Goldwin's French was atrocious. She inclined her head stiffly to de Brize and set the pitcher of ale down on the workbench. 'I am sorry, we have no wine,' she said without really meaning it.

'No matter, I'm learning to like ale,' the Norman replied with a smile. 'Your husband has sold me a mail coif and promised me a new helm.'

Here, in the small, cramped forge, the Norman's vigour was almost indecent. Ailith moved closer to Goldwin, seeking sanctuary. 'Norman business?' she said a trifle sarcastically to her husband. 'A coif and a helm?'

Goldwin cleared his throat and his complexion darkened. 'I would have been stupid not to accept what he offered me for my services. I made the coif for a Saxon thegn who never returned from Stamford Bridge. It's been lying in the workshop for two months now; the Norman is welcome to it. I thought that you wanted me to collaborate?'

Ailith glanced at de Brize from beneath lowered lids. He was watching her with scarcely veiled amusement in his greenish eyes. 'I do,' she said. 'I was just surprised, that's all.' She turned to leave, but Goldwin stopped her and lifted the swaddled baby out of her arms.

'This is my son,' he said proudly to Rolf. 'One day all this will be his. I will teach him everything that I know, and he will become the greatest weapon smith in England.'

Reluctantly Ailith translated Goldwin's boast. Harold wailed weakly and at the sound of his cry, milk began to leak from her overflowing breasts and stain her gown. She saw de Brize stare, and the forge became even smaller so that there was no room for Goldwin or the baby in its confines, just herself and the red-haired Norman. Her breathing quickened, her heart thumped in panic against her ribs and she knew that if she did not escape, she would be crushed. Snatching the baby from Goldwin's arms, she muttered an excuse about burning stew and fled the forge.

The men looked at each other and both of them suddenly smiled in rueful, masculine companionship. 'Women!' snorted Goldwin, shaking his head.

Felice sat upon the birthing stool, her legs splayed, her face contorted in agony as she strove to push the baby from her womb into the world. For two full days she had been in labour, but it was only in the last few hours that the bag of water had broken and the baby had begun to descend down the birth passage. The pain had been relentless, but she was so exhausted now that she was beyond fear or caring. 'I don't want to die,' had become 'Let me die, let me have peace!'

'Push!' cried Sister Winfred fiercely. Before becoming a nun, she had borne six children of her own and had the most experience of midwifery. 'Your womb is tiring. You must push for your life, and the life of your child!'

'I can't!' Felice sobbed, then cried out sharply as the nun slapped her.

'Of course you can. Would you deny your husband his son!'

Felice bit her lip and closed her eyes.

'Come now, you are almost there, you must not give up!'

Felice had always prided herself on her indispensable skills as a wife, and one of those skills was producing a living child. If Ailith could do it, then so could she. Drawing a deep breath, she bore down.

For another hour Felice struggled to deliver her child, and at last, Sister Winfred cried that the head was there, that one more effort would see the baby born. Hearing the hope in the nun's voice, Felice clenched her teeth and bore down with the last of her strength. An infant's indignant wail filled the room.

'Just listen to the lungs on him!' declared Sister Winfred, smiling broadly as she lifted a thrashing, bawling baby from between his mother's bloody thighs.

'A boy!' Felice panted triumphantly, and raised herself against the bolster to look at him. 'I knew it would be a boy! Let me hold him!'

Smiling broadly, Sister Winfred cut the cord, wrapped the child in a towel and gave him to his mother. Then she took another towel to staunch the blood that was trickling from Felice's womb. The linen reddened all too rapidly. A frowning Sister Winfred summoned another nun to help her and sent a third to fetch the grains of black rye from the infirmary.

Ailith stared numbly at the swaddled little body lying on her bed. The baby's forehead glistened where the priest had anointed it with holy oil. His eyes were closed and he looked as though he were only asleep. Two hours ago he had ceased to breathe and time for Ailith had stopped too. She would not allow him to be dead. If she prayed hard enough for a miracle perhaps he would open his eyes and look at her. Had not Jesus restored Lazarus to life?

She touched the baby's cold, soft skin. 'Harold,' she whispered softly, 'Harold.'

'Aili, he is gone, come away.'

She felt Goldwin's hand on her shoulder and heard the hoarse grief in his voice. He had been beside her when Harold died. In her mind she could still hear the drawn-out groan of anguish he had uttered and see the despair in his eyes. Initially, she too had wept and wailed, clinging to Goldwin, but after the first storm had passed, she had discovered the welcome numbness of disbelief. There was still milk in her breasts and fresh swaddling bands warming near the fire. Her baby was only sleeping.

'I cannot leave him,' she said distantly without looking round. 'What if he wakes up and I am not here?'

'He is not going to wake up ever again.' Goldwin's voice cracked. 'Jesu, Aili, don't you see?' He tried to draw her away from the bed, but she resisted him.

'I am his mother, I will not yield him to the soil!' she said determinedly. 'Go if you must, but I will sit here until he rouses.'

'Aili, he's dead!'

The word rang brutally around the room and threatened her numb cocoon. She stared obdurately at the baby's still form and gripped her hands together.

'I cannot bear it!' Goldwin choked and flung out of the room. She heard him descending the loft ladder, his voice downstairs, harsh with grief, and then silence. She did not know for how long she sat. For her, like Harold, time had no meaning. Sigrid brought her a bowl of gruel and replenished the small portable brazier with fresh lumps of charcoal.

Hulda came visiting and removed the bowl of gruel, now cold, from the coffer. She sat beside Ailith for a long time, holding her hand, saying nothing, but at last she gently broached the subject of Harold's burial.

'But he's not dead.' Ailith's voice quavered.

'No-one who lives in the love of our dear Lord Jesus Christ is ever dead,' Hulda said gently, 'but he has no need of his earthly body. Ailith, you have to let him go. You have a husband who is as sorely wounded and frightened as you. Seek him out. Take comfort in each other.'

'I do not know where he is.'

'When he returns then. I will sit with you in vigil until he comes.'

Hulda's firm, sensible tone, the compassion in her eyes, reached across the barrier of Ailith's defensive numbness. And when Hulda said softly, with tears in her old eyes, 'Poor little mite,' Ailith's composure shattered, and she flung herself down on the bed beside the dead baby and wept and wept.

Hulda let her cry, knowing it was the best thing she could

do, and tip-toed to the loft opening to tell Wulfhild to find Goldwin.

Rolf's best tunic had emerged somewhat crumpled from his baggage, but it did not matter. Only the all-important gold-embroidered hem would show beneath his quilted gambeson and mail shirt. He dragged a comb through his hair, cupped his jaw to satisfy himself that he had made a smooth enough job of shaving his stubble, and tucking his helm under his arm, went outside to his horse.

Aubert was already mounted and waiting, but then the merchant had not had to spend time donning armour and weapons. Indeed, Rolf knew that Aubert had not been to bed at all, and apart from a change of tunic and a rapid sprucing, had made very little preparation for the coronation of Duke William at Westminster.

Aubert's wife had borne him a son. Apparently the child was healthy enough, but Felice had been brought to the brink of death by heavy bleeding at the time of the birth. Aubert had told Rolf that as soon as he had witnessed the crowning, he intended returning to St Aethelburga's to watch over his wife and newborn heir, for whom the nuns were seeking a wet nurse.

Rolf mounted Sleipnir. The grey had been groomed to perfection. Although there was no shine on his thick winter coat, it was whiter than the frost which had thickened overnight, and his full tail glittered like spume from a waterfall. Ears pricked, he sidled restively, eager to be away. A groom handed up Rolf's banner. Attached to a spear, a raven spread its black wings on a crimson field. He had found it on Hastings field the day before they marched away. The fact that it had survived unplundered for several days, together with the exquisite embroidery, had made him desire it for his own. The Dane axe would hang on the wall of his English hall and the raven banner would become his emblem.

Together he, Aubert, and their small entourage, rode out onto the Westminster road. Already a procession of people,

English and Norman, were heading towards the abbey in order to witness the coronation of the new king.

Rolf was riding past the armourer's dwelling when the older maidservant emerged from the garth and stood at the side of the road. Her hands were set in fists upon her meaty hip bones and there was an anxious expression on her face. Her gaze fell upon Rolf and Aubert. Tightening her lips, she took a step backwards into the stiff silver grass on the verge as if to avoid being contaminated by their proximity. Rolf glanced at her curiously. He did not think that she was standing in the road for the purpose of gawping at the people on their way to the abbey.

She hesitated, then arriving at a sudden decision, addressed Rolf. Rolf knew that the woman must be aware that he spoke no English. Obviously she wanted to talk to Aubert, but since her master had declared the merchant *nithing*, she could not approach him directly. Playing along, Rolf looked over his shoulder at Aubert and raised his brows.

'She asks if either of us has seen Master Goldwin,' Aubert said neutrally. 'She thought perhaps he had come this way since he is not in his forge.'

'No,' Rolf said. 'Last time I saw him was yesterday morn in his workshop. Is there something wrong?'

She shook her head at Aubert's translation and made to return to the house.

'Wait,' Aubert called to her. 'Will you tell your mistress that Felice bore me a son in the early hours of this morning.'

Wulfhild gave him a glittering look compounded of unshed tears and loathing. 'I will tell her nothing,' she said, and turned her back.

Rolf whistled softly through his teeth and urged Sleipnir forward on the road. Aubert followed, his dejection tangible and tinged with anger. 'No more,' he vowed stiffly. 'I will try no more.'

Goldwin tilted the cup against his lips and in a single, angry gulp, drained the mead remaining in it. He had no appreciation for the honey-sweetness of the brew; he wanted only to buy oblivion from thinking. But the more mead he drank, the less control he had over his thoughts. They kept dragging him back to the lifeless little form on the bed. All the hopes that Goldwin had begun to nurture were mocked. He would never guide a small hand upon a blacksmith's hammer or watch a curly head crouch over a pair of bellows at the forge. It was all dust, his dreams as dead as the swaddled baby over whom Ailith was keeping such a fierce vigil.

He knew that he should be with her now, but he did not think that he could shoulder the burden of her grief on top of his own. Well-meaning neighbours would visit and tell them that they would have other sons in the fullness of time, but Goldwin was afraid that the injury he had sustained at Stamford Bridge had rendered him impotent. Not once since his return from the battle had his manhood risen and stiffened with desire. Even when his thoughts strayed down erotic paths, his organ remained limp and unresponding. Perhaps he ought to ask Hulda for one of her remedies; but what good were her simples when she had been unable to save his son?

The alehouse was becoming crowded with Englishmen seeking refreshment and courage on their way to bear witness to the coronation of the new Norman King at Westminster. It had not occurred to Goldwin in his grief that this was the day that Duke William was to be crowned, but he realised it now as another crowd of men surged into the alehouse and demanded a pitcher of mead from the harassed landlord.

Vacating his trestle, Goldwin stumbled outside. A conroi of Norman soldiers rode past, stirrup to stirrup. Goldwin scowled at the arrogant manner with which they forced themselves a path, but at the same time, his armourer's eye admired the quality of their mail and weapons.

More soldiers followed, and then a haughty-looking priest riding beside a magnificently clad Norman upon a superb golden-red stallion. The nobleman's hair was dark and thick, his features rugged and crude. It was a face that had been used time and time again to batter other men beneath its owner's will, and Goldwin realised that he must be looking upon the great William of Normandy himself. His gut churned with revulsion while his mind acknowledged that here was a power which would dominate all others and bring them subservient to the Conqueror's will.

The road home to Ailith was filled with the glitter and pomp of the conquering Norman army. The other drinkers were all emerging from the alehouse to watch the procession ride past.

'God curse him,' Goldwin heard someone mutter softly from behind. These sentiments echoed Goldwin's own, but he was enough of a realist to know that there was no Englishman who for one moment could match the abilities of the Norman Duke.

Goldwin was borne along with the tide towards the abbey, and after a brief struggle of body and conscience, he let his feet take the path of least resistance.

When Duke William entered the abbey, Goldwin stood outside with the crowd of English, waiting for the roar of assent which would announce that the crown had been placed irrevocably on a Norman head by an English prelate. The Duke's soldiers patrolled the crowd, their eyes hostile and uneasy. The Saxon who had uttered the curse outside the alehouse stood close to Goldwin, his legs planted apart and a belligerent expression on his face.

'Should be an Englishman who sits on England's throne,' he muttered, and there were growls of assent from his companions. Goldwin started to feel hemmed in and sick from the quantity of mead he had consumed. Two Normans halted their destriers close to him and spoke to each other rapidly in French. One man was heavily mailed and carried a stout iron mace with a flanged head. The other sat astride a dappled stallion and was more lightly armed, although his equipment was of no less calibre. The soldiers finished their conversation and the one on the dappled horse made to ride on. Then, by chance, his eye caught Goldwin's, and with a smile of greeting, he raised his hand.

Goldwin nodded brusquely at Rolf de Brize and turned

aside. Laughing with the man in the privacy of the forge was one matter, but publicly acknowledging him in this volatile situation was quite another. To Goldwin's horror, de Brize pursued him through the crowd, and when Goldwin would not heed him, shouted out in very rough English, 'Saxon, you are sought at home!'

Reluctantly Goldwin turned round. He knew that the other people in the crowd were watching him. 'I know!' he snapped. 'Go away and leave me alone!'

'Aye, Norman pig, go home!' spat the Saxon from the ale-house. 'Crawl back to your French sty!'

De Brize could not possibly have understood the rapid English, but the explicit tone made the sentiments all too obvious. The Norman gave the troublemaker a hard, contemptuous stare, and turned the grey around.

'Friendly with the bastards, are you?' the Saxon sneered, and the moment de Brize was gone, shoved Goldwin's shoulder.

'No, he's billeted close to us, that's all,' Goldwin responded. He was shoved again. Angrily he thrust the man away, the slow burn of anger kindling within him to a brighter flame. 'It is no concern of yours. I was the personal armourer of King Harold himself and my wife's brothers died on Hastings field. I'll not be insulted by a loud-mouthed empty brain such as you!'

The man raised his fist to strike Goldwin, but was diverted by the enormous shout of approbation that rippled outwards from the abbey. '*Fiat! Fiat! Long live King William!*' The first cries were in Norman French, but soon the English took up the cry in their own tongue.

Beside Goldwin, the Saxon lowered his fist, took a deep breath, and bellowed forth the English war chant from Hastings field. '*Ut! Ut! Ut!*' It was taken up by his companions and the contagion spread like fire. Goldwin knew beyond doubt that it was time to make his escape.

'*Ut! Ut! Ut!*'

The Norman soldiers spurred through the crowd, bludgeoning with maces, striking with shield and sword, creating panic. The small core of troublemakers were targeted and ridden down.

Goldwin tried to run, but there was nowhere to go, he was trapped on all sides. He saw the steaming nostrils of a bay stallion, the decorated chest band, the sharp glitter of a spear before it plunged. The Saxon who had originally started the chant made a bid to escape by slamming the heel of his hand into the middle of Goldwin's spine. Goldwin was catapulted forward, straight beneath the hooves of the oncoming warhorse. He saw the steel curves of the horseshoes and the short overlaps of white hair on the bay's pasterns. And then the weight striking down. Goldwin screamed and struggled until his voice was cut off by the blood filling his lungs. The horse plunged through the crowd. Panicking Saxons leaped or tripped over Goldwin in their efforts to flee. Time and again his body was kicked and buffeted, but he did not feel the blows. His last sight was the banner of a raven on a blood-crimson background raised in the distance above the multitude, his last thought that his turn had come to feed the carrion birds of the battlefield.

Order was swiftly restored, but not before the coronation ceremony had been marred by the violence of several English deaths and the burning of some nearby buildings by an overzealous conroi of Norman mercenaries. To placate the English, and because his own sense of justice dictated it, the new king had the bodies brought to a side room at the abbey, where their relatives could come and claim them, and he ordered recompense to be paid for the accidentally burned houses.

Rolf yielded ground to two Saxons who staggered past him into the abbey, bearing the weight of a bloodstained corpse between them. Although its face was badly battered, Rolf still recognised the armourer. He crossed himself, feeling a pang of shock and regret. He had liked the small, pugnacious Saxon from the little he had known of him.

It occurred to Rolf that someone would have to bring Master Goldwin home to his widow. She was but recently out of childbed and would not be permitted to enter a church until she had been cleansed. From what he knew of her background, she had no living relatives to perform the task for her. He wondered irritably where Aubert was. They had ridden to Westminster together, but had parted company shortly after their arrival. The onus, no matter how unpalatable, was upon himself to lay claim to the body.

Giving Sleipnir to one of his grooms, Rolf followed the Saxons into the abbey and waited until they had laid Goldwin on the floor beside the bodies of four others who had been trampled in the riot. More victims were still being brought in.

A middle-aged monk stooped over Goldwin and set about composing the dead man's limbs and straightening his garments.

'Do you speak Norman?'

The monk raised his head and fixed Rolf with a sad brown stare. 'I am Norman,' he said, 'although sometimes I come close to denying it.' His gaze wandered sorrowfully over the mounting toll of bodies. 'How can I assist you?'

'This man, the one you are attending — I know him and I will take the responsibility of bringing him home to his family.'

'You know him?' The brown gaze widened.

'He's a master armourer — my billet makes us neighbours.' Briefly Rolf explained why it would be best for him to claim the body and bear it home to the widow. 'It is such a waste,' he added with a grimace. 'He should have stayed at home, the fool.' Fishing in his pouch, he withdrew two silver coins. 'Will you have masses said for his soul? I would not want him to find a lesser place in heaven since he died unshriven.'

'It is not shriving or silver that places a man's worth in God's eyes,' the monk rebuked gently, but nevertheless he took the coins. 'If his heart and soul were true, he will find eternal peace. But I will have the prayers said. Take him now if you wish.'

With a heavy heart, Rolf lifted Goldwin's body, positioning it across his shoulders like a dead deer, and carried it outside to his horse.

Dusk was falling, the sky over the new abbey was a sultry pink hemmed by a border of ragged slate-blue. Out in her garth,

Ailith shivered and rubbed her arms, but had no desire to
return to the empty warmth of the house. She had fled its
cheerful nothingness for the starker ruins of her garden which
were far more in keeping with her state of mind.

Harold lay sewn in his shroud, his little body surrounded by
myriad flickering candles. Tomorrow he would be buried and
all her hopes and joys with him. Hulda had said that she would
stay, but had been called away to a difficult birth. There was still
no sign of Goldwin, and Ailith was growing anxious. She had
heard rumours of violence at the Norman Duke's coronation;
some of the onlookers had been trampled and killed.

At first she had convinced herself against the possibility of
Goldwin being among the crowd, but the darker it grew, the
more her confidence was shaken. *I will go and make sure that the
hens are properly shut in*, she thought. *And when I turn round he
will be there.*

But when she had checked the fowl run and for good measure had walked twice around her ruined vegetable plot, her
eyes met only the encroaching darkness of the empty path.
She walked slowly down to the road. Perhaps if she stared hard
enough, she would see Goldwin coming towards her with that
slow, halting gait of his.

At first the road was indeed empty. The Normans had
imposed a curfew on the city and it needed a very good excuse
to be abroad after dark without facing arrest and punishment.
The wind was bitterly cold and the puddles bore diamond patterns of ice. Ailith shivered and tightened her cloak around her
body. Her breasts ached. Hulda said that her milk would soon
begin to dry up, but that was no comfort now.

'Goldwin,' she muttered through teeth that were clenched
with cold, and stamped her feet. 'Oh, Goldwin, please hurry.'

And then, in the distance, she saw a man on foot leading a
silver-white horse, its colour intensified to a gleam by the dusk.
The man wore a frosting of chain mail and as he drew closer,
the waxen glimmer of the rising moon gave her enough light
to see that it was the knight Rolf de Brize.

Her stomach turned over. She wanted to run to him and at

the same time she wanted to run away and between the two found herself unable to move at all. He came on and she saw that his expression was sombre. The horse bore a burden over its saddle – an indeterminate dark mass. She could not tell what it was, for it was covered with the Norman's cloak. As he drew level with Ailith she cleared her throat.

'God save you, Sir Rolf, have you seen my husband?'

He halted the horse, his hand sliding up the bridle to the curb chain. 'I am sorry,' he said. 'There was nothing I could do except bring him home.'

Ailith's glance flickered to the mounded bundle on his saddle and her unease intensified to become stark fear. 'What do you mean, bring him home? Where's Goldwin, has he been injured?'

'I am sorry,' he repeated. 'Some of the crowd at the coronation ran wild and the Duk . . . King's knights had to charge to disperse them. Your husband was trampled . . . He is dead. I am sorry.'

Ailith stared glassily at him. The chill of the night seeped into her mind, numbing it. The words *trampled*, *dead*, and *sorry* were laid across the numbness in thicker cords of ice.

'Shall I bring him to the house?'

She stood aside and gestured him to enter the garth. Her composure was solid enough to walk upon, but she was trapped beneath it, screaming.

He tethered the horse to a tree and unfastened the bundle. Ailith saw the dark smears on the cloak that could only be blood. In silence she watched him heft the bundle and carry it into the house. It could not be Goldwin, she told herself. The Norman had made a mistake, it was someone else. She followed him within to tell him so, but it was too late. He had set his burden down on one of the sleeping benches along the far wall, and the cloak had slipped from the dead man's face. Ailith gazed upon her husband's battered nose and mouth, the dead eyes and blood-caked hair. The ice encasing her thickened.

Wulfhild let out an enormous wail, and then stifled it with her fist. Sigrid, who had been kneeling in a candlelit corner, came forward. 'Master Goldwin,' she whispered, and her eyes flew from the body, to Rolf, to Ailith.

'Go and fetch the priest, girl,' Rolf commanded.

She looked at him blankly.

'Bringeth thu y preost,' he said in mangled English.

Sigrid grabbed her cloak from a peg on the wall and hurried out, a frightened look on her face and tears filling her eyes.

'It is too much,' Ailith said in a distant voice and knelt at Goldwin's side. 'My brothers, my baby, my husband. What more is there to take?' She stared up at the Norman, but he had no answer for her. A look of appalled comprehension dawned on his face and his eyes went to the corner where her baby lay, surrounded by lighted candles on his last night above ground.

'Christ have mercy, I did not know.' He crossed himself.

'I do not need your pity,' Ailith said, as she felt her frozen shell begin to crack under the pressure of his scrutiny. 'I want you to leave.' She touched Goldwin's cold, rigid hand.

Rolf de Brize remained where he was. Although Ailith did not look up at his face, she could see the firm stance of his legs. Her eyes fixed upon the toggles of rolled leather that fastened his nearest boot, upon the herringbone pattern on his twill cross-garters. She set her jaw. 'Please go.'

For a moment longer he held his ground. Then he said a third time, 'I am sorry,' and walked away.

The crack froze over and Ailith sank back beneath the protecting layers of ice, but with her she brought a shard of disappointment that he had not ignored her plea and remained to bring her kicking and screaming to the surface.

CHAPTER 16

In the hour before dawn, Rolf ceased tossing and turning on his pallet by the fire and conceding that sleep was impossible, rose to start his day. Tomorrow, he promised himself, he would find a woman to keep his blankets warm. That always helped.

Apart from his grooms and retainers, he was alone. Aubert had elected to spend the night at St Aethelburga's guest house with his wife and the new baby. Rolf grimaced. Small wonder that the armourer's maid had rebuffed Aubert's tidings of Felice's safe delivery yester morn.

Rolf broke his fast on a heel of bread dipped in a bowl of thick gruel, his mind dwelling on the memory of Ailith's face and the way she had said *'My brothers, my baby, my husband. What more is there to take?'* The image was too powerful and disturbing to dismiss and unsettled him into restless motion.

Collecting a horn lantern from the storeroom, he went to the stables and the makeshift shelters that had been hastily erected to house the extra horses. Sleipnir was dozing, a rug thrown over his back, but when he saw Rolf, he nickered a greeting and rapidly perked up. The man fussed the horse for a while, scratching the whiskery jaw, rubbing the questing muzzle before setting to work with the grooming tools. As Rolf worked, a memory came to him and made nothing of the years between himself as a ten-year-old boy, and the man of seven and twenty working on the thick silver hide of an Iberian warhorse.

It was autumn at Brize-sur-Risle, a day of dripping mist, the leaves drooping on the trees in tints of burnt orange, ochre, and weld-yellow, spider webs festooning the bramble bushes in clear, sprang-work designs. The surface of the great river was veiled in curling tendrils of its own breath, and every sound was muffled to grey distance.

It was the day they brought his father home across his horse.

Rolf could remember his mother growing ever more agitated as she waited for her husband to return from hunting a stray mare and foal in the forests on the south side of their estate. She had alternated between railing at her husband for being the greatest fool on God's earth, and praying aloud, that he would be safely restored to her. When he was not home by a drizzling, smoky dusk, she had flung on her cloak, and auburn hair uncovered, torch held high, had climbed to the wall walk as if her eyes could pierce the murk and guide him home.

One of the search parties had brought him in.

His horse had shied and thrown him against a tree. That he was not dead was due entirely to luck and the hardness of his skull. As it was, he was out of his wits for a full three days. Rolf had never forgotten the sound of his mother's high-pitched wail as her lord was brought to her across his saddle, had never forgotten the swoop of dread in his own gut. He should never have left the Saxon woman alone last night.

With a hiss of irritation, he finished grooming Sleipnir and went outside. Tiny flakes of snow starred the wind, and the ground underfoot was brittle and white. He shivered and slapped his arms. His cloak was still next door at the armourer's house. Blood-smeared it might be, but it was also double-lined and trimmed with coney fur. Self-interest said that he should fetch it before he froze to death. Besides, it was an expensive garment. Conscience said that he should make sure that the widow was all right.

By the light of a rush dip in the storeroom, he found the older maid mixing batter to make griddle cakes. She let out a scream when she saw Rolf, then clapped her hand to her mouth and stared at him wide-eyed.

He told her in halting English that he had come for his cloak, and with a nod, she wiped her hands on her apron and hurried to fetch it.

'Where is your mistress?' he asked when she handed him the garment.

The woman pointed outside. 'The privy,' she said.

Rolf had walked past the privy and knew that Ailith was not there. The withy screen surrounding the hole in the ground only came a little above waist height, and he would have seen her. Explaining this to the maid, however, was beyond him. He thanked her and left. His fingers discovered a damp patch on the cloak. In the strengthening light he saw that the blood had been cleaned away – or most of it. A stubborn trace still remained. He swept the garment around his shoulders and took the fastening pin from his pouch.

Of their own will, his feet took him not back down the garth past the destroyed vegetable garden, but towards the forge where only two days ago he had shared ale with the dead man and watched him work his magic to make a living thing out of an inanimate piece of metal. As he drew closer, he saw a light glimmering through a gap in the hide window covering, and heard a voice whimpering softly in grief.

It was her, he knew it was, and his scalp prickled at the emotions the sound raised in him. He halted in mid-step, deliberating whether to advance or retreat. *My brothers, my baby, my husband.* The words came back to him as they had done all through a sleepless night.

He pushed the workshop door open and stepped quietly inside. The air still bore a residue of heat from the forge, although the fire had died on the same day as its owner. She was leaning against the bench. Her right hand held an unfinished scramaseax blade at a cutting angle to the wrist of her left, and in contrast to yesterday's composure, her face was tear-wrecked and wild. She had looked up at the sound of his entry, and now, her eyes upon him and her breath shuddering, she forced the knife into her flesh.

'No!' Rolf roared and strode across the room. She tried to

run from him, but he was too fast and caught her against the heavy brick side of the forge. She was tall for a woman, and strong. He was surprised by her strength as he tried to disarm her. Thigh braced against thigh they struggled, both of them becoming smeared with the blood that was trickling down Ailith's wrist. At last Rolf succeeded in taking a grip on the knife himself, and with a wrench and a twist, tore it from her hand and flung it across the room.

'Let me be!' Ailith screeched. 'Leave me alone, I want to die and be with Goldwin and my baby!' She struck at him furiously. Rolf seized her wrists to make her stop, and at the same time he squeezed her left hard to control the bleeding.

'If you kill yourself, you will go to hell and never see them again!' he said brutally. 'The priests won't bury you in hallowed ground either. You would probably fetch up in the town ditch!'

For a moment longer she struggled, and then the fight went out of her and she slumped against him as if she were boneless. The sound of her noisy weeping filled the forge.

'I have nothing to live for,' she sobbed into his cloak.

Rolf was completely at a loss to know what he should do. Arlette had never behaved like this. His only experience was of careful, dutiful composure. Perhaps his wife cried in private, but if so, she had never shown him. And of other women, Rolf knew only their welcoming arms and parted thighs. 'Of course you do,' he said awkwardly, and wished that her maids would come to investigate, or the priest, or even Aubert, damn him.

'Name it,' she challenged.

Rolf trawled his mind but caught nothing. So that when she died she would be reunited with her loved ones was a goal too distant and sanctimonious. The Normans held London, her own menfolk were all dead. To tell her that she would find a new husband and bear other children might earn him nothing but a kick in the shins and renewed hysterics. And then, another idea surfaced, one that was so obvious that he had almost overlooked it. He grasped it joyously in both hands.

'Your husband and child are dead, I am sorry for that.' He

spoke the words quickly, without any great degree of sincerity because they were only an approach and he wanted to get to the core of the matter. 'But there is another child, a newborn infant, in great need of your help. Two nights ago, Aubert de Remy's wife bore a son. She was too badly mauled by the birth to be able to suckle him herself and Aubert has been searching for a wet nurse ever since.'

She sniffed loudly. 'Why should a Norman child be a reason for me to live?' she challenged in a watery voice.

'Because if you do not, he will die.'

'I do not believe that.'

'Already two women with babies of their own who could have fed Aubert's son have refused – or found excuses not to come to the convent. They are English, you see, and as you so rightly say, he is a Norman child.'

'My husband called Aubert de Remy *nithing*,' Ailith said. Her voice still quavered, but it was steadier now, and Rolf felt safe enough to release her.

'But you did not, and as I understand it, you and his wife were good friends.'

She said nothing. His hands were red and his cloak looked as if it had been dragged through a butcher's shambles. Blood trickled slowly down her wrist now he had released his pressure. He retrieved the scramaseax blade from the dusty floor of the forge and placed it gently on the bench.

'He has been christened Benedict, and I am told that he has dark eyes and hair and a squall on him fit to blow the thatch off a roof,' Rolf added, his voice soft and persuasive. It was like coaxing a mare to accept a foal not her own. If he had mentally to drape Felice's child in the dead baby's skin he would do so.

She turned away to face the cold forge, but he saw her right hand go to her injured wrist and press down hard on the line of the cut. Even before she spoke, he knew that his battle was won.

'I cannot go looking like this.'

'Then change your gown and make yourself decent.'

'But Goldwin . . . and my son . . .' Her voice faltered and her eyes started to fill again. 'I have to see them properly buried. How will I do that?'

'Leave that to me. I will make all the necessary arrangements with your priest.' He tried to keep the impatience out of his voice. *Tread softly*, he told himself. *Imagine that she is one of your mares.* 'Then he can come to St Aethelburga's and tell you all that you need to know.' He went slowly to the forge door and held it open.

'The child is two days old,' he said. 'Fortunately he is strong, but the weather is so cold.'

She followed him to the door. 'Benedict, you said?'

'For Aubert's father, although fortunately for his future, the babe resembles his mother's side.'

She lifted her smudged, suffering eyes to his. Although heavy with tears, they were quite lucid now. 'Do not expect my gratitude for this,' she said shakily.

'It is Aubert's gratitude I expect,' he answered, his tone wry.

The nun opened the door and ushered Ailith into a spartan, clean room, its walls whitened with lime daub and given light through an aperture at shoulder height. The only furniture consisted of a crude wooden coffer and a bed. Aubert was sitting on its coverlet of woven wool and was holding his wife's hand, watching her as she slept. When he heard the door open, he turned round.

'Ailith!' His weary features lit with pleasure, but in the next moment sobered as he rose and hastened towards her. 'What are you doing here? Has Goldwin relented?'

'Goldwin is dead.' Ailith felt each word like the slash of a knife. Why couldn't Rolf de Brize have minded his own business instead of forcing her to remain and endure this hell? 'He died at the coronation of your precious Norman Duke.'

'Ah, Ailith, no!'

'Do not touch me!' She took a rapid back-step. 'My husband called you *nithing*, and if it were not for your wife and the child . . . and the intervention of Rolf de Brize,' she added with a grimace, 'I would not be here now.'

'Rolf?' Aubert looked more baffled than ever. He rumpled his hand through his unkempt grey curls and rubbed his eyes.

'He says that you have a son in need of a wet nurse?'

'Indeed so. He will die unless we can find a woman to suckle him. Do you know of one?' Aubert looked at her hopefully.

'Yes, I know of one.' Advancing to the bed, Ailith stared down at Felice. The glossy black hair had been neatly braided and arranged, but it only emphasised her pallor.

'She almost bled to death,' Aubert said. 'Even now the nuns are not sure if she will live. Certainly she is unable to feed the baby.'

Ailith could scarcely remember the pangs of her own labour. It was the aftermath that had caused her own mortal wounds. 'I too might have bled to death,' she murmured, touching her bandaged left wrist.

As if aware of Ailith's brooding scrutiny, Felice stirred and licked her lips. Her eyelids fluttered open and then her hand groped for Ailith's.

'I'm so glad you have come,' she whispered. 'I have a son too . . . born on the eve of the feast of our Lord. Aubert will show him to you. The nuns have put him in a separate room because his crying disturbs me . . . I am not strong enough to feed him. We have to find a wet nurse.'

Ailith squeezed Felice's narrow fingers. A deluge of words were held back by the sight of Felice's weakness. Ailith could see that even the effort of speech had exhausted her. The new mother's eyelids were drooping and her grip was limp. 'That is why I am here,' Ailith said softly. 'Later, when you are better, I will tell you.'

Felice nodded. 'Tired,' she mumbled and her head lolled on the bolster. 'So tired.'

Ailith gently withdrew her hand and turned to Aubert. 'Take me to the child.'

He led her to a room at the other side of the courtyard. It was warmed by two charcoal braziers and an elderly nun was keeping watch over a cradle containing a swaddled baby while she spun wool. He was asleep, but as Ailith went to the cradle, his small face puckered and he began to grizzle.

'We cannot keep him silent, the poor little scrap,' said the nun. 'He's that hungry, and at this time of year, there is scarcely even cow's milk to be obtained. We managed to buy a jug yesterday, 'but he just sicked most of it up.'

The grizzle became a wail and the wail a full-fledged bawl of indignation. Pain stabbed Ailith's vitals. He was so like Harold, and yet so unlike, a reality instead of a grey little shadow. Her breasts tightened and tingled. Bending over the cradle, she lifted the baby out and sat down on a low stool near the brazier. When she removed her cloak, took the neck pin out of her overgown, and began unlacing the drawstring on her shift, Aubert's eyes widened in startled comprehension.

'Yes,' she said in a voice that was low, but intense with emotion. 'I lost my son too. He was weak from the moment of his birth, and even before that inside my womb, I think. No, do not speak. There is nothing you can say that will be of comfort, and if you offer me your pity, I will hate you.'

Aubert compressed his lips, and after a single look, schooled his shocked expression to neutrality.

Ailith ignored him. The baby demanded her attention. He was dusky-red in the face with frustration and the room echoed to the sound of his screams. The drawstring unlaced, she pulled down her shift and offered the infant her exposed breast. Furiously, Felice's son rooted back and forth, seeking so frantically that several times he missed her nipple altogether. Finally, with some adroit manoeuvring by Ailith, he discovered what he desired. A blissful silence descended, punctuated only by the sucking noises of the baby. Feeling the powerful tug of the small jaws, and the warm weight of him in her arms, Ailith realised how feeble Harold had truly been. Her eyes brimmed, but her tears, although of sorrow, were tears of healing too.

Benedict emptied one breast, belched happily, and demanded to be given the other side too. Rolf was right, he did look like his mother, Ailith thought as she shrugged up one shoulder of her chemise and pulled down the other. His hair was black and he had Felice's feathery eyebrows. His eyes were going to be brown too.

'He is more handsome than you,' she jested to Aubert who had been watching the baby feed with a mixture of relief and apprehension.

'That is not difficult,' Aubert answered with a pained smile. 'Ailith, I know you do not want me to say anything, but I am forever in your debt.'

She shook her head. 'I do not want to talk of debts. It is too complicated to decide what is owed and what is owing.'

The door opened and Rolf strode in. Immediately the size of the room seemed to diminish. 'Has she . . .' he started to say, then his eyes fell on Ailith and the greedily sucking child. 'Yes she has,' he finished for himself with a satisfied nod.

Ailith felt uncomfortable beneath his scrutiny. The only man to have seen her naked breasts before today was Goldwin. With Aubert it had not seemed so awkward because all his attention had been on watching his son take sustenance. The look in Rolf de Brize's eyes was rather more predatory, and lingered a little too long before he raised it to her face. His colour heightened as he saw the contemptuous awareness in her expression.

'He has taken to it well,' he said.

Ailith nodded stiffly in response. For the moment, because of what had happened at the forge, because of his gaze just now, she could not bring herself to speak to the Norman. He half-turned so that the swollen globe of her breast was no longer in his direct line of vision, and began talking to Aubert.

The baby finished feeding and drowsed in sated, milky pleasure. Ailith gently prised him from her nipple and covered herself, but the act did little to diminish her feeling of vulnerability.

CHAPTER 17

It was a raw day at January's end when Rolf rode into Ulverton at the head of his troop, and was tendered submission by a group of sullen, resentful villagers. Their lord had died fighting the Normans on Hastings field, and with him had perished a third of the young men from the seventy-strong community. Others had returned injured and heartsick. They had no mind to accept a Norman lord, but were forced by their circumstances to do so.

Rolf discovered that the hall had been abandoned after the great battle, and that it had been stripped to a shell. Not so much as a cooking pot or trestle table remained. The English lord had been a widower, with no children to grieve his passing. All that greeted Rolf was the musty smell of a place several months dead. The floor rushes were dank and mouldy, and near the hearth where the lord's seat should have proclaimed its owner's status, there were bits of bone and fruit stones from feasts long gone. On the wall, outlined in white against the grey of old limewash, was the space where a battle axe had hung until recently. Rolf imagined his own weapon sitting there, and snorted at the irony of placing an English war axe amidst such squalor.

Yet, despite the shortcomings, he was pleased with his new estates, of which Ulverton was the main settlement. They were easily as large as Brize-sur-Risle and had just as much, if not more potential. The lands were situated on the south coast of England, five days' ride from London, and included several fish-ing villages and a fine, ocean-going harbour along the shingle shoreline. There was excellent grazing for his horses, as well as for the large population of sheep which the rich downland supported. Rolf recognised the value of the limestone soil for producing sound bones in the animals he intended to breed here.

In the time of King Edward, Ulverton had been wealthy, and the difficulties that Rolf encountered were only recent and certainly reversible. He threw himself into the task with determination. The hall was patched up to make it habitable while he set about finding a site on which to build his keep. He soon chose a fine slope overlooking the village and backed by high sea cliffs. The villagers were none too happy at having to dig the mounds and ditches of the castle, but had little choice except to comply. Besides, they frequently heard tales from other communities about the harshness of the new Norman masters, and could only be thankful that their own, while not being Saxon and therefore of considerably less calibre than the former lord, was neither unfair nor tyrannical in his dealings with them. Indeed, he permitted them to retain their old laws and customs with very little interference.

Ulverton settled down to a state of truce. The castle mound continued to grow, and with it grew the relationship between the people and their new lord. He looked more Norse than French, they said, and unlike the other Normans over the hill, he spoke some English and strove to learn more at every opportunity.

Rolf treated his new peasants in much the same manner as he treated those on his Norman lands. He was of the opinion that to obtain the best from any tool, be it a spade, a piece of harness, a horse or a man, you had to treat it well. Oil and polish, kind words and discipline, a listening ear. It was not altruism, but self-interest that motivated him.

In March, King William announced his intention of returning to Normandy to parade his English victory throughout his duchy, and Rolf felt secure enough in his position at Ulverton to leave the lands in the charge of a deputy and make the journey too. But first he travelled to London, to the house of Aubert the wine merchant in order to pay his respects to the family: to Felice who had only just been rising from a protracted childbed when he went to claim his lands, to the thriving, rosy-cheeked baby to whom he had the serious honour of being Godfather, and to Benedict's wet nurse . . . Ailith.

Ailith sat in a puddle of sunshine, carding the last of the previous year's fleece ready for spinning. The day was so mild that she was beginning to believe that spring was actually on the threshold. There were often black days in her existence when she felt so full of grief and anger that she did not care about the weather or any other circumstance of her life, but today was a good one. She could feel the sun's warmth in her bones, and appreciate the comfort with which she was surrounded.

For a month, before coming to live in Aubert's house, she had dwelt at St Aethelburga's while Felice slowly regained her strength; a month in which her own wounds had begun to heal. On her second day at the convent, Rolf de Brize had taken her to witness the burial of Goldwin and Harold within the same grave. Although she was but recently out of childbed and not allowed within the hallowed confines of a church, still she was permitted to stand at the graveside. That had been one of the black days. She remembered it patchily, but the most disturbing part was her vivid recall of the Norman's strong, wiry grip holding her steady at the graveside, preventing her from falling in as the labourers began shovelling earth back into the hole.

Ailith liked Rolf de Brize, but she preferred to keep her distance. There had been an incident at the end of January just before he left when she had sought him in Aubert's stables to say that food was ready, and discovered that he had not heard the dinner horn because his face was buried in the ample bosom of Gytha the Alewife from down the road. Ailith had backed away quietly before either of them saw her, and had informed the household that Rolf was busy and would eat later. A whole candle notch later as it happened, his lids heavy with satiation. His appetite had been enormous – he had devoured all the chicken stew which Ailith had set down before him, and more bread than herself, Felice and Aubert put together.

'Ailith said you were busy in the stables,' Felice had told him.

Rolf had looked sharply at Ailith, and then a slow, incorrigible smile had spread across his face as hers reddened. 'I was,' he had replied without elaboration. No, he was neither to be trusted nor encouraged.

Ailith considered the foamy pile of carded wool in the basket beside her and decided that she had enough now to begin spinning. But first she had to see to Benedict. He had been gurgling in his cradle, delighting himself by trying to grasp the motes of dust suspended in the splash of sunshine, but his voice had become more querulous by degrees and she could almost feel his growing hunger in her own stomach. Her breasts filled as they always did at the sound of his cry. She lifted him from the cradle and crooned to him, her face radiant with love, and Benedict responded with a gummy smile.

Ailith settled down to feed him, freeing one of his hands from the swaddling so that she could play with his tiny fingers. She knew that it was dangerous to love so hard, but Benedict had bridged the aching chasm left by Harold's death. Her own son lay in the soil, but it was so easy to imagine him living on in Benedict. With his brown eyes and dark hair, he could have belonged to her and Goldwin.

When the baby had finished suckling, she laid him down on a soft pile of raw fleece to change his linens. He crowed at her and kicked his legs high in delight at being freed from the tight binding of the swaddling bands and the bulk of the soiled tail clout. This led to an accidental discovery that he could suck his toes, and he undertook the new skill with great gusto.

Laughing at his antics, Ailith fetched a fresh linen napkin from where it had been warming near the firepit. It seemed a pity to cover him up when he was enjoying himself so much, and she decided to let him kick for a while in the fresh air. The fleece was unwashed as yet, and it would not matter if he stained it.

Ailith glanced up to see Felice descending from the sleeping loft where she had been napping. She had made a slow recovery from Benedict's birth and still tired very quickly. 'Are you feeling better?'

'A little.' Felice finished securing her wimple and sat down on the stool which Ailith had vacated to tend the baby. Idly she picked up a mass of carded wool and ran it through her fingers. 'Should you not cover him up? He will catch a chill lying there.'

'I thought he would like to lie and kick for a while. The sunshine is lovely and warm.'

'All the same I would rather you covered him. A small baby should be swaddled so that his limbs will grow straight later on.'

Ailith lowered her eyes and bit her tongue on the response that Hulda said such stories were so much nonsense, that no animal ever swaddled its young.

Sometimes Ailith found herself sorely tried by living with Felice and Aubert. When Goldwin had been alive and King Harold new on the throne, Ailith had held the same, if not higher social status than her neighbours. Now, with a conquering Norman King commanding their lives, her husband dead, and his business sold off to a Norman armourer, she was an English widow, dependent on the de Remys' goodwill. It did not matter that they were in her debt, that they tried to treat her as one of their own, Ailith knew that the gulf was too wide to bridge. Since Felice had to spend so much of her time resting, the burden of domestic duty had inevitably fallen upon Ailith's shoulders. Sometimes she was the servant, sometimes the mistress. It was inevitable that whichever role she played, either she or Felice felt resentful. And then, she thought grimly, there was the unspoken battle of wills over Benedict.

Silently Ailith folded a fresh linen square between the baby's legs and rebound him in clean swaddling. Benedict complained loudly at being confined. Giving Felice an *I told you so* look, Ailith presented her with the wailing infant. In a moment, she was sure that Felice would hand him back, lacking the confidence to cope.

But Benedict, made curious by a different but familiar smell, by the sound of a voice that belonged to the warm womb-darkness before his birth, responded with a smile to his mother's overtures, and then a gurgle.

Ailith felt a stab of vicious jealousy as she watched Felice play gently with Benedict, encouraging him to laugh, talking to him in soft, high-pitched Norman French.

'Isn't he beautiful, Ailith?' Felice's dark eyes were burning with love-light. 'And so good-natured. You are!' she crooned to the baby, making a kissing sound. 'Yes you are! Oh just look at him!'

Ailith could not bear to watch. She wanted to snatch Benedict out of Felice's arms and keep him all to herself. Filled with bitter envy, knowing that it was wrong, she murmured that she had to visit the privy, and fled outside.

Rolf de Brize was tying a chestnut stallion to a bridle ring nailed in the wooden stable wall, and the yard was filling up with an entourage of grooms and retainers. Ailith hesitated. She had left the house to find a breathing space and perhaps to cry; there was that kind of pressure behind her eyes. Instead she encountered the vital red-haired Norman, and space of any kind was denied to her.

He raised his head and saw her standing in the doorway. A look of pleasure brightened his face and he strode up to her. 'Ailith, it is good to see you!' he declared warmly, and before she could move, he had kissed her on both cheeks in greeting.

Her face flaming, Ailith stepped away from him. 'We did not know you were coming to London.'

'I thought I would pay a visit before taking ship; I'm bound for Normandy on the next Rouen trader out of Dowgate.'

'Oh.' Ailith felt a surge of relief followed closely by a sensation that was almost disappointment. She was about to usher him into the house when Felice herself came out to investigate the commotion, Benedict cradled in her arms.

Again Rolf's face lit up and he kissed Felice on both cheeks too. 'You look well,' he said. 'Much better than you did in January.'

'And I am beginning to feel well too,' Felice assured him, a flush to her cheeks and her brown eyes sparkling. 'What do you think of your Godson? Hasn't he grown?' She held out the baby for his inspection.

Ailith watched Rolf take Benedict into the crook of his arm and agree gravely with Felice as to the child's progress. 'One day he will be as handsome as his mother is beautiful,' he charmed, causing Felice to blush harder than ever. 'Aubert's a lucky man. Is he home?'

'Soon,' Felice said, preening at her wimple. 'He's attending to a cargo down at the wharf.'

'Good, I need to buy some wine for Ulverton, and I know Aubert will give me the best price.' He returned Benedict to his mother. 'Not that I'll need it until I return from Normandy.'

'Normandy!' Felice had not heard that part of his conversation with Ailith, and looked at him with raised eyebrows. Benedict, tired now, began to cry fretfully.

'Shall I take him?' Ailith held out longing arms.

Felice shook her head. 'No, he's not hungry, you fed him not long since, and his swaddling is clean. I'll sit down and nurse him awhile until he falls asleep. Perhaps you could oversee the meal now that we have guests to provide for?'

Ailith nodded. 'Of course,' she said, her lips tightening. Rolf looked thoughtfully between the two women but made no comment, and when Felice linked her free arm through his to lead him back into the house, he smiled and yielded her his full attention.

The hearth smouldered softly, bathing the woman and baby in a dull red light. Awake, Rolf lay on his pallet and watched Ailith suckle Benedict in the hour when everyone else was sound asleep. Her hair was braided in a loose sheaf and secured by a simple ribbon. She had freed the baby's limbs and a little hand clutched her plait as the infant sucked. Rolf quietly enjoyed the scene. He had never witnessed Ailith off her guard before and the softness in her face as she played with Benedict was a revelation.

He had not had much opportunity to speak to her since his arrival. At first she had been busy with the maids preparing food, and when she had sat at table, the conversation had all been in rapid Norman French and she had been unable to follow it and join in – or perhaps she had not wanted to. He had seen a look of strain on her face as the evening wore its way down the candle notches.

There was no strain now. She finished feeding the baby and covered her breasts. Quietly he left his pallet and crouched down at her side before the banked fire. He felt her silent surprise, but she accepted his company.

'How are you faring?' he enquired as she set about changing Benedict's swaddling. Her fair braid swung forward. The movement of her breasts was heavy and fluid within her chemise. After one, rapid glance, he kept his eyes on her face, but she did not look at him, preferring to busy herself with the baby.

'Well enough. I still miss Goldwin and Harold terribly. It is an ache that will never go away.'

'But you are no longer tempted to take a knife to your wrist?' His voice emerged sharper than he had intended.

'I am tempted every day, but I manage to resist,' she answered.

He eyed her thoughtfully. While the child needed her for sustenance, he could see that she was sufficiently fulfilled to think life worth living. But what about the future? He had seen the unspoken tension between her and Felice and how it stemmed from mutual jealousy over Benedict. Sooner, rather than later, he thought, the battle to wean the baby would begin.

Having saved her life in the forge at midwinter, Rolf felt that he had a responsibility for Ailith's welfare, one that he would rather have foregone. In the normal course of his life, he would have tumbled her joyously in the warm stable straw without a second thought and then gone on his light-hearted way. And if she refused him, which occasionally happened, he would have shrugged and found someone else to lighten the heaviness in his groin. Now, burdened, he was at a loss.

'How long will you be gone in Normandy?' She returned Benedict to his cherry wood cradle and set it gently rocking with her toe.

'For the spring and early summer. I have to look over the new foals at Brize and decide what is to be done with the yearlings. I'm going to bring some horses back to England with me as breeding stock for Ulverton. It was the reason the King granted me the lands – to raise warhorses for his stables. I may go to Flanders too. They raise heavier animals there, ideal for blending with my Spanish grey. Breeding the perfect warhorse is not easily done, but I have always relished a challenge, and I suffer from the wanderlust,' he added with a smile.

'Is that what brought you to England? Your wanderlust? The challenge of another man's grass?'

Rolf shrugged uncomfortably beneath her stare, which was almost accusing. 'In part, yes,' he confessed, 'but King William had need of my skills and no-one ever denies his will – not if they want to live.'

'And did you leave a family at home in Normandy when you crossed the narrow sea?'

Rolf sighed down his nose. He had known the question was inevitable, and would have preferred not to answer her. Normandy was Normandy, and England was England. 'I have a wife and child,' he said.

Ailith's expression became closed and wary as he had known it would. 'It must be hard for you, being apart from them for so long,' she murmured.

'Sometimes it is.' He picked up a twig of stray kindling from the floor rushes and peeled at the bark with his fingernail. 'I was married to further the interests of Brize-sur-Risle – for wealth and land and politics. My father was the most astute of men when it came to such dealings. I had no choice. Not that it mattered. Arlette was suitable in every way and there was no-one else.' He poked the twig beneath the smouldering logs in the hearth. 'She is a good wife,' he said, his tone wry. 'Near to being perfect.'

The kindling smoked at the tip and turned black. The bark writhed away from the pith and suddenly bright flame licked intensely along the twig and consumed it. Rolf stared at the blackened, crumbling fretwork. 'Perhaps that is why I have a need to play with fire,' he said softly.

CHAPTER 18

Rolf fondled the bay mare's soft muzzle. A leggy red-gold yearling butted jealously at his hand, seeking attention, and the mare's new chestnut foal stretched his neck to discover if he was missing anything. The dark January night of a year and a half ago when Rolf had struggled to save the yearling's life seemed to be from a different lifetime, so much had happened since.

'England,' said Arlette. 'You are taking them to England?' There was anxiety in her voice. 'But she is your best mare, Rolf.'

'I want to breed her to Sleipnir,' he answered. 'And there is no way on God's good earth that I am bringing him back across the narrow sea. Once was enough. She has mated well with Orage, I won't deny it, but I want to see the result of putting her to the grey. There are some other mares I have a mind to take too.'

Her eyes clouded. 'That means you will be spending much of your time in England.'

'For a while, until the lands are more settled, and the breeding established.' He ceased stroking the mare and sat down on the river bank where Arlette had organised a picnic. In the village he knew that his people would be dancing around the maypole and indulging in various pagan rites connected with the celebration of the fertility of spring. Father Hoel would be among them, scattering blessings and holy water in a vain

attempt to Christianise the proceedings. Rolf would have preferred to join the dancing and oversee the feast he had provided
for his people, but Arlette, full of righteous disapproval, had
suggested the alternative of dining by the river in the sunshine,
adding that in the month he had been home, they had scarcely
been together except at retiring time.

He had complied, for it gave him the opportunity to inspect
his horses, nor was he averse to a lazy hour beside the peace of
the river. Besides, the May celebrations would go on all day,
and well into the night. And the night was usually the best part.

Watched closely by her mother, Gisele toddled about on
the grass, constantly plumping down on her fat little bottom.
Delicate pale gold curls escaped the edges of her linen bonnet
and framed a dainty face that was Arlette's in immature
miniature. Rolf took her on his lap, but she struggled free
immediately.

'Want Mama,' she whined, and tottered over to Arlette.
Shrugging, Rolf dug a stone out of the ground and threw it at
the water. It vanished with a plop, leaving only the ripples
radiating downstream. Arlette directed a squire to pour him
wine from the stone bottle that had been cooling in the
shallows.

'Perhaps I could go with you to England,' she suggested
tentatively as she settled Gisele on her own knee.

'No!' Rolf snarled, surprising himself as much as his wife
with the vehemence of his denial. He realised, as her great, grey
eyes rested on him in shock, that he did not want her bringing
her dainty ways, her mouse-like attention to detail, to the
robust simplicity of Ulverton. England belonged to his spirit
and he did not want his wife interfering, no matter how good
her intentions. 'No,' he modified his tone. 'It would be too
dangerous.'

'But other Norman women are there,' she objected. 'What
about Felice de Remy?'

'Felice de Remy almost died in England,' Rolf said impatiently. 'Even when I sailed, she had not recovered her full
strength. And not every Saxon is as good-hearted as the one

who saved her life and that of her child. It is no place for you, Arlette.'

'But I want to be with you. How will I bear sons for Brize-sur-Risle if you are never here?'

'I am here now,' he said. 'Every night for a month I have sown my seed in your furrow. It is not for want of my attention that you have begun your flux.'

Her pretty mouth drooped and she lowered her eyes. 'I know, Rolf. I wish I conceived more easily. If only we could . . .'

'I need you to govern Brize in my absence,' he forestalled her plea. 'It is unwise for us both to be away. What if there was a storm in the narrow sea and we both drowned, or our ship was attacked by Dublin pirates? What would become of Brize-sur-Risle then?'

'I'm sorry, Rolf, I didn't think.'

He rose jerkily to his feet and walked along the river bank a little way. What he had said was true, but it was an excuse to keep her away from England. He did not want her finely manicured fingers meddling in that particular pie. He felt a twinge of conscience. Perhaps he would take her to William's court. The Duke was currently accepting the adulation of his populace at Fécamp with a bevy of English hostages in his train and a treasure house of English booty – artefacts of gold and silver, heavily crusted embroideries, books and church ornaments. Arlette would like that. She would be able to wear her new gown of green silk damask and the gold Saxon round brooch he had brought her from Ulverton. In fact, he would quite enjoy parading her before his fellow Normans. Not having borne many children, her figure was supple and slender, well suited to the new fashion for closer-fitting garments. Other men would admire her demure prettiness and feel envious of the man who possessed its obedience.

Arlette and Gisele returned to the keep, and Rolf joined his villagers in their May Eve celebrations. A huge bonfire had been kindled on a low slope above the village and the people capered around it, their blood warm with cider and the vigorous surge of springtime currents. A man and a woman, each with a tabor, beat out an ancient, insistent rhythm while alternate circles of women and men performed the sacred dance, and all of them wore at least one item of green to symbolise the clothing of the earth in new life.

The light faded from the sky, leaving a teal luminescence. Older women carried querulous, sleepy children home to bed. The unmarried, the unattached and the drunk remained to dance in the Beltane ring, honouring a religion far more ancient than the one that the poor, isolated priest was trying to uphold.

Rolf accepted a cup of rough, golden cider from a grinning villager, and watched Father Hoel depart in the direction of the keep, there no doubt to commiserate with Arlette about the blasphemous collection of pagans who made up his flock.

Rolf joined the dancers, linking his arms with his overseer and Brize's blacksmith. They faced the fire, circling, stepping to the beat of the tabor. Then they faced the women and circled in the opposite direction. Three times the move was repeated before the men separated and the women were passed through in a handfasting figure of eight to become the inner ring. The links were reforged and the dance continued.

Rolf's eye fell upon one of the village women. Her tossing corn-blonde hair was bound back from her brow by a crown of white hawthorn, the symbol of the fertility goddess. Her face was flushed with exertion and her breasts and hips jiggled suggestively as she twisted and turned in the motion of the dance. Hand over hand, Rolf passed her from inside ring to outer. The side of her breast, heavy and soft, brushed against his arm; the musky scents of hawthorn blossom and sweat filled his nostrils. His loins began to burn.

In and out, weaving the darkness with a living thread. The drums and the cider banished all thought and left only touch. A dark-haired girl, slender as a weasel, swept her hand across Rolf's groin in a feather-light touch that left his manhood as huge and hard as the maypole at the foot of the slope. Her eyes glistened; she drew a thick tress of hair across his face and arched her spine, offering him the thrust of her small, pert breasts.

Rolf swung her round into the arms of one of the village men and sought the blonde woman instead. She seemed momentarily surprised to be chosen, but when his hands settled on her hips and he pulled her out of the dance, she went willingly into the shadows with him.

Her breasts were large and soft from the suckling of several children, there was a gentle roll of fat on her belly and her hips were wide and meaty. But Rolf saw none of this. His only care was that she spread herself willingly to accept him. All sensation was concentrated in his swollen shaft and aching cods. He grasped her ample buttocks and plunged in hard. Her thighs gripped him; she struck her heels on the ground and circled her hips to meet his thrusts. Blonde hair tossed in Rolf's face. He felt the surge of power rising inexorably within him. He tried to slow his thrusts and prolong the pleasure, but the woman urged him on, kneading his back with her hands, pumping her hips in a relentless, slick rhythm, and making small, inarticulate cries.

It was too much. Rolf jammed into her, his spine arching. 'Ailith!' he sobbed through his teeth as his seed pulsed from his body into the woman beneath him.

He roused to the flickering light of the bonfire behind his eyes, to the shouts and laughter of the people who still danced, the whispered moans of those who had succumbed to the lure of 'wearing the green' in the form of grass stains on their clothing. Slowly he withdrew himself from the woman and tucked himself back inside his braies.

'What was that word you shouted, my lord?' His partner tugged her bunched-up skirts back down over her legs and sat up beside him. Her fingers combed through her coarse blonde hair and she straightened the hawthorn crown on top of her head. 'Was it a charm?'

Rolf shook his head. He had not intended to cry out at all, but the intensity of his climax, the fair hair, the body arched beneath him in passion, had roused a powerful spectre from his imagination and clothed it with life. 'A charm,' he repeated and smiled with irony. 'I suppose you could call it that. An English one.' He tugged a strand of her hair and grinned. 'Riding always gives me a thirst. Go and fetch a jug of cider, there's a good lass.'

She wove unsteadily away to do his bidding. Rolf reclined on the grass, pillowed his head on his hands, and looked at the stars.

The worse for drink, old Ragnild tottered out of the shadows and regarded Rolf with gleaming, weasel eyes. 'You will get what you desire, Rolf de Brize.' She nodded as if listening to an invisible presence. 'But not without a reckoning. Break your faith, and the axe will break you.'

He jerked to a sitting position, intending to ask her what she meant, but his companion returned with a brimming jug of cider and plumped herself down beside him. Ragnild rummaged in the pouch at her waist and brought out a scrap of linen which had been twisted and tied to hold herbs. 'A pinch is all you need,' she cackled, dropping it in Rolf's lap so that it landed over the area of his genitals. 'Keep you firm as a quarterstaff all night if you've a mind to pleasure.' With a lascivious roll of her hips and a wink, she moved on towards the bonfire.

Rolf swore and hurled the scrap of linen after her, but later, in the aftermath of a second, more leisurely mating, he retrieved it from the grass and stowed it in his pouch. His head spinning with the force of the cider and the Beltane scents of crushed grass, sweat and sex, he wondered what Ragnild had meant about the axe and breaking faith.

CHAPTER 19

DECEMBER 1067

'It is time you ceased mourning and thought about finding another husband,' Felice told Ailith. The two women were sitting around the winter hearth peeling withies to make rush dips. It was past Yuletide and the days would gradually begin to lengthen, but there were still a three full months between now and the warmth and light of spring. 'I know that you miss Goldwin, but it is more than a year since he died. A man and household of your own would make you miss him less. And in the fullness of time you would have children too.'

'I do not want another husband.' Ailith made a conscious effort to keep her voice firm and steady. 'I am not ready yet. And Benedict still needs a wet nurse.' She glanced at the black-haired infant playing on a fleece rug near their feet. He was sturdy and strong, on the verge of taking his first steps. Morning and evening he still suckled at her breasts, and for comfort when he was tired, but more and more, urged by Felice, he was relying on other foods for sustenance, on bread smeared with marrow jelly, on wheat porridge, buttermilk and whey.

'But by the summertime he will not.' Felice added her stripped rush to the pile at her side and frowned at Ailith. 'You are welcome to live here as long as you choose, you know that. I am only thinking that it will be difficult for you. If you had a home of your own again, it would give you a new sense of purpose.'

Feelings of hostility and panic rushed through Ailith as she heard these words. Felice was making it obvious that once Benedict had dispensed of the need for a wet nurse, she intended taking full responsibility for him, and that there would be little room for Ailith.

'Perhaps I could find somewhere down by the wharves and take in washing for the sailors,' Ailith suggested cuttingly.

'Don't be so foolish!' Felice snapped. 'I said that you were welcome here – for the rest of your life if need be.'

'If you have to support me you mean!'

'Ailith, I do not wish to quarrel.' Felice's voice took on a conciliatory note. 'I just want you to think about the future. Look at us now. Will it get any better?'

Ailith blinked. She could not see to peel the rush in her hand for a sudden film of moisture. 'No,' she shook her head. 'No, it won't.'

'Oh don't cry, you will make me cry too!' Felice's own eyes filled with tears. She gave Ailith a warm, pleading hug. Ailith accepted it passively and wiped her eyes on her under-tunic sleeve. Benedict came to join in, clawing himself to a standing position at Ailith's knee, demanding to be taken on her lap. She lifted him in her arms and nuzzled his hair, drinking in his warm, heartbreaking infant smell. How could she give this up? And yet she knew it was inevitable. The child came first, she could not put her own needs before his. She had once heard a priest recite a story from the Bible about a great king called Solomon who had been asked to judge between two women as to who was the mother of a disputed infant. He had commanded that the child be cut in two and each claimant be given a half. One woman had relinquished her right so that the child might live, and she had been deemed the true mother. Ailith knew that she could not let Benedict be torn in two. She had to let him go.

Felice allowed her to cuddle Benedict and with a sigh, returned to stripping the withies. 'Aubert is bringing a guest home to eat. I thought when we have finished this, we could prepare the food.'

Ailith nodded dully. 'As you wish,' she said.

Felice pursed her lips, then added nonchalantly, 'It's Wulfstan the Goldsmith – do you remember, he was here last month?'

Ailith started to say that no, she did not remember; Aubert and Felice were always entertaining guests of one kind or another, but then an image did come to her – a tall, blond bear of a man with twinkling grey eyes and hands that he could not keep to himself. 'Yes, I know him. He palmed my rump when I took his cloak.' She had quickly disabused him of the notion that she was a serving wench with whom he could take liberties.

'That is just his way,' Felice dismissed with a wave. 'He's a superb goldsmith, the best in the city, and he's so rich. Aubert says that Wulfstan is having a grand house built near the Fleet river and that he owns a half-share in a merchant galley too.'

'Being rich does not give him the right to grope and fondle at will,' Ailith said tartly.

Felice sighed again, and expression pensive, let the subject lie.

That evening, to her displeasure, Ailith found herself seated next to the goldsmith and forced to share her dish with him as was the custom. The scented oil he had used on his beard and hair cloyed her nostrils. His tunic was crusted with gold embroidery and the belt encircling his ebullient waist was elaborately tooled with gold leaf. Rings cluttered his broad fingers. She noted that his nails were trimmed and clean. He had obviously taken great care with his appearance, and to his own taste, no doubt thought himself magnificent. Ailith thought that he looked as if he had just staggered out of the dragon's cave in one of the tales of Beowulf, laden with the monster's hoard. She smiled to herself at the whimsy, but then, feeling Wulfstan's thigh insistently brushing against hers, she thought with a chill of fear that perhaps Wulfstan himself was the dragon.

He expertly carved the small roast fowl that they were sharing, and laid the choicest breast slices on her trencher; he plied her with Aubert's best wine and kept up an amusing flow of conversation. There were deep laughter lines surrounding his grey eyes, but the eyes themselves were assessing and shrewd and never relaxed for a moment.

''Tis good to eat such fine food in good company,' Wulfstan rumbled in his gruff, bear's voice. 'Since my wife died, my own household's been mighty dolorous.'

A lump began to constrict Ailith's throat and after a few bites of the chicken, she was unable to eat any more. She sipped the wine and glared at Felice and Aubert. How dare they try and pair her off. She had not the slightest interest in Wulfstan; indeed, she found his attentions distasteful.

'You must visit more often,' Felice said sweetly, adroitly avoiding Ailith's despairing, furious stare.

'That is most kind of you, mistress,' the goldsmith acknowledged. His hand slipped beneath the table and squeezed Ailith's knee.

She could feel the hot spread of his fingers through her garments and jerked her leg away, hard-pressed not to stab him with her eating knife. Wulfstan smiled at her, hunching and releasing his shoulders as if he found the entire situation a game which he intended to win.

'I will not sit at table with that odious man again!' she hissed furiously to Felice when Wulfstan finally went on his way, promising that he would visit again soon. 'He seemed to think I was a part of the feast the way he prodded and poked at me!'

'He's lonely,' Felice excused. 'He needs the comfort of touch. His wife died last autumn of a bloody flux from her womb and he has been a long time in mourning for such a vigorous man.'

'So it is excusable for him to paw me?' Ailith asked with an ominous air of calm.

'You should not take so much offence. He likes you. He's good-humoured, wealthy, and one of Aubert's best customers.' Felice gave an impatient cluck. 'Life moves on, Ailith, you must not let yourself become enslaved by the dead.'

'It is better than being enslaved by the living,' Ailith retorted waspishly and stalked off to her pallet in the corner of the hall, pulling the wool curtain across, thereby curtailing all further conversation.

'Horse,' commanded Benedict, bouncing up and down in Ailith's embrace and opening and closing his small, fat hands. 'Want horse.'

Leaning down from the saddle, Rolf swept the child up in his arms and sat him on Sleipnir's back. Benedict laughed and grasped handfuls of the wiry silver mane. Sleipnir flickered his ears, but otherwise stood as docile as an ass. Rolf touched him lightly with his heel and rode him round in a slow circle.

It was May once more, a year since the festival at Brize-sur-Risle. This time Beltane had found him at Ulverton where the celebrations had been very similar, although the symbol of a hobby horse had featured prominently in the English rites. The fact that Rolf intended breeding horses at Ulverton had impressed the villagers considerably; indeed, they had seen it as an omen of good fortune. Rolf had joined them at the dancing, but had stopped short of taking one of their women in the grass. Although the people cautiously approved of him, he knew that he was still considered an outsider and a usurper of the rightful lord.

That had been at the beginning of the month. Now, at the end, he had travelled to London to attend the crowning of William's wife Matilda at Westminster, and as always, had billeted himself upon Aubert and Felice.

Ailith was much slimmer than the day of their first encounter, and he was not sure that it suited her. Her face was gaunt, and the tiny lines at the corners of her eyes and between mouth and nostril were not of laughter as they should have been in a young woman. Surely she was not still pining for her husband and child?

'More!' cried Benedict as Rolf drew rein before Ailith. She was anxiously biting her lip, but doing her best not to speak out.

'He loves it!' Rolf chuckled.

'And the Lord alone knows what his mother will say if she

sees you!' Ailith answered, but a smile curved her lips. 'Sometimes I think that the only word she knows is "don't".' Then she shook her head. 'I'm sorry, I'm being a shrew. It is only because she cares for him so much, and the midwives told her that she would never be able to bear another child.'

He took the baby on another circuit of the small yard and then, returning him to Ailith, dismounted.

'How old is your own child, your daughter?' she asked curiously as he led the grey towards his stall.

'Almost three years old.'

'And you have no others?'

'Arlette does not bear children easily. She miscarried again just before I left for England.'

'I am sorry.'

Benedict was clamouring to pat the horse. Rolf took him from Ailith's arms and held him close to the stallion's head so that the baby could touch the dark grey muzzle. 'She was making a good recovery,' he said, 'but she was not well enough to journey across the narrow sea with the other Norman ladies to watch the crowning of the Duchess Matilda.' It was a blessing in disguise, he thought, but said nothing aloud to Ailith.

'She must be very disappointed.'

'A little.' He shrugged uncomfortably, for he did not wish to talk about his wife.

They were both startled by the sound of a deep voice raised in demand. 'Ailith? Ailith, where are you, sweetheart?'

Rolf stiffened at the possessiveness in the tone. Beside him, Ailith stiffened too, and he saw the colour drain from her face.

'Who seeks you?' he asked.

'Wulfstan the Goldsmith. He's a friend of Aubert's,' she murmured in a low voice which would not carry beyond the bounds of the stable.

'But not of yours?'

She looked at him with the eyes of a hunted animal and shrank into the shadows.

'Ailith, my love?' The voice came closer.

Benedict squealed loudly and Ailith made a small sound of

despair, half-gasp, half-sob. Then she swallowed, and taking Benedict from Rolf, stepped from the stables into the warm spring daylight. 'I'm here, Wulfstan. What do you want of me?'

Rolf heard the defensive note in her voice and an edge of fear, but there was more to it than that. She had spoken to him in both those tones in the past, but never had he heard that third strand of loathing trembling there too.

'Pour us a cup of wine, my girl, and I'll tell you. Are Felice and Aubert not here?'

'No, they've gone to visit a client together, but they'll be here soon if you want to see them.'

'I suppose I do in time, but it's really you I've come to see, chicken.'

Rolf grimaced. *Sweetheart? Love? Chicken?* The goldsmith spoke as if he wished to devour, and Ailith was indeed behaving like a hen about to be necked for the pot. He followed her out into the yard and saw a blond bear of a man towering over her, his stance intimidating because he stood so close. The visitor's attention diverted from Ailith as Rolf strode into the yard, and immediately, the grey eyes narrowed and the lips tightened within the full, gold beard. Rolf could almost see the man's thoughts. Felice and Aubert absent and Ailith lurking in the stables with another man. Rolf smiled pleasantly. He had no intention of disabusing the visitor.

Looking anxious, Ailith said, 'Wulfstan, I want you to meet Rolf de Brize, a household guest. Rolf, this is Wulfstan, a business friend of Aubert's.'

Rolf extended his hand. The goldsmith grasped it and forced a smile onto his face. His beard bristled, revealing his tension and hostility. 'Are you in London for long?' he asked with a show of teeth which could hardly be termed a smile.

Rolf glanced at Ailith. 'For the coronation of the Duchess Matilda, and to conduct a little business before I return to my lands. Benedict is my Godson, I like to visit him when I can.'

Wulfstan continued to smile, but he did not relax. 'A fine little chap,' he said, chucking Benedict under the chin with a meaty forefinger. 'I hope when the time comes, my own sons are as robust and good-natured.' He looked indulgently at Ailith, as if they shared a secret. She bit her lip and Rolf saw her jaw clench. He wondered if the goldsmith had intentionally arrived when Felice and Aubert were absent.

The men followed Ailith inside the house and in silence she served them with wine and honey griddle cakes. Rolf took Benedict onto his knee and gave him one of the cakes to chew. Wulfstan waited until Ailith went to check and season a pan of frumenty that was simmering on the hearth bricks.

'I have been courting Ailith since the Yule feast,' he said, leaning close to Rolf and lowering his voice so that his words would not carry. 'It has been hard; she still grieves unnaturally for her dead husband and child, but I think I am beginning to wear her down. She is foolish to reject my suit. I have two fine houses, one in the city attached to my business, and one near the Fleet river with a little land. I can afford to dress her in silk and gold. She can have whatever she desires. Felice and Aubert believe that the match cannot be bettered and have given me their blessing to seek her hand in marriage.'

Benedict generously offered Rolf a well-sucked piece of griddle cake. He persuaded his Godson to eat it himself and wondered what he should say to the goldsmith. The man's face was open and pleasant, but there were several contradictions that made Rolf uneasy. Having learned to read the impassive features of William FitzOsbern during their dealings in Normandy, other men were seldom a mystery to him. He concluded that Wulfstan had been born with the advantage of amiable, generous features just as some men were born looking mean even if they were not. Wulfstan used his physical bulk and his wealth to intimidate people and he was accustomed to getting his own way. Rolf only had to look at the manner in which the man's hands made constant little grasping motions to know that.

'Why Ailith?' he asked in a voice of mild curiosity, although inwardly he was filled with alarm. 'Surely there are other women more suitable?'

'There are other women, yes,' Wulfstan answered, recoiling with a grimace as Benedict tried to share with him the mangled remnants of his griddle cake. 'But Ailith is my preference. She is good and broad in the beam. Aubert de Remy's son has thrived on her wet nursing. I need a competent woman, one whom I can breed upon and who will be a buxom armful in bed. My first wife was a whining bag of bones.'

'But Ailith's first-born child was weak and died soon after he was born.' Rolf eyed Ailith up and down. Competent and buxom. Yes, both applied to her, but he did not see why her attributes should be wasted on a complacent boor like Wulfstan.

'Bad seed, nothing to do with the soil in which it was planted,' Wulfstan snorted. 'She wants a real man in her bed.' His fingers flexed and grasped again.

Rolf watched Ailith remove the frumenty from the hearth and cover it with a lid. No wonder she shrank from Wulfstan's attentions.

'I thought it best that you knew my intentions,' Wulfstan continued as Rolf said nothing, his eyes thoughtfully upon Ailith. 'I hope that come the next Yuletide, we will be man and wife. The child will not require a wet nurse by then. Indeed, look at him, he scarcely needs one now.'

Rolf brushed the smears and crumbs of Benedict's meal from his tunic. 'You think she will have you?'

'In the end she will have no choice,' Wulfstan said. 'I will make sure of that.' A sly look entered his eyes, serving to increase Rolf's alarm. Ailith rejoined them to take Benedict from Rolf's arms and Wulfstan's expression cleared. He bestowed a benign smile on Ailith.

'I have an interesting surprise for you, sweetheart,' he announced, and patted the trestle bench beside him, indicating that she should be seated.

By a supreme effort of will, Rolf succeeded in maintaining a neutral façade. Wulfstan sounded like a man in a brothel about to whip his cock out in front of a whore. Ailith looked dubious. She seated herself sideways so that she was facing away from Wulfstan, and busied herself with Benedict.

'You are going to attend the coronation of the King's Duchess in Westminster itself. With me. Wear your best gown and I will give you some gold to go with it.' He leaned towards her and squeezed her knee.

Ailith shook her head. 'I thank you for your generous offer, for thinking of me, but I cannot go, it is impossible.'

'Oh, come now, of course you can!' Wulfstan laughed, but the note was brutal, containing little of humour. 'I have discussed it with Felice and Aubert and they think it an excellent idea.'

Ailith's face was ashen. She swallowed several times. 'Felice and Aubert are not my keepers.'

'They only have your good at heart, as I do,' Wulfstan said self-righteously. 'You need jolting from the rut you are wearing ever deeper for yourself.'

'You do not understand.' She shook her head, biting her lip in distress. 'Goldwin died at William's crowning, and as you must well know, my best gown is my wedding gown. It would seem like a betrayal.'

'Nonsense, it would seem like bravery!' He shook the knee that he was squeezing. 'You don't have to answer now. Tomorrow will do, when you have had an opportunity to think it over. You'll see that I'm right. If you do not want to wear your wedding gown, then I will buy you another.'

Despite his instinctive dislike of the man, Rolf could not help but admire the goldsmith's powers of persuasion. He was relentless, refusing to take no for an answer. Rolf could see that when the time came, Wulfstan would take Ailith to wife simply because she would accept him in order to have some peace. *I will wear her down,* he had said. Wear her out, more likely. Rolf did nothing to defend her from Wulfstan's assault, but his mind was very busy, nor did it cease working on the problem when Felice and Aubert returned, rather their presence and their response to Wulfstan gave him additional food for thought.

CHAPTER 20

Matilda, Duchess of Normandy and now Queen of England, was a diminutive, slender woman. Her head, even bound by a crown, did not reach her husband's crimson-clad shoulder as she paced beside him, but for all that, those who watched her could feel the strength of her personality.

Standing beside Wulfstan in the crowded abbey, Ailith forgot her misery and apprehension as she watched the new queen walk past on the arm of her adoring husband. Rolf had told her a little about Matilda — how in the days when William had sued for her hand in marriage, she had refused him, saying that she would not mate with a bastard, and how William had dragged her from her chamber and thrashed her with a riding crop in front of her father's court. They had married, their passion had changed direction, and still powerfully dominated their marriage. She had borne him nine children, the youngest still an infant in the cradle, but her figure was as slim as a honed blade and well suited to the tightly laced, deep-red gown that glowed beneath her cloak as she walked. Watching her, Ailith wondered dubiously how much of Rolf's tale was embroidery for the sake of a better story. Certainly if Goldwin had come wooing like that, her father would have thrown him out on his ear.

In procession before and behind the royal couple came the archbishops and high prelates of the Church, followed by the powerful secular lords, most of them Norman with a scattering of

ill-at-ease English among their number. The lesser barons followed. Rolf was easy to find, his auburn hair marking him out.
He was wearing a knee-length tunic of the darkest blue wool, the
colour in itself a display of his rank since it was so expensive to
produce. The undertunic was of a lighter blue, and both were
banded with scarlet braid. Around his neck an ornate silver cross
glinted. So did a pagan hammer of Thor and a coloured stone on
a leather cord. He wore bracelets today, in honour of the great
occasion.

His eyes met hers briefly as he filed out of the abbey, and she
managed a wan half-smile, wishing that she could file out with
him. Instead she had to wait out the turn of her common rank
beneath Wulfstan's devouring stare. She was still not sure what
she was doing here in the goldsmith's company, only that it had
been easier to yield to the pressure rather than continue the
instinctive refusal.

'You do not have to go, of course you can stay here,' Felice
had said, taking her gently on one side. 'I know it might cause
you distress. But if you keep burying your head beneath the
covers, how will you ever manage to rise and face the day? I
believe it will do you good, even if you do cry.'

Badgered, bullied and coaxed, Ailith had found herself
dressed in her rose and blue wedding outfit. Wulfstan had tried
to give her a gold cross and a large round brooch to wear on
her mantle, but she had refused him with dignity, choosing
instead to wear her own jewellery – the glass beads that
Goldwin had given her on the occasion of their betrothal, and
bracelets of twisted silver and bronze wire.

Ailith was glad that they had persuaded her to come. It was
indeed a long time since she had had any horizon but the de
Remy household. To awake to the world was to face the pain
of colours and sounds that seemed too bright and sharp, but
were only caused by the fact that she had in truth been burying
her head beneath the covers.

She had seen enough now. What she needed was to go
home and sit in silence to digest it all; but Wulfstan had other
plans. In honour of the coronation, he had thrown open his

new house on the Fleet, to friends, relatives and fellow crafts-men, and declared a day of feasting. He had also insisted that Ailith attend. She knew that for her own wellbeing she should dig in her heels and refuse, but she was too tired to put up a stubborn resistance. Besides, she did not want to dampen the occasion which Felice was so obviously enjoying.

She capitulated and set herself to endure, the true Ailith retreating to a far corner of her mind and yielding control to the smiling, compliant Ailith whom Wulfstan and the others wanted her to be.

'Is Ailith all right?' Felice nudged Wulfstan as the goldsmith sought a fresh cup of mead from the pitchers set on trestles against the wall. 'Her eyes look glazed. You shouldn't give her any more to drink. She's not used to it.'

Wulfstan shrugged his powerful shoulders. ''Tis a day to celebrate, and she has been in the doldrums for far too long. Besides, look at the smile on her face. She's enjoying herself!'

Felice frowned, not so sure. She felt a little guilty. They had all pushed Ailith to attend this feast when perhaps she was not yet ready. Earlier, at Queen Matilda's coronation, her friend's face had been animated, and there had been interest in her eyes as she absorbed her surroundings. Now Ailith's expression was fixed and distant. The smile was not really a smile at all.

Wulfstan was a good customer of Aubert's. He enjoyed wine and bought copious quantities of it to impress his friends and curry favour with the Normans. He had also given Aubert several valuable contacts within the merchant and craft frater-nities. From a social and business viewpoint, a marriage between Ailith and Wulfstan was ideal.

Felice gnawed her lip. They owed Ailith far more than they would ever owe Wulfstan. Perhaps they ought to take Ailith home and cease pushing her to accept Wulfstan's suit. Before she could act on the thought, however, one of Aubert's friends claimed her attention. He was accompanied by his wife, newly arrived from Normandy. The couple were from the same quar-ter of Rouen as Felice and the woman had a store of recent gossip. Felice gladly set the conscience-troubling dilemma of

Ailith to one side, promising herself that she would deal with it later.

Ailith sat on a sun-warmed wooden bench in the small, but pleasant orchard garden. There were dense beds of herbs and tender green salat crops, there were strawberries still tight and green, and raspberries beginning to show a tinge of pink upon a trellis against the wattle fence of the dividing boundary. Blinking, disoriented, Ailith stared around. The sound of conversation and loud laughter assaulted her from the house. She saw a harassed serving maid hastening out to the well in the yard to fill her wooden bucket.

'Here we are, sweetheart, a cup of fresh mead to set you up. Are you feeling better now?' Wulfstan sat down beside her on the bench, too close for comfort as always, and pressed a small, beautifully turned wooden beaker into her hand. 'Drink up, my girl.'

She took a sip of the sweet, golden liquid and felt faintly nauseated. 'Your garden is well tended,' she managed to say. Her tongue felt too large for her mouth, almost as if she was drunk. 'I like gardening. Rolf's warhorse ran amok through my winter cabbages once, and I took a besom to the beast.' She was aware that she was speaking far too quickly, and that Wulfstan was sitting almost on top of her, the calculating grey eyes bright with lust. Her throat closed; she struggled to swallow.

'Ailith,' he said tenderly, 'don't be afraid. I won't hurt you, I swear.' His lips crushed down on hers, forcing them open, and one powerful hand grasped the back of her neck, holding her still. His beard scraped her face and his mouth was wet with saliva as if he were about to enjoy a meal. Ailith tried to pull away. His tongue stabbed and probed indecently. She raised her hands to strike him, to push him away, but he was swifter, grabbing them and forcing them down. This meant, however, that he had to release her head, and she was able to break the kiss and scream for help at the top of her lungs.

'Wait!' Wulfstan panted, his face congested. 'Ailith, wait! I want you to marry me!'

She wrestled with his greater strength, trying to free herself, half-weeping with the futile effort and the shock. 'I would not marry you even if you were the last man alive, you lecher!' she sobbed. 'Let me go!'

Lust and wine-anger thickened Wulfstan's voice. 'You will have no choice in the end, you know that. I could ruin your reputation if I so choose, as easily as doing this!' Releasing one of her hands, he yanked her wimple from her head, baring her braids. Ailith screamed again. Hot pain streaked through her neck and panic through her body. No respectable woman ever went forth in public with her hair uncovered. To have her head covering snatched off was tantamount to accusing her of being a whore.

'I have been patient with you beyond my usual scope,' Wulfstan said, breathing heavily. His gaze lingered upon the heavy golden lustre of her plaits before he returned the wimple. 'That was just a warning. I will have your reply by the end of the week.' His voice softened and he stroked her cheek. 'It is for the best, my Ailith, you'll see. I drive a hard bargain, but I can be generous too.'

Ailith drew a shuddering breath. Odious pig! He was so full of self-conceit that doubtless he truly believed he was being generous and patient. She started to tell him that she would rather be a whore than wife to such as he, but he stopped her, one hand across her mouth, the other wagging an index finger back and forth.

'Say nothing that you will later regret,' he warned, and raising his glance, let her go. 'Here's Felice, looking for you, I suspect.'

Shakily, Ailith draped the wimple over her braids and arranged the loose end across her shoulder. She saw Felice eyeing her and Wulfstan as if trying to decide whether she had interrupted at the right or wrong moment.

'Are you ready to go home?' she asked. 'I don't like to leave Benedict with the maids for too long.'

Ailith nodded. She could not speak, but the relief burned in her eyes.

'By the end of the week, my love,' Wulfstan said in a tender voice and bowed them both farewell. His eyes lingered possessively on Ailith.

'What did he mean "by the end of the week"?' Felice wanted to know as they sought for Aubert among the throng of guests.

'He wants me to marry him,' Ailith said dully. 'I have until the end of the week to decide.'

'What will you say?'

Ailith shook her head and gave no outright answer. She did not want to marry Wulfstan, but what if he made it impossible for her to do otherwise?

'There will be several noses put out of joint if you do accept him,' Felice said with a glint of relish. 'I know quite a few merchant families who have been throwing their daughters in Wulfstan's direction. He's still quite young, he's rich and he's handsome, a fine catch.'

'He is a conceited bully,' Ailith retorted shortly. 'You know it as well as I do. I want to go home, I feel sick.'

CHAPTER 21

In the yard, a cauldron simmered over a low fire. Ailith poured a beakerful of lye soap into the hot water, stirred the brew with a stick, and then dumped in a pile of soiled linens. These she attacked vigorously with a forked pole, prodding down billows of fabric as they rose to the surface, her sleeves pushed back and an old apron saving her working gown from the worst of the splashes. In her mind's eye, each time she thrust with the pole, she was drowning Wulfstan the Goldsmith. Nor did she intend confessing such sinful fantasies to a priest because they gave her great satisfaction and she was in no way repentant. If he thought he could harry her into his bed, he was mistaken. And yet, at the same time she was afraid of the depth his persecution might reach at her continued resistance.

'What has that shirt done to you that you should treat it so viciously?'

Ailith gasped and spun round to face Rolf de Brize. He was dressed less elegantly today. Like herself he wore his working clothes – a plain tunic, slightly threadbare, dusty leggings, and a short cloak with a round pewter pin. 'You have to pummel the washing hard to remove all the dirt,' she replied somewhat breathlessly. 'It is no different to beating it out on the rocks down at the river bank.' Red-faced, she blotted her brow on her freckled forearm. She could see from his expression and the way he lingered that he was sceptical.

'Felice was telling me just now that you had the misfortune

to receive a proposal of marriage from the illustrious Wulfstan.'

Ailith resumed her task, thrusting the pole down to the bottom of the cauldron. 'And if I did?' she asked defensively.

'You think it no business of mine, I can see, but as it happens, I do have an interest, since his intentions clash with my own.'

Ailith's heart lurched, and then commenced pounding in hard, swift strokes. She slammed the pole up and down a few more times, then stopped. Her breath was shaking, so were her hands. 'But you already have a wife and child,' she said to the bubbles of linen sitting on the scummy surface of the water.

'Yes, in Normandy,' he said gently.

Ailith almost laughed at the irony. Wulfstan said that if she would not marry him, he would ruin her reputation. And here was Rolf offering her that ruination. She contemplated assaulting him with the hot, soapy forked pole. 'I am no man's whore,' she said stiffly. 'I'll not argue the point with you. Just go away.'

'I haven't finished speaking – you misconstrued my meaning,' Rolf responded patiently and came around the side of the cauldron until they stood eye to eye and she was forced to look at him. His features were marred by the shadows of yesterday's excesses, and lack of sleep. He had not returned from celebrating the coronation until almost dawn, and Ailith knew that he had not been to bed – at least not to his own. 'I need a chatelaine for Ulverton, someone to bring order to the chaos of my household.'

'Then ask your wife.' She remained unbending.

'Arlette has responsibility for Brize-sur-Risle, and she speaks no English.' He grimaced. 'Besides, I don't want her at Ulverton. She would make the household a replica of Brize, and I do not think I could bear that.'

'You think I could better a great Norman lady?'

'I know you could. Look, it would only be the same as managing Aubert's house, or the one you shared with your husband, but on a larger scale. I always feel a sense of belonging when I come here, far more than I ever do at Brize.'

Ailith began to feel a treacherous glow of warmth at his flattery. She imagined herself dressed in the tightly laced Norman fashion, with a huge hoop of keys hanging from the belt at her waist. 'But Wulfstan has offered me marriage and wealth and high status.' She pounded the pole, forcing him to step back.

Rolf folded his arms. 'I offer you your freedom,' he delivered triumphantly. 'From Wulfstan, from all that hems you in. If you come to Ulverton as its chatelaine, all that I require of you is that you run my household. I will expect no more than that. Indeed, it may be in the fullness of time, you will find yourself another English husband from among the people there.' He gave her his white, sharp, smile. 'Of course you will have a deal of competition. Since the great battle, there are more women than men. It has been on my mind to make you the offer for a long time; I would not have you think it is done lightly.'

Ailith stared at him, trying to see through his ingenuous expression. If all he did indeed desire was a housekeeper, then his offer was heaven-sent. 'You swear on your soul that the position will be an honourable one?'

Had Goldwin been making the proposition, he would have been mortally offended by her doubt of his intentions. Rolf, however, smiled ruefully.

'On my soul.' He signed himself with the Cross. 'As proper as you choose.'

She chewed her lower lip and stared at him. She had many doubts, but they were accompanied by a spark of anticipation. No Wulfstan licking his lips and rubbing his hands. She and Felice could become friends again instead of rivals . . . No Benedict. Her breath caught in her throat and she looked at Rolf with stricken eyes.

'The baby, I cannot leave him, he is still taking suck.'

'He is well grown and he has his teeth. He only takes sustenance from you for the comfort, and for that, surely he should turn to his natural mother. Ailith, I do not mean to be cruel, but you have to let go a little. If you do come to Ulverton, it does not mean that you will never see Ben again. I am his Godfather and that means I have a duty to visit him. You can come with me as often as you want.'

Ailith shook her head, her mind filled with the vision of Benedict's laughing, rosy features. 'I . . . I do not know what to say.'

'I leave for Ulverton in two days' time with a wain load of supplies. Indeed, there are still some things I need to buy. When you have finished murdering those linens, perhaps you might accompany me to Chepeside?'

Wulfstan had given her a week to think upon her decision. Rolf, in his generosity, was giving her no time at all. Nor, she discovered, did she need it. There had been too much time of late to brood and fear. 'This will take until prime,' she said, not wishing to appear too eager.

Rolf nodded in a businesslike manner, but there was a gleam in his green agate eyes. 'I'll be in the stables,' he said, and without further ado, walked away.

She watched his lean, retreating form and began methodically beating the washing once more. She still mistrusted him, but she was aware of trusting Wulfstan's solid, mercantile bulk even less. Rolf had sworn on his soul that the position at Ulverton was an honourable one, that in time if she wished to remarry, she could choose her own mate. And she would not be losing Benedict entirely. Ailith began singing to herself as she worked, and thought that she would need to change her gown if she was to go visiting the markets of Chepeside.

Felice emerged from the house, her hands occupied by a drop spindle, her eyes by Benedict, who was toddling along at a merry pace in pursuit of a soft leather ball. He squatted, laboriously picked up the toy and threw it with a giggle, then lost his balance and plonked down. Laughing, Felice stooped and set him on his feet. Then, alerted by a sound she had never heard before, her gaze flickered to Ailith and widened.

'Your mood has changed somewhat since yester evening,' she said cautiously.

'What?' Ailith glanced round, her expression startled. She

had been so deep in thought that she had not noticed Felice approach.

'I said your mood has improved since yesterday. I do not think I have ever heard you sing before.'

'Was I singing?'

'As loudly as a songthrush at dawn. I never knew that your voice was so true.'

Ailith smiled a little at the compliment and reddened too. Her singing had been for her own ears and she was embarrassed that Felice had heard it.

'Does this mean you have changed your mind about Wulfstan?' Felice raced after Benedict as he toddled towards the dung heap.

Ailith's generous pink lips tightened. 'No,' she said with quiet dignity. 'I will never change my mind about Wulfstan. As it happens, I have received another offer, one I intend to accept.'

'Another offer of marriage? Who from?' Felice grabbed her son and stared at Ailith in astonishment. 'I did not even know that you were courting!'

Ailith reddened. 'It is not an offer of marriage. Rolf wants me to be his chatelaine at Ulverton. He says that his wife has enough on her trencher with Brize-sur-Risle. He has promised that I will be treated with all respect and honour,' she added hastily as she saw the look on Felice's face.

Benedict began to cry, his face growing dusky with temper. Felice set him down once more. 'And you believed him? Oh, Ailith, you goose!'

'Why should I not?' Ailith said defensively. 'He has never behaved less than honourably towards me. He swore an oath on his soul that there would be nothing improper about the arrangement.'

'Rolf's ideas of improper tend to be somewhat liberal,' Felice said dryly. 'He has no morals below the level of his belt.'

Ailith fished a linen napkin out of the cauldron and began to wring out the water. 'I know that,' she said with a toss of her head. 'I once caught him in the stable straw with Gytha the

Alewife, and from the tales I have heard, there have been many
others. I know I must be careful, but I am not afraid of Rolf as
I am afraid of Wulfstan. Rolf will only take what is willingly
offered. Wulfstan will seize what he wants without thought. I
know to which man I would rather trust my virtue.' She
dropped the napkin in the large basket beside the cauldron and
gave Felice a challenging glare. 'I know that it would be more
convenient for you if I married Wulfstan, and for that I am
sorry. If he was a good man in the mould of Goldwin, I would
do so, but he isn't and there is nothing more to say.' Her chin
started to quiver and she turned back to the cauldron and fished
out another piece of linen.

A moment later, she felt Felice's hand on her shoulder.
'Ailith, I'm sorry, you must do as you see fit. I just don't want
to see you hurt any more than you have been already.'

Ailith draped the linen over the side of the cauldron and put
her arms around Felice, hugging her. 'Then let me make my
own mistakes,' she said, and then with a small cry of alarm, she
pushed out of the embrace and ran to the dung heap to snatch
Benedict out of the muck and straw.

The baby squealed his delight at being swung up in Ailith's
arms. 'Oh, you rascal!' Ailith could not help but laugh as she
cuddled him. Her eyes filled with moisture. The baby would
be the hardest thing to leave behind despite Rolf's assurances
that she would still see him often. But as she carried him back
to his mother, her decision was made and her heart was filled
not only with determination, but a new sense of purpose.

Wulfstan's shop occupied a prime position in the heart of
London's goldsmiths' quarter. The frontage was more generous
than usual for business premises in the heart of the city.
Morning sunshine gleamed on the whitewashed walls and the
open counter with its cover of dark green cloth. Two apprentices were erecting a canvas awning to provide shade for the
customers since the day looked set to be hot.

Rolf dismounted from Sleipnir and handed the reins to the
accompanying groom. Then he asked one of the apprentices

for Wulfstan. The lad appraised him, and quickly realised that Rolf was Norman and rich. Sensing new and valuable custom, he hurried into the living quarters at the back of the shop.

Rolf leaned on the counter and studied the various items hanging on the wall behind it. To one side there were pincers, snips, and engraving tools, each neatly hung in its set place. Directly before his eyes were the samples of merchandise. Their style reflected their creator. All the pieces without exception were heavy and opulent, the sort of items that said *Behold, I am wealthy and to be respected.* Rolf grimaced at a large disc brooch so crusted with gold that it looked like a bubbling griddle cake, and wondered how much some city burgher, eager to show off his status, was going to pay for it.

Wiping his hands and lips on a napkin, Wulfstan emerged from the rear of the shop. The apprentice followed him and returned to helping his fellow with the awning. Wulfstan looked at Rolf and the pleasant, slightly obsequious expression fell from his face and was replaced by narrow-eyed wariness.

'Lord Rolf,' he acknowledged. 'What can I do for you so early this morning? Do you wish to break your fast with me?' He gestured towards his living quarters.

Rolf shook his head. 'Thank you, but I ate at dawn. I am leaving for my lands today; indeed, my baggage wain left the city at first light. As soon as I finish my business, I'll be following it out. And when I tell you why I have come, I do not believe that you will want to offer me hospitality of any kind.'

Wulfstan's eyes flickered. He put the napkin down on the counter. 'This concerns Ailith, I think?' he said coldly.

'Yes, it concerns Ailith.'

'If you are here to warn me against pursuing my suit, you are wasting your breath. I intend to have her.'

Rolf's dislike of the goldsmith deepened towards loathing. 'But she does not want you,' he said more sharply than was polite. 'To that end she has agreed to become chatelaine of my English lands. She left this morning with the baggage wain.' And then he added softly, each word biting and distinct, 'She is mine, Wulfstan, and always will be.'

The goldsmith stared at him. Then he began to shake, and uttering a roar of rage, he seized Rolf around the throat and started to squeeze. Rolf scrabbled for his dagger. The groom abandoned the two horses and ran to help his master, snarling at the gaping apprentices to pull Wulfstan off.

Passers-by hurried to help, and after a struggle, Wulfstan was finally prised from his victim. The Saxon fought against the restraining hands whilst Rolf wheezed and choked on his knees.

'May you and she be damned for eternity!' Wulfstan snarled. 'Whoremonger and whore!'

Rolf regained his feet. The goldsmith's rage was that of a child denied its own way. There was no point in continuing the scene. Wulfstan was beaten and Rolf was finding it difficult enough to draw a clean breath without the added burden of speech.

Ignoring Wulfstan, which only added another dimension to the Saxon's fury, Rolf mounted his horse and rode away. He had done what he intended, and the road ahead was clear.

CHAPTER 22

On a bright spring noontide, five days after setting out from London, Ailith came to Ulverton. On this final day, they took the road from Wareham where they had rested for the night and headed over the undulating greenery of the chalk downs towards the coast. The sky was blue, the air sparkled; so too in the distance did the sea, its horizon haze-grey. Ailith narrowed her eyes the better to focus. Everything was so different. Before this, the furthest she had ever been from London was the village of Tottenham, just a few miles from the city's hub, where she had lived before her marriage. She had never seen forests as huge and dark as the ones which had engulfed her journey, could never have imagined such vastness. The bursting Maytime greenery overwhelmed her senses, made her feel humble and afraid, but at the same time she was charged with exultation.

Now the forests were behind them. The three cobs pulled sturdily in the shafts of the baggage wain, their step brisk and their ears pricked. The driver was a taciturn little Saxon named Osred, whose speech consisted of positive and negative grunts in response to her curious questions. He had a scrawny neck and stringy arms which seemed on first glance incapable of controlling the three lively horses, but his wiry frame was deceptively strong. Wulfhild, who had opted to remain with Ailith, declared that he only required feeding up, but she said that about everyone less plump than herself. Sigrid had remained in London with Aubert and Felice, for she was soon to marry an armourer's journeyman from Southwark.

The sea vanished from sight as they entered a low dip, reappearing as the wain gained the brow of the slope. It was closer now, a glittering swell of darkest blue stretching as far as the eye could see, and filling the bay of the nearer vision. A village was cuddled down in the folds of the hills. Standing a little apart from it on another slope that showed an edge of raw earth, stood a wooden tower surrounded by a palisade of sharpened stakes, and beneath the main hill, a raised bank of earth creating a fortified compound filled with a variety of thatched wooden buildings.

Rolf appeared suddenly at the side of the wain. He had been riding Sleipnir ahead and behind all morning – to scout so he had said, but Ailith had sensed the restless anticipation that made keeping still a torture. 'Ulverton,' he announced, pointing towards the village. 'I have other holdings, of course, but this is the main one, your new home.'

Ailith set aside the disturbing thought that these lands through which they travelled were only Rolf's by right of conquest. An English thegn had died by a Norman hand on Hastings field so that Rolf could take possession. 'Do I live in that place up there or in the village?' She looked dubiously at the crude wooden structure on top of the hill. If it was habitable, that was the most which could be said about it.

'The castle, you mean?' He sounded wryly amused at her doubtful tone. 'The village is too far for you to trudge every day. When I first arrived here, the old English hall was stripped and derelict, not worth renovating, so I began afresh. A castle is far more secure from attack. Don't worry, there's a perfectly liveable hall in the lower bailey; the tower is just in case of dire necessity.'

Ailith noticed that his voice was stronger today. When he had joined the baggage wain on the road after departing London, he had been scarcely able to speak. She had learned in a roundabout manner from one of the grooms that Rolf had gone to see Wulfstan and that there had been violence. Rolf himself had not spoken of the incident, and Ailith had seen no reason to seek the details. 'Do you fear attack?'

Rolf smiled and shook his head. 'Not from these people. They have accepted me with a remarkably good grace. I wear no armour to come to them – a sword at my hip, yes, it is a mark of my rank, but I have no need of further protection.'

Ailith returned his smile. 'A wolf in sheep's clothing,' she said.

Rolf laughed aloud at her sally. 'Better than a sheep in wolf's clothing,' he retorted.

The 'castle' owned a sketchy garrison consisting of two knights and eight footsoldiers, all of whom were at work on building tasks as the wain rolled across the wooden bridge built over the ditch.

'I can't afford the luxury of keeping men purely to fight,' Rolf explained as he dismounted. 'Those who are too proud to dirty their hands, work for other masters.' He moved to help Ailith from the wain, setting his hands around her waist to give himself purchase as he swung her round and down.

She felt the curious stares of the men – both Rolf's troops and the English labourers. From her eye corner she saw one soldier nudge his companion, mutter something from the side of his mouth, and laugh. She had done nought but allow Rolf to assist her from the wain and already they were speculating and coming to the wrong conclusions.

'Come,' said Rolf, 'I will introduce you.'

Ailith thought, *Why bother, they already think I am your whore.* Her lips narrowed. She would show them the meaning of respectable.

The men were amenable enough and prepared to be polite to her face, although she could not help but wonder what they would think and say of her behind her back. It was the Saxons who eyed her the most doubtfully. While they could come to terms with a Norman lord in their midst, they were perturbed that he should bring a stranger of their own race into his house-hold. Although the word *'traitor'* was not uttered, it hovered in the air as clearly as the word *'whore'*.

And yet she had to take charge of these people, command their obedience and respect if she was to succeed in the duties Rolf had proposed that she carry out.

Ailith set her jaw and resolutely followed Rolf across the bailey to the long wooden hall standing close to the eastern palisade.

'They will soon grow accustomed to you,' he said over his shoulder. 'They looked at me like that for the first month or so until they realised I was no ogre come to eat their children.'

'You are not English,' Ailith answered in a subdued tone.

'Would you rather have yoked yourself to that bullying goldsmith?'

'You know I would not.'

Rolf paused on the threshold of the hall and turning, took her by the shoulders. 'I know it is hard,' he said. 'But time will make it easier, trust me.'

She removed his hands and shook her head. 'When you touch me in front of everyone, when you look into my eyes and laugh and make private jests, the people here are going to construe far more than friendship and obligation. "Ah yes," they will say. "Lord Rolf and his Saxon whore. Why should we do as she bids us?" You swore that my position in your household would be an honourable one. Well in Jesu's name, I pray you set about establishing it now before it is too late!'

His face darkened. Ailith stared him out. She had never seen him angry before, but she knew that her own anger and fear were any match for his.

'You insult me,' he said huskily.

'By showing you the truth?'

'You want to live like a nun?' he bit out. 'Then so be it. I'll have your cell prepared.'

Ailith nodded vigorously. 'With a bar on the inside of the door. And I want one of the village women to sleep with me at night, so that everyone will know that I am virtuous. Until then, I will sleep in the main hall with everyone else.'

'God's death, you're as stubborn as a mule, and you know how to kick like one – straight in the teeth!' Rolf growled, but reluctant humour began to gleam in his eyes.

Ailith stared him out without responding to his humour. This point of principle was very important to her.

Clearing his throat, Rolf shouldered past her into the hall. 'Well then, Abbess Ailith,' he declared with a sarcastic flourish, 'let me show you around your new convent.'

Driven by a boisterous wind, sunshine and shadow chased each other recklessly across Ulverton's beach. Gulls wheeled and screamed above the limestone cliffs, or foraged along the shore-line where the tide had flung up a bounty of dark seaweed. A donkey stood in the lee of a cliff and munched hay from its nosebag, while two women culled mussels from the beds exposed by the retreating sea.

Muddy sand squished between Ailith's bare toes. She had drawn her gown between her legs and looped it through her belt as the fisherwomen did, and because a full wimple would have hampered her, she had pinned her braids in a coronet and cov-ered them with a simple triangular kerchief. Her knife cut through the threads securing a clump of mussels to a rock and she dropped them in the basket beside her. Her hands and feet were numb with cold, but nevertheless she was enjoying herself.

She had been nervous of the sea at first, but in the five months since coming to Ulverton, she had learned to appreci-ate its moods, both fierce and calm. Sometimes she would take her spinning and stand in the high tower of the keep with the soldiers on guard to watch the waves roll into the bay. On other occasions she would use the excuse of gathering driftwood to walk along the beach with the donkey harnessed to a small cart. Today she had decided that as it was Friday, they would observe the fish-only rule by dining on mussels. During her days in London, Felice had taught her a way of cooking them in a stock of garlic and wine, and she knew that it was one of Rolf's favourite dishes.

She already knew many of his likes and dislikes from his sojourn in London, and in truth he was easily accommodated. He enjoyed food, had a voracious appetite that showed not at all on his lean, active frame, and he liked his meals to be served in good quantity with the minimum of fuss. In that respect, he was so much like Goldwin, that despite her determination to remain aloof, Ailith found herself looking forward to the dinner hour each day, to the conversation and the pleasure of watching Rolf devour everything that she prepared.

There was a proper bakehouse now in the lower compound with a magnificent brick bread oven, the rival of any in London. The villagers, if they wished, could bring their dough to be baked, providing that they paid for the service with a portion of that dough. Ailith often supervised this particular duty herself, for it gave her an opportunity to speak to the village women and disabuse them of any notions they might have concerning herself and the Norman lord. She had also given Wulfhild free rein to gossip and make friends with the women, for Ailith knew they would believe far more of her maid at this stage than they would of her. She had ensured too, that the village wife who was paid to sleep across her bolted chamber door at night was a talkative biddy who would delight in telling everyone in Ulverton how matters were ordered up at the castle, that its English chatelaine was a woman of stout moral fibre.

This guardian of her virtue was with her now, helping her to cut mussels from the sand. Edgith was at least threescore years. According to hearsay, mostly her own, she had been a great beauty in her youth, and having lived so long, there were few folk remaining who could contradict her. Her wizened face did indeed possess regular features, although they were somewhat marred by the decayed state of her remaining, worn-out teeth. Still, her eyes were bright with a zest for life. She had been married to a fisherman, but he had been lost in stormy seas some eight years ago. Four brawny sons she had borne, and they were all fishermen too.

Edgith dropped another bunch of mussels into the basket and pressed her hands to the small of her back. She unstoppered the water bottle hanging from the tie at her waist and took a drink.

'Did your husband fight in the great battle against the Normans, Mistress Ailith?' she asked curiously as she dug around in her pouch and brought out a small, flat griddle cake saved from the breaking of fast.

Ailith shook her head as the old woman offered to share, but she too stopped work for a moment. She licked her wind-dried lips and tasted salt. 'No, he was badly wounded fighting the Norse in the north. On the day of the great battle he was lying in his bed raving with fever. I had two brothers though, and their bones lie bleaching on Hastings field. They were members of King Harold's bodyguard. Lyulph was only in his nineteenth year.' Her voice started to tremble. Abandoning the muddy sand, she went to rinse her feet in a shallow channel of running water that was carving a path to the sea.

Edgith chewed carefully on her griddle cake and drank her water, her old eyes fixed shrewdly upon Ailith. 'So, if you had so much grief from the Normans, what be you doing with this one?'

Ailith turned sharply.

'Oh aye,' Edgith nodded sagely. 'I know that you are a respectable woman – and so does the village. Most of 'em are sick to the back teeth with being told that you and the lord do not bed together. But you be friends with him and you speak the Norman tongue uncommonly well for an English woman. How came this to happen when your own kin died for King Harold? Doesn't it disturb you to sit down at his table and see those two great battle axes on the long wall? Don't you ever wonder about who he killed to get them?'

Briefly, with a hint of defensive irritation, Ailith told Edgith about her friendship with Felice and Aubert, and how she had come to know Rolf. 'I do not allow myself to wonder,' she concluded. 'I do not look at those axes – to me they do not exist.'

Edgith made a non-commital sound and returned to harvesting mussels.

'Do you think I am wrong?'

'It is not for me to say, Mistress Ailith.'

'No, I want to know. Do you think I am wrong?'

Edgith straightened once more. 'They do exist,' she said. 'So does his hunger for you and yours for him. You can pretend all you want, but neither will go away just because you have buried yourself in the sand. One day you will be dug out of your hole.'

'I do not hunger for Rolf de Brize!'

'The defences you have built say that you do, that you fear him, and rightly so I think.' Before Ailith could reply, she nodded behind them. 'Visitors, mistress. Perhaps we should gather extra mussels for the table.'

Perturbed by Edgith's words, which held an alarming ring of truth, Ailith turned to see a troop of horsemen advancing along the shore towards them. She could tell that they were Normans from their manner of dress. Eight grown men she counted, and a blond-haired boy. A like number of bay and chestnut horses followed on leading reins.

One of the riders detached himself from the party and kicked his mount to a canter. The man's hauberk glittered like fish scales, the sun glanced off the sharpened tip of his spear. He drew rein before the women, pulling the horse in tight so that it danced on the spot. Ailith looked up into a square, powerful face with long dimples in the cheeks and a wide expanse of chin.

'Which way to Ulverton?' he demanded in appalling English. Another Norman rode up beside him, a younger man porridged with spots.

'Look at the udders on that, Tancred!' he enthused coarsely in French. His eyes lingered on Ailith's breasts before dropping to her exposed legs. He smacked his lips.

The older man snorted. 'God's eyes, is that all you ever think about?' There was indulgent humour in his tone. 'You haven't got time today to go swiving in the dunes. Still, I see what you mean.' He looked Ailith appreciatively up and down.

Ailith glared at the two men. 'Ulverton is that way,' she said in immaculate French and directed with her arm. 'Follow the track for half a mile and you will come to the castle. Lord Rolf, I am sure, will be fascinated to know what you think about his chatelaine.'

The square-faced man blinked rapidly, then bit his lip, stifling his amusement. The younger one blenched. Ailith turned her back on both of them and resumed picking mussels.

'I am sorry, my lady. If we had known your status, we would have been more polite,' said the first Norman.

'Is a fisherwoman not as entitled to as much courtesy as a

'lady of rank?' she said scathingly without bothering to look round. Beside her, Edgith glared at the two men, her knife held ready in her hand.

Without reply, the men sheepishly withdrew, and when Ailith raised her head, it was to see them riding off the beach in the direction she had indicated.

'Visitors indeed,' she muttered through her teeth to Edgith.

'I encountered your "chatelaine" down by the shoreline,' Tancred said to Rolf.

Rolf had been examining his new mares and deliberating whether to graze them on their own for a while, or introduce them immediately to Sleipnir. Now he turned and looked at his overseer.

'I thought she was nought but a fisher-wench, but she soon set me and Arnulf to rights.'

Rolf grinned. He had seen Ailith set out for the shore with Edgith and the donkey. She had been wearing an old, patched homespun gown, ancient shoes, and a plain linen kerchief over her braids. 'I can imagine that she would.'

Tancred eyed him soberly. 'Arnulf's a randy pup. He made certain crude remarks concerning her figure. I agreed with him before I realised she could understand us. I did not know that she was yours. There was no insult intended.'

Rolf resumed his inspection of the mares. 'Do not assume that because she is my housekeeper, she warms my bed too,' he said as he assessed a small, perky chestnut. 'I wish that she did, but Ailith has her own thoughts on the matter. She is a respectable widow and intends remaining so.'

Tancred looked nonplussed. 'Then she is not your mistress?' he said with an air of astonished disbelief.

Rolf shook his head regretfully. 'Not at the moment,' he said, and then suddenly grinned. 'But who knows what the future holds?'

The three weeks which Tancred and his party spent at Ulverton were the most uncomfortable of Ailith's life, and she was not sorry to see them leave before the winter storms began to make the crossing of the narrow sea too treacherous an enterprise.

In defence of that first encounter on the shore, she had made sure that in their presence she was always dressed properly and in the high Saxon style, which meant layer upon layer, so that not so much as an outline of breast could be discerned. She had fastened her belt loosely so that there was no emphasis on the trimness of her waist. Nor had she worn a kerchief again, but had replaced it with the full wimple and circlet, a brooch pinning its folds secure for good measure. And she had kept her distance, conspicuous by her absence at the high table. It had been less embarrassing for all concerned.

Now that their visitors had returned to Normandy, Ailith applied herself to the task of packing the travelling chests for the Christmas visit to London. She was greatly looking forward to seeing the city again. Although she had settled at Ulverton, she still harboured longings for the bustling markets of Chepeside with their unrivalled selection of commodities, for the smoky, smutty, greasy smell of the city's heart. She wanted to see Felice again, and most of all, in order to fill the empty hole in her heart, she had a fierce need to hold Benedict in her arms.

Her own chest was packed and contained a plain working gown, her best, wedding outfit, and a dress of plain green wool decorated with embroidery. The linens for her monthly bleeds, leg bindings, woollen socks, spare combs and jewellery pins had also been included. There was nothing else she required.

Rolf would be attending the court to make his report to the King, so he would need his best robes. Tancred had brought gifts across the narrow sea from Rolf's wife, including a beautiful tunic of expensive dark blue wool embroidered with thread of gold. His old court garment was of almost the same colour. Rolf wore a great deal of blue, and it suited him, but Ailith thought that a change might gladden the eye. To that end, before Tancred's arrival, she had purchased two bolts of fabric, one of rich tawny, the other a smoky green that matched Rolf's eyes, and during the last three weeks of withdrawal from open company, she had made Rolf two very fine tunics that were just as worthy of his rank as the blue.

Ailith had dared not explore the emotions behind her determination to make as good as, if not better a task of the tunics than his wife had made of the blue. Nor was she proud of herself for the way she examined the blue robe in strong light, searching for flaws. Those were acts that smacked of jealousy and how could she be jealous of that which she did not desire?

All the same, as she folded Rolf's clothing in his baggage chest, she placed the blue robe in the bottom and laid everything else on top, finishing with the two tunics she herself had stitched, together with a shirt of fine, soft linen.

'I see you are well ahead,' Rolf said from the doorway.

Ailith jumped guiltily and turned round. He was leaning against the door jamb, watching her, his arms folded. She wondered how long he had been there, and if he had seen her lingering touch when she carefully laid the tunics and shirt within the chest.

'It seems only sensible to be ready in good time. Tomorrow dawn with everyone waiting in the bailey is no occasion to be packing baggage.'

'No,' he agreed with a smile, and pushing himself upright, advanced into the room, which was, after all, his own.

'You can come out of hiding now that Tancred's gone. I have never known you to be so industrious in far-away corners,' he teased. 'He was as embarrassed as you were.' He tilted his head to one side. 'Tancred is a good friend and the best overseer a man could have. When the time comes, his son Mauger will inherit his father's place. I could not wish for better people to serve me, even as I could not wish for a better chatelaine. I expect you and Tancred to forget that first day and rub along together if circumstances demand.'

Ailith had watched Rolf and Tancred drinking together, had seen their camaraderie and the way each man reacted upon the other until they degenerated into silly little boys. She had also heard them discussing horses and bloodlines in the yard with a fluid expertise that left her a baffled outsider.

'If it is important to you, I will do my best,' she said.

He eyed her thoughtfully. 'Fetch your cloak,' he said suddenly. 'I want to see how good a rider you are these days.'

Ailith shook her head. Since arriving at Ulverton, she had been coaxed by Rolf into learning how to ride on her own instead of going pillion behind him or a groom, or taking a seat in the baggage wain, but she knew herself an indifferent horse-woman. 'I haven't the time,' she excused lamely.

'Then make it.'

Before she knew what was happening, Ailith found herself down in the lower courtyard outside the stables. A groom led out a small chestnut mare with sharply pricked ears, a bright eye, and a high-stepping action.

'She won't be mated until the spring.' Rolf gave Ailith a gentle push in the mare's direction. 'She is yours until then.'

Ailith swallowed, not at all sure that she desired such a splendid gift.

'Do not you dare to say that she is beyond your station or moralise on what people will think of you,' Rolf forestalled her protest. 'You will not shame me before everyone here by refusing.'

Ailith smiled nervously. 'I fear that I will shame myself. 'How will I stay in the saddle when I am only accustomed to the plodding paces of that old brown cob?'

'You'll learn between here and London,' he said cheerfully, and cupping his hands for her foot, boosted her into the saddle. The young mare shied and almost unseated Ailith. She clung grimly to the reins, gripped with her thighs, and after a few fraught moments, managed to bring the horse under control. She glared at Rolf. He just grinned.

'You will never see anything but the ground unless you lift your eyes to the horizon,' he told her. 'Live a little, Ailith, cast yourself into the wind.'

Ailith drew in the reins as tight as she could. 'At the moment,' she retorted, 'I am more concerned with not casting myself beneath the hooves of this horse.'

CHAPTER 23

Whistling to himself, Rolf came in from the cold and sat down at the fire beside Aubert. The wine merchant was recovering from an attack of winter ague, and although over the worst, was cosseting himself before his hearth, using his blocked nose as an excuse to drink hot, cinnamon-flavoured wine.

Rolf rubbed his hands and held them out to the flames. 'Tell me I am mad,' he said.

'You do not need me to tell you that!' Aubert snorted. 'What have you done? Wagered your fortune on the throw of a single dice? Courted another man's wife beneath his very nose?'

Rolf laughed. 'Neither of those, although they were both possibilities. No, I'm going north next week with Robert de Comminges. The King has granted him the lordship of Durham – it's a city close to the Scots border.'

'Ah, your incurable wanderlust.' Aubert looked at him side-long. 'I did not know Robert de Comminges was a friend of yours.'

'He isn't, but he pays well for his horses. I've seen nothing of England north of the Trent, but I have heard that they breed fine, sturdy ponies in the north parts of the old Danelaw.'

'You intend breeding ponies?' Aubert lifted a curious brow.

'There are plenty of buyers for good sumpter beasts. Think of all the English wool that has to be carried to the ports for shipping to Flanders.'

Aubert nodded at the sense of the statement and stroked his bristly jaw. 'You talk like a merchant,' he said dryly.

'I am, although not as adept as you if what I hear of your business ventures is true.'

Aubert shrugged modestly. 'I invest in vessels and cargoes, and thus far, they've all had the good fortune to return me a profit.'

'A handsome profit. I understand you've invested in property too.'

'Here and there, mere dabblings to provide security. I want to leave Benedict well provided for when it comes his turn to inherit.'

Rolf doubted the veracity of Aubert's claim to 'mere dabblings', for that was not Aubert's way. He suspected that his friend's ventures were making him a very rich man. Before he could decide how to fish further, however, the door was flung open and Felice and Ailith bustled into the room, their arms loaded with Chepeside purchases.

Felice looked as beautiful as always, her cheeks rosy-bright, her dark eyes sparkling, but it was Ailith who held Rolf's eye – and tugged at his heartstrings. The alchemy of laughter transformed her entire face and made of it a bewitching new territory that he longed to explore with a wanderlust almost as powerful as that which drew him towards the north.

'You know,' murmured Aubert, 'Felice and I were deeply concerned when you took Ailith to Ulverton, but I can see now that we were wrong. Ailith needed to break away from the life she was leading with us, and from what I have seen and heard, she is very happy in her new position. I misjudged you, Rolf.'

Rolf slowly shook his head. 'You did not misjudge me at all,' he said softly, watching Ailith as she removed her cloak and hung it on a wall peg. 'Sometimes I am hard pressed not to fling her down on the nearest mattress and fill her to the hilt. The only thing that prevents me is the thought of what would happen afterwards, and I am coming closer and closer to saying be damned to the consequences.'

'So that is why you are going north – because you cannot scratch your itch?'

Rolf pursed his lips to consider. 'No,' he said after a moment. 'Whether I had bedded her or not, I would still take the road to Durham.'

Aubert grunted. 'Then you are not as much in thrall as your body thinks.'

'And there are bound to be willing women along the way,' Rolf added with a self-mocking grin. He rose and stretched, his glance meeting Ailith's across the room. Benedict in her arms, she smiled and hastened over to him.

'Have you spent all my money?' he teased.

'Do not judge me by your own standards,' she retorted smartly. 'I have brought you home a full bag of silver.'

'Hah, then what did you buy?'

'Linen for shirts and shifts, needles and threads and herbs. A loaf of sugar.' She ticked off the items on her fingers while Benedict rested in the crook of her arm and grinned at Rolf as if he was party to a great jest. 'Some pottery cups for the high table. They stack one inside the other according to size, so they'll be easier to store than the ones we've already got. I bought myself a new belt since my old one is almost worn through, and two dozen weaving tablets. Oh, and this.' She gave him Benedict to hold and delved into the pouch at her waist. 'For you,' she said, reddening a little as she presented him with a silver cloak brooch in the shape of a six-legged horse.

'It is bought with my own coin from the sale of Goldwin's forge. It is to thank you for all you have done for me, and to bring you good fortune. I know you set score by your talismans.'

Rolf looked at the token in his palm – Sleipnir, the legendary mount of Odin the all-father. He was touched and proud. He also felt more than a little unworthy. Stooping slightly, he kissed her cold cheek. 'It is more than I deserve,' he said.

Felice joined them, taking Benedict from Rolf's arms. 'Is it not pretty?' she asked, nodding at the brooch. 'The moment Ailith set eyes on it, she was determined to buy it for you.'

Pretty was not the word Rolf would have used to describe the stark, spartan lines of the clasp, but he nodded all the same.

'While we were discussing the price with the silversmith, we saw Wulfstan and his new wife,' Felice added.

'His new wife?' Rolf looked up in surprise. He touched his throat, remembering Wulfstan's fist squeezing there and the spittle of rage on the Saxon's beard. 'He recovered from his disappointment soon enough.'

'The damage was to his pride, not his heart,' Felice said darkly and wagged a salutary forefinger. 'Do not think he has forgiven and forgotten? He hasn't spoken to us since you took Ailith to Ulverton.'

'Small loss,' Aubert grunted from his seat by the fire.

'And you say he's married now?' Rolf asked.

'In the autumn to the daughter of another goldsmith. Wulfstan must have got her with child on their wedding night because she is showing as round as a barrel and he is at pains that everyone should see the results of his prowess.'

Rolf pinched his upper lip between forefinger and thumb. 'Did he speak to you?'

'He didn't see us,' Ailith said quickly. 'We hid our faces until he had passed. I felt sorry for his poor wife. She was dressed in so much finery that it was weighing her down, and I could tell that she was longing to be sick. When I think that it could have been me . . . ' A little shiver ran through her.

'But it isn't,' Rolf soothed. 'You are safe forever from such as he.'

Aubert spoke up, trying to dispel the sombre atmosphere that had suddenly settled, 'Out of the frying pan and into the fire, I would say.'

Ailith reddened and excused herself to the safe stowing of her purchases. She heard Rolf say something reproachful to Aubert, although she did not catch the words, and then Aubert's hearty laugh, which terminated in a bout of coughing.

Moments later, Rolf joined her in the corner of the hall where her pallet and belongings lay. 'I'm going north for a few months,' he announced.

'North?' Ailith stopped what she was doing and stared at him. 'Where?'

'To Durham with Robert de Comminges. He's been appointed earl in Gospatric's place. I have heard that there are good sumpter ponies to be bought in Mercia and Northumbria.'

She was gripped by a cold feeling of dismay. 'The north has not been tamed. My brothers used to say that the peoples beyond the Humber saw King Harold as a foreigner. They look to the Norse for their succour. Their language and their ways are different.'

'I know,' he said without concern. 'My own family were once Vikings. I am told that my great-grandfather was as fluent in Norse as he was in French.'

She shook her head. 'You will be putting yourself in great danger.'

'No more than I ever did by joining the English expedition in the first place.'

Her lips tightened. She turned away and began folding the yards of bought linen into a coffer. 'You have responsibilities that you take as lightly as your care for your own life,' she said without looking round.

Rolf snorted. 'I know my responsibilities. Christ, you sound like my wife!'

'Then follow your whim up the great north road,' she retorted stiffly, 'and pray that your gains outweigh your losses.'

'What is that supposed to mean?' He grasped her arm and dragged her round to face him.

Ailith shook him off. 'You fool. Do you never stop to think that the green on the other side of the hill might be nothing but a quagmire?' She glared at him, banged down the coffer lid, and stalked away.

Rolf had not bargained for such a hostile response. Several emotions assaulted him at once. He was angry at the manner in which she had spoken to him, and that in turn made him all the more determined to travel north. He had wanted to take her in his arms and brutally cover that furious mouth with a kiss. Lust, frustration, the need to possess. Most unsettling of all, as he stood staring at the coffer and the empty pallet, a treacherous thread of reason told him that he should heed her opinion and bide here in the south.

A sharp pain in his clenched fist caused him to look down and see that the pin on the silver cloak clasp had come unfastened and stabbed his palm.

CHAPTER 24

North of York, two days' ride from Durham, Rolf took his leave of the Norman army and its arrogant commander Robert de Comminges. Partly this was because Rolf desired to investigate the types of horses and ponies that these northern climes bred, but the other part of the decision was caused by Rolf's irritation at the attitude of his fellow Normans.

They treated the lands through which they rode as conquered territory, not asking, but taking what they wanted with a rough hand. Any who made complaint or resisted found themselves looking down the blood gutter of a war sword. In their wake, de Comminges' army of mercenaries left a smouldering resentment, and the further north they rode, the brighter grew the embers and the less cowed became the people. Here, the majority of the local lords were still of the native Anglo–Danish blood. They owed their allegiance to the English earls Edwin and Morcar, and to Waltheof, son of the great Siward of Northumbria. These powerful English lords might have bent the knee to William of Normandy, but what they really wanted to do was spit in his face.

'We have to show them with an iron fist that we are the masters,' Comminges said to Rolf. 'If they think for one moment that we are weak, they will be upon us like a pack of wolves.'

Rolf grunted and tightened the cinch on his chestnut's girth. Dawn had broken a hole in the slate-coloured sky, and a half moon was lingering to greet it. 'I have no doubt you are right,' he replied, thinking of the dark scowls they had received along their way.

'You should not be leaving us to ride alone.'

Rolf raised his brows at de Comminges. The man had a florid complexion that was threaded with a hard drinker's broken veins. The upright stubble on his scalp, short-shaven at the back, gave him the look of a man who spent all his time in fights, most of them disreputable. But Robert de Comminges, for all his brutality and arrogance, was no mindless vandal. He had a brain when he chose to use it. 'You have your horses,' Rolf said to him, 'and I have my money. I doubt that Durham will be any safer than the villages round these parts.'

'Yes, but there are more of us.'

'And a greater native population in Durham,' Rolf pointed out. 'Do not worry about me. I can take care of myself.'

De Comminges looked sceptical. 'There are bound to be refugees from Hastings up here.' He scowled. 'You'll be dead before you're even out of the saddle.'

'The sword is a language that every man understands,' Rolf answered. 'But so is trade. Wherever one goes, so does the other.' Catching up the reins, he swung across the chestnut's back. 'I will see you in Durham town, within a seven day.'

De Comminges snorted. 'I'd wager on that boast if I ever thought I'd see the colour of your coin.'

'How much?'

De Comminges pursed his thin lips and rubbed the back of his shaven neck. 'The price of a good warhorse.'

'Agreed.' Rolf reached down from the saddle to seal their bargain with a handclasp. De Comminges had a meaty palm and solid, fleshy fingers. Even now, in the chill dank of a winter dawn, they were moist and slightly warm.

Rolf's were cold. As he rode out of the Norman camp, he pulled on his sheepskin mittens. They were proof that, despite the difficulties, trade was possible with the natives of northern England. He had bargained for the mittens in York with a shepherd's wife. While she had made her contempt of all

Normans obvious, she had not scorned his silver. It was in York too that he had learned of a horse-trader who might be willing to deal with him.

The sounds from the Norman camp dwindled. Soon, when he looked over his shoulder, Rolf saw nothing but bare, black trees and the dull green and brown of a dormant winter countryside. The sky lightened to a uniform, dreary grey with a heavy border of darker cloud menacing the direction in which he and his men were heading. The road was well used, for tracks had been laid upon tracks, and picking out one particular set from the morass of trampled mud was impossible.

They came to a wayside shrine, but it was not a Christian one. The rain-weathered features of the Norse god Odin glared out at them from an oak-wood effigy. At the feet of the crude representation, there were offerings of bread and mead. One of Rolf's men made the sign of the cross and muttered a Christian charm against the evil eye. Rolf, however, fingered the hammer of Thor at his throat and, dismounting, took a chunk of bread from his saddle bag and laid it beside the other offerings. He might believe in Christ, but he believed in the power of the old gods too, and if the people here were pagans, then he was quite willing to respect their ways.

His groom looked at him askance.

'For luck,' Rolf said, and smiled.

'But, sir, it is blasphemy!'

Rolf twitched his shoulders, which were aching beneath the weight of his hauberk. 'One day the priests will come and set a cross in Odin's place. Do not tell me that there is only one door to heaven.'

'But, sir . . .'

Rolf held up his hand to silence the man, for he could hear the sound of a masculine voice raised in song on the track ahead of them. A moment later, a swineherd rounded the bend, driving perhaps a dozen pigs towards them. His large fawn hound saw Rolf's troop first and gave warning by darting towards the Normans, its black gums bared and savage growls rumbling from its throat. Rolf tightened his hand on the reins as the chestnut backed, coiling its haunches to shy. The swineherd saw the Normans and stopped. His eyes widened and he gripped his staff in both hands, holding it horizontally across his body.

The pigs meandered from side to side of the track, snuffling and rooting, advancing unconcernedly on the horsemen.

'Call off your dog,' Rolf said in Saxon, hoping that the man would understand. 'We come to trade, not to plunder. I seek Ulf the horse-dealer.'

The swineherd swallowed, and his eyes darted over the rank of glittering mail and casually held spears, the slung shields. His dog snarled and made a rush at Rolf's horse. The stallion reared and whinnied. The dog avoided the pawing forehooves and nipped at the chestnut's hocks.

Rolf strove to control his horse. Normally he would have slackened the rein and let the stallion kick the brute, either that or draw steel and strike it himself, but he was here to trade and he had only six men at his back.

The swineherd turned and fled back down the track. Untended, his pigs strayed hither and yon. The dog, after a final sally, abandoned the fray and raced after its master.

'For luck?' the groom muttered sarcastically under his breath, but not quietly enough, and Rolf glared at him.

'How else do you expect to be greeted?' he snapped. 'With smiles and open arms?'

'No, sir, I . . .'

'Have you ever herded pigs before?'

'No, sir.'

'Well here's your first opportunity.'

By the time Rolf and his men had persuaded the pigs with a combination of whistles, yells, riding whips and spear prods to turn in the direction of home, the swineherd had succeeded in rousing a welcoming party. Every able-bodied man in the village waited to greet the Normans, a motley collection of spears, pitchforks, hoes, and axes brandished on high.

The village leader was a tall, bearded man in his early thirties with hair as red as Rolf's own, but flowing to his shoulders. He wore a mail shirt with short sleeves in the old style, and a bright new helm. Held competently in his large fists was a Danish broadaxe very similar to those that held pride of position in Rolf's hall at Ulverton. The man's feet were planted wide, and his mouth was grimly set. Nor did his expression change when he saw the pigs that Rolf's men were driving before them.

'Greetings,' Rolf said. 'We come in peace. I am looking for Ulf the Horse-trader. Do any of you speak the Saxon tongue?'

There was a silence. Then the red-haired leader raised his axe. 'I speak it,' he growled. 'You are not welcome here. We have nothing to trade.'

'I will pay good silver.'

'We have no need of your tainted silver, Norman.' The man spat from the side of his mouth.

'I was told in York that Ulf has the best horseflesh in all of the north country. I have come a far distance to discover if this is true, such is his fame. If you do not want to trade then we will ride on, but I pray you, let Ulf speak for himself if he is among you.'

The villagers remained obdurately silent. The swineherd broke from their ranks to take charge of his pigs. Someone else gripped his snarling fawn hound by the collar. Rolf sighed heavily and turned the chestnut. Behind him he was aware of a rapid conversation being conducted in the Norse–English tongue of the region. His shoulder blades tingled. He imagined the curved axe blade sinking between them and dragging out his lungs on the return stroke.

'Wait!' shouted their leader gruffly. 'Ulf does speak for himself.'

Rolf stopped and looked over his shoulder, but he did not turn his horse lest he appear too eager. 'Then where is he?'

The warrior lowered his axe. 'I will take you to him,' he said. 'He is my father. Come.' He gestured with the haft of the weapon.

Rolf exchanged glances with his men. He knew that they might well be riding into a trap from which they would never emerge save as butchered corpses. What had the rapid conversation been about? Nothing gambled, nothing gained. He dismounted.

The palisade guarded some fifteen dwellings. The stakes would not have kept a serious attacker at bay, being more of a territory marker than anything else. The paths between the houses were thick with winter mud. Straw had been thrown down to make rough walkways through the morass. The houses were made of timber, the spaces between the spars filled in with crude daub plaster. Their roofs were thatched; some in good repair, some in a state of mossy dilapidation. The axe warrior led Rolf to one of the larger and sturdier buildings. Its walls were constructed of stout timber logs and there were even carvings on the gable ends.

'You can rest your horses in yonder barn,' said red-beard.

Not without some misgivings, Rolf delivered his reins to his groom.

The warrior stooped under the lintel, and drawing aside a heavy curtain, entered the house, ushering Rolf and his men within. Then, without another word, he left. Rolf was not reassured. He knew full well that they had been invited into the village because their leader had decided that it was unsafe to let them leave. He also knew with the sharpness of instinct that in one of the other huts their fate was about to be discussed by the rest of the villagers. All this crossed his mind in the time it took to strike spark from steel, and then his attention was occupied by the man who sat warming himself before the hearth, his splinted and bandaged leg resting upon a stool.

His long grey hair was bound back from his brow by a woven band of scarlet and gold wool and his eyes were bright and shrewd as he inspected Rolf and his men.

'Are you Ulf the Horse-trader?' Rolf asked, approaching him. As he advanced into the room, a movement caught his eye and he saw a young woman sitting at a table skinning a hare, two copper-haired children at her side.

'Who seeks me?' The voice was a hoarse growl, which owed more to a winter ague than permanent nature, Rolf thought.

'Rolf the Horse-trader from southern parts,' he replied. 'I desire to buy sumpter ponies of the highest quality to breed on my own lands.'

'Hah, the south is soft!' The older man rubbed his leg. Now that he was closer to him, Rolf could discern dingy streaks of red among the grey locks. 'Your accent is not that of a south Saxon,' Ulf added suspiciously. 'I've met enough of them in my time.'

'It is Norman,' Rolf said, taking a gamble. He had no doubt that a charade was being played out here, that he was being tested. It was inconceivable that Ulf had not been told of their visitors when the village had been roused to arms. 'I trade in war stallions, but there is a need too for sturdy pack animals. I was told in York that I could obtain them from you.'

'Norman, eh?' Ulf said, more than half to himself. 'A breeder of warhorses.' He looked Rolf up and down. 'Why don't you stay on your own lands instead of meddling with what is ours?'

Rolf could have mouthed the standard reply that the crown of England belonged to William of Normandy as of right, but it had not been his own reason for crossing the narrow sea. And having seen Ulf's son and the manner of Ulf's dress, he knew the right answer to give. 'I am a Viking at heart.'

The small eyes narrowed and Ulf rubbed his broken leg faster. Again his gaze probed at Rolf, and fastened upon the various objects he wore around his neck – the cross, the red toadstone, and the hammer of Thor. Then he came to a decision, and shouted over to the woman. 'Inga, bring bread and ale for our guests, and fetch the bacon flitch from the store.'

The woman wiped her hands on her apron and rose from the trestle. Two plaits of shining, wheat-silver hair rippled from beneath her kerchief. Rolf watched her, reminded of Ailith. Without being aware, he touched the horse clasp pinning his cloak.

'My daughter-in-law,' Ulf said sharply as he saw Rolf's scrutiny. 'And my son is a proud and jealous man.'

'If I was staring, it was because she reminded me of someone close to my heart,' Rolf said and immediately dropped his gaze.

Ulf grunted. 'I said that your accent was not south Saxon, but still, you speak the language well for a foreigner.'

'Sometimes words will unlock a door where a sword will only snap off in the keyhole,' Rolf said, and thought of the times that he and Ailith had sat before the hearth, each learning the other's language, exasperated and delighted by turns.

'Aye, I suppose it is more diplomatic to oil a lock with a long tongue than it is to thrust a sword in it, but I have no trust in empty words. Rather the truth of the sword than a larding of falsehood.'

'Amen to that. I bring good silver with which to trade.'

Ulf sucked his teeth and nodded slowly. 'You are either a very brave or a very foolish man. We are not dullards or cowards to be duped or frightened into giving you what you desire. It may be that you will not leave here alive.'

'I have felt so much in my gut,' Rolf agreed. 'But you have given me the protection of this house by offering me food and drink. The laws of hospitality are sacred. And I judge to look at this place that you are not only Ulf the Horse-trader, but Ulf the Thegn, the leader of this village. Your people will do as you bid them.'

Amusement glinted in the deep-set eyes. 'You are wily, Norman,' Ulf conceded. 'It will be a pleasure to bargain with you over the animals you desire to buy, but you should temper your confidence. My leg is broken, and for the moment my son Beorn wears the mantle of leadership.'

The woman returned with a woven basket containing flat loaves and a shallow wooden bowl holding fatty slices carved from a bacon flitch. Her daughter bore a pitcher of ale with laborious care, and the boy carried yet another container that held a collection of drinking cups, their wood still dark and damp from having been recently washed. With lowered eyes, the woman set about serving the men. Rolf studiously avoided looking at her, but he was aware of her presence nevertheless.

Ulf eyed him. 'My son fought the Norwegians at Stamford Bridge, and he fought the Normans far to the south,' he said.

'He was one of the fortunate ones, he managed to escape in the confusion at dusk when King Harold fell. I am told that we have a Norman overlord now, but we have never seen him. As far as we are concerned, the north is still free.'

Rolf made the sign of the Cross over the bread in an absent-minded fashion born of automatic habit, accepted a sprinkle of coarse salt as he broke the crust, and returned Ulf's piercing glance. 'Your son Beorn, he greeted our party in full battle-kit?'

Ulf's expression was suddenly cautious. 'What of it?'

'He must have been dressed that way before we came. There was no time for him to arm up between the swineherd crying the alarm and our arrival. Surely he does not keep order in the village by wearing a mail coat and brandishing a battle axe?'

'My son thinks you are a spy from the Norman army. We hear that one has crossed the Humber.'

'Indeed it has. I travelled with it for protection along the way.' Rolf tried to sound nonchalant as he helped himself to a chunk of the greasy bacon. It tasted much better than it looked.

'You need have no fear,' he added with a brief glance at the woman, who had stiffened and drawn her children into her arms. 'They will not approach this village. Indeed, their commander told me that I was mad to leave the beaten track and seek you out.'

'He was probably right,' Ulf said grimly, 'but he is no less mad himself to venture into these parts. You asked me why my son wears his battle-kit? I say that it is no business of yours. Only be thankful that you are not still travelling with the Norman soldiers. Now, eat and drink, and we will talk of trade.'

Spring bulbs were pushing blunt green shoots through the black soil beds in Ulverton's kitchen garden. Some of the more precocious plants were in bloom. Ailith regarded with pleasure this sign that the dark winter season was ending. The months following Yule were always the most difficult to bear.

Tancred had arrived from Normandy yester eve with messages for Rolf and a delivery of some yearling mares. But his lord was still absent. There had been no word of his whereabouts since the New Year when he had ridden north with Robert de Comminges.

Ailith was worried, although she tried to keep her fears to herself. As a child, a native Saxon child, she had always harboured a fear of the northern parts. Fed tales of savage Vikings by her brothers, there had been a time when she had woken screaming every night, certain that a murderous Norseman was going to burst into the sleeping loft and separate her head from her body with a dripping sword.

Ailith could feel Tancred's eyes on her in speculation as they sat down in the hall to break their fast after attending mass in the chapel. Since their first, unfortunate encounter on the shore, she had been unable to fault the man's behaviour. He was unswervingly polite, treating her with a grave courtesy that was so correct she wondered if it was false. His son was of an unsmiling, serious mien, but hard-working and unobtrusive. With his snub nose and wide, grey eyes, he could easily have been mistaken for a Saxon child, and Ailith had accepted him with an easiness that was totally absent in her dealings with his father.

'Perhaps Lord Rolf will be here today,' she said, partly from courtesy, partly to voice her concerns before they exploded within her. 'He knew that you were due before the feast of the Virgin.'

Tancred smiled wryly. 'When Lord Rolf is on a trail, nothing else matters to him. There is no-one as keen-scented as he when it comes to seeking out a good horse. If you showed him a hundred destriers, all looking much alike, and asked him to pick the best, he would know straight away which animal to choose. It is an instinct of the gut, and few men have it.'

'What does his wife say of his long absences?'

Tancred eyed her warily as they sat down before the hearth to eat their griddle cakes. 'She is not pleased, of course, but it is the lot of many Norman women whose husbands are still in Duke William's service over here. She knows that my lord is working to increase his fortune and standing, and that his endeavours can only benefit their daughter when it comes time for her to wed. 'And of course,' he added neutrally, 'Lady Arlette knows that whatever indiscretions her lord may commit, he will always return to her. It has been so since the day they married.'

Ailith coloured at his implication and finished her food in hostile silence. She was torn two ways. One direction led to vexation that Tancred should consider her an 'indiscretion' when nothing the least indiscreet had occurred between Rolf and herself. The other led to a surge of jealous insecurity over the information that Rolf always returned to his wife. She stood at a crossroads, torn and aching. Into her mind there came a picture of Goldwin, solid and dependable, his eyes alight with a love that was hers alone to command, and then she saw Benedict as a baby, suckling at her breast, depending on her for his very life. All that lay in the past, her memories both a salvation and a curse.

Irritated with herself, she repaired to the stables and ordered the groom to saddle up the small chestnut mare. Elfa, as Ailith had named her, pricked her ears and whickered through her soft muzzle. The young woman fed her a crust of bread left over from the morning meal and followed it with a wrinkled apple from the store. Elfa crunched the treats greedily and searched for more. When the groom led her out of her stall, Ailith saw with misgiving that the little mare was already too fat. *I should ride her more often*, she thought. Rolf would be annoyed when he saw her. None of his horses was allowed to carry surplus flesh or lose condition for want of exercise.

The groom held Elfa steady at the mounting block while Ailith gained the saddle. The leather was cold on the bare skin of her upper thighs between her long hose and her loin cloth. She found the stirrups and kicked with her heels. Elfa broke into a reluctant trot. The thrust and fall of the mare's spine set up a tingling between Ailith's thighs and she shifted uncomfortably, disturbed by other memories of herself and Goldwin in the early days of their marriage, by imaginings of how it would be with Rolf. Was the bush of his manhood as red as his hair? The thought made her blush at her own boldness, but not enough to abandon her speculation.

Rolf's grey stallion was at grass with his mares in the fields below the castle mound. Ailith halted Elfa at a safe distance, not desiring Sleipnir to give chase. The grey's thick winter coat was as silver as frost. In the summer he was darker, with dapples like charcoal bubbles on his quarters and belly. Rolf said that he was proving a potent sire. Almost every mare he had covered the previous season was heavy with foal. It only remained to be seen over the next few years if he had bequeathed his own excellent qualities to his offspring.

She rode away from the stud herd and took the stony path down a gully to the shore. The mare's hooves crunched on shingle and then thudded hollowly on firm sand. Spindrift blew off the tops of the waves and tingled Ailith's lips with salt. Beneath each curl of white crest the sea was a cold, clear green. Ribbons of weed, dark as blood, trailed in its glassy coils. Ailith urged the mare first to trot, and then eased her into a canter.

Her hooves skimmed the edge of the waves, her mane flew like a banner, her tail undulated behind, and as the mare stretched herself, Ailith began to feel a sense of freedom. She flew with the horse, became part of her motion, and it was all too soon that Elfa's stride slackened as the mare became winded. Ailith slowed her to a walk and made the resolution to exercise Elfa every day until the gallop along the beach was twice as long.

When, eventually, she rode into the bailey, she saw that a groom was rubbing down a mud-spattered bay which looked as if it had been hard-ridden.

'A visitor rode in while you were gone, mistress,' the man responded to her anxious query. 'The seneschal and Sir Tancred are with him in the hall.'

While he was speaking, Ailith's eyes travelled again to the weary horse. There was something familiar about it, and in a moment she recognised it for the one that Aubert rode when he had business abroad.

'The visitor, what does he look like?'

The groom shrugged. 'Not above your own height, mistress, and dressed in a brown cloak and brown English cap. Bushy eyebrows too.' He made this last remark to thin air for Ailith was already off the mare and running across the bailey. She was filled with a terrible sense of foreboding, and when she burst into the hall and saw Aubert standing before the fire with the other two men, a fortifying cup of mead in his hand, she knew from the look on his face that her fears were about to be borne out.

She had gathered her skirts and raised them to her shins, the better to run, but now she let them drop and advanced to the hearth. 'Aubert, what has happened? Is it Benedict or Felice? Tell me!'

Aubert's eyes were suspiciously moist. 'No, no, Felice and the babe have never been better . . . it is about Rolf that I have come.'

Ailith stared at him. 'About Rolf?' she repeated, and clenched herself, knowing that she was about to be dealt a mortal blow.

'Do you want to be seated, Ailith?'

'No, tell me,' she said with wooden composure. 'Now. Is he dead?'

Aubert's heavy brows drew together across the bridge of his nose. 'I do not know, but it is more than likely. Robert de Comminges and the main body of his troop were slaughtered in Durham by English and Scots rebels. De Comminges and his bodyguard were chased into the bishop's house and the place was set alight around them. There were very few survivors, none of Rolf's men among them. The news arrived in London four days ago. King William is mustering an army to go north and quell the rebels, but the damage is already done.'

'Rolf went north to buy horses, he might not have been in Durham at all,' Ailith said. There was a cold ache in the pit of her stomach that no fire would ever dissolve. She recognised the sensation from the night when Goldwin had died. It had been with her ever since that time, but she had been learning to ignore it. Now it reclaimed her attention, threatening to freeze her in solitary confinement.

'No, he might not,' Aubert agreed, but not as if he really meant it. 'We'll know more in a few days. The reports from the north are very fragmented.' He looked at Ailith. 'If Rolf is dead, then you know that you have my protection, and my roof to comfort you.'

Ailith nodded stiffly. 'Thank you, Aubert, but I know he still lives,' she heard herself say in a voice that was calm, without hint of a tremor, 'and I have my duties here at Ulverton. Indeed, I should be preparing a feast to celebrate his return.' A feast to honour a hero's safe deliverance, or a wake for a man who had flirted with danger once too often. She knew to her cost that refusing to believe in the death of a loved one could not bring that person back to life. She touched the thin, pink scar of an old knife wound on her left wrist and not for the first time, wished that Rolf had not found her that winter's day in the forge.

CHAPTER 26

Rolf was impressed by the ponies that Ulf showed him. Propelling himself about on a wooden crutch, the village leader instructed one of his people to load a black pony with two sizeable panniers of stones. The animal bore the weight easily and trotted along without any signs of labouring. 'Yon beast will carry the burden of such as you or my Beorn in full armour, thirty miles a day for a full seven-night,' Ulf declared with quiet, sure pride. 'You'll find nowt better if it's stamina you want.'

Rolf was inclined to agree, but kept a straight face and indifferent manner the better to haggle. Ulf was shrewd and equally determined to obtain the best bargain possible, but finally they reached an agreement, and Rolf found himself the owner of six mares – two maidens and four in foal, and a young bay stallion with sweeping black mane and tail.

'Take my advice,' Ulf said after the coins had changed hands and they were sealing their agreement with a cup of mead. 'Make your way homewards now. The north is no place for Normans.'

'I have a wager to settle in Durham with Robert de Comminges,' Rolf protested. 'I will owe him a warhorse if I do not go.'

'Forget your wager. Tonight it will snow. Turn south.'

Rolf heard the note of urgency in the horse-trader's voice. Ulf knew far more than he was telling, and whatever his knowledge, it boded ill for Robert de Comminges. 'I will heed your warning,' he replied gravely, 'but let me in my turn warn you. If you resist King William, he will make you pay. I do not speak as your enemy, but as a fellow trader concerned for your future and that of your village. I know William of Normandy. He is a powerful man and you have no-one of his strength to unite the north now. If he comes seeking retribution, his wrath will be black indeed.' His glance flickered to Beorn's attractive young wife and the two children.

Ulf followed Rolf's gaze. 'If he comes,' he answered evenly, 'we will be ready.'

Rolf opened his mouth.

'No,' Ulf said brusquely, 'I will hear no more. Tonight it will snow. Tomorrow, you will turn south.'

Ulf was right and Ulf was wrong. That night it did snow, but in the morning, any hope that Rolf had entertained of going anywhere was abandoned to the blizzard which howled some of the flimsier dwellings out of existence and buried others up to the tops of the shuttered windows. Animals huddled in pens at one end of the long houses and humans huddled at the other around the smoky warmth of their hearths. Every time anyone ventured out to fetch more kindling from the wood pile or to squat in the snow, the fire would flatten and belch out great gusts of smoke, and all the rush lights and candles would be extinguished.

For three days and nights the storm held Rolf and his men prisoners in Ulf's long house. The fourth morning brought still, cold sunlight that glittered a bleached yellow splendour on a landscape of undulating, brittle white.

Rolf aided the villagers to dig paths to the stream and the village well. He helped to repair the damage wreaked by the storm and resigned himself to the fact that he would have to stay here for several days more until the roads were passable.

During a respite in the snow shovelling, Beorn's wife Inga served him with ale, a chunk of new bread and slices of smoked goose.

'I do not see your husband.' Rolf tucked his mitts inside his tunic and bit ravenously into the food. Indeed, he had not see Beorn since the evening of first arrival, nor half the young men of the village.

'He has business to attend elsewhere,' she said, her manner cool, verging on the hostile.

'Fortunate then, that you have some Normans on hand to lend you aid.

She looked at him. Her eyes were a pale gold-green, the colour of the most expensive French wine. Cat's eyes, set on a slant, utterly bewitching, and utterly cold. 'Some would say that.'

'Are you one of them?'

'I keep my own counsel,' she answered and gestured brusquely. 'Eat your food. The servant will collect your bowl when you have finished.'

He watched her walk away, admiring her proud carriage, disgruntled by her frigid response.

Four evenings later as he sat at Ulf's fire, making his preparations to leave the next day, Beorn and the village men returned from their 'business', floundering through the snow on several fine Norman warhorses. As well as bearing a man, each horse also carried an assortment of plunder — mail and weapons, cups, belts, brooches and other personal effects.

'We have wiped out the stain of Hastings field!' Beorn declared, his eyes alight, his flowing red hair burnished with gold from the flames of his father's hearth as he swept his arm around a fierce, smiling Inga. 'The Normans have been slaughtered to a man in Durham town!' His stare fell upon Rolf and fingered the haft of the Norman langseax hanging at his belt. 'Every last one, horse-trader, what do you say to that?'

Rolf stared at Ulf's huge, handsome son and thought of the huscarl on Hastings field whose axe now hung on Ulverton's wall. There was a sick emptiness of fear in his gut. He was among wolves and they would eat him if he displayed the slightest sign of weakness . . . as they had eaten Robert de Comminges. 'Do you wish me to cry out in terror or admit that your prowess is beyond compare?' he declared far more

boldly than he felt. 'Robert de Comminges is not William of
Normandy. If you can defeat him, *then* you will have reason to
exult.'

Beorn's eyes narrowed. 'You have a bold tongue. Perhaps I
should cut it out with your countryman's seax.'

Rolf regarded him impassively. 'That would silence me,' he
agreed.

'Beorn, sit down!' Ulf snapped. 'Your own tongue wags
too much for its own good. The rules of hospitality apply and
Rolf de Brize has repaid them more than fairly with the way
he and his men have toiled to clear the snow. By all means
celebrate the victory at Durham, but this man will go on his
way unmolested.'

Beorn's lips tightened. There was a long silence while stubborn will met stubborn will, but finally the younger man
capitulated with a sulky shrug and releasing his wife to her
duties, sat down cross-legged before the fire.

That night, lying on his sheepskin, Rolf dreamed that the
entire north country was covered in a thick, vellum layer of
snow, and lying upon it, inscribing its pristine pages with crimson scrawl, were the bodies of men, women and children. The
bare trees were roosts for flocks of ravens, their bodies plump
with feeding, their plumage sheened with blue and purple like
the rotting corpses on which they gorged. One bird, larger than
the rest, launched itself into the still air. Its wings blocked the sun,
and Rolf saw that its terrible red eyes were those of his King.

In southern parts, the promise of spring retreated beneath a sifting of snow and a new, bitter, deep cold. Sitting on top of the
fire in Ulverton's hall, Ailith abandoned the pretence of working on a delicate netting bonnet and stared into the flames.
King William and the core of his army, his hardened mercenary
troops, had struck to quell the rebels. This much she had heard
from a pedlar who had seen the army ride past on the great
north road.

They were going to avenge, not to rescue. 'Too much
blood has been shed already,' she muttered to herself and

glanced with revulsion at the battle axes hung in pride of place above Rolf's empty chair at the end of the hall. Rolf called them his luck. But the luck of the battlefield was fickle, and someone always had to lose.

Unable to sit still any longer, she put her needlework aside and went to lift her cloak from its peg. Tancred raised his eyes from the game of tafel he was playing with his son and glanced at her, but he offered no comment. He had voiced his intention of returning to Brize-sur-Risle if there was no news by the end of the week. 'For if there is none,' he had said to Ailith, 'I think we must assume that my lord has perished in Durham with Robert de Comminges.'

Tancred's was the voice of reason. She had seen in his eyes that his lingering was only a matter of form, that he had already resigned himself to the belief that Rolf was dead.

Leaving the smoky hall, Ailith crossed the moon-silvered bailey. Ice crunched beneath her shoes and she felt the cold pierce the soles of her feet as she climbed the wooden walk lining the palisade. Her breath emerged in puffs of white vapour. The only sound was the soft whispering of her feet on the rime of the wall walk, echoing the muted swish of the sea. The water was visible as the faintest glimmer of moving darkness patterned by a road fashioned of narrow slices of moonlight. She paused to stare, drawn in by the beauty and tranquillity of the deadly elements of black and white cold, deep and dark, air-bright and fragile. For a long time she stood in silence, absorbing and being absorbed, the chill seeping into her bones until she was a frozen part of the night, an icicle.

A sound chimed gently against her brittle shell and vibrated upon a remaining strand of her consciousness. She blinked and shivered, and the enchantment shattered into a million crystal fragments. Her hands were numb, her lips and cheeks and feet. Ailith turned round, intending to make her way back to the hall, but the sound came again, arresting her motion. She heard the clink of harness and the voices of men, the clop of hooves on an iron-frost road. Her heart started to thump and she stared out into the night with eyes stretched so wide that they ached.

It had been full dark for two hours now. It was almost time to set out the sleeping pallets and bank the fire for the night. No visitors would be on the road so late. And an enemy would use more stealth. That left but one alternative. For a moment Ailith was unable to move, her body and mind disconnected from each other, but then they slammed together with a jolt so strong that all previous inhibitions were hurled aside and with a small cry, she sped towards the bailey gates.

He was the first to ride through them on his familiar chestnut horse, and he was closely followed by his men and several dark-coloured ponies, some of them laden with packs. Ailith saw this with a distant part of her mind, but the force of her attention was focused upon Rolf. He dismounted and handed the stallion's reins to the groom who had come running at the summons from the gate guard. And then he raised his eyes to the wall walk and saw Ailith.

Her impetus carried her rapidly forward until no more than a body's length separated her from Rolf. She halted, swaying slightly. Torchlight flickered over him, brightening his hair, emphasising the lean bone structure. He was as thin and muscular as a wolf, and as dangerous too, she thought, but it was probably too late for caution to be of any use.

'We thought you were dead.' Her voice was a dry croak and her swaying resulted in another pace forward. 'Aubert brought us the news about the massacre in Durham.'

'I did not go to Durham.' He spoke the words absently, a matter of rote without any thought behind them. Ailith saw the narrow glitter in his eyes, the rapid rise and fall of his chest. The ice encasing her heart melted away beneath the fierceness of his stare and her knees turned to water.

Rolf caught her, his arm hard about her waist. 'Jesu,' he groaned softly as she came into his embrace. And then, a moment later, 'Jesu forgive me,' as he bent his head and took his first taste of her lips.

Ailith lay across Rolf, her head upon his naked chest, her fingers toying with the downy stripe of auburn hair running from the base of his breastbone to the bush at his groin. The latter was indeed red as she had once wondered. The feel of him upon and within her had been one of completion, of a dull ache banished by the fierceness of their loving. Her body now held a gentle, diffusing warmth. Her smoothing fingertips encountered tiny droplets of sweat, the faintly raised line of an old scar, the hollow of his navel.

'I wish this was a dream,' she said softly. The words had been spoken more than half to herself, she had thought him drifting into sleep, but he stirred beneath her hand and his muscles tensed.

'Why should you wish that?' he asked.

Ailith was silent for a while. Then she said pensively, 'There is no retreat from what we have done . . . from what we are doing. If this were no more than a sinful dream, I could keep it to myself, it would not matter.'

'Is what we have done sinful? Look at me, Ailith.' He grasped a handful of her hair, making her turn to his will. 'It would have been a sin to deny our love.'

'You have a wife.' Ailith had the misgiving that the word 'love' came too easily to his tongue, that to his way of thinking, it was just a more courtly word for 'lust'. And she had no right to throw it in his face, for her appetite was as great as his, if not greater, for she wanted more.

'My wife is in Normandy. Our marriage bed is cold and she does not have the spark to set it ablaze. I have wanted you for a long time, Ailith. You may have anything of me just for the asking – a wife's rights if you will, although there can be no sanction from the church. If anyone looks at you with the slightest degree of contempt, I will have the hide off him, I swear it.'

'And he will hate you all the more and it will not change his opinion.' Ailith tossed her head.

'And his opinion matters so much to you.'

Ailith sighed, wondering how she could explain her feelings to him when plainly he did not see her dilemma. 'Yes, it matters, because in their eyes I see the reflection of my opinion of myself. I do not want to be just another casual tumble in the straw, a mare serviced along your way. I need your respect too, Rolf.'

He raised himself up on one elbow and trapped her stare with his own. 'Have you not had proof of that over and again?' he reproached her. 'Have I not yielded to your wishes at every turn – a room with a bolt on the door and a village woman to sleep across the threshold? I fully admit they are of small use now, but at the time they were freely granted. You have my respect, you have all of me.' His voice softened and he stroked her naked shoulder where it gleamed through the strands of hair. 'Now give me all of you, Ailith. I swear on my soul that you will never have cause for grief.'

She looked upon him and was lost by the tenderness and desire that shone in his eyes, by the warm curve of his mouth and the tiny, coppery glints of beard stubble. There could be no withdrawal from this situation. They had to go on together. She would make sure that he never so much as looked at another woman again. In place of his cold marriage bed, he would have this one with her, and she would brand him beyond bone to the spirit itself.

Slowly she sat up. Tossing back her hair, thrusting out her breasts which were still firm despite the suckling of a child, she straddled his thighs. His response was gratifying and instantaneous, but she had no intention of granting him release just yet. She teased him, rubbing against his trembling shaft, pulling away, circling her hips, always just out of reach, until he groaned with frustration and arched his body.

The Valkyrie image filled her mind. It had first been created for her by Goldwin, but she had long since made it her own. Now, here with Rolf, she was all-powerful and she would pluck him from his writhing mortal state and show him the home of the gods.

And so she sheathed his straining flesh and heard with triumph his long moan of pleasure, relief, and renewed tension. She undulated slowly, keeping his frantic body at fever pitch while her own pleasure swelled and tightened. She rose and fell more swiftly. His hand was on her breast and then between her thighs. He grasped her buttocks with the other one, holding her hard, and thrust up powerfully into her body. A battlefield cry tore from his throat as he filled her, and Ailith caught her breath, her head thrown back, all her consciousness centred in the exquisite pulsations radiating from her loins.

Rolf's vision was filled with the sight of Ailith glorying in her climax, her strong, beautiful body arched with pleasure and a pink flush mantling her face and throat and breasts. He had never seen anything so magnificent, had never felt such intensities of emotion and physical sensation. This was how it should be.

Ailith's head came forward. Panting, gleaming with sweat, she gave him back stare for stare. Her hips still swayed gently and there was an exultant smile on her lips.

'By Christ and by Odin I love you.' His avowal was whispered with tenderness and awe. 'It is forever, Ailith, forever.' And he thought that he meant it.

She leaned over him, her full breasts grazing his chest, the tips of her hair tickling his skin. 'Forever,' she repeated, and sealed the bargain, her mouth on his, their bodies still one flesh.

CHAPTER 27

His wanderlust temporarily sated and sobered by his experience in the north, Rolf was content to dwell at Ulverton, to oversee the breeding of his destriers and the new sumpter ponies, to watch the farmlands turn beneath the plough and the fishing boats bring home their catch. And to be with Ailith.

They played like children in the snow, they stayed abed whilst the weather howled around them, and made long, slow love. When the season warmed into true spring, she rode beside him to look at the stud herd, and he accompanied her into the village. At first, because of her earlier determination to be chaste, she was embarrassed to go abroad among the people, but they treated the change of circumstance up at the castle with tolerant amusement and knowing looks which said that they had known all along how it would eventually be, and they were not displeased.

The uprising in the north had been summarily quelled, and King William celebrated Easter in Winchester, where Rolf repaired briefly to present him with his tribute of a dozen warhorses and payment in silver in lieu of his personal presence on military duty in the King's service. He was only away from Ailith for a week, but it seemed like a year and he hastened home to her side and did not stir from it again until the land was covered in bursting, soft greenery on the borders of April and May.

The world could not be shut out forever, even if his oath to

Ailith had been made for all time. As the season progressed, a niggling voice ate at Rolf's contentment, telling him that whatever his indifference toward his wife, he still had a duty towards her and his daughter. And for all Tancred's competence, the herds at Brize-sur-Risle still required his attention.

It was May eve and the green fertility of the land was being celebrated with enthusiasm. The village blacksmith, hidden within the fluttering skirts of a hobbyhorse costume, flirted with the maidens and became blatant with the married women. Mead and ale were consumed with true, Saxon capacity, and the three pigs slaughtered especially for the occasion vanished as rapidly as the bread and broth accompaniments.

Ailith joined the festivities with a childlike enthusiasm. Seeing her standing among the village women, eating slivers of roast pork with her fingers, and laughing at the antics of the blacksmith, Rolf contrasted her behaviour with Arlette's prim coolness, and was filled with a warm glow of pleasure, followed quickly by a feeling of depression.

Raising her head, Ailith caught him in the act of scrutiny. Their eyes locked. She left the crowd and hurried over to him, her freckled face aglow. The spring evening was as mild and warm as new milk and she wore only her shift and her best undergown, of blue wool. Her hair was decently covered by a light wimple, held in place by a chaplet of white May blossom. He rested his fingertips gently on the garland.

'In Normandy, at Brize, a chaplet like this would signify your willingness,' he murmured.

Ailith stooped to wipe her greasy fingers on the grass and looked up at Rolf through her lashes. 'My willingness to what?' she asked saucily.

Rolf drew her to her feet and then against him. 'To honour the May with the gift of your body to any man who asks.'

'Then it is a blessing we are not in Normandy, for if so, you would have to wait your turn behind the blacksmith.' She giggled and then hiccuped and put her hand to her mouth. 'I mustn't drink any more mead, it's too strong.'

Her mention of the blacksmith, a lusty, dark-eyed fellow,

sent a pang of jealousy through Rolf, so unaccustomed, that it thoroughly unsettled him. The thought of leaving her for the duty of Normandy grew even less palatable. She was looking at him with an air of provocative mischief that sent an unbearable ache through his groin. He needed to possess her, here and now.

She seemed somewhat surprised at his sudden urgency, but followed him willingly into the shadows, where he spread his cloak and pulled her down onto it.

'I cannot wait,' he groaned, tugging at her gown and shift. 'I will burst!'

She laughed, the sound low and throaty with power, almost a purr. 'My, you have taken the May fever badly,' she said, but altered her position to smoothly accommodate his desperation. Her hands upon him were cool, her thighs too, as she clung to his flanks and returned each hard surge of his body. It was a primitive lovemaking, befitting the rites of the May Eve. There was no finesse, only the raw power of the mating instinct. The plough in the furrow, the sowing of the corn, the begetting of new life.

In the aftermath, as their heartbeats slowed and their breath grew quiet, Rolf traced the contours of her strong, honest face with his fingertips and thought her beautiful, and yet the releasing of physical tension had given no ease to his mind.

'Ailith, I have to leave for a while,' he said, gently following the outline of her lips with his forefinger. 'There is a horse fair in Paris that I must attend, and other matters at Brize-sur-Risle that I cannot leave to Tancred.'

Her half-smile faded and her eyes opened to search his face. 'Other matters? Your wife and child, I suppose?'

'Don't look at me like that.' He shifted uncomfortably. 'I owe them my duty, you know that. And I have to make decisions about the horses – I'm not going for the sole purpose of seeing Arlette and Gisele. Christ knows, I would rather be with you.'

Ailith sat up and smoothed her rumpled garments. 'I know you must go to them,' she said with dignity, 'and that you must find horses to breed, to buy and to sell. It would be foolish of me to cling and weep, to beg you not to go. I only wish that you had had the wisdom to tell me on another occasion. First you take me in the grass like a stag in rut, then you announce that you are going to your wife. Or were you afraid that I would deny you once you had spoken?'

'Yes, I was.' He threw his arms around her, and although she averted her head, she did not shrug him off. 'All I could think of a moment ago was that I did not want to leave or lose you, but that I might do both. You looked so beautiful and I wanted you so much.'

Her manner softened and with a light sigh, she turned in his arms and laid her head on his chest to hear the steady thud, thud of his heart. 'When must you go?'

'As soon as I can find a galley to take me across the narrow sea.' He grimaced as if his mouth was full of sour wine. 'The sooner there, the sooner home to you.'

CHAPTER 28

At harvest time, Felice and Aubert escaped from London's heat and an outbreak of the spotted fever, and came to spend a month at Ulverton. Although Aubert had visited on several occasions, it was the first time that he had brought his wife and son. Ailith was both delighted and pensive as she greeted the family and made them welcome. Rolf was still across the narrow sea and she was filled with anxiety. What if he chose not to return? What if he sent Tancred in his stead? He had only been away for three months, but it seemed more like three years. She was in half a mind to confide her doubts and fears to Felice, but she held back, unsure as to how her friend would respond. But four days after their arrival, the decision was forced upon her.

She and Felice were walking by the shore, both women keeping a sharp eye upon Benedict as he skipped along the beach at the very edge of the waves. His pudgy baby fat was melting to reveal coltish, slender limbs. He had his mother's quickness and grace, her sparkling dark brown eyes and regular features. His impish grin, however, was all Aubert's.

'Aubert is never going to make a wine merchant of him.' Felice laughed indulgently as the little boy lifted a stone and threw it as far into the waves as he could. 'I might almost believe he were Rolf's the way he loves horses.'

Ailith tried to smile and respond naturally, but she knew that her attempt was poor. Her stomach felt like a cauldron full of boiling broth. The breeze off the sea did nothing to cool her hot brow.

'Still,' Felice added, her gaze upon her son, 'we have plans for him that will take him far beyond the wine trade.'

Ailith tried to look interested.

Felice eyed her sharply and halted. 'Ailith, what's wrong? Are you ill?'

'It is too hot.' Ailith swallowed valiantly. 'If I can just sit down in the shade of that rock for a moment, I'll feel better.'

Felice called Benedict to her side, and taking Ailith's arm, drew her up the beach to sit down. Ailith leaned against the cool, dark stone, her head thrown back and her breathing shallow while she fought her nausea. Felice eyed her critically. She knew that Ailith possessed the stamina of an ox and in the normal course of her life was seldom hampered by illness of any kind. A niggling suspicion at the back of her mind began to gain ground.

'Ailith, are you with child?'

Ailith swallowed again, and flickered a sideways glance at Felice. 'Is it so obvious?' she asked weakly.

'Only because you are never sick. I noticed this morning that you broke your fast on dry bread and ale, and there are shadows beneath your eyes as if you have not slept for a week. It must be Rolf's,' she added with certainty. 'I knew when I saw you both at Yuletide that it was only a matter of time before you became lovers.'

'It happened in February when he returned whole from the north.' She looked sidelong at her friend. 'I love him. Are you going to rail at me and call me foolish?'

Felice clucked her tongue. 'Where would be the point?' she said with some exasperation. 'I tried to warn you once before in London, and you almost bit my head off. I know how stubborn you are.' She shook her head slowly. 'I remember the way Rolf used to look at you when you were feeding Ben. He has desired you for a long time.' She was not so cruel as to add that from what she knew of Rolf, the hunt was frequently more important than the capture. Surely Ailith must have that intuition too. And who was to say that Rolf had not finally found what he was looking for? 'All I will say is that you must be careful. Do not give him everything, for I know that he will never return it to you.'

Ailith placed her hand upon her belly and her smile became wry. 'It is too late for that. And besides, in a way, I belong to him.'

Felice saw Ailith lightly touch a narrow pink scar on her left wrist. Often she did that when discussing Rolf. The action reminded Felice of the way other women fingered favourite pieces of jewellery, or the nuns at St Aethelburga's their crosses while they prayed.

'He is in Normandy now, with his wife,' Ailith murmured. 'It is very hard for me to think of him with her. I try not to be jealous. What does she have of him but brief visits of duty?' She looked up at Felice, a haunted expression in her eyes. 'When I was married to Goldwin, I knew that he was mine alone. Had it not been for the war between England and Normandy, we would have lived out quiet, companionable lives. Instead, I find myself tied to the tail of a comet. I have never been so happy, or so lonely and afraid at one and the same time.' She lifted Benedict onto her lap and cuddled him, seeking the comfort of his warm, small body.

Felice could think of no reassurances to offer to Ailith. Indeed, she was inclined to agree with her that she had tied herself to the tail of a comet. 'When is the child due?' she asked. 'Do you want me to be here for your lying in?'

'In February.' Ailith gave an ironic smile over the top of Benedict's glossy black hair. 'At the feast of the Virgin. And I would be more than pleased if you were there.'

'Of course I will!' Felice declared with more enthusiasm than she felt. Having almost died giving birth to Benedict, she had little desire to attend at a childbed. But she owed Ailith too much to refuse her.

The sea breeze was fresh and the galley frisked through the waves like a two-year-old colt, bucking exuberantly and leaping high.

Rolf watched the English shoreline approach. The first grey-blue smudge of sighting had yielded to striated gleams of marble cliff topped by green pasture. Gulls and cormorants wheeled above the vessel's striped sail. His heart was filled with anticipation like the bulging linen canvas. He was returning to Ailith, to the harbour of his heart. If he looked back, he would view only sea, the coast of Normandy was far beyond the horizon now.

He thought briefly of Arlette, of the tears in her eyes as she bade him Godspeed, Gisele clinging to her hand and obediently waving. Returning the gesture, he had felt relief and guilt. He was a visitor, bidding polite farewell to strangers whose hospitality he had shared on his road to a greater destination. Arlette was no fool, she knew that something had changed. At one point, it had been on the tip of Rolf's tongue to tell her about Ailith, but those wounded grey eyes had chained him to silence.

'Ah God,' he cursed softly to the salt-splashed deck.

A sound behind him caused Rolf to abandon his brooding and turn round. Tancred's son Mauger was retching over the galley's side, his face a suffering greenish-white.

'Won't be long until we make landfall,' Rolf said encouragingly.

'I'm all right, sir,' Mauger said defensively and wiped his mouth. He was small for his age, but what he lacked in stature he made up for in stocky breadth which gave promise of bull-strength in later years. He had a mop of sun-streaked blond hair and eyes of a woodsmoke blue-grey. The distance between his nose and upper lip was short, and like his father, he had a wide expanse of chin.

Rolf leaned against the tall mast of the galley and felt the creak of her ropes and timbers as if they were a part of his own body. He narrowed his eyes towards the coastline, and although his stance was nonchalant, his blood was fizzing with impatience.

'Do you think we're safe?' the boy asked.

'Safe from what?' Rolf smiled and cast his eyes to the solid blue of the sky and the rapid progress of white clouds.

'That Danish fleet we were told about in Honfleur. What if their ships are here in the narrow sea?'

'They'll be headed for the north lands, for their allies in the old Danelaw,' Rolf said. 'And like as not, the King has already gone there to deal with the threat.'

'But that merchant said there were upward of two hundred warships.'

'That is not as many as we brought to Hastings, and even Swein of Denmark and the sons of Cnut are not match enough for William. Stop fretting, lad, we're almost home.'

Mauger spun to heave over the side of the galley again. As far as he was aware, they had just left home, and their destination could never aspire to that title. His apprenticeship to his father was finished. He was now to serve Rolf, and hope to prove Tancred's expectations. It was a heavy responsibility and Mauger had only just turned thirteen years old. Sick, miserable, he stared at the white churn of the wave crests three feet from his nose and longed for the familiar haven of Brize-sur-Risle and Fauville. His imagination, not usually vivid, was peppered by visions of the boat capsizing in a sudden squall, and of himself drowning in a high and murky sea. Even when the lookout perched on the mast cried landfall, the terror remained, and Mauger was taken with a fresh bout of retching.

'A baby?' Rolf stared at Ailith as if she had addressed him in old Norse. He looked her up and down, but she was wearing her loose Saxon garments again in which she could have been a full nine months round and a pregnancy would not have shown.

'I wore the white hawthorn on May Eve,' she said, 'there are two women in the village due at the same time as me. Are you not pleased?'

There was an anxious note in her voice. Rolf strove to compose himself. 'Yes, of course I am, but grant me a little space to recover from my surprise. When I left you, you were as slim as a wand.'

'Well I'll soon be as round as a pease pudding,' she retorted.

'I'm twice the size I was when I was carrying Harold, and I have quickened already.'

Her tone was hostile, as if she was blaming him for her condition when the begetting had been a mutual pleasure. Rolf slipped his arm around her waist and drew her against him. He had embraced her on the harbour side, but that had been in front of a host of villagers and castle folk, and without benefit of information, he had not noticed her increased girth. Now he ran his hand lightly over her belly and easily detected its round swell.

'February?' he repeated, mentally counting the months and feeling dismayed, for whenever Arlette was pregnant, she insisted that they must not lie together because it was against the teachings of the Church. Besides, there was always the danger that she might miscarry. And even after the child was born, the Church declared that a man might not lie with a woman until she had been out of childbed for forty days.

'Rolf, what's the matter? Why are you scowling?'

He deliberated for a moment, then told her. 'I am selfish, I know, but I cannot bear to be near you and not touch you.'

The anxiety cleared from her brow and she laughed with relief. 'Is that all?' She patted her belly. 'Well I might be growing by the day, but I'm not too huge yet, and when that time comes . . .' She cocked her head on one side. 'Well surely there are other ways?'

Rolf laughed too and shook his head. Just when he thought he had her measure, she would surprise him anew. 'Do you recall in your first months at Ulverton, when I used to call you Abbess Ailith?' he chuckled. 'You would not even let me lift you down from a baggage wain without scolding my ears off!'

She had the grace to blush. 'That was before I yielded up my common sense,' she murmured, looking at the floor.

'And found your reason,' he retorted, unpinning her wimple to nibble at her ear and her throat; and from that moment, all conversation ceased for no small time.

*

'Keep an eye on Mauger for me,' Rolf requested in the lazy aftermath of their lovemaking, his long body stretched at ease beside hers in the great bed, the palm and fingers of his right hand spread upon her stomach to feel the tiny, flutterings of the life she carried within her. 'He was sick all the way across the narrow sea, and he's homesick too.'

'I will do what I can,' Ailith murmured, and rolled into the warmth of his body, savouring the feel of his flesh against hers. 'But I am not his mother.'

His shoulder moved beneath the web of her hair. 'She died soon after he was born, and Tancred's never taken another wife. The lad's only ever known wet nurses and the women of the castle. He never complains, but a matronly eye would not go amiss.'

'And you think I have a matronly eye?' She snuffled at him, inhaling his scent – the sweat of love-play, the tang of woodsmoke from the hall. Her tongue came out. Her teeth playfully nipped at his bicep.

'Certainly you have a matronly figure.' The palm of his hand gently rubbed; his fingers arrowed lower with delicate precision and she caught her breath.

'Whose fault is that?'

'Mine, I suppose,' he murmured, and once more they ceased to talk.

CHAPTER 29

Julitta of Ulverton was born a little after sunrise on a bright February morning in the year 1070. Having kept her mother awake all night with severe labour pains, she shot into the midwife's spread apron and announced her presence to the world in no uncertain terms. She had a fuzz of dark red hair and a face to match, although that soon became a more healthy pink as each resounding cry cleared her airway.

'And I thought Benedict was loud,' Felice remarked as the baby was cleaned of blood and mucus and wrapped in warm swaddling. The sight of Ailith labouring had swept her on a flood of memories to her own travail, and at the moment of Julitta's birth, she had been unable to watch. Nor was she at ease until the midwife, Dame Osyth, a woman with nine children of her own, had delivered the afterbirth and pronounced that the blood Ailith had lost was 'nought but a smidgin'.

'She resembles Rolf,' Felice said, giving the howling bundle to the exhausted, but happy mother.

Ailith laughed. 'God grant that she does not act like him. Two of them is more than I could bear!'

'You do not mean that!'

'Could you imagine Rolf in female form?' She put the infant to her breast. The baby found her nipple immediately and set to with a voracious will. 'But I fear you are right,' she added wryly. 'She certainly has his appetite.'

'I'll go and fetch him,' Felice said as the midwife set about tidying the room, putting the afterbirth and bloodstained bed-straw in a basket for burning and covering them with used linens.

Ailith gazed down upon her new daughter, enchanted by the fragility of her skin and the coppery-gold lashes lining her half-closed lids. She was long of limb, and since both her parents were tall, would doubtless grow to match them. Ailith spoke softly to the baby and her eyes opened. They lacked focus and were an indeterminate horizon-blue, but they followed the sound of the voice and seemed to study Ailith curiously. She felt a pang of protective love so fierce that it brought tears to her eyes.

'Julitta,' she murmured, testing the strange, Norman name on her tongue. At Yuletide she had made a bargain with Rolf beneath a kissing bunch of mistletoe. If the baby was a boy, she had requested that he be named Lyulph in remembrance of her younger brother. Not Goldwin, for that was a name too sacred and painful to her heart. Rolf had agreed on the condition that if the child was a girl, she should be named after his mother, Julitta.

'She did not have very much out of me or my father during her lifetime,' he had said with a shrug, 'and I know that she would have liked you.'

'Why didn't you give her name to your . . . your wife's daughter?' Ailith had asked, the word 'wife' sticking in her throat.

Rolf had smiled. 'I did think about it, but Arlette desired to call Gisele after her maternal grandmother, and I knew that I could have the naming of any sons. Besides, it did not seem to matter. When I saw Gisele lying in her cradle, I knew immediately that she was no Julitta.'

'And are you a Julitta?' Ailith asked her newborn daughter, and was answered by a loud sucking noise. The tug of the baby's lips on her nipple sent waves of cramp through Ailith's loins.

The hangings across the doorway moved, and she propped herself up and put a smile on her face for Rolf. The curtain billowed again, and instead of the anticipated lean, red-haired man, there entered a bright-eyed small boy.

'I've come to see the new baby,' announced a confident Benedict de Remy.

The midwife set her lips and started towards the child, but Ailith stopped her. 'No, let him come and look. He does no harm.'

Benedict sidled past the village woman and ran up to the bed. He stared solemnly at the sucking infant and very gently placed his finger on her downy red hair.

'Except for your mother and Wulfhild, and Dame Osyth here, you are the first person in the castle to have seen her,' Ailith told him.

Benedict nodded. 'She's very small,' he said, frowning.

'You were too when you were born.'

'I want a brother, but Mama can't have any more babies. What's her name?'

Ailith told him, and he repeated it carefully. A bright little imp was Benedict, full of life and filled with a ruthless quest for knowledge. In her tired state, he quite overwhelmed Ailith. She was rescued by Felice, who hurried into the room, looking exasperated.

'I'm sorry, Ailith, he gave me the slip. I should have known he would come straight here to you. Ben, leave Ailith alone, she's exhausted.'

The little boy pulled a face and refused to move from his post at the bedside, but he ceased his chatter.

'Where's Rolf?' Ailith asked of Felice. 'Could you not find him?'

'He's gone out to one of the horses. Mauger summoned him in a panic so the steward says, about half a candle notch since. Something about a broken leg.'

'Oh.' Ailith nodded and tried not to feel disappointed. She knew that his horses came first, that she should not expect him to be waiting in the hall on the whim of his child to be born, but nevertheless, weak tears filled her eyes. She blinked hard. Supposing Sleipnir had broken a bone, Rolf's prize stallion? Or what if it was Elfa, her own little mare?

'He'll be back soon,' Felice soothed with the false heartiness of a sickbed nurse. 'Try and sleep, so that you'll be refreshed when he does arrive. Come on, rascal, you can see the baby again later.' She took her son's hand and drew him firmly away while the midwife came to tend to Ailith and take the satiated baby from her arms.

Ailith gave Julitta to Dame Osyth and wearily closed her eyes. She knew that she was being irrational, but knowing did not prevent her from feeling as if she had been deserted.

Several hours later, a sound woke Ailith. The baby was no longer in her cradle where Dame Osyth had placed her, and of the midwife herself there was no sign. Ailith pulled herself up on her pillows and stared round the room. There were cramps in her belly and the entire area of the birth passage was no longer numb, but decidedly sore. The sound resolved itself into Rolf's voice talking softly near the shutters, and she saw that in his arms he was gently cradling the swaddled baby.

'Rolf?'

He turned as she spoke, and came to the bed. She saw that his face was slack and tired, as if he too had not slept all night. Certainly he had not shaved, for his lips and jaw were outlined in garnet stubble.

'Did I waken you?' Leaning over the bed, he kissed her.

'It does not matter. I am glad that you're here.' Her eyes filled with tears again. It was a weakness of women the days immediately following childbirth, or so Dame Hulda had told Ailith when she bore Harold. 'Is she a Julitta?' she managed to choke out. 'Does she meet with your approval?'

'She is a princess,' Rolf said softly, and brushed away her tears with the hand not occupied by his daughter. 'And yes, she is a Julitta. My mother was the one responsible for the red hair in the Brize bloodline, and I can see that this little one has it.' He seated himself on a stool at the bedside. 'Down her back it was, a mane of wild curls. But I think that her namesake is going to be even more beautiful.'

His words were a soothing balm on Ailith's earlier feelings of rejection, and a watery smile emerged through her tears.

'And I think that last night is only the first of many sleepless ones that she will cause us,' she teased.

Rolf acknowledged the truth of her words with a grimace. As if indignant at being maligned so young, Julitta set up a fractious wailing, and when rocking her only brought forth louder roars of protest, Rolf hastily handed her to Ailith for feeding.

'Felice said that you could not come when our daughter was born because you had gone out to tend a horse?' Ailith settled Julitta at her breast and hoped that her tone had not sounded petulant.

His grimace lost its humour. 'The bay pony stallion, the one I bought in the north,' he sighed. 'Put his leg in a mole mound this morning while Mauger was trying to catch him, and snapped the bone clean through.'

'Can nothing be done?'

'It was a hind leg; he would have been useless for breeding – no strength to mount the mares. The break was too severe to even try to save him. I had to kill him.'

'Oh, Rolf, I am sorry!' She touched his hand in sympathy with her free one and was ashamed at the anger she had felt earlier. 'And you had such hopes!'

'It just means I'll have to go north and buy another stallion.'

Ailith tightened her arm around the suckling baby and was filled with fear.

'Oh not yet,' he said as he caught the look on her face. 'Next month perhaps, or early in April when the roads are fit for travelling. I have learned my lesson about visiting those parts in wintertime.'

'Do you think there will be anything left up there to seek out?' she demanded with some agitation.

'What do you mean?'

'Oh you know as well as I do. The traders who come to Ulverton tell dreadful tales of what your king has done in the north lands; of the villages he has wasted. People say that if peace lies over England, it is the peace of death.'

If he noticed her say 'your king' as opposed to 'the King', he did not remark upon it. 'Pedlars always exaggerate,' he said uncomfortably. 'And the north was in rebellion – the Scots, the Danes, several English earls. What was he supposed to do? They had received warning enough already.'

She said nothing, but bit her lip and paid undue attention to the feeding baby. She did not have the strength to quarrel.

'I won't find another pony stallion of the bay's stamp in these parts. Nor will I know what I can obtain in the north unless I go and look for myself.'

'You will do as you please,' she said stiffly. Here he was, watching his newborn daughter suckle at her breast, and he was contemplating leaving her. It was a bitter morsel to swallow. Was this how his wife felt when she saw him for a few brief weeks each year? The land on the horizon was always better than the land he possessed. From feeling bathed in love, she returned to feeling desolate and frightened. The midwife would say that it was the effects of giving birth that were making her emotions swing from high to low like a falconer's lure, but Ailith knew differently.

'You need to sleep,' Rolf said, leaning over her to brush his lips lightly against her temple and cheek. 'I'll come back later.'

She watched him make his escape, treading buoyantly to the door, and wondered if that was what he always said. One day, she thought, he would 'come back later' to a cold hearth.

CHAPTER 30

Rolf had been prepared to see a scarred and punished land, but he could never have envisaged the devastation which greeted his eyes as he, Mauger, and eight retainers crossed the Humber and headed into what remained of the Yorkshire Danelaw.

Entire villages had been scorched to the ground, their livestock butchered and their crops destroyed. Charred bodies lay where they had fallen, and many of them were human, with no-one to bury them decently. The few living people they did encounter either fled at their approach on famine-thin legs, or accosted them in desperation, begging for food. They had nothing to sustain them, not even hope, for William had destroyed everything. There was no seed to sow crops, no fruit trees to provide winter stores, no animals to salt down.

Occasionally Rolf found a village which had escaped more lightly than the others, but even here there was a lack of men to do the work. Every male over the age of fifteen had been slaughtered. Terrible indeed had been William's vengeance upon the rebels. It was almost as if he had decided that he could do without the troublesome population of northern England, and with a determined swipe of his iron fist, had swatted it from existence.

Mauger began to have nightmares and Rolf found himself touching the talismans he wore around his neck and praying more than he had done in a long time. The loyalty he felt towards King William remained as staunch as ever despite the atrocities, but the admiration which had long been attached to his loyalty died, and in its place grew a cold disgust. He saw starving women and infants and tried not to think of Ailith and Julitta, but his imagination would not be commanded. Time and again he saw their ghosts in the gaunt, skeletal faces cursing their tracks as they rode towards York. Obtaining a single pony stallion suddenly seemed futile, a paltry speck on the road of his life. In his black mood, he would have turned back, but he was so close to Ulf's village by then, that he knew he had to go on. For good or evil, he had to know what had happened.

They approached the village on a hazy spring afternoon, the sun a misty halo in a pale sky. The track was muddy and Rolf was encouraged to see the print of hoof and foot gouged in the mire. Neither pigs nor swineherd materialised to greet them, and at the place where the Odin statue had stood sentinel, there was nothing but a lush growth of nettles. Rolf drew rein and saluted his respect as if at a grave before riding on.

The palisade of wooden stakes was commemorated by a charred circle of ashes, blurring black into the soil. It surrounded fewer than a dozen houses, and these were new structures of fresh thatch and green timber. More black smears and twisted black beams revealed what had happened to the other dwellings. Ulf's village had not escaped the attentions of William's Norman mercenaries. It had been seriously mauled, but it had not been utterly destroyed.

A woman carrying a large water jug from the well was the first person they encountered. Her eyes widened, but she did not panic as the swineherd had once done. Instead she put down the jar and went straight into one of the huts, her step swift but graceful. Rolf recognised Inga, Ulf's daughter-in-law. Moments later Ulf himself emerged from the building. He walked with a stick, his limp severe, but the same iron will was in evidence.

Rolf dismounted and walked over to him.

'So,' Ulf jutted his silver and rust jaw at Rolf, 'your Viking instinct brings you back to see what the ravens have wreaked?'

Rolf drew a deep breath. 'I am grieved for what my countrymen have done, but I tried to warn you what would happen.'

'Aye, so you did,' Ulf said without warmth. 'What do you want?'

'If you still have ponies, I have come to trade for another stallion. The one you sold me broke his leg before he had covered more than one season of mares.'

'Aye, I still have ponies.'

'Will you trade?'

Ulf stared at him for a long time with eyes of winter ice. Then abruptly he swept his arm towards his hut. His tunic sleeve fell away to reveal heavy bracelets of incised silver and bronze on his wrists. 'Enter within and partake of what meagre hospitality I can offer. I am one of the fortunate ones, I still have a roof over my head.'

Once more Inga brought food for the guests, serving Rolf and his men coldly, her mouth tucked in a severe fold and her cat-hazel eyes downcast. The bread was gritty and impure, the boiled stockfish salty and tough. Mauger pulled a face and almost gagged, but a glare from Rolf made him choke down his food and murmur his thanks.

'Your community has survived,' Rolf said, forcing himself to eat, knowing what a sacrifice the old man was making in his pride.

'After a fashion,' Ulf growled. 'There are no villages left hereabouts with whom we can trade. We have to go to York for our provisions and that costs silver. But it is due to you that some of us are alive to grumble about our lot.'

'Due to me?'

'As you said earlier, you warned us about what your Duke would do. I heeded your words above those of my own son and I had our people take all of our winter supplies and animals into the woods and hide them. When the Normans arrived, they found the village already deserted. All they had to burn were our empty houses.'

Rolf ate in silence. There was nothing he could say apart from that he was sorry. He was being thanked and hated at the same time, and the sensation was disquieting. His eye fell on Inga as she went about her duties. She looked beaten down and weary. Her son sat on the floor playing with a chicken's foot, fiddling with the guiders to make the toes move. Of the little girl there was no sign. 'There were many more houses when I came before,' he said to Ulf.

'My son Beorn and our hot-headed young men died fighting a Norman patrol on the York road at the beginning of the troubles. And then, around the time that we had to hide in the woods, many of us took sick of a pestilence and very few recovered. Inga's daughter was among them.'

'I am sorry.' Rolf's glance flickered again to the young woman. He would have pitied her, but her self-contained manner forbade such a sentiment.

'Being sorry will not bring the heart back to this place,' Ulf grunted sourly. 'Have you finished? Then come, I will show you the ponies.'

The new stallion was a glossy, pine-pitch brown which hovered just short of being pure black. He was more sturdily made than the previous bay Rolf had purchased, for he was three years older and in his prime. Fine hairs feathered his hocks and pasterns, but his leg action was high and clean.

'I was saving him for myself,' Ulf announced, 'but there is no-one in this wilderness with the money or need to buy a horse unless it be to eat, and for that they will steal. I keep him close to the compound; I know if I do not, he will finish his life upon some poor wretch's table. Silver is of more use to me now. I can buy seeds and supplies to start anew.'

They settled down to haggle a price, although Rolf did not haggle very hard, for he could see the older man's need. Blood money, he thought, the price of feeling less guilty for the sin of being a Norman.

'There is one other thing I desire of you,' Ulf said as Rolf counted the silver coins out of his pouch.

'There is?' Rolf was alerted to caution by the sudden gruff note in the other's voice.

'When you leave, I desire you to take Inga and the lad with you. There is no future for them in this village save that it be from hand-to-mouth.'

Rolf stopped counting and looked at Ulf in surprise. 'You would entrust them to a Norman?'

'To save them from being killed by other Normans. What if your king's mercenaries should return and ravage again?' Ulf shook his head, his shoulders drooping. 'Even if that does not happen, Normans will still come and lay claim to what is ours, and we are too weak to stop them. What was "Ulf's land" will become Osbert's or Ogier's.' He spat the French names with contempt. 'How will my grandson fare against them, do you think?'

'You believe they will fare better in the south?'

'They could not fare worse,' Ulf said scathingly, but then moderated his voice. 'You are a man of honour, I trust you to see them safely settled.'

Rolf looked thoughtfully at the old horse-trader. 'And what will you do?'

'I do not need a place of sanctuary. My roots are too deeply buried here to be torn up and planted elsewhere, and there are others in the village of my ilk who will need my counsel in the months to come. For Inga and Sweyn it is different. The boy is still thistledown in the wind. He could settle anywhere.'

Rolf inclined his head. 'Then so be it,' he said. 'My roof is theirs.'

Inga perched silently on the baggage wain, her posture resembling a drawn purse concealing its contents. Her arms were folded across her breasts, hugging a thick, rectangular cloak to her body. Her fists were clenched, her mouth was pulled tight, and barely a word had she spoken during all the long first day of the journey towards Ulverton. Her son, Sweyn, by contrast, was riding with Mauger and talking nineteen to the dozen, his eyes bright with the joy of adventure. Rolf harboured no qualms about him settling to a new life. His mother, however, was cause for concern.

He rode up to the front of the wain where she was huddled beside the driver, her expression remote and enigmatic. Her bones were more dainty and precise than Ailith's, her beauty more exotic than Arlette's. Her coldness piqued and intrigued him. He rode closer, intending to speak to her, but a loud honking and a clattering of imprisoned wings caused his mount to shy, and he spent several precarious moments preventing himself from being thrown.

Inga had insisted upon bringing her geese to Ulverton, or at least the means to begin a new flock from the original birds. They would be her livelihood, she said. No-one could smoke gooseflesh as succulently as she did. They would provide her with an income and they would be a reminder of home.

Much of the disturbance was caused by an aggressive young gander, still in the brown plumage of adolescence. He had been hissing threats ever since being latched inside his wicker cage at the journey's outset. Rolf eyed the bird with disfavour and hoped that it would soon be consigned to the smoke-house.

Inga regarded him coldly as if she could read his thoughts. 'I chose the strongest,' she said, 'because only the strong survive.' The words held a note of challenge.

Rolf inclined his head. 'Then you must be strong too,' he said.

'And my husband was weak?'

'He was faced by men more ruthless.'

'Hah,' she said with scornful dismissal and looked away. 'He was worth ten Normans, my Beorn.'

The goose beat its wings against the wicker bars and continued to threaten Rolf and his mount. The horse sweated and pranced, thoroughly upset. 'He's worth nothing now that he's dead,' Rolf replied, stung by her contempt, and he rode off to join his men.

CHAPTER 31

AUTUMN 1075

On the day that Julitta fell in love with Benedict de Remy, she was five years old and playing a game of pretend. It was early autumn, the leaves gowning the trees in tints of tawny, amber and flame. Ulverton's razor-backed swine rooted in the moist ground beneath the canopy for a pannage of acorns and beech mast, and the villagers gathered firewood against the harsher months to come.

Julitta had slipped away from her mother and Wulfhild who had been too busy and harassed preparing a feast to notice her absence. The de Remy's were expected from London, and all had to be made ready for their arrival. Julitta hoped they would come soon. She liked Aubert; he had a face like a hoary tree trunk, with deep smile lines either side of his mouth. Aunt Felice, as she respectfully called his wife, was beautiful. She always wore lovely clothes and she smelled delicious – of roses and spice. They had a son, a big boy of nine years old, named Benedict, and sometimes he would play with her.

This particular morning, Julitta had sneaked some hazel nuts from one of the bowls laid out for the feast and had dropped them into the small draw-cord purse attached to her belt. Her father would sometimes ruffle her tangled dark auburn curls and call her a squirrel because of her delight in hoarding small objects in unexpected corners – marbles, feathers, little coloured stones. Today, Julitta had decided to be that squirrel.

The autumn gold of the trees beckoned and the nuts in her pouch were to be her food.

The tree she chose was a young oak growing beyond the castle ditch close to one of the dew ponds. The prevailing winds had caused it to lean to one side, and its tilt had been further exaggerated by the attentions of sheep and cattle using it as a scratching post. There was a branch at just the right height for the reach of Julitta's legs, and in no time at all, she had pulled herself onto it. The next branch was a little further away, but after a determined struggle and a scraped knee, she succeeded in reaching it. She sucked the graze, tasting the saltiness of damaged skin, and having reassured herself that the injury was not great, she sought for the next hand- and foothold. She was a quicksilver squirrel, whisking her way through the branches, her long red hair, a busy tail.

Light although she was, her progress dislodged amber showers of leaves. A thrush which had been roosting in the oak took wing in twittering alarm. Julitta discovered a nest which had been well used during the spring and summer. It was comfortably rounded into the shape of a bird's breast and from somewhere the former occupant had filched some bright red embroidery wool and used it for part of the lining. Julitta was captivated and gently dislodged the nest from its position in the fork of two branches. Perhaps her mother would let her keep it.

She settled herself against the rough main trunk, wriggling back and forth until she was comfortable, and then removed one of the nuts from the pouch. Her teeth were too small to pierce the glossy brown shell. She tried striking the hazel on the tree trunk, but her blows were not strong enough, and finally she just had to pretend to eat the nut. She was not really hungry anyway, having devoured bread, honey and a beakerful of buttermilk whilst sitting on her father's knee before he rode out to inspect his horses. Frequently he would take her with him, but today he had been too busy, and Julitta felt secure enough in his love to let him go without too much protest. There was always tomorrow.

A sound began to encroach on her thoughts, distant at first

and barely a disturbance, but as it grew louder, Julitta's sense of wellbeing turned quickly to apprehension. She was a steadfast, confident child, afraid of very little. Her father's great grey stallion Sleipnir gave her not a moment's qualm, although one kick from a careless hoof could have killed her. She romped with the dogs in the hall, she played among men whose trade was the war sword, but for all her boldness, she was utterly terrified of Inga's flock of greylag geese. One of the birds had pecked her when she was tiny, and the memory, although not clear, had left its legacy. She was frightened of Inga too. Unlike the other village women, Inga never smiled at her or said how pretty she was, but treated Julitta in a cool, offhand manner that spoke of disapproval.

Inga was herding her geese to graze on the lush grass around the dew ponds. If she saw Julitta up the tree, she would certainly tell her off and command her to come down. The child hugged herself for comfort and peeped down through the gaps in the golden foliage at the numerous geese waddling beneath the oak, their plumage a glossy, variegated brown, their blunt orange beaks promising vicious bruises. Julitta could almost feel them on her flesh. Geese couldn't climb trees, could they? She listened to their aggressive honking as they waddled towards the water. Inga passed beneath the tree, a gnarled stick swinging loosely in her hand. A small, rough-coated terrier trotted at her heels. Now and then she encouraged the birds with a command in a guttural language that Julitta had been told was the English of the north, the place where Inga had come from. Her son Sweyn spoke like her too, but Julitta quite liked him. He lived in one of the fishing villages, where he had a share in a boat, and he was always laughing and cheerful.

Inga's dog snuffled at the base of Julitta's tree and then barked. The woman glanced round and, with irritation in her voice, called him to heel. He barked again, but only in parting as he obeyed the command.

Julitta watched Inga and the terrier walk on across the field, leaving the geese to their grazing – leaving her alone with them, perhaps until dusk. Someone was bound to come seeking her.

But then she would be in trouble for running off and her mother might make her miss the feast in punishment. The very thought of such deprivation filled her eyes with tears of self-pity. She wiped them defiantly on the sleeve of her green dress and gulped back a sob.

The remedy was to climb down from the tree by herself and run away as fast as she could. If she was lucky, the geese might not see her until she had put a safe distance between them and her. Terrified but resolute, the child started to descend from her perch. She scraped her knee again and added a long scratch to her shin. The distances between hand- and footholds seemed far greater than on the way up. By the time she reached the last branch, her arms were hot and aching, and as she lowered herself to the ground, she lost her grip and fell.

It was not a hard enough landing to break any bones but Julitta was shaken. The pain in the shoulder and side which had borne the brunt of her fall made her cry as she sat up. She knuckled her eyes with grimy fingers, smearing grey bark stains over her face. Her hair was tangled around her shoulders in disarray, and a ripped side seam in her dress revealed an ominous amount of undershift.

She struggled to her feet, and immediately her hiccuping sobs turned to screams of terror as Inga's huge greylag gander ran at her, beating its clipped wings, darting its long neck and hissing. She spun frantically and tried to scramble back up the tree, but fear had turned her legs and arms weak.

The goose lunged at her, its beak clacking within a fraction of her arm. Screaming, she ran round the tree. The bird chased her, honking belligerently. Julitta's shrieks became hysterical; nothing existed beyond her terror.

Then suddenly there was a boy on a sleek bay pony. He yelled at the gander, and tugging his cloak over his head, whirled it round and round to distract the bird. The enraged goose flapped to face the new intruder on his territory, thoroughly prepared to do battle. The pony gave a startled snort and bunched its haunches. Seeing that the gander was not to be intimidated by loud noise and vigorous movement alone, the boy swung his cloak a final time, casting it upwards and out-wards like a fishing net. It landed squarely over the bird, engulfing it.

'Hurry, before he escapes!' he shouted at Julitta, his dark eyes flickering between her and the goose. He urged the pony over to the tree and leaning gracefully down, extended his hand to her.

She was still sobbing hysterically, but at her core, a final spark of reason responded to the boy's gesture. She grasped his hand, set her foot upon his in the stirrup, and let him pull her up before him across the pony's neck.

Tangled within the cloak, the gander hissed and honked. Its head surged free and then a flailing wing-tip. Abandoning the garment, the boy kicked hard with his heels. The pony, his head tilted at an angle by the awkward position of his extra burden, cantered valiantly away from the danger.

After several glances over his shoulder, the boy slowed his mount to a trot, then a walk, and at a safe distance, finally drew rein. 'It's all right now,' he reassured Julitta. 'He's won free, but he's not chasing us, see?'

Having been jounced over uneven ground across a pony's withers, Julitta felt thoroughly sick. She wanted the security of her mother's arms desperately. To look back and see if what he said was true, she had to relinquish her tight grip on the pony's mane and slide to the ground. Her legs refused to hold her up and she crumpled on the dusty grass. The gander had indeed chosen to abandon the fight and was waddling in high dudgeon towards the other geese grazing near the dew pond. Julitta gave a loud, mucous sniff and pressed her hand experimentally across her midriff to decide if she really was going to be sick.

'Does your mother know where you are?'

Julitta shook her head and began to cry again. 'I want her,' she sobbed miserably. 'I was only playing squirrels, but it all went wrong.'

'Sit behind me then, and I'll take you home.'

Julitta gazed up at the boy through her tears, and recognition suddenly dawned. He had thin, black brows, liquid brown eyes, and black hair, glossy as a raven's wing. Her stare took on the intensity of a religious mystic granted a vision of God. He returned the smile she gave him and held out his hand again.

She was still a little unsure of the state of her queasy stomach, but found the strength to rise and clamber up behind him, across the pony's satin-dark rump.

'Hold tight to my belt,' he said.

Julitta needed no prompting. She grasped the leather at his waist and leaned her tear-streaked cheek against the comfort of his spine. 'Ben,' she murmured, suddenly feeling very sleepy.

It was not long before they happened upon the adult company of Benedict's parents, riding towards Ulverton at a more sedate pace than their son, who had been making forays ahead and playing at reconnaissance for the past several miles.

'Blessed Virgin!' declared Felice in horror as she took in the draggled state of the little girl riding pillion behind Benedict.

By this time, Julitta had fallen soundly asleep, but although her head lolled against Benedict's tunic, her fingers remained firmly gripped in his belt, and Felice deemed it wise to let her remain thus until they reached the castle.

Ailith watched her small daughter stir her spoon slowly round and round in her bowl of frumenty. Julitta's naturally fair skin was paler than usual and there were dark shadows beneath her eyes. To her mother's concerned stare she looked like a wilting bluebell. Ailith knew that she should not have yielded to Julitta's pleading, nor to Rolf's gruff comment that it would be unjust to put the child straight to bed when she had been so looking forward to this feast. The fact was that Julitta was too exhausted by the day's ordeal to enjoy any of this celebration. She had barely eaten a morsel, and her usual vivacity was entirely quenched.

Most of the story of the incident with Inga's gander had come from Benedict. Ailith had been horrified and filled with self-reproach to hear how far Julitta had wandered; she could have fallen in the pond, or been pecked to death by that vile bird. It was so difficult to keep an eye on her all of the time. She had her father's quicksilver, curious nature, and a way of

making opportune escapes. Trying to hold Julitta was like trying to trap a mote of sunlight. The minute you clenched your
hand around it, the light went out.

'Deep thoughts?' Felice asked, nudging her lightly.

Ailith gave a pensive smile and shook her head. 'I was
brooding upon what might have happened,' she said. 'Rolf is
always complaining that I worry about her too much. I suppose
it is because I lost Harold, and since bearing her, I have not
conceived again.'

'It is the way I feel about Benedict,' Felice sympathised with
a fond glance at her son. In contrast to Julitta, he was demol-
ishing the food on his trencher with a healthy gusto. 'But I try
not to clip his wings too much. Of course,' she added quickly,
'he is older than Julitta and a boy.'

'It would have been simpler if Julitta had been born male.'
Ailith sighed. 'She would rather be out among the horses or
romping in the mire than learning to spin and sew and brew
and bake. I know she could do those things if she applied her
mind. She does not lack the wit, just the desire.'

'It will come in time.' Felice nodded sagely. 'Besides, it is
not given to all women to be paragons of domestic virtue, and
it does not suit all men to have wives who are such. She will
have fire and beauty enough to catch any man she wants.'

Ailith grimaced. 'That is no comfort,' she said.

Just before Julitta's face drooped into her frumenty dish,
Rolf caught her, and lifting her from her place, drew her into
his lap. She put her thumb in her mouth and snuggled tightly
against him.

'I'll take her to bed now.' Ailith held out her arms. She
could not help but give Rolf an 'I told you so' look.

'I'll carry her.' Rolf returned her look with a sharp one of
his own, and setting his other arm beneath Julitta's knees, rose
and walked down the crowded, smoky hall to their sleeping
quarters. Ailith followed him, and when he laid Julitta down on
their bed, she stripped her of tunic and undergown to leave her
clothed in her best linen short shift. Once more, her eyes were
drawn to the scratches and livid bruises on Julitta's slender legs.

'It is not the first time that Inga's gander has attacked some-one,' Ailith complained as she gently drew the covers over their daughter. 'Wulfhild was telling me that the shepherd's youngest son was badly pecked at midsummer. I know that Julitta should not have been out on her own, but those birds are a danger to anyone who walks near the dew ponds.'

Rolf was silent for a while. 'The geese are her livelihood and her independence,' he said at length. 'She will not easily give them up.'

'Just that gander.'

'Him least of all.' Rolf grimaced. 'She brought the bird from the north as a gosling. He represents all that used to be hers.'

'And her sensibilities are reason enough to let everyone else go in fear?' Ailith curbed her anger with difficulty. Of late there had been a lack of harmony between herself and Rolf. She sensed a restlessness in him like the swallows that gathered at harvest time in preparation to fly away. It burned her to think of him with his wife and daughter when he went to Normandy, and she was frequently waspish to him despite her best intentions. He had ceased to argue with her or give her reassurances. Instead he would calmly shut her out and go about his work with the horses as if she did not exist, or spend yet more time away, visiting clients.

And then there was Inga; cold, fair-haired Inga who was as indifferent to Rolf as she was to everyone else. Ailith could sense how much it irked him, itching away beneath his skin.

'I did not say that,' he replied with laboured patience. 'Of course she must be held accountable for her flock. I will speak to her.'

'For all the good that will do,' Ailith said witheringly.

'More good than speaking to you,' Rolf retorted, and walked out of the room.

Ailith closed her eyes and bit down on her lower lip. The promise of forever was bleeding away and she did not know how to staunch it.

Rolf replenished his cup and sat down before the hearth with Aubert. The women had retired, and although the servants and retainers had laid out their pallets along the walls or rolled themselves in their cloaks to sleep, to all intents and purposes they were alone.

'Ailith was quiet tonight,' Aubert remarked.

Rolf shrugged. 'She was brooding about Julitta.' He pulled a face. 'I sometimes think that all women are the same, not a hair to choose between any of them.'

Aubert raised his brows, inviting confidences.

Rolf drank from his cup and let out a deep sigh. 'I love Ailith, but sometimes she is so impossible that I cannot bear to be in her company. It is like being caged.'

'And of course your own nature is so perfect that you are never the cause of her contrariness,' Aubert said neutrally.

'I know I have my faults, but of late, whatever I do or say is wrong in her eyes.' Rolf scowled at his cup, and then at Aubert. 'You said you wanted a word in private. If it's about myself and Ailith, I might as well take myself off to bed.'

Aubert just looked at Rolf and beneath the sharp, hazel stare, Rolf's indignation crumbled to be replaced by embarrassment. 'Very well,' he said with a grudging smile, 'I have no redeeming features and the fault is all mine.'

'Just have a care, Rolf. Some broken hearts mend, but I doubt that Ailith's would, or yours for that matter. And there endeth my sermon. I'm not here to preach what you already know. Besides, I need you in a listening humour and not out of sorts with me.'

'Indeed?' Rolf raised an eyebrow and felt a pleasant curiosity. Conversations with Aubert, whatever else, were never boring. Although Aubert had mostly given up the more questionable activities attached to his wine trade, he still dabbled here and there at the request of the King. But what Aubert said next took Rolf completely by surprise.

'I have been deliberating upon approaching you for no small time; I would not have you think this is lightly suggested out of a moment's folly. I have a business proposition to put to you concerning Benedict's future.'

'Oh?' Rolf folded his arms.

'What would you say if I offered for your daughter Gisele in marriage on his behalf?'

At first Rolf could only gape at Aubert in astonishment. He did not know what to say; then several things, all contradictory, crowded onto his tongue at once and rendered him incoherent, which was just as well since some of the comments would have irrevocably sundered the friendship between himself and Aubert.

'Gisele and Benedict,' he finally managed to croak out. 'You aim high indeed.'

'My son is never going to be more than a mediocre wine merchant; he has no interest in the trade, but it is as if he was born knowing horses. You have seen it yourself.'

Rolf rose to replenish his cup and remained standing, for Aubert's words had kindled his restlessness. His friend was wily; he would not have broached the subject without first considering it from all angles and weighing up the risks of rejection. 'I have noticed that Ben does have a talent that way,' Rolf said cautiously, 'but how far it will develop is a point of chance, nor is it a recommendation I can give to my wife. I have always promised Arlette that our daughter will make a great marriage. I cannot go to her and say that for the sake of friendship I have accepted the offer of a Rouen wine merchant.'

Aubert drew himself up. 'I do not ask you as a boon for friendship's sake. I know full well that you have the wealth and position to make a high marriage for Gisele. While I cannot match your rank, I can easily match your wealth, so I count the scales even. You were never one to stand on ceremony, Rolf.'

Rolf's eyes became dry with staring and he blinked rapidly several times.

Aubert hunched forward in his seat and eyed Rolf intently, his own gaze unwavering. 'You know that I have risked my neck for William both as Duke and King. After the great battle at Hastings, he rewarded me in coin and English booty and I bought land and houses in London and Rouen. People pay me rent and my wealth increases. I have two wine galleys, one trading out of London, the other out of Rouen, and a merchant vessel, the *Draca*, to be ready in the spring. Benedict will be very rich one day, but I would like him to be content too.' Aubert shrugged, and spread his hands. 'That is why I made you the offer. If you do not think that our differences are negotiable, I'll look elsewhere and take no offence.'

Rolf shook his head, totally bemused. 'God's nails, Aubert, I need time to think, and for that I have to gather my wits, which you have scattered to the four winds.'

Aubert smiled, a decided gleam in his hooded hazel eyes. 'I knew that one day, I'd see you at a loss for words.'

Ailith felt Rolf raise the covers and slide into the bed. One sinewy arm came across her body, and he pressed close, touching the tip of his tongue to the tiny hairs on her spine. Ailith had been pretending to be asleep, but a small, sensuous shiver gave her away and with a sigh, she rolled over to face him.

He nuzzled her throat. 'We shouldn't have parted in anger earlier,' he murmured.

Only moments before Rolf had come to bed, she had been imagining a scene where she necked Inga's cursed gander herself, and perhaps Inga too into the bargain, but she grasped Rolf's olive branch eagerly. 'I'm sorry I was a shrew. I was worried about Julitta.'

'I was too thin-skinned myself. Call it even. I promise I will speak to Inga and make her do something about those geese.'

Ailith snuggled against him, breathing in his familiar scent. He stroked her hair, her spine, her breasts, and she felt his erection strain against her belly.

'Aubert desires a marriage between Benedict and Gisele.' His words came muffled as he buried his lips in her cleavage. 'I do not know whether I should accept or not. What do you think?'

'Benedict and Gisele?' she said, as surprised as Rolf had been. 'Are they suited?

'As well suited as any couple are when their parents arrange a marriage. Aubert, as it turns out, is a very wealthy man, and I like the boy's spirit. Gisele is like her mother – biddable, pious, and very pretty.'

'Perhaps you should let them meet and see how they respond to one another.'

'That would not be so bad an idea, and in the meantime, I could give the proposition due consideration.' He moved lower, softly pinching her skin with his lips.

She touched his hair, feeling beneath her fingertips the springy curls that he had passed on to Julitta, making her longer tresses such a bane to comb. 'But they will meet on Norman ground, you will not bring your wife to Ulverton?' she said, suddenly anxious.

He ceased what he was doing, and the muscles tensed across the back of his neck. 'I am not a complete fool,' he murmured against her flesh.

'I could not bear it if you did bring her,' Ailith whispered.

He sighed, and for a moment she thought that he was going to turn away as they trammelled the same old ground whose ruts they both knew because they had worn the path so often and so painfully before. 'I won't,' he said. 'On my soul I swear I won't.'

'It is forever.' Her hands remained in his hair, gripping him. 'Say it is forever.'

He hesitated again. 'It is forever,' he repeated, and broke her hold, pinning her beneath him, assaulting her senses until she sobbed aloud, half with pleasure and half with pain.

CHAPTER 32

Two days later, Rolf gave Mauger instructions to spruce up a young grey stallion which was to be inspected for the royal stables by a representative of King William, and rode out in the misty, gleaming dawn to keep his promise to Ailith.

Smoke twirled from village cooking fires and the people were already up and about their daily business. He was greeted according to each individual's adjustment to the fact of a Norman lord, but mostly with respect. Curious stares followed his progress down the village street to the house at the end where dwelt Inga, the woman from the north, and eyebrows were raised when he dismounted and tethered his horse to the low palisade surrounding her property.

Inga herself was just emerging from her house. She had a knobbed walking stick in one hand, although she had no need of it, the item was just a matter of habit, a prop to make people keep their distance. Over her other arm was draped a fine, dark blue cloak. Her small terrier growled at Rolf, but she commanded it to silence. Her cool hazel stare assessed him.

'How may I help you, my lord?' Her voice was cool too, but like Scots usquebaugh, it possessed an afterburn that set his nerves tingling.

'I want to talk to you about your geese . . . about your gander in particular.'

Inga pursed her lips. Her gaze flickered beyond him to the interest being generated in the village street and turning back, she reopened her door. 'Then you had best enter,' she said and commanded the dog away to his kennel in the yard.

Feeling uncomfortable, Rolf followed her into the house. The beaten earth floor had been stamped solid and covered with a layer of rushes. There was a bedding bench along one wall, piled with goatskins, and shelves upon the wall boasted an array of jars and pitchers. It was far from poor, but much less than that which had been her due in the north.

'They don't like me, your villagers,' she said, depositing the cloak, and gesturing him to be seated on the bedding bench. 'I don't fit in with their customs or their ways.'

'You don't try to like them,' he answered. 'Your son Sweyn has been accepted easily enough.'

'He's a man now, and they're short of men. I'm a rival for the few available – my own house, an income of sorts. They're jealous.' She reached down a flask of mead and poured a mea-sure into a round wooden cup, then held it out to him. 'What about my gander? I suppose Widow Alfric's been complaining again.'

Their fingers touched as Rolf took the cup from her hands. Cool, with an afterburn. He was playing with fire and he knew it. 'Widow Alfric would have taken her complaint to my reeve first,' he said. 'This comes closer to my own threshold. Two days ago, your bird attacked my daughter Julitta, and she has the marks on her body to prove it. If my Godson Benedict had not happened along on his pony, she might have been killed. As it was, the gander attacked him too, and he had to throw his cloak over the thing to save himself.'

Inga's face became ivory pale, but she maintained her com-posure. 'I am sorry to hear that,' she said in her clear, astringent voice. 'It is in the bird's nature to protect his territory. Belike the children came too close. Was there no-one there with them?'

He saw through her attempt to turn the tables and his lips tightened. 'It is not his territory, Inga. And what you say wan-ders from the point. It could have been anyone crossing that land – Widow Alfric for example. You know as well as I, that this is not the first time your gander has made an attack. If you value him as much as you say, then you had best keep him penned up and make sure he causes no more trouble. If he does, I will come here and neck him myself.'

Inga eyed him stonily. 'It will not happen again,' she said. He gave her his empty cup, but instead of setting it aside, she poured it full again from the mead pitcher and fetched another cup for herself. 'And if the gander is to be necked, I will do the deed. He is mine, not yours to destroy.'

Rolf knew that he should refuse the drink and escape, but his body would not obey his conscience, preferring to remain and play her game, whatever it was. And he thought he knew.

She drank her mead swiftly, like a man, tilting, swallowing, setting down. 'But then you're a Norman, aren't you?' she added when he did not speak. 'You do not care what you destroy.'

'Is that what you truly think?'

'Why should you care?'

Rolf shrugged. 'It might explain why you are so hostile. I do not believe I have ever seen you smile or utter a glad word.'

'What reason do I have?' She eyed him scornfully. 'You come here to complain of my geese, my livelihood, and expect me to smile you fair.'

'No,' he answered dryly. 'I did not expect you to "smile me fair". I expected you to behave exactly as you are.'

Colour tinted her creamy skin and her eyelids narrowed. 'So then, my lord Rolf, do you truly desire to know what I think?' She moved closer as she spoke, and now she unpinned the two brooches securing her overgarment in place. It puddled in the rushes at her feet, plain brown fabric enlivened by a braided border of scarlet, green and gold. She pulled off her kerchief and shook down her long, flaxen hair, and her eyes held his, golden-green, clear as mead and set beneath finely sketched tawny brows.

The attraction had always been there, as dangerously beautiful as the blade of a well-honed knife. Once her flaxen hair had reminded him of his ache for Ailith when he was in a strange country. Now it made him ache for the freedom to tumble a woman out of lust with no thought beyond the present. Off came tunic and shift, hose and shoes. Her figure was firm and lithe, her shape sleeker than Ailith's. She took his hands, placed them over her breasts, drew them down to her waist, and held them there while she straddled him upon the bed of piled skins. Uttering a soft groan, Rolf yielded to her demands, and was soon making demands of his own, his conscience cast aside with the same rapid urgency as his clothes. And as they thrust against each other with the fierce greed of lust, he discovered that she was right. For the moment he did not care what he destroyed.

'Where's Ben?' Julitta demanded. She could not pronounce his full name and so had shortened it to the one which only his immediate family were privileged to use.

Ailith was kneading enriched dough to make a spiced fruit bun, but now she stopped and regarded the small curly red head at her side with exasperation. Felice's son had become Julitta's talisman. She followed him everywhere, demanding his attention, wanting him to play with her. The boy had excellent manners, and despite a slightly martyred air, also possessed exceptional patience. Rolf's instinct was right; Benedict de Remy would make an admirable son-in-law. The pity was that he was going to marry him to the wrong daughter.

'He's gone with your papa and uncle Aubert to look at the horses,' Ailith replied and scattered some more flour on the trestle. The large, spiced fruit bun was a tradition that had been handed down in her family from the time of her great-grandmother, each woman teaching her daughter so that the fragrant, wheaten delicacy should gladden the table at every feast and holy day. Julitta, however, was a less than apt pupil. It was not that the child was incapable – she had nimble fingers and an equally nimble brain – it was just that, to Ailith's chagrin, she was not in the least interested.

'Will he be back soon?' Julitta prodded her finger into her own small lump of dough and watched it slowly spring back into shape.

'I expect so.'

'Can I go and look for him when I've done this?'

Ailith pummelled the main batch of dough. 'You know what happened the other day with Inga's geese. I want you to stay here with me.'

'But I don't want to stay!' Julitta's hyssop-blue eyes darkened stormily and she stamped her small foot. 'I hate making bread.'

'You cannot always have the world for the asking,' Ailith retorted with asperity. 'The sooner you learn it, the better.'

Julitta scowled ferociously at her mother. Her bottom lip pouted and she attacked the spiced dough with a clenched fist. 'Hate it, hate it,' she repeated with each smack.

Ailith sighed. 'What am I going to do with you?' she asked, her voice a mingling of love and exasperation.

Her daughter continued to thump the dough. Each punch sent a small ripple down the cascade of dark auburn curls. Ailith wondered guiltily if she was clipping Julitta's wings for her own peace of mind rather than for the child's good. As always she was torn both ways. She should seek to control rather than confine – but how to yield a little without letting Julitta think that she had won? Knowing Rolf only too well, she also knew his daughter.

'That looks about right.' She nodded at Julitta's lump of dough. 'Leave it to rise now, I want you to go and give these scraps to the hens. It will help them to keep on laying now that the days are growing shorter.' She took a shallow wooden dish of chopped-up cabbage leaves, stale bread and old, stiff pease pudding, and gave it to Julitta.

The child wrinkled her nose at the sight of the leavings, but after the merest hesitation to consider rebellion, took the dish with suspicious meekness. Ailith was not ignorant of the swift, calculating glance that was flashed in her direction before Julitta turned carefully away.

'And mind you don't take too long,' Ailith warned. 'Don't go outside the bailey, or I shall have to tie you to my apron with a rope.'

'I won't, Mama.' Julitta half-turned and gave her mother a

smile that was as bright as a May morning – a blinding smile to dazzle the uninitiated.

Watching Julitta go out of the door, Ailith gnawed a pensive lower lip. It was going to be a such a fine line between how many hearts her daughter broke, and how many times her heart was broken.

Julitta emerged from the chrysalis of the kitchens and stood in the open air, blinking and absorbing her surroundings while her crumpled wings grew dry and strong, preparing her for flight.

The hens came running greedily at her first call. For a brief instant Julitta panicked, remembering the gander, but she held her ground and the moment passed. These were her mother's birds, and she had watched some of them grow from damp, warm eggs into self-important speckled hens. She gripped the edges of the wooden bowl and gave a vigorous toss. The scraps of food flew into the air and scattered far and wide, the hens scattering with them, squabbling vociferously.

She ventured further into the bailey. A playful breeze snagged at her curls and gently pushed her in the back as if urging her on. She glanced over her shoulder towards the kitchen. It had taken her no time at all to feed the hens; her mother would not expect her back inside yet. She could see Mauger grooming Apollo, a handsome grey colt which she had often fed pieces of apple, turnip, and crusts of bread.

She approached Mauger and stood watching him until he became aware of her scrutiny and raised his head.

'Shouldn't you be inside with your mother?' he asked in a voice that had overcome the trauma of early adolescence and settled into a stolid baritone.

'She said I could come outside for a while.' Julitta had already learned the advantage of telling as much of the truth as suited the circumstances without actually lying. 'Can I have a ride on him?'

'No, your father wants him prepared for someone to look at, someone important.'

'Is Apollo going away then?'

'Probably.' Mauger stepped back from his labour and blotted his brow on his forearm. His cheeks were red with exertion, making his grey eyes seem very bright. His hair was blonder than barley straw and cropped above his ears.

'Let me ride him.' Julitta gazed up at him beseechingly. 'If my papa does sell him, I'll never be able to sit on him again. Just for a minute.' She glanced over her shoulder toward the kitchens, then back to Mauger. 'Mama said I wasn't to be long.'

The youth folded his arms and his wide brow developed three horizontal creases. 'I don't know that I should.'

Julitta hopped from foot to foot and never took her eyes off him. Mauger could be moody and difficult, but more often than not she could cozen him round.

'Oh come on, quickly then,' he capitulated with a sigh, and swung her up across Apollo's broad, dappled back. The horse snorted and glanced round at her as if to ask what she thought she was doing. Julitta patted him and giggled. From the vantage point of his withers, she could see far more of the world and in turn let the world see her. Mauger obligingly untied the horse and with a click of his tongue, began to lead him on a circuit of the ward.

'Give me the rein,' Julitta commanded. 'Let me ride on my own.'

Mauger shook his head. 'I don't think that is a good idea, young mistress.'

'Just for a minute.' She tossed her head. 'Papa lets me, you know he does.'

Mauger sighed again. 'Just one circuit,' he said, 'and then you go straight back to your mother.' He handed her up the reins and Julitta took them competently, her small face filling with pleasure. Her father had introduced her to a saddle almost before she could walk. When she was two, he had bought her a tiny Hibernian pony in London and by the time she was three, she was riding the larger animals he had brought from the north with total confidence. A warhorse was still slightly out of her scope to adult opinion, but Julitta had no such reservations. Besides, she and Apollo were old friends.

She trotted him around the palisade and reached the far side away from the gateway. Turning him, she was in time to see her father, Aubert and Benedict coming back from their ride. Julitta bounced up and down and shouted across to them, but they were too wrapped up in their own conversation to pay heed. Her high-pitched cry startled Apollo. He half-reared, and took off as if a bee had stung his rump. Julitta clung to the reins and gripped with her thighs. His bare back was slippery and her legs were short, making her seat more than precarious. She saw the ground blurring beneath his hooves, saw Mauger's white, horrified face, his mouth open in a square yell. The grey thundered past him and he was forced to jump aside or be ridden down.

Now she had the attention of the company by the gate. Her father's expression was one of furious incredulity, Benedict's one of astonishment. Squawking hens scattered frantically. A woman flattened herself against the side of the well, her hand cupping her mouth. Someone screamed. Julitta pulled on the reins to stop the horse, leaning back, using all her weight, but she might as well have been a feather on his back. Apollo swerved to avoid a wheelbarrow of dung, struck the side of a storage shed and stumbled. Julitta was flung from the saddle to the dusty bailey floor. By a miracle the horse kept his feet, and staggered to a halt, sweating and trembling.

Julitta lay stunned, unable to move. She had bitten her tongue, and a thin trickle of blood ran from the corner of her mouth, convincing the onlookers that she was more badly hurt than was the case. In a daze she saw Benedict's worried face bending over her. She tried to smile at him and speak his name, but her wits were still numbed and all that emerged was a bloody croak. Then the boy was pushed roughly aside by her father.

'Princess?' he said, and then she heard him swear softly under his breath. He ran his hands over her, the way he did over his horses, gently but firmly seeking for broken bones. 'Can you sit up?'

'I . . . I think so, Papa.' She took his hand and pulled herself up. The world tilted up and down a few times, then settled on a level. A pile of stable sweepings had cushioned her fall; the smell of dung and urine overpowered her nostrils.

'Open your mouth.'

She did so, and saw a look of relief cross her father's face, followed swiftly by a darkening anger. 'Little harm done to you at least,' he pronounced. 'What were you doing riding Apollo in the first place?'

Julitta stuck her finger in her mouth, touched the bitten edge of her tongue, and then looked at the thin streak of blood. She saw Mauger's bleached face among the crowd of onlookers and knew that she had got both of them into terrible trouble. Then, beyond him, she saw her mother forcing her way forwards, her gown dusty with flour. Julitta started to sob for Ailith, knowing full well that the more she could manipulate her mother's heartstrings, the less severe the punishment was likely to be.

Ailith snatched her daughter up in her arms and Julitta clung to her like a little limpet, burying her face in the soft haven of her mother's neck.

'Can't you keep that child in your sight for more than a minute!' Rolf snarled at Ailith. 'God's sweet life! First you let her wander off by the dew ponds, now I come home and find her almost killing herself and a costly warhorse into the bargain. Don't you have eyes in your head, woman?'

Ailith recoiled from the force of his anger. 'I asked her to feed the hens for me. When I looked out she was holding the empty bowl and talking to Mauger, so I judged it safe to go and put some bread to prove.' Her reply was calm, but her body trembled with the effort of remaining so. Her eyes flickered to the crowd of witnesses before whom she was being humiliated.

'Not safe enough, it seems.'

'My trust was misplaced.'

This time it was Rolf who recoiled as if she had slapped him. Ailith turned her back on him and walked with dignity towards the kitchens. Julitta perched on her mother's hip, one frightened blue eye peeping out from sanctuary at the havoc her impulsive act had wrought. The witnesses to the incident quickly melted away. Aubert took Benedict by the shoulder and tactfully withdrew.

Rolf cursed and dug his fingers through his hair in exasperation and anger, more than half of it self-directed. He ought to go after Ailith and make peace between them, but in his current state of defensiveness and tension, that was impossible. He would only bellow at her. Her remark about misplaced trust had struck at the core of his hidden guilt. If she could not trust Julitta, how much less could she trust him after what had happened earlier this morning at Inga's cottage? In his mind's eye he saw Inga lying upon her narrow bed, her body drenched in the sweat of pleasure, a frown contorting her face as she twisted and writhed. It had been a battlefield, each sound and gesture of need a blow, and neither of them willing to be merciful. Even to think of it now made him shiver.

Swallowing manfully, Mauger stood before Rolf to take his punishment. 'It was all my fault, my lord,' he owned, standing to attention. 'I should have known better than to let her ride Apollo.'

'Yes, you should.' It would have been easy for Rolf to vent his rage upon Mauger's hapless shoulders; too easy. He bit his tongue and began to examine the grey for damage.

'She . . . she said that you permitted her.'

'Not without a leading rein, but I do not suppose she told you that.'

'No, my lord.' Mauger cleared his throat. 'I'll know better in future.'

'We all will,' Rolf said, and left it at that.

The day continued to be fraught with near-disaster and frayed tempers. Scarcely had Rolf checked Apollo and found him none the worse for his experience than the royal representative arrived to look at the horse, and turned out to be none less than King William's eldest son Robert. He brought with him a sizeable entourage of young knights and hangers-on, all of whom had to be extended Ulverton's hospitality. They were clients and future clients, the men who put the bread on Rolf's table. That occasionally they must eat it was well understood.

Ailith, still simmering from the altercation in the yard and with Julitta underfoot, was fit to be tied. Rolf avoided her, apart from issuing curt instructions concerning the provision of a meal for their guests. She snapped at him that she was perfectly capable of preparing food without his interference, after which everything conspired against her. The milk curdled, the griddle cakes burned, the meat was as tough as saddle leather. Stony-faced, Rolf presided over a meal that had nothing to commend it apart from the mead which was served at the merciful end with fresh fruit and nuts which at least could not be ruined.

Robert of Normandy was a charming young man, light-hearted and exuberant. He treated the shortcomings of Rolf's table as a huge joke and being familiar with the superb order of the household at Brize-sur-Risle, baited his host mercilessly about the differences.

'I suppose heaven is all the sweeter when you've experienced hell,' he grinned, eyeing a charred griddle cake, and then a flustered, red-faced Ailith. 'But you're a strange one to prefer the second for ten months of the year.'

'It is not always like this,' Rolf muttered, feeling thoroughly humiliated beneath Robert's heavy-handed jesting. He glowered at Ailith. His wife would never have been caught out like this. Arlette, whatever the difficulties, would have provided a superlative meal and maintained her grace before the guests. Felice was doing her best, but her efforts only made Ailith appear all the less competent. She looked as if she belonged in a byre, and Rolf was ashamed.

By the time Robert of Normandy departed, Apollo in the care of one of his grooms, Ailith was tearful with exhaustion and Rolf was ready to explode. Instead of comforting her and trying to mend the breach that had opened between them, he saddled up a horse and rode out alone, shunning all company.

'Forget today,' Felice advised, and with her own hands prepared Ailith a calming blackberry tisane and made her drink it in the quiet of the solar. Despite Ailith's worried protest, she sent Julitta out with Benedict to play. 'You cannot cage the child,' she gently admonished. 'Rolf only shouted at you from his own fear this morning. It was unjust and he knows it.'

Ailith sipped the drink. 'Then why hasn't he come to me and told me himself?'

'He didn't have a chance. The Lord Robert arrived right on top of Julitta's prank. Neither of you were expecting so important a visitor. Tempers were bound to be frayed.' She gave Ailith a consoling pat on the shoulder. 'It will blow over like a summer squall. Tomorrow you will both laugh at yourselves.'

Ailith digested this in silence and then looked up at her friend with troubled eyes. 'Sometimes I think that he is tiring of me.'

'Ah no, Ailith, never!' Felice said quickly. 'Men have their moods just as women do. God knows, sometimes I want to kill Aubert more than he wants to kill me!'

Ailith gave her a wan smile. 'You're a true friend.'

'Who speaks the truth. Stop worrying, Ailith. Dab that rose scent I brought from London between your breasts and loosen your hair for him. You'll soon see whether or not he's tired.'

'That's what I'm afraid of,' Ailith said.

CHAPTER 33

SPRING 1076

Mauger had been drinking for more than half the day and in that respect was little different from most of the men among the company at Brize-sur-Risle who had gathered to celebrate the betrothal of Rolf's daughter Gisele to Benedict de Remy. Unlike the older men, however, Mauger, at eighteen, had not yet learned to hold his drink. The wine was yellow, the kind that was reserved for feast days and holy days in preference to the rougher red draughts of everyday usage. Its effect upon Mauger was to turn him from a taciturn, polite young man, into a loud and slightly aggressive individual. Twice he had almost begun quarrels which his irritated father had had to dampen down.

At Lady Arlette's side, Gisele sat like a votive statuette removed from a church aumbry to preside over the feast. A jewelled circlet was bound around her tightly plaited fine hair. Her blue silk gown was lavishly embroidered and decorated with braid, and on her narrow wrists there clinked a fortune in silver and gold bracelets, some of them betrothal gifts. Mauger studied her calm, glazed façade and saw no resemblance at all to her little firespark of a half-sister who had almost got him crucified back in the autumn with that trick on Apollo.

'Nothing like Julitta, is she?' he commented over-loudly to the ten-year-old prospective bridegroom, and filtered the dregs of his final cup of wine through his teeth, Tancred having banned him from consuming any more.

Benedict smiled and looked uncertain. He was an assured

child, but not confident enough to deal with Mauger's drunken meanderings. He looked round hopefully for his parents, but they were engrossed in conversation with other betrothal guests. Rolf had taken himself off to talk business to another horse-breeder, and Tancred was with him.

'Who's Julitta?' Gisele asked curiously.

'Lady Ailith's daughter.' Mauger suppressed a belch. 'A wildcat if ever there was one.'

'She doesn't mean it,' Benedict said uneasily. He had been primed by his parents before this visit to Brize, to say as little as possible concerning the domestic situation at Ulverton.

'Oh I think she does,' Mauger retorted. 'Mark me, Lady Ailith has lost the battle with that one. If her father does not deal with her now as she deserves, he'll reap trouble later.'

At this point, the volume of his voice alerted Aubert to the indiscretions being spouted, and with consummate diplomacy, he excused himself from his conversation and took command of Mauger, persuading the young man that it was time to visit the latrines and ease his bladder. But the damage had already been done.

Arlette lay in bed waiting for Rolf, listening to the sound of Gisele's soft breathing on the pallet close by and watching the flicker of the night candle create shadows on the whitewashed walls of the great bedchamber. She brooded upon Mauger's words at the betrothal feast. They had caught her awareness, but not her surprise.

Rolf had planted unease at the back of her mind several years ago with his insistence that establishing his trade in England was just as important as nurturing his existing trade in Normandy. The crux of the matter was that Brize-sur-Risle had ceased to be Rolf's harbour and she his anchor. Even when he was here in body, she sensed that his mind and spirit were elsewhere. Arlette accepted that Rolf was unfaithful to her; his ruttings were an overspill of his restless nature, but she could no longer tolerate being ignored and taken for granted the times that he was home.

Instead of a great marriage for Gisele, he had arranged a match to a merchant's son, albeit that the merchant was very rich, high in King William's favour, and could have bought himself titles a hundred times over if he so wished. It still went against the grain. Rolf had expected her to bow her head and acquiesce, and like a milksop she had done so. 'Yes, Rolf, you are right, it will be a good match.' But not what she had wanted.

And now Mauger had mentioned Lady Ailith's daughter Julitta. Arlette had heard very little about the English widow Ailith — too little in hindsight. All she knew was that the woman's husband had been an acquaintance of Aubert de Remy's and had been killed at the time of Duke William's coronation. The young widow had entered the de Remy household as a wet nurse to Benedict. Then Rolf had offered her the position of chatelaine at Ulverton to save her from the attentions of an unwanted suitor. No further information had been forthcoming, although Arlette had deduced certain things for herself.

Among Rolf's baggage there were garments that had been painstakingly sewn by another woman, and not just as a duty or chore. The tones suited Rolf's colouring perfectly, the stitches were skilled, and more damning than that, Arlette could feel the loving care that had gone into the making of the tunics, shirts and chausses. The Widow Ailith, whoever she might be, whatever she might look like, had cast her net and snared Rolf by the gills, of that Arlette was positive. And she had borne him a daughter, for Julitta was the name of Rolf's mother, and no Saxon woman was going to call her child by such a blatantly Norman name, unless she had good reason.

Rolf entered the room, treading quietly so as not to disturb the sleepers in the ante chamber through which he had to pass. He glanced at Gisele's sleeping form, and then at the bed. Arlette met his look evenly. She was very tempted to confront him and demand to know the truth, but she checked herself. He was adept at skirting issues he did not wish to discuss, and if she pushed him too hard, he would only turn the tables and deposit all blame on her shoulders.

'I expected you to be asleep,' he murmured.

'I was thinking.'

'About what?'

'About today, about the future.' She watched him undress. At seven and thirty, his body was still lean and hard. The first glints of silver had appeared in his hair, and the fine lines at his eye corners had deepened into permanent creases, but he remained a handsome, vital man. Aware of her scrutiny, he paused, a questioning half-smile on his lips, but she shook her head.

'The feast went excellently,' he remarked, seeming to assume that her thoughts of today and the future consisted of thoughts about the betrothal. 'I can always trust you to rise to an occasion.'

Smiling modestly, she thanked him, both pleased and surprised at his compliment. It was not usually within his scope to realise how hard she worked to grease the wheels of the household so that they turned seemingly without effort. 'Perhaps Gisele and I could come to England with you and see what Aubert de Remy has accomplished for himself in London,' she suggested.

He made a non-committal sound and busied himself unwinding his cross garters.

'I would like it very much,' she emphasised.

'I will give it some thought,' he said, without raising his head. 'It is not something to be decided in a moment.'

Arlette narrowed her eyes, but permitted the subject to drop, commenting instead upon how well the two children had conducted themselves during the betrothal ceremony and the feast that followed. The fact that he was quick to follow her lead, his expression relieved, compounded her suspicions and brought her to a decision of her own.

CHAPTER 34

Suitably dressed in an old patched gown and apron, her hair tied up in a kerchief, Ailith prepared to give Ulverton's hall a thorough scouring to remove the detritus of a hard winter and wet spring. It was early May now, the worst of the bad weather over so she hoped, and the warmth of the sun allied with the bright birdsong had filled her with a powerful energy.

All the trestles were carried outside and stacked against the wall where the village carpenter started sorting through them and mending any damaged ones. The rank, mouldy floor rushes were broomed vigorously out of the door into the bailey and removed by the barrowload to the midden where the hens descended upon them in high delight.

Ailith saw Rolf grimace at the industry as he swung into the saddle and caught up the leading reins of the two destriers he was taking to the royal stables at Winchester, three days' ride away.

'It will be finished before you return,' she told him irritably. He would soon complain if she left the rushes as they were to harbour all manner of pests and stinks in the summer heat.

'That's a relief.'

Ailith compressed her lips.

Rolf made as if to ride on, but changed his mind, and bringing his horse around, drew rein in front of her. He looked her up and down, from the frayed edge of her kerchief, to the scuffed toes of her old shoes. 'I remember the first time I saw you, standing over your cabbages with a besom in your hand,' he mused. 'You were angry then too.' Impulsively, he leaned down to stroke her cheek.

Ailith felt the bitter-sweet touch of his fingers. 'And you were the most handsome man I had ever seen, and still are,' she responded with a wounded smile.

They stared at each other, as if trying to peel back the accumulated layers of familiarity that had been laid down season after season, tarnishing and obscuring.

Ailith held her breath, waiting for him to fling down from the horse, take her in his arms and tell her that Winchester could wait, that 'forever' still remained. But he did not move. Locked to the ground by her own doubts and fears, neither did she, and the moment passed, becoming another layer upon the debris.

'God be with you,' he said, and turned his horse around.

'God speed you,' she responded. The feel of his fingers on her cheek lingered like an echo as he rode out of the gate.

Ailith returned to work, venting her emotions in vigorous sweeps of the besom. Julitta came running from her lesson with Father Goscelin. The priest was the younger brother of one of Rolf's knights and Rolf had been persuaded to take him into his household as a chaplain until Goscelin could be recommended to a parish of his own. The young priest had been given the task of teaching the castle children their letters. Only boys were to benefit from his lessons, but Julitta had whined and demanded so persistently that at last she had been given a place among the sons of her father's retainers, and was proving more adept than most of them.

This morning, however, there were tears on her lashes and her face was flushed with temper. From the corner of a vigilant eye, Ailith saw seven-year-old Hamo run to his mother, bawling loudly. A stubby finger pointed accusingly at Julitta.

'What have you done now?' Ailith sighed.

'Hamo told a lie, and when I said it wasn't true and his tongue would drop off, he said it was so, and I was a stupid little bitch. So I kicked him.' Julitta's face was red with indignation.

Ailith eyed her daughter with a mingling of love and exasperation. Hamo's mother was cuddling her fat, pasty-faced son and glowering across the hall at Julitta. 'You should not have done that.'

'He deserved it!'

'Still, you should not have struck the first blow.'

'But he called me a name and he told a lie!' Julitta cried, beside herself with fury. 'He said that Ben was going to marry someone in Normandy. It's not true, he's going to marry me!'

Ailith winced and bit her lip. The child had been bound to discover the truth sooner or later, but she had not bargained for quite so much vehemence. 'Julitta, it was wrong of Hamo to call you names, but he told you no lie. Benedict de Remy has been betrothed to someone in Normandy, a girl of his own age.'

Julitta stared at Ailith with huge, stricken eyes. Her lower lip trembled and she shook her head from side to side with gathering speed.

'Sweetheart . . . ' Ailith reached for her.

Julitta threw down her slate and stylus and ran away down the hall, her red curls flying and her sobs trailing behind her like a ragged banner. Ailith hastened in pursuit. As she did so, one of the hide thongs securing Rolf's battle axes to the wall gave way, and both weapons clashed down onto a small trestle holding jugs of ale and trencher loaves. One axe landed harmlessly on its side, but the other sank into the table as if the wood was made of moist butter.

Ailith halted. A feeling of dread raised the hairs on her nape and seeped through her pores, chilling her to the marrow. The luck of Ulverton was down, and the way the axe had sundered the wood was an omen. She stared at the still quivering haft and tried to shake off the notion. The thongs were rotten after more than ten years aloft, she told herself; it had been bound to happen. But as she hurried on beyond the exclaiming witnesses to find Julitta, her heart was pounding with fear and the dread remained.

The little girl had thrown herself down upon her small pallet in the main bedchamber, her entire body shaking with grief. 'It's not fair, it's not fair!' she sobbed.

Ailith gathered Julitta in her arms. Life never was, she thought as she smoothed the unruly hair and kissed the hot temple. 'Benedict is like a brother to you,' she murmured. 'Girls do not wed their brothers.' She half-expected Julitta to be awkward and demand to know why, but the child said nothing. Her sobs diminished to sniffles and the occasional body-shaking hiccup.

'So Hamo was telling the truth,' she said in a quavering, forlorn voice.

'Yes, sweetheart, I'm afraid he was. It doesn't mean he is a blameless innocent,' she added grimly. 'I can imagine the pleasure he took in telling you. Ah, Julitta, why is it so easy to make enemies and so hard to make friends?'

Julitta sniffed loudly, and sitting up, dried her face on the kerchief that Ailith gave her. 'What's a whore?' she asked.

Ailith's blood turned to ice. 'Who told you that word?'

'Is it a bad one?'

'Who told you, was it Hamo?'

Julitta swallowed. 'He said that I would never make a good marriage because you were nought but Papa's stupid English whore and that Papa had another proper wife and little girl somewhere else.' Julitta twisted the kerchief viciously in her fingers. 'He said that Benedict was betrothed to her. I didn't believe him. Mama, what's a whore?'

'Merciful God,' Ailith whispered and turned her head aside, her lips pressed tightly together and her eyes closed. Was this what it had come to? Rolf had been more cruel than he had known that frosty morning in the forge when he had prevented her from cutting her own wrists.

'A whore is a woman who lends herself to a man for money,' she said, forcing herself to speak for the sake of the bewildered child. 'I gave your father everything for love, and we made a pledge to each other.'

'But does he have another, proper wife and a little girl somewhere else?'

How did you explain such things to a precocious six-year-old, Ailith wondered, when you could not explain the wherefores and whys to yourself? The bedchamber walls seemed to be hemming her in, stifling her. With sudden decision, she stood up, tugging Julitta by the hand. 'Come,' she said, 'we're going out for a ride. Elfa needs the exercise, and the fresh air will make us both feel better.'

'But, Mama . . .'

'You can ask me things as we ride along, and I will do my best to tell you.'

In the hall there was no sign of Hamo, or his mother. Ailith wondered where the boy had picked up his notions and prejudices. Did the other Normans at Ulverton look upon her with resentment as Rolf's 'stupid English whore'? Surely she would have felt such hostility.

Someone had pulled the battle axe out of the trestle and laid it to one side. Ailith gave it a wide berth, issued brief instructions to the servants to continue the spring cleaning, and went outside. But despite the soft spring warmth, she was cold.

'Yes, your papa does have a wife,' she told Julitta as they rode their mounts down the coast path and came to the long expanse of shoreline, bordered by the hissing suck and murmur of the sea. 'But she lives in Normandy and he does not see her often.'

Julitta stared over the glittering plumes of spray to the line where the blue of sea merged hazily with the blue of sky. 'Does he love her?'

'I do not know. It was a marriage arranged by their parents when they were both very young.'

'Like Ben's, you mean?' Julitta looked at her mother, the sea-sparkle reflecting in her blue-green eyes.

Ailith saw the trap waiting to swallow her. If she said yes, then she was condoning the breaking of marital law. If she said no, she was a hypocrite. 'Every arrangement is different,' she fenced. 'If my husband had not died, or your tiny half-brother, I would never have given myself to your father. So much depends on chance.'

As they rode along the beach, Julitta held herself to a listening silence that was unusual for her bright, impatient nature, and Ailith found herself talking to the child as if she were an adult.

She told her about the past, about Goldwin and the forge for which he had nurtured such plans; about Aldred and Lyulph, Julitta's dead uncles, their stature and prowess. About the baby she had lost, and her eyes filled with tears.

Julitta was only just six years old and did not understand all that Ailith told her, but she sensed that her mother had suffered greatly, and that the thin, often broken thread-of-gold which her father had woven into her mother's life had been the reason for her survival. She still did not really understand what a whore was, nor why her beloved papa should go and betroth Benedict to his other little girl. Perhaps he loved the other one more. The thought frightened her, and suddenly Julitta did not want to understand. She kicked her heels against her pony's sides, making him canter, and then gallop, as if she could outrun her fears.

Mother and daughter returned by way of the village, where they were greeted cheerfully by those folk not absent in the fields. The carpenter's wife gave Julitta a drink of milk fresh from the cow and a piece of bread smeared with honey from her own hives.

At the end of the village they came to Inga's house. It stood a little apart from the other dwellings and was surrounded by a palisade of stakes to contain her flock of geese when they were not out grazing on the common. Julitta craned her neck nervously, but there was not a single goose, gosling or gander to be seen. Inga's door was open, and as Ailith and Julitta rode past, the little brown terrier came hurtling out to bark at them, its stumpy little legs almost leaving the ground with the force of the noise.

Elfa flickered her ears and sidled. The dog made several dashes as if to attack the horses, but stopped short each time, barking ever more frantically.

Then, faintly, Ailith heard a woman's voice calling for help. For a single, appalling moment, she was tempted to ignore the voice and ride on. So strong was the urge that she actually heeled Elfa's flanks, although her hands remained firm on the reins. The confused mare snorted and turned in a circle.

Julitta watched her mother with wide eyes. After last

autumn's incident with that horrible gander, she had privately christened Inga the 'goose witch' and would lief as not go anywhere near the cottage – although sometimes she dared herself just to prove that she wasn't really afraid. The cry came again, thin with pain and terror.

'Stay here,' Ailith commanded, and rode Elfa towards the stockade. Still yapping, the terrier ran ahead of the mare. Julitta deliberated between being adventurous and remaining obedient, and, after a moment, inevitably chose the former.

Ailith dismounted at the door of Inga's cottage and went inside. It was dim within for all the shutters were barred. The hearth in the centre of the room was cold and the sweet reek of blood filled her nostrils. Inga lay on her bed of skins against the side of the room. She was wearing nothing but her shift and this was bunched up around her waist. Her thighs and belly were smeared with blood and there was a glistening red puddle on the beaten earth floor. In her arms she held a tiny baby, and in her eyes there was the terror of a stricken animal. 'Help me,' she croaked.

'Merciful God!' Ailith gasped. Her legs threatened to give way and her stomach heaved. The baby was dead; she could see that it had been born with the cord wrapped tightly around its neck. Its head lolled, its eyes half-open. Its scalp was covered by a fuzz of dark red hair. Between Inga's thighs, she saw the cord of the afterbirth quivering like a bluish-white tail. 'Where's the midwife?'

'No-one knew I was with child. None of their meddling business.' Another spurt of blood reddened Inga's thighs and spilled down the sheepskins to increase the puddle on the floor. 'The afterbirth's stuck.'

Ailith heard a muffled cry from the door and whirling, saw Julitta standing there, her eyes as huge as moons. 'I told you to wait outside!' she shouted at her daughter and moved rapidly to blot the scene from the child's sight. 'Go back into the village. Fetch Father Godfrid and tell him that it is urgent. Hurry now!' She gave Julitta a sharp push. White-faced with shock, Julitta scrambled to untether her pony.

Ailith found a jug and went outside to fill it with water from the well. She poured a beaker for Inga and helped her sit up to drink it. And all the time the blood dripped from between the woman's legs. Ailith pulled the blood-soaked shift down over Inga's belly and took the baby from her to wrap it in a shawl. Images of her own son flashed through her mind, and then, more disturbingly, images of Julitta.

Inga watched her from the bed. The woman's breathing was rapid and shallow, her skin beaded with cold sweat. 'Are you not going to ask me who fathered him?'

'It is none of my business,' Ailith said in a stiff parody of Inga's earlier words.

An arid smile twisted Inga's lips. 'Oh, but it is,' she said, 'or at least it would have been your lord's business had the babe been born alive.'

Ailith looked at the soft red down on the baby's head, at the shape of his cold little hands as she tucked them inside the shawl. She laid him down beside his mother, her mind frantically calculating. Nine months ago it had been autumn. She remembered Rolf saying that he would speak to Inga about the gander, his furtiveness around that time, his sudden absences and the way his moods had been more mercurial than usual. It seemed that he had done more than just speak. 'I suppose he swore you undying love,' she said in a choked voice.

Inga laughed. The sound had a harsh rattle to it. 'Undying lust perhaps. My husband was a vigorous man; I wanted to prove to myself that a Norman could not better him, but I was wrong. I told your man that his kind did not care what they destroyed, and I was right, was I not?' The laugh became a sob. She drew her knees towards her belly as her womb cramped in a vain spasm to evict the afterbirth.

Ailith swallowed, fighting her nausea, her world shattering around her. The dog barked and she heard the sound of running feet. A breathless Father Godfrid hurried through the door, and just as Ailith had done, stopped short in horror.

'Quickly,' Ailith commanded him. 'Shrive her before she dies so that her soul may have peace – more peace than mine.' She pushed past the priest and ran round the side of the cottage where she was sick beyond anything that lay in her stomach. How could Rolf betray her like this? It was unbearable, a waking nightmare.

'Mama?' Julitta's frightened small voice pierced through her soul-sick misery. Swallowing and swallowing again to prevent herself from retching, Ailith straightened and turned to face her daughter. How easily it could have been her own self lying in that hut, she thought. How easily it could still be.

'Mama, is Inga going to die? Is that why you sent me for Father Godfrid?'

Ailith hesitated. Julitta's gaze, although scared, was steady. 'Yes, sweetheart. Sometimes a birth can go wrong, and Dame Osyth wasn't there to help her.'

Julitta nodded and chewed her lip. 'Does that mean the gander can be necked now?' she asked.

Ailith did not know whether to laugh or weep in despair at her daughter's remark which revealed how close in nature Julitta and Rolf were. 'It means,' she said, 'that it is finished.'

Julitta gave her a puzzled look, but before she could speak, Father Godfrid emerged from the hut, his face grim. Ailith did not have to enquire if Inga was dead.

'She should have sought aid in the village,' said the priest. 'But she always held herself aloof. I believe that her heart was still in the north lands.'

Ailith bit back the comment that to leave a heart you had to have one in the first place. What did she know about Inga? Very little, save that she had lain with Rolf and the act had finally destroyed her.

After arranging with the priest for the decencies to be observed concerning washing and shrouding the bodies of mother and child, Ailith took Julitta back to the castle. The spring-cleaning she had left in such haste was still underway, but her heart was no longer in seeing a thorough job done. From the kitchen sheds there wafted a delicious aroma of meat and onions. Ailith's stomach turned over and she had to clench her jaw. Julitta's hunger was unaffected by the traumas of the day and as soon as she had dismounted, she skipped off to cozen a griddle cake and a beaker of buttermilk from the cook.

Wearily Ailith entered the hall. She parried Wulfhild's two-pronged assault concerning how well the servants had worked in their mistress's absence, and her complaint that Hamo's mother should be rebuked for the rudeness of her revolting son. Ailith was too tired and heartsick to care. 'It doesn't matter any more,' she cut across her vociferous maid and sat down heavily at the trestle where Rolf's battle axes had fallen. Ignoring the food that Wulfhild tried to set before her, she requested instead a cup of mead. Tight-lipped, muttering to herself, the woman retreated.

The weapons still lay on the board. Someone had cleaned and oiled them in preparation for their return to the wall. The luck of Ulverton; the misfortune of some poor English warrior on the field of blood. Wulfhild returned with the mead and lingered anxiously until Ailith gestured her to go away with a sharpness unusual to her character.

The mead was sweet and strong with an underlying clover tang to the honey. It slipped down Ailith's throat and warmed a delicate trail to her belly. She turned the axe over. Rolf's pride and joy. Perhaps if he had loved her enough to make a talisman of her, he would have kept the faith. Salt burned her eyes even as the mead burned in her stomach. She blinked fiercely, and as her focus returned through the tears, saw several markings incised upon the socket of the axe. It was unmistakable. Beneath some letters which she could not read, was cut the shape of a swan, Goldwin's mark. The weapon was of her former husband's making.

Rolf had told her that he had won the axe on Hastings field, and that it had saved his life when he was attacked by a looter whilst lying wounded after the battle. But whose had it been before then? She drank more mead, her hands shaking.

When Julitta came into the hall with crumbs around her mouth and a moustache of buttermilk, Ailith asked her to read what the letters said.

'William,' said Julitta without hesitation, proud of her ability to read. And then she pointed to another, lighter row of scratches. 'And this says . . .' She peered closer. 'This says Lyulph.'

Ailith fell into a deep, black gulf. She heard Julitta scream and Wulfhild's cry of concern. Hands supported her and bore her up. The mead cup was forced against her teeth and her nostrils were filled with the stink of burning feathers. Goose feathers probably, she thought, from Inga's flock, and heard herself laugh. When Wulfhild tried to urge her to lie down on the great bed, Ailith became hysterical, insisting that she would never sleep there again.

The afternoon was a bright, sun-washed gold. A skylark bubbled in the blue air above the heads of the woman and child travelling on the dusty road towards Wareham. All that Ailith had to show for her nine years at Ulverton were her red-haired daughter, the mounts they rode, and the sumpter pony with a bundle strapped to its back. For protection Ailith carried a sharpened, oiled battle axe, her brother's name carved on the steel behind the biting edge of the blade.

She had told Julitta very little. As far as the child was aware, they were going on a visit to London, a visit that somehow involved the battle axe and Inga the goose-witch. Ailith had used the word 'visit', but she meant forever. Nor did she look back as they crested the rise and rode down into the dip that would take Ulverton from their sight. Her spine was held haft-straight, her hands were steady on the reins, and her eyes were fixed unswervingly on the horizon.

Ahead of them a swirl of dust rose from the road and Ailith reached quickly for the axe. Even if there was a reluctant peace in England, and men were wary of the King's wrath, a woman and child travelling alone were always vulnerable. The cloud resolved itself into a small band of Norman soldiers escorting a horse-drawn litter. Ailith and Julitta drew aside in politeness to let them pass, but Ailith received the strong impression that the Normans expected it of right. The litter drew level and stopped. The heavy curtains parted to reveal a richly dressed woman and a girl on the verge of adolescence.

'How far are we from Ulverton?' asked the woman in a clear, silvery voice.

'About three miles,' Ailith replied. 'You will see it as soon as you gain the top of that hill.' Her French was now without accent and she saw the woman's delicate brows lift in surprise.

'We live there,' Julitta volunteered, her gaze on the pale-haired girl. 'My papa's the lord. He's got other lands too, but Ulverton's his favourite.'

The brows remained high and the woman's delicate colour grew ashen. She stared at Ailith intently, absorbing every tiny detail, whereas a moment before she had been content just to glance. And then her gaze transferred to Julitta, as if seeking a confirmation.

Realisation struck Ailith as she witnessed the Norman woman's response to Julitta's remark. Her stomach churned with a fresh surge of nausea, but at the same time, the appearance of Rolf's wife confirmed her decision to leave Ulverton as the right one.

'He is in Winchester, but he will be home within the week,' she heard herself say woodenly.

'Home?' The word seemed to agitate Arlette de Brize. The wide pewter eyes were suddenly narrow. She touched her throat.

Ailith had neither the energy nor the inclination to fight with Rolf's wife. 'You need not vex yourself,' she said with cold dignity. 'My daughter and I are leaving, and we will not return.' Clicking her tongue to Elfa, she eased the mare past on the verge, Julitta following.

She half-expected the soldiers to ride in pursuit and take her and Julitta into their custody, but nothing happened. On looking over her shoulder, she saw that the litter curtains had swung back into place and that the small entourage had resumed its journey.

'Who was that?' Julitta asked curiously.

'A visitor for your father. She does not want or need our presence. Ah Jesu, enough now,' she added as Julitta opened her mouth to ask another question. 'Let me be, I can bear no more!'

Ailith wanted to weep, but the grief was too deep and the tears would not come. They remained inside her, vitrified and dagger-sharp, wounding her beyond hope of healing.

CHAPTER 35

In Winchester, Rolf bought an amber necklace for Julitta and a gold ring for Ailith, upon which he requested the goldsmith to etch in runes the symbols for love and good fortune. On impulse too, with humour and a feeling of wistfulness, he purchased a new besom of birch twigs.

His conscience was rife with guilt where Ailith was concerned. Of late he knew he had been wayward, taken up with his pastime of investigating other pastures. Once or twice his quest had taken him into fields dangerously close to home. He had not regretted lying with Inga at the time, it had vented a heat which had been kept beneath a lid for far too long, nor did he regret it even now, but it was finished. He would give Ailith the ring, he would invite her to jump over the broomstick in the age-old tradition of hand-fasting – unless she wanted to brandish it about his head – and they would start anew.

His mood was optimistic, as bright as summertime as he topped the hill and saw Ulverton curled in the valley like a sleepy cat upon a blanket. Behind the village, the sun dazzled on the sea. He imagined Ailith walking along the beach with Julitta, her feet bare and her gown kilted through her belt.

He was smiling when he dismounted in Ulverton's courtyard, but it was the last occasion he was to do so for a very long time. No auburn-haired child shot out to dance around him, demanding to know what he had brought her; no tall, handsome woman emerged from the kitchens or brewery, wiping her hands on her apron, her eyes alight. His groom took his horse and with lowered eyes, led it away. A feeling of unease swept over Rolf like a cloud across the sun. The village priest emerged from the hall with a woman, the pair of them deep in conversation. It took a moment for Rolf to recognise Arlette. This was the last place he expected to see her, but when he did, his unease turned to outright fear.

He strode across the bailey, reaching her before she had taken more than two paces of her own. 'What are you doing here?' he snarled. 'Where is Ailith?'

Arlette's grey gaze widened and she clenched her hands upon the fabric of her gown, but she held her ground. 'I arrived after she had gone,' she said truthfully, 'and I took up the reins because everyone was galloping around in aimless panic. She has left you, my lord. You may ask her maidservant if you do not believe me, since she did not take the woman with her.' Briefly she returned her attention to the speechless, staring priest. 'I am sure that my lord will pay to have masses said for the souls of the dead woman and her baby. Perhaps if you would return later and dine with us?'

Father Godfrid took the hint, and with a furtive glance at Rolf, inclined his head and made himself scarce.

'What dead woman and baby?' Rolf demanded. 'What do you mean, Ailith has left me?' His gut somersaulted.

Arlette took his stiff, resisting arm in hers. 'Come inside, my lord, we can talk better there.'

He shook her off. 'Tell me, or by God I will mount up and ride out of here now!'

The colour drained from Arlette's face, but still she stood up to her husband. 'And then you would never know,' she retorted. 'Besides, your threat has no power over me. All I have seen of you this past ten years is your back as you ride away from me. Please yourself.' Turning from him, she walked towards the hall.

Rolf glared round. Everyone was suddenly very busy. The priest was a dwindling figure on the wooden bridge over the ditch. Hunching his shoulders, Rolf put his head down like a bull and strode after his wife.

The hall was clean and tidy. New rushes yielded up a scent of sweet dried grass as he crushed them beneath his boots. Arlette paused at a trestle before the hearth, poured wine into a goblet, and brought it to him.

'Gisele is here too, but I bade her remain in the chamber beyond until we had spoken together. What you must know is not pleasant, and I did not want her to see and hear.'

Rolf took the cup from her hands. His sense of unease was increased by his wife's changed attitude. She had become more assertive. Her gaze met his squarely, without the deference to which he was accustomed.

'There was a woman in the village with whom you dallied, so the priest says, a woman from the north?'

Rolf went cold. 'Inga?' he said involuntarily, and his hand tightened on the stem of the goblet.

'That was the name the priest gave to me.' Her lips tightened, and she nodded to herself as if a distasteful rumour had just been confirmed. 'You do not deny it then?'

'I don't need your pious condemnation!' he snapped. 'No, I do not deny it, but she was nothing, a means to scratch an itch.' He took a mouthful of wine, swilled it around his cheeks and swallowed. 'What has she been saying?'

'She was nothing to you before, and she is nothing now, because she is dead,' Arlette said brutally. 'She bore your child six days ago, and it was your mistress who discovered her bleeding to death in her cottage with the baby birth-strangled in her arms. That was why the priest was here. He would rather have spoken to your English mistress about such matters, but she rode out of here on the day of the discovery.'

'It could have been anyone's child,' Rolf said huskily.

'The baby had red hair and the woman confessed all of her sins on her death bed,' Arlette said grimly. 'You are never content with what you have, and now, because of it, you have nothing, not even that with which you started.'

Rolf raised his fist. Arlette blenched, but stood fast. He looked from her face to his clenched fingers, and with an oath, turned from her to hurl his goblet at the wall. Wine spattered down the pale linen of an embroidered hanging like drops of blood. His eyes had followed the goblet's path, and now he saw that, on the wall above the spot where it had crashed, one of his battle axes was missing – the Hastings one, the luck of Ulverton.

A huge hole seemed to open up in his belly and his heart and lungs dropped through it. If Ailith had taken the axe then this was no foolish pet of jealous temper; she truly had flown. Ignoring his wife, he gazed frantically round the hall until he located a plump, grey-haired woman desultorily peeling rushes to make tallow dips.

'Wulfhild!' He almost ran to her. 'Where is your mistress, where did she go? In God's name tell me!'

The old woman looked up at him with bleak and bitter eyes. 'She would not confide in me, save to say that she would never let you find her. I wanted to go with her, but she said I was too old to take to the road. You betrayed her, lord, more than you will ever know.' Her double chins wobbled and she quickened her movements, splitting the withies, exposing the creamy-white pith.

'But how can I make amends if I do not know where to find her?' he demanded with desperation, an edge of fear in his voice.

Wulfhild shrugged. 'She don't want you to find her after what you done, and it ain't just because o' the goose woman in the village, although that's a mighty part of it.' Wulfhild folded her lips inwards until they almost disappeared. When he remained stubbornly in front of her, his expression a mingling of bewilderment, anger and loss, she shook her head and sighed. 'Your precious axes fell down during the spring cleaning. My mistress returned from the village. She was already distressed because she'd just found Inga all bloody and dying alone. Then she looked at your axe, the one that's missing.' She made small chewing motions.

'And?'

'She recognised some marks on the blade.' Wulfhild raised her eyes to his. 'That axe of yourn was made by Master

Goldwin, and it belonged to Mistress Ailith's brother Lyulph. All these years she has been sharing the bed of her own brother's murderer. She has called you *nithing*.'

'It was in fair fight,' Rolf protested. 'He would have killed me had not my spear taken him first! I did not know he was Ailith's kin, I swear it!'

Her gaze held mute contempt. He flung away from her and drove his fist at the wall with the same violence that he had flung the cup. His skin split and the splits filled with blood. His mind howled and his voice howled with it.

Arlette ran to him, her cold composure broken by real fear. She grasped his arm and held on like a terrier. He heard her screaming at him to stop, and when he tried to shake her off, she refused to relinquish her grip. His blood smeared her gown of fine, pale blue linen. A streak of it lay like a long gash on her pale cheek.

His breath choking harshly in his throat, Rolf turned his back on the wall and slumped against it. Arlette snapped at a gawking servant to bring another cup of wine, and pulling her kerchief from her sleeve, bound it around his bleeding knuckles. But although the injuries were efficiently staunched, Rolf knew that he had suffered mortal wound.

CHAPTER 36

'Mistress Ailith?' Sigrid opened the door of her low-roofed, simple thatched house. An infant riding on her hip, she stared at her former employer with wide, astonished eyes. A soft drizzle shaded the summer dusk, and blurred outlines with a hoar of fine droplets.

'Can you provide us with sleeping space for the night?' Ailith asked. 'And a place to shelter the horses?' She tried to smile at her former maid, but she was so tired and heartsick, that for the moment she was beyond more than a meagre stretching of the lips.

'Of course, come within.' Recalling her manners, Sigrid stepped aside and ushered Ailith and Julitta over the threshold. Putting the baby in its cradle, she set about rousing the fire beneath the cauldron. 'You'll be wanting to eat,' she said. 'Is bread and broth enough for tonight?'

Tears prickled behind Ailith's lids at Sigrid's goodness. The young woman had always been quietly efficient in her capacity of maidservant, never saying much, totally ungiven to gossip. 'Bread and broth will be a feast, but you need not trouble yourself.'

'It is no trouble,' Sigrid said serenely. Once the fire was burning to her satisfaction, she went out to attend the horses. Ailith insisted on accompanying her, and Julitta was given a cup of milk and left to keep an eye on the baby.

The two women led the horses round to the back of the

house and set about unsaddling them. 'You are no longer my servant, you do not have to do this,' Ailith said.

'But you are my guests, and in need of help, I think.' Sigrid heaved the saddle off the chestnut mare's back. 'If this had been an ordinary visit, you would have come here during the day, and you would have been lodging with the de Remys.' She gave Ailith a single, shrewd look, but did not press further and continued quietly with her task. It was this very undemanding silence that led Ailith to speak out.

'I have left Rolf,' she blurted, 'and I don't want him to find me – ever.'

'I thought as much when I saw you.'

'That is why I cannot go to Felice de Remy. It is the first place he would look for us. Even here it is dangerous. Your husband knows Rolf and the de Remys.'

'Edwin's away on a commission in Dover,' Sigrid soothed. 'He won't be home for ten days at least. And he knows how to keep his mouth closed.'

'I don't know what I'm going to do!' Ailith's voice quivered with a note of panic. 'I have got some silver, and we'll sell the horses, but that won't keep us for a lifetime.'

'But for long enough until you find something,' Sigrid said practically. 'Here on the Southwark side there is always work. We can think tomorrow about what to do. Tonight you must rest. I have never seen such dark shadows beneath your eyes.' A note of concern entered her voice.

Ailith looked bleakly at the saddle marks on Elfa's sweaty chestnut back. 'I thought when I lost my brothers, my son and then Goldwin, that my life was ended. I thought that no grief could ever cut more keenly than that. But I was wrong. That was just death. This is betrayal.'

Julitta sat on the floor, a wooden bowl between her knees, a heap of pea shucks at her side. Her thumbnail was green from splitting the pods and pushing the peas into the bowl. Some would be cooked and eaten fresh with mint from Sigrid's herb plot, the rest would be dried for winter use. Sigrid's baby was asleep in its cradle, and sunlight shone through the open door-way, striping the floor rushes with gold, and burnishing Julitta's hair to a rich garnet-red.

Earlier that afternoon she had asked her mother when they were going home, and had been told that for the time being they weren't, that they had to find somewhere to live here in Southwark. Julitta wrinkled her nose. She did not mind living here with Sigrid, but it was cramped and poky, and she missed the luxuries of her life at Ulverton, and her father's careless, proud affection. And then she remembered that her papa did not really love her or her mother any more, and that was the reason they were here.

A woman had come to collect some mending and laundry that Sigrid had done for her, and was now in earnest conversa-tion with Ailith. Julitta had met Dame Agatha two days before when the woman had brought the clothes to be washed and mended. She was as comfortable and plump as a hen, double-chinned, florid of face and cheerful of manner. Julitta quite liked her, for Dame Agatha had made a fuss of her, admiring her beautiful hair, and giving her a piece of almond paste to suck. Julitta, in turn, had admired Dame Agatha's gaudy rings and a cross of real gold that she wore on her ample bosom. The woman had chucked her beneath the chin and laughingly sug-gested that Julitta and Ailith should come and live with her. Julitta had thought it a jest, the kind that adults often made to children, but now, eavesdropping, she discovered that Dame Agatha was in earnest.

'My business is so hectic at the moment, that I do not have the time to be collecting laundry and mending. I should be home now, seeing to my guests and preparing for the others. It is often beyond curfew before I can shut my doors, and some-times I find customers waiting on my doorstep at the crack of dawn.' She bewailed her difficulties with complacency, a bright brown eye cocked upon Ailith.

'What kind of business, mistress?' Ailith responded politely.

'Oh, I run a bathing establishment, with a hostelry lying next door. It's not a brothel, I have nothing to hide,' she added quickly as she saw Ailith's look. 'I'm a respectable widow, and that's what keeps me in clients.' She sucked her teeth and folded her arms beneath her copious breasts, hitching them up beneath her chin. 'I heard that you were looking for somewhere to stay and occupation for your hands, and that you too are a respectable widow, indeed with a daughter to provide for.' Her glance went to Julitta, who quickly dropped her gaze to the task of pea-podding. 'No-one asks too many questions round here. That way, no-one never gets told any lies.'

Ailith coloured beneath the older woman's sharp scrutiny. The Southwark side of the Thames was outside London's jurisdiction, although in distance it was no more than a short boat journey or walk across the bridge. Here, bathing establishments had begun to flourish, some legitimate, others concerned with providing services less innocent than cleanliness of the body. She was not sure into which category Dame Agatha's premises fell, despite the woman's vehement reassurance. On the other hand, the offer of employment and a place to live seemed God-given.

'What kind of occupation for my hands?' she asked.

Agatha gave her a wintery smile. 'You're a suspicious one, aren't you?'

'Life has taught me not to trust.'

'Sometimes you have to take things on trust,' Agatha said. 'What I want is a someone to help me run my house and my business. Sigrid hasn't told me much about your life, but she says that you have worked in the households of a wealthy wine merchant and a Norman lord, and that you speak the language of the Franks fluently.'

Ailith nodded stiffly. 'That is true.'

'All to the good, since my clients are frequently Normans, and always rich.' Agatha tapped a ring-heavy forefinger against her prominent front teeth. 'You and the girl can have a chamber of your own, and I will pay you according to my profits – say five shillings a week and your board.'

Ailith knew that she had little choice, but all the same, for the sake of her pride, she was determined to hold out just a little. 'I will think on it,' she said.

Agatha's small eyes narrowed, but she nodded her approval. 'A day's grace I will give you, no more. I do not have the time, and neither, I think, do you.'

Exhausted, soaked to the bone, Rolf entered the de Remys' fine new house by the Thames, sat down at the trestle near the hearth, and put his head in his hands. 'I am never going to find her,' he said desolately to Aubert. 'For three months I have searched. I don't know where else to look.'

The merchant set a cup down in front of his friend.

'Drink,' he said. 'And give me your cloak.'

Rolf did so, and tasted the burn of ginevra mingled with the wine. He knew that he could remedy the hollowness within him by downing measure after measure of this concoction, that warm oblivion could be his for the swallowing, but only for a brief time. And payment was always exacted on waking.

'Then perhaps you should stop looking,' Aubert said. 'If Ailith had thought the better of running away, she would have returned by now – either to Ulverton, or to myself and Felice.'

'I could have made things right. She didn't have to go.' He listened to the heavy beat of the rain against the shutters. It had been spring when she left and now autumn was on the threshold.

'No, she didn't.' Aubert sat down opposite Rolf and joined him in a drink. 'But she chose to, and I doubt that you could have made things right even had she stayed. You would be asking too much of her heart – that is what Felice says, and I am inclined to agree.'

'She took our daughter too; she had no right.' Rolf ground an agonised fist into the trestle. 'God knows the kind of life Julitta might be leading!'

Aubert eyed Rolf sombrely. 'I know that is no small part of your torment,' he said. 'But it is something that you must learn to bear. It is right to mourn, but not at the expense of everything else. You still have a wife and daughter. Arlette has been at your side through thick and thin – even if you have not wanted her. It is time you acknowledged that particular debt.'

'You sound like a priest!' Rolf snapped savagely.

'I am sorry. I only meant to be your friend.'

'Ah God, I'm the one who is sorry,' Rolf grimaced and gripped Aubert's arm across the table. 'You present me with truths that I don't want to swallow.'

Aubert gave him a pained smile and returned the grip. 'I miss her too,' he said.

Rolf closed his eyes, squeezed them tightly shut, but Aubert's words were the key that unlocked a bitter flood of yearning and grief, and he lowered his head and wept until he was wrung dry of all emotion, and only a stone-like numbness remained.

PART II

JULITTA

CHAPTER 37

LONDON
1084

Merielle was a whore, although she preferred to call herself a courtesan. The truth was somewhere in between. She did not frequent the houses and bastions of the city's wealthy burghers and French-speaking nobility; they came to her in clandestine fashion, ferried across the Thames by knowing boatmen to the Southwark side and appointments with their lust.

Merielle was tall and shapely with flawless skin, huge blue eyes, and a pouting red mouth. In the six years since becoming the chief attraction of Dame Agatha's bathhouse, she had not once conceived, and the blessing of her barrenness made her very popular with men who had no desire to add the complication of bastard offspring to their family line, but urgently required the services that only a Southwark bath girl could perform. Merielle was ambitious and professional in her work. She was also a prize bitch.

'You stupid little slut, you're not currying a horse! Can't you be more gentle!' she snapped at the girl with the comb. Her voice, which was musical and throaty for her customers, was ugly and petulant now.

'I'm sorry,' Julitta said, not in the least. 'There was a tangle, it's out now.' She drew the comb down through Merielle's silky golden hair and thought grudgingly how beautiful it was. Her own hair was an uncontrollable mass of wood-shaving curls, and the colour was disastrous. 'Like raw liver – disgusting,' so Merielle was always telling her. But then Merielle never had a good word for anyone unless they were rich and male.

'That will have to do. You're too slow, there's no time now.' Merielle swiped Julitta's hand aside. 'My robe, bring me my robe.' She snapped her fingers.

Julitta curbed the urge to return the gesture in Merielle's overfed face. Her rebellious nature had already earned her several reprimands this week, and Dame Agatha was not patient at the best of times. With her mother sick, Julitta could not afford to incur any serious disfavour.

Eyes lowered, she brought Merielle a gown of blue linen to cover the light chemise. It was of a fashion typical to nursing mothers, its deep neck opening fastened for modesty by a simple clasp at the throat. Julitta, at fourteen, was not ignorant as to the purpose of the dress in Agatha's bathhouse. On more than one occasion she had seen a bellicose merchant thrust his hand inside Merielle's bodice and squeeze her breasts like a housewife testing bread dough. It was always a preliminary to yet more intimate pawing, and she was not ignorant about that either, despite the protective efforts of her mother.

She helped Merielle to don the blue gown, and arranged the blonde hair over it in a sheaf of sultry gold, her emotions vacillating between contempt and envy. The young whore pushed her dainty white feet into a pair of soft leather slippers, added an extra dab of rose oil perfume to her generous cleavage, and was ready to go down to her client, a corpulent gold merchant called Edmund.

On the threshold, she turned imperiously to Julitta. 'Tidy this up,' she commanded, waving her arm to indicate the scattered debris of her preparations. 'Then come and help below. And mind you make haste.' Her dainty nose wrinkled. 'And tie your hair back too, you look like something out of the wild woods!' With which parting sally, she minced forth.

Julitta swore at Merielle's retreating back and with a toss of her head, wound her fingers through her hair, deliberately entangling it further. She looked like something out of the wild woods because she *was* something out of the wild woods, trapped in a noose and slowly strangling to death. It was no use complaining to Dame Agatha. There were other girls who worked at the bathhouse, but Merielle was the prize asset, and if it came to a choice between the whore and the housekeeper's rebellious fourteen-year-old daughter, Julitta knew who would win.

Julitta's memory of a secure existence was a distant, unreal point of colour like a passage from a bard's winter song. Once there had been a little girl, a princess who lived in a rich hall and had everything she wanted, horses, servants, fine clothes, the world at her beck and call. A witch from the north lands had changed all that, setting a blood curse upon the girl so that she was changed into a beggar maid. It was a fantasy to which Julitta often returned, promising herself that one day the beggar maid would regain her true inheritance. But not today, she acknowledged to herself with a disgusted glance around the cluttered room.

Julitta tidied Merielle's debris with nimble speed and a bad grace. Edmund the Goldsmith had bought his mistress a hand mirror in which she could admire her flawless beauty. Julitta picked it up to put on the coffer, and paused to study her own reflection. Her hair kinked in unruly close waves, its colour the dark, pure red of a Lothian garnet. The face returning her stare was of balanced proportions, the nose fine and straight, the eyes almond-shaped and of a deep, green-flecked blue, the jaw stubborn and slightly angular. She bore small resemblance to her mother lest it be in the generous curve of her lips and the width of her brow. Everything else, so she was told, was a feminine version of her father's.

'You are so like him,' Ailith would mutter, shaking her head. But Julitta had no true idea what her father was like. She remembered being swept up in strong arms, and a deep voice, bright with laughter, she remembered the deliberate nuzzle of stubble on her cheek making her squeal with delight, and of riding with him to look at a meadow full of grazing horses, her small finger pointing, following his. But such memories were inextricably twined with other, darker ones that she preferred not to explore. If he was so wonderful, why had her mother left him and gone into hiding like a wounded animal?

Abruptly Julitta turned the mirror over and placing it on the coffer, went down to the bathhouse, her hair falling to her hips in eldritch tangles.

Dame Agatha was the widow of a Galwegian mercenary who had made his fortune by changing sides to be on the right one at the right time. In their turn he had served Hardraada of Norway, Harold of England, and William of Normandy. With the profits of his plunder, he had built a bathhouse in Southwark and lived to retire and die of apoplexy.

The premises boasted six private bathing cubicles, each supplied with a large oval tub on a tiled floor, with sufficient room for a charcoal brazier to keep the bather warm, and a dressing couch, which had certain other uses. Dame Agatha's also contained a popular public steam room. The widow's husband had owned the foresight to build a cookshop next door to his bathhouse, so that his clients could send out for hot food, should their exertions make them hungry.

Ailith appeared, carrying two buckets of scalding water.

'I'll do that, Mama.' Julitta held out her hands, but Ailith shook her head.

'I'm almost there now,' she panted. Entering the nearest cubicle, she dumped the buckets on the floor. Immediately Julitta took over the task of pouring the water into the huge bathtub. She saw that it would take at least another three journeys to fill it to a sufficient level, and knew that her mother would make herself ill if she did not rest. The cough which had bothered her throughout the winter had not eased with the advent of spring, and Julitta had become alarmed at how gaunt her once robust mother had become.

Whisking the empty buckets from beneath Ailith's nose, Julitta was gone before her mother could protest. When she returned, the buckets full to the brim and steaming, Ailith was scattering herbs into the tub to scent the water. From the main room, where guests were greeted and made at home, they heard Merielle's alluring voice and the laughter of men.

'I thought she was only entertaining Edmund?' Julitta said, eyeing the tub which, although capacious, was certainly not large enough for three. Perhaps they would all go into the steam room together.

Ailith coughed harshly. 'Agatha told me he'd brought a friend with him. She's sent for Celestine to provide him with hospitality.'

Dame Agatha would be pleased, Julitta thought as she journeyed to and fro with the buckets to fill the bath. Edmund was one of her best customers, and if he was introducing all his rich friends to the location, then so much the better for business. Celestine was Agatha's second-best girl, and like Merielle, only involved herself with the wealthiest clients.

Julitta's assumption of Dame Agatha's delight was correct, for when the proprietor came to discover if the bath was prepared for their guests, her plump face was wreathed in smiles and she presented Julitta with a silver penny for herself. 'You're a good lass,' she declared, patting Julitta's cheek. 'I know I shout at you oftimes, but it's more bark than bite. You're a good worker. Now, I want you to go round to the cookshop and bring back two roast capons, a manchet, and a dish of pepper sauce.'

Julitta turned to leave on her errand just as Merielle emerged from the main room with the two clients. Edmund's arm was around her waist, his hand fumbling at her breasts already. His friend was red in the face and kept touching his crotch. When he saw Julitta staring at him, he grinned, and striding forwards, snatched hold of her wrist in a grip heavy with rings.

'How much is this one?' he demanded of Dame Agatha.

Dame Agatha looked slightly taken aback, but she rallied quickly. 'I am sorry, Master Wulfstan, but Julitta is my housekeeper's daughter. She does not serve as a bath maid.'

Julitta struggled against the biting grip on her wrist, but he only tightened it. 'I want her,' he said. 'How much?'

Dame Agatha's chins wobbled as she swallowed. 'Celestine is very accommodating and trained to the arts,' she said. 'I am sure you will find her more to your taste.'

'I think not. This one's a virgin? I'll pay you double for her maidenhead.'

'Leave my daughter alone!' Ailith burst furiously upon the

little group, her hand dropping to the haft of the all-purpose knife at her belt. 'Let her go,' she snarled at Wulfstan, 'or I will geld you!'

The merchant recoiled, and Julitta was able to snatch herself free. Rubbing her wrist she ran to her mother's side for protection and stood panting and wide-eyed. The man gazed upon her and Ailith, his eyes narrowing. His hands went to his hips and a smile suddenly curved beneath his full, grey-gold moustache. 'Well, well,' he said softly, 'I always knew you would end your days in a brothel, Ailith. What happened, did your lover abandon you when your belly came between him and his pleasure?'

Ailith stared. An expression of loathing contorted her features. 'Wulfstan!' she almost retched.

'Aye, sweetheart, Wulfstan.' The goldsmith's smile grew mocking. 'You should have accepted my offer all those years ago. My wife dresses in silks and sables. She is the mother of four lusty boys, and mistress of a great household.'

'And her husband visits bathhouses on the Southwark bank,' Ailith retorted with contempt.

Wulfstan's complexion darkened, but he kept his smile. 'Aye, visits,' he sneered. 'I need not resort to living in one.'

Ailith tried to stare him out, but she was seized by a violent paroxysm of coughing that doubled her over. Her ribs felt as if they were going to tear apart. Blood filled her mouth.

'Mama!' Julitta put her arm around her mother, supporting her while she choked and spluttered.

Wulfstan eyed the two of them, then turned decisively to Edmund, who had been watching the proceedings with astonishment. 'Go on, get in the tub before it goes stone cold,' he said. 'You've paid enough for the privilege. I want a private word with this good dame here.' He smiled at Agatha, but the expression was far from pleasant.

'Of course,' she said faintly, then rallied herself. 'If you'll come this way to my solar. Julitta, take your mother to your room and let her lie down awhile. You had best take over her duties for tonight.'

Wulfstan followed Dame Agatha into her sanctum, but not

without casting a look of malice over his shoulder at mother and daughter.

'Mama, who was he?' Julitta asked with a shudder of revulsion as she helped Ailith to their chamber and sat her down on the bed.

Ailith spat blood into her kerchief. Mercifully the cough had eased. 'Wulfstan the Goldsmith. He courted me once and tried to force me into marriage. Your father intervened by offering me a position at Ulverton. Wulfstan was humiliated and he is not the kind to forgive and forget. He will joy in exacting vengeance.' Ailith bowed her head. 'Jesu, I am so tired, and my head is spinning. I do not know what to do.'

Julitta was frightened. Her mother was usually so uncomplaining and resourceful, a rock to which she could cling when life threatened to engulf her. To see her like this made Julitta realise that she must either learn to swim on her own, or one day drown. She struck out in anger, as she had struck out as a small, spoiled child when learning against her will to make bread.

'I hate it here!' she cried. 'Why did you ever leave my father? At least he would have taken care of us!'

Her mother's face was waxen. 'I left your father because I did not respect him any more. He had dragged me through the mire once too often.'

'And we are not being dragged through the mire now? Jesu God, Mama, you had an entire keep at your command, and you gave it up for a bathhouse?'

Ailith sighed. 'Oh Julitta, Julitta,' she said wearily. 'If only it were that simple. Many is the time I have thought about swallowing my pride and returning to him, but it would be too late, I know, the bitterness is carved too deep. Do you remember that time I took you across the river to that big house with the wharf at the back?'

'Of course I do,' said Julitta without hesitation. 'We went to visit the de Remys but they weren't there. You bought me some green hair ribbons from a market stall on the way home.'

'You really remember it so well?'

'I thought I was going to see Ben again, I wouldn't stop crying.'

Julitta looked sidelong at her mother. 'Yes,' she said softly. 'I do remember it well.' The bitter disappointment, the anger. 'Why didn't we visit another time?'

'Because I should never have gone in the first place,' Ailith said wearily. 'It was after Sigrid moved away to Southampton. I felt so alone, that I was tempted to try and make contact. When the de Remys were absent, it seemed to be a sign from God that I should leave well alone.' She began to cough again, and the kerchief in her hand grew red. 'It doesn't seem so important now. Perhaps I was wrong.'

'Mama!' Alarmed, Julitta crouched at her mother's side, feeling as helpless as a straw in a gale.

The paroxysm eased. Her face grey, Ailith wiped bloody foam from her lips. 'Tomorrow,' she whispered. 'Tomorrow, you will go to the nuns at St Aethelburga's, and they will send for your father.'

'But I . . .'

'Do not argue with me, child, I haven't the strength. I should have done this long since.'

Disobeying the hoarse command, Julitta began to protest in earnest, but Dame Agatha barged into the room like a ship in full sail, and rendered her silent. The woman puffed to a halt at the bedside and folded her arms, hitching her pendulous breasts up beneath her chin, always a sign that she was prepared to do battle.

'I have had words with Master Wulfstan,' she announced to mother and daughter, her eye fixing on Ailith in particular. 'He says that he is willing to overlook what happened earlier, if you are willing also.'

'Then Wulfstan is the only leopard who has ever changed his spots.' Ailith dabbed the kerchief at her mouth.

Agatha frowned. 'I don't say as I like him, but he's rich and he has influence. I cannot afford to turn a customer like him away from my door.'

'You once told me that this was a respectable establishment,' Ailith croaked.

'So it is!' Agatha's cheeks fattened with indignation. 'There's no thievery or evil doings. This place is clean and well ordered – just as respectable as any of the homes my clients come from. I set my standards high!'

'But not high enough to deny Wulfstan the Goldsmith.'

'You make too much fuss,' Agatha sniffed. 'You've been glad enough of a roof over your head and a place to hide these last eight years, have you not? Don't preach standards at me, my girl!'

Ailith bowed her head and said nothing. Agatha's bosom surged again, and she rounded on Julitta. 'I had to send one of the other girls out to the cookshop in your stead. There's a tub needs filling downstairs, and the couch making up. Best be sharp about it. There's other customers arriving soon.'

'But my mother . . .' Julitta gestured at Ailith. 'I cannot leave her like this!'

'She will be all right. You can check on her between tasks, and I'll look in myself,' Agatha said not unkindly, but with a determined glint in her eye. 'Go on, girl, the sooner gone, the sooner back!' She flapped her hands in a shooing motion.

Julitta did not want to go, but she had little choice. With a final, worried glance at her mother, she went reluctantly from the room and down to the bathhouse.

For the next quarter candle notch, she heaved the pails back and forth, back and forth until the tub in the end cubicle was filled to two-thirds of its depth and the steam rose from its surface as thickly as river mist. Her wayward hair developed a wilder curl, and her face glowed with effort. She scattered fragrant herbs in the tub and made up the couch. Her mind watched her body at work, focusing upon the red hands, the damp, wild curtains of her hair as she leaned forward, the stoop of her spine. The cruelty was knowing that there was more to existence than this. She was bursting with life and all the vital force was being wasted in bearing pails of water and watching fat merchants grope smug whores . . . in watching her mother die by inches before her very eyes. Julitta thumped the bolsters and shook the coverlet vigorously in the same way that she had once attacked the bread in the kitchens at Ulverton.

That memory mauled her now, springing from its forgotten

corner to sink its claws into the present. She could clearly recall the gritty feel of the flour on her small palms, the smell of yeast, the sunlight patterning the kitchen shed floor; her mother's voice gently chiding, and her own tantrum in response. The princess never knew what she owned until she was made a beggar.

There were tears in her eyes as she picked up the empty bath pails and prepared to leave the room. Wulfstan the Goldsmith was blocking the doorway. She gasped in surprise, and her stomach clenched with fear as he drew the curtain across, blocking the safe view of the passage and main room beyond.

'Put the pails down,' he said gently. 'You won't be needing them for some little while.'

His bulk was firmly planted between Julitta and escape. Her eyes flickered, seeking a way out, and finding none. Retaining the pail in her left hand, she relinquished the one in her right and drew her eating knife. She held it close in to her body, tilted at a wicked angle. Even at fourteen, her uncertain life had taught her the skills of survival.

The merchant smiled indulgently but his grey eyes were cold as he unpinned his cloak and wrapped it around his arm. 'Put that toy away,' he said in the same mild, comfortable voice. 'It would be a pity to hurt you.'

His tone raised the hairs at Julitta's nape. She could see in his eyes that despite his words, he intended to hurt her very much.

Wulfstan took a step forwards. 'I kissed your mother once, but I'll wager that your lips are the sweeter. No-one else has tasted them, eh?'

Julitta shifted her stance, trying to keep the bathtub between herself and Wulfstan. There was a new coarseness to his breathing and his complexion was darkly flushed. She had heard men speak of being 'hot for a woman' and now she knew what they meant, could almost see the heat shimmer of Wulfstan's lust. Her legs were suddenly weak and her heart banged against her ribs like a prisoner hammering to escape.

'Please, Jesu, please let me go!' she cried.

Wulfstan cocked his head on one side. 'I tell you what,' he said, moistening his lips, 'I'm a fair man. Some might hold my softness against me, but I'm prepared to give you a sporting chance. If you can win past me and through that curtain, I'll let you go and not pursue you further. What do you say?' Smiling, he stepped aside and spread his arm in invitation.

The mild voice was now gently playful, but Julitta knew that she was trapped. She had once seen a cat catch a bird and then toy with it, letting it flutter free then batting it to the ground before its mauled wings could carry it to safety. And when the cat had tired, it had unsheathed its claws and sunk them deep to kill. But like the bird, Julitta's terror still made her struggle for that impossible freedom.

'Don't you want to escape?' Wulfstan hitched up his tunic and loosened the drawstring on his braies. 'You want me, is that it?'

In one swift motion, Julitta scooped up a bucketful of the bath water and flung it over Wulfstan in a sparkling deluge. He staggered backwards, spluttering, and she made her bid for escape, clawing frantically at the curtain. Wulfstan caught her around the waist and dragged her back into the room where he flung her down on the floor and pinned her there with his weight. One large hand crushed over her right wrist until she was forced to relinquish her grip on the dagger. His soaking hair and beard dripped on her face. 'You little bitch!' he snarled, and his tone now was neither mild nor playful. She could hardly breathe for the pressure of his well-fed weight on her slender body. Against the juncture of her thighs, through her clothes and his, she felt the swollen pressure of his erection and she screamed. The merchant pressed his hand over her mouth and nose, cutting off her air. She bit him as hard as she could on the fleshy side of his palm and he released her with a bellow of enraged pain. Julitta screamed again. Wulfstan fetched her a clout on the side of the head that made her ears ring, and sent black stars wheeling across her vision. Muttering curses at her and encouragement to himself, the man set about dragging up her skirts and forcing her legs apart. Julitta heaved and struggled. He had to release her while he freed his turgid organ from his braies, and Julitta made her right hand into a claw and gouged a deep line of scratches from his cheekbone to the growth of beard on his jaw. He reared back, blood welling from the wounds, and Julitta once more displayed her uncommon education by seizing his exposed testicles and twisting with all her strength.

It was Wulfstan's turn to scream. The noise rebounded off the walls and sank into the curtain. He rolled off her hand, doubled up, twisting back and forth, howling in agony. His erection deflated more rapidly than it had risen, and he clutched himself.

Gasping in terror, Julitta scrambled to her feet and groped at the curtain. Wulfstan's voice ceased abruptly in mid-howl and suddenly he was choking and struggling for air, his face turning a ghastly greyish-blue. A spasm shuddered through him and his body arched. His irises disappeared, leaving blind eye-whites. Julitta stared, knowing that she should make her escape, but rooted to the ground by sheer horror.

Wulfstan shuddered again, his entire body rigid. His final breath wheezed in his throat and his body slumped. The white stare locked upon Julitta in accusation. She clutched the curtain for support, not understanding what had happened, her legs made of jelly.

'In the name of all the saints, what goes forth here?' Dame Agatha came puffing down the line of cubicles. 'What were those dreadful sounds?' She pushed past Julitta into the room, then stopped and clapped her hands to her mouth. 'God on the Cross!' She sucked a breath through her fingers.

'He . . . he pounced on me,' Julitta said weakly. 'I tried to fight him off and suddenly he started choking for breath and turning blue . . . I was only trying to stop him . . .' Her voice wobbled. She swallowed, struggling for composure.

'Well, you have certainly done that, my girl.' Agatha's expression was grim. She stooped to check Wulfstan's body for signs of life, then, shaking her head, stood up. 'Reckon as he had a seizure. I seen it oftimes before. A rich man in his middle years comes seeking excitement and 'tis more than his body can stand.'

'Is he dead?' Julitta gave a small shudder.

'As a Norman's conscience,' Agatha confirmed. 'It'll ruin my custom as soon as this news hits the city. What did you have to claw him for? Them marks on his face will make it look as if he died of more than just a seizure!'

'He . . . he was going to rape me,' Julitta said. 'I . . . wanted to stop him, not to kill him.'

Agatha's ham-like arms folded around each other and hitched the mountainous bosom. The good dame pushed out her lower lip and scowled thoughtfully. 'His family won't want this cried abroad, that's for sure. I suppose there's profit to be had out of that along the way, but you and your mother must leave. I can't afford to have you here if the law comes calling. As this is, it won't do my reputation no good. I run a proper house.'

'Go?' Julitta looked at her, nonplussed. 'But my mother is too sick to make a journey.'

'She won't get any better staying here.' Agatha unfolded her arms and removed the leather money pouch from her belt. 'Here, take this silver to tide you over.'

Julitta stared at the bag of coins dangling from Agatha's fat fingers.

'Go on, take it and get you gone, before worse befalls you,' Agatha commanded. 'Do you want to be stripped naked and paraded through the streets of Southwark in an open cart before you finish on the gibbet for the murder of a prominent townsman? Well, do you?'

Julitta shook her head, her mind filling with a vision of herself standing in a ladder-sided cart, no garment save her wild, red hair, while jeering crowds threw stones at her and clods of dung, their stares a combination of lust and contempt. She knew that no-one would think to plead for an insignificant Southwark whore. The closest to mercy she was going to come was this bag of coins and the leeway to make her escape across the river to the nuns at St Aethelburga's. If only her mother was strong enough to bear the journey. If only she was strong enough herself.

CHAPTER 38

'Ever been to a Southwark bathhouse, Ben?'

Benedict de Remy paused in his examination of the dappled brood mare he had purchased at London's horse fair, and resting one hand lightly on her neck, looked across the stable at Mauger. Mauger, at eight and twenty, held a full ten years of seniority, a fact that he was fond of shoving down Benedict's throat. The younger man knew the reason, and being of an amiable nature, made allowances. Mauger worked like a Trojan, and because of his dedication, was a solid, if uninspired successor to his father as overseer at Brize-sur-Risle. In contrast, Benedict possessed the natural talent to spot a likely horse by eye alone, and one day, through his link with Rolf's daughter Gisele, he would be Mauger's employer and overlord.

He shook his head. 'No, but I've heard all about them.' A smile curved his lips. He was a good-looking young man, dark of hair and eye, his thoroughbred features taken from his mother and given character by the expressive mobility he had inherited from Aubert. At the moment, despite the smile, there was a hint of wariness in his eyes.

'Hearing's not seeing.'

'Have you ever been then?'

Mauger pursed his lips. 'On occasion. I thought I might go this afternoon – I'm free of duties and a man must have some pleasure.' He emphasised the word 'man', and thrusting his broad, square hand through his cropped blond hair, added,

'I've never asked you before because I've always thought you too young, but if you can cut yourself free of the apron strings for a while, I thought we might seek a little sport together.'

Benedict shrugged nonchalantly as if Mauger was offering him a mild diversion, but a surge ran through him, part apprehension, part excitement. 'Why not?' he said. Actually, he could think of a dozen reasons why not, and only one in favour, but he would rather have cut out his tongue than say so to Mauger. Besides, he resented Mauger's remark about the apron strings. As Rolf's apprentice, Benedict had long since learned independence. Affection and respect he still possessed for his parents, and it was only natural that he should lodge in his mother's house while the family was in London. Soon enough his parents would be returning to Rouen, and he would be riding on to Ulverton with the grey mare and coin from the sale of four sumpter ponies and two geldings at the fair. He resumed his careful examination of his purchase.

Mauger seemed nonplussed and not a little disgruntled by Benedict's sanguinity. 'Ever been with a woman before?' he asked like a challenge.

Benedict ran his hand down the grey mare's slender foreleg, pleased at the strength of bone and the set of the limb. He thought about not answering, but knew that Mauger would immediately jump to conclusions that had little to do with the truth. 'Yes,' he said without looking up. 'But I don't make a habit of blabbing it abroad. You know what Lord Rolf is like.'

'He wasn't always that way. Morals of a tom cat at one time. Rutted his way through all the towns in Normandy and half of England.'

Benedict looked up. 'He took me on one side once and delivered me a lecture about the perils of sowing wild oats in furrows too close to home. Everyone at Ulverton knows about the tragedy of the woman from the north and the Lady Ailith.' He gave the mare a final slap on her muscular shoulder and wiped his hands on a wisp of hay. 'I wonder what happened to her and the little girl? Do you think they're still alive?'

'God knows!' Mauger snorted. 'He searched far and wide in

the early days, but found neither hide nor hair.' He gave an impatient shrug as if the subject bored him. 'It's of no consequence now.'

Benedict frowned at Mauger's indifference. He did not remember the Lady Ailith well himself, but he knew that his mother had grieved and worried as much as Rolf when she vanished. Indeed, it had taken her a long time to forgive him for what he had done.

Benedict's memories of Lady Ailith's daughter were a little more focused. The impulsive, headstrong nature, the tantrums, the adoration she had poured out upon him. Without knowing, his expression softened as he remembered the day he had saved her from the greylag gander, and she had fallen asleep on the saddle behind him. How old would she be now? Growing into womanhood, surely? Was her nature still as wild, her hair still as curly? More to the point, was she still alive? Small wonder that Lord Rolf tortured himself.

The bath was hot, the woman's hands slow and sensual as she sat behind Benedict and massaged his soapy shoulders. 'Mauger tells me that you have not been to Southwark before?' Her voice was low and sweet with a strong Flemish accent. She had a lush figure, glossy brown plaits, and her name was Gudrun.

'Not to Southwark,' he murmured. 'But there are places like this in Rouen and Falaise.'

'You are well travelled for one so young.' Her hands came forward, slowly soaping his smooth chest. Despite his dark colouring, Benedict possessed very little body hair. Indeed, although fully developed in all other ways, he only needed to barber his face with a blade twice a week.

'So have you to judge from your voice,' he retorted. 'Ghent, I would say.'

Gudrun laughed and her hands plundered lower, exploring the firm bands of his stomach muscles, and then, with mischievous discovery, the equally firm length of his erect shaft which had risen to the occasion with adolescent joy. 'Bruges, my young lord,' she contradicted, 'but close enough. I was a simple townsgirl who followed my soldier lover across the narrow sea. When he abandoned me, I had to make my living as best I could.' Her hands stroked with exquisite gentleness and Benedict closed his eyes. The sensations were extremely pleasant, but not as yet unbearable.

'So Mauger visits often?' he queried.

'Whenever he is in London. He always asks for Aaliz, she's his favourite.' Her voice took on a curious note and she paused in her ministrations. 'Are you apprenticed to him? I heard him tell Aaliz that you were learning his trade.'

Benedict smiled somewhat sourly. 'I am apprenticed to the same master who taught him.' His spine stiffened with resentment. Gudrun, sensing that she had asked the wrong question, ceased speaking and resumed her fondling. Before she could bring him to his peak, he grasped her hand to stop her motions and directed her to join him in the tub. Casting off her linen robe, she straddled him. Water sloshed rhythmically onto the floor as Benedict practised what he had learned in the establishments of Rouen.

Whilst he was dressing, Gudrun tugged on a loose linen robe and went out to replenish the pitcher of wine. Glancing at the girl, then round the comfortably appointed room, Benedict had to admit that Mauger had sound taste. He wondered if the overseer had had to work as hard at acquiring that taste as he did at selecting breeding stock for the stud at Brize. It was an uncharitable thought and he was surprised to find it lurking in his mind when his body was so at ease.

Gudrun returned with the wine and a small bowl of raisin cakes. 'There has been trouble at one of the other bathhouses tonight,' she told him breathlessly. 'A good thing Mauger didn't take you across the way to Dame Agatha's.'

Benedict took a swallow of the wine she poured for him and raised his brows in silent question.

'Do you know Wulfstan the Goldsmith?'

'Vaguely.' Benedict's curiosity sharpened. His parents often moved in the same company as Wulfstan, but they were not on speaking terms due to some quarrel in the past that had never been explained to him. 'Why?'

'One of the other girls has just told me that he's lying stone-dead on the floor of one of Dame Agatha's cubicles. A seizure so she said, but there's another rumour that one of Agatha's girls killed him.' Gudrun's eyes glowed. 'It'll be all over the city by tomorrow. Wulfstan was well feared, but not well liked. No-one'll likely mourn him, not even his wife.'

Benedict digested this information while he finished his wine and blotted up some of its potency with a couple of raisin cakes. He could almost hear Rolf saying *As ye sow, so shall ye reap*, and having just sown a few wild oats of his own, he felt a little uneasy. When he departed, he paid Gudrun from the depths of his niggled conscience, and her eyes widened at the amount of silver he pressed into her hand. When she made to exclaim, he put his forefinger to her lips and glanced quickly over his shoulder at Mauger who was making his own farewells.

'Say nothing,' he whispered. 'Just put it away against a time when you might need it. My friend . . . he wouldn't understand.'

Gudrun nodded. Her eyes flickered to Mauger. Aaliz said that he was as solid and unimaginative between the sheets as he was out of them, and not particularly generous. She contrasted that description with the good fortune withdrawing from her own arms now.

'Will you return?' Her fingertips slipped the length of his sleeve, the final contact of flesh, hand upon hand, and then the space of air between them, wealthy young man and riverside whore. He drew a breath, and this time it was she who laid a forefinger to his lips. 'No, do not answer that,' she said quickly. 'It was a foolish question.'

'Ready?' Mauger nudged Benedict. Gudrun stepped back, a professional smile on her face. There would be other customers as the darkness thickened and the night grew older.

Benedict returned her smile and walked away, turning to wave once before he lost sight of the bathhouse. It was drizzling, the twilight soft and murky and the air pungent with the smells of wet earth and smoky cooking fires. The two young men made their way down to the river and sought along the bank for a boatman to row them back across the water to civilisation.

'Was it worth it then?' asked Mauger, a slightly patronising smile on his lips.

Benedict murmured a reply and hoped without much optimism that Mauger was not going to demand a detailed account of his experience. He knew that the older man, having introduced him to the delights of Southwark, would feel entitled to know everything and be aggrieved at anything less.

They found a boatman within minutes. He was tying up his craft with determined tugs on the mooring rope whilst arguing with a slender young woman. An older female sat on the ground, her cloak bundled around her body, which shook with spasms of coughing.

'I tell you, I be finished for the day. I been rowing this hulk back and forth across the river since afore cockcrow this morn. Do you think I've no other life to live?' the boatman snapped.

'My mother's sick, she can't go any further. You must take us across!' The girl compounded her frustration by stamping her foot.

The gesture was familiar to Benedict, but he could not remember from where or why. The girl wore a dark cloak and a hood of paler, gold wool, the colour dim in the twilight. Escaping from its edge were several strands of curly dark hair. He could not see her face.

'I must do nothing, wench,' the man growled and started to walk away. In desperation, the girl leaped in front of him and clutched at his sleeve. Benedict was granted a swift vision of delicate features marred by the pinch of exhaustion and despair.

'Please, for the mercy of God!' Her young voice trembled on the verge of breaking.

Benedict intervened, stepping across the boatman's path as the man tried to shake her off and go determinedly on his way.

'I would make it worth your while,' he said. 'How much for the four of us? Come on, man, it's only one more journey there and back. Think of your profit!'

'I can't enjoy me profit if I'm dead from overwork!' the boatman snapped, but ceased trying to push past Benedict and put his hands to his hips instead, indicating that he was prepared to bargain.

Mauger rolled his eyes heavenwards and shook his head at what he saw as complete lunacy on Benedict's behalf. There were other boatmen further along the bank who would not cost the earth to hire. Let these women fend for themselves, they were of no importance. 'You are paying,' he said grimly to Benedict as an exorbitant sum was agreed.

Benedict drew the coins from his pouch. 'We cannot just leave them here,' he said. 'How would you feel if it was your mother or sister stranded here and sick?'

'Neither my mother nor my sister would be sitting on a riverside at dusk in a neighbourhood like this,' Mauger retorted.

Benedict's mouth tightened. 'Then for simple Christian charity, or don't you comprehend that either?'

Mauger gave him a fulminating look. 'You may think you know everything, but you don't,' he said curtly.

The boatman took the coins, made sure that they were genuine, and still grumbling to himself, set about untying the mooring rope. Benedict and Mauger glared at each other for a long moment, the hostility no longer sheathed but bare and bright.

It was the girl who broke the bitter eye contact by laying her hand on Benedict's sleeve, and pressing a silver penny into his hand. 'Thank you,' she said with heartfelt gratitude.

'No, keep your money.' He tried to push it back at her, for he could see that her cloak was patched and that a silver penny must mean far more to her and her mother than it did to him.

'Fair is fair,' she said, refusing to take it back, and turned away to help her mother to her feet.

They were all seated in the boat, and its grumpy owner had begun to skull out into the current, when the girl's mother raised her head and thanked Benedict with quiet dignity. He murmured a disclaimer, feeling uncomfortable. A sense of familiarity nagged at him, but pinning it down proved elusive, and it was Mauger, his arms folded across his chest and his gaze fixed broodingly upon the women, who made the discovery, his disgruntled expression becoming one of astonishment.

'Mistress Ailith?' he asked uncertainly. His glance flickered disbelievingly to the girl. 'Julitta?'

The older woman coughed into her blood-sodden kerchief and examined Mauger as intently as he was examining her. 'It's Mauger, isn't it?' she said weakly.

Benedict's sense of familiarity came home to rest with a breathjarring thud. He saw his own emotions mirrored in the expressions of the others, but individually tinged by their different characters. The older woman's gaunt, sick features wore a mingling of relief and fear. The girl was still bewildered, uncomprehending, but she had braced herself as if to resist a blow. Mauger's discomfort made him brusque and annoyed, while Benedict knew that his own features must display a fierce curiosity. Where had they come from? Where had they been? It was a return from the dead.

'It is impossible.' Mauger shook his head and his glower deepened. 'Lord Rolf searched high and low for the both of you. He thinks you are dead!'

Ailith grimaced wearily. 'He is not far wrong. Is he in London?'

'He is at Ulverton with his wife and daughter.'

'But my parents are in the city,' Benedict added quickly. 'Felice and Aubert de Remy.'

Ailith looked at him, and he saw a glimmer of recognition kindle through the pain in her eyes. She tried to smile. 'Benedict, I should have known you at least, since I suckled you at my breast for the first year of your life. You have your mother's eyes.'

'I remember you now,' Benedict said, a note of uncertainty in his voice, for the encounter had put him off his stride. 'But I would not have done so in passing.'

'And no surprise,' Ailith said with a wan smile. A cough shook her body. 'For the sake of old kindness, I ask you to take us to your mother. We have nowhere else to go and as you can see, my time is short.'

'Mama, you'll soon be well.' The girl clutched her mother's arm. The thread of fear in her voice reminded Benedict of a time long ago when he had dragged a terrified auburn-haired child across his pony's rump.

'Oh aye,' the woman said. 'I'll soon be free of pain.' She huddled into her cloak, retching.

Julitta bit her lip and swiped the heel of her hand across her brimming eyes.

Rain spattered into their faces. The boatman dipped the brim of his hat and clucked through his teeth, making his displeasure known. When they reached the London bank of the Thames, it was immediately obvious that Ailith's failing strength was not equal to walking the short distance along the bank between the mooring and the de Remys' house.

Mauger, being the stronger of the two men, lifted Ailith in his arms and carried her to their destination. In the past, he might have been hampered by her robust build, but the affliction of her lungs had wasted her to skin and bone. She lolled against him, only semi-conscious, the flesh surrounding her eyes so dark that it looked bruised.

'Your mother will soon be safe and warm,' Benedict reassured Julitta, as behind them the boatman clambered into his craft and sculled out into the black water, heading at last for home.

Julitta nodded and continued to chew her lip.

'Do you remember me?'

Julitta blinked through the rain. How could she ever forget? 'Yes, I remember. I was a princess then.' Suddenly it was hard to set one foot in front of the other, as if all her will had trickled out through the worn soles of her shoes. Her mind kept filling with the vision of the fat gold merchant turning blue on the floor at her feet. She could still feel the pressure of his body on top of hers, crushing out her life. But it was he who had died. She looked sidelong at Benedict. Once, in another world, he had saved her from being pecked to death by a goose. 'What were you doing in Southwark?'

He checked his long stride to accommodate hers which was slow with exhaustion and hampered by her wet gown. 'Visiting a bathhouse,' he said after a moment and avoided her eyes. 'I've never been to the Southwark side of London before.'

'I work in a bathhouse.' Julitta cast the words at him like a sharpened spear. 'Or I did until tonight.' The vision of the merchant hit her again, full force, and the weapon she had flung at Benedict rebounded and sank into her own breast. She would have run from the look on his face, but she stepped awkwardly on a stone in the road, wrenched her ankle, and fell with a cry.

He stooped over her. Julitta squeezed her lids tight and hung her head so that she would not have to meet his gaze. Besides, her twisted foot was agony. She heard him shout out to Mauger to wait. Gentle hands removed her clutching one and carefully examined.

'I don't think it's broken,' he said, 'but certainly you cannot walk on it. The flesh is puffing up faster than a batter pudding. I'll have to carry you.'

Julitta was dazed and exhausted, unable to reason any more, unable even to think. Risking a glance at his face, she saw that his recoil at her words had been replaced with an equally dangerous expression of pity. She tightened her lids again and bowed her head, holding her breath on tears. When he lifted her in his arms, she had to link her own about his neck to support herself. The smell of rain-wet wool filled her nostrils, and underlying it, rising directly from his smooth, olive skin, the herbal scent which came from long soaking in a bathtub.

CHAPTER 39

Julitta sat in Aubert's chair before a blazing hearth. A stool supported her swollen ankle and a cup of strong, hot wine comforted her hands. Her mother had been given the great bed in the sleeping loft and was now being tended by Felice de Remy. Mauger had been sent back out into the wet night to fetch a priest – just a precaution, Aubert de Remy had said, but Julitta knew better. She sipped the wine. Its colour was as rich and dark as the tendrils of hair drying in a frizzy cloud around her wan face.

'Do you want to eat?' asked Aubert. He had been sitting at her side in silent vigil, but now seemed to think that since she displayed no inclination to speak, he should take matters into his own hands.

Julitta shook her head. Her stomach was a clenched fist of misery and fear. Even to swallow the wine was an effort. She stared at the logs in the firepit, their undersides a translucent orange edged with flaky grey. Her eyes began to burn and then to fill.

The man sighed heavily. 'I wish that your mother had come to us before . . . such a waste.'

Julitta looked dully at the merchant, at his fur-trimmed tunic and small, smug paunch. How often had she seen such family men queuing outside Merielle's door? 'We did come here once, but the house was locked up and we heard that you were in Rouen. Mama never tried again.'

'So where were you bound tonight?'

'Mama said that after what happened, the only thing we could do was seek my father's protection. We were going to the convent at St Aethelburga's.'

'What do you mean, after what happened?'

The outside door banged shut and Benedict advanced to the hearth, raindrops beading his cloak and sparkling in his hair. In his right hand he carried the pig's bladder which he taken out to fill with cold water from the well in the yard. Now he knelt at Julitta's feet and arranged the bladder around her ankle with gentle skill. 'It always works on the horses,' he said cheerfully. The curve faded from his lips as he looked between his father and Julitta. 'What's wrong?'

Julitta scarcely felt the soothing relief of the cold compress and the competent touch of Benedict's hands. All her attention was focused upon Aubert, as if he was the predator and she the prey.

Aubert too ignored his son. 'Julitta, what happened?' the merchant repeated in a gentler voice. 'You can tell me, you need not be afraid.'

'I had to stop him,' she whispered. 'He pounced on me like a dog on a bone. I didn't mean to kill him.'

Aubert blinked rapidly. 'Kill who?'

Benedict sat back on his heels and stared at her, his hand resting forgotten on the pig bladder and his dark brown eyes full of appalled comprehension. 'Dame Agatha's,' he said. 'Is that where you worked?'

'Yes, but not as a whore. Mama was Dame Agatha's house-keeper, and we helped out when she was busy. He tried to rape me, so I hit him in the cods, and then he had a seizure.' She shuddered at the memory.

'Hit who?' Aubert demanded, beginning to sound impatient. 'What do you know about all this, Ben? Who's Dame Agatha?'

Benedict reddened. 'She owns a bathhouse on the Southwark side. Mauger and I heard tonight that one of her clients had died there – Wulfstan the Goldsmith.'

'What?' Aubert jerked upright in his chair.

'That was his name,' Julitta nodded. 'Dame Agatha said he was a very important man and that if Mama and I did not leave immediately, we would finish on a gibbet. I didn't mean to kill him,' she repeated with a pleading look at Aubert. 'But he was hurting me.'

Benedict resumed his ministrations, turning the bladder over and smoothing its colder side around her ankle. 'You might hurt a man beyond your imagination by kicking him in the bollocks,' he said sensibly, 'but it would take a mighty blow to render him dead. There's no more meat on you than a sparrow. Even a full-grown man would have difficulty in felling Wulfstan. It was his own lust that brought on his death I would wager.'

'But still, whatever the cause, he is dead.' Aubert cupped his chin and thoughtfully appraised her. 'I do not believe that anyone will come looking for you or your mother. Wulfstan being so prominent a figure among the city merchants, it is likely that the circumstances and whereabouts of his demise will be kept as quiet as possible and all rumours denied.' He clucked his tongue. 'A bathhouse,' he said softly to himself. 'What was Ailith thinking of?' He looked with heavy perplexity at the slender, auburn-haired child. One of Felice's old gowns clothed her like a sack, drawn in at the waist by a braid tie. She was an eldritch waif, but he could see that one day she was going to be more beautiful than the Queen of Faery herself. A premonition of danger raised the bristly hairs at Aubert's nape.

'Tomorrow,' he said to Benedict, his voice abrupt with urgency, 'tomorrow you will go to Ulverton and bring Rolf here.'

Felice threw the shutters wide to admit a stream of bright spring sunshine into the room. It flooded across the greenish-gold rushes lining the floor and spilled upon the counterpane of the bed where Ailith lay propped upon several pillows. Warmth danced across Felice's face and illuminated the fine lines etched upon her olive skin. She was eight and thirty, the same age as her dying friend, but she could pass for a younger woman, while Ailith had aged to resemble a crone.

The fresh pink complexion had become a patchy grey; folds of skin draped loosely over gaunt bones; the fine blue eyes were sunken in their sockets and the thick blonde hair was now a sparse, dull yellow. Never would Ailith regain the smooth-fleshed bloom of earlier years. Her death was upon her, and in defiance, Felice had flung wide the shutters.

The sound of birdsong filled the room, the harsh, poignant screaming of gulls, Benedict shouting at one of the grooms as he made ready to leave.

'You are sending for Rolf, aren't you?' Ailith's voice was a weak whisper.

Felice returned to the bedside and sat down on the woven coverlet. She took Ailith's shiny, work-roughened hand in hers and felt the brutality of bone through the skin. 'Benedict is riding out this morning, but it will be more than a week before Rolf arrives.' *And you cannot hold out for that long*, she thought to herself. Her unspoken words must have shown in her eyes, for Ailith gave the ghost of a smile and shook her head.

'I do not want to see him, not even one last time. And if he should arrive before I am sewn in my shroud, do not show him my body.' Her throat worked and the smile became a brimming of tears. 'Let him remember me as I was . . . Promise me.'

Felice was torn by a surge of grief. Her own eyes filled, and it was a moment before she could find the control to speak. 'I promise.' She gripped Ailith's hand and watched her friend, the lovely, generous woman who had saved Benedict's life, turn her cloudy gaze to the bright aperture of light.

'Could you not have forgiven him?' Felice had only a vague knowledge of the circumstances in which Ailith had left Rolf, but she had been a witness to the torment that the action had caused, and was still causing.

Ailith coughed. 'I forgave him long ago,' she said wearily. 'It was not as if I did not know his nature, or that I was a snared innocent. I was deliberately blind, and when I was forced to see, I could not bear what my eyes looked upon.' Her gaze turned to Felice. 'It was easy to forgive Rolf, but I have never been able to forgive myself.'

Felice did not know what to say beyond her first, pitying exclamation of denial. Whatever Rolf had done, Ailith had taken the blame and guilt upon her own shoulders and punished herself. Not only herself, but the child downstairs too.

'I committed adultery with my brother's murderer,' Ailith said into Felice's struggling silence. 'I bore Rolf's child from the rites of the Beltane fires. The priest yesterday . . . he was in half a mind not to shrive me even though I swore bitterly that I had repented.'

Felice could see the tragedy as if it was laid out before her like the great embroidery recently commissioned by Bishop Odo of Bayeux. 'Ailith stop it,' she said sharply. 'It avails you nothing. Perhaps if you had repented less bitterly and with more under-standing, you would not have come to this pass now. And the same goes for Rolf,' she added half under her breath.

Ailith's stare returned to the brightness of the window. 'The path home was too hard for me to find,' she whispered. 'All the familiar places had disappeared.'

The door opened, and Julitta stood hesitantly on the thresh-old, a huge jug of spring herbs and flowers clutched in her hand. As the girl approached the bed, Felice saw that Benedict's cold compresses had worked wonders on the injured ankle, for Julitta was scarcely limping. Today the wild auburn hair was severely tamed in a thick plait and there was a little more colour in the pallid cheeks.

'Ben . . . Benedict said that it was all right for me to pick these from your garden, and that you seldom use this jug,' Julitta said hesitantly.

Felice eyed the handsome glazed pitcher. She seldom used it because it was her best one, kept for special occasions – but then was this not a special occasion? Feeling unworthy, she set aside her irritation. 'Of course it is all right, child. The flowers look beautiful, don't they, Ailith?'

'They do,' Ailith agreed, her eyes brightening on the collection of flag irises, lilies and honeysuckle with a mingling of pleasure and sorrow. 'I used to love my garden at Ulverton.'

A delicate perfume filled the room as Julitta set the jug down on the coffer at the bedside. Clearing her throat, Felice excused herself to other duties below stairs, leaving mother and daughter alone.

Julitta went to the window and looked down into the yard. The grooms had finished saddling Benedict's horse and the young man had emerged from the house to mount up. Her eyes fed on him for a moment, drawing sustenance from his graceful, competent movements. She leaned out a little to watch him collect the leading rein of a grey mare and circle round to leave. Then he chanced to look up and saw her watching from the room above. A smile broke across his face and he saluted her. Julitta felt an uplifting surge of emotion and waved in return as he passed beneath the window. Standing in the stable doorway, Mauger was party to the exchange, and directed a censorious glance in Julitta's direction.

Suddenly self-conscious, she put her hand to her hair to make sure that it was still contained within its severe braid, smoothed her sack-like gown, and withdrew into the room. Her mother had been watching her too, and Julitta blushed. 'I was waving farewell to Benedict,' she said defensively, and found it pleasurable to taste his name on her tongue. Hastily she sat down on the bed, and as Felice had done, took Ailith's hand in hers.

Her mother swallowed, making the effort to speak. 'Benedict is betrothed to your half-sister,' she warned. 'Have a care where you spend your affection, Julitta. I would not have you repeat my mistakes.'

'I did no more than wave, I haven't done anything wrong.'

'Would you have waved for someone else?'

Julitta scowled, and stared at the embroidered counterpane without answering.

'It will be your father's task to dower you and find you a suitable husband, and for that, you must be above reproach.'

'You haven't even considered if I want to go to him at all!' Julitta cried resentfully. 'You said you no longer respected him. Why should I do his bidding!'

'Would you rather the convent or the gutter?'

'You chose the gutter above him!' Julitta spat, and was immediately contrite. The indignant colour left her face and she chewed her full, lower lip. 'Mama, I'm sorry,' she said in a voice thick with tears and pressed Ailith's hand to her own hot cheek.

Ailith's fingers uncurled in a tender caress. 'So am I,' she said. 'More than you will ever know. And so tired.' She struggled to gather her failing strength. 'I know it is hard for you to understand, Julitta. I wanted more from your father than he had it in him to give . . . it was like donning a shimmering gossamer cloak and expecting it to keep me warm even in the deepest winter. For you, it may be that the cloak is lined with fur. You are of his blood and you will not be sharing his bed, lying there, waiting for him to come home from the arms of another woman. That is why I tell you not to grow too fond of Benedict de Remy.' She subsided against the pillows, her energy drained, and when she spoke again, her lips formed the words, but she scarcely possessed the breath to utter them. 'You are so young, and I won't be here to protect you from yourself.' Her eyelids fluttered and closed.

Julitta leaned over her mother, sick with terror, thinking that she had died, but Ailith's hand moved, groping blindly for hers. Julitta grasped it and squeezed with all the desperate strength in her bursting young body, and knew herself as powerless as a straw twirling on the surface of a flood.

CHAPTER 40

It was the middle of the afternoon when Benedict arrived at Ulverton. The late May sun dazzled on the sea and clothed the new green of the land with an eye-aching intensity. On the castle's outer defences, a group of labourers were digging foundations for a stone curtain wall to replace the wooden palisade. They worked bare-chested, their skins reddening beneath the first onslaught of the sun that year. The chink of their spades and mattocks, their salty language, followed Benedict through the gates and into the sun-basked lower bailey.

His thirsty horses were eager to plunge their muzzles into the stone water trough. He let them drink, but only for a short time as a precaution against the colic. A groom came over to take them in hand.

'Is Lord Rolf here?'

The groom fixed his gaze on a point beyond Benedict's shoulder. 'No, sir,' he said and quickly lowered his eyes.

Turning, Benedict found himself facing Gisele, his betrothed. Their wedding was set for the autumn, her mother having finally decided that at nineteen years old, her daughter was robust and mature enough for child-bearing. 'My father is riding by the shore,' she said. 'Do you want to come within?'

Gisele was attractive to look upon, being tall and slender with fine, silvery-brown hair and clear grey eyes. Her nose was dainty and sharp, her cheekbones high. Her mouth was small with a tendency to purse when she thought she was being put

upon, or when, like her mother, she was judging others and
finding them lacking. Benedict had been graciously permitted to
kiss that mouth once or twice and had made his own judgements. He did not attempt to kiss it now, not in public before
the groom.

'No, I have to see him, it's urgent. But if you could bring a
cup of cider out?'

She nodded and started to turn away, but not before he had
seen the curiosity in her eyes. 'I can't tell you,' he said. 'Not
until I've spoken to your father.'

Alarm joined the curiosity. Ignoring it, he swung to the
groom and commanded him to saddle up Cylu the grey. By the
time Gisele returned, Benedict had stripped his cloak and tunic
and was already astride the fresh horse. Leaning down, he
accepted the brimming cup from her hands and downed the
contents in a few fluid swallows of his strong, young throat.
The taste was acid and clean, clearing the dust from his mouth,
stinging slightly in his nostrils.

'That's better,' he said gratefully and handed the empty cup
back down to her.

Although Gisele smiled at him, it was with a closed mouth
and he saw her nose wrinkle fastidiously. He was immediately
aware of the stale condition of his garments – five days on his
body without a change, and since the episode in the bathtub at
Southwark, he had washed nothing more than his hands and
face. The horse swung its head, hooves dancing eagerly. Flecks
of foam spattered from the bit. Gisele trod hastily backwards
before her immaculate blue linen gown could be smirched.

'While you're gone, I will have the maids prepare a tub,' she
announced. Although she was looking at him through her
lashes, the glance was far from provocative; her lips were
pursed. And when he did step into the tub, he knew that the
proprieties would be rigidly observed. No taking liberties until
the nuptial knot was securely tied, and probably not even then,
he acknowledged wryly. Still, the thought of a warm tub and
fresh raiment was fortifying, and he smiled his gratitude at her
before turning the horse.

Cylu was fresh and responded to the touch of his heels with a half-buck and an exuberant breaking of wind. The slight wrinkling of Gisele's nose became an outright grimace of distaste and sent her in full retreat back to the hall. Grinning, Benedict patted the muscular, glossy neck, and urged the horse to a pacing trot.

Rolf was riding Cylu's sire, Sleipnir, along the path which led between Ulverton and one of the small fishing communities beholden to the main village. Benedict, having enquired first of the miller and then the reeve, caught up with him on the dark stone cliffs, negotiating the track which meandered down to the sand and shingle beach. Some of the downland was cultivated with maslin, the green shoots of wheat and rye rippling in the warm wind blowing off the sea. Gulls wheeled and spiralled, and a white-tailed eagle soared on spread pinions. Sheep grazed the clovery turf, watched over by an elderly man, his weathered faced tanned a deep soil-brown.

Rolf looked over his shoulder and reined to a halt. 'I thought that I heard hoofbeats,' he said, and having looked Benedict up and down, his eyes narrowed. 'Is there a reason for such haste?'

There was just room for two horses to ride abreast on the track and Benedict joined his lord. The sun was bright on the older man's face, emphasising the deep creases at the eye corners and between nostril and mouth. Threads of silver were beginning to dim the garnet brightness of his hair, but enough fire remained to reveal from whence Julitta had inherited her colouring. 'Sir, there is indeed,' Benedict replied, and wondered how he was going to tell Rolf what had happened in London, that the woman and child over whom he had long grieved were resurrected. There was no easy way.

'Well, what is it, spit it out!' Rolf snapped impatiently as Benedict hesitated. 'If you've bought a sow instead of a mare at Smithfield, or sold those nags I entrusted you at a loss, you might as well say so.'

'No, sir, I fared excellently at the horse fair.' Benedict deliberated a moment longer, and as they reached the flat ground of the sandy path behind the beach, inhaled deeply. 'You must come to London immediately. Lady Ailith and your daughter are at my parents' house near Dowgate, and Lady Ailith is grievously ill with the lung sickness.'

The horses continued to pace forward, tossing their heads towards each other, swishing their tails against the flies. Rolf's hands were relaxed on his mount's bridle and his face was expressionless.

'Sir, I . . .' Benedict stuttered with a degree of alarm.

'I heard you,' Rolf answered shortly. His eyes were fixed on the silver forelock between Sleipnir's ears, but without focus. 'By grievously ill, I suppose you mean dying?'

'Yes, sir.'

Silence again. They came to half a dozen fishermen's houses beyond the high tide mark, and the hulls of two small boats upturned on the shingle. Out at sea, Benedict's keen eye could just pick out the masts of three fishing craft. The houses were deserted, for the womenfolk were out in the fields tending the crops. Rolf drew rein and stared at Benedict, forcing him to hold eye to eye when the young man would rather have looked away. 'How came they to your father's house?' he demanded. 'Tell me.'

Benedict searched his mind to pick out what could be told and what was better left unsaid. 'Mauger and I were looking for . . .' he began.

'I will have the truth,' Rolf interrupted harshly. 'Do you think I have not learned how to live with it these eight barren years? Do not presume to pity me, boy, or judge what is and is not fit for me to hear.'

Benedict felt himself redden beneath Rolf's fierce green stare. The ability to read the faces and almost imperceptible body gestures of other men was a great advantage and Benedict had done his best to learn from Rolf. But he would never be able to flip the coin onto its other side and dissemble with ease.

Trepidation in his eyes, he began again, but out of pride, made sure to use the same opening words. 'Mauger and I were looking for a boat to row us across the river from the Southwark side . . .'

As his tale progressed, Rolf's set expression grew ever more rigid until his face might have been carved of stone. Only once did he move, and that was to steady the horse by taking a firmer grip on the reins.

'Wulfstan is dead,' Benedict added when he had finished the tale. 'Of a seizure at home, so the rumour goes. Already his family has moved to disguise what really happened. On my way out of the city I was stopped twice and told the news by people who knew that he and my parents were acquainted.'

Rolf neither moved nor spoke and Benedict grew concerned. 'Sir, shall I . . .?'

He saw Rolf make the effort to tug free of the immobility of shock. 'Leave me alone awhile to think,' the older man said, his voice slow and careful, as if he were treading in deep water and feeling for each footstep. 'Return to the keep and tell the women not to wait dinner on me.'

'Shall I tell them anything else, sir?'

'No.' Rolf shook his head. 'I will tell them myself.' He tugged on the reins and the grey stallion turned. Out to sea the fishing boats were closer now. Benedict could see the men on deck and the dark shape of a net draped over the side of the nearest craft. He hesitated for a moment, watching the boats, inhaling the warm salt wind, and feeling totally out of his depth. With a final, worried glance at Rolf's solitary form, he kicked Cylu in the direction of the keep.

A series of mental visions spilled like blood from an opened vein as Rolf rode the old stallion along the beach. He saw Sleipnir trotting towards him, ears pricked and tail carried high, Ailith in pursuit, a birch besom brandished in her fist. He saw her in the forge, a knife poised to take her own life, and he watched himself wrestle that knife out of her hand and cast it across the room. Instead of the swift mercy of the blade, he had given her the long, slow death of loving him. And then he had turned that knife on himself and twisted it deep.

The horizon was suddenly blurred. He dashed his sleeve

across his eyes and swallowed. He saw her feeding Benedict, her blonde braid heavy in the firelight, watched her furiously pummelling a tub of laundry while he asked her to become chatelaine of Ulverton. That first, frozen moonlit kiss that dissolved into molten urgency, searing them both to the bone. Her hair spread upon the pillow, grasped in his hands; the beauty of her strong, generous body which had given him such pleasure to possess and had bestowed on him the gift of a fire-haired child. He wiped his eyes again, but his vision blurred almost immediately. Ailith and Julitta eking a living in the stews of Southwark. Eight years. He had thought in his stupidity that even if he had not found peace, he had at least discovered a degree of equilibrium, but he had been deluding himself. He had discovered nothing, and still had so much left to lose.

He could ride no further. Halting Sleipnir, he dismounted, and seating himself on a flat, sun-warmed rock, put his head in his hands.

'A bathhouse?' Arlette's shocked gaze flickered rapidly from Rolf to Gisele, as if worrying that the very mention of the word would corrupt her daughter's purity. 'What were they doing in a bathhouse, or perhaps I should not ask?'

Benedict, who had been invited to share in the discussion that was taking place in Arlette and Rolf's bedchamber, cleared his throat. 'Not all bathhouses are dens of iniquity,' he defended, thereby earning himself a glare from his future mother-in-law, and a prim lip-purse from Gisele. 'Besides,' he added doggedly, 'from what Julitta told me, her mother was the housekeeper of the place, they were never actually involved in the private bathing of the clients.'

Arlette sniffed scornfully. 'That is as maybe,' she said. 'And it is only Christian charity to pity the woman and the child. But what is to be done with them? You say that the mother is dying of the lung sickness? Aye well, perhaps that is a blessing in disguise. But the girl . . .'

'My daughter,' Rolf interrupted, his voice almost a snarl, a dangerous glitter in his eyes. 'Julitta is my child as much as

Gisele. Bridle your tongue when you speak, or by God I will do it for you.'

Arlette paled. 'I was only going to say that you need to take careful thought for the girl's welfare. She has known such an uncertain life, that there are bound to be difficulties.'

Rolf's eyes remained suspiciously narrowed, but he leaned back in his chair and slowly rubbed his forefinger back and forth across his upper lip while he considered her words.

Benedict glanced around the family and tried to imagine Julitta settling into the household. From what he remembered of Julitta the child, and from what he had seen of Julitta the budding woman, there was going to be precious little peace in the bower. Just the sight of Julitta's wild red hair would be enough to send Arlette running for her shears and a thick linen wimple to tame and cover such wanton glory.

'I am more than willing to take her under my wing, indeed I am,' Arlette added piously.

'*More* than willing?' Rolf asked in a wintery voice. 'I would have thought the opposite.'

His wife compressed her lips. 'As you say, she is your child, and I have always done my duty as your wife to the best of my ability. If I cannot love her, then at least I can see that she is prepared for marriage to a husband of your choosing . . . unless you had the Church in mind for her?'

Rolf scowled and bit viciously at his thumbnail. 'Not the Church,' he said.

Benedict agreed. If anyone should enter a religious establishment, it should be Arlette, the amount of time she spent on her knees. 'She will need gentle handling,' he said aloud, thereby earning himself another glare from the women. It was impossible to explain Julitta to them, the paradox of toughness and vulnerability that had so moved him. 'As you say,' he appealed to Arlette, 'she has known an uncertain life, has had to fight to survive.'

'I am sure I am capable of taking that into account,' Arlette said, but her expression softened slightly at his acknowledgement of her own wisdom. 'After all, I have raised a daughter myself.'

She looked proudly at the young woman sitting at her side, her posture echoing her mother's. Neat, prim, upright.

Although it did not show on his face, Benedict's foreboding increased.

'What is my sister like?' Gisele asked Benedict. Driven by avid curiosity, by what he had not said in front of her parents, she had followed him into the hall.

Benedict shrugged. He glanced round. Most people had settled down for the night, drawing their pallets close to the banked fire. One or two still lingered over late games of tafel or completed small personal tasks by the grainy light of small rush dips.

'Is she pretty?'

Benedict reached out, placed his arm around Gisele's supple waist and drew her towards him. She resisted for a moment, glancing round, then deciding it was all right, capitulated. 'No,' he said, 'I would not call her pretty.' That was a word that conjured up a picture of safe, conventional attractiveness. He had known many pretty girls, his betrothed among them, but Julitta was like none of them.

'Then she is ugly?'

He nuzzled Gisele's warm throat and sought her lips. 'That neither,' he murmured. 'She . . . she resembles your father, and of course she has scarcely left childhood.' He stroked a tentative hand up her side towards her breasts. Usually this was forbidden territory, but tonight, Gisele's insecurity permitted him the liberty. She yielded passively to his questing touch, a slight frown between her eyes.

'You'll meet her soon,' he said, an undercurrent of impatience in his tone. 'Then you can judge for yourself.' And knew as he spoke that any judgement Gisele made would be based on that of her mother. He felt her nipple bud beneath his fingers and in that same moment she pushed herself out of their embrace, a flush creeping over her throat and mounting her cheeks. Benedict started to speak, but Arlette entered the hall, carrying a wax taper on an iron spike.

'Gisele, are you coming to bed?' It was an order framed as a question, terse with reproach

'Yes, Mama,' Gisele said as meekly as a child, and without even a parting word or glance for her betrothed, pushed out of his arms and hurried towards the taper's glimmer.

Benedict sighed, scooped his hair off his brow in a gesture of frustration, and sought his pallet, ignoring the amused glances of the tafel players.

CHAPTER 41

Julitta curled up in the hay loft above the stable and hugged herself, moaning softly. The grief was a physical pain in her stomach, doubling her over, surging through her, filling all the spaces that had been blank with shock.

At first, gazing down on her mother's body, shrunken in death, the flesh clinging to the sharp bones and pitiful hollows, she had been filled with a merciful numbness. That state had remained and carried her through the first day and night following the death. She had slept beside Felice, clinging to her for comfort, while Aubert bedded down on a pallet in the hall. Then, this morning her mother had been sewn in a shroud and taken away to the parish church of St Martin. There had been some dispute with the priest over Ailith's right to be buried within its precincts. Officially she was a resident of Southwark and Aubert had been forced to pay an indemnity of silver to have her remain.

These considerations of etiquette had passed over Julitta's head. She only knew that they were quarrelling about her mother's body as if it were a scrap of carrion to be devoured by kites. That was when the numbness had begun to wear off. The pain had attacked her vitals in earnest when they finally reached an agreement and removed Ailith to St Martin's. Suddenly the house was bereft of her presence. Standing in the bedchamber, looking at the stripped mattress, awaiting the attention of Felice's maids, at the withered bunch of flowers in the glazed pitcher, Julitta had realised that her mother was truly dead, that a great empty chasm had opened in her life and although others might create bridges across it, it would never go away.

Footfalls sounded on the hayloft ladder and the trap was thrown open. A pitchfork was tossed through the hole. A mop of hair, blonder than the straw, appeared, then a tanned face with wide-set grey eyes.

'Who's there?' Mauger demanded suspiciously.

Julitta jerked her head from her makeshift hay pillow.

'Oh, it's you,' he grunted. 'I thought for a moment it was that accursed stable lad and his wench again. It wouldn't be the first time.'

Julitta sat up and dragged her sleeve across her swollen eyes. Mauger stepped into the loft and, frowning slightly, picked up the fork. He was not much above average height and chunkily muscled. His brows were heavy, his face square in shape with slanted cheekbones and a considering mouth that seldom smiled. Julitta was wary of him. She had the vaguest recollection of teasing him, of being very naughty and leaving him to bear the brunt of the punishment. He had been about Benedict's age then, perhaps slightly older. Now he was a grown man, dour and solid.

Mauger advanced to stand over her, his boots crackling on the warm, meadow-scented hay. Clearing his throat, he said gruffly, 'I'm sorry about your mother . . . and about what I said when Ben and I found you on the Southwark bank. Lady Ailith was always kind to me.'

'I . . . I thought you didn't like us,' Julitta snuffled.

Mauger's frown intensified. 'That's foolish!' he growled. 'What reason should I have to dislike you?'

At fourteen, on the verge of womanhood and armed with the knowledge that came of dwelling in a bathhouse, Julitta could have told him the reason for his brusqueness with her. She was Eve and he was scared of temptation. But at the moment, she was no more than a frightened, grief-stricken child. 'You're always scowling. You never smile or try to be nice.'

'You are Lord Rolf's daughter. I mind my manners and keep my distance, unlike others who should know better,' he said with heightened colour and strode away to unbar the large doors at the end of the loft. Throwing them wide to admit a torrent of sunshine, he began pitching forkloads of hay down to two stable hands below. Julitta watched him work, his movements forceful and jerky beneath her scrutiny. Patches of sweat glued his linen shirt to his body, and she knew that, but for her presence, he would have removed it.

Suddenly he stopped work, and leaned on the pitchfork stale. 'Your father's here,' he announced, and half-turning, looked her up and down. 'Best clean yourself up. You don't want him to get the wrong idea about you.'

Julitta scrambled to her feet. Stalks of straw adhered to her gown, which was the threadbare one of her first arrival with a large patch near the hem where the original fabric had been scorched by a cinder. Her face, she knew, would be grimy with tears, and a rapid exploration of her hair revealed that, as usual, it had begun to escape its braids and it too was tangled with straw. She was imbued with a feeling of panic at the expectations being laid upon her, one after the other, in layers so thick that she was in danger of losing herself. What indeed was her father going to think of her after so long? And surely if he could not accept her as she was, his love was flawed, if he loved her at all. Perhaps she was just an inconvenience to him, a *nithing*. These thoughts flashed bewilderingly through Julitta's mind as she hurried down the rungs of the loft ladder. Suddenly she did not want to see her father lest he should be *nithing* in her eyes.

Mauger's warning and her escape were not, however, swift enough. As she emerged from the stables, her skirts gathered above her shins the better to run, she was almost knocked down by a rangy dappled stallion. The man astride cursed and wrenched on the reins. The horse plunged across the path of the rider behind and he in his turn had to back and control his own mount.

Her breathing swift and shallow, her stomach flopping over and over, Julitta watched the leading rider bring his horse to a stand. Her eyes fixed on the sinewy working of his fingers and wrists, the green linen cuff with its edging of blue and buff braid. And then she lifted her gaze beyond the mundane detail and met the furious glare of the man. The strong, clean features of her half-buried memory were overlaid with harsh lines of care. The laughing green eyes were stormy and opaque.

'Have you no more sense than a hen to run out beneath the hooves of a horse?' he snarled at her.

Behind him, Benedict de Remy, the second rider, drew breath to speak, a look of alarm on his face.

Julitta was in no fit state to answer. Filled with dismay that this bad-tempered, harsh-faced stranger, so familiar and yet so different from her memories, now had responsibility for her life, she uttered a gasp and fled, her movement so abrupt that it set the grey horse off again. By the time Rolf had steadied the animal down, she had made good her escape.

'These kitchen wenches are all the same,' Rolf snapped contemptuously as he dismounted. 'Their brains are only ever in one place!'

Benedict cleared his throat. Rolf's temper had worsened with every step they took towards London. This morning he had been unbearable. Benedict could almost see apprehension sitting on his lord's back like a large, grey demon armed with nine-inch claws. It was not entirely Julitta's fault that the horse had played up. The beast was only responding to Rolf's tension. 'That was Julitta, sir,' he said neutrally.

'What?' Rolf glared round at him. 'That raggle-taggle waif is my daughter?'

'Yes, sir.' Avoiding Rolf's stare, Benedict dismounted. 'My mother has commissioned a sempstress to make Julitta some new gowns, but for the moment she only has the clothes in which she came to us, and a dress of my mother's that has been cobbled to fit. Do not think too badly of her. Perhaps you surprised her and she was hurrying to make herself presentable.'

Rolf's mouth tightened. He continued to glower, but Benedict sensed that the disapproval was more self-directed than aimed at him. He took Rolf's bridle and made to lead their two horses into the stables.

Rolf grimaced. 'Ah God,' he said, 'why should it take a lad

of eighteen to show me the road when I have been on it so much longer?'

Benedict paused, half-expecting a reprimand, but Rolf sighed heavily. 'You are right. At five years old Julitta was not capable of sitting still for a moment. I used to call her Squirrel because she was so quick and inquisitive.' A painful half-smile curved his lips. 'A different scrape every day, and I never had the heart to punish her because she was so independent and funny. I should have looked beyond the straw and tattered gown to recognise her.'

Perhaps he had known it was her, Benedict thought, but had not wanted to believe it. The sight of Julitta running around like a hoyden in rags was all too close to Arlette's expectations of what he would find – a Southwark 'bath girl'. 'I think you should go and find her, sir,' he said with respectful neutrality.

Rolf eyed him. 'So do I,' he said. 'You've a wise head on your shoulders, Ben.'

Benedict looked modestly down, feeling a not unnatural glow of pride. He was quickly brought to earth by the sight of Mauger descending from the hay loft, a pitchfork in his hand and his sweat-soiled shirt slung around his bull-strong neck. The glow of hard work oiled his well-muscled body, and bits of chaff clung to his damp skin. His chausses had slipped down and hung on his hips, exposing a border of crisp pubic hair. Stalks of straw were snagged in the fabric. Mauger and Julitta in the loft together? It was a preposterous notion, but that did not prevent it from occurring to both Benedict and Rolf. A flush broke across Mauger's cheekbones at their scrutiny.

'I did not remove my shirt until the lass had gone,' he said with dignity before Rolf could challenge him. 'I had no idea she was in the loft until I went to fork some hay.'

'I do not doubt your honour,' Rolf rectified quickly. Mauger said nothing, but his grey eyes revealed that he was not deceived. With dignity, he shouldered the pitchfork and walked on.

Rolf pushed his fingers through his hair. ' "As ye sow, so

shall ye reap",' he quoted wryly to Benedict. 'What worries me is that not every man would have the honour to leave his chausses on, let alone his shirt.'

Felice wiped Julitta's tear-swollen face with a cloth wrung out in herb-scented water. 'Come now, come now,' she murmured. 'You can't greet your father like this. Dry your eyes and sit up, there's a good girl.'

'I don't want to see him!' Julitta flung. 'And he doesn't want me. I'm a burden, that's all!' Her lower lip jutted mutinously, but she obeyed Felice and raised herself from the bed.

'Oh, that isn't true! He searched high and low for you and your mother all those years ago. Of course he wants you. You're his daughter!' She smoothed the wavy masses of hair with a gentle hand and wondered what had brought Julitta bolting into the hall like a terrified horse. It had taken all Felice's persuasion and not a little physical struggle to make the child abandon the idea of grabbing her cloak and a loaf and running away. 'It is what your mother wished for you, did she not?'

'Only because she had no choice!' Julitta spat.

'That is not true either.' Felice fetched a bone comb and began to tidy Julitta's hair, plucking out fragments of straw and cleaning it of hayloft dust. 'She had several choices, and she judged your father to be the best of them in the end. I know that she talked about it to you before she died.'

Julitta gripped the coverlet in her fists and submitted for a moment to Felice's soothing ministrations. But in the end her fear and anger could not be contained. 'I don't want to see him!' she repeated and jumped to her feet. 'I won't go with him! It's all his fault that my mother is dead!'

'Julitta!' Felice stood up too, her dark eyes beginning to flash with anger.

'She is right,' Rolf said from the doorway, standing foursquare, banishing all Julitta's hope of escape. 'Had I heeded my conscience and had more self-discipline, Ailith would be with me yet, and none of this need ever have happened.'

Julitta's knees weakened and she sat down abruptly on the bed, her eyes lowered and her head averted.

Felice looked anxiously at Rolf. 'I do not know what to do with her,' she said.

'Leave her to me.' Rolf touched Felice's arm. 'I am indebted to you for your care . . . '

Felice smiled, but the gesture did not reach her eyes, which were troubled. She laid her hand over Rolf's, gave it a brief, sympathetic squeeze, and went out, leaving father and daughter alone together.

Rolf advanced two uncertain paces into the room. Julitta's head remained averted.

'I know that you want me to go away,' he said, 'but that is something I cannot do. You have haunted me for far too long. If I could change the past, I would, but since that is beyond me, I can only offer you the future.'

She was aware of him moving closer, could feel the warmth and vibration of his body now. 'You called me a hen,' she said in a low, aggrieved voice. 'You shouted at me.'

'You almost ran beneath the hooves of my horse, you could have killed us both. Besides, that is not the true reason you will not look at me.' He reached out across the last few feet of space between them and tilted her chin on his fingers, turning her to face him. 'It is because of your mother, is it not? You think I betrayed her?'

Julitta's thoughts and feelings were so tangled that there was not the slightest possibility of her being able to unravel them into coherence. All she knew was that she was angry at her mother for dying, and because the dead were inviolate, she had to take her anger and misery out on the living. And her father was a prime scapegoat.

'Didn't you?'

'Yes,' he admitted, 'I did betray her, and myself, and there is not a day that has gone by since then that I have not wished it undone. I won't betray her memory. Julitta, I want you to come with me to Ulverton. I want to do my best for you now.'

'And if I don't want to go?' She tossed her head defiantly, shaking off his touch. 'You'll make me, won't you?'

Rolf went to the window where only a few days before a jar of blue and yellow irises had blazed with brave colour. Now the top of the coffer was bare. He stood against the chest, arms folded, and looked out on the bustling yard, and beyond it, the wine wharf jutting into the Thames. 'Do you remember anything of your life before?' he asked. 'Do you remember Ulverton?'

Julitta stared at her father's turned back. His hair was unruly like her own, but maintained in cropped order, and the colour was neither as rich nor as dark, and diluted with wings of silver. Her mother had said that she resembled him as much in character as in looks. Did she remember Ulverton? Dear Jesu, if she tried, she could remember far too much. 'Not really,' she said with a sulky shrug.

'Your mother loved the sea,' he mused. 'At the slightest excuse she would take herself down to the shore in the summertime and go wading barefoot in the shallows. And in winter she would put on her cloak and watch the waves come pounding in for hours on end. She had never seen the coast until I brought her to Ulverton. I can still see her collecting driftwood with the other women, and you running between them, your hair like a banner in the wind.' His voice shook and he sucked an unsteady breath through his teeth.

Julitta bit her lip, fresh tears scalding her eyes. 'Yes, I do remember,' she whispered. 'And you came down and spoke to my mother, then you took me on your shoulders, and I could see so far that I thought the world was mine.'

'It still is if you want it.' Her father turned round and held out his hand once more, but this time he did not advance and touch. 'Princess?'

The word leaped at her and she was smothered by all its promise and heartache. His hand was quivering, perhaps just with the stress of position, but she thought not. There was a tension in his face that spoke of control on the verge of cracking. Her own composure broke beneath his gesture, his stare,

and the memories he had invoked. Rising from the bed she ran
to him. His arms closed about her, one hand convulsively
grasping and smoothing her hair. 'Julitta!' he said hoarsely,
almost weeping. 'Oh Christ, Julitta!'

Julitta pressed her cheek against the rough linen of his tunic.
Hard, harder, forcing belief into her soul. She would go with
him to Ulverton and piece together the shattered dream.

When they had both recovered somewhat from the emotional hammerblows, Julitta detached herself from her father's
arms and going to a corner of the room, lifted the edge of a
half-folded cloak, and withdrew a Danish war axe.

'My mother always kept this by her. She said that it was hers
by right of blood. I remember it hanging on the wall at
Ulverton, and falling down on the day that we left. I know that
it once belonged to my uncle Lyulph and that he died on
Hastings field. It was made by Mama's husband, the armourer.'
Julitta gave a little shiver. 'I wish she hadn't kept it.'

'The luck of Ulverton.' Rolf took it from her, hefting its
once familiar weight. Or perhaps its misfortune, cleaving in
twain the lives of all who touched it. Christened with blood. 'I
wish it too,' he said with a grimace, and stretched out his free
hand. 'Come with me.'

Julitta took it, feeling the security of the warm grip, the ten-
sile fingers. Her own hand was damp with cold sweat. 'Where
are we going?' she asked as he led her down the outer stairs and
across the yard toward the wharves.

'To the river to make an offering.'

'What sort of offering?'

'In times gone by, when a warrior died, his weapons often
went to the grave with him, or were flung into the nearest river
or lake as an offering to the Gods. That is what my grandfather
used to tell me, and he had it from his own grandfather who
was a pagan.'

Julitta was aware of people stopping work as she and her
father went by. From the corner of her eye, she saw Benedict
and Mauger standing together, their mouths open. The wharf-
side was bustling with labourers and sailors as a Rouen wine

galley was disembowelled of her cargo. The rumble of wooden tuns over the stones was deafening. Vinegary fumes from an accidentally broached cask assaulted the air.

Tugging Julitta in his wake, Rolf strode out onto a wooden jetty which currently had nothing but shallow boats moored to its sides. The smell of wine was replaced by the smell of the river as it slapped against the posts, grey and green, frilled with white foam. Gulls wheeled over their heads, and a single, black-winged bird that might have been a raven.

'Stand back,' Rolf said to Julitta, and when she was clear to his satisfaction, he began to whirl the axe around his body in double circles, faster and faster until the weapon was a gleaming blur. Then on a final surge he released it, crying out, and the axe sailed upwards and outwards in magnificence, the head flashing over and over in the sunlight as though it were on fire, before plummeting into the choppy water of the Thames to be quenched forever.

'It is neither good luck nor misfortune now,' Rolf panted, staring down at the opaque green wavelets lapping the posts of the jetty, and then at his daughter. 'It is nothing.'

Later, Julitta and Rolf visited Ailith's grave, the place a scar of fresh, raw earth in the cemetery. Rolf stared at it, still unable to believe that she was truly dead. He had not seen her, therefore it could not be. Even though he had disposed of the axe and its ability to strike, the wounds it had left were deep beyond healing.

Julitta knelt at the graveside and laid a fresh bunch of irises on the soil. Rolf swallowed, watching her. She had her mother's width of brow and generous mouth. There was also a touch of Ailith's stubborn jaw and more than enough of her mannerisms to give Rolf constant twinges of pain whenever he looked at Julitta. The past was an open grave from which the dead stretched out to touch him no matter how he tried to lay the ghosts. Ailith, his beautiful, betrayed Ailith.

'Come,' he said abruptly as Julitta rose from her knees and wiped her eyes on the back of her hand. 'Leave her to sleep. We have a road to travel.'

CHAPTER 42

'So you are Julitta?' said Arlette de Brize. It was more than a plain statement. The woman's grey eyes examined the travel-dusty girl without warmth. 'Be welcome.'

A groom led away the docile chestnut gelding on which Julitta had made the journey from London. She shook out her creased gown and briefly met Lady Arlette's cool stare, doubting that she was welcome at all. Her father's hand firmly grasped and squeezed her shoulder, imparting the reassurance that she badly needed.

Julitta flickered a brief glance around the bailey. It was all so strange, and yet so familiar. She was tired from a journey that had been as much emotional as physical, and was far from over. She did not remember her father's wife from their chance encounter eight years ago, and the woman was nothing as she had imagined. Arlette de Brize was composed, attractive, and immaculately groomed, the sort of person who could walk along a muddy track without so much as smirching her dainty shoes. Julitta was aware that her own appearance, although much improved since London by new clothes, fell far short of the older woman's approval. But then, she thought mutinously, she had no need of that. She raised her head, and unconsciously tightened her jaw.

Arlette turned to the demure young woman standing at her side. 'Gisele, greet your sister,' she commanded.

The girl hesitated, then stepped forward with obvious

reluctance. 'Be welcome,' she said in a monotone and kissed the air beside Julitta's cheek.

Julitta inhaled the astringent scent of lavender. This was Gisele, Benedict's betrothed. She was filled with the hazy memory of herself in a rage of infantile disbelief that her father should have destroyed her dreams and betrothed him elsewhere – to her own sister.

'Benedict told us all about you,' Gisele said sweetly, displaying that she possessed claws, no matter how dainty the paws that sheathed them, 'that he rescued you from a bathhouse.'

Red heat flooded Julitta's face.

'Actually it was from a grouchy Thames boatman,' Benedict interrupted easily from his place among the escorting soldiers and grooms. 'They think they own the world.'

Julitta gave him a grateful look, Gisele a narrow one.

'Come.' Arlette took Julitta by the arm as if she were taking the lead of a recalcitrant puppy. 'Let us go within. You will want to wash away the dust of travel and rest before we eat in the hall. Gisele, see to everyone's comfort and then join us.'

'Yes, Mama.' Gisele's voice was a dutiful chime, sweet and slightly high-pitched. Julitta imagined that given the chance it could be shrill and whiny. She longed to remove her arm from beneath Arlette's and gave an experimental tug. The slim white fingers tightened and the grey eyes silently warned her to do no such thing. Julitta yielded, but if anything, the spark of defiance kindled by Arlette's reception, was only fanned to a flame.

'I can see that Felice de Remy has done her best for you, but you need taking in hand,' said Arlette. They had retired to the privacy of the chamber above the hall. It was divided by a wattle and daub partition into two rooms, one being the main bedchamber, the other Arlette's working domain. The orderliness of her character was reflected in the precise arrangement of every item of furniture. The upright loom was placed just so to gain light from the window aperture. A dark oak bench leaned against the wall, its positioning exactly central. Julitta wondered if Arlette had used a measuring stick. Everything was neat, dust-free and firmly put in its place. More to be admired than used, Julitta thought.

Arlette walked round Julitta, examining her as if she were a doubtful piece of ware that she had been duped into buying by a travelling pedlar. Her fingers plucked at the sage-green linen of Julitta's over-dress which had been completed in a rush on the night before she set out from London. Some of the stitches, mostly her own, were over-large, and Arlette clucked her tongue over these.

'Sewing and weaving, baking and brewing,' she declared like a devotional plainchant. 'I do not suppose that your mother had much opportunity to teach you any of those. Well, you'll soon learn. You have your father's looks, so I suppose you must have his quick wits too. If you are to be of any profit to Brize when your marriage is arranged, it is my duty to make a silk purse from a sow's ear . . . and it is your duty to learn.'

Julitta's eyes flew wide at the words *profit*, *marriage* and *duty*. She knew it was the lot with which most women were burdened, but she had lived outside its conventions for most of her life and was filled with horror at the thought of conforming. 'My father did not bring me to Ulverton to be groomed for sale like one of his mares,' she said with a toss of her head.

Gisele looked primly horrified at Julitta's rebellion. Arlette's stare was cold. 'Your father at least acknowledges *his* duty,' she said icily. 'He could have left you in the gutter. Think about that, my girl, before you open your mouth to be ungrateful. I'll not have you shaming the proud name of Brize-sur-Risle.'

Julitta blinked hard, fighting tears. She would not cry in front of her half-sister and her father's wife. At the moment she hated both of them, and she knew without a doubt that they hated her. 'What makes you think I would rather not live in the gutter?' she said hotly.

Arlette's thin eyebrows rose to meet her wimple. Her face wore an expression of fastidious distaste. 'Certainly your manners smack of such habitation,' she replied, and terminated the exchange by returning to practical details. 'You will sleep in here with Gisele and the maids. You did not bring many belongings from London, but what you possess, you may store in that coffer.' She indicated an oak chest standing next to a neatly arranged stack of mattresses. 'Tomorrow we shall see how much you know and what you can do.'

Julitta opened her mouth to rebel again, but thought the better of it. Whatever she said would only fetch a rebuke. She had to use guile. Arlette and Gisele had already formed their opinions as to her character and worth, but there were others she could win to her cause, chief among them her father. So instead, she composed her expression meekly and lowered her eyes as if she had been cowed into submission.

Watching over Julitta as she put her few belongings in the coffer, Arlette uttered a horrified squawk when she saw the size of the honed dagger that the girl laid across the top of her spare gown and short shift.

'Surely that is not your eating knife?'

Obviously it was not, for Julitta's small, bone-handled meat-blade was hanging in the leather scabbard at her belt. 'It was my mother's,' she said.

'Your mother wore a murderous thing like that?' Arlette's voice remained horror-struck.

'Sometimes.' A devil in her prompted Julitta to lay her hand to the hilt of polished antler and slowly draw the blade forth from its sheath. 'She always kept it sharp. See, I have her whetstone too.' In her other hand she held up a stone suspended from a small belt cord. 'I know how to hone the edge,' she said confidently and ran her thumb along the blade, 'but it doesn't need it just now.' She gave Arlette a feline smile.

'Put that thing away!' Arlette said hoarsely, one hand at her throat as if she expected to be assaulted. 'It is no fit possession for a girl of your breeding to own. I shall speak to your father about this!'

Julitta shrugged. 'He knows I have it. He saw it in London and he let me keep it. It was made by Mama's husband. He was a master armourer in the days before King William.' She sheathed the dagger and replaced it in the coffer. 'We got rid of the battle axe though.'

Arlette's eyes almost popped out of her head and she did not ask to have the last statement explained. 'Your father is frequently too soft for his own good,' she snapped. 'Keep that thing from my sight. I hate to see weapons in my bower.' A small shudder of genuine aversion ran through her.

Julitta wrapped her shift around the weapon. There were chinks in the armour if you knew where to probe. With satisfaction, she knew that, if necessary, she could give as good as she got.

Being the implicit believer in duty that she was, Arlette had prepared a feast to welcome Julitta into the household. Sitting on the high dais, surrounded by embroidered napery, glazed earthenware vessels, an elaborate aquamanile and matching silver salt dish, it was difficult for Julitta not to feel intimidated. At the bathhouse she had eaten off a plain trencher of wood or stale bread, and the food had been simple – pottage more often than not, or a split loaf served with butter and curd cheese. At the de Remys' she had grown accustomed to dining in a little more style, with a cloth on the trestle for the main meal, and a wider choice of dishes, but this was overwhelming.

She looked at a platter of roasted songbirds that had been placed close to her right hand. They were something she had never liked. Their tiny size always filled her with feelings of grief for their death. She could not bear the feel of their frail bones in her fingers. To her left a shoal of trout adorned a flat wooden dish, overlapped one upon the other, their skins brown-silver in the candlelight, their boiled eyes milky-white.

'Are you not hungry?' her father asked with concern.

Julitta shook her head. Her stomach was empty, but the fare set before her had killed her appetite, as had the formality. She would far rather have sat among the servants in the main body of the hall and shared their soup and stewed meat.

Rolf eyed her thoughtfully. 'It is too much, isn't it?' he murmured quietly, so that Arlette's sharp ears should not hear.

'My mother never gave me food like this,' Julitta said. She knew that she was being petulant and ungrateful, but it had come to her as she sat down to the feast, that in the old days her mother would have sat in Lady Arlette's place. Although Julitta's memory of those times was hazy, she did know that the meal would have been edible and the atmosphere warm and informal.

'Oh, but she did,' Rolf said with a wry smile, 'but never presented in quite the same way. This is how we would eat at court. You are done a great honour. You like fish, don't you?' He deftly removed one of the trout from the serving platter, set it down on a spare trencher, and with a few practised motions of his eating knife, removed the head and filleted the body, turning it over to expose the moist pink flesh. Then he transferred it to her trencher. 'I can promise you it tastes good.'

Julitta hesitated, then flaked a piece of trout off the skin and put it in her mouth. He was right, the fish was indeed succulent and delicately flavoured. As she chewed, her stomach came to life, leaping and craving.

'I would not have thought it of you to be squeamish,' Rolf said curiously.

Julitta shrugged. 'It is easier to eat things if they do not look as if they might still be alive.'

Rolf almost choked on his laughter and had to take a swift gulp of his wine.

Julitta ate the fish and glanced through her lashes at her father, waiting her moment until he had recovered and was ready to give her his attention again. 'May I ask you a boon?'

'Ask me anything you want.'

Julitta flickered a brief glance at Arlette who sat on Rolf's other side daintily nibbling one of the songbirds. She could almost see the woman's ears extending like trumpets to listen. 'Can I ride out with you tomorrow to see the horses?'

His eyes gleamed with pleasure. 'Of course! It would give me great delight to have you keep me company.'

'Only Lady Arlette says that I have to begin to learn how to become a lady for the profit of my future marriage. I did not know if I would be allowed out of the bower.'

Rolf's mouth compressed. He glanced at his wife, whose face

had paled as Julitta spoke out. 'No-one will confine you to the bower.'

'She is twisting my words,' Arlette said angrily.

'I'm not, you did say it!' Julitta protested, her voice rising so that other people stopped eating and looked towards the family gathering with curiosity.

'Most certainly your behaviour is a disgrace at the moment. You deserve no favours.'

'Peace, both of you,' Rolf commanded in a tone that caused the witnesses to look elsewhere and pretend attention to their food. 'I will not have this bickering. Julitta, I do not expect you to air your grievances before all and sundry. You are no longer a small child to throw tantrums if your will is gainsaid . . . or perhaps you are?'

Heat scorched into Julitta's face. She shook her head and looked down at her trencher.

Rolf turned to his wife. 'There is time enough for her to learn from you what she does not know. Tomorrow she will ride out with me and Benedict to see the breeding stock.'

Arlette's lips became a narrow line. 'As you wish, my lord,' she said quietly, a wealth of unspoken resentment in her response. 'Do I have your permission to retire?'

He gestured brusque assent. Arlette rose. So did Gisele, lending moral support to her mother.

Julitta was alarmed. 'I don't have to go too, do I?'

Rolf sighed. 'Better if you remain here for a while to let the dust settle,' he said wryly. Julitta smiled with relief. 'I wasn't lying,' she declared as Gisele and Arlette left the hall. 'She truly did say those things.'

Rolf poured more wine into his cup. 'She has your welfare at heart, you should not take against her so. She is right that you have things to learn.'

'Does that mean I'm to be trained like a horse and then sold off to the highest bidder?' she demanded.

'Selling you off is the last thing on my mind, Princess. I've only just found you again.' He looked at her sidelong. 'Think of acquiring skills, whatever they might be, as armouring yourself against the world. You have learned to survive, to be independent and think for yourself. Now you must learn control; to bite your tongue when it is unwise to speak out. Lady Arlette can teach you a great deal, do not reject her out of hand.'

Julitta nodded sensibly. Her father patted her head affectionately and turned to talk to one of his retainers. A sudden pang of loss swept over her. She desperately wanted her mother, the comfort of her arms, the warmth of her unconditional love. Instead, all she had was the hostile, dutiful care of Arlette de Brize. Her father, for all his kindness and appearance of understanding, was a man and a stranger, self-centred at his very core. He could not even begin to comprehend.

Muttering an excuse about needing to visit the privy, Julitta escaped the hall. Her father's was not the only gaze to follow her hasty exit. Further down the main trestle, Benedict watched her with troubled eyes, and so too did Mauger, a deep frown between his brows.

CHAPTER 43

'She hates me, I know she does!' Julitta mutinously dragged off the wimple that Arlette had said she must wear whenever she ventured out of the private quarters, and tossed it aside.

Benedict paused while saddling up Cylu to admire the glossy tumble of her curls. The July sunshine burnished the strands to a bright garnet red. She was seated on a heap of straw, her legs parted in most unladylike fashion, her modesty preserved by the full folds of her blue riding gown. He knew that, like casting off her wimple, the pose was in deliberate defiance of Arlette. She and Julitta never quarrelled in front of Rolf these days, but it did not mean that the battle between them had ceased.

'She doesn't hate you,' he contradicted. 'You exasperate and baffle her. More than half the trouble that comes your way is your own fault, you know. You should learn to compromise.'

Julitta glowered at him, but Benedict ignored her expression and resumed harnessing the horse. He was learning how to deal with her moods and had discovered that paying her no heed was the swiftest way to bring her out of a sulk. Besides, he was fond of her, and aware that he was the one to whom she turned to air the frustrations and upsets which she kept to herself on the battlefield.

The straw rustled and a moment later Julitta came to the gelding's head, stroking the soft grey muzzle and muscular cheeks. 'She wants to turn me into a copy of Gisele. She wants me to live my life in that room above the hall with nothing in my head but needles and thread and weaving patterns. I feel as if I am in a prison.'

'Gisele has more in her head than just sewing and weaving,' Benedict defended his betrothed. 'Perhaps it is that you do not want to see beyond it.'

Julitta gave him a glittering look, her expression one that he could not define. 'She doesn't like me either,' she said.

'And you don't like her.' Benedict led Cylu out into the fresh early morning. Already saddled in the bailey was Julitta's small chestnut mare. 'Each of you should appreciate the other for her particular skills.'

'Did you never think of becoming a priest?' Julitta snapped waspishly and led her mare to the mounting block.

Benedict laughed. 'What, and become a martyr?'

Side by side they rode out of the yard. Rolf was absent, delivering three young mares to a client in Winchester; Mauger had returned to Normandy; and thus, for three days, Benedict held responsibility for the stud at Ulverton. He was accustomed to such weight, for it had devolved upon his shoulders before – for the first time when he was sixteen. He was a calm, level-headed young man with a maturity far beyond his years – a maturity that occasionally lapsed if not yoked to the plough of serious occupation.

He looked at Julitta's profile, the daintiness of her nose and cheekbones, the sensual cushion of her mouth. He knew well why Gisele did not like her half-sister. It was a matter of jealousy, simple and hot. Gisele's silvery attractiveness became watery and insipid beside Julitta's raw beauty. Men looked at Julitta in a way that they never looked at Gisele, himself included. And God on the Cross, she was not yet fifteen. He tried not to think about that. She turned her gaze to him now, her eyes a dark sea-blue, flecked with green.

'Anyway,' she tossed her head, 'I've found a way of escaping from the hall and still keeping in Lady Arlette's good graces.'

'You have?'

'I'm learning bee-keeping. The hives are out in the meadow

and Arlette never visits them. She hates bees even though she values the honey, and besides, all the grass makes her sneeze and her face swells up.'

Benedict compressed his lips, forcing himself not to chuckle at her resourcefulness. 'The bees will suffer if you slack your duties,' he warned.

'Oh, don't be so pompous,' she scoffed. 'I like tending the hives. Did you know it takes three weeks for a bee to grow from a grub to a worker?'

Still suppressing a grin, Benedict shook his head. 'I know nothing about bees except that they make honey and there is no taste like it straight from the comb with new, warm bread. Even the thought makes my mouth water. I remember your mother giving me a piece of honeycomb when we came to stay at Ulverton in the old days.'

'My mother used to like bees too.' Julitta's eyes grew distant. 'She used to tell them everything of importance that ever happened in the hall.'

'What for?'

'So that they would not fly away, of course!' She looked at him as if he were simple-minded. 'If you forget to let them know who has died, or who is to be married, or when a baby has been born, they will swarm.'

Benedict raised a sceptical brow.

'Well that is what the old lore says.' Julitta shook back her hair. 'Of course they swarm when the queen gets old or the hive becomes too crowded, but it's still best to talk to them. Besides, there is no danger that they will carry tales. I can tell them what I think of someone and they won't scold me or lecture me on how I ought to behave.'

'And I suppose they taught you how to sting too,' Benedict said with a wry grin.

Julitta wrinkled her pert nose at him. 'They die if they sting,' she said after a moment. 'The barb lodges in whatever they attack and they cannot free themselves.' A small shiver ran down her spine.

The destrier herd was spread out over the lush midsummer

grasslands, mares, foals and yearlings grazing together under the watchful eye of a powerful silver-grey stallion, a son of Sleipnir.

Confidently, Benedict pointed out to Julitta the best horses in the herd, and indicated which yearlings would be kept for breeding and which would be sold and for what purpose. Julitta was an interested listener and an apt pupil with a born eye. She forgot to be prickly and defensive, her natural personality sparkling through.

'When we lived in Southwark, one of our neighbours had a horse that came from Spain. It was a stallion, but apparently it had no seed – no mare it covered had ever quickened. He still kept it though, just to parade on. I have never seen a horse so beautiful, nor so intelligent or good-natured.'

Benedict felt the excitement take and squeeze him as she spoke. 'That is what I want to do with this herd in the future,' he confided with enthusiasm. 'I want to introduce a strong vein of Andaluz blood, put more fire in their hooves. Oh, they're excellent animals now, you'd have to go all the way to Spain to find anything better, but I want the name of Brize-sur-Risle to shine as the best. To do that, we need to buy stock from the infidel lands, but for the moment, that's nought but a dream. It is almost impossible to get the Moors to part with a stallion unless there is some defect – as your neighbour in Southwark discovered. And for now I still have to prove myself to your father.'

Julitta eyed him, her own face flushed. 'But you will go one day?' she said breathlessly. 'When you are able?'

'Yes, I will,' he said with determination. 'Once I have learned all I can from your father, and once I've fulfilled my obligation to Brize by marrying Gisele and begetting an heir to continue the line.'

The animation left Julitta's face. Abruptly she pulled her mare round and dug in her heels.

Benedict was startled at her change of mood, but dismissed it as Julitta just being her mercurial self. He knew that she was changing rapidly from child to woman. In the months since he had found her, her scarcely budded breasts had developed an alluring roundness, and her hips a gentle curve. She had grown too, was going to be tall for a woman, perhaps even reaching his own height, which was a little short of two yards. But with the changes to her body, came difficult fluctuations of mood. He had endured a similar stage himself as an uncertain youth of fourteen summers, his voice slipping from high to low, like a file across a sword blade, his burgeoning private parts a source of wonder, embarrassment, and pleasure. Of course, it was different for girls, but he still thought he understood, and held back to give her a little space. Or perhaps the space was for himself.

CHAPTER 44

BRIZE-SUR-RISLE,
SEPTEMBER 1084

'He's marrying my sister today,' Julitta announced to the industrious bees circling around the entrance of the basketwork hive. It was a glorious autumn morning, and although the insects were not as active as they had been in midsummer, there was still late pollen to be gathered and harvested. 'I know I should have told you before, but I did not want to believe that it was real.' Lightly she spread her fingers against the side of the skep. 'I wish it was me,' she whispered, her throat closing with tears.

Earlier that morning she had helped Gisele to dress in a wedding gown of palest blue silk, cut in the new fashion which moulded to the body. Gisele's supple, boyish figure was well suited to the style, and the colour was a perfect foil for her clear grey eyes. Her fine, silver-brown hair had been washed in chamomile and brushed down to her hips in token of her virginity, and a chaplet of wild flowers crowned her brow. Gisele had always been pretty, but today, attired for her wedding, she looked breathtaking, and Julitta had been filled with bitter jealousy. In the end, to avoid being physically sick, she had fled the chamber full of chattering, gossiping women, and escaped to the sanctuary of her bee skeps.

The morning dew had soaked through Julitta's thin, gilded shoes, darkening the leather. The hem of her dress was damp too. Lady Arlette would scold her, but Julitta did not care a bean for the woman's opinion. Indeed, just now she hated her. Julitta's attire for the wedding had been carefully selected by her father's wife. The gown was cut in a similar fashion to Gisele's, but not quite so closely moulded, so that Julitta's delectable curves were not displayed to their best advantage. While the over-dress was not expensive silk like Gisele's, it was nevertheless of a superb quality linen, heavy and close-woven. Arlette could scarcely be accused of parsimony. Julitta had never owned such a fine gown, but the bright orangey-yellow colour of the fabric was disastrous against her pale, satin skin and rich garnet hair. She looked as if she was suffering from an excess of the yellow bile. Julitta had been more than tempted to take from her coffer the knife of which Arlette so disapproved, and use it to slash the offending garment to shreds.

Julitta was not vain by nature – usually she did not care what she wore, but she was accustomed to seeing admiration in men's eyes, in Benedict's in particular, and was mortified to know that today he would look nowhere save at his bride.

'It isn't fair,' she muttered to the bees. 'Ben should be mine.'

'Found you at last,' said Mauger impatiently. 'They're all looking for you. It's time to go to church.'

Guiltily, Julitta whirled to face her father's overseer. He was dressed in a tunic of dark blue wool trimmed with scarlet braid. His heavy blond hair had the feathery look of recent washing, and there was even a gold ring on one of his fingers. It was easy to forget when his daily garb consisted of plain shirts, worn tunics and dusty chausses that he was a landholder in his own right. Today he was the lord of Fauville, and wore his rank boldly.

'Lady Arlette said you'd be here,' Mauger added when she continued to stare at him without speaking, torn between resentment and surprise. 'She says you always visit the hives when you're out of temper.'

'I'm not out of temper,' Julitta snapped.

Silently Mauger held out her cloak. It was a slightly darker orange than her dress and equally disastrous to her complexion. Gracelessly, she snatched it from him and put it on.

Mauger observed her from beneath his brows. 'Lady Arlette says that you're to stay with me until we reach church,' he said

brusquely, and led her to his tethered horse. 'You're to sit pillion.' He gathered the reins and gained the saddle, then reached
down for her hand to pull her up behind him. Julitta perched
on the horse's rump and grasped his belt to hold herself secure.
Mauger's neck reddened, and he shifted uneasily in the saddle
as if there was a thorn under his buttocks. The proximity of his
lord's young and nubile daughter performed a disturbing
alchemy on his body.

They rode in silence. Julitta was in no mood to make conversation and Mauger was more taciturn than ever, his mind
occupied with ambitious thoughts, not unconnected with the
discomfort of his half-erect manhood.

When they arrived at the church in the village, he dismounted and helped Julitta down from the horse. Her body
grazed against his as he set her on the ground and involuntarily his hands tightened. Jesu, it was almost more than a man
could bear.

Julitta pulled away from him, disliking the dampness of his
palms and the look in his eyes. He reminded her of Merielle's
clients at Dame Agatha's bathhouse and she did not want to be
with him. She stared round, saw Felice and Aubert de Remy,
and in relief hastened over to them. Mauger wrapped his fists
around his belt and followed her, his head slightly lowered,
giving him the aspect of a charging bull.

Felice greeted Julitta with a warm hug and sound kisses on
both cheeks. 'Let me look at you, child! My, haven't you
grown!'

Julitta grimaced and plucked at the skirt of the dress. 'I hate
this. She did it deliberately. I'd rather be wearing that old blue
gown you gave me in London!'

'Nonsense! Look at how rich and heavy this material is.'
There was a hint of censure in her voice, as if she thought
Julitta was being ungrateful.

'Yes, so I'll have to wear it as my best gown for ever and
ever!' Julitta's eyes darkened. 'She didn't even ask me if I liked
it, just chose and bought it herself from the mercer. She doesn't
want me to compete with Gisele.'

Aubert raised a wry brow at his wife, cleared his throat, and excused himself, pausing only to put his arm across Mauger's shoulders and tactfully lead him away too.

Felice tried to soothe Julitta's ruffled feathers, but with little success, for she was only uttering platitudes and both of them knew it.

'Perhaps you could dye it another colour,' Felice suggested, cocking her head on one side. 'If you could darken it a few shades, it would go well with your hair.'

Julitta's eyes brightened at the thought of stuffing the gown in a vat of water with leaves of lady's bedstraw and pummelling it viciously with a pole. Perhaps she could arrange something next time the homespun wools were being dyed.

'Anyway,' Felice added softly, 'this is Gisele's day. You would not want to outshine the bride, would you?'

Julitta lowered her gaze without speaking. She wanted to be the bride.

Felice eyed her compassionately. 'You are very young,' she said. 'Too young to know your own mind, but old enough to think you do and feel the pain. It will pass, believe me.'

Julitta shook her head. She had known her own mind since she was five years old, and she had given up believing a long time ago.

The marriage ceremony took place in the porch of the church as was the custom. Bride and groom clasped hands in the presence of the priest and the wedding guests, and spoke the formal, binding words, neither of them faltering, both firm and clear. Benedict was resplendent in a tunic of rich crimson wool and blue chausses, the colours setting off his dark good looks. Julitta had never seen him appear so handsome, nor Gisele so beautiful. She heard other guests murmuring what a well-matched couple they were, how fortunate the families were in having such fine heirs.

Julitta watched Arlette fuss and preen at the compliments, saw the pride in her father's eyes as they followed the bride and groom towards the waiting horses. Beside Julitta, Felice was sniffing and dabbing at her eyes.

'Are you ready to return to the castle, Mistress Julitta?' Mauger said at her elbow. His face, at least, reflected no emotion. She nodded and silently followed him to his mount. As he drew her up behind him, she discovered to her dismay that they were alongside Benedict and Gisele. The couple were pressed close together upon the same horse, Gisele smiling at the unaccustomed pleasure of being the centre of attention, Benedict's optimistic nature made exuberant by the atmosphere of celebration. Averting her eyes, Julitta grasped Mauger's belt and leaned against him, pressing her face against his solid back and closing her eyes as she had once done behind Benedict when he had saved her from the geese.

Bathhouses had taught Benedict several valuable lessons when it came to the art of making love. He knew that such knowledge sat quite at odds with what Gisele had been taught by her mother, and was not a little perturbed. It was like being invited to a feast and then being told that you could not eat any of the food spread before you. And where was the pleasure in that?

Gisele looked at him nervously. The sheets were drawn up to her chin, concealing her pale, slender nakedness. He sat up beside her, his own olive skin tanned deep brown from his busy outdoor life. They were alone and the door was barred, but the sounds of celebration still drifted through the wood. Some folk would stay up until dawn, reminiscing round the fire, talking and singing. He half-wished he was with them now, a guest himself, but he and Gisele had a duty to perform and a bloody sheet to present in the morning in token of that duty accomplished. And the other half of his wish was watching him fearfully for any sudden move.

He reached with a gentle hand to brush at a wisp of silvery hair lying on her cheek. 'You look as if you have just stepped from the land of faery,' he said softly, 'so beautiful and delicate. Look at the difference in our skin.' Adroitly he peeled aside the sheltering covers, exposing her satiny shoulder, and laid his fingers there, warm brown upon white.

Gisele looked and shivered, small goose bumps rising on her

flesh. 'I won't hurt you,' he murmured, 'I promise I won't. Just let me touch you for a moment. Here, rest against me, you're cold.'

Although Benedict would not be nineteen until Christmastide, it had been more than three years since he had lain with his first woman, and in that time he had learned that to light a blaze in a cold hearth, you had to pay great attention to setting the fire. You could not brutally thrust a torch into the kindling and expect it to burn. The flames had to be coaxed and fanned.

Of course, he also knew that he could throw Gisele flat on her back and take her within a matter of seconds to sate his own lust, that it was his marital right to do so, but Benedict's was a sensual nature. He derived as much pleasure from the slow spiralling of his senses as he did from the core of the act itself. He wanted Gisele to feel as he did, wanted to see her eyes grow hazy with desire and then widen in astonishment, wanted to hear her gasp as she arched against him. He could not allow her mother's shadow to have the dominance of their wedding bed.

He continued to whisper how beautiful he thought her, and moved his hand up and down her spine in a slow, stroking rhythm that warmed and soothed. After a while she began to relax and he persuaded her to drink some of the spiced wine that had been left on the night table in case they became thirsty at their endeavours. Benedict set his lips to the place where she had drunk, holding her eyes while he tilted the cup. And then, handing it back to her, he was deliberately clumsy and spilled some of the sweetened wine upon her shoulder. Gisele jumped with surprise, then raised an edge of the bed-sheet to dry herself. Benedict quickly set the cup down on the coffer and grabbed her hand before she could accomplish her intention. Bearing it down, he leaned over her and began to kiss and lick the wine from her skin, following the track of the droplets from shoulder to armpit, to the small swell of breast and the roseate crown of tight nipple, by which time Gisele had given up all resistance, permitting him to have his way.

Benedict led her slowly through the labyrinth of desire

towards its core, pausing here and again to explore and savour. She came with him, eager, and at the same time reluctant. Even as she arched towards the feather-lightness of his touch between her thighs, her breath hissing through her teeth, she kept her eyes tightly closed, protecting herself. And although she put her arms around his neck and her fingertips dug furiously into his shoulders, she refused, even at his gentle coaxing, to touch him intimately in return. It was as if he was asking her to place her hand upon the devil's branding iron.

And then, beneath his sure, soft stroking, her closed eyelids tensed and she began to gasp and buck. Benedict entered her then, and as her flesh enclosed him, he felt the exquisite closeness of release and relief. He had been holding himself in check for a long time while he concentrated on bringing Gisele to a state of excitement that would overcome whatever pain there was, and now she had reached the pinnacle, he let his body have its way, and quickly, before she descended from the height of her own pleasure. The barriers in his mind dissolved, there was nothing but her smooth, tight sheath, and himself filling it, bursting. Her throat arched, her short fingernails imprinted half-moons of lust across his shoulders and she sobbed once aloud, the sound caught back and smothered behind her teeth.

Finally, Benedict caught his breath. Bracing his weight on his elbows, he looked down at her. Still her eyes were closed. Her breathing was short and swift, and a rosy flush illuminated her face, throat, and breasts. He dipped his head to nibble her shoulder and tasted a residue of wine, salty now with sweat.

'That wasn't so bad, was it?' he murmured.

Wordlessly she shook her head, and the colour mantling her face darkened as she blushed.

'You can open your eyes, you know.'

Reluctantly she did so, avoiding his dark gaze as if they had done something shameful.

'Pleasure can be God-given too.' He rolled off her and lay down at her side. 'We are man and wife, we have not sinned.'

She nodded agreement, more to please him, he suspected,

than from true belief. She raised the covers and looked down, checking that there was blood between her thighs and that some of it had smeared on the sheet. 'It didn't hurt,' she said in a puzzled, almost accusing voice.

'I suppose your mother told you it would?' he said neutrally.

Gisele frowned and shook her head. 'She said that it might, but not to worry, it would soon be over. But Father Hoel says that it is a woman's lot to bear pain for the sin of Eve, that anything else is lust.'

'Father Hoel is a sapless old stick,' Benedict snorted. 'I could have given you more than enough pain to satisfy your guilt, but I wanted it to be good for you.'

She bit her lip and was silent for a while. 'It was,' she said in a small, tentative voice, and pulled the bedclothes back up, covering herself from his gaze.

Benedict felt a surge of irritation. What was good was obviously not necessarily right. He drew her against him, his hand sweeping over the curve of her spine and her buttocks. He had intended going to sleep, but a different resolve grew inside him as he witnessed her reaction to his lovemaking. 'Next time,' he said a trifle grimly, as if responding to a challenge, 'will be even better.'

And as Gisele twisted and wept beneath the relentless onslaught of his tongue and fingers, Julitta lay in the bower with the other women, and twisted and wept too in anguish of her own. And alone with his hand, so did Mauger.

CHAPTER 45

Julitta stooped, formed a snowball from the thick white carpet at her feet, and hurled it at the young squire who had just struck a direct hit on her cloak. Her missile hit him on the side of the neck and showered in crystalline fragments down his tunic and shirt to find his skin and make him bellow. Julitta shrieked with delight and pressed home her attack. The youth rallied and chased her. Giggling, she fled across Brize's lower bailey for the safety of the stairs, but her skirts hampered her, and the squire caught her by the arm and spun her round to face his handful of snow. Half-screaming, half-laughing, Julitta fought him off, her hair untwisting from its braid.

Mauger paused at the top of the wooden stairway linking the keep with the lower bailey and stared down on the tussling pair. His mouth tightened, and his hands clenched into fists. 'Arnaut!' he bellowed furiously. 'Arnaut, who gave you permission to leave your duties?' He thumped down the steps and strode over to Julitta and the squire. 'What do you think you are doing?'

The youth released Julitta as if she had suddenly become a scalding ingot, and looked guiltily at Mauger. 'I was on an errand for Lady Arlette,' he stammered. 'I didn't mean anything, it's only bit of fun.'

Her hair more than half undone, Julitta beat snow from her cloak and looked at Mauger through lowered lashes.

'A bit of fun?' Mauger said incredulously and cuffed the lad across the ear. 'More important than your errand, eh?'

'No, sir.'

Mauger cuffed him again. 'Then see to it, and if I catch you dallying again, I'll have you forking dung with the stable lads for the next month!'

'Yes, sir.' The youth fled.

Mauger rounded on Julitta, his hands planted authoritatively on his hips. Since the autumn she had been wilder than usual, as uncontrollable as the steep seasonal winds that came blustering off the Normandy coast scattering everything before them with a wanton disregard. She had no sense of the impropriety of wrestling in the courtyard with one of the junior squires. Good Christ, she was almost fifteen, far too old to be romping like a puppy, far too much of a woman to be a child.

'You should not encourage the lad,' he growled. 'It is not seemly.'

Julitta tossed her head. 'There was no harm in it.'

With some difficulty Mauger bit back the comment that she was no longer a street-hoyden and that she had to learn to behave with decorum. 'Does Lady Arlette know where you are?'

'Yes.'

The word was spoken with such defiant bravado that Mauger knew Julitta was lying.

'You are in her charge while your father is away in Flanders,' Mauger said sternly, 'and you should obey her will.'

'Why should I?' Julitta glowered at him defiantly. 'She only wants to sit me down with a pile of smelly fleeces and make me spin while informing me how much better Gisele would do it if she were here!'

'But you don't even try,' he said. 'I have seen the way you bait her and flout her rules. Do you think your mother would joy to hear and see you now?'

Julitta continued to glare at him, but now her eyes brimmed with tears and her jaw trembled. 'I hate you!' she spat, and whirling round, ran towards the hall, stumbling and slipping in the ankle-deep snow.

Mauger did not pursue her, except with his eyes. She needed a firm hand, he thought, more specifically, the hand of a firm man who would brook no waywardness. Not her father; he was too scarred by the past to deal with her effectively. Head bent in thought, he continued on his way to the stables.

By the time Julitta arrived at Lady Arlette's bower, she was unusually meek and silent, for Mauger's words had chastened her. What indeed would her mother think? Ailith would have laughed at the snowball fight with Arnaut and seen no harm in it, of that she was sure, but Julitta's certainty wavered when she thought of other aspects of her recent conduct. As she silently picked up her drop spindle and began to twirl the raw wool into yarn, she admitted to herself that she was often badly behaved for the sole purpose of spiting Lady Arlette and a world that had treated her ill.

It was a moment of painful revelation to Julitta, as she faced herself and realised that she did not like all that she saw. And when she sought her mother's image in her mind's eye for comfort, she discovered that she could no longer see her face. Her eyes filled and her hands trembled on the spindle, but she continued to ply the thread with determination so that Arlette would not notice and pounce upon her distress.

Arlette, however, had distractions and problems of her own, and although her gaze fell upon Julitta as she worked, in actual fact, she was less aware of the girl than usual. Her thoughts were all for her absent daughter.

She had not wanted Gisele to cross the narrow sea in November with her young husband, it was far too dangerous. A stubborn line to his mouth, a frown in his dark eyes, Benedict, however, had insisted, and Rolf had supported him.

'I cross the narrow sea all the time,' he had answered her protest. 'You have to let her go. She has to stand in her own light, not your shadow.'

It was the truth and it hurt like the cut of a sword, but even more painful was the being apart. Gisele was not only Arlette's daughter, she was her friend, confidante and ally. Not for one instant would Arlette have considered opening her mind to the child who was left for her to tend. Julitta was a cuckoo in the nest. Even to tolerate her was a chore.

Arlette had never quite forgiven Rolf for arranging the marriage to Benedict de Remy when they could have negotiated a match to a family of high Norman blood. Benedict was handsome, diligent and, according to Rolf, so talented that he could spot a good horse with his eyes blindfolded. But to Arlette's mind, he took his pleasures too seriously, and his responsibilities not seriously enough. Quite simply, he was not good enough for her daughter. He could have been a saint and still he would not have measured up to her standards.

Her brooding was interrupted as a maid entered the room and informed her that Lord Rolf had returned from his journey to Flanders. Arlette set aside her sewing and went down to greet him. She was more than halfway to the hall before she realised that Julitta, usually so eager to fling herself upon Rolf, had remained in the bower at her spinning.

Grimacing at the pain in his knees, Rolf eased his legs forward beneath the trestle and wished for spring. He was forty-six years old and in fine summer weather, he was still a young man. But on days like this, after a gruelling journey through bitter wind and snow, his joints told him that this was not so, that if he looked over his shoulder, he would see his youth disappearing towards the horizon.

'Once I helped to dig an English village out of the snow after a blizzard,' he said ruefully to Mauger as he raised his cup. 'I worked all day, and then sat around the elder's fire telling stories and drinking mead all night. The winter of 'sixty nine it was, the year before Julitta was born. It seems like yesterday, but it is more than sixteen years.'

He and Mauger had been discussing the progress of the stud during his absence. People were preparing to retire for the night, dragging pallets towards the warmth of the fire, shaking out blankets cloaks. Outside, the wind whistled like a demon.

Mauger nodded and fiddled with his empty cup. Rolf eyed the young man thoughtfully. Their business was concluded, and Mauger was not usually one to linger for the purposes of conversation. Had it been Benedict here instead, Rolf might have stayed talking all night as he had done round the fire six-teen years ago, and forgotten his aching knees, but Mauger was not cut of the same cloth.

'What is on your mind?' he asked. 'Is there some problem with the horses you have not broached to me?'

'No, my lord.' Mauger shook his head and drawing a deep breath, looked Rolf in the eye. 'It is about your daughter, Julitta, that I would speak.'

'Julitta?' Rolf eyed him with surprise which quickly darkened into worry. 'What has she done now?'

'Nothing, my lord, I am not bringing a complaint.'

'Then what? I haven't got the patience tonight to play at riddles.' Rolf rubbed his leg a trifle irritably.

Mauger swallowed. 'I know that I am breaking the rules of convention by approaching you myself, that I should have a mediator, but there was no-one I felt I could trust. The task would have fallen to my father were he still alive, God rest his soul, but since he is not, I have no alternative.' Mauger paused, took a deep, steadying breath, and said, 'I am asking you to consider me as a suitor for Julitta's hand in marriage.'

Rolf was nothing short of astonished. Mauger and Julitta? 'Has she given you any encouragement?' he asked faintly.

'No more than to any man,' Mauger answered, and then reddened. 'No, my lord, she has not, but I would give her a safe and steadfast home where she would be her own mistress, and not want for anything.'

Rolf eyed the young man warily. Mauger was stockily handsome. Blond and strong. His best attributes were persis-tence, endurance, and foursquare solidity, his worst, that he had a tendency to be sullen, and when he got stuck in a rut, it took an almighty shove to remove him. Until now, Rolf would have said that Mauger was incapable of taking a risk, but then perhaps he had never wanted anything badly enough to do so. Wanting his lord's daughter to wife, especially a girl like Julitta, was more than a calculated risk, it was downright dangerous. Rolf knew that he was well within his rights to dismiss Mauger as his overseer for such presumption, although he could hardly banish him from tenure of his ancestral holdings at Fauville. Mauger might be his vassal, but his bloodline was just as noble and respected as that of Brize-sur-Risle.

'I have no intention of betrothing Julitta anywhere yet,' Rolf said with caution. 'After all the upheaval in her life, it is too soon to unsettle her again. Since she has given you no encouragement, then neither can I, and I would advise you to look elsewhere for a wife if that is your need.'

Mauger nodded, his expression carefully neutral. 'I understand,' he said. 'But I had to ask, and now you see why I had to do it in person. It is between you and me. No-one else knows.'

'I understand too,' Rolf said. 'For your father, whom I loved as a friend, and for yourself, whom I value, I will take no offence.'

Mauger gnawed his lower lip, rose to leave, and then turned back. 'One of the reasons that I came to you is that I am concerned for her, my lord.'

'In what way?'

'It worries me to see her running around the keep the way she does.'

Rolf's eyelids crinkled. 'You think she should be at her distaff like all good women, eh?'

Mauger's face suffused with colour. 'I am worried that not all men are honourable, Only this morning I had to reprimand Arnaut for horseplay in the snow with Mistress Julitta. She made light of it, but young squires – ' he screwed up his face, 'they need very little encouragement.'

Rolf eyed him thoughtfully. 'I take your point,' he said, 'but you do not tame a wild thing by stifling it. Julitta will always be a little different because of her upbringing. You mention marriage. I say it will take a special man to know how to treat her, to yield at the right moment and yet maintain control.' He rose to his feet and limped stiffly in the direction of the bedchamber. 'She knows how to defend herself,' he said over his shoulder to Mauger. 'Besides, while I am the lord of Brize-sur-Risle, no man will dare to lay a finger on her unless he wants to be a gelding.'

CHAPTER 46

Julitta stood beside Mauger in the bailey, silently watching him inspect some horses that a hopeful trader had brought up from the regions far to the south. He said that he was on his way to Paris, but having heard of the fame of Brize-sur-Risle, he thought he would bring his stock here first.

In Julitta's opinion, his prices were far too high for what she considered to be very ordinary beasts. Her father or Benedict would not have entertained the thought of purchasing any of them. Mauger was being slow and deliberate as he examined each one. She knew that he would reject them too, but it would take him twice as long as the other men to make up his mind.

Julitta walked over to the horses which Mauger had rejected earlier before she emerged from the confines of Arlette's bower to watch him. For the most part they were mere nags, basic riding beasts that would serve well enough in ordinary domestic situations where excellence was not desired. The trader had brought his wares to the wrong market. Her father was no bucolic dabbler in the art, but a man who bred, bought and sold top quality horse-flesh for the high nobility. From what she could hear of the conversation between Mauger and the trader, Mauger was expressing those sentiments precisely, and not mincing his words. Lately, Mauger had been more irascible than ever, and she avoided his company unless, like now, the lure was too great. On the other side of the coin, he seemed to be doing his best these days to avoid hers.

Among the rejected horses, Julitta came across a cream-coloured mare with a filly nuzzling at her heels. The mare was nothing to look upon, although the journey she had travelled whilst carrying and then bearing the foal was a testament to her endurance. The colour of her coat was unusual, exactly mirroring the thick, yellow cream that was skimmed off the milk in the dairy each summer evening. Still, Julitta would have passed her over with only a minor second glance, were it not for the foal.

Her colouring was even more striking than her mother's, for instead of being a dappled grey, she was a dappled gold, or would be when her baby fuzz had grown into true, glossy horsehide. She had the sharp, pricked ears, the intelligent eye and the fluid lines that suggested her father at least must have come from Andaluz stock. An aristocrat, lost among the peasants, so small an aristocrat, that Mauger had overlooked her.

Julitta was not so naive as to call Mauger over and make a fuss about purchasing mother and daughter. If they were fortunate, they could obtain both for a bargain price. She sauntered back to the men. 'Are you going to buy any?' she asked Mauger.

He eyed her suspiciously. 'Why?'

Julitta pointed at a jet-black yearling which she knew Mauger had discarded as being too weak in the chest and spindly of leg. 'He's nice,' she said to the coper. 'Can you trot him up and down again?'

The coper agreed with alacrity, scarcely able to believe his luck. Mauger, full of his own disbelief, faced Julitta. 'What do you think you are doing?' he hissed furiously. 'That animal's not worth a bag of beans!'

'I know,' Julitta said calmly.

Mauger glared. 'Then why did you . . .'

'Oh, be quiet and listen! I asked to look at the yearling to distract the trader so that I could talk to you about that mare and foal over there without him suspecting. The mare's ordinary, but look at the foal, look at the breeding in her.'

'I've already looked,' Mauger said coldly.

'And you were not impressed?'

His eyes flickered to the trader who was trotting the black up and down. 'I won't waste your father's coin for your foolish whim,' he growled.

'It's not a whim, it is sound sense!' Julitta's eyes flashed angrily. 'There's Spanish blood in her. Do you think I cannot recognise quality when I see it?'

'You are saying that you know more after one year than I do after nine and twenty?' Mauger's nostrils flared.

'I am saying that you overlooked the foal because the mother is not what you want.'

'I overlooked nothing,' Mauger said through his teeth, clinging grimly to control. 'Even if the sire is pure-bred Andaluz, the mother's blood will bring it down. Your father entrusts me with the management of his horses, not some flighty wench who should be at her distaff.'

Julitta recoiled as if she had been punched. Mauger might have more knowledge than her, but he did not possess the vital spark of intuition. To be slapped down when she knew she was right was a blow that left her first speechless, and then hot with indignation. 'Then he entrusts a jackass!' she spat, and turning her back on him, faced the trader who had given up all pretence of showing the black's paces and was staring at the two of them in astonishment.

'How much do you want for the cream mare and her foal?' Julitta demanded, all subterfuge flown.

The coper drew breath.

'You bargain with me, or not at all,' Mauger snarled furiously. 'I am responsible for my lord's bloodstock. The girl has no authority, and furthermore no coin. And I wish to buy neither mare nor foal.'

Julitta whirled round and glared at Mauger, loathing him.

'Scowl all you want, your tantrums will not change my mind,' Mauger said brutally.

She wanted to kick him, she wanted to scream abuse in his face, but she saw that the deeper she wallowed in fury, the more he gained. Gathering the tatters of her dignity around her like a threadbare cloak, she swept out of the bailey, and only when she was out of sight did she stoop to pick up a stone and hurl it as far and as hard as she could, to the accompaniment of language purloined from Dame Agatha's bathhouse.

For the rest of the day she kept to the bower, twirling raw wool on her distaff with a vengeance while she wondered how many other opportunities Mauger had let slip through his fingers during the twenty-nine years of experience he claimed to his advantage.

In the late afternoon just as the candles were being lit, a servant hurried into the bower to inform Arlette that Benedict de Remy and the Lady Gisele had ridden in.

Arlette's face shone so brightly that they scarcely required the candles, and she leaped to her feet. So did Julitta, her heart bumping against her ribs, her stomach queasy with anticipation. She had tried to banish Benedict from her thoughts since his marriage at Michaelmas, but she had no control over her dreams. Time and again he would invade them and torment her with his smile.

Full of anticipation, full of dread, she followed Arlette out to the bailey. Gisele had been travelling by litter, she had never been keen on riding, and as the contraption was set down, she drew aside the curtains, stepped out and flung herself into her mother's arms. Weeping, the two women embraced. Julitta stopped dead, her gaze held not so much by the sight of Benedict, lithe and strong with a new maturity to his features, as by the cream mare and golden-dapple foal attached by a leading rein to Cylu's saddle.

She stared and stared. Arriving to greet the visitors, so did Mauger, his complexion growing dusky and his grey eyes brightening with rage.

'How did you do this?' he hissed furiously at Julitta.

'I didn't do anything!' she retorted. 'I've been "minding my distaff" as you suggested.'

Glowering, Mauger shouldered forward to confront Benedict. The young man drew breath to speak, but Mauger stole his space.

'Where did you get this mare and foal?' he demanded. 'Did she put you up to it?' An aggressive forefinger stabbed at the staring Julitta.

Benedict looked astounded. He glanced briefly at Julitta, then back to his fuming accuser. 'Put me up to what?' He shrugged. 'I've only just arrived, and this is the first time I've set eyes on Mistress Julitta since Martinmas. 'I met a horse-trader driving his animals towards Honfleur and I stopped to look over what he had.'

'Surely you must have known that he had been here first, and that I had rejected his stock as unfit for Brize?' Mauger said huskily.

'Of course I knew. I guessed even before he told me. And since you had rejected them,' Benedict added silkily, 'I judged myself perfectly within my bounds to buy the mare and foal for Ulverton. The mare's ordinary, I grant you, but the foal shows promise, and if she carries the stallion's line so well, she will probably make an excellent brood mare. The trader was disappointed at having sold you nothing, so he made himself feel better by letting me have these two at a very attractive price.' Benedict tilted his head. 'What's wrong, Mauger? To look at you, anyone would have thought I had squandered a hundred marks on a broken-winded ass.'

Mauger clenched and unclenched his fists as if contemplating using them on Benedict. He brought himself under control, and making a sound of pure disgust, turned on his heel and stormed off. Benedict stared at his retreating back, and then at Julitta, seeking an answer.

'I asked him to buy the mare and foal, but he turned stubborn on me and refused. We had a furious argument right in front of the horse-trader. Mauger thought he had won.' She said all of this in a neutral voice, but then her eyes began to sparkle and her mouth to curve. 'I could not believe it when I saw them on leading reins!' She approached the mare and foal, her hand outstretched. 'Perhaps prayers are answered after all.' She threw Benedict a dazzling smile.

He caught his breath at her beauty. She was so spontaneous,

so different to Gisele who carefully weighed every action, each word and gesture, tempering them all to what was correct. 'Not Mauger's,' he said with an answering grin. It felt strange to smile. There had been little humour in his life these past few months. Sometimes he thought there would be more joy in becoming a monk.

Arlette appeared at his side and greeted him with a cool peck on each cheek. 'Welcome, son,' she said formally. 'Will you come inside?'

Benedict returned her stilted embrace. He and Arlette were never going to be more than tepid with each other. She resented the rights he had over her daughter, rights that enabled him to take Gisele far away from Brize if he so desired, and for his part, Benedict resented the hold Arlette had over Gisele, that made of his young wife nothing but a pretty, hollow shell without a mind of her own.

'In a moment, Mother,' he said. 'I want to see the mare and foal safely bedded down first.'

'I'll come with you,' Julitta ventured quickly, gambling that Arlette would not refuse. Usually she would have done, but with Gisele home at Brize after an absence of five months, Julitta was certain that mother and daughter would want to talk in private without the constraint of other ears.

Arlette gave her a hard look, obviously torn between her desire to be alone with Gisele and the inadvisability of letting Julitta out of her sight. The former won, but only just. 'Do not be too long,' she said sternly and waggled a smooth, white forefinger to emphasise the point.

'No, Madame,' Julitta said meekly, barely able to conceal her fierce delight.

Benedict watched the small, golden-dappled foal curl up on the straw of the stall and immediately fall asleep. Her mother dozed too, replete with the feed of oats she had been given.

'She's a little beauty,' Benedict said, admiring his purchase.

'I could have killed Mauger.' Julitta watched the foal too. 'I sometimes wonder how he finds his face to shave!'

Benedict laughed, but felt forced to speak up in Mauger's

defence. 'Anyone can make a mistake. And it doesn't do a man's pride any good to admit to a girl of fifteen that she is right and he is wrong.'

'Well he didn't do much for my resolution to be of a sweeter nature in the future,' Julitta answered ruefully.

'You? Sweet natured?' Benedict snorted as if he thought such a notion preposterous, and Julitta swiped at him.

'I suppose,' she said wistfully, 'that you'll take her back to Ulverton when you return?'

'You don't think I'm leaving her here with Mauger, do you?'

Silently she shook her head and looked longingly at the foal.

Benedict pursed his lips, considering. 'I tell you what,' he said, 'I'll keep her for you at Ulverton. When your father returns, I'll tell him that the horse is yours. He'll understand when he sees young Freya here.'

'Freya?'

'One of your father's Norse Gods, or should I say Goddesses.' He smiled.

'And you are saying she is mine?' Julitta's eyes began to shine.

Benedict nodded. 'I bought her for Ulverton, but if not for Mauger's foolishness, she would have been yours first.'

Julitta gave a small, joyous cry and flung herself into his arms. 'Ben, thank you!' she cried, hugging him enthusiastically. He hugged her in return. His nostrils were filled with the scent of her, his hands with the feel of her soft, supple body, and his breathing quickened. For an instant his grip tightened as if to hold her, but then he changed direction and pushed her gently away.

A groom entered the stables and Benedict released her completely. 'As I say,' he repeated, clearing his throat, 'I'll tell your father about the arrangement.' He drew a deep breath, and as the dangerous moment receded, his tone lightened and his manner became more natural. 'Besides, I have advanced the prestige of Ulverton tremendously this winter season. Your father cannot help but be delighted.' A note of pride entered his voice.

Julitta watched him, fascinated by every movement, every facet: the shine of light on his heavy black hair and the planes of his face, the cadence of his voice, his lips shaping the words. The place between her legs, the place that Arlette said was forbidden and sinful to think about, was leaden with heat. 'What have you done?' she heard herself prompt.

Benedict moved towards the door and the safety of the open bailey. 'The King's sons came to Ulverton to look at our horses. Robert and Rufus and Henry on my threshold, I could not believe it. Their father has always come to yours for his mounts, but this is the first time that his sons have shown an interest of their own. They wanted to see your father, but of course he is in Paris, so they had to deal with me. Actually, I think it sat better with them to talk to a younger man than with one of their father's years. They bought several animals and promised to return in the summer – and I think they will. Robert was particularly interested in my desire to import Iberian horses for breeding. He is a great believer in their qualities.'

Julitta followed him into the bailey, her eyes upon his spine, his rangy body. Sometimes she thought she would go mad cooped up at Brize and made to live the life of a gently bred Norman young lady. She was none of these things. Her blood was fierce and nomad, and just now, provoked by Benedict, it was fizzing in her veins.

'I know Robert of Normandy,' she remarked. 'He's handsome and very generous.'

Benedict turned and looked at her with surprise. 'You know Robert of Normandy?' he repeated.

Julitta smiled at the look on his face. She enjoyed being the centre of attention and she had certainly grabbed Benedict's. 'Oh not well, although he spoke to me kindly, and to my mother too. He used to visit Dame Agatha's bathhouse when he was in London – he had taken a great fancy to Merielle, one of the girls there. He gave me a silver penny to buy ribbons for my hair, and chucked me beneath the chin. I thought he was nice, but I also thought that he had no more depth than a puddle in sunshine.'

Benedict shook his head in bemusement. *She did not belong here*, he thought. *She was like a caged animal.* 'Robert is always surrounded by beautiful women,' he said. 'Already he has one son to his name.'

Julitta put her hands behind her back and gently swayed her body. 'If I had stayed at the bathhouse, who knows, I might have become his mistress too,' she said provocatively.

Benedict muttered something beneath his breath which she did not ask to have repeated, but the heat at her core pulsed gently in response. 'I wonder what he would think if he could see me now,' she murmured. 'I do not think he would remember me . . . but sometimes I think I would go with him if he asked.' She glanced at Benedict for his reaction, but his expression was carefully controlled.

'You are fortunate,' he said dryly, adding what at first seemed like a *non sequitur,* 'his brother Rufus prefers men.'

'Why am I for . . . ?' She broke off, unable to continue. It would probably be tactless to ask him if Rufus had made advances when he came with his brothers to look at Ulverton's bloodstock. It was not given to every young woman to know about the preferences some men had for other men, but her upbringing had shown her facets of life that would have horrified Arlette and Gisele. King William's own son, the heir to the throne. 'Oh,' she said.

Benedict smiled without humour. 'Gisele could not understand his interest, but I see that you do.'

'Did you yield to him?'

The smile became a short laugh. 'I spent my time with Robert – and you know all about his particular lusts. I took them to a place I know on the Winchester road, where they cater to all tastes. Gisele thinks that we went to a monastery to discuss an endowment. In a way we did. The place is commonly known as "The Convent".' Benedict's expression changed, becoming a trifle perplexed. 'I feel I can tell you anything,

Julitta, and you won't leap to condemn me. It's like having a confessor and not having to do the penance. If I told Gisele any of this, she would run to the nearest priest in horror and go down on her knees for my soul.'

Julitta gazed across the bailey. Mauger was approaching them, leading two mares by halter ropes. 'Who else is there to shield Gisele from life but her mother and God?' she murmured. 'I have neither.'

She and Benedict had to step aside to let Mauger pass. His features were set in a heavy scowl but nothing was said, making his hostility all the more tangible.

In the darkness, half-asleep, Benedict rolled over and threw his arm across Gisele's sleeping form. She was wearing her linen undershift, and had covered her hair with a net cap, signalling that tonight, like so many other nights, her body was out of bounds. He sighed and nuzzled his lips into her soft nape anyway. Her breast was beneath his fingers, the curve of her buttocks a cushion to the growing pressure in his loins.

Gisele woke up. 'Stop it,' she whispered fiercely. 'Do you want to wake my mother? Have you no sense of decency?'

'I only wanted some comfort,' he hissed back.

'Aye, and I know what sort. You're always at me!'

'And you always turn away.'

'You expect me to yield to your lust in the very same room where my mother is sleeping?' Her spine was rigid. She shrugged him off, punched the bolster and rammed her head down into it. The covers were dragged over her ears.

Benedict turned on his back. From the great bed there was silence, but he knew it was not the silence of sleep. Arlette was listening. He thought about inviting her with sarcasm to join their argument. She was the reason behind most of their problems as it was. *My mother wouldn't approve*, had become the bane of his life. He had thought that the months away from Arlette in England would give Gisele time to develop a mind of her own, but instead she had pined, complaining all the time about how much she hated England, the people, the weather, the food. He had tried being patient, he had tried being the stern husband, neither to any avail. In the end, defeated, he had brought her back to Brize, to her mother. That decision had its dangers, not the least of them Gisele's half-sister with her knowing innocence. He sat up.

'Where are you going?' Gisele whispered.

'To the hall,' he answered, not bothering to lower his voice. 'There is no point in staying here.'

She lay in silence for a while after he had gone, biting her knuckles, not knowing whether to feel anxiety or relief. At length, she too rose from the bed, but not to follow him. She clambered in beside her mother and curled up against her, seeking a comfort that would not compromise her soul.

CHAPTER 47

Father Jerome was a Cluniac monk from the foundation at le Bec, and distantly related through a cousin to Arlette. He was erudite, ambitious, and delighted that his house had been invited to found a convent on lands granted to them by the lord of Brize-Sur-Risle.

He sat in Arlette's private bower, his powerful hands resting upon his knees, while his hooded blue eyes took in the wealth of the tapestries and hangings warming the walls, the glazed cups, the superb pale wine, which was far more expensive to produce than its rough, red counterpart. He remarked upon its excellence to his hostess.

Arlette blushed with pleasure and thanked him. In her gown of sombre-coloured, heavy linen, a silver cross shining on her breast, she was the image of the pious aristocratic lady, nor was it a disguise donned to impress the monk. It was her habitual garb. And when the time was ripe, she intended to retire behind the walls of the convent she was founding. 'My son-in-law's father is one of the foremost wine merchants in Normandy and England,' she replied. 'Doubtless you have heard of Aubert de Remy.'

'Yes indeed, my lady. He is a generous benefactor of our order, as was his father before him.'

'I trust the tradition will continue,' Arlette replied. 'Benedict is heir to a considerable fortune, albeit that the wine-trading will be conducted by Aubert's nephews.' She frowned at the sound of shouting below the window and the hollow thumping of drums.

'Gisele, close the shutters,' she said stiffly.

The young woman left her embroidery and went to do her mother's bidding.

Father Jerome raised a questioning brow.

Arlette cleared her throat. Even through the shutters the beat of the drum could still be heard as a muffled thump, thump. 'The villagers are celebrating May Eve,' she said with distaste. 'I know that it is unchristian, a terrible pagan thing, but I can do nothing while my husband permits it to flourish. Time and again I have entreated him to give it up, but he refuses. He says that it is tradition, that the villagers expect it. I have tried all ways to cure the people of their ignorance, but they pay no heed. Perhaps when the convent is built and they are set an example by the nuns, they will be deterred.'

'Perhaps, but most of humanity are weak reeds, easily swayed by the pleasures of the body,' said Father Jerome, and without the slightest twinge of conscience, took another deep drink of the wine. He was a worldly man, who knew the right words to say in the right places, the correct balance to strike with each person. He desired Arlette's patronage, but not at the expense of alienating her husband, or Benedict de Remy, who stood to inherit a great deal of wealth, and who, if he lived to a ripe age, could be milked for the next forty or fifty years.

'What then should I do?' Arlette pleaded.

The priest eyed mother and daughter, pale, nervous, moth-like women. The younger one was fiddling with what he took to be her wedding ring, tugging it on and off her finger. 'Let them celebrate,' he said.

'But . . .'

He held up his hand to prevent Arlette from speaking further. 'But let it be in God's name. Let them give thanks for His gift of the new season. Let the tradition prevail, but let the rejoicing be in God's name. Year by year you can make gradual changes until it becomes nothing but a harmless ceremony with none of the old power remembered. For today, if you wish, I will bless the Maypole in the name of Christ, and exhort them to celebrate in ways which will not displease the lord.'

Arlette's expression brightened slightly. 'I suppose it is a beginning.'

'Of course it is,' Father Jerome said heartily and draining his wine, levered himself to his feet. He was a tall man, who walked with a natural bounce in his step despite his bulk. 'Let us go down now, and begin the blessing. When we return, we can discuss the matter of your convent's dedication. Perchance the Blessed Virgin, or the Magdalene. She is always a favourite for returning fallen women to the fold, and of course, she symbolises spiritual rebirth.'

The cider brewed by the villagers of Brize-sur-Risle was sweet and strong. Julitta sipped from the drinking horn that one of them had given her, and moved among the throng gathered around the dripping oxen and pig roasts, the coneys and chickens skewered across small firepits, gleaming with yellow dripping. There were singing and merriment, jocular conversations, rude riddles, looks exchanged and promises made as dancers flung themselves down to rest for a while before returning to join hands around the Maypole.

Up on the hill, the castle was a silhouette in the twilight. Julitta knew that she ought to be there, closeted in the bower with Arlette and Gisele, praying for the erring souls of the villagers, but unless someone actually came and fetched her, she had no intention of leaving the celebrations. Her father was somewhere amongst the revellers, as were Benedict and Mauger. What harm could possibly come to her? No-one was going to lay his hands on Lord Rolf's own daughter. The atmosphere was magical. Not even that self-important Cluniac monk had been able to dampen the festivities with his warnings about what was and was not pleasing to the eye of God as he sprinkled the Maypole with holy water from the church font.

Julitta sipped the heady brew and topped up her horn from a jug standing on a trestle. She saw Benedict and her father laughing together. Her heartbeat quickened. Benedict had only been back at Brize for two days, delivering some English bloodstock, and she had had no opportunity to talk to him. His visit to Brize in the early spring, when he had bought the cream mare and her foal, had been fleeting. He had not stayed above a week, and had returned to Ulverton before Rolf arrived from France. Gisele had not gone with him, nor, from what Julitta had seen, had their reunion been more than tepid now that he was back. Between Arlette and Benedict, the courtesy was as sharp as a honed knife.

A plump village woman waddled up to Julitta and crowned her garnet braid with a chaplet of white hawthorn. 'You has to honour the Goddess on May Eve, young mistress, if you wants the corn to grow!' she chuckled.

Julitta laughed and finished the horn of cider so that she could put it down while she secured the chaplet to her hair. The woman grabbed her arm and tugged her towards the Maypole, its rounded phallic tip thrusting at the sky. 'Come, dance the sacred dance!' she exhorted.

Julitta found herself whirled into the steps of the Maypole jig. The cider coursed through her blood and filled her feet with magic. She stepped and turned in motion with the other dancers until she felt as if their movements, their very limbs were her own. The beat of drum and the skirl of bagpipes filled the night, the notes flinging skywards like the long orange sparks from the bonfire. Two circles of men and women, weaving in and out, forward and back. The sweaty paw of Brize's miller grasped hers, swung her round and passed her on to one of the grooms from the castle. She saw the flash of his white teeth, smelled his animal scent, and was whirled away to the next man in the line while the music beat relentlessly on, pulsing to the hammerbeat of her own blood.

The next man in line grasped her hand in fingers warmly strong, only a little damp, revealing that he had not long joined the circle of dancers. Benedict pulled her against him, hip to hip, and instead of spinning her round and passing her to the next man, drew her out of the dance and into the flamelit shadows at the side of the great bonfire.

Dizzy, her brain still in motion despite the fact that her feet had ceased to move, she swayed and staggered, then looked up at him.

'Shouldn't you be up at the keep with the other women?' he asked.

Julitta adjusted the crown of May which had skewed over one eye during the energetic steps of the dance. 'What other women?' she challenged. 'All the village wives and their daughters are here. If you mean with Arlette and Gisele, then no, I shouldn't.' She tossed her head defiantly. 'I suppose you want us all safely locked away so you can go "wearing the green" with whomsoever catches your eye.' She leaned across him to reach for the jug of cider, for the dancing had given her an inordinate thirst.

Benedict grinned. 'I was going to say that it is neither safe nor respectable for a young woman of your rank to be here tonight, but I know that you'll only stamp on my foot. The rules do not apply to you. Perhaps I should just warn you 'o have a care. Men do indeed come here to "wear the green" and you are a sight to make any of them forget his reason.' His voice grew croaky on the last words.

Julitta drank straight from the jug and then offered it to him. 'Even you?' she asked provocatively.

'Especially me.' He drank and set the jug back down on the trestle with a wobble and a bang that revealed his own senses were blurred by the potency of the drink. 'You are beautiful and wild, like the May herself.'

Julitta's knees weakened at the timbre of his voice. Her whole body quivered. She was poised with the anticipation that he was going to touch her, and the fear that he would not. She did not dream of running away. Benedict might be Gisele's husband, but he had always belonged to her.

Slowly she raised her hand and laid her palm upon his chest, uncaring who saw. Tonight was May Eve, and people's eyes were dazzled. Even Mauger, her watchdog, had gone into the shadows with one of the village women, and there was no sign of her father.

Benedict swallowed and clasped his fingers over hers. 'Your father said that I was to bring you home in a while,' he murmured, and pulled her tight against him, hip to hip, groin to groin, then spun her away in a muted rhythm of the wilder dance around the phallic pole.

'But not yet.' Julitta stepped lightly, a smile on her face, her breathing pleasantly short as he drew her against his body once more. They arched together, side-stepped and parted, maintaining the link of hands.

'No, not yet.'

They danced and drank, drank and danced. Julitta's hair began to wisp free of her braid and with an impatient twist of her fingers, she shook it free. The crown of May blossom slipped down again, and she would have cast it away, but Benedict caught her hand, and taking the chaplet from her, replaced it delicately on her brow.

'Queen of the May,' he said softly and traced one forefinger gently down her cheek. Julitta lifted her face, mutely offering him her lips. He took them, meaning only to salute the new season, but the spark engendered was beyond all his knowledge, and within moments, beyond his control.

When he was with Gisele – the times she permitted – there was nothing, a pale, cold flame that gave off little warmth despite all his efforts to kindle it to a more robust heat. This was true fire, blood-red of flame, molten-white at its core, beating with the night. Julitta's lips clung to his, sweet and warm, tasting of cider. Her body followed his, as fluid as a shadow, a mirror-image. Whatever his hands did, so did hers, and her lips and her tongue; without hesitation, without shame, until they were both incandescent with lust.

By mutual need, they moved deeper into the shadows, playing out the ritual of the deeper fertility dance. She wound her hair round him like the ribbons on the Maypole. His fingers wove a pattern of desire over her flesh, the cold silkiness of her thighs, the stems of grass between them. Her hips, the dark triangle of the Maythorn gateway. And then his own thighs over and between hers, and the first sure, blood-hot thrust.

Her throat arched and her fingers clutched convulsively at his sleeves.

'Did I hurt you?' He ceased moving, although it was torture to do so; his entire groin was one magnificent, swollen ache.

'Yes,' she whispered, but clasped him to her and raised her hips. 'But if you stop now, I will kill you.'

'Then I won't stop,' he said breathlessly. 'This is a far better way to die.' He lowered his mouth to hers, teasing the outline of her lips, then covering her mouth, enclosing the cry in her throat. The kiss moved in concert with the surge of his hips. She pushed down upon his swollen flesh, desiring to be one with him, and although it hurt, it was the pleasure that was almost too much to bear. She broke the kiss to cry out and clutch at him. She pressed her hot face against his throat. 'Ben!' she wept. 'Oh, Ben, please . . .' Striving for she knew not what, only that she would die without it.

Panting harshly, Benedict knew that he could wait no longer. Julitta's voice, the wild innocence of her need brought him to the edge. He braced himself on one forearm, and sought down between them to the sensitive little nubbin above the passage he was filling. Once, twice he stroked it, and Julitta suddenly caught her breath and went rigid in his arms. Removing his hand, he pushed forward hard, and groaning her name, burst within her. He felt the ripples of her climax swallow over him, drawing each surge of his own pleasure into her body until both of them were spent. But even then, they could not bear for it to be finished, and lay in the grass together, touching and stroking, while around them the celebrations continued, and above them the stars glittered like salt crystals. The enormity of what they had done lay heavy on both their minds, but neither of them was willing to break the joy of the moment by admitting that a world beyond themselves existed.

'Is it always like that?' Julitta asked after a while.

Benedict smiled and drew a tendril of her hair through his fingers. 'No, not always,' he said with a gentle wryness, knowing that nothing would ever be able to match tonight. May Eve, the soft spring earth and a beautiful virgin. And yet it went much deeper than the venting of springtime heat. Julitta, his lovely, wild Julitta. His throat ached with poignant grief.

Julitta sat up. 'Then it gets better?' she asked with spurious innocence as she shook back her hair and tidied the disordered bodice of her gown.

Benedict's eyes widened. For one brief instant he was taken in, and then he realised that she was teasing him. He lunged at her. She squealed and tried to escape, but not very hard. Accidentally on purpose, her hand brushed his now flaccid manhood, enchanting it into immediate hardness. She wriggled and squirmed but not to escape.

Benedict had intended returning her to the castle before the night grew much older and questions began to be asked, but he could not resist the lure of her body. This time they took each other with laughter, with breathless, snatched kisses and teasing touches. Julitta was an apt pupil. As the moment of crisis approached, she stopped moving, lay perfectly still until it had passed, with Benedict, scarcely breathing, poised within her. And then, when it was safe, they began to build again. Higher, faster, hotter, until they were molten. And then, the moment before they were welded into one, Julitta saw her father standing in the shadows, staring at them in disbelief, and with him was the Cluniac monk whom Arlette had been entertaining earlier.

Julitta stiffened, the fire turning immediately to ice. She pushed at Benedict, whimpering, and when he only groaned and gripped her closer, she cried out in panic and struggled to free herself.

Benedict opened his mouth to ask her what was wrong, but Rolf pre-empted him, his voice a soft snarl.

'I should kill you,' he said. 'Get up.'

Benedict closed his eyes. Beneath him Julitta was shaking. He bent his head, took a deep breath. 'Will you turn your backs?' he requested.

'For decency's sake?' Rolf bit out acidly, but turned away, drawing the monk with him.

Benedict rolled off Julitta and adjusted his clothing. He

pulled her skirts back down to cover her legs. She struggled to
fasten her gown, but her fingers were shaking so badly that she
was unable. Benedict in contrast was calm and controlled.
Leaning over her, he tied the drawstring on her shift, kissed her
cheek in reassurance, then rose and joined Rolf and Father
Jerome.

'It is my fault,' he said. 'Do not punish her.'

'The lust of Eve is common to every woman,' said the
Cluniac. His eyes roved the scene of May revelry. 'My son, to
the peril of your soul, you have yielded to the temptations of
the flesh. You have sinned greatly against God and nature.'

A muscle worked in Benedict's jaw as the monk spoke.
There was an open wound. Salt had to be ground vigorously
into it. Rolf stood rigid as stone. Feeling sick, Benedict faced
him. 'I will take all the blame. It was not intentional between
us; it just happened.'

Rolf nodded viciously and ground his teeth. 'It just happened,' he repeated. 'Came out of nowhere, hit you so fast you
did not know?'

'I . . .'

'Christ Jesu, Ben, nothing "just happens" without our will!'

Julitta came unsteadily to Benedict's side. Her hair was
loose, her clothes burred with bits of grass, and fear trembled
through her body. 'It is as much my fault as his,' she owned
with a stubbornly lifted chin. 'As Ben says, it was not intentional at the beginning, but I am not sorry, and I will gladly pay
the price.'

'Harlot, have you no shame?' thundered Father Jerome in
outrage. 'Your own sister's husband!'

'He was mine first,' Julitta retorted, her lips curled back
from her teeth in a snarl. 'I do not care what you do with me.
Now and forever it was worth it!'

'Then you are more foolish than I ever believed.' Rolf seized
her arm in a grip of iron. 'You are coming back with me now
to the keep. Tomorrow, I'll decide what is to be done with
you. Benedict . . .' His jaw worked, the sinews cording in his
throat. 'Just get out of my sight.'

'Sir, it wasn't her fault,' Benedict repeated, his voice cracking. 'Don't punish her.'

'You should have given thought to the consequences before you lowered your braies!' Rolf said contemptuously.

Benedict was not drunk, but he had consumed liberal quantities of the villagers' rough, potent cider. As well as loosening his moral inhibitions, it also served to unchain his tongue. 'As you gave thought when you took and then ruined her mother?' he retorted.

Rolf flinched. His grip on Julitta's arm tightened until she gasped aloud with the pain and then bit down on her lower lip. 'I said get out of my sight!' he hissed. 'Or I swear on the Cross of Christ and the Tree of Odin that I will personally geld you!'

Father Jerome frowned at the profanity of Rolf's pagan oath. He took Benedict by the arm, much as Rolf had hold of Julitta. 'Come,' he said coldly. 'You may spend the night with me in the church before the altar, praying for God's forgiveness, for I doubt that human forgiveness will be forthcoming.'

Benedict tried to shake him off, and go after Julitta and her father, but the monk's grip was tenacious. 'You young fool,' he growled. 'Can you not see that if you pursue this matter now, blood will be spilled? Will you add that to your conscience too?'

Benedict heard the monk as if from a distance, but nevertheless the urgent tone reached him, and he subsided within Father Jerome's brisk grasp. 'It wasn't her fault,' he repeated. 'How do I make him understand?'

'Tomorrow, when tempers have cooled, there will be an opportunity to have your say, although if I were you, I would keep my mouth closed. You have others to think of besides yourself and the girl.'

Benedict eyed the monk. The man's grip was still tight on his arm, and the face was severe, but he had detected the faintest note of sympathy in the voice. 'She is not a harlot,' he said.

'But she has given her body, and she is no longer a virgin,' answered Father Jerome. 'And what is more, the giving was on the eve of a pagan feast. It does not matter who is to blame. In the end, the consequences come to roost where they will, and God sees and knows all.'

Benedict said nothing. They entered the stone coldness of the church, standing amidst but aloof from the May Day celebrations, the hall of God, so different from the vast, starlit hall of the Goddess. He had worshipped at the altar of one; now he came to do penance at the altar of the other, and his heart was a stone within him.

Dragged by her father, Julitta stumbled over the rutted road towards the castle.

'If you have no shame, at least I would have credited you with more sense!' he said between panting breaths as he drew her onwards with the pace of rage. 'You're not some simple village girl to mate where she chooses on a whim!'

'It wasn't a whim!'

'Don't answer me back. I've never taken a whip to your hide, but one more push will break me, Julitta. If it wasn't a whim, do I dare to think that you have been plotting this for some time?'

'Since I was five years old!' she answered, and cried out as she twisted her ankle on a stone and fell at her father's feet, her wrist still locked in his grasp. Her breath sobbed through her clenched teeth. 'Since I was five and you went and betrothed him to Gisele!' She began to cry harder, and blamed it on her sore ankle.

Rolf released her wrist. Hands on his hips, he looked down at her. He was filled with anger, and guilt, sympathy and exasperation. How did he deal with her? The sight of her body writhing in pleasure beneath Benedict's still tortured his mind's eye. He saw more than just the ruination of two lives. For how long had it been under his nose, and he too blind to see? You don't take the whims of five-year-olds seriously; nor of adolescent daughters unless they make it impossible for you not to.

He reached down and helped her to stand. She limped

gingerly on the damaged ankle, and made small, sobbing sounds. Rolf resisted the urge to comfort her.

'Your sister and her mother must never hear of this,' he said grimly, as they began a slow progress towards the keep. 'For the sake of everyone you have ignored in your lust, you will hold your peace, and so will Benedict.'

'But . . . but what about the people who saw us?'

'They were drunken villagers. They were mistaken. Father Jerome will confirm this if he desires my patronage.'

They walked in tension-filled silence for a while, Julitta limping and sniffing on tears, Rolf's face set like granite facing a storm. 'I thought to give you time,' he said as they approached the huge wooden gateway. 'I see I have given you too much. You tell me that you will gladly pay the price – those are just words. Do you think you can stay under the same roof as Gisele after this? Even if she lives in ignorance, you will not. And what if you have conceived a child this night? Are you ready to face the world with your brother-in-law's baby in your arms and say that you will pay the price?'

Julitta shivered. 'I do not regret lying with him,' she said. 'Whatever you throw at me, you will not make me change my mind. Done is done, and yes, I will pay what is due.' Her jaw was set defiantly, but the wobble of her chin gave her away. She was very frightened.

'You have no choice.' Rolf's jaw was set too. 'As you say, done is done.'

Benedict awoke to the glimmer of a milky dawn. He was lying on the floor before the altar of the village church where he had knelt to pray last night, before finally succumbing to exhaustion of body and spirit.

His tongue was cloven to the roof of his mouth and his stomach churned like a dyer's vat. He blinked and wondered with momentary bewilderment what he was doing here. Then it all came flooding back and he put his face in his hands and groaned.

The sound that had awoken him from stiff sleep was that of

a horse being ridden up to the church door and the chink of harness as the animal was tethered to the bridle ring in the wall. Now, the heavy, iron-barred door creaked open. Rising to his feet, Benedict watched Rolf pace down the nave towards him. His father-in-law's expression was bleak, but the fury of the previous evening was stonily controlled.

Rolf halted when he was several yards away, and the two men stared at each other.

'I won't waste my breath by telling you what a fool you are, or how angry I am,' Rolf said. 'There would be no point, and we need to deal in practical terms this morning, not lose our heads. Agreed?'

'Yes, sir.' Benedict felt queasy. He longed to sit down, but knew that he must face Rolf in order to hold his ground. Already he was at a disadvantage. 'If I could undo last night, I would.'

'That is not what Julitta says,' Rolf said with a grimace. 'I could whip her skinless and still she would not repent. Christ, I don't know, perhaps neither of you ever had a chance.' He looked at Benedict from eyes that were bloodshot and pouched with weariness, for he had not slept, having used that time instead for pondering the solution. 'How long has this been going on beneath my nose?'

Benedict swallowed. 'It hasn't, sir. Last night was the first time.'

'No fire without kindling,' Rolf growled. 'You did not just join up to mate like two animals in the wild.'

'No, sir. I . . .' Benedict closed his eyes. A nauseous headache beat behind his lids with a similar tempo to the drum beats of the night before. 'I married Gisele in good faith. There was nothing between myself and Julitta then, I swear it. Nor would there be now if . . .' He broke off and swore beneath his breath. 'I tried to keep my distance, but last night . . . it was too much.'

'Too much indeed,' Rolf said and dug his fingers through his hair. 'Best I think if you leave for a while. I have decided that you can take over my work, search out new clients and good bloodstock, visit the established ones. You need more experience on that side of the trade, and I'm becoming too old to spend so much time on the road. In other words, I am sending you out of temptation's way and giving the dust time to settle. You will leave this morning as soon as you have collected what you need.'

It was a practical solution and Benedict felt a pang of relief, closely followed by one of regret and misgiving. 'What about Julitta?'

Rolf's lips tightened. 'She is my daughter,' he said. 'I will deal with her fairly. That is all you need to know.'

'But I . . .'

'Perhaps you ought to consider your other responsibility, your wife,' Rolf added, his eyes hard.

'Does she know?' Benedict swallowed, feeling utterly wretched. If only Julitta had been his wife in the first place.

'Not the entire truth, although you will come out of it with a whiter fleece than ever you deserve. She thinks that you took part in the revels with one of the village women, and then, overcome with remorse, you spent the remainder of the night in the church, praying for forgiveness.'

'And I suppose she is prepared to forgive me too?' Benedict said angrily.

'I suggest you make your peace.'

Benedict snorted. Making peace with Gisele was like wading neck-deep in carded wool. The best peace he could make was a peck on the cheek, a mumbled apology, and a rapid departure. The shocking notion came to him that perhaps he could elope with Julitta. There were lands beyond Normandy and England, and he had a skill at his fingertips. His soul would be damned, but he would find ways to redeem it through the years. The anger left his face, and a spark kindled in his eyes.

'I'll make my peace,' he agreed. 'I had better speak to Julitta too.'

'You can't,' Rolf said, and there was no triumph in his eyes, only a great weariness. 'She is not at Brize. I sent her elsewhere, this morning, before I came to you. Knowing you, and knowing my own past, I judged it for the best. As far as Arlette and Gisele are concerned, Julitta was indiscreet last night, but they do not know how far. Nor shall they from me. Let them believe that she went no further than drunken fondling.'

'You are building on lies.' The gleam in Benedict's eyes had turned to anger once more, and mixed with it, chagrin, that his intentions should have been less obvious to himself than they had been to Rolf.

Rolf sighed heavily, and genuflecting, knelt before the altar. 'Only because I can find no firm foundations for the future in outright truth,' he said.

CHAPTER 48

Julitta was accustomed to either riding or walking everywhere she went, and found Arlette's litter both claustrophobic and uncomfortable. Every rut in the road threatened to jolt her bones out of their sockets despite the padding of tapestry-worked cushions stuffed with duck down. The excuse of making her travel by litter was that her twisted ankle would not benefit from being stressed by a stirrup, but she knew that the real reason had more to do with keeping her out of sight and under control.

Where she was bound, she did not know, her father had not told her. Nor had she asked questions, still being in too much of a daze. Sorry and not sorry. Stubborn and frightened. Ready to brazen it out and ready to yield. And between all these conflicting directions, she found herself paralysed. Within the litter, she curled up on the cushions, her ears filled with the creak of the wooden wheels and the plod, plod of the horse's hooves as they drew her further and further away from Brize-sur-Risle, and from Benedict.

Nursing the devil of a headache, Mauger avoided breaking his fast in the hall, and went on a slow round of inspection. There were few people about, for it was not much after dawn, and most adults were only just stirring from the surfeits and abuses of 'wearing the green'. His own recollections were hazy, but at least he had remained sober enough to find his way to bed.

Some folk still snored where drink and dancing and lust had felled them.

Mauger was busy examining a mare and her new chestnut foal when he saw Benedict de Remy emerge from a stall and lead a fully saddled Cylu towards the mounting block. Two laden pack ponies were tethered nearby, and a groom appeared with another saddled horse and two chestnut yearlings.

'Early business?' Mauger enquired.

Benedict glanced his way. His fine dark-eyes were red-rimmed for want of sleep, and his olive skin had a greyish tinge. The natural curve of his mouth had been banished to a tight line, and it tightened further in response to Mauger's query, forbidding a reply.

'I thought Lord Rolf was going to take those chestnuts himself?'

'He changed his mind.' Benedict stepped from the mounting block to Cylu's dappled back, and gathered up the reins.

Mauger tried to remember what Benedict had been doing last night, who he had been with, but that part of his recollection was not good. He had been too interested in his own pursuits then. 'Why'd he do that?'

Benedict's fist tightened on the reins, his knuckles showing a glimmer of white, and Cylu pranced, opening his mouth against the bite of the bit curb. 'Why don't you ask him?' Benedict snapped, and dug in his heels, making the grey clatter away from the mounting block with a grunt of indignant surprise.

Hands on hips, Mauger watched Benedict leave the keep, and then, with a superior shake of his head, returned to his duties. He had not been working much above ten minutes when Rolf joined him, and dismissed the grooms with a flick of his wrist.

'Are you sober?' Rolf demanded.

'Yes, my lord.' Mauger managed to keep from sounding indignant. Had the question been asked a few hours ago, he would not have been able to answer so positively. Still, it was a strange thing for Rolf to ask.

'Good, you need your wits about you for what I'm about to say.' Rolf drew Mauger away to a wooden bench leaning against the gable end of the stable wall and bade him be seated. Feeling uneasy, Mauger did so. Rolf was not just going to question him about some mundane matter concerned with the horses.

His overlord drew a deep breath. 'Some months ago, you came to me and offered for Julitta. At the time I refused, but . . . matters have changed. If you still want her, she is yours.'

Mauger's eyes widened upon Rolf and the breath left his body as if he had been physically punched. He did not quite believe what he had heard. 'You are offering me Julitta?' he said in a strangled voice. 'To wife?' His eyes narrowed. 'Why?'

'Because you are the best I can do for her.' Rolf met Mauger's astonishment for a moment, then looked away. 'She is wilful and strong, Mauger, fond of her own way, and taking it without thought for the consequences – like me, some people would accuse, and say that it is only my sin coming home to roost.' He scooped back his silvering curls and gave a harsh laugh. 'I am not making sense, I know.'

Mauger thought, a chill running down his spine, that Rolf was making perfect sense. 'Has Mistress Julitta taken her own way into disgrace of some sort?' he prompted, as certain as any man could be that he already knew the reply.

'That would about sheath the sword,' Rolf said heavily. 'Last night, May Eve. She drank more than she should, and, well . . . enough to say that she is no longer a virgin. It was a regrettable accident. For all her wild ways, I know that she is not indiscriminately promiscuous.'

Mauger was not surprised. He had only to remember her romping in the snow with Arnaut the squire, to know that the potential had been there. And a life in a Southwark bathhouse would hardly have stiffened her moral fibre. He felt a flicker of irritation. If Rolf had not rejected his offer three months ago, this would never have happened. Now Rolf was the one making the offer, and of damaged goods. He imagined the dark red hair spread upon his pillow, Julitta's naked body at his side in the marriage bed. Julitta's naked body beneath someone else last night.

'So the man with whom she lay was known to her? She did not go with anyone at random?'

'He was known, and he regrets it too. It will not happen again, I swear it.'

Mauger dug at a soft spot on the wood with his thumbnail. He thought of Benedict saying *Why don't you ask him?* and he knew the identity of Julitta's lover without having to ask. And that, too, came as no surprise. He had seen the way she looked at Benedict.

'You said that you could give her a safe and steadfast home where she would be her own mistress,' Rolf added when Mauger continued to dig at the wood without answering. 'You can see how difficult it will be to keep her under the same roof as my wife and daughter. They grate upon each other as it is. Life will be made impossible for Julitta now. I have no alternative but to find her a husband, or put her in a nunnery. I know that there are many families I could approach with a view to negotiating a marriage – a good dowry will usually overcome the gravest misgivings, but you offered for her before, and I am giving you the opportunity to have her before I seek elsewhere.'

'How large a dowry?' Mauger asked.

Rolf named a sum that caused Mauger's steady nerves to lurch. It was guilt money, he thought, a sweetening of the sour. It made Rolf's suggestion impossible to refuse, and yet, he hesitated. He had taken his life in his hands three months ago to offer for Julitta, but now the stakes had changed. How much for a virgin's honour? 'What if she is with child? You would not expect me to raise it as my heir?'

'If she is with child, then Father Jerome will admit it to the Cluniac order for a career in the church.'

'So Father Jerome knows?'

'He was present when Julitta was discovered. He needs the patronage of Brize-sur-Risle for his new convent, and he's not the stuff of which holy martyrs are made. Expedience first, religious considerations second. If you take up my offer, he is willing to wed you to Julitta this very day, before he returns to Bec.'

Mauger did not like thinking on his feet. He preferred to go away somewhere quiet and mull things over to himself until he was sure that he had made the right decision. But he could see from the glint in Rolf's eyes, the twitch of his fingers, that the answer was required now. Julitta, he could have Julitta. His blood thumped in his head like the tabors had thumped out the dancing rhythms last night around the Maypole. Julitta and a dowry that outstripped his imagination. Another man's leavings. Payment for sweeping embarrassing debris out of sight.

'Supposing she will not agree to the marriage?' he asked. 'You cannot force her.'

'Oh, she will agree,' Rolf said, the grim line returning to his mouth. 'And I won't have to force her. The alternatives are the convent or a life confined to Arlette's rule in the bower. Faced with those, I doubt she will baulk.'

Mauger nodded. He supposed that it was a compliment that he would be preferred above Church and father's wife, but it sailed dangerously close to an insult. He chewed his underlip, his grey eyes narrow with thought. Powdery green fragments from the bench darkened his thumbnail. Once Julitta was his, he could mould her, bring her around to his way of thinking and behaving. Rolf was not strict enough with her, half the reason for her waywardness. With a household of her own to run and a husband to keep her in order, she would not have time to play the hoyden. And perhaps, in time, as her personality matured and steadied, she would come to love him, and thank him.

'Then I agree to your offer,' he said slowly to Rolf. 'I have no family to consult on the matter, only myself to speak for.' He stood up and dusted his hands down his tunic. 'I'd best change my garments, if I'm to stand before witnesses.'

Rolf let out a deep sigh, although it was difficult for Mauger to tell if it was of relief or resignation. The older man slapped him on the shoulder. 'Tancred was always a good friend to me, as well as my vassal and overseer,' he said. 'And you have served me unstintingly. I welcome the opportunity to call you son.'

Mauger nodded stiffly and mumbled a polite reciprocation. Words did not come easily to his tongue the way they did for Rolf and Benedict. He felt clumsy and uncomfortable, nor did it make it easier that he and Rolf both knew that Rolf was trying his best to make a silk purse out of a sow's ear.

'Julitta isn't here,' his future father-in-law added as they set off together towards the hall. 'I sent her away before dawn — better for all concerned. She is waiting at your manor of Fauville.' He spread his hands in a gesture both wry and apologetic. 'I gambled that you would agree to the match. You can be married in the chapel there, and I will give you a month's leave from your tasks at Brize.'

A honey month, a time for settling into the married state . . . or a time of siege. Mauger thanked Rolf for what could either be a blessing or a curse, and went to change his garments. Rolf had asked him if he was sober. Mauger rather wished that he had been sodden drunk.

CHAPTER 49

Julitta stood in the road and watched her father, the Cluniac monk who had married her to Mauger, and the small entourage of knights and servants, ride away from Fauville. It was very difficult to know who was the betrayer, and who the betrayed. Her father said that he had done his best for her, that she would see it in time, and had admonished her to start her life afresh and be a good wife to Mauger.

Her new husband stood beside her in the road, one arm raised in farewell, the other in heavy possession across her shoulders. She was his property now, her father had relinquished his guardianship when the vows were pledged. Julitta was still unable to believe that she had spoken the words so meekly. It was not what she wanted. Inside she was screaming.

Even before the horsemen were out of sight on the road, Mauger lowered his arm and drew her round to face her new home, her prison. She twisted her head and stared over her shoulder, willing her father to turn around, but the distance continued to grow and Mauger's urging grew more insistent.

'Come,' he said brusquely. ''Tis no use looking back.'

'What reason have I to look forward?' she retorted, and tried to shrug him off. 'I did not want this marriage, it was forced upon me.'

Mauger's grip tightened. 'By your own folly,' he said tightly. 'What you want is not always what you receive.'

'You seem to have landed upon your feet.'

'Do you think my dream is to have a wife who cannot see beyond her own selfish whims?'

'I don't care what your dream is,' Julitta said defiantly, and then cried out as Mauger's fingers dug into the apex of her shoulder with bruising force.

'Then you had better begin caring,' he snarled. 'I won't stand for your sulkiness, and I'm not a soft fool like your father or Benedict de Remy to cast myself at your feet to be trodden on. I am the master of Fauville, and my word here is law!' His voice gained power, the last five words hard and vehement. He fixed her with his stare, imposing his will. When he spoke again, his tone was flat and cold. 'Disobey me, and I will beat you. Please me, and I will please you. I'm a simple man, I live by simple rules.'

Julitta thought of another scathing retort related to his simplicity, but caution jailed it in her head, and a twinge of shame caused her to cease glaring at him and lower her lids. If she was being horrible to Mauger, it was because life was being horrible to her. Was it selfish to want what she could not have, or just unfortunate? Tears thickened in her throat and prickled her eyes. *I will not cry*, she told herself and clenched her jaw.

'Do you understand?'

Unable to speak, Julitta just nodded. Mauger grunted, the sound accepting, but doubtful, and led her into the hall.

Fauville was a fortified manor house, built in stone at the time of Mauger's grandfather. There was a stone tower too, for defence, but this was more as a last resort and was used mainly as a storeroom for surplus provisions and basic weapons such as spears, shields, bowstaves and arrows. If war did come to the lands of Fauville, then the population would remove six miles to the greater security of Brize-sur-Risle.

The manor house possessed a vaulted undercroft to the ground floor, again for storage of supplies. On the first floor, with access by stone stairs and a rope hand rail, was the hall, a handsome room with arched windows and a fine, raised dais at the end away from the door. There was a narrow wooden staircase up to the loft, which ran the length of the hall below, and served as a bedchamber and personal room for the lord and lady should they wish for a little privacy. It was here that Mauger brought Julitta as the day yielded to a mild spring dusk.

The air was dusty and cobwebs festooned the beams. Although the bedding had been hastily aired by two maids, it still smelled musty and stale, as if it had not been washed from its last occupant, who had died here more than six years ago. There were yellow creases in the linen and a nasty brownish blotch on the exposed bottom sheet. Julitta wrinkled her nose. Although she and her mother had lived a perilous existence in Southwark, they had always kept themselves and their belongings clean. She could still see her mother vigorously punching their bed linen up and down in a barrel of hot water, and smell the stinging aroma of the lye suds. And Lady Arlette was meticulous to the point of obsession. The maids were always whisking the sheets away to be washed, and the linens in the coffers were strewn with dried lavender and rose petals to keep them sweet.

Mauger kindled some more rush dips to light the gathering gloom. 'This room hasn't really been used since my father died,' he said. 'I know it is a little shabby, but nothing that a good broom cannot set to rights. You can start tomorrow.'

Julitta stared at him, the resentment plain in her eyes.

'It is your right as the mistress of Fauville,' Mauger said. 'And your duty.'

'Ah yes, my duty,' Julitta repeated flatly. She did not want duty. She wanted love and light and laughter . . . and Ben. Selfish, *selfish. Do your duty, be approved of.* She sat down on the grimy bed, the rushlight shadows lumbering around her, and removed her veil and the circlet of twisted silk which held it in place. Her braids, each a handspan thick and tightly plaited, framed her pale face, the determined mouth and blank eyes. Fumbling, she reached to the pin at the neck of her gown. Dear Christ, was it only last night that Benedict's fingers had lingered there, and then upon her breasts?

Breathing heavily, Mauger began to undress too. From long habit he took time to fold his clothes neatly and place them on the single coffer in the room, and then he advanced to the bed.

Julitta's vision was filled with the sight of his flat belly, the stripe of blond hair running down into his pubic bush and the burgeoning length of his penis. She averted her head.

'There is no need to pretend shyness,' he said. 'You are not a virgin.'

'And you hold it against me. I can hear the anger in your voice.'

'Why should I be angry?' He shrugged, and pulled her to her feet so that he could remove her undergown and short linen shift. 'I'm the one who has you now. You're my wife, and honour-bound to obey me, as I am honour-bound to care for you.' One calloused hand closed over her breast, the other pressed her close to his body and he rubbed himself against her, his organ hot upon the juncture of her thighs. Julitta closed her eyes and prepared to endure.

The mattress was lumpy under her spine, and Mauger's eager weight crushed her down. His mouth was everywhere, wet and searing. His hands rubbed and pawed. 'Open your legs,' he demanded. 'Open for your husband.' Julitta complied. She had no desire to fight him and increase the level of his vigour, which already bordered on violence. Mauger searched for a moment, poking and prodding, then with a grunt, found her sheath and thrust himself forward with the force of a bull. Julitta clenched a scream behind her teeth and arched her body.

'Ah, you like it, do you?' Mauger panted. 'Is mine bigger than his, eh? I know what you need.' He set to with a will.

Julitta bit her lip. The force of his thrusts cramped her inside, but every time she tried to wriggle away, he would grip her buttocks and command her to lie still and take what was due. As his crisis approached, he pounded into her as if he hated her. At the moment of his climax, Julitta's scream blended with his roar of triumph and despair.

In the aftermath, he lay upon her, his chest and belly heaving rapidly, slippery with sweat. Julitta felt the thundering of his heart and heard his breath roaring in her ears like the roaring of a wild beast on top of its bloody prey. Slowly he withdrew himself, and she stiffened at the scalding pain.

Mauger's hand pawed over her body in a clumsy caress. 'I'll keep you so busy, that you'll have no time for thoughts of other men,' he said thickly.

Julitta said nothing. Her thoughts were the only private thing left to her now. She was not going to allow Mauger to violate them as well.

He lay down beside her, continuing to fondle. 'We're man and wife in every way now.' There was satisfaction in his voice, but something else too, as if saying the words aloud would make their union more convincing. 'You enjoyed it, didn't you?'

Julitta longed to slap his hand away. 'You hurt me,' she said.

'You'll grow accustomed. Probably I am much bigger than he was, a man, not a boy.'

Julitta closed her eyes and turned her head away. 'You do not dance,' she murmured, thinking of the weaving of the May ribbons. 'You trample.'

'Meaning what?'

'Oh, Mauger, I'm so tired and so sore. Can't I just go to sleep?'

The pawing hand stopped on the crown of her breast. In the weak glow of the rushlight, Mauger leaned over her. She felt his stare but did not open her eyes. 'I suppose I was a little rough,' he admitted gruffly. 'I wanted to prove my vigour. Julitta, don't turn away from me.' His hand left her breast. She felt a light caress on the side of her face. 'Yes, go to sleep,' he said in a softer tone than he had used to her all day.

If Julitta had looked at his face, she would have seen bewilderment and tenderness fighting for a place among the masterly emotions which Mauger considered fitting to his manhood. But she had reached the end of her tether, and could only feel a deep relief, untinged by any gratitude that he was going to leave her be. Turning on her side, she drew the musty coverlet over her shoulder and curled herself up like a child in the womb.

Mauger lay on his back, staring at the loft beams, and as the rushlights burned down and sputtered out, he wrestled with himself, trying to understand his internal conflicts. And the more he wrestled, the more he tied himself in knots, until anger and resentment were the only outcome.

CHAPTER 50

'Married to Mauger? Is Rolf out of his wits?' Benedict demanded of his father.

They were seated in a cookshop on the banks of the Seine in Rouen. Two of Aubert's wine galleys were in dock, loaded and ready to sail for London. A third vessel was imminent from Corunna, with a cargo of southern wines and citrus fruits.

'Rolf is not the only one without wits, it seems,' Aubert said with a pointed look at the young man. 'In the circumstances, I would say that Rolf did his best for the girl. At least she was not carrying a child from her exploits. That would have complicated matters.'

Benedict toyed with the engraving on his cup. It was October, five months since the folly of May Eve, and not a day had passed that he had not regretted the incident, or wished with fevered blood that it could happen all over again. He felt as if he had done Julitta a grievous wrong, and Gisele too, for all that they were not on easy terms. Rolf had sent him away, but perhaps he ought to have refused and ridden out the storm, rather than running for the harbour of absence. And now Julitta was Mauger's wife. Dour, unsmiling Mauger.

'How much do you know?' he asked.

A serving girl placed a basket of new bread in the centre of the trestle and followed it with two wooden trenchers, each holding a whole flat fish, which had been cooked in a skillet with butter and herbs. Aubert leaned back to permit her to set the dish before him, and drew his eating knife from his belt. 'Rolf told me everything. He knows that I am not a blabber-mouth, and besides, as the father of the other party involved, it was my business.'

The fish stared up at Benedict out of milky eyes and his appetite, such as it had been, vanished. His stomach was still rolling from his journey across from Ulverton. The narrow sea had not seemed so narrow with the wind inciting the waves to buck like wild horses, and the rain striking the deck in freezing silver lances. Besides, thinking of Julitta always made him queasy. 'I love her,' he said.

Aubert busied himself with his fish, deftly filleting flesh from bone. 'I gathered as much. Or should I say, less charita-bly, that to think of my son taking his wife's younger sister in drunken lust was more than I could bear to contemplate of your character.'

'It wasn't drunken lust, nor was it deliberate.' Benedict met his father's eyes, willing him to understand. 'It just happened, and while it was happening, it seemed right. It was not until afterwards that we realised it was wrong, and before we could gather our wits or decide what to do, the consequences were upon us. Mauger,' he said with anguish. 'I do not believe he has married her to Mauger.'

'Rolf says that she appears to have settled down and is mak-ing a good wife. Perhaps she has been given what she needs – responsibilities and a husband who is as solid as a rock.'

Benedict winced inwardly. That was hardly a description that could be applied to him over the past several months. *Responsible, solid.* A pang of jealousy had seared through him as his father spoke of Julitta being happy. How could she be con-tent with an overbearing dullard like Mauger? It was not the Julitta he knew. What had they done to her?

'I have to see her,' he said. 'I have to set matters right between us.'

Aubert laid down his knife. 'If you love her, you will let her be,' he said forcibly. 'A wound never heals if you keep poking a blade into it and stirring it around. You already have a wife.

Set matters to rights between you and her. No, do not look away.' He grasped Benedict's wrist. 'You have a duty to Gisele, and a debt owing to Rolf. These you will pay, and that payment involves remaining apart from Julitta. I know what would happen. And would you still be able to say that it "wasn't deliberate"?' He withdrew his hand. Benedict stared down at the cooling, untouched fish on his trencher. He knew that his father was right, but his words of advice were almost as unpalatable as the food. Never see Julitta again? Her tumbled hair, the look in her eyes that had haunted him for five long and lonely months. He could not bear the burden, and yet the alternative would impose a greater burden still.

'I cannot eat this,' he said, and pushing the trencher aside, walked out of the tavern into the cold, damp air.

The lord of Fauville owed military service to the lord of Brize-sur-Risle in exchange for his lands, and in his turn, the lord of Brize owed military service to the Duke of Normandy. So it had been since the time of the first Duke, and so it continued, although Rolf had commuted some of his obligation by the payment each Michaelmas Day of five warhorses to the ducal household. He still, however, had to provide three knights and twelve footsoldiers for a forty-day period of each year. Sometimes he would take command of the duty himself, but now that he was growing older, he preferred to delegate, and so Mauger was given the responsibility.

Julitta helped her husband to pack his baggage for the forty days that he would be absent. Two linen shirts, two tunics, trousers, hose, leg bindings. A spare, short cloak and coneyskin cap. Her movements were calm and methodical, and her face wore no particular expression. She was being the good and dutiful wife that Mauger expected her to be. Inside, where he could not reach to look, she was fizzing with delight at the prospect of an entire six weeks without him.

People thought that she was happy, that sixteen months of marriage had given her steadiness and purpose, but they were only granted a view of the outside, even her father. Sometimes, if she pretended hard enough, she could even fool herself too. It was like playing at squirrels when she was a little girl. The harder she believed, the closer to the truth it became. It was a defence, protecting her from Mauger by giving him what he wanted. She had ceased to fight him with her tongue. There was no point, for anything she inflicted only rebounded unpleasantly upon herself. For the first month she had wallowed in misery. Her flux had been late, and she had dared to hope that she was carrying Benedict's child. The first morning that she was sick, Mauger saddled up one of the more unruly horses and took her out riding. She had been jounced up hill and down dale for the better part of the day, and when they returned, he had taken her to bed, and continued to ride, vigorously, throughout the night. The next morning, instead of being sick, she had begun to bleed.

'A good thing you've bled,' Mauger had grunted at her. 'We can start again once you're clean, breed some true heirs for Fauville.' Sick and groggy though she was, Julitta had raged at him and he had beaten her until she could not stand up. Then he had put her to bed, tended her bruises lovingly, and explained that he had only punished her for her own good, and that if she obeyed his rules as the head of the household, she need never be beaten again.

And so she obeyed his rules, and Mauger was good to her. And beneath the pretence she hated her life. The only alternative was to run away, but her years in a Southwark bathhouse had given her the practical knowledge of how vulnerable she would be, and so she stayed chained at Fauville – paying the price.

Mauger entered the bedchamber now. He was dressed in his quilted gambeson, the undergarment worn beneath mail to protect the wearer from the bruise of a blow, and from the chaffing of the thousands of iron hauberk rivets. His mail coat was rolled up in a corner of the room and beside it were his sword, shield and spear.

'Have you finished, wife?' he enquired. Unconsciously, he took up a dominant pose, legs spread apart, fist clutching his belt close to the long knife hanging on his hip.

'Yes, Mauger.' She fastened the straps on the heavy linen satchel. 'I think you have everything you need.'

He stared at her, a frown between his thick blond brows. 'I don't like leaving you,' he said belligerently, as if it was her fault that he had to perform his military service.

She met his grey eyes briefly, then looked down at the counterpane of their bed. It was a new one that he had bought from Rouen as a guilt offering after he had beaten her. Three shades of blue wool intricately woven with a chevron pattern. Against her will, she liked it. 'It will not be for long,' she murmured, wishing that it were eighty days instead of forty.

'You think so?' he growled. 'It will seem like purgatory for me. Will you miss me?'

'Yes, Mauger, of course I will.' She looked at him again. To have remained staring at the counterpane would have given her away. And indeed it was the truth. She would miss him watching her every move. She would miss being stifled. The thought of such freedom was as heady as strong wine. 'I will pray for you every morning at mass.'

He took her in his arms and kissed her with that strange, disquieting mixture of need and anger. She submitted dutifully, knowing that she was caught in a cleft stick. If she responded too much, he would doubt her integrity; if she did not, then she was failing in her role as tender wife. Perhaps a life at Dame Agatha's bathhouse would not have been so difficult after all.

Once Mauger had gone, Julitta set about loosening her bonds and rediscovering herself. It was not an immediate transformation, but came slowly and painfully over the weeks. The carefree, devil-may-care Julitta had joined the past together with the princess and the beggar maid. Now the coveted wife peered out from between her cramped prison bars and contemplated freedom.

A fortnight after Mauger had gone, Julitta felt emboldened enough to remove her wimple, shake loose her hair, and bathe herself in one of the laundry tubs, filled to the brim with hot water and a scattering of herbs. Mauger viewed such pastimes with suspicion; they spoke to him of a past that was better buried. Julitta had learned to love the luxury of a tub at Dame Agatha's and it was something that she had sorely missed. She knew without a doubt that someone would carry tales to her husband concerning her relapse into decadence, but retribution was over a month away, and in that time she could think of a believable excuse.

She spent an hour in the tub, until the skin of her fingers and toes was crinkled and the water was becoming cold. Her maid Eda helped her to dress in a clean linen undershift and gown, topped by an embroidered dark green tunic, and looked at Julitta askance when she requested her cloak.

'You be going out, mistress?' she enquired as she fetched the garment.

Julitta twisted her damp hair into a loose braid, secured it with a strip of silk, and topped it with a wimple. 'Don't look so frightened. My husband might not approve of the bathtub, but he will find nothing wrong in my destination.' Which was why she had chosen it. She would spend an afternoon of free- dom, blowing the dust from the old Julitta, refurbishing her, and the tale-tellers would have very little to relate. 'You can accompany me. We are going to visit the new convent and see how the work progresses.'

'The new convent, mistress?' Eda repeated, looking sur- prised. It was the first interest Julitta had ever shown in Lady Arlette's project. As far as the maid was aware, Mistress Julitta had no strong leanings towards religion, unlike the other women of her family.

'Don't just stand there, put on your own cloak,' Julitta said impatiently, having no desire to discuss her motives with the woman. Eda, although not overly bright, was shrewd, and could usually follow a trail to its conclusion unless quickly put off the scent. 'Lord Mauger has told me about it; I want to see it for myself.'

Without waiting for Eda, Julitta pinned her cloak across her breast and swept out of the room to order a groom to saddle her horse.

Rolf had granted a wooded ridge to the east of his keep at Brize-sur-Risle for the building of the Cluniac convent dedicated to the Magdalene, and with that grant, he had bestowed the revenues from one village and the rights to take tolls on the road that wound its way along the foot of the ridge towards Honfleur. It was a generous endowment, but then the lord of Brize-sur-Risle had a position to maintain among his peers, where religious endowment was fashionable, and even had he been inclined to let fashion pass him by, he had a pious wife, who was determined that he would do his duty to God and the Church, and glorify his own name in so doing.

The air was redolent with the golden feel of autumn. There was a sense of wistfulness lingering among the harvest stubble and the ripening bramble bushes as the year gathered speed towards its ending. Julitta savoured each moment of freedom, storing it in her mind against the barren times to come. She rode her mare at a faster pace than Mauger would have approved, and Eda squeaked in fear as she clung precarious pillion to the one of the escorting men-at-arms.

The ridge had been felled of its trees, and a new pathway ran like a white scar to the building site. Nuns, masons and labourers had arrived in the early spring, and now, almost seven months later, the foundations had been laid, the service buildings mapped out, and the main structure of the convent had begun to rise from the landscape in white Caen stone. A mason's apprentice with a hod load of mortar passed in front of Julitta, and ran lightly up a withy walkway to the craftsmen working on the walls. The chink of chisel on stone carried like the chime of a chapel bell, and the air was powdery with dust. In the midst of it, a brawny cook stirred a cauldron of pottage for the workforce. Julitta gazed round at the activity. People who thought Arlette de Brize had a gentle nature should come here, she thought. Every stone was a testimony to her determination to have her way.

As if her thought had summoned the image, Julitta's attention was drawn to a small travelling wain that had been drawn up in the shade of two oak trees on the edge of the bustling site. A servant was watering the two horses between the shafts, and another man was helping Arlette de Brize descend from the rear of the wain.

Julitta pulled a face. This, she had not bargained for. She and Arlette had seen very little of each other in the months since Julitta's marriage, and the arrangement had suited both parties very well. *Dear Jesu*, she prayed, her stomach knotting, *please don't let Gisele be with her.*

Another woman descended from the wain, but it proved only to be Arlette's serving woman, and Julitta's stomach unclenched. She could not have faced Benedict's dainty blonde wife with any degree of equanimity. Clicking her tongue, she urged her mare in the direction of the wain, knowing that she would have to make a polite greeting whatever her private dismay.

Arlette de Brize had been talking to the master mason, but when Julitta approached, she broke off her conversation, and stiffened her spine. Julitta could tell from the gesture that Arlette was as uncomfortable as she about the encounter.

'It is a fine afternoon to ride out,' Julitta said, and gestured at the bustle. 'I came to see how work is progressing.' In her own ears, her excuse sounded lame and she felt her face grow hot beneath the other woman's cool scrutiny.

'It is progressing very well,' Arlette responded. 'I did not know that you had an interest.'

'More of a curiosity.'

Arlette pursed her lips. 'I see,' she murmured.

Julitta had the disturbing impression that Arlette did see, all too clearly. 'When will it be completed?' she asked quickly, and kicking her feet from the stirrups, dismounted.

Arlette frowned at Julitta's lack of propriety in not waiting for her groom to help her down as etiquette demanded, but passed no comment. 'It is to be consecrated at Easter of next year, but of course, work will continue for many years yet, to the greater glory of God. Come,' she took Julitta by the arm. 'You say you are curious. Let me show you what you say you have come to see.'

Julitta glanced at Arlette's hand where it gripped and guided, and was surprised at its boniness. Surely the rings had not hung so loosely before, or seemed too large and bulky for the fingers? Arlette's breath had a stale, sick smell too, and Julitta had to keep holding her own in order not to inhale the rank odour. Arlette led her through the chapel, refectory, cloister, chapter-house and dorter, and the further they walked, the slower Arlette became, and the more she leaned upon Julitta's arm.

Her father's wife stopped in what was to be the guesthouse, with rooms set aside for women who wished to retire from the world without necessarily taking holy vows. 'One day, I intend living here myself,' she announced, gesturing around a room that was no more than a mere outline in ashlar and rubble. 'In a year or two.'

Julitta gazed at the view of undulating fields and woods. In the distance, she could just see the stone battlements of Brize-sur-Risle. Nostalgia stung her eyes. It was more than a year since she had dwelt within its embrace, and danced in the May meadows outside its gates. Perhaps she would never enter its precinct again. She was desperate to enquire after Benedict and knew that she must not. *You are Mauger's wife*, she told herself, *and you should not even be here. Decorum is everything*.

'Is my father at Brize?'

'Is your father ever at Brize?' Arlette responded a trifle tartly. 'No, he has gone to a horse fair in Bruges. I am alone. Gisele is with Benedict.'

Julitta swallowed. 'In England?' she asked, when she was sure of her voice.

Arlette shook her head. 'Gisele hates crossing the narrow sea. They are in Rouen, to make an offering at the tomb of St Petronella.'

'Why St Petronella?' Julitta was forced to ask. As a child, she had paid very little attention to her saints' days, and knew only the most important ones.

'She can work miracles. Women who offer at her tomb, often quicken with child within a month of the visit. I prayed there nine moons before Gisele was born.'

It was on the tip of Julitta's tongue to say that women who wore the green on May Eve frequently quickened within a month of the event too, but she held her tongue. That avenue was fraught with thorns of personal pain. Nor did she want to think of Gisele and Benedict lying together. 'I wish them well,' she managed to say.

'Perhaps you and Mauger should do the same. It is more than a year since you were married.'

Julitta said nothing. She did not want children who looked like Mauger. She wanted children who looked like Benedict. And that opportunity had bled away.

'You have settled well to the yoke of marriage.' Arlette gave her a sidelong look. 'There were times when I despaired of you, but Mauger seems to have tamed your wildness.'

Julitta compressed her lips. Caged, not tamed, she thought, and to emphasise the point to herself moved away from Arlette in the direction of her mount. A long gallop on the way home would dispel some of the frustration. Arlette followed her, but after no more than three paces, desisted with a gasp and pressed her hand to her side.

Julitta turned at the sound and was just in time to see Arlette stagger and fall. She hastened back to her and dropped at her side. Arlette's features were twisted with pain. Her right hand was pressed over her lower stomach and her breathing was short and distressed.

Julitta did not ask what was wrong. Arlette was so consumed by the agony that she was obviously incapable of answering. From the manner she was clutching her abdomen, it was clear where the problem lay and there was nothing Julitta could do except soothe, reassure, and summon help.

Arlette's maidservant wrung her hands at the plight of her mistress, and began to blubber. 'She's had the pains since Easter time, but never as bad as this before!' the woman sobbed, kneading the end of her wimple for comfort. She refused to touch Arlette, and Julitta realised grimly that even threats of a beating or dismissal would not coerce her into helping. The woman had a mortal fear of sickness, that was a sickness in itself.

'Go and plump up the cushions in the wain for your mistress,' Julitta snapped, 'then take one of the grooms and ride on ahead to let them know at Brize. Don't just stand there gawking like a codfish, go on!' She shooed a furious hand. The woman swallowed, dipped a curtsey, and fled. 'Eda, Simon, help me raise her into the litter,' Julitta commanded her own servants.

When the young serjeant raised Arlette from the ground, she screamed and doubled up, and he almost dropped her. Lifting her into the wain was a struggle, but he succeeded, and laid her clumsily down upon the cushions. Arlette lolled, semi-conscious, a continuous low moan issuing from her throat.

'What shall we do, mistress?' Eda's voice was a frightened whisper.

Julitta gnawed her lip. Panic was infectious. In a moment, all the servants would be baulking. She realised that the responsibility for seeing that they did not, was hers, and almost baulked herself. Then she drew a deep breath and steadied down. 'Simon,' she called to the young serjeant, who was waiting at the side of the wain.

'Mistress Julitta?' He stood to attention, all brawny two yards of him. Everyone liked Simon. He was intelligent, good-humoured, and quietly dependable. Even Mauger, who could usually find reason to grumble, had never said anything against the young man.

'Return to Fauville and let them know what has happened. I am going to ride on to Brize with Lady Arlette. There is no-one of authority there, so I will remain until either my father or Lady Gisele returns.'

He departed straight away. Julitta grimaced. Now she was more alone than ever.

The journey to Brize was no more than two miles, but it seemed to take forever. The wain travelled slowly and the driver was careful, but each time the wheels rumbled into a rut on the road, Arlette would groan and clutch her belly. Julitta sat beside her, holding her hand, trying to comfort her. She suspected that Arlette would only become quiet when she was given a potion to deaden the pain. Syrup of poppies usually worked, although too much could kill. Perhaps that would be a blessing in disguise, she thought, watching Arlette twist and struggle like an animal in a trap. How thin she was, nothing more than skin and bone. Reminded of her own mother, Julitta had to struggle with a sudden upsurge of grief. Arlette de Brize did not have the coughing sickness, but something just as deadly was eating her away. Julitta wondered if her father's wife would live to see her convent consecrated, let alone live within its confines as its patroness.

Arlette opened her eyes and her gaze wandered around the chamber, drifting and resting and drifting again like a leaf blown by the wind. Julitta leaned over her, and saw the eyes struggle to focus. Poppy syrup not only served to quieten pain, it also impeded a patient's vision and coherence.

'Gisele?' Arlette licked her lips and strove to sit up.

'No, it is Julitta. I do not know if you remember, but you fell ill at the convent and I brought you home.'

'I want my daughter.'

'She will be here soon, I am sure,' Julitta soothed and plumped the pillows at Arlette's back. 'Are you still in pain?'

Arlette's hand travelled to her abdomen and briefly explored. 'It is still there,' she said, 'but it gnaws quietly now.' She plucked at the embroidered coverlet. 'Sometimes it is worse than others. I should not have travelled out as I did, but I wanted to see the convent.' Her cloudy gaze perused the room once more before returning to Julitta, and although unfocused, her eyes were shrewd. 'People say that you are your father's daughter; you have his looks, his ways about you, but I do not believe that is the entire story.'

'Do you not?' There was a touch of hostility in Julitta's tone. She had heard Arlette's opinion of her worth several times in the past and was wary of any new pronunciations.

'You need not have brought me home to Brize and seen me to my bed. You need not have stayed to see me wake. I do not delude myself that there is any tender emotion between us, but the fact remains that you are here. That is more than I have ever been able to say of your father. You have a steadiness that he lacks, and that must surely come from your mother.'

'A steadiness in me?' Julitta stifled a bitter laugh. 'I think not.'

'It is true.'

Julitta shook her head. 'If I have more steadiness,' she said, 'then I also had more wildness, and that too comes from my mother.' And quickly changed the subject as she was assaulted by a prickling of tears. 'Is there anything you need?'

Arlette sighed and moved her head restlessly on the pillows. 'I need to see my daughter,' she said. 'May God speed her home from Rouen. A word with Father Hoel will do for the moment. I am in need of spiritual comfort.'

Julitta inclined her head and went to the door. She could have sent one of the maids, but she wanted to escape from the claustrophobic grip of the sick woman's presence. It was not Arlette de Brize lying in that bed, it was her own mother, and with that association, came all the other memories of those terrible days.

She was crossing the bailey in search of Father Hoel, when the riders entered through the gateway, a westering sun gilding their silhouettes. There was a large travelling wain drawn by four horses in single line, and a small escort of men-at-arms. Julitta stood aside to let the wain draw into the yard, and raised her hand to shade her eyes against the glint of the low sun.

Benedict dismounted from Cylu, his favourite grey, and handed the reins to an attendant. His black hair was wind-ruffled, and his features were clear-cut, etched in sun-gold. Her eyes traced every facet and nuance, remembering, and memo-rising. The expressive eyebrows, the quick, dark eyes, the Hellenic nose and the mobile mouth. She thought that he looked tired and a little grim. Perhaps the tomb of St Petronella had been an ordeal. He was wearing a soldier's quilted gambe-son and a sword hung at his left hip, but these were his customary travelling clothes. A soldier, so her father always said, was less likely to be attacked on the road than a merchant, and he had drilled it into all who served him.

The moment came when their eyes met. His widened, and he silently formed her name on his lips. She saw him struggle with the shock and a sudden assault of emotions. 'Julitta?' he said, this time aloud, and his gaze devoured her, as hers had earlier been devouring him.

They were in full public view, and Julitta was horribly conscious that all eyes were upon them. At the moment they saw nothing but the lord's daughter doing her duty to her brother-by-marriage, but that could soon change, especially in the light of rumours from the village concerning a certain May Eve celebration. She decided against kissing him on both cheeks. Better to keep a distance between them, both physical and emotional. It was the 'steadiness' in her which Arlette had earlier identified. She tore her gaze from his. 'Is Gisele with you?'

His brows twitched together. She could tell that he was wondering what to read into the question. 'Yes, in the wain.' He gestured brusquely.

Avoiding him, Julitta went round to the rear of the travelling cart. An attendant was helping Gisele to descend from the cushioned interior. One slender hand rested on the man's sleeve, the other grasped the skirts of her gown and tunic to prevent them from impeding her progress. As usual, she was immaculate, looking almost like a statuette of the Virgin in a well-endowed chapel. There was nothing rumpled about her to suggest that she had just arrived from Rouen after a day on the road.

Gisele set her feet on the ground, released her grip on the attendant, thanked him with a cool little half-smile the image of her mother's, and then stopped and stared as she saw Julitta. The half-smile faded. 'Sister?' she said politely, and leaning forward, kissed the air near Julitta's cheek. 'What brings you to Brize?'

'Your mother was taken sick at her convent,' Julitta said without preamble. 'I was there too, so I brought her home and promised to stay with her until you came. I was looking for Father Hoel when you arrived.'

'Father Hoel?' Gisele's face paled and she closed her fist

around a silver cross and a small phial of holy water lying on her bosom. 'Is she so sick?'

Julitta shook her head. 'I do not know. All she said was that she required spiritual comfort. And of course she wants you.'

Gisele swallowed. 'I must go to her,' she said, and looked at her husband, as he came around the side of the wain. 'My mother . . .' she started to say.

'Yes, Doucette, I heard,' Benedict's tone was carefully neutral as he stepped aside to let her pass.

'If I had known how ill she was I would never have gone to Rouen!' Her fist still clenched on her religious jewellery, Gisele hurried towards the hall, her cloak billowing behind her. Julitta quickly turned to follow her, keeping a distance between herself and Benedict. She did not even want to feel the warmth from his body.

'Julitta, stay a moment,' he entreated.

His eyes were upon her spine; she could feel them as surely as if he had touched her. Against her better judgement she stopped, but she did not turn round. 'For what?' she asked the busy courtyard before her eyes. 'What is there to say?'

He made a wry sound. 'Too much, I don't know where to begin.'

'Then don't.' She bit her lip. 'It has taken me a long time to find my balance on this sword edge. I don't want to be cut again.'

'I'm sorry. Perhaps that should come first.'

Someone was unhitching the horses from the wain and the baggage was being unloaded. An attendant approached Benedict with a query, and he answered with distracted impatience.

Julitta briefly closed her eyes, summoning her strength. 'There is no point to this,' she said. 'I cannot bear it.' And walked briskly away from him, forcing each foot down upon the bailey floor, welcoming the sting of pain.

Benedict watched her and stamped his foot too in frustration. His first impulse was to stride after her, grab her arm and spin her round to listen to him, but he curbed it so that it was only an image of the mind. There were too many witnesses for what needed to be a personal discussion. He dug his hands through his hair in a gesture he had unconsciously picked up from Rolf, and cursed softly through his teeth. On that fateful May Eve they had both jumped into the river, had been tossed and churned in its turbulence, and finally, washed ashore on opposite banks. Now he had to build a bridge across the torrent so that at least they could have a meeting point without danger of falling in again. Perhaps it was impossible. He was fully aware that he had more than one bridge to build, not least between himself and his wife.

In Rouen, he and Gisele had knelt and prayed at the tomb of St Petronella. It was almost three years since they had wed, and in all that time, Gisele had never quickened. Of course, he admitted to himself, he had often been apart from her, and the times they did share a bed, Gisele was adamant on church strictures concerning the act of copulation. Never in Lent or on a Holy day; never in daylight. Even candlelight was shameful, and it was better to remain clothed. If he forced her to go against these rules, she became tearful, and would go remorsefully to confession, imploring him to do the same for the sake of his mortal soul.

Her mother's recent ill health had changed matters somewhat. Arlette had wistfully hinted about holding her first grandchild in her arms. Prayers had been said, and Gisele had taken to drinking potions of betony and figwort in the belief that these would help her to quicken. And although not particularly enthusiastic, she had made herself a more willing bedmate. Without success as yet, hence the visit to St Petronella.

Benedict left the attendants to finish unloading the wain and went to the hall. A rapid glance around the main room revealed no sign of Julitta. The household was dining on an evening meal of meat stew and flat loaves. The seats at the high table were occupied by several of the Brize knights and their families, but the heavy carved chairs at the head of the board were empty. He could have sat there and presided over the meal, but he owned neither the desire nor the appetite.

Leaving the hall, he climbed the outer stairs to the rooms above. Julitta was not here either. He walked past the loom, the polished bench, the precisely placed coffer on which stood a small basket containing hair ribbons and fillets, and a carved antler comb. He pushed aside the curtain which partitioned off the bedchamber, and entered its private sanctum.

Arlette was propped upon a mountain of pillows. Against the linen of her chemise, her face was positively yellow, and the bones of her face were gaunt. Benedict was shocked by her appearance. He knew that her health had been poor, but it had always seemed suspicious to him that it deteriorated whenever Gisele had to give her attention elsewhere. Now he could see her mortality written in her eyes.

Gisele sat on the bed, holding her mother's hand and talking quietly, but she ceased when Benedict entered and glanced at him with worried eyes. To one side, her maid was making up a truckle bed with clean linens and sorting Gisele's bedrobe from the travelling coffer that had been lugged up the stairs from the bailey. Benedict eyed these signs with depressed resignation. So much for St Petronella.

Advancing to the bed, he leaned over and kissed Arlette on her hot, dry cheek. 'Mother,' he acknowledged dutifully and resisted the urge to wipe his mouth on the back of his hand.

'Son.' Arlette's own response was tepid.

Benedict knew the rules of the women's domain. It was his duty to pay his respects and then depart. The only men who had access to the bower and bedchamber were those of the family – Rolf, himself, and Mauger at the limit. Arlette had always made it clear that he was tolerated rather than welcomed.

'I am sorry to hear that you are unwell.'

Arlette shrugged. 'It will pass,' she said wearily. 'It always has before.'

'You need sleep, Mama, and plenty of rest with someone to look after you.' Gisele patted the hand beneath her own. 'I am here now, and I promise not to leave your side until you're better.'

'You're a good child.' Arlette's gaunt face brightened slightly. Then she looked at Benedict. 'I asked Julitta to bring Father Hoel to me, but I think she must have forgotten. Will you go and see if you can find him?'

Benedict complied with alacrity, as glad to leave the room as Arlette was to see him go. On the outer staircase he inhaled deeply of the crisp September air, cleansing his lungs. A full, silver moon was rising, in a clear, star-bright night sky, beautiful and cold.

At the foot of the stairs, he encountered Father Hoel on his way up. Obviously Julitta had not forgotten. When he enquired as to her whereabouts, the elderly priest spread his hands.

'I do not know. I only met her in passing in the bailey. You could ask the guards.'

'Thank you, I will.'

Within the keep torches, candles and rush dips shed their light and shadow over plastered walls, embroideries and hangings. Hazy ribbons of blue smoke layered the hall and meandered without any great haste towards the vent holes.

Viewed from the wooden stairway connecting the upper and lower sections of the castle, the river Risle possessed the black sparkle of a jet necklace and the surrounding land was an ocean of soft, dark-blue hummocks. He heard the snort of a dozing horse, and the intermittent creaking of a storeshed door.

The guards on duty near the gates in the lower bailey were warming themselves at a brazier filled with firewood. One of the wives had brought out a covered iron container of pottage for their supper, and her husband was setting it to keep warm. Benedict's query was met with shaken heads and frowns. No, she had not left the keep. Yes, she had been in the bailey talking to the priest, but they hadn't taken much notice of where she went after that.

Benedict did not want to make too much of an issue of his search and arouse unwelcome curiosity. 'If you see her, tell her that I will be in the solar or the hall,' he said casually, and turned away.

A child belonging to the soldier's wife had wandered across his path and he almost tripped over the infant. Its face and hands were shiny and sticky from the piece of honeycomb it had been sucking with total absorption. A glistening smear dripped down the expensive blue wool of Benedict's tunic. Mortified, the mother grappled her offspring away, apologising profusely.

Her words fell upon deaf ears. 'Of course, the bees,' Benedict said with a gleam of comprehension, and to the bewilderment of the gathering around the brazier, set off in the direction of Arlette's garden. It was built against the outer wall, a haven of retreat, a pleasant suntrap, where Arlette and Gisele came in fine weather to sew and listen to moral fables and readings from the scriptures. The garden was surrounded on three sides by walls, with a gated entrance to prevent animals from wandering in and destroying the plants, of which Arlette was inordinately proud.

The moonlight cast a luminous, silverish light over trees and shrubs, herbs and flowers. Scents assaulted him, sweet, bitter, astringent, muskily soft. Drugged moths floated from flower to flower, and above his head he heard the shrill squeaks of hunting bats. He followed the path to the well which was the garden's focal point. The gardener had left a hoe leaning against its side, and a wooden dibbing stick, the soil dark on its tip. Benedict continued along the path until he came to the corner against the outer wall, his footfalls and breathing cat-light.

She was there, standing beside the straw bee skeps, her hand lightly pressed against the nearest one, and she was talking in a low voice, too low for him to hear what she was saying. Her hair was loose, curling to her hips, and her discarded wimple was draped over the chamomile seat at her side.

'Talking to the bees again?' he said softly. 'I thought that I would find you here.'

She gave a small cry and spun to face him, her hand going to her throat.

'I didn't mean to startle you,' Benedict said swiftly, 'but if I had made my presence known before, I feared you would run away.' He straddled the path, blocking her exit.

Julitta lowered her hand. 'And not without cause,' she said, but made no move to try and escape. Her eyes gleamed in the darkness. The rich tendrils of her hair framed her face. He could see the rapid rise and fall of her breasts and knew that her breathing was no less rapid than his own.

'I haven't spoken to you . . . God's eyes, even seen you since that last May Eve we were together.'

Her jaw tightened. 'I thought that there were reasons for that, good reasons.'

'Oh yes, the reasons were good,' he answered grimly. 'I was given them from all directions until I was nearly out of my mind. I have reached the conclusion that I have no reason where you are concerned. You have left your footprint on my soul.'

She drew a shuddering breath. 'You have always had a way with words.'

'It goes much deeper than words. May Eve . . . was more than lust. We both know that.'

Almost without realising, she swayed a step towards him, then checked herself as he reached for her. In a moment she would be lost. 'What purpose does this serve?' she said hoarsely.

He spread his hands. 'I just wanted to see you in the flesh and . . . and talk the way we used to.'

'Talk.' Julitta fixed on the word as if it were an anchor in the midst of a stormy ocean. Half-turning, she sat down on the turf seat and spread her wimple across her knees – symbol of respectability, a married woman's prop. 'Very well,' she said, a quaver in her voice, 'sit down and talk to me.'

Benedict hesitated, then sat down gingerly beside her. 'Where do I begin?' he said. 'Are you happy with Mauger?'

Julitta stared out over the moon-silvered garden and deliberated her reply. Benedict's shoulder was almost touching hers. She could feel his breath, his body; the danger of the moment. How easy it would be. 'I have been happier in my life,' she said at length, 'but also I have known more grief. There is a roof over my head, I am mistress of my own household, saving Mauger's word, and he provides well for me.' She looked at him from beneath her lids and wound her wimple around her fingers. 'It must be the same between you and Gisele – not what you want, but enough to keep you from starving?'

Benedict laughed bitterly. 'Enough to keep me from starving,' he repeated, as if the word was a great jest at his expense. 'Ah God, Julitta, you are as much Rolf's daughter as she is Arlette's. How much love is enough to keep me from famine?'

Julitta bit her lip and looked away, her fingers tightening in the cloth.

Benedict's grimace deepened. 'Did you know that we were in Rouen for the purpose of praying at the tomb of St Petronella?'

'Arlette said as much.'

'I tell you, if prayer was the way to fruitfulness, we would have half a dozen offspring by now. St Petronella might grant a miracle, but how I can sow seed when the garden door is barred, is beyond my understanding.'

'Do you mean Gisele is unable to bear children?'

'No, just unwilling to beget them,' he said dryly. 'An immaculate conception would suit her. That is why I say she is Arlette's daughter. Everything she is has been learned by rote from her mother, nor can she be persuaded to question the rule. Mama says so, therefore it is true . . . but then I suppose you know most of this already. You used to dwell in the bower.'

'They tried not to involve me in their conversations.' Julitta laughed shortly. 'I used to disrupt them with my "bathhouse" morals. I do admit that I cut off my own nose to spite my face by saying truly outrageous things just to see how horrified I could make them, so that they took to ignoring me. A blessing in disguise, I think. Arlette used to try and curb my excesses, but I would just escape to you and Papa.'

'Yes, I remember,' Benedict said softly. He took a lock of her hair between forefinger and thumb and played with it. 'And then your poor father would have to keep the peace.' He was smiling as he spoke.

'It wasn't my "poor father" who had to live among them,' she retorted. 'He scarcely spent any time in the bower. And neither do you, I hazard.'

'No,' he admitted reluctantly, 'not at Brize, although I do at Ulverton. Many men do not dwell in their wives' working chambers.'

'Mauger does.'

'So would I in his place.'

The conversation was becoming dangerous, Benedict's proximity even more so, and Julitta knew that she must make an end of the meeting for both their sakes. 'But you are not in his place,' she said, and would have risen to her feet except that he still held her prisoner by her hair. 'Benedict, let me go.'

'I cannot,' he whispered. 'God forgive me, I cannot.' And set his mouth upon hers.

Julitta quivered beneath his touch. Torn between the urge to yield and the need to fight, she remained where she was, trapped like a moth dancing in a candle flame. And then the flame began to consume her, licking delicately at first, but growing hotter, beginning to singe. Her mouth responded to his; she set her arms around his neck and dug her fingers into his hair. His hand opened and trailed its way down the strand of hair he had been grasping. Light as a feather, he touched her breast, and Julitta gasped, stiffened, and then pressed herself closer. It was wrong, she knew that it was, but now she too could only think 'God forgive me.' Her tongue followed his, then took the initiative. He reached to the brooch fastening the neck of her gown. Her hand went to his belt, and then travelled below it. Benedict groaned and pulled her into his lap. Julitta wriggled, seeking out the hard length of his manhood, her own desire heightening with each shifting movement.

'Ah God, Julitta,' he said hoarsely, and clutched her in an agony of pain and pleasure. 'Julitta, please.' His hands cupped her buttocks, assisting her to rise and fall against him. Her head went back, her throat arching, and her red curls stroking his knees.

Outside the haven of the garden, the gate guards shouted a challenge, were answered peremptorily and immediately set about opening the great wooden barriers to the troop demanding admittance. Fresh torches flared, illuminating the progress of mounted knights and footsoldiers.

Through a haze of sensation, Julitta heard the cries of the guards, the clatter of hooves and jink of armour. Her mind shrieked danger! even while her body sought its pleasure. Benedict had heard it too, for his hands gripped her now to hold her still, and his harsh breathing was suddenly held silent, the better to listen.

'Who could it be at this hour?' he asked. 'Surely not your father. He has no such troops with him, unless he has gathered them on his way home.'

The clattering and shouting continued. They heard the rumble of iron-shod wheels on the bailey cobbles, denoting the arrival of a baggage wain.

Julitta scrambled from Benedict's lap and rapidly shook out and smoothed her gown. 'Whoever it is, I will be sought to find them bed and board,' she said in a flustered voice. She flung her wimple over her head, secured her circlet, and drew the loose end of cloth through the loop.

Benedict watched her rapid movements and gnawed his lip. 'Julitta . . .'

She darted him a rapid glance through her lashes. 'No, Ben, say nothing. It would have been like the last time – great pleasure, and then great grief.'

'I only wanted to . . .'

'So did I,' she interrupted, her eyes suddenly bright with tears. 'It is not wise for us to be alone together. I do not trust you, Ben, but most of all, I do not trust myself! No, do not follow me,' she snapped. 'What will be said of us if we are seen emerging from the garden together at this late hour?'

She hurried down the garden path, still smoothing her gown and checking her wimple. Benedict cursed and struck his fist upon the soft turf of the seat. Some of it was natural frustration at the untimely interruption, but most of the anger was directed at himself for handling the moment with such crass clumsiness. He had intended seeking her out to smooth the ground between them, and ended up strewing yet more thorns. 'Fool,' he muttered to himself, and rising, went slowly to the silent bee hives. 'I am a fool,' he reiterated, and laid his hand against the side of the woven skep. A sense of the enclosed energy of the insects throbbed through his palm and along his fingertips. When a suitable amount of time had passed, he left the garden quietly, and went to discover whose arrival had both saved and stranded himself and Julitta.

Julitta closed the garden gate behind her, took several deep breaths, and then walked briskly towards the bailey entrance. There was a sick feeling in the pit of her stomach, a combined broil of thwarted lust, guilt, relief, and disappointment. She knew exactly how far she and Benedict would have gone without this interruption, and that she ought to be grateful. But no such emotion beat in her blood just now. With loins that still flickered, and with aching breasts, she went forward to perform the duty of respectable chatelaine.

A man clad from head to toe in chain mail was dismounting from a stocky chestnut stallion. The horse's neck was crusted with sweat and the scars of recent wounds were dark scabs upon its hide. Julitta's heart lurched and she almost screamed aloud in fear.

'Mauger!' Her hand went to her mouth, to her lips still full and red from Benedict's kisses. 'What . . . what are you doing here?'

He gave the reins to a groom and turned round. 'I could ask the same of you,' he replied while removing his coif and arming cap. There were dark shadows beneath his eyes and a short, deep cut under his left cheekbone.

'I, I . . .' she stammered, hoping against hope that Benedict would not leave the garden now beneath the full suspicion of Mauger's jealous gaze. Dear Jesu, what if the troop had arrived just a little later into the night. Her face flamed. She sought swiftly for a means of escape. 'Oh, that is easily explained, but surely you will be more comfortable if you come within and let me help you unarm.'

His eyes narrowed, but he nodded stiffly and consented to follow her towards the keep.

'You look as if you have ridden hard,' she said to engage his attention, and forced herself not to crane her neck in the direction of the garden.

'I have.' He rubbed a weary hand over his face. 'There is news, grave news from Rouen. Your father must be summoned, and Benedict too.'

Julitta's entire spine prickled with cold. Somehow she managed to keep moving. To have stopped and stared at mention of his name would have given her away. 'Benedict and Gisele are already here,' she said, averting her face so that he would not be able to read her eyes. 'They rode in from Rouen just before vespers. Neither of them mentioned anything about grave news.'

'No, they would have departed the city before Duke William arrived.'

'It concerns the Duke?'

They climbed the stairs of the motte slope together. Mauger's breathing grew laboured beneath the weight of his mail and Julitta had to slow for him. At the top of the steps, he paused to regain his wind, one hand pressed to the stitch in his side.

'The Duke is dying,' he panted. 'We went for the throat of the French, attacked Le Mans and set fire to it. His stallion, the chestnut your father gave him last year, it stepped on a burning ember and shied. The Duke was thrown upon his saddle pommel and it has torn him somewhere inside – mortally torn him. Messengers have gone out. All the tenants-in-chief who are able, are summoned to Rouen to hear his dying wishes for his lands.' He removed his hand from his side and straightening, walked slowly towards the hall.

Julitta now hastened before him and chivvied the servants to bring food for the returning men. Fires were stirred to life, and people poked to wakefulness. Julitta threw herself wholeheartedly into the duties of chatelaine, hiding her anxiety within her attention to domestic detail.

Mauger eyed her bustle with pride. Her behaviour these days was all of his doing. He had been right when he told Rolf that all she needed was a household of her own and the guiding hand of a firm husband. And yet the pride was mixed with a certain amount of doubt. She was a little too meticulous in her observations of duty, and he was not sure whether it was deference or fear that caused her to keep her lids lowered and avoid his gaze.

'That is my reason for appearing so suddenly at Brize's gates,' he said as she helped him remove his armour. 'But you have still not told me yours.'

She had fine, milky skin that coloured easily. Even though the solar was only illuminated by candlelight now, he could tell that she was blushing. Her lower lip chewed from side to side and she quickly turned away from him to set his discarded garments upon coffer.

'You said there was a simple explanation,' he said, watching her closely. 'Perhaps it is as simple as Benedict de Remy.'

He saw her stiffen for an instant before she turned round. This time, although her colour was high, she looked him straight in the eyes. 'Gisele and Benedict did not ride in here until sunset. I came to Brize because Lady Arlette had need of me. That is the truth, and you may ask anyone to confirm what I say.'

Mauger eyed her broodingly. Clad in the old, sweaty tunic he wore beneath his armour, he sat down at the solar trestle which was adorned with a spread of cold meats, a raised pie, bread, cheese and honey cakes. There was also a flagon of wine. He stabbed a sliver of meat on the point of his knife, and eyed the length of her legs beneath her garments. His loins tightened with pleasurable anticipation. Leaning over, he placed his left hand possessively on her thigh and squeezed.

'I hated every moment of soldiering in the Duke's army,' he

declared. 'Jesu, I almost went mad of a night thinking of you alone at Fauville. You were alone, weren't you?'

Julitta looked down at the trestle, at his hand upon her thigh. 'Yes, Mauger, I was alone.'

He reached to the flagon, filled his cup and drank. 'But wishing you were not,' he said, and kneaded her thigh. She blushed again. Smiling, Mauger drained the cup, then drew her towards him. 'Show me,' he said huskily, 'show me how much you missed me, and I will show you how much I missed you.'

'Here? In the solar?' Her eyes darted. 'Someone might disturb us.'

'Let them. We are husband and wife.'

'But . . .'

Mauger's expression was tense with desire. 'I laid not so much as a finger on the whores of the Duke's army camp,' he said through clenched teeth. 'I haven't had a woman since I left you. We are alone, and you'll not deny me. Do as you are bidden.'

With shaking hands Julitta reached to the neck fastening of her tunic. Mauger watched her fumble. She looked as if she might cry. He thought that either he had done an excellent job of teaching her modesty, or that she did not want to lie with him, and because the latter was damaging to the image he had of himself, he chose the former.

'Come, come,' he cajoled. 'Pretend that we are at home, that this is our bedchamber. Leave that.' Pushing her fingers away from the clasp, he laid her down on the solar floor with its thick covering of straw, and raising her skirts, mounted her. Julitta gasped as his weight covered her. Mauger groped within his braies and his erect organ sprang free, purple and bursting. Once, twice, he jabbed at her, and then he thrust home, full and strong. She was ready for him, he could feel by her moistness that she was. Mauger closed his eyes and savoured. Two weeks had seemed an eternity. He held onto the exquisite sensations burning in his groin. Two hard thrusts and he would be home, but he wanted to prolong the agonising pleasure, and so he checked himself, holding his breath and moving just the barest fraction. Lifting himself a little, he was able to fondle Julitta's breasts. He almost wished that he had let her undress so that he could caress them unhindered. Beneath the slow rubbing of his palm, he felt her nipple bud and harden and heard her breathing quicken. Usually she was passive, as befitted a dutiful wife, but tonight he felt a change in her, as if she had caught the scent of his own desire.

Mauger had found his rhythm now, a gentle rocking that kept him on a plateau beneath the pinnacle and allowed him to explore his wife's body. Now and again she whimpered softly. Her eyes were closed, and there was a slight frown marking the smoothness of her brow. Her hips began to rise and fall against his, urging him to more vigorous motion.

Had Mauger but known it, he was only completing what Benedict had started in the rose garden. Julitta's earlier arousal had left her body receptive to Mauger's intrusion. And Mauger himself, by exerting more control than usual, had brought her to fever pitch.

Her hands clenched upon his spine, and her legs parted further. The whimpers rose in volume and became a drawn-out cry. Unable to resist any more, Mauger seized her buttocks and plunged, his body shuddering in the throes of climax.

He was still pushing lazily in and out, responding to the twinges of aftermath when Benedict walked into the solar. The young man stopped dead and for a shocked moment stared at the two of them. Mauger did not rise off Julitta, or try to conceal himself. Instead he smiled at Benedict with triumph in his eyes. Julitta, her eyes still closed, made a soft sound and rotated her hips, seeking further pleasure. Benedict whitened. Without a word, he turned on his heels and left.

Julitta's lids fluttered as she felt the swirl of cold air from the disturbed curtain.

'It's all right,' Mauger said, 'nought but a draught.' Then he gave a rich, self-satisfied chuckle, and pinched her thigh. 'I see indeed how much you have missed me.' He withdrew from her, and did not turn away as he usually did to tuck himself back inside his braies. Mauger's sexual confidence had increased by leaps and bounds during the last quarter candle. The look upon Benedict's face had been the gilding on the moment though.

Julitta stood up and shook down her rumpled, straw-decked skirts. Her legs felt shaky; her woman's parts still quivered and pulsed. She had closed her eyes and imagined that she was still in the garden with Benedict; that the floor was made of crushed herbs, not straw and that the body to which she was joined, owned a slender, wiry strength, instead of a stocky bullishness. Indeed, she had almost sobbed Benedict's name aloud as Mauger brought her with him to the moment of supreme pleasure. It was the first time he had ever done so. She thought she knew the reasons, and yet she was disturbed by the very sensuality of her own nature. Perhaps any man would suffice to satisfy her if she just imagined him wearing Benedict's face. She just wanted to be left alone, and was too relieved to be resentful when Mauger told her to go and join the other women while he attended to 'men's' business.

'Were you looking for me a moment ago?' Mauger asked innocently as he joined Benedict before the fire in the hall. He chuckled. 'You must forgive us. Julitta was as eager to greet me fittingly as I was to greet her. Time apart whets the appetite.'

Benedict gazed down at his hands and fought the urge to clench them into fists and punch the supercilious smile off Mauger's face. If a man could enjoy bedding with different women, then it must work the other way around too. He did not blame Julitta, but he was brimful of jealous pain all the same, and he did not need Mauger's heavy-handed boasting. He made a non-committal sound and shrugged. 'I was told that you had ridden in with the tidings that the Duke is dying?'

The smirk left Mauger's face as he was recalled to the wider arena of the political world. 'It is true. I saw him after his horse trod upon the burning ember in Le Mans, since I was the one summoned to deal with the crazed beast. Our lord Duke is not long for this world. He was in such pain that they had to bear him in a litter to Rouen. He has summoned all his vassals. You will have to represent Rolf if he does not arrive in time.'

Benedict did not miss the curl of Mauger's lip. Not only Julitta sat like a poisoned cup between them. So did the fact that Benedict was Rolf's heir, while Mauger, although he was Rolf's son-in-law too, was only a vassal. Benedict knew that Mauger thought him a jumped-up merchant's son whose only claim to nobility was through his marriage into a higher blood-line. And he, in his turn, saw Mauger in a less than favourable light and was all too willing to denigrate any good points that the man possessed. 'Certainly I will go,' he replied, 'but I hope to God that Rolf will be able to represent Brize himself. He knew the Duke well; I only saw him from a distance.'

Mauger nodded. 'It was always Rolf's prerogative to select William's mounts.'

'Oh, I have selected horses for the Duke before now. His tastes were predictable – the larger and meaner the better, but Rolf always did the negotiating himself. The Duke was not fond of younger men. I think he had been soured by the behaviour of his sons. I wonder what will happen now,' he added thoughtfully.

'What do you mean?'

'Well, if William is dying, what will happen to his lands? Will they remain whole in the possession of one son alone, or will they be divided up? And if they are, will Rolf find himself owing allegiance to more than one man?'

Mauger gently fingered the scabbed cut on his cheekbone. 'I had not thought about it,' he said. 'I suppose that by tradition the hearth lands will go to the eldest son, and the conquered lands to the second one. Robert for Normandy, Rufus for England, and whatever scraps remain to young Henry.'

Benedict pursed his lips. Mauger was probably right. Albeit that William's eldest son, Robert, was currently in rebellion against his father, the young man would doubtless inherit Normandy, and William Rufus would take England. It was a worrying prospect. The relationship between Robert and Rufus was a stormy one, compounded of brotherly love and brotherly hate in equal proportions. It would be laughable if it were not so frightening, that one day the men of Brize and the men of Ulverton might be called upon to fight against each other. Himself against Mauger. He chewed his lip on the thought. It would be all too easy. Between them there was no love to temper the hostility, only sense, and he knew how easily that was lost.

CHAPTER 51

On the ninth of September 1086, William, Duke of Normandy and King of England died at St Gervase on the outskirts of Rouen. To his eldest son, Robert, he bequeathed the duchy of Normandy; upon his second son William Rufus, so called because of his ruddy complexion, he bestowed the kingdom of England, and to his youngest son Henry, nineteen years old, he gave five thousand pounds of silver from the treasury, and his blessing.

None of the brothers was pleased with his share of their father's inheritance, the word 'share' in itself a stumbling block. Each desired the whole, and the Norman barons who had served the Conqueror faithfully found themselves having to choose between his sons. As Benedict had foreseen, men such as Rolf with lands on both sides of the narrow sea, had no option but to break their faith with one of their disgruntled overlords.

'In Normandy I will serve Duke Robert for the fealty owed by Brize,' Rolf told Benedict at William's funeral in Caen. 'In England, I will serve William Rufus, since his father designated him king. And if they come to blows, I will commute all my military service to payment in coin and let them fight it out between themselves. I have no desire to be torn in two.'

Following the funeral, Rolf repaired to Brize for the winter season. His wife was slowly dying, and he knew that he had to be with her, as he had not been with Ailith. When Benedict crossed the narrow sea to Ulverton, Gisele remained at Brize to nurse her mother, although she dutifully sent her husband an embroidered belt as a Christmas gift.

Benedict presided over the Yuletide feast in Ulverton's long hall. Despite the presence of the villagers, the priest, retainers, soldiers, grooms, servants and anyone else who could squash into the festively decorated room, he felt utterly depressed. The revelry which he had always taken pleasure in before, now seemed trivial and garish.

A villager capered beneath the high table. He wore a fantastic costume composed of shredded fabric in different shades of green – pea and emerald, sage and olive. His face was smeared with the colour too, and a pair of antlers crowned his shaggy brown hair. He was The Green Man, Jack-in-the-Green, denizen of Maytime and Yule alike.

Benedict desired no reminders of the month of May. Once it had dwelt like fire within him. Now there were only ashes. Taking a flagon of wine, he left the hall and went to his solitary chamber. To think about Julitta increased his depression. Not to think of her was almost worse. Torn between one and the other, he sat in a grey haze of self-pity while Christmas, season and spirit, passed him by.

Late the following month, he was out in the fields, inspecting the mares soon to foal, when King William Rufus arrived at Ulverton unannounced, and demanded to see the blood-stock. Summoned by a groom, Benedict hurried back to the wooden keep, and bent the knee to the monarch who still sat upon his horse, his pudgy hands toying with a decoration on the saddle pommel.

'Get up, boy,' Rufus commanded.

Benedict concealed his irritation at being addressed as 'boy' and rising, went to hold the grey stallion's headstall whilst the King dismounted. 'Sire, this is an unexpected pleasure.'

'I have no doubt that it is,' Rufus answered with an edge to his voice. It was gravelly and harsh, suiting the scoured, ruddy features. He was smaller than the Conqueror, but possessed the same stockiness of build. A barrel on bandy legs was how Rolf had once described Rufus, and the comparison was entirely appropriate. Benedict was slightly above average height and Rufus's eyes were on a level with his mouth, and this the King stared at for a long moment, before his gaze drifted down Benedict's body in a fashion that men usually used when they were eyeing women.

It was not the first time that William Rufus had made his interest known. Glancing round the group of retainers accompanying the King, Benedict caught the pouting scowl of the current court favourite, a slender young man with a bright blue Phrygian cap set at a rakish angle on his blond curls.

'Will you come within, can I offer you food and drink, Sire?' Benedict enquired, thinking that it was all Rufus was going to get.

'It will do for a start,' Rufus answered, 'although I'm hoping for more . . .' He let the ambiguity hang in the air for just a moment too long, before adding, 'I've come to look at your horses.' A half-grin at the pouting youth. 'Time I had a new mount.'

Benedict stretched his lips in the semblance of a smile, gave the King's horse to his senior groom, and led the way towards the hall. At least Rufus had not brought his entire court, for they would have eaten Ulverton clean down to the bone. Here was just a minor entourage consisting of the King's favourites and hangers-on. No sign of the venerable Archbishop Lanfranc to lend dignity to the proceedings. This was a private jaunt. Probably the main court was keeping warm in the royal hunting lodge in the great forest to the east. Still, it was uncomfortable and annoying. He wondered if Rufus intended paying for the horse he chose. The royal stables always received a quota of beasts each autumn as part of Brize and Ulverton's feudal dues. Perhaps Rufus was going to increase his demands. He was known to have a grasping, avaricious nature.

'Where is your father-by-marriage?' Rufus asked, as he was given the lord's chair in the hall and served with the best wine. His hazel eyes roved the plastered walls with their embellishment of embroidered hangings and bannered lances. 'Skulking at Brize, I suppose, and licking my brother's boots?'

'He is indeed at Brize, Sire, for the winter season. His wife is sick unto death and he is there for her sake too.'

Rufus snorted. 'It would be the first time!' he said nastily. 'Unless he's changed his spots, which I very much doubt.'

'Even so, it is true,' Benedict said with quiet dignity.

Rufus snorted. 'And pigs nest in trees,' he scoffed, and drank down the wine in five hard gulps, wiping his mouth on his gorgeously embroidered sleeve. 'Your father-in-law knows a good excuse when he sees one!'

'Do you blame him?'

Rufus stared at Benedict as if he had been pole-axed. Around him, his sycophants held their breath, awaiting the explosion of the royal rage. The red cheeks darkened, the barrel chest expanded, threatening to rip the stitches on the crimson, fur-trimmed tunic. Benedict found himself wondering what would happen if someone stuck a cloak pin in Rufus's belly. Would he pop like a Yuletide bladder?

'You have a bold tongue to say that when you are scarce out of tail-clouts!' Rufus growled. It was significant that it was a growl, not a full-throated bellow. It meant that for the moment he was prepared to find Benedict's insolence intriguing. 'I wonder how bold you truly are.' He tapped his forefinger against his square front teeth, and abruptly jerked to his feet. 'Come, show me your horses,' he said. 'I need one fit for a king.'

Benedict rose too. 'A destrier, Sire?' he enquired. 'Or a palfrey?'

Rufus shrugged and hitched at his belly where it hung over his embossed belt. 'I want a beast that will make my brother Robert's eyes pop out with jealousy,' he said, and his pugnacious jaw jutted. 'The best.'

Benedict discovered that the King's taste in horses was about as dubious as his taste in clothes and cronies. Gaudy not good, brash not brilliant. He was drawn too much by markings and colour, and all the superficial cladding that meant nothing when it came to stamina, quality, and endurance. Benedict tried to interest Rufus in a young dappled grey stallion of sound conformation. The horse was alert and confident without being too spirited to handle, but Rufus dismissed it with a wave of his hand as being 'naught but a peasant's nag' – a totally unfair remark, since even the meanest horse on the stud was worth more than a peasant might earn in an entire year.

Rufus tried several animals, and declared them all unsuitable. Finally his eye settled upon a steel-grey stallion which was giving the grooms a deal of trouble, backing and sidling, rolling its eyes. Foam lathered its neck, matching the glittering white of its mane and tail, the latter switching angrily from side to side.

'That one,' Rufus said, and his lower lip joined the outward jut of his jaw. 'I want that one.'

'His temper is uncertain, Sire,' Benedict warned.

'So is mine, we'll match well.'

Benedict could not argue with that. 'He is not saddle-trained, Sire,' he said, adding a rapid 'thank Christ' beneath his breath. The last thing he needed was for Rufus to try the brute out and get tossed into the midden.

'I've got grooms enough to break him.' Rufus approached the stallion and despite being held by two attendants, it still managed to lunge at him, teeth bared, one forehoof pawing in threat. Rufus laughed buoyantly. 'Satan!' he cried. 'I will call him Satan!'

His paramour tittered behind his hand. Benedict knew the King's reputation of disrespect for the Church. There was even the whispered rumour that he followed the old religion. Still, the name was more than appropriate to the animal. The only way to remove the devil from his nature was to geld him, and he very much doubted that Rufus would do anything so sensible.

The King went on to examine the destrier herd, and then the ponies which Rolf had brought out of the north so many years ago, and for which Ulverton was now justly famous. 'Ponies!' Rufus snorted, eyeing the sturdy, ugly little animals which contrasted so strongly with the proud, graceful warhorses. 'What in the world possessed your father-by-marriage to invest in them?'

'Is it not better to have more than one dish on a table, Sire?

Rich and powerful men come to purchase warhorses, palfreys and coursers from our stock. Between times, we take the custom of merchants and carriers. And in times of war, rich and powerful men return to us to buy our ponies for sumpter work. They look nothing, I know, but they have an endurance beyond all believing. I would wager with confidence that one of those ponies bearing two pannier-loads of rocks could outpace a destrier in the course of a day, and still be fit on the morrow for another dawn-to-dusk trek.'

Rufus looked thoughtful. 'In times of war,' he repeated and eyed Benedict. 'Does Rolf breed ponies at Brize?'

'No, Sire, only at Ulverton.'

'Then I will buy what you have.' He nodded to himself with satisfaction, a gleam in his eye at having access to something that his brother Robert did not.

His paramour loudly cleared his throat to attract the King's attention. 'Sire, would I not look divine beside you on this one?' He pointed a lily-white finger at a horse which had been grazing among the ponies and now had come in curiosity to examine the visitors. It was a mare of a good average size, with neat, sharp ears, intelligent liquid eyes, and proud carriage. Her colouring was a glorious golden dapple, beautiful and rare.

Rufus just stared, his small eyes widening and widening in covetous greed. 'Saving the best until last?' he said, and moistened his lips. 'I should have expected such. You horse-traders are all the same, whatever your rank.'

The effeminate young man made kissing noises at the mare and she snorted gustily at him before walking directly up to Benedict with a nicker of greeting. Benedict stroked her cheeks and rubbed her soft muzzle. 'She is not for sale, Sire.'

'I want her,' Rufus said as if that was the end of the matter. 'Name your price.'

'There is no price, Sire. Even if you offered me her weight in gold, I would not sell. I purchased her as a gift for someone else.'

The King's eyes narrowed. 'You seem eager to bring hardship upon yourself. I could take my custom elsewhere.'

Benedict braced his shoulders as if to withstand a blow. 'That is your prerogative, Sire,' he said quietly.

Rufus glared. His pretty boy pouted. 'Make him give you the horse, Sire,' he challenged in a light, spiteful voice, and posed dramatically with his hand on one hip, his white, pretty fingers tapping on the decorated hilt of his eating dagger. The King's eyes flickered from Benedict to his favourite.

'Be quiet, Godfroi,' he snapped, and took a step nearer to Benedict. 'So, you deny me this horse?' If he had intended to intimidate the younger, slightly built man by the force of his presence, he was disappointed.

'With regret, Sire, I do,' Benedict answered without flinching. He could smell the wine on the King's breath, see the broken veins spidering the ruddy cheeks, and the dewdrops of sweat in the receding chestnut hair. Godfroi was looking at his fingernails, his cheeks sucked in to display his affront.

'You will do more than regret,' Rufus snarled, and barging past Benedict, called for his grooms. Benedict watched him warily. He did not believe that Rufus would order anything so crass as an armed assault upon Ulverton, but one did not stand in the path of a wild boar with impunity.

The King mounted up and thrust his feet into the stirrups. He snapped his fat fingers and two equerries fetched the steel-grey destrier. Ignoring their struggles to control the beast, he turned his own horse in a semi-circle and reined him in hard before Benedict. Rufus's eyes were narrow and bright, his nostrils flared with a mingling of choler and lust, and it was all Benedict could do to stand his ground. 'It is a fine line between honour and stupidity,' Rufus said, and slapped the leather down on his horse's neck. The horse lumbered forwards and Benedict was forced to leap aside to avoid being trampled.

The King cantered out of the keep gates. His *bon ami* followed at his heels, nose cocked high, chin puckered.

Benedict held himself straight until the last man had ridden from sight, and then sat down weakly on the lowest step of the mounting block, and closed his eyes.

★

Julitta crossed herself and rose from her knees. Before her, on the altar in the chapel of Arlette's convent, the creamy wax candles gleamed with translucence. Between them, a cross of silver-gilt, amethyst and rock crystal commanded the congregation to worship. Father Jerome, resplendent in robes of scarlet and crimson silk damask performed the blessing, his fingers eloquent and lean, contrasting with the bull-like solidity of his body.

The chapel itself was a place of contrasts, of practical, sturdy arches and intricately decorated columns, the reliefs brightly painted to war with the natural gloom of the thick stone walls. And yet everything blended with harmonious individuality. Julitta's attitude to religion was dutiful rather than devoted, but here, today, at the convent's consecration to the Magdalene, she felt uplifted.

At her side, Mauger was listening intently to Father Jerome as if he understood every word of Latin spilling from the priest's lips. She glanced at her husband sidelong. He was wearing his best blue tunic with the red braid, and his pale hair gleamed like barley in the chapel's soft light. He had been different of late, more at ease, she thought, and her own life was more bearable because of it. Mauger was still gruff and brusque, not given to conversations beyond the practical, but he permitted her a larger degree of freedom than in the early days of their marriage, and their bed was no longer a battlefield on which he sought to subjugate her to his will. Indeed, sometimes Julitta even derived pleasure from the encounters. If she could never come to love Mauger, then at least she no longer hated him. The thought of Benedict was like an aching tooth that could not be pulled, but she was disciplining herself to live with the pain.

Benedict was not here now for the consecration of the convent's chapel, and she was both disappointed and relieved. What would they say to each other after their last meeting? She had not seen him after that incident in Arlette's garden, not even to bid farewell before she returned to Fauville the following morning. He had not come seeking her again and she had avoided him. It was safer that way. Even a meeting of their eyes would have betrayed them.

The witnesses to the chapel's consecration had all been standing throughout the ceremony. Arlette, due to her frailty, sat on a bench at the front of the nave. Her condition had improved a little recently, but it was caused more by the knowledge that her convent was close to completion than by any return to health. She was painfully thin, her bones almost poking through her skin, and her eyes were feverbrilliant in their sockets.

Gisele looked ill too, her complexion pasty-white with puffy welts of exhaustion beneath her eyes. Julitta knew that it was not the nursing that was taking its toll, but the sight of her mother growing progressively worse, no matter how hard Gisele tried. Julitta felt genuine pity for her half-sister. She knew what it was like to lose a mother, to be powerless in the inexorable face of death.

Back at Brize, sitting with the women in the bower, Julitta listened as one of the consecration guests held forth upon the wonders of her recent pilgrimage to Santiago de Compostella in Galicia, where the remains of the blessed apostle St James were supposedly interred. The woman's name was Matilda de Vey. She was wealthy and devout, a combination of great benefit to the Church. She was also garrulous and loud, and with the aid of a couple of goblets of Aubert's fine wine was sailing very close to being outrageous. Julitta found herself longing to giggle, something that she had not done in a long, long time.

'I tell you, my dear,' she shouted at Gisele, who actually flinched, 'you have not lived unless you have been on a proper pilgrimage – not just to Rouen, but further afield. It not only does wonders for the soul, it bestows wisdom and understanding!' She plumped herself down on the bed where Arlette was resting. The entire mass sagged to the left beneath her exuberant weight. Her face reflecting the red of the wine she had so liberally consumed, Matilda pushed at her wimple which had come askew. 'On my way to visit the blessed saint, we stayed in Toulouse, at a pilgrim hospice, and there was a priest who owned a piece of the True Cross. We were all permitted to touch it.' She waggled a forefinger at her bemused audience. 'My hands were swollen up with the dropsy, but when I laid them upon that tiny piece of wood, within moments my fingers were as thin as they were on the day that I was married. I swear it to you.'

Julitta wondered why the miracle had stopped at the fingers. If Matilda had been truly blessed, then her figure would be sylph-like too. She wondered how much the woman had paid the priest for the privilege of touching the relic. Benedict had told her that he had encountered many corrupt clergymen on his journeys, who would sell anything to the gullible. 'I have seen enough nails from the True Cross to shoe an entire conroi of cavalry!' he had laughed.

'And this,' Matilda continued, delving in her ample bodice and withdrawing a small, wooden box threaded upon a leather cord, 'holds the nail clippings of the blessed St James himself!'

The other women clustered around the bed to gasp and exclaim over the dubious contents of the box. Julitta remained aloof, and busied herself replenishing the cups with wine. *Am I mad, or are they?* she asked herself, and grimaced to wonder whose nail clippings really occupied the little box. Why did all these saints have nails, hair, bones and clothing to spare, but never the more intimate parts? The Virgin Mary's right nipple from which the Christ child sucked? Her left one for good measure? Julitta almost choked on the thought, torn between mirth and horror at her own blasphemy. Jesu, if those biddies by the bed knew what she was thinking she would be locked up in a penitent's cell on bread and water for the next month at least!

The Lady Matilda continued to hold forth, and her audience hung on her every word. Julitta had to admit to herself that the woman possessed a story teller's skills. Her descriptions brought places and incidents to colourful life in her audience's imagination. Julitta could smell the dust of the road, feel the blaze of the sun on her spine, and taste the sweetness of the bloomy cluster of grapes that the pilgrims had eaten as they rode through the vine fields on their road to Compostella. Arlette seemed to derive pleasure from the minute details of the many churches which Matilda had visited along her route, with the various legends and saints attached to them.

'I wish that I could have seen them,' she said wistfully. 'It is too late now, my time is too short. When I was younger I wish . . .' Her voice trailed off and she stared into the distance and sighed heavily.

The garrulous Matilda was temporarily silenced, but quickly regained the use of her tongue, having loosened it in a long swallow from her replenished cup. 'Oh indeed, it is too late for you,' she said with a total absence of tact, 'but it is not too late for your daughter. Mayhap if you send her to pray for you, the blessed St James will grant a miracle.' She smiled at Gisele, who could only stare at her in mute shock. 'Besides,' Matilda added practically, 'she could seek out a relic to grace the new convent and bring it prestige and respect. I know places in Compostella where such things can be obtained. One of our number, a merchant from Caen, obtained a vial of the Holy Virgin's milk. Think how such a thing would glorify your convent!'

Julitta spluttered and turned the sound into a cough. The Holy Virgin's nipples suddenly did not seem so far-fetched. 'Forgive my ignorance,' she interrupted, 'but surely there are many dishonest traders in these relics. How will she know that she is not being cheated?'

Matilda stared down her nose at Julitta. 'Of course there are many dishonest traders, child. You should always ask a priest's advice before you purchase anything.'

'Oh, I see,' Julitta nodded slowly. 'Ask a priest,' she repeated.

'And use your common sense.' Matilda's eyes flashed at Julitta, daring her to speak again. 'That goes without saying, I would have thought.'

'Oh certainly.' Julitta took Matilda's advice and retreated from the confrontation. There was nothing wrong with her own common sense.

CHAPTER 52

Benedict sat at a trestle in his chamber at Brize, and counted the silver he had brought with him from Ulverton. Payment for horses by clients, the coins displayed a wide variety of mints, monarchs and petty rulers. Eric Bloodaxe, Harold Godwinson, the Confessor, the Conqueror, and even a recent William Rufus, bright as a fish scale. Benedict had deemed it prudent to remove not only himself from England, but the bulk of Ulverton's surplus coin, and if that was treason, then so be it. Rolf had entirely endorsed his decision, but his look had been wry and not a little irritated.

'You have a nose for trouble,' he had commented with a sigh and a scowl.

'Should I have yielded to him?' Benedict had retorted. 'What would you have done?'

His defence had elicited a grimace from Rolf. 'Ach, I don't know. Probably I would have promised to geld him.'

Benedict smiled at the memory and stacked another pile of silver at his right hand. Reaching to a tally stick by his left, he made a notch in it. It was not really funny. He was as good as banished from Ulverton for the immediate future. To return now would be like jumping up and down in front of an enraged bull and hoping that it would not charge.

The silver clinked gently upon the trestle, the sound comforting to his merchant blood. Raising his head he glanced across the room to his wife. She was sitting near the brazier,

quietly stitching at a garment, an undershift by the looks of the
fabric. Even in the privacy of their own chamber, she still wore
her wimple, and the scrubbed, bleached linen did nothing to
enhance her wan complexion. She was biting her lip, and as he
watched her, he saw two tears trickle down her cheeks. She
sniffed and reached surreptitiously into her undergown sleeve
for a square of linen on which to blow her nose.

'Gisele?' He set aside the coins and rose to his feet.

She made a small sound of dismay at being discovered and
shook her head, gesturing him to sit back down, but the tears
came faster and harder, as if his notice had released a well-
spring.

He crossed the room and set his arms around her like a cradle, and he let her cry. It had been a long time since he had
held her – since he had held any woman come to that. The
casual, joyous tumbles of his adolescence seemed a lifetime
away, and besides, they had owned a different purpose entirely.
His moments with Julitta were far too distant and far too close.
And Gisele had always kept him at arm's length until she had
driven him away. Now, here they were, in the same chamber,
alone, with not even a maid as witness, the only disturbance the
rain driving against the shutters.

Her shoulders were bony beneath his fingers; she had no
more meat on her than a starved sparrow. She took too much
upon herself, he thought, acting out the role that her mother
had assigned to her, flavouring each moment with guilt if it was
not spent in duty. He knew what she was going to say even
before she calmed enough to speak.

'Mother says that she is going to take Holy vows and enter
her convent at Eastertide,' she gulped. 'She has discussed it
with Father Jerome and Father Hoel. She says . . .' sniff, sob,
'she says that it is her wish to die as a nun.' A fresh flood of
weeping.

Benedict could see nothing so dreadful in that. In fact, it
seemed like an excellent idea considering Arlette's preoccupa-
tion with the Church. Not only that, but if she entered the
convent now, it would be the task of the nuns to nurse her, and

not Gisele who was clearly drooping beneath the burden. 'What does your father say?'

'He says that it is what she wants, and that it is a wise decision.'

'And is it not?' he asked gently.

'Oh I know it is,' Gisele croaked, 'I just don't want to think of her dying. And when she enters the convent it will be like bidding farewell. She doesn't want me with her at the end.' Gisele wrung the kerchief between her fingers and laid her head upon Benedict's chest. 'I am crying for myself. I feel so frightened!'

Benedict felt the damp of her tears through his tunic and shirt. He made soothing noises and stroked with his hands. 'It is not a burden you need bear alone,' he murmured. 'You know that I am here.'

'But you wish you weren't, and I do not blame you!'

Benedict winced and tightened his hold on her narrow shoulders. Indeed he did wish to be elsewhere, but then he would only be fulfilling her expectations and contributing to his own self-disgust. 'I am here,' he repeated firmly.

Gisele chewed on her lower lip. Her lashes, spiky and wet, clung together. She sniffed loudly, then blew her nose again. 'I . . . I know I have not been much of a wife to you recently . . .'

He shook his head. 'Do not go down that road. I have not been much of a husband either, have I?'

There was a taut silence, broken only by the howl of the weather outside the shutters. Breaking it, Gisele said, 'I know about you and Julitta.'

Benedict stiffened. His heart began to pound and he knew that Gisele was sensing it against her own body.

'I know that you love her, and that she feels the same way about you.'

'It is in the past,' he said when he was sure his voice would serve him. 'And it was only the madness of springtide blood. She is content with Mauger now . . . and as I have told you, I am here . . . for you – but you must do the same for me. If a home hearth is cold, a man is bound to seek elsewhere for warmth.'

She looked up at him from drowned eyes, their grey colour strangely enhanced by the red rims. 'I will try,' she said unsteadily.

'We will both try.' Benedict kissed her cheek, and tasted the salt of her tears. He kissed her lips too, but did not linger.

Gisele lay against him for a while as they silently acknowledged the new pact between them, then she lifted her head and said softly, 'My mother wishes me to do something for her, and I promised I would.'

'Oh?'

'Last month, when you were in England and the convent was consecrated, one of the guests talked a great deal about pilgrimages and holy relics. Mama wants me to go to Compostella to pray for her soul and she desires me to bring back a relic to donate to the convent in her name.'

Benedict pursed his lips. He tried to imagine Gisele making a pilgrimage as far as northern Spain when he knew that she hated travelling. The ordered life of the castle was for her. Spinning, weaving, supervising; regular, organised meals and prayers in a safe environment. No surprises. Even journeying to Rouen, or, God forbid, Ulverton, was a trial to her. Small wonder that she had found reason to weep. But if it was her mother's will, then nothing on this earth would prevent her from going to Compostella, not even her own fear. To reason with her was useless. Not that he intended reasoning with her this time. It would be the discharging of a final duty to Arlette, a seal to put the past where it belonged. And he had his own reasons. His arm tightened around her at the sudden leap of his thoughts.

She looked at him with anxious eyes, seeking his face for anger or impatience, but he gave her a reassuring hug and smiled.

'I will take you to pray at the tomb of St James, and if I see horses fit for purchase, I will buy them,' he declared. 'Spanish destriers are the best in the world.' A spark of relish gleamed in his eyes. Gisele would have her saint's bones and prayers by the bucketful; he would obtain his wish to inspect Spanish horse-flesh at close quarters. And it was a legitimate excuse to avoid William Rufus for several months until the dust should settle and royal interest drift elsewhere.

Gisele wiped her nose a final time and tucked her soggy ker-chief back inside her sleeve. 'Do you truly mean it, that you would accompany me to the tomb of St James?'

He heard the lost note in her voice. Gisele was always seek-ing for approval and reassurance. She had very little sense of her own value beyond that which was reflected in her mother's eyes. It was up to him to imbue it in her. 'I would not have spoken otherwise,' he said, and kissed her damp cheek.

At Easter, shortly before he departed on pilgrimage with Gisele, Benedict paid a visit to Fauville. The road was soft with mud, and the wind bit through his cloak. A watery April sky fur-nished brightness but little warmth, and the trees wore only the most delicate tippets of green.

Within its palisade, Fauville's hall faced the world with a stone solidity, its slate-tiled roof attesting that its lord was com-fortable for funds, thatch being the norm of all lesser men. The windows faced the muddy bailey and the shutters were thrown back to admit the April daylight to the interior. Down the long side of the hall a herb bed had been planted and the soft greens of sage and lavender blended with the yellower tints of rue and fronds of early dill. Two hens scratched among the plants, clucking importantly to each other.

'And stay out, you thieving, mangy cur!' a woman shrieked. A tan deerhound shot out of the hall door on the end of the vicious sweep of a birch besom. A large chunk of blood pud-ding stretched its jaws, and had it been human, triumph would have glowed in its eyes. It clattered down the steps, streaked past the startled man, and scattering the hens in squawking high dudgeon, disappeared in the direction of the gates.

'I swear to you, my lady, if Ernoul Huntsman don't keep that hound of his under control, I'll have him with this broom too!'

'All right, Eda, calm yourself. I'll talk to him.' Julitta's voice came from within the hall, her tone bubbling with amusement. Benedict's stomach jolted just to hear her. Suddenly he wondered whether his visit had been such a good idea after all.

'It isn't the first time! Naught but trouble, that dog!' The maid poked her head out of the door to make sure that her quarry was not lurking on the stairs awaiting another opportunity to sneak in and steal again. She saw Benedict and jumped with surprise. Her round face reddened. She dipped him the merest curtsey and spoke rapidly over her shoulder.

Benedict dismounted as Julitta came to the doorway. She wore a homespun tunic of brown wool over an undergown of cream linen. A plain leather belt was passed twice around her waist, and from it dangled the household keys, a small pair of shears in a case, and her knife in a tooled leather sheath. Her hair was bound up in a kerchief tied with braid, and at her throat there was a simple bronze cross upon a leather cord. Her complexion had an alabaster luminosity, and her eyes were the dark blue of sapphires. She gazed at him and a pink flush crept slowly up her face.

'Will you come within?' She gestured through the open door of the hall.

Benedict smiled and shook his head. 'Thank you, but no. I am not even sure that I should be here at all.'

She folded her arms and leaned against the door post. 'Then why are you?'

'Among all the things I have taken from you, there is one that I can return. I know Mauger will not approve, but you can probably see your way to persuading him to accept it, since I know that you and he are on better terms these days.'

Her flush deepened. 'I had also heard the same about you and Gisele. Mauger says that you are departing on a pilgrimage together.'

He nodded. 'Within the month. I came to bid you farewell.'

'Yet another parting?' She raised a mocking eyebrow.

Benedict flinched beneath the look she gave him. He cleared

his throat, and stepped aside to reveal the golden-dappled mare tied on a leading rein. 'I came to bring you the mare. King William Rufus wanted to buy her and I refused him – one of the reasons I'm making myself scarce for a while. I thought I would give her into your custody before I left. It would not have been safe to leave her at Ulverton.'

Julitta stared at the young mare and then at him. 'Freya?' she said. 'This is Freya?'

He nodded. 'What do you think?'

Julitta ran down the steps to the courtyard to examine the mare at close quarters. 'Oh, she is beautiful!' she declared as she walked around the young horse and ran her hand over fluid muscles and sturdy bones. 'I told Mauger that she had breeding.' She stroked the plush nose, noting how quietly she stood to be inspected. 'Is she saddle-broken?'

Benedict smiled and gave a flourish. 'Of course.'

'Give me a leg up.'

Benedict's smile became a poignant grin. Here was the Julitta of his most precious memories, moved by enthusiasm to discard convention. He cupped his hand and boosted her across Freya's bare back. There was a cracking sound as a side seam gave in her undergown. Julitta clucked an irritated tongue and hitched her garments up, exposing her green hose almost to the knees. Benedict unknotted the long rein and presented it to her with a gallant bow.

Julitta laughed at him, and lightly kicked her heels against the mare's flanks.

Freya moved off across the courtyard, her gait silk-smooth. Benedict watched the two of them, deriving both pleasure and pain from the sight. Julitta rode superbly; there was something of her father's casual arrogance in the way she sat a horse. He could almost imagine her in chain-mail and helm, a sword at her hip and a kite shield upon her left arm. Or perhaps a wild Valkyrie, sweeping down from Valhalla to claim heroes for the eternal feast hall. He did not know that it had been one of Ailith's favourite self-images, nor that she had unconsciously imbued her daughter with much of its fire.

Julitta rode back to him, her eyes shining and a flush on her cheeks. 'She's perfect, Ben.'

'You'll have to test her over a longer distance before you can say that.'

'Oh, I will do, but I know already that she'll be as clear as a bell. How could she not in your care?' She slipped down from the mare's back with lithe ease and dusted down her skirts. 'You say William Rufus wanted to buy her?'

'Yes, for his catamite.'

Julitta considered him with pursed lips. 'I'm glad you refused, but it has made trouble for you?'

He shrugged and smiled ruefully. 'No more than usual. Rufus will forget, and his pretty boy will fall from favour. They never last for long. Rufus treats them like meals to be eaten – chews them up and throws away the bones.'

Julitta turned to stroke the mare's face and strong, arched neck. 'You once told me that Rufus wanted to make a meal of you.'

'He still does, but I have no intention of lying down across his table. Let his *bons amis* and the churchmen wrestle for his soul. I am well out of the broil and on my way to God's grace in Compostella.' He gathered Cylu's reins and set his foot in the stirrup before the temptation to say that yes, he would enter the hall, became too great.

'I did not think that you really cared about God's grace,' she said, watching him narrowly.

'No, but Gisele does, and who is to say that she is not right?'

Julitta shrugged. There was a brief, awkward silence.

'Besides,' Benedict continued, 'my own concern is with Spanish horses. I'm going to buy some good breeding stock for your father – Iberian stallions and mares. We need an influx of new blood.'

Julitta nodded and folded her arms as if protecting herself. The spontaneity had died. She was a polite hostess bidding farewell to a sometime visitor. Her eyes looked at him and through him.

'Wish me good fortune,' Benedict said, and turned Cylu

towards the gates. Suddenly he was desperate to be gone, as if the air of Fauville's courtyard was unbreathable. He clicked his tongue and drove in his heels, and Cylu sprang into a startled canter that took man and horse swiftly away from Julitta and the mare.

'A safe journey, and a safe return!' she called after him, but he was already beyond hearing, the pounding of hooves and the snort of Cylu's breath wasting the words torn from her. She gathered up her skirts to run after him, but as he reached Fauville's gates, Mauger came riding in on his stocky chestnut work horse, and the moment was lost. She dared say nothing in front of her husband.

Mauger eyed Benedict and then cut his gaze to Julitta standing poised in the ward.

Benedict reined back to let Mauger pass. 'It's only a fleeting visit,' he said to the other man's scowl. 'I brought a leaving gift for Julitta. If you've any sense, you'll accept it with goodwill.'

'You're a fine one to talk of sense!' Mauger growled. 'Every time you show your face a storm brews. You were leaving, were you not?' He gestured over his shoulder at the open gateway.

Benedict quelled the urge to make a snide reply, and without a word, rode out of Fauville. Mauger continued on into the bailey and dismounted.

'What did he want?' he demanded brusquely.

'To say farewell before he leaves for Compostella,' she answered evenly while she tried to judge his mood. The scowl on his face meant nothing, it was a habitual expression – a great pity, since it marred the handsomeness he would otherwise have possessed.

'He said that he had brought you a gift.'

'Yes.' Julitta indicated the mare. 'I do not suppose you recognise her?'

'Should I?' Mauger handed his own mount to a groom and came to look at Freya. He ran his hands down her legs, picked up her hooves and studied the undersides, measured her proportions with an experienced eye. Grudging admiration flickered upon his face. 'Should I?' he repeated, for Julitta had not answered.

Watching him carefully she said, 'Do you remember that day when I begged you to buy that mare and foal and you refused?'

'No, I don't, I . . .' he said, and then stopped as he did indeed remember. 'And this, I suppose, is the foal,' he said after a moment.

Julitta nodded silently.

'I don't like him giving you gifts, and sneaking around Fauville when I am not by.'

'One gift, and one visit?' Julitta was stung to reply. 'He did not even stay for refreshment. Ask in the hall if you do not believe me.'

His eyes narrowed. 'Perhaps I will,' he said, and then, folding his arms, added, 'You know by law that what is yours belongs to me.'

'You will not take her away!' Horrified and angry, Julitta rounded on him.

Mauger rubbed the knuckle of his forefinger beneath his nose. 'That is for me to decide, not you to command,' he said stiffly.

'She is mine.' Julitta threw caution to the wind. The leash of duty could only accept so much strain before it snapped. 'If Benedict can see it, why can't you? Are you less than him, or perhaps you are afraid, is that it?'

Mauger's complexion darkened angrily. 'Mind your tongue, or I'll have you clapped in a scold's bridle!' he snarled. 'Benedict de Remy is a weak fool, a *nithing*. I count him beneath my contempt. I fear no man.'

'Then prove he is nothing to you, let me keep the horse.' Julitta raised her chin a notch and challenged him with her eyes and her posture.

'And is he nothing to you?' Mauger took a step towards her, his breathing swift. She saw the brightness of lust in his eyes, of doubt and the need to believe.

'He is nothing to me,' she lied in a steady voice, and

although she could not prevent hot colour from flooding her face, she held Mauger's gaze. 'You are my husband.'

'And you obey me.' Mauger took her by the arm and steered her up the stairs and into the hall.

'Can I keep the mare?'

Mauger paused at the second set of stairs to the sleeping loft and pulled her against him. Julitta made herself pliantly passive, modestly willing as Mauger preferred. 'That depends,' he said again, but she saw that once his appetite was sated, he would yield.

CHAPTER 53

It was going to rain. Benedict glanced at the sky, which an hour since had been a brilliant summer blue. Now, clouds were piling in grey, fleecy layers over the High Pyrenees and billowing fast towards the pilgrims on the open road which twisted its way from the splendour of the mountains, down to the sun-baked plains of the kingdom of Castile.

Although it was still midsummer, the mountain winds could still cut ice-sharp through garments, and heavy rain turn tame streams into savage torrents. Landslips were not infrequent upon the tortuous road, and more than one traveller had come to grief before reaching the safety of the plains.

Had Benedict been alone, he would have travelled on one of his father's wine galleys, but Gisele hated the sea. She only needed to set her foot on a deck for her stomach to curdle. In defence of the overland route she had argued that a true pilgrimage to Compostella should involve paying respects at various abbeys, shrines and cathedrals along the way, lighting a candle at each one for her mother's soul.

So now, here they were, descending from the mountains, their offerings lighting a chain of devotional wax beacons that stretched back seven hundred miles to the cathedral in Rouen. Arlette's passage to heaven was assured.

The first drops of rain spattered down as heavy and cold as the small silver pennies in Benedict's pouch. Gisele exclaimed in dismay and pulled her broad-brimmed pilgrim's hat down over her ears. The other pilgrims with whom they were travelling for safety's sake, sought among their own packs for cloaks and hats.

'How much further to the hospice?' a merchant from Bordeaux demanded of their guide, a wiry little Basque who went by the name of Pons.

'Another hour, perhaps two.' The man gave a casual shrug. His accent was strong and difficult to follow. 'We arrive before dark.' He hitched the coil of rope on his shoulder, and continued along the path, his step light and arrogant.

The merchant hissed with irritation and rolled his eyes at Benedict. 'He's being paid enough to guide us through the passes. These mountain people, they are not to be trusted. Sooner cut your throat than give you respect.'

Benedict said nothing. Pons was indeed a rogue with more than a touch of the light finger about him, but the Bordeaux merchant was a pompous windbag and his attitude did not merit respect. All the way from Bordeaux he had blustered his own self-importance abroad. Everyone knew how rich he was, how influential, how intelligent a business man. Benedict, whose own wealth and connections put the merchant's in the shade, could not be bothered with such petty conflict and avoided the man as much as possible.

Receiving no response from Benedict now, the merchant sought approbation among the other travellers. There were a dozen in all, ranging from three Cluniac nuns and a priest, under Benedict's and Gisele's patronage, to a travelling musician with an extensive repertoire of songs, both sacred and profane, with which he regaled the company at intervals. Now he placed his precious harp in a waxed linen bag, and drew his hood up over his tawny curls. The nuns twittered nervous agreement with the merchant. The priest, like Benedict, held aloof, retreating into the depths of his cowl and thrusting his hands into the wide depths of his sleeves.

Without any warning except a brief, wind-snatched shout from Pons, the road narrowed, becoming a bitten white ribbon with a grass-tufted rock wall on one side, and a sheer drop on the other. Through a bluish haze of rain, Benedict stared at the stiff green spears of pine trees, at the jagged thrusts of stone, grey as solidified cloud, and in the chasm below, the thin, white twist of fast water, menacing and beautiful at one and the same time. He perceived it with the eyes of an eagle, yet he knew that if he flung himself into the void, he would drop like a stone.

The company had been riding two abreast, but now the line was forced down to single file. Gisele sat rigid upon her mare, her face averted from the steep emptiness beyond the crumbling track. Her lips were bloodless, so hard were they compressed by her terror. Benedict thought it ironic that she could worship God so thoroughly in the edifices built by man, but when confronted by God's own elements, she shrank in fear.

Thunder rumbled in the distance behind them, and the clouds were an ominous purple. The merchant's horse whinnied and sidled, its ears flickering. Loose stones skittered from beneath his hooves and tumbled over the road's edge, bouncing and rebounding into rain-driven oblivion. The nuns began to pray, their voices thin and puny against the power of the storm. The priest joined them, his baritone more powerful, but still as nothing. Lost voices in a vast cathedral.

Lightning daggered the boiling clouds and the thunder cracked overhead. The merchant's mount squealed and bucked, its hooves striking solidly in the chest of the following pack pony. The smaller beast shied, lost its balance, and slipped over the edge with a scream of terror. The pony's lead rope was wrapped around the merchant's saddle cantle, and now the falling weight slewed the larger horse around, dragging it towards the chasm. Soil-loosened stones bounded down the steep sides. The merchant's mouth widened in a silent scream.

Without pause for deliberation, Benedict leaped from Cylu's back. As he reached the merchant, his knife was already in his hand. He laid his hand on the taut lead rope and slashed. Fibres parted, the final thread clinging for what seemed an eternity before it snapped and the pack pony's weight surged free with a catapulting jar. The sound of the animal's falling flesh smacking on stone rose through the rainfall until, with a final bump, there was silence.

Soaked to the skin, his hair plastered to his skull, Benedict grasped the merchant's cob by its headstall, and held the beast steady. 'Get off and walk,' he snapped to its corpulent rider, and stared round at the rest of pilgrims who were looking on with shocked eyes. 'All of you, dismount. At least if another horse goes over, you won't be sitting on its back.'

Frightened and miserable, they did so. Tremors shook the merchant's vast bulk and his legs would scarcely support him. 'You did not have to cut the rope!' he cried.

'No, I didn't!' Benedict responded tersely. 'I could have left you to go over the edge.' He thrust the cob's wet reins into the merchant's slack fingers and turned away to deal with his own horses.

Pons was unmoved by the incident when he came to see what was keeping his charges so long. 'It happens,' he said, spreading his hands and shrugging. 'Lucky he was only a pack animal.' And then he looked shrewdly at Benedict. 'You cut the rope?'

'There was no time to do anything else.'

'You think on your feet, Frank,' Pons said. 'You are not such a fool as the others.' Swinging round, he began to slog onwards through the rain. Benedict received the impression that the guide's words were not by way of a compliment.

The journey continued, the weather growing murkier by the moment. No more horses were lost over the edge of the path. Within a hundred yards, it widened slightly, allowing room to breathe, and soon they were descending into the valley. But no-one dared to remount. Cold, dispirited, soaked to the bone, they plodded on. The beauty of the mountains was screened by thick curtains of rain.

Hampered by her skirts, Gisele tripped and stumbled.

'Tuck your gown through your belt,' Benedict said impatiently as yet again she almost went to her knees.

'It wouldn't be seemly,' she protested tearily.

'Who's to see in this?' he growled. 'Do you think anyone besides yourself cares? Do it now, before you fall.'

With trembling chin, Gisele fumbled beneath her cloak and tugged the merest token of dress through her belt. Benedict clamped his jaw on his irritation. It was at moments like this that he longed for Julitta, for her forthright, practical nature. She would have hitched her gown without a qualm, perhaps even have donned a pair of men's breeches. The word 'seemly' would not have disturbed her, unless it was being yelled at her by a purple-faced Mauger.

The pilgrims' hostel that greeted their arrival in the valley was a low-roofed timber dwelling with a balding thatched roof. The heavy rain had advanced the dusk and at first the proprietor did not want to admit them for the place was already bulging with travellers. There were no beds to spare, or even spaces in beds. At last, however, he was persuaded to sell the late arrivals floor space around the fire in the main hall. The merchant was furious, but no amount of railing made any difference to the proprietor's assertion that he had no beds.

'Even if you was the Queen o' Sheba, you'd sleep on the floor!' he declared. 'If you want to go higher than that, then you can sleep in the stables like our Blessed Lord.'

Complaining, the merchant opted for the main room, the smoky fire, and sleeping space on the filthy, trodden rushes. Benedict chose the stables, where the bedding was marginally cleaner, and the company more wholesome.

Gisele disappeared behind a stack of hay to change into dry garments from their pack, dry being a relative term, for even the fresh clothing was damp to the touch. Benedict stripped down to his loin cloth and set about making a thick, deep nest in the hay, then spread out the spare garments from his own pack to air, so that in the morning they might seem slightly drier.

The watery stew in the main room had not appealed to him, and he delved amongst his pack rations to see what he could find. There were small, hard cakes made of oats, raisins and honey, dried figs, a small cheese purchased from a shepherd's wife along the way, and some salty, spiced sausage from the same source. To wash it down there was wine mixed with water from a mountain stream. It was hardly a feast, but it was an improvement on the meal being served in the main room across the courtyard.

Gisele emerged from her hiding place and looked at Benedict with startled eyes when she saw his near-nudity.

'It will be warm enough beneath the hay,' he said. 'I don't want to sleep in damp clothes. If you had any sense, you'd take yours off too.'

Her colour heightened and her right hand rose to clutch at the silver cross hanging round her neck, and beside it, the reliquary she had bought in Toulouse. The small box with its facing of polished agates and emeralds purported to contain three eyelashes belonging to Mary Magdalene, who had, apparently, lived out her latter years in Southern Gaul. It had cost as much as a top quality warhorse, but Gisele had thought it worth every last silver penny. Benedict knew what he thought, but had reserved comment. The matter of the relic for Brize-sur-Risle was not his concern.

'Sit.' He gestured at the food.

Gisele abandoned her clutch on the reliquary and did as he bade her, tucking her gown neatly around her legs. Her gaze flickered over his shoulders and chest, the narrow smudge of hair running from nipple to nipple, and the fine line feathering down over the firm bands of stomach muscle and disappearing into the linen loin cloth. Her colour remained high. She nibbled daintily on a fig and sipped at the watered wine.

Benedict ate hungrily. The cheese was excellent, the sausage revolting, but he was famished and devoured both. Gisele ignored her portions, preferring instead to chew slowly on a honey cake. Her delicate stomach echoed her sensibilities.

The end of their meal was interrupted by Pons, who entered the stables with a laughing woman in tow, her brown hair indecently loose and her bodice in disarray.

Pons jerked to a halt when he saw Benedict and Gisele, and his foxy face became sharp with hostility. 'I thought everyone was in the hall. I always sleep here when I am guiding people through the passes.'

Benedict gestured around. 'There is room enough,' he said.

The woman with Pons murmured in his ear, detached herself from his embrace, and disappeared into the night. Pons scowled furiously at the interlopers. 'It is not safe out here. You should stay with the others.'

Benedict arched his brows. 'I'll take my chance.'

The Basque glanced over his shoulder at the stable entrance, then back at Benedict and Gisele. 'You Franks,' he sneered contemptuously. 'You think that you own the world.'

Benedict almost laughed at the irony of the statement. He wondered if Pons had ever listened to his own words. Mountain guides were notoriously arrogant. He said nothing, meeting the angry black stare with indifference.

Pons made to leave, but changed his mind and paused, his shoulder leaning against the door jamb. 'Travelling does not burden you the way it does some of the others,' he remarked. His posture remained hostile, but there was curiosity in his voice too. At his belt there were two knife scabbards, one sheathing a nine-inch hunting dagger, the other a smaller meat knife. Pons drew the latter and began paring his nails.

'I am accustomed to making long journeys.' Benedict tried to appear nonchalant, but he kept a wary eye on the knife. Beside him, Gisele was rigid with fear.

'Then you are a merchant?'

'Of sorts. I breed horses – destriers and sumpter ponies.'

Pons nodded and looked over the curve of his knuckles at Benedict. 'In Castile and Navarre, you will find the greatest horses on God's earth.'

'Yes, I know.'

'You come to buy?'

'Perhaps.'

The Basque sucked his teeth. 'These horses, they are expensive.' He rubbed his fingers and thumb together. 'Perhaps you do not have enough silver.'

'We shall see.'

Pons nodded. His eyes were still narrow, but the edge of anger had vanished, replaced with a glint of what might have been amusement. 'I am a merchant too,' he said. 'My whole family, they trade between our lands and yours, Frank.' He wiped the knife blade on his breeches and stabbed it into its sheath. 'I'll leave you to sleep now. Marisa and I will find somewhere else.' Bestowing a mocking flourish upon Benedict and Gisele, he disappeared into the night as silently as a cat. Like a dog, Benedict's hackles rose.

'As soon as we reach the plains, we'll hire a different guide,' he murmured to Gisele.

She clutched the reliquary at her breast, her grey eyes filled with fear. 'I don't like him,' she whispered.

Benedict made a wry face. 'And I don't trust him.'

The morning dawned bright and golden, with not a single cloud to mar the stunning blue of the sky. Shabby became quaint, primitive became rustic. The pilgrims took genuine pleasure in breaking their fast at the trestles set up in the meadow behind the hostel. Woodsmoke from the cooking fires hazed the air and carried upon it the smells of frying ham and batter cakes. There was milk and buttermilk to drink, and the air was clear and pleasantly warm.

Pons, who had not been in evidence for morning prayers, nor the main part of the meal, appeared as folk were rising from the tables. He snatched some left-over bread from a basket, speared a brown batter cake off the griddle iron on the point of his knife, and taking alternate bites from each one, set about mustering his charges.

He was in high good humour, whistling and singing as if the weather itself had entered his veins. But there was a tension about him too, like a storm building behind the sunshine.

'The road is easier today,' he announced. 'And the weather is fine. We'll make good progress.'

The pilgrims did indeed make good progress. The road was easier, but it was still narrow and stony with sharp outcrops of rock on either side. As the morning wore on, the pleasant warmth of the sun melted into a beating bronze heat. Water bottles were thirstily depleted; outer garments were removed. The Bordeaux merchant, his face the same mulberry shade as his robe, kept up an incessant litany of complaint, directed at the landscape, the weather, his fellow pilgrims, and most of all, at Pons.

The little Basque bore the merchant's tirade in silence, but his countenance steadily darkened, and he kept his fists clamped around his belt in an obvious effort to prevent himself from using them.

'I left civilisation when I left Bordeaux,' grumbled the merchant. 'If I did not love God and the blessed St James so much, I would not be here at all.'

Pons ceased walking and turned on the path to regard his charges. His dark eyes narrowed, his chest rose and fell rapidly, but it was with the effort of control, not because of the pace he had set. 'There is a wide stream beyond the next bend,' he said. 'Water the horses and fill your bottles. I'll join you in a moment.' He started to leave the path.

'Where do you think you are going?' The merchant's voice was like a whiplash.

Pons spread his hands. 'You want I should open my bowels in front of you? Do they do that in Bordeaux?' He gave the merchant a mocking stare and continued on his way, his step light and swift. Within moments he had vanished.

The merchant blustered and spluttered, his deluge of vocabulary temporarily arrested by the sheer insolence of their guide.

Benedict concealed a smile behind the pretence of wiping sweat from his face. He might not like or trust Pons, but that retort had hit the mark beautifully.

The stream was a stony mass of boulders and gravel, divided into several channels, some deep and narrow, others shallow and broad. The pilgrim company were only too pleased to dismount, water their horses and take a rest. The water was as clear and cold as glass, the pebbles on its bed shining like jewels. Gisele refilled the water skins whilst Benedict supervised their mounts, making sure that they did not drink too much.

One of the nuns daringly raised her habit above her ankles, revealing skinny white legs, and waded into the first, shallow channel. She uttered a small squeal at the coldness of the water and looked round at her sister nuns. They watched her dubiously for a moment, and then throwing caution to the wind, followed her example. The monk remained on the bank, washing his hands and face, and soaking a linen cloth to give cool respite to his sun-burned tonsure. The merchant removed his mulberry tunic, and puffing through his heavy jowls, sat down in the shade of a large rock.

He was the first to die. Silently, his windpipe severed. 'You were right about me,' Pons whispered as the merchant slumped. 'I would sooner slit your throat.'

The first Benedict knew of the attack were the two arrows that hit him, one through his side, the other through his left arm. The force spun him round and dropped him like a stone in the water. Gisele screamed and ran to him, floundering through the stream. Then she screamed again, the sound cut off before it had reached full pitch.

The water turned red and the colour eddied away down the current like scarlet fairing ribbons. Benedict was aware only of burning pain, of a weight across his body, driving that pain into every vital part of him. He tasted blood, and then the cold swirl of the water. It entered his nostrils and mouth, choking off his breath. He jerked his head up, gasping and gagging, and the pain redoubled. Gisele stared into his eyes, an expression of utter bewilderment on her face.

He tried to cry her name, but all that emerged was a wordless croak. To lift himself was agony. He pushed himself half-way to a sitting position, but the pain was too great, and he slumped back upon his wife's dead body, darkness claiming him.

CHAPTER 54

Faisal ibn Mansour, a Moorish physician in the employ of a Christian lord, Rodrigo Diaz de Bivar, had his mind on more pleasant thoughts than the stony route beneath his mule's hooves, when he and his escort came upon the scene of the massacre.

One moment, he was imagining the pleasures of home – the comfort of a couch, as opposed to the chaffing of this saddle, Maryam's quiet smile as she rubbed his feet, the laughter of their children in the room beyond – the next he was gazing at the bodies, strewn around the crossing place like so many discarded rag dolls.

'Allah be merciful!' he gasped, and drew rein so abruptly that the mule threw up its head and sat back on its haunches, almost unseating him. Kites and buzzards circled in the sky above, and as the new travellers approached the river, two black griffon-vultures took ponderous wing from the body they had been tearing apart. The birds flapped to the nearest tree and sat in the low branches, biding their time.

Faisal scrambled down from his mule and hastened to examine the bodies to see if anyone still lived. They were Christian pilgrims, he could see at a glance. Nuns and a monk, a minstrel, merchants and traders. Their clothing was sober, but of good quality. None of them wore a purse, nor was there any jewellery to be seen. There were hoofprints in the soft earth of yesterday's rain, but no sign of any horses. It was plain to Faisal that these pilgrims had been murdered by one of the bands of robbers that preyed on groups heading through the mountains towards the shrine of St James.

He shook his head in dismay as he moved from one to the other, laying his hand against their throats to check for the life-beat, holding a small mirror before their lips to see if they breathed, although in his heart of hearts, he knew that none would.

Generally, Faisal had an optimistic view of human nature. When you served such a man as Lord Rodrigo, whom the Moors knew as El Cid, you could not help but see your fellow man as worthy, but sometimes, such as now, the small, grey-bearded physician would wonder at the savagery which lurked in human nature too. Even with all his medical skills, it was not something that Faisal could cure.

Two soldiers of Faisal's escort had pulled some more bodies out of the water. A man and a woman, both of them arrow-shot. Shaking his head, tugging at his neat beard, Faisal went to inspect them. The woman had taken an arrow beneath the left shoulder blade, straight through the heart. Probably she had died even before she had hit the ground. She was slender, with a delicate, oval face and dainty features. The robbers had plundered her corpse as they had done all the others, but they had missed something. Her right fist was tightly clenched, and when Faisal gently prised it open, he discovered a small, jewelled reliquary pressed against her palm. The Christians, he knew, set much store by these objects, often reverencing them more than they did their God. He could understand that they were a focus and a comfort, but was glad that his own belief required no such props.

He shook his head over her body, and, having tugged out the arrow head, laid her flat and composed her limbs. Then he turned to the final corpse, and discovered with a sudden lurch of his stomach that the young man was still alive and watching him out of glazed, dark brown eyes.

'Bring me blankets, quickly!' Faisal commanded over his shoulder. 'This one lives, but I do not know for how long!' He knelt down in the grass beside the young man and laid his lean palm against the water-dewed neck. The pulse was steady, if somewhat slow, and was cause for reassurance. The Moor drew a sharp, curved knife from his belt.

'No, no,' he soothed, pressing down firmly with the flat of his hand as the brown eyes widened and the young man fought to rise. 'I am here to help you.' His tone, if not the meaning of his words, was understood, for the wounded pilgrim ceased to struggle and lay still except for the rigours of cold which shook his body.

Faisal eyed the two arrow shafts quilling the victim's tunic, one in the arm, the other in the side, and briefly deliberated whether to remove them, or leave them *in situ*. The one was likely to cause poisoning, the other excess bleeding, depending on angle and internal damage. He was accustomed to dealing with this kind of injury; he had cut his surgeon's teeth on just such wounds when travelling with Lord Rodrigo's army.

The soldier returned with the blankets. Faisal spread them over the pilgrim's right side, leaving the left bare to the exploration of his knife. The Moor cut away the blood-soaked sleeve, and slit the side seam of the tunic and shirt so that he could assess the damage. The arm injury was obviously a flesh wound. The tip of the arrow had pierced skin and muscle, but Faisal could tell from the amount of blood on the tunic that it was not too serious.

'This will hurt,' he said, and when the young man looked at him with a questioning frown, repeated the words haltingly in the language of the Franks.

The dark eyes flickered, the throat moved in a swallow. 'Do what you must,' the pilgrim said huskily.

Faisal gripped the arrow shaft firmly in his two hands and smartly snapped it off. The young man arched, his breath catching and then hissing raggedly through his teeth. Faisal reached into the pouch at his waist, withdrew a small flask, and removing the stopper, dripped a clear liquid onto the site of the wound which had begun to ooze blood under the movement of the arrow shaft. This time, the injured man's body leaped like a bounding gazelle.

'I am sorry to hurt you,' Faisal said, 'but this will keep your wound clean until I have time to probe the rest of the arrow from your flesh. I must look at the other one now.'

Faisal did not know if the pilgrim had heard him through the pain. His eyes were clenched shut, and his breathing was a series of unsteady sobs.

The soldier who had brought the blankets, a man in his thirties whose name was Angel, squatted on his haunches and looked across the body at the physician. 'Is he going to live?'

Concentrating intently upon his patient, Faisal did not look up. 'It is hard to tell. He is strong to have survived thus far, and he is conscious, he knows what I am doing and he is able to respond. It depends upon how much more punishment his body can take. He is chilled to the bone, and I can do no more for him now except remove the length of these shafts for travelling and keep him warm. I dare not start probing for the arrow heads out here.' Although talking to the soldier, Faisal was also talking out his thoughts for his own benefit.

'Will he be able to sit a horse?'

'He will have to. He is not heavily built. I will sit behind him on the mule and hold him in place.' Faisal's strong, brown hands moved dextrously to the second arrow shaft, buried in the young man's side.

Angel grimaced. 'Is he gut shot?'

'I do not think so, he would be screaming and writhing if he were, and his condition is too good for a man with a pierced belly. I think,' he added slowly, his words keeping pace with his examination, 'that he is very lucky. It is like the arm wound – through the skin and flesh of the side without touching any vital organ.' He broke off the second shaft, and then leaned over to sniff at the site of entry. 'I feared that perhaps the point had entered a kidney, but there is no smell of urine,' he muttered. 'Yes, it may be that he will survive.' Faisal proceeded to anoint the second wound with the clear liquid, and again, his patient reacted strongly, then shuddered and was still.

Angel looked anxiously at Faisal. The physician checked his patient's wrist and then the bare young throat. 'He is merely unconscious, and better so, I think, if we are to journey with him.' He fingered the rich woollen cloth of the pilgrim's tunic, typical of the finest fabric that the northern Franks produced, and then frowned as he felt something flat, hard and round under his touch. It was a token, or a coin of about the circumference of his little fingertip. He found more of them, identical in size, spread throughout the lining of the tunic. Robbers might have seized his money pouch, but it seemed that the young man was still not without his resources, and Faisal was willing to hazard that the coins would amount to a small fortune.

Angel had been watching the physician's exploration with ever-widening eyes. 'I wonder who he is.'

'If Allah wills it in his mercy, he will live to tell us.' Faisal rose to his feet, and tugged thoughtfully at his beard. 'He looks to me like a Frankish merchant, and a wealthy one. Nor would I say that the pilgrim road was his only business in our country. A handful of silver would be more than enough to see him comfortably to Compostella. I think that Lord Rodrigo should involve himself with this one.'

Benedict tried to move and found that he could not. Someone had taken two nails, each a foot long, and driven them through his body, pinning him to the ground. He could hear shouts and screams, cries choked off in blood as those around him died. He tried to shout for help, but his voice remained locked in his throat. Gisele fell beside him and he saw her die before he died too, and woke to find himself in hell.

There was a devil with black eyes and a trim, grey beard who kept poking and prodding at his wounds with a sharpened knife, and muttering to himself in a strange language full of hawkings and words that sounded like '*Beelzebub*'. Sometimes the devil would attempt to communicate with him by speaking in halting French, but Benedict would pretend not to hear, and close his eyes. There were others, his minions, who came and went. On several occasions, Benedict was visited by a priest wearing a dark brown habit, a heavy silver cross hanging upon his breast. The priest urged him to repent of his sins so that he might be shriven. Benedict could not remember revealing anything to him, but he must have done so, for he could still distinctly feel the slick anointing of the holy oil between his brows. Were there confessions and anointings in hell?

Cautiously he raised his lids and looked around. On this occasion, no-one leaned over him to pronounce judgement. His eyes met cool, whitewashed walls and a high, wooden ceiling, a cupboard of dark oak, and an arched aumbry above it in which stood a terracotta oil lamp. A path of sunlight streamed through the shutters of an open window and traversed the foot of his bed, brightening the colourful stripes on the coverlet of woven linen. Three ripening oranges glowed on the sill, drawing his eye with their intensity of hue. He frowned. Wherever he was, it was certainly not the hell of his fevered dreams; nor yet was it heaven. And there was pain. His entire left side from armpit to groin felt like a bar of red-hot iron.

He strove to sit up, and quickly discovered himself so stiff and sore that he was as stranded as a beetle cast over upon its back. Then, right-armed, he eased back the sheet and coverlet to look at himself. Layers of linen bandage were wrapped around his upper left arm and secured with a small cloak pin. On his torso there were livid bruises, and another wad of bandage which covered his left side from his lower ribcage to his protuberant hip bone. He had never carried much meat on his body, but now there was scarcely enough for a vulture to pick clean.

The thought of a vulture sent unpleasant images jolting through his mind. Bodies strewn on a river bank, and huge birds descending to feast, while he watched, powerless to move. Human vultures stalking among the dead, knives like beaks rending and tearing.

The door opened, and amidst a rustling whisper of silk robes, the devil of his dreams with the hawk nose and black eyes of a bird of prey stood over him. This time, however, Benedict was lucid enough to see that he was a man of Moorish extraction in his early middle years, slender and small. His loose tunic was of striped silk in deep citrus shades that complimented his dark skin.

'Ah, you are awake,' the Moor said in careful French and smiled, revealing a gleam of white teeth. 'I was beginning to think that I might lose you. You must be wondering who I am and where you are?'

Benedict swallowed. 'I thought I was in hell at first.'

The smile became a wry chuckle. 'You would not be the first. My name is Faisal Ibn Mansour, and I am a physician in the employ of Lord Rodrigo Diaz de Bivar, who is also known among my people as El Cid, the Lord – may Allah grant him many blessings and a long life.'

Benedict struggled with the names. The Moor was watching him as if expecting the titles to mean something. He thought that he might have vaguely heard of Rodrigo Diaz in a hostel along the way, but at the time he had taken small notice.

'You are in one of Lord Rodrigo's castles on the road to Burgos,' the Moor continued, and the black eyes softened. 'We brought you out of the river beyond Roncevalles, half-dead with cold and suffering from arrow wounds. You were the only one of your company to survive. I am sorry.'

Benedict drew a deep breath and released it shakily. So that part of his nightmare had been true. 'My wife,' he said. 'She was in the river with me, filling our water bottles . . .'

The physician shook his head sorrowfully. 'She was shot to the heart. One arrow. It is a dangerous road through that pass.'

'We were on pilgrimage to Compostella, to pray for her mother's soul. She hated travelling. It was only because it was her duty . . . her accursed duty.' Benedict's eyes burned and filled. He looked through a polish of tears at the Moor. 'I was with her; she thought that she was safe.'

'Do you desire to speak to a priest for comfort?'

'No!' Benedict almost choked on the word. 'That is the last thing I want to do.' He bit his lip, struggling for control, and when he had mastered himself, looked at the physician, who was eyeing him the way he might eye a strange creature in a cage. 'I want to sit up, but I cannot move.'

'Small wonder, the size of the hole in your side. Allah be praised that the arrow did not pierce a fraction deeper, or you would now be dead.'

'Allah be praised?' There was a note of cynicism in Benedict's voice. Just now he was not sure whether living was a blessing or a curse.

'Allah be praised,' Faisal ibn Mansour repeated firmly, and grasping him by the right arm, manipulated him gently upright, supporting his spine with more pillows. The pain was briefly blinding and it took Benedict a moment to recover, leaning back, his eyes tightly closed. When he opened them once more, the older man was staring at him curiously, his hands folded within his sleeves.

'You see that you are wearing nought but a loin cloth,' he said. 'That is to help your wounds heal. If you wish to leave your bed, clothes can be found for you. Your tunic, the one you were wearing when we fished you out of the river, is locked in the chest in my chamber. If you had a money pouch, I fear it has been robbed.'

Benedict's gaze sharpened. The pain had sufficiently diminished for him to be aware of the reason for the Moor's curiosity. It was not every pilgrim who carried a fortune in silver sewn into the lining of his tunic. 'I did have a money pouch,' he said slowly, 'with enough in it to give alms to the poor and pay out for our board and lodging where necessary, but as you have realised, that is not where the bulk of my wealth was stored.'

The physician unfolded his hands from his robe and went to the cupboard, returning with a jug of wine and a cup. He filled one from the other. 'Drink,' he commanded. 'You must restore your strength.'

Benedict took several swallows, and rested his head against the heavily stuffed pillows. His left arm and side throbbed painfully. 'How long have I lain here?'

'You have been three days on the road, and three days in this bed. This morning is the fourth.'

Benedict tried to order his thoughts. It seemed as if eternity had passed since the attack, and conversely, no time at all. 'My wife,' he said hesitantly, 'and the others. What happened to them . . . I mean, what did you do?'

Faisal spread apologetic hands. 'We were only a small party, we could not carry them with us, but we composed the bodies decently, and spoke to a priest as soon as we met habitation. He promised that he would attend to the matter of their burial. I will take you to the village when you are recovered, if you wish.'

'Thank you.'

Faisal cocked his head on one side. 'We still do not know your name, or how we should address you. Outside this room, they call you the Young Frank, but there is more to you than that, I think.'

Benedict's mouth curved in a bleak half-smile. 'I prefer the simplicity of being "the Young Frank",' he said, 'but if you desire to know my name I will tell you. I am Benedict de Remy and I call Normandy and England my home. My father is a prosperous wine-merchant, and my father-in-law breeds horses for the Duke of Normandy and the King of England.'

'Ah,' said Faisal, looking interested, but not particularly impressed. A man, as El Cid was always saying, should be judged on what he is, not who his forefathers were. Although a breeder of horses might take exception to that theory. 'But what of yourself?' he asked.

The half-smile deepened. 'I would not blame you if you thought I had been sent on a pilgrimage to stiffen my character – it is something that rich fathers do for their decadent sons.'

'I make no such judgements. Only Allah sees what is in a man's heart.'

Benedict shrugged, not entirely in agreement, but did not argue the point. 'You ask what of myself,' he said after a moment. 'The easiest reply is that I too breed horses, that I am an assistant to my father-in-law. My wife came here to visit the shrine of St James at Compostella, and I elected to escort her because I wanted to buy Spanish horses to improve our blood-stock in the north. It is my desire to breed the best warhorses in the Christian world.'

'Even if the best warhorses of the moment are Moslem bred?' Faisal asked mischievously.

Benedict smiled. 'I am willing to learn. A man's religion should not stand in the way of knowledge.'

Faisal nodded with cautious approval. 'When you are well, will you still pursue your intention?'

Benedict closed his eyes for a moment, mustering his strength. 'If I do not, then everything will have been wasted. No matter how much I want to crawl into a corner and cover my head, it is no respect to the dead to live a life of mourning. I will still go to Compostella, and fulfil her vow, and I will still find my horses.'

Faisal pursed his lips and nodded slowly. 'That is good,' he pronounced. After a pause, he added, 'When we found your wife, she was still clutching a reliquary in her hand. That too is in my coffer with your tunic. I know that you Christians set great store by the relics of their saints.'

'Some of us,' Benedict said, and his voice was tired and bitter. 'Gisele believed that they would take her unharmed through fire and flood. I was the unbeliever, and yet I survive. Perhaps, as they say, the devil looks after his own.'

CHAPTER 55

The interior of the tiny chapel glowed like a jewel. Slender wax tapers twinkled in pyramid clusters, lighting the cool stone darkness, giving the pilgrim a feeling of intimacy with God. Upon the altar, a cross of inlaid silver-gilt reflected the flames until its surface rippled like water. A statue of the Virgin Mary, blue-robed and serene, smiled down upon the worshippers. A plump Christ child sat in the crook of her arm and raised his painted wooden hand in blessing to all who knelt before him. At his mother's feet lay a treasure house of pilgrim offerings, from simple wreaths of flowers and cheap tokens in plaster and wood, to bracelets and crosses of silver and bronze inlaid with semi-precious stones, belts and cups, and even a carved cedarwood box containing myrrh.

Benedict knelt before the silver-gilt cross and the statue with its improbably coloured pink flesh. The stone floor was cold beneath his knees; the scar in his side was sore from the strain of riding and then kneeling. It was less than a week since he had risen from his sick bed, and he knew that he had pushed himself too fast and too far in his need to make atonement at the place where Gisele was buried.

He tried to concentrate on the chapel's gentle atmosphere rather than his own aches and pains, to project himself beyond the mire of the physical. *Ave Maria, Regina caelorum, Beata Maria* . . . The Virgin's smile filled his vision. He clutched Gisele's small reliquary in his hand, his thumb moving over its edges, the raised cold bumps of agate and emerald. He was going to leave her here, in this small, intimate hamlet on the road to Compostella. Every day pilgrims would come to pray. If her spirit chose to linger, she would not be lonely. He could not bear the thought of disinterring her body and bearing it home to England. Mile after mile it would drag like a lead shackle upon his conscience. Let her lie here, undisturbed. *Benedicte.*

Behind him, someone gently cleared his throat. Turning, he saw the soldier, Angel. Hat in hand, the man knelt before the altar, genuflected to the statue, then addressed Benedict in a hushed voice. 'I am sorry to disturb you, Señor, but Lord Faisal says that if you have had enough time, we must be riding on to reach our destination before dark.'

Benedict looked down at the small box in his hand. 'I am ready,' he said, and rising stiffly to his feet, stepped forward to the statue and laid the reliquary at its feet. It belonged to Gisele, was no part of him. He remembered the look on her face when she first held it in her hands, the hunger; the wondering delight that such an object could actually exist and belong to her. He crossed himself once more, and then turned and walked out of the chapel without looking back. Nor did he visit the graveyard. What was there to see but a mound of earth?

Faisal was waiting for him, holding the bridle of a cream Andalusian gelding, a steady horse, almost beyond its prime and docile, suited to the needs of an invalid who was recently and inadvisedly out of his sick bed. The Moor's dark eyes were compassionate as he handed up the reins, but he did not speak. Neither did Benedict. His heart was too full; his throat ached, his eyes stung.

They rode in silence, the cream horse smoothly pacing the miles of dusty road, worn into a rut by the tramp of pilgrim sandals. The ache in Benedict's chest eased. He blinked the moisture from his eyes, and at length turned to his silent companion.

'I did not love her,' he said with quiet intensity, 'but she was a part of me, and now it is as though that part has been cut out.'

Faisal nodded compassionately, but recognising Benedict's need to talk, said nothing. A wound had to be cleansed before it would heal.

'We were betrothed when we were children. My father could see that I was better with horses than I was with barrels of wine, so he secured me a future with the best breeder of horses in Normandy, who was also his very good friend.' Benedict grimaced at the Moor. 'The trouble was that in his enthusiasm, he betrothed me to the wrong daughter.'

Faisal arched his brows. 'Your wife has a sister?'

'A half-sister. Gisele was the fruit of Rolf's legal marriage. Julitta was born to his Saxon mistress.'

'Mistress?' Faisal frowned, the word evading him.

'Concubine . . . although she was more like a wife.'

'Ah.'

Silence descended again and persisted for several minutes. Then Benedict drew a shuddering breath. To speak of Julitta was difficult, although she dwelt in his memory far more brightly than did Gisele. 'She used to follow me round when I was a boy, chattering nineteen to the dozen, being a nuisance as little girls are – I am four years older. On one occasion, I rescued her from a vicious gander, and from that day forth I became her hero. She was funny and high-spirited, always into mischief – and not much of that has changed,' he added wryly. 'I tolerated her, treated her like a little sister.'

Faisal sucked his teeth. 'You are going to tell me that this changed as you grew up.'

'There was a gap of many years when we did not see each other. Julitta's circumstances changed, and when I did meet her again, she was just turning into a woman, and I had been betrothed for more than eight years to Gisele. The gap had been too long; I could not see her as my sister any more.' His expression grew bleak as he told the silent Faisal the remainder of the tale. 'I thought that perhaps this journey with Gisele would bring us together as husband and wife . . . You can see where it brought us.'

Faisal looked thoughtful. 'To a crossroads,' he said, 'from

which you go on alone with your burdens. The time will come when you will shed them, I think, but for now, you must bear them as best you can.'

'The wisdom of the prophet?' Benedict blinked moisture from his eyes. Self-pity would only weigh him down further. He wondered if Faisal knew that in the Frankish lands, cross-roads were places where the dead and the living were reputed to be able to meet.

'No, the words of a friend.'

Benedict managed a tight smile. '*Inshallah*,' he said, murmuring the customary Arabic words of protection. 'If God wills it.'

'*Inshallah*,' Faisal responded gravely, his hands together in a gesture of prayer.

Rodrigo Diaz de Bivar, better known as 'El Cid', looked every inch his title. He was tall, with the wide shoulders and narrow hips of an athlete. His tanned face was wide at the brow, with a long, powerful jaw, and prominent cheekbones. Swept-back silver-black hair was trimmed just above the collar of a crimson silk tunic crusted with gold embroidery. It was court dress and not at all customary. Faisal and Benedict could as easily have found him wearing a warrior's quilted gambeson and his swordbelt.

Benedict stared around the great hall as they were led by an equerry towards Lord Rodrigo. It was not so different from the hall at home; although larger and more sumptuous. The architecture was similar, but the painted designs on the plasterwork were bolder and bore a Moorish influence, and on the dais, a brightly coloured rug had been spread on top of the rushes.

Two white and gold Balearic hounds with broad hunting collars trotted up to Benedict, and sniffed him thoroughly. Faisal they accepted with wagging tails and a joyful dance of paws. Faisal laughed and fussed the dogs, sending them into wriggles of ecstasy.

The Lord Rodrigo glanced up from his business on the dais,

saw the physician and, with a smile, beckoned him forward to the high table.

Benedict hung back out of courtesy, but Faisal took him by the arm and drew him to the dais. The dogs gambolled underfoot, making it difficult for the men to walk, and a squire hastened to grab the animals by their collars and bring them to heel.

'Well,' said the Lord Rodrigo as Faisal and Benedict bowed the knee before his ornate chair. 'You have finally decided to return, eh? I give you leave to gather herbs in the mountains and attend a sick friend, and you disappear from the face of the world.'

The tone was strong and controlled, bearing no particular inflection. Benedict risked a glance from beneath his lids to see if Rodrigo was angry, and was reassured to perceive a glimmer of dry humour in the dark, almost black eyes.

'It grieves me deeply not to have been here sooner, but there were grave doings that kept me from your court, my lord.' Faisal bowed even further, almost as he did when he faced the east to pray to Allah.

Rodrigo looked down and concern coloured his next words. 'Lord Pedro is well, I trust?'

'I left him in good health, my lord. His chest will always pain him somewhat, but I have given him a medicine to take every day, and if he obeys, he will yet live out a long life.'

Rodrigo's expression softened. 'Then it is well. Both of you, rise and sit by me a while.' He indicated the cushioned bench beside his carved chair. A squire was summoned. Food and drink were brought, and while Rodrigo finished his business with his officials, Faisal and Benedict ate and drank.

Benedict had not had much appetite these last few days on the road. Wrestling with his thoughts and his conscience had left very little room to be concerned for bodily sustenance. Now he realised, as he dipped his bread in a bowl of seasoned olive oil, that he was ravenous. He forced himself to chew and swallow at a measured pace and not to overeat, although that was difficult, since the food was the best he had tasted in a long time – succulent roast lamb with mountain herbs, pigeons served with a peppery sauce of wine and garlic, biblical fruits, and small, sweet fritters.

Lord Rodrigo finished his business and turned his attention to the diners, helping himself to a fig from the bowl of fruit. 'Now, then,' he said with a sharp glance at Benedict, 'to grave doings. Your name is?'

Benedict hastily swallowed his mouthful of fritter. 'Benedict de Remy, my lord, from Rouen in Normandy.'

'We came across him almost dead from exposure and arrow wounds,' Faisal explained. 'He was the only one of his pilgrim group to survive. It was an organised attack by Basque hill men. His wife was among the dead. I have been caring for him these past few weeks, and now I bring him to you.'

The Lord Rodrigo's face had turned to stone as Faisal spoke of mountain robbers. 'Such men are beneath mercy,' he said, his lips curling back from his large, white teeth. 'To rob and murder pilgrims bound upon errands of prayer is an act beyond salvation.' He looked at Benedict with anger and compassion. 'I am sorry that you should bear such a burden of grief. Rest assured, I will pursue this matter. The mountains are beyond the reach of my writ, but I will do what I can to influence those who do have jurisdiction.'

'Thank you, my lord.'

'I know it is small comfort to you. The loss of your wife must be a great sorrow.'

Benedict lowered his eyes and said nothing. He did not want to talk about Gisele. He had said enough to Faisal. Nor did he wish to speak of the attack. He remembered very little except the horror of the vultures settling to feed, and Gisele's dead weight stirring back and forth against him in the water's current.

'Do you continue on to Compostella?'

'In time, my lord.' Benedict relaxed slightly. 'It was my wife's intention to pray at the shrine, and I will do so to honour her. But I also came to your country to buy horses. My father-by-marriage is a famed breeder of destriers in Normandy and England. Iberian bloodstock would enhance his reputation even more . . . and mine.'

Rodrigo looked him up and down. He saw a young man, handsome and slender. The eyes were careworn, the mouth held in the tight line of recent suffering, the hands lean and clever. A horse breeder of repute, so he said, and yet he scarcely looked old enough to grow a beard. Rodrigo could imagine him dallying in the company of women with a harp and pretty love songs, but not assessing warhorses in a dusty tiltyard. Appearances could be deceptive, and Faisal certainly seemed to have taken to the pilgrim, but Rodrigo had learned from bitter experience never to take anyone by word alone.

'I can find you horses,' he said. 'When you are rested, I will show you the herds on my own estates.'

The weariness lifted slightly from the young man's expression. A spark kindled in his eyes and he thanked his host in a tone less dull than his previous exchanges.

Rodrigo shrugged his powerful shoulders. 'It will be my pleasure,' he said, and perused Benedict once more. 'Are you a fighting man? Have you ever been trained to arms?'

Benedict pinched his upper lip between forefinger and thumb and considered the reply. 'I am not sure how to answer, my lord. I know the rudiments of sword play and I can use a spear and shield as well as any footsoldier, and I am competent with both on horseback. I have to be for testing how a partic-ular horse will respond to the weight of an armed man on his back. Not every animal of destrier stock is suitable to become a warhorse.'

Rodrigo nodded. Deceptive appearances again. Perhaps a deceptive tongue too. He reserved his judgement.

The young stallion's hide flowed like molten-bronze, rippling over powerful muscles and strong bones. His mane and tail were an attractive contrast of silver-blond, the latter sweeping to the ground.

Rodrigo smiled inside his mouth at the rapt, almost stunned expression on Benedict de Remy's face as a groom led the animal up and down. 'He is yours,' he said. 'A gift to replace the mount you lost when you were robbed.'

Benedict stared at the vision before him, and was mute with longing, delight, and awe. Cylu, beloved even though he had been, would have fetched only half the worth of this horse in trade. 'My lord, I can never repay you,' he said huskily. 'I know many a lord in Normandy who would give his teeth for a such a horse to use in the hunt.'

'Let me hear no talk of repayment,' Rodrigo said with a shrug. 'What I give, I bestow freely without obligation. Other horses on this stud you may buy, but this one is yours to do with as you wish. He comes from the south, from the Andaluz, and he has a pedigree that goes back to the bible . . . or so my overseer tells me.'

Benedict stepped up to the horse, approaching it from the side so that it could obtain a full view of him. The liquid eye appraised. The head swung and the nostrils drank in Benedict's scent. In preparation for a morning of examining Lord Rodrigo's horses, Benedict had filled his pouch with dates. Unerringly, the horse extended his neck and snuffled at the leather bag hanging from Benedict's belt.

Rodrigo laughed. So did Benedict as he stepped adroitly to one side and turned his back while he removed two dates and laid them across his palm. The horse followed him, tugging against the groom, until its head rested over Benedict's shoulder. An insistent muzzle quested, and the dates vanished in short order. The horse tossed his head up and down as he chewed, see-sawing the poor groom like a man stuck on a bell rope. As daintily as a nun in a refectory, the horse spat out the cleaned fruit stones, then looked round for more.

Benedict took the bridle from the groom, and setting his foot in the stirrup, swung across the saddle. The wound in his side twinged, but it was an uncomfortable rather than incapacitating pain. The stallion grunted as Benedict's weight came down in the saddle, a sound out of all proportion to the light bulk of the man, and gave a vigorous back-kick of protest. Benedict rode with the move, keeping his body supple, and began to draw in the reins. He recognised the stallion's temperament. The spectacular bronze hide and silver mane and tail were for show and these antics were merely an addition, a way of ensuring attention. *Look at me, am I not fine.* Benedict had met people who said that a horse was a horse. If it was sound and capable of doing the work for which it was purchased, what more was there to consider?

Benedict thought of gentle Cylu, even-tempered and with the endurance of a rock, of the sparky bay pony of his childhood, and the stubborn pied gelding which had replaced it as he grew. Sleipnir, Cylu's sire, old and whiskered, nigh on thirty years old, a veteran of the great battle on Hastings field. And Freya, Julitta's golden dappled mare. If she was mated to this stallion beneath him, the offspring would likely be beyond price. His mind flooded with the possibilities.

'Does he have a name?'

Rodrigo nodded. 'Kumbi.'

'Kumbi?' The stallion's ears flickered at the familiar sound and he bucked again, more vigorously. Benedict tightened in the reins hard, letting him know who was master, and the warning issued, slackened them slightly.

'It is a trading place, far, far from here; across the sea, across a vast desert larger than an ocean; a market for the gold that is mined in a kingdom the Moors call Gana. Horses, smaller than this, but of great endurance are to be found in the desert.'

Benedict smiled. 'My father-by-marriage would be interested to know of such lands. He has always had a wanderlust for new places and new experiences.'

'You say he is a renowned breeder of horses on his own lands. I am surprised that he has never travelled beyond the Pyrenees himself.'

'It has always been on his horizon, a "one day" destination,' Benedict said. 'The last dream when all others have been broken.'

Rodrigo raised his eyebrows, but Benedict did not offer to elaborate. The golden horse, sensing the division of concentration, tried to play up again and for the next few minutes

Benedict was occupied in exerting his authority. The stallion put up a struggle, but finally settled down to perform as the man commanded. Benedict asked for a lance and a shield, and when the two were handed up to him, he threaded his left arm through the leather shield straps, and couched the lance in his right. His control of the reins was now negligible, and he had to command the horse through leg pressure and tone of voice. This was where the sensitivity and intelligence of the animal was important. Kumbi possessed full measure of both, and beneath Benedict's gifted handling, performed magnificently.

Rodrigo watched man and mount. Benedict rode like a Moor, he thought, light in the saddle, supple and deadly. The young man knew his trade, of that now Rodrigo had not a single doubt. His look grew thoughtful, but when Benedict drew rein and dismounted, his face flushed with pleasure, the lord of Bivar said nothing of what was on his mind. Instead, he praised Benedict and the horse, and took his guest to meet Sancho, the overseer.

Sancho was wizened and leathery. There was no telling how old he was, but to Benedict, he looked as if he had already been embalmed so closely did his features hug the contours of his bones. Most of Sancho's teeth were missing, and those that survived were twisted yellow pegs. One eye was milky, almost blind, the outer rim of the other was encircled with white, and yet their gaze on Benedict managed to be as sharp as a blade. Looking amused, Lord Rodrigo distanced himself from the confrontation.

'You are a horse breeder in your own country, eh?' Sancho challenged in a cracked voice. 'That doesn't even set you on the first rung of the ladder in Castile.'

'I learn fast,' Benedict replied, maintaining an even tone. 'And I have always been taught well . . . in the past.'

The old man hawked and spat. The eyes gleamed like opaque stones. 'What makes you think I want to teach you?'

Benedict shrugged. 'What makes you think I want you to teach me?'

They stared at each other, the small, wrinkled veteran of

more than sixty burning Iberian summers and the limber young man, supple as a young tree, full of rising sap.

'I know horses, I know men,' Sancho said. His tone was less hostile, as if in that last, examining stare, he had discovered something of interest.

'So do I.' Benedict's gaze flickered to the Lord Rodrigo who was supervising the encounter from the corner of his eye, a half-smile twitching his lips. Sancho glanced too, and his own seamed, thin scar of a mouth began to curve.

'And no-one knows men better than El Cid,' he said. 'He must think you worthwhile in some way to bestow on you a horse of Kumbi's value, and promise you the pick of this stud. What it is he sees in you I do not know, but perhaps I should find out.'

Benedict returned the smile. 'I was of the same opinion about you,' he retorted.

CHAPTER 56

Arlette de Brize died on a shining midsummer morning in the convent of the Magdalene. She was at peace, and as Rolf looked down on her waxen, closed face, he could almost detect a smile on her lips. Her last words of an hour since lingered with him, causing a shiver of discomfort. 'I am going to be with Gisele,' she had said. Not God, but Gisele.

During her last week when the pain had been great, the nuns had drugged her with poppy syrup. The nostrum had taken the pain and brought lurid visions in its stead. In her waking moments Arlette had spoken in a trembling voice of beautiful gardens and angels brighter than the morning sun. She had also cried out at visions of blood and death, growing agitated despite the heavy sedation.

Rolf was glad that her suffering was over. He wished that he could grieve, but for the moment he only felt numb, as if he too had drunk of the poppy's narcotic. They had been married for almost thirty years, and she had been a constant in his life – too familiar to be noticed until there was a cold space where her presence had once stood. It was nothing compared to the frozen landscape occupied by Ailith's ghost, but still he was aware of how threadbare his life was becoming.

He meditated beside her body for a respectful period, and then left her to the ministrations of the nuns. She belonged to them now. They would care for her far more diligently than he ever had. He departed the chapel, a greying man almost fifty years old, the wiry grace of his youth now set in a more solid mould, his features still handsome, but showing the marks of time.

He rode home to Brize in a reflective mood, his mind dwelling on the bitter-sweetness of the past. If only Arlette had yielded a little more; if only he had been more patient. If only . . . And the name his mind spoke was suddenly not his wife's.

When he arrived at Brize, he was still preoccupied, heavy of heart, and it took him a while to realise that he had visitors. It was the sight of his grooms more than usually busy in the stable area and his automatic eye for a good horse that jerked him belatedly out of his reverie to ask what was happening.

'Duke Robert's here, my lord,' replied the man, nodding his head at the glossy chestnut stallion that an unfamiliar squire was watering at the trough. The horse's bridle and saddle were of rich, embossed leather. The breast band was decorated with red silk tassels and so was the brightly woven saddle cloth. Rolf cursed to himself. The last thing he needed now was a serving of Duke Robert's heavy-handed jocularity at his table.

'Did he say anything to you?'

'No, lord, only to find stabling for his horse and those of his men. They did not bring a baggage wain, but they all had full saddle rolls.'

Which meant at least an overnight stay on the road to Rouen, and not just a passing visit. Rolf nodded to the groom, mentally armed himself, and went forth to battle.

The first thing he heard as he approached the hall was Robert's loud, hearty laugh, and a woman's voice chiming softly beside it. Julitta, he thought, and felt a little less beleaguered. And if Julitta was here, that meant Mauger was around somewhere.

Robert, Duke of Normandy, eldest son of the Conqueror, was a well-built man of medium height. He had russet hair, slightly protuberant grey eyes, a good, straight nose, and a sensuous, full-lipped mouth. The overall effect fell just short of handsome, and was certainly attractive. His nature was attractive too, providing you were not hoping for hidden depths. There weren't any. Robert of Normandy was shallow and unreliable. He always meant to keep his promises, but somehow he seldom did, and given such a lead, his barons felt free to break their oaths to him. It led to confusion, to dishonesty, doubt, and even war.

Robert was seated at the high table at the end of the hall where he had been furnished with food and wine. Mauger, his expression stonily controlled, sat a little to one side with the Duke's retainers, and in the lord's seat, beside the Duke himself, was Julitta. She appeared to be keeping him amused, but then beautiful women were another of Robert's weaknesses, no matter that they belonged to other men.

'My lord,' Rolf bent the knee to the Conqueror's son. It was a matter of form. When he had knelt to the old Duke, it had been out of genuine respect.

'Oh get up, get up,' Robert gestured magnanimously. 'No ceremony among friends! Come, sit down, it's your hall!' The Duke indicated the bench at his left hand side, and hitched his chair closer to Julitta's.

'You will pardon me if I seem a trifle distracted,' Rolf said, warning Robert before he started his usual back-thumping, all comrades together routine, 'but my wife died at the convent of the Magdalene this morning – it was expected, but nevertheless,' he made a small hand gesture serve for the remainder and sat down heavily.

Julitta poured him a cup of wine and looked at him anxiously. He managed a half-smile for her and an almost imperceptible grimace in the direction of the Duke. Her eyes kindled with understanding, and she pulled a face of her own. 'Papa, I'm sorry.'

Rolf shook his head. 'She was at peace,' he said, and raised the cup to his lips.

'My condolences,' Robert's open features sobered at the news. 'Your lovely daughter told me that you had gone to visit your lady and that she was mortally sick. I will pay for the priests to say a special mass for her this very day, God rest her soul.' He crossed himself vigorously. 'She was a gentle, pious lady, you will miss her sorely.'

'Yes.' Rolf examined his wine, its colour the dark red of his daughter's hair. Robert of Normandy might be vainglorious and selfish, but the words, for what they were worth, were genuinely meant.

'That makes it all the more difficult for me to impose upon you, but impose I must,' Robert added with a theatrical sigh, and leaned back in his chair.

Rolf shook his head and murmured a polite, half-hearted disclaimer. He did not own the stamina today for Robert of Normandy's impositions. 'Must' in the new Duke's case was frequently a cover for the more indulgent 'want'.

'My father was accustomed to buying all his horses from you,' Robert said, 'and I see no reason to change that. Of course,' he added, his eyebrows puckering, 'I am not entirely at ease that you should continue to trade with my brother William. It seems to me a conflict of interests.'

Rolf took a slow drink of wine and rolled it around his mouth, while he wondered how to reply. If Robert's imposition was a demand that he cease selling horses to Rufus, then he knew he could not, nay, would not meet it. 'In England, I am your brother's tenant, in Normandy I am yours,' he said after a moment, his tone polite, but firm. 'Many of us with lands on both sides of the narrow sea are divided in our loyalties and obligations. But you and your brothers have always looked to Brize and the new farm at Ulverton to provide you with warhorses. If you and Rufus come to friendly terms and I have refused to trade with one or the other of you, where does that leave me? No, my lord. I will conduct my business as I see fit.'

Robert continued to frown. He drummed his thick fingers on the table. 'You don't even like Rufus,' he growled.

'No, my lord, but he has my pledge for my English lands since your lord father designated him the heir.'

'Is that why you are here, Lord Robert?' Julitta interrupted. 'To persuade my father to change his ways?' She regarded the

Duke with limpid eyes, her face turned towards him in a pose that almost invited a kiss, yet retained an air of innocence.

Mauger almost choked on his food, and Rolf on his wine, both men wondering what devilry she was at. The Duke was partial to pretty women, and she appeared to be playing up to his weakness.

Robert cleared his throat, and his complexion grew ruddy. 'Well partly, yes,' he said. 'It isn't a good idea for a man to have two masters.'

Julitta nodded, as if Robert's words were pearls of ineffable wisdom. 'What about two mistresses?' she asked saucily.

Robert threw his head back and laughed. 'That neither!' he chuckled, and glanced at Rolf. 'She has a sharp tongue, your daughter!'

Rolf said nothing, his eyes slightly narrowed as he pondered her outrageous behaviour. Beside him, he thought that Mauger was going to have an apoplexy.

Julitta said, 'I am like my father, so I am told.' She leaned a little closer to the Duke and made good use of her eyelashes, lowering them, looking at him through them. She wanted to put Robert of Normandy off the dangerous subject of oaths and loyalty. She knew the man, had watched Merielle manipulate him like warm clay at Dame Agatha's bathhouse, and was thoroughly confident that she could do the same.

'Your father does not delight me half so much!' Robert warmly flirted in return.

Julitta gave him a look of playful reproval. Then she tilted her head to one side. 'So what is the main reason for your visit, my lord?' Her voice was rich and low now, inviting confidences. And by suggesting that his complaint to Rolf was only a trifling side matter, she was able to dismiss it from Robert's mind. He might remember it later, but by then he would be so bedazzled that he would let it lie, or else, knowing him, would be too lazy to turn back and settle the issue.

Robert basked in the light from Julitta's eyes, in her attentive expression, the slightly parted lips. 'I have come to ask your father to obtain some stock for me. I want a Spanish stallion such as my own father rode.' He patted Julitta's hand where it lay on the trestle. Then he looked at Rolf. 'Do you think that you can find one for me?'

Rolf shifted in his chair. 'A Spanish stallion,' he said slowly.

'I'm not saying that those you breed are not good enough,' Robert added hastily, 'but my father always had a Spanish stallion for the most important occasions, a sort of mark of prestige, and I want one too.'

Rolf rubbed his jaw, where stubble, silver and red, was beginning to poke through the skin. *But you will never be even half the man your father was*, he thought. *If you were, the King of Castile would have sent you such a horse by now.* 'I daresay I could find what you want, but it would not come cheaply.'

Robert took his meaty paw from Julitta's hand, and gave a profligate wave. 'Don't worry, you will be paid.'

Rolf's lips tightened. With what? he wanted to ask. Robert's spendthrift nature was notorious. Already he was in debt to the moneylenders, and it was not even a year since his father had died with a well-stocked treasury. In silence he finished his wine. It was too much of an effort to enquire of the fine details such as colour and weight, broken or unbroken. He wondered to himself if Benedict would bring anything back from his pilgrimage that was suitable, thereby saving the need for a further excursion.

'Well?' Robert demanded. 'Will you fulfil my commission, or shall I look elsewhere?'

Rolf passed a weary hand across his forehead. 'Forgive me, my lord, I am tired and in a state of grief. I shall be pleased to fulfil your commission if there is nothing at Brize that takes your eye.'

Robert's gaze admired Julitta. 'There is always something at Brize to take my eye,' he said with double meaning, 'but I still want a Spanish warhorse.' He allowed the squire serving at table to replenish his cup.

'There is a horse fair in Bordeaux in two months' time. Belike I could find you something there. Spanish stock is frequently traded, and at better prices than in the north.'

'As you wish.' Robert's concentration remained on Julitta. 'I am sure that I have met you before now,' he said with a puzzled frown between his russet brows.

Julitta had known that there were dangers inherent in flirting with Duke Robert. If he remembered that he had previously encountered her in a Southwark brothel, there would be no constraints on his lechery. 'Probably when I was a child, my lord,' she said lightly. 'I was always underfoot in the stables.'

'Yes, perhaps.' Robert pinched his chin between forefinger and thumb. 'But I cannot help thinking it was elsewhere that I saw you.'

She gave him a smile and a shrug, and towed the conversation into safer waters by asking him about the kind of Spanish horse he wanted. Basking in her attention, Robert followed her lead with enthusiasm, and the subject lasted them until the servants began clearing away the trestles in the main part of the hall and stacking them neatly down one wall.

Robert gently squeezed her knee beneath the table before he rose to visit the latrine. 'You are a beautiful woman,' he murmured. 'Would that I could have more of your company.'

Julitta had been expecting this particular move all evening, but it did not prevent her stomach from lurching now that it was played. 'You honour me, my lord,' she said demurely, and thought that his intention was more in the realm of 'dishonour'.

'I speak no more than the truth. Perhaps you would like to visit the full splendour of my court?'

Julitta lowered her lashes. 'That is most generous of you, my lord,' she murmured. 'But I have my position and duty as a wife to consider.'

'I am sure something could be arranged,' Robert said with a slow, meaningful smile.

Something was arranged, and in short order. Mauger found himself consulted on the matter of Spanish bloodstock by Duke Robert, who then insisted that Mauger should be the one to go to Bordeaux and bring the required warhorse back to Normandy. It made perfect sense. Rolf could not go, he had a funeral to arrange and his wife's affairs to set in order.

'Why did you encourage him in the first place?' Mauger snarled at Julitta as the Duke's retinue rode out of Brize the following noontide. 'Or perhaps you want to parade yourself at his court, show yourself off as his latest whore!'

Julitta whitened. 'How dare you say that to me!' she said icily, and stalked away towards the hall. Mauger caught up with her and spun her round.

'Do you think I do not know why he demands that I go to find his blessed horse? It is so that he can have free rein to do as he likes with you!'

'And you think that I would have anything to do with a strutting cockerel such as him?' she said scornfully.

'What am I to think after your behaviour at table last night? God's death, you were almost in his lap!'

'That was because he was hounding my father, who was in no fit state to respond to him. If I had not intervened and distracted him, Duke Robert would have insisted that Papa yield him sole fealty and abandon his oath to Rufus. There would have been hot words for certain!'

'It was not proper or decent!' Mauger raged through his teeth, his complexion dusky.

'No it wasn't!' Julitta retorted, her own voice rising to match his. 'And neither is this!'

Mauger glanced around the bailey and saw that they had an interested audience of castle folk. Beneath the weight of his scowl they dispersed, but he knew that they would watch and listen from a distance, and that the tales would carry.

'I ought to whip you,' he muttered.

'Is that your answer to everything?' she demanded scornfully. 'Will whipping me set everything to rights, or will you just salve your wounded manhood at the expense of my hide?' She tried to shake him off, but Mauger maintained a bruising grip on her arm.

'It is holy writ that a woman should submit to her husband!'

Mauger said through his teeth. 'I will have your obedience!' His face thrust down into hers.

Panting, they glared at each other. Then, with an oath, Mauger covered Julitta's mouth with his own, and kissed her forcefully.

Julitta struggled, but he held her fast. His tongue invaded, his hands clamped their bodies together. 'Holy writ,' he repeated, as he surfaced for air. 'Willing or unwilling. You are mine.'

Willing or unwilling.

Aching, sore, Julitta stared at the rafters. Mauger lay upon her, his breath thundering in her ears, the driving rhythm of his buttocks reduced to spasmodic twitches. This time he had not even tried to prolong the act or give her pleasure. It had been purely for his own release.

She shifted beneath him, trying to ease her cramped muscles, trying to breathe. There was no flab on Mauger, but he was solid and heavy-set.

He raised his head, and looked down into her face. An expression of bewilderment crossed his own. Almost tender now that the force of his passion was spent, he touched her dark red braid. 'It would be easier for you if you were not so wilful,' he said. 'You anger me . . . you make me lose control.'

She was not surprised to hear that it was all her fault. Mauger had never admitted to a single mistake in his life. She said nothing; there was no point.

Frowning slightly, he withdrew from her. His colour high, he straightened her skirts which he had dragged up around her waist in his desperation to be at her. Then he turned his back to adjust his own clothing. Modesty now had precedence over lust. 'You're not going to Duke Robert's court,' he said brusquely as he retied his loin cloth. 'I won't permit it.'

'You would defy the Duke?'

'It was an invitation, not a command.'

Julitta looked at her husband's broad back and thick,

muscular neck. 'Then what will you do?' She sat up on the bed. 'Refuse outright?'

'You are a dutiful wife, are you not?' Mauger's tone was sarcastic. He turned round to her once more. 'It is your obligation to provide me with an heir of my blood, and that cannot happen if we are apart. I am taking you with me to the Bordeaux horse fair.'

Julitta slowly covered her braids with her wimple. Many women would have leaped at the opportunity to visit the court of the Duke of Normandy, but Julitta's breathing quickened at the mention of the horse fair. She loved such gatherings, the sights, sounds and smells; the thrill of the chase, of finding gold among dross.

'You truly mean that?' she said to her husband in a tone much brighter than that of a moment since.

His eyes narrowed and she saw him try to gauge her response. 'My mind is made up. I'll not have Robert of Normandy sniffing around your skirts like a dog after a bitch while I'm conveniently absent.'

Julitta tucked the end of her wimple through her circlet and stood up. Her body was sore from Mauger's rough lovemaking, but she put the discomfort to the back of her mind. For once, in his jealousy, he was giving her what she wanted.

'How soon do you want to leave?' she asked. 'Shall I begin packing the saddle rolls?'

Mauger rose to adjust his belt and tunic. 'As you wish,' he said. His voice was gentler now, for her eagerness had mollified him. Her smile was for him, and the sparkle in her eyes. Robert of Normandy could go whistle.

CHAPTER 57

Benedict spent two months with Sancho, learning his ways, which in many did not differ from Rolf's, learning to handle the spirited Iberian horses, becoming acquainted with Kumbi. His injuries ceased to pain him and the bright, raw colour of the scars faded to pink. The wounds of the mind healed a little too. Two months lent distance to the memory of the attack. He still relived it when his mind was unoccupied, but he could fight down the waves of sick panic now. Nightmares continued to plague him, but Faisal said that in time they would fade.

Learning from Sancho involved living with him for much of the time. The Lord Rodrigo, for all his interest in Benedict, was a man with deep political concerns, a great landholder, a vassal-in-chief of Castile's King, a warrior lord. Although welcome at Rodrigo's court, Benedict knew that his way was more or less his own to make. One day soon, he knew that it must be to Compostella, and then home, to Brize-sur-Risle as the bearer of bad tidings. As the days passed, and the need to leave grew more pressing, so did Benedict's reluctance.

He liked Iberia, the land, the people, their rich and varied culture. Christian fought Moor, but weaving between the flash of sword and cut of scimitar was great knowledge, religious tolerance, and a wealth of trading opportunities such as would have made his father weep with envy: the patterned silks of Andalusia; the gold, ivory and hides of Africa; perfumes, spices and rare books in the Arabic text on philosophy and medicine. Rice, long-storing wheat, oranges, lemons, figs and pomegranates. The opportunities begged to be grasped in both hands, and Benedict's merchant origins stirred with excitement.

Living with Sancho was not as difficult as he had thought. Benedict had never possessed a grandfather, but Sancho came close to fulfilling this role. The old man was cantankerous and difficult, especially in the early morning and late at night when his joints were stiff, but he possessed a vast store of wisdom, and a dry, salty wit. By turns, Benedict was aggravated, amused, or goaded to do better. Sancho liked to talk about himself and possessed a seemingly endless fund of anecdotes, and yet he was a good listener too, with more than a streak of natural curiosity.

Benedict told him about his past, about Julitta and Gisele. Sancho snorted and called him a young fool with no brains above his belt. Sancho's daughter, Lucia, a widow in her middle years who now looked after her father, brought Sancho a cup of the spiced red wine of which he was so fond, and went quietly away to pick up her distaff. She was fine-boned, graceful of carriage, with masses of black hair coiled upon her head, and almond-shaped green-hazel eyes. She was handsome now. In her youth, Benedict thought that she must have been quite beautiful.

'Did the same thing myself with her mother,' Sancho declared, and took a noisy sip of the wine, washing it around the yellow stumps of his teeth. 'Leilah was Moorish – Christian convert married to a fat merchant. It was lust at first sight, the love came later.'

Benedict eyed Sancho. It was hard to imagine any woman falling for him, but perhaps he had been handsome long ago. Put the teeth back in his mouth, whiten them, add flesh and eyesight, banish the wrinkles and a presentable rogue might emerge. 'So you had a future together?'

'Oh aye.' Sancho ran his tongue around the inside of his mouth. 'We eloped in the middle of the night, with all our belongings in a bundle. Spent three months on the road running from place to place. It was hard, I tell you, especially on her. A respectable married woman going off with a stallion man. If they had caught us, I would have lost my balls, and her the skin off her back. Not surprising that we didn't know much tranquillity those first few years. It was worse after Lucia was born. Leilah was worried what would happen to her if we were caught. We never really had peace of mind, but we had each other.'

'Would you do it again?'

Sancho glanced at his daughter spinning, her face rapt with concentration. 'Yes,' he said gruffly, 'I would. But I don't know about Leilah. She's been dead these past twenty years. I think she would say yes, but you never know with women. That is their beauty, and their flaw.'

Benedict smiled wry acknowledgement, and saw that Lucia was smiling too, her look quietly indulgent on her grizzled father.

Two days later, Benedict finally made the decision that he must leave for Compostella before it became too difficult to leave at all, and from there return to Brize.

Inspecting one of the herds of brood mares with Sancho, he told the overseer of his intentions.

Sancho heard him out in silence, his jaws working on a piece of liquorice root, manipulating it from one side of his mouth to the other in search of teeth with which to chew. Black juice oozed on his lips. 'You must do what is necessary for your conscience,' he said. 'A man works best without a burdened soul.' He cocked his head on one side. 'But you will return here, I think, when you have shed your load.'

Benedict looked sharply at the old man. 'Are my thoughts so obvious?'

Sancho gave a laconic shrug. 'It does not take a grand wisdom to see that you have settled here, and when you talk of Normandy, your face grows troubled and you bite your thumbnail.'

Involuntarily, Benedict cast his glance down to the hands which gripped Kumbi's reins. With a grimace, he concealed his thumbs within his palms. Sancho saw and his lips curved in a black-stained smile.

'I have been wondering when you would go. You have been restless these past few days.'

'And yet you have said nothing?'

'I have watched and listened.' Sancho spat over his mount's withers and resumed his chewing. 'You cannot go alone,' he said after a moment. 'You will need protection and escort over the mountains.'

Benedict drew a deep breath. He did not want to think about that part of his journey, retracing his steps to the place of attack. 'I intended hiring soldiers from Lord Rodrigo.'

Sancho nodded. 'Wise,' he said.

Benedict thought that the conversation had ended there, but that evening as they sat over a game of merels, Sancho carefully positioned one of the small clay balls on the board and rolling another between his palms, said thoughtfully, 'I think I might see you part of your way home.'

Benedict stared. 'Why should you do that?'

'Why should I not?'

Bemused, Benedict shook his head. 'I could give you a host of reasons, but surely you already know them.'

'The dangers of the mountain roads, my advancing years,' Sancho said with a cackle of amusement. 'Let me tell you, I've been as far as the cities of Constantinople and Nicaea in my time in search of bloodstock. I have travelled throughout Andalusia and the Moorish kingdoms.'

'But that was long ago.' Benedict looked at the wizened, leathery face across from him, the milky eye and scrawny throat.

'Not that long. Even at my time of life, a man can still have itchy feet. Besides,' he added, 'there is no need to cross the mountains. Galleys are easily hired in Corunna to make the journey up the coast. There's a huge horse fair in Bordeaux before the summer's end and I want to do some trading. In previous years I've sent younger men, but I don't see why I shouldn't indulge myself one last time.'

'It might well be your last time,' Benedict could not help but say. And yet the thought of the old man's company was comforting, and there was no conviction in his protest.

Sancho shrugged and smiled. 'It is my choice.' He gestured at the merels board. 'Your move.'

CHAPTER 58

The *Draca*, one of Aubert's wine vessels, docked in Bordeaux, having sailed down the French coast from Rouen. The late summer journey had been beset by unseasonable winds and some minor squalls. Mauger, never a good ocean traveller even in the calmest of conditions, spent a great length of time leaning over the gunwale, his complexion a delicate shade of green.

Julitta, in contrast, revelled in the brisk weather and the freedom from being tied to the quiet domesticity of Fauville. She took up a favourite position on the raised decking by the prow, and stood for hours on end, watching the *Draca* carve her way through the glistening green waves with their white netting of foam. If conditions grew too rough and she found herself becoming saturated by the spume, she would retire to one of the benches in the hold which lay amidships, and keep Aubert's cargo company. He was exporting barrels of English mead, and hoped to bring home a cargo of leather and strong southern wine. Not that he was personally on board the vessel, but one of his senior overseers was – a black-bearded, hearty soul named Beltran who had been sailing these waters for the better part of twenty years.

Beltran took Julitta and Mauger to the lodging house where he himself usually stayed when he was in Bordeaux and within moments secured them a bed for the night and the promise of a substantial meal. At the mention of food, Mauger compressed his lips and excused himself, declaring that all he wanted was a bed that did not move.

Beltran and Julitta exchanged amused, pitying glances, and guided by their landlady, a talkative, tiny woman with sallow skin and beady black eyes, they descended from the sleeping loft and entered the main room below.

Gulls screamed overhead. The sounds of the bustling, dusty streets percolated through the cool stone walls, which kept out the worst of the day's burning heat. Their hostess brought them a jug of wine, a loaf, and earthenware bowls of steaming fish soup. 'Are you on a pilgrimage?' she asked curiously as she set the food down on the trestle.

Julitta shook her head. 'We are here to buy horses at the fair.'

'Ah.' The woman absorbed the information, and if anything, her curiosity increased. 'I think you are newly married then? He does not leave you at home with your children?'

Julitta half-smiled a response and curbed the impulse to tell the woman it was none of her business. Let her believe that this as a journey undertaken by an ardent groom and his new bride.

'You should travel down to Compostella,' advised their hostess. 'Ask his blessing.' She patted her belly, her meaning obvious.

Julitta reddened. At Dame Agatha's she had learned how to protect herself against the fate of pregnancy. Merielle, in one of her rare spurts of benevolence, had shown her the method employed by the cannier whores. You took a small piece of moss or sponge, soaked it in vinegar, and inserted it into your passage. So far the method had worked remarkably well and Julitta desired no intervention from St James.

'Me, I have eight sons, and twenty-four grandchildren,' the woman declared proudly, and proceeded to regale Julitta with all their names and circumstances. Julitta ate her soup, which was delicious, and tried to look interested. She was aware of Beltran's amusement and wondered why on earth he chose to lodge here. He did not strike her as a man who liked having his ears talked off, even for the sake of good cooking.

Finally the garrulous old biddy removed their dishes to rinse them out by her well in the yard. Julitta wondered which was worse, retreating to lie down in bed beside Mauger, or remaining here to be verbally assaulted by her landlady.

'How far is the horse fair?' she asked.

Beltran's lips twitched. He wiped his palm across his bushy moustache and beard. 'Not far,' he said.

They left the lodging house, and walked along the banks of the Garonne. Numerous trading galleys were moored along the wharves and the vinegary smell of split wine casks pervaded the air, reminding Julitta of the time spent at Aubert's house in London.

'Clothilde means well,' Beltran said. 'Usually she gives lodging to ships' masters and the like. It is not often that she plays host to another woman.'

Small wonder, Julitta was tempted to say, but she managed to curb her tongue.

They walked past other moored vessels, including Italian and Byzantine horse transports. At one of them, she saw a small, leathery old man guiding a mare and colt down a ramp. He issued orders in rapid Castilian Spanish to a groom. From between his clamped lips there protruded a stick of liquorice root.

'Iberian horses,' said Beltran. 'Your husband will be spoiled for choice.'

Julitta admired the mare and foal and stepped forward for a closer look. The man with the liquorice root swivelled milky eyes in her direction and looked her up and down. His stare was disconcerting, for although he looked blind, Julitta could tell that he saw her perfectly well.

'They are fine horses,' she said to him.

'Aye, that they are, my lady.' His tone was dour.

'Are they to be sold at the fair?'

'No, they're already spoken for – just resting them a couple of days before we sail on.'

'Do you have others?'

'Already taken to the market place.' He gave a nod of

dismissal, spat a wad of black saliva at his feet, and recommenced talking to the groom as if Julitta did not exist.

That was the drawback with Spanish horses, Julitta thought. They were so much in demand that those who sold them could be as objectionable as they liked and still reap a profit. Even if she told this particular trader that her husband was commissioned to purchase a horse for Duke Robert of Normandy, she doubted that it would increase the level of his courtesy.

Julitta moved on. A glance over her shoulder for a final look at the mare and foal caught the small trader in the act of staring after her and Beltran, a thoughtful look on his wizened features.

The horse-dealer's name was Pierre, and he dealt in war stallions, brood mares and endurance horses for distance travelling and the hunt. He was the last in a long line of dealers visited by Mauger and Julitta that morning. It was close on noontide now, the sun high and hot. Mauger wore a frown, and his eyes were heavy. He was still suffering from the aftermath of the sea journey, and the red heat of the sun, the dust and the market place smells, had all combined to give him a nauseous headache.

He had never looked at so many horses and discovered so many nags. The southern lands might be famous for their bloodstock, but he had seen precious little so far. Scrubby ponies, cow-heeled knock-kneed jades, broken-winded hacks; the parade had been endless, yet he had seen nothing to suit the tastes of Duke Robert of Normandy. The problem with looking for gold was sifting through the dross to find it.

Pierre was short and stocky, of a similar build to Mauger, but larger and softer in the gut. He had curly blue-black hair and the skin of his face was deeply pitted. Shrewd black eyes assessed his potential customers and he spread his hands towards his merchandise. 'You want warhorses?' he enquired. 'You have come to the right place.'

Julitta had heard that opening gambit several times and was not impressed; however, she kept her eyes modestly downcast and hung back a little. Pierre flashed her an assessing glance as if considering the points of a young mare ripe to be serviced.

'I will be the judge of that,' Mauger said tersely. 'Let me see what you have.'

Pierre shrugged and smiled with his mouth but not his eyes, and gestured his groom to bring forward a cream-coloured stallion.

Mauger began an examination, running his hands lightly over the horse in search of lumps and defects. He looked in its mouth, discovered that it was around eleven years old, and shook his head. A younger animal was brought forth, a skittish bay with black points. Julitta went to cast her eye over the rest of Pierre's stock. Some animals were quite presentable, but there was nothing better than what they had at Brize or Ulverton.

Her eye was caught by a dappled grey courser standing quietly at the end of the line. It was a little short of fifteen hands high, its mane and tail pure silver against the smoky grey rings of its hide. Beside it stood a smaller, chestnut mare with a white star marking on her forehead and a white sock on her offside hind leg. Julitta admired the two horses, thinking that they were the best she had seen thus far, although sadly neither was of the type to turn into a destrier. They looked extremely like her father's horses, she thought, the mare from Brize, the gelding from the grey herds at Ulverton. Suddenly, despite the heat of the day she was cold.

'Cylu,' she said softly and approached the grey.

Immediately he turned his head, and with ears pricked, nickered to her. Julitta's stomach plummeted. She had expected the horse not to respond, or to turn a different face towards her, but there was no mistaking the small coronet of hair on Cylu's forehead that grew against the grain, nor the pink splash on his otherwise dark grey muzzle.

She compressed her lips, feeling sick. Pierre's groom gave her an anxious look. 'My lady?' he questioned. 'There is something wrong?'

'That grey horse, where did your master buy him?'

The groom shrugged. 'Master Pierre bought him and the mare from a Basque trader last week. Do you like him?' He smiled and patted Cylu's smooth dappled neck. 'A fine riding horse, and still young.'

Julitta would not have called ten years old still young, but the groom's small lie was swamped by the greater tide rising in her mind. She flung away from him and marched up to the horse-trader, who was in the middle of expounding the virtues of the young bay to Mauger. 'Master Pierre,' she interrupted, her voice and expression full of urgency, 'I want to ask you about the grey gelding and the chestnut mare over there.'

The man stared at her as if she had spoken in a different language. He was not accustomed to having his deals interrupted by women, and this one looked as if she was about to turn into a blazing termagant.

Mauger's lips tightened and he frowned at Julitta. 'Can you not see that we are busy,' he growled. 'Where is your modesty?'

'It flew out of the window the moment that I saw Cylu and Gisele's chestnut mare,' Julitta hotly retorted and pointed towards Pierre's other horses. 'Look for yourself.'

Mauger opened his mouth, shut it again with a snap, and glowered his way over to the line of animals. He walked around the grey gelding, while the bewildered groom looked on, and Pierre stood frowning, his hands on his hips and his moist lower lip thrust out.

'The same age,' Julitta declared. 'The same forehead mark and pink star on his muzzle. The groom told me that he and the mare were bought from a Basque trader.'

Mauger studied the chestnut mare too, and rubbed his aching forehead. 'Perhaps Benedict sold them,' he said to Julitta.

'Ben would never sell Cylu!' she declared with certainty. 'They have been together too long!'

'You cannot know Benedict's every thought,' he snapped irritably and turned to the trader who was watching them with wary eyes. 'We know these horses. They belong to my wife's sister and her husband.'

'They do not belong now,' Pierre said sharply. 'I bought them in Arachon from another trader who gathers his horses from far and wide.' He spread his hands in a choppy, aggressive gesture. 'Even if these horses did once belong to your kin, they do not any more. If you desire them, you will have to buy them the same as any other beast at this fair.'

'How much do you want?' Julitta demanded, her own tone easily matching Pierre's belligerence.

Pierre's complexion grew ruddy and his jaw made chewing motions. 'I do not deal with women,' he growled.

'And I do not deal with thie . . .'

'How much do you want?' Mauger's voice cut across Julitta's final word. He seized her by the arm and twisted it so that she could not break free without snapping a bone. The pain made her writhe, but it also silenced her.

Mauger purchased Cylu and the mare, abandoned all intention of buying any other horses from Pierre, and in grim mood, drew Julitta away.

'You shame me!' he retorted. 'I will become a laughing stock.' He shook her arm upon which he still retained a savage grip.

Julitta gasped at the pain. 'Is that all your care?' she retorted in a choked voice. 'Does it not worry you to find Benedict's and Gisele's horses in the care of a trader?'

'Of course it does,' he snapped. 'But I hope I have more sense than to antagonise that trader by calling him a thief. You heard him. He bought Cylu and the mare in Arachon.'

'Something is wrong, Mauger, you know it is!'

He rolled his eyes. 'I have come to buy horses for the Duke of Normandy, not to pursue a niggling doubt hither and yon.' He gestured brusquely. 'Knowing Benedict, whatever has caused him to part with those two, he has landed on his feet. Not even a cat could better him at that game.'

'So you are going to do nothing?'

Mauger drew her on through the throng of people and horses. 'You are quite right,' he said grimly. 'I am going to do nothing.'

'But . . .'

He swung her round to face him, his light eyes showing a red rim of temper. 'Enough, Julitta. Push me no further.'

People were turning to look. Amusement glinted at the sight of an argument between husband and wife. Mauger's eyes flickered. He tightened his lips and with sudden purpose, dragged Julitta out of the market place and away in the direction of the lodging house. 'I should never have brought you with me this morning,' he growled, shouldering his way through the traders. 'Until we leave, you can stay with Madame Clothilde, and mind your distaff. I will not tolerate any more of this.' He yanked on her arm and tears burned her eyes, but they were of rage and pain, not self-pity or remorse.

Mauger deposited her at the lodging house, gave strict instructions to one of his grooms that she was not to leave the premises, and strode back to the horse fair to conduct his business alone.

Clothilde looked at the young woman sitting on a stool near the neatly swept hearth. She was rubbing her arm and struggling not to cry.

Clucking like a mother hen, Clothilde approached to comfort her, thinking that she had just witnessed the end of a young couple's tiff. 'There now, there now,' she soothed, setting her arm across Julitta's shoulders. 'Don't you fret, he'll be back, and you'll soon mend things between you.'

Julitta drew a shuddering breath. She raised her head and looked at Clothilde with brimming, burning eyes. 'I don't want him to come back!' she spat.

'Oh, come now, you don't mean that!'

Julitta sprang to her feet, thrusting off the woman's embrace. 'If I never saw him again it would be too soon!'

Clothilde uttered a horrified gasp and pressed her hands to her mouth. Mauger's groom was tying Cylu and the chestnut mare to a bridle ring in the wall. Now and then he cast a dark look towards the house.

Julitta narrowed her eyes, her mind racing with the speed of her temper. She drew a deep breath to steady herself and tepping outside, approached the grey gelding and the mare.

The groom eyed her sidelong. 'Mistress, Lord Mauger said that you were to stay within,' he said doubtfully.

'Surely there is no harm in this?' She stroked Cylu's sleek, grey neck and half-contemplated making her escape across his dependable back, but she knew that she would be conspicuous in a crowd. Besides, he was not wearing a saddle so her seat would be precarious.

She made a fuss of the horse, scratching behind his ears, and then the tender spot at his withers. The groom's watchfulness eased and a half-smile played at his mouth corners. He made the mistake of turning his back to fetch a bucket of water. Immediately Julitta untied the two ropes and slapped both horses on their rumps, sending them clattering around the small courtyard. As the groom turned round from the well, his mouth open in surprise, Julitta fled out into the street.

She heard the groom's shout of alarm, and Clothilde's shrieks. The sound of footsteps in pursuit lent wings to her feet. She grasped her skirts in both hands and raised them to her knees the better to run. A narrow alleyway leading to another street presented itself on her left and she plunged down its dark throat. A mongrel dog ran out of a doorway and snapped at her. Two half-naked children ceased their game of knuckle-bones to stare after her. She splashed through a puddle, noisome with mud and trampled dung, and felt the cold seep into her shoe and splatter her leg.

From the alley she emerged into another thoroughfare, filled with merchants, hucksters and market-day crowds. It seemed as if the entire population of Gascony had converged upon Bordeaux. A street pedlar waved a bunch of scarlet hair ribbons beneath her nose. A woman tried to sell her a length of cheap woven braid. She shook her head and ploughed grimly on through the throng, not daring to look back.

Finally, she stopped and leaned against a house wall to regain her breath. She did not know where she was or how far she had run. People were looking at her curiously. She gulped another breath and began to walk slowly, trying to blend with the crowd.

And then her arm was grabbed from behind, and at the same time, she heard the groom shout across the heads of the people in the street.

Generally, Mauger was slow and thorough in his purchase of horses. He took his time, and was prepared to reject a beast rather than take a risk. But his blood was up, his anger simmering, and it made him incautious. He swallowed convulsively, the lump in his throat so huge that he felt it would choke him. Julitta's contrariness drove him to distraction. Why couldn't she be a proper wife to him? Why did she always make him feel clumsy and inferior? Did she not realise that if only she ceased fighting him and accorded him the respect that was his due, he would give her the world? Perhaps he ought to tell her, but Mauger was wary of the gentler emotions, especially his own.

He watched a Spanish trader trot a bay colt up and down, and forced himself to concentrate upon the horse rather than imagining Julitta's lovely white throat beneath his hands. Even if he did tell her, she would probably toss her head and ignore him. He could see the expression on her face now.

'You like, my lord?' demanded the trader of Mauger's deep scowl.

'No, show me something else, something with more fire.' Robert of Normandy wanted a warhorse. Well and good, he would find Robert of Normandy such a beast. A savage glint in his eye, Mauger set himself to find a stallion that matched the state of his temper.

It was an hour and ten traders later that he came across the young, unbroken black colt which the Catalan dealer's lad was striving to calm. Sweat creamed its neck along the line of the bridle, and it fretted at the sharp bit, specks of blood mingling with the foam at its mouth corners. Its hide was a glossy jet-black, its mane and tail in contrast a dazzling silvery white. Usually Mauger would have kept his distance, but now he plunged into bargaining with a vengeance.

*

The merchant's wife escorted Benedict to the door of her handsome timber house, and stood with him on the threshold. She was thickly set, with a florid complexion and heavy-lidded brown eyes. Her gown was of the thickest, costliest wool to mark her rank, but the sweat stains encircling the armpits had ruined the fabric. In the room behind her was a family gathering of adult sons and daughters, and several noisy grandchildren. Benedict was not sorry to leave. Out of charity he had made enquiries and brought them the sad news of the death of the family's head on the road to Compostella.

There had been a suitable amount of dramatic wailing for effect, but no deep-seated grief as far as he could tell. The merchant had not been the kind to engender affection, even among those closest to him. Oh they would do all that was necessary to mourn him, exalt his position amongst Bordeaux's merchant fraternity by staging sumptuous masses and giving freely of alms, but it would all be for show.

'Thank you for bringing us the tidings,' the woman said formally.

Benedict bowed. 'It was my duty, Madame.' He did not say 'Christian' duty, since it was Christians who had murdered the pilgrims, and a Moor who had enabled him to be here to give the news.

The woman stepped into the street, gave him directions back to the main thoroughfare and wished him Godspeed. Benedict bowed again and set out. He was in no particular hurry and took his time, admiring the fine merchants' houses which a prospering wine trade had funded. There was a mixture of wooden shingles, thatch and tiles on the roofs. Many had fine first- or second-floor galleries. Women stood gossiping outside their doors, their fingers busy twirling raw wool into yarn on their distaffs. Young children played. Older ones were employed in household tasks. Various cooking smells wafted past his nostrils, and once the stink of burned pottage, where a wife had been so busy chattering that she had forgotten to add more water to her cooking pot.

Without conscious thought he strolled towards the wharf-side where the wine galleys bobbed at anchor. He could see the vessel in which he and Sancho had sailed from Corunna; a Byzantine horse transport, three-decked, sturdy and large. It had been Sancho's idea to commission her in Corunna and sail her up the coast, rather than face the dangerous trek over the mountains. She was specifically designed to carry livestock, with large holds in her port hull. Once he and Sancho completed their business in Bordeaux, they would take her on up the coast to Rouen and disembark the horses there.

He stepped back to admire her lines and thought about discussing with his father and Rolf the possibility of building one of these vessels for transporting stock between Iberia and Normandy. Ordinary trading vessels could carry horses over short distance, but they were no use for longer sea voyages.

Pondering the thought, he continued along the banks of the Garonne, passing other transports, Mediterranean round ships, northern narrowboats, and Flemish cogs. And then he saw the *Draca*, his father's wine galley, bobbing at anchor, its great mast and canvas sail lying along the deck, its oars neatly stacked across the rowing benches. There was no cargo in her mid-deck open hold and no members of crew on board guarding her. She was obviously at rest and waiting to be reloaded.

Benedict knew that it was unlikely his father was here in Bordeaux. Aubert seldom made the journey; he said that the sea was bad for his ague, but Beltran was almost certain to be in port somewhere, purchasing a cargo for the return trip to Normandy. Benedict's heart lightened, and for the first time in several days a smile came to his lips.

He walked on, intending to visit the horse sales and inform Sancho of his discovery, but he had scarcely changed his direction when he saw a young woman burst out of an alleyway like a hunted doe and join the main thoroughfare, her soft shoes scarcely making any sound as she ran. A veil of light silk covered the top of her head, but not the heavy, dark red braids which snaked from side to side with her motion.

'Julitta,' he said in astonishment. It was her, he would have recognised her anywhere. But what was she doing in Bordeaux? Obviously she must have sailed in on the *Draca*. But why?

A man was chasing her, shoving his way rudely through the crowd. Benedict recognised Austin, Mauger's chief groom, and in a regular rage to judge by the glower on his perspiring features. Shock had rooted Benedict to the spot, but now he regained the use of his limbs and set off in pursuit of Julitta, determined to reach her first and discover what she was doing and what was wrong.

He cut diagonally through the bustle, weaving and dodging, making breathless apologies. At first he thought that he would lose her, for despite being hampered by her gown, she was as swift as an arrow, and nimble too. But she had been running for longer than he, and gradually he gained on her. At last, she stopped for breath, leaning against a house wall, her hand pressed to her side, and he was able to catch her.

She flung round at the touch on her arm, her blue eyes immense with fear and fury. Her foot drew back to kick her assailant in the shin, and was arrested in mid-motion. 'Benedict?' she gasped, and then her eyes flooded with tears and instead of launching an attack, she threw herself into his arms and hugged him tight. 'You're safe! Oh thank God!'

Austin arrived then, his breath whistling in his throat, and his face the hue of an over-ripe raspberry. He was too exhausted to speak and could only glare at the two of them.

Julitta raised her head from Benedict's chest, tears brimming. She bit her lip. Her own breathing was still rapid and uneven. 'I quarrelled with Mauger – about you as it happens, and he confined me to our lodging house with Austin as my guard. So . . . so I ran away.'

'Where is Mauger now?'

'At the horse market – I think. Either there, or in a drinking house.'

'And your quarrel was about me?'

'I thought you were in trouble. He said that you were like a cat – always landed on your feet, and that he did not have the time to seek you out just to discover that you were all right.'

Benedict's lips twitched at her summary of Mauger's response, but there was pain in his smile too. 'Like a cat,' he repeated, and shook his head. 'He is right and he is wrong. I have landed on my feet, but not before being first beaten to my knees.'

By now, Austin had recovered enough to stand straight and his complexion was less congested. 'Mistress Julitta, you must return to the lodging house,' he panted.

'Mistress Julitta must do nothing unless it be her will,' Benedict said sharply to the groom.

The man clamped his jaw. His eyes were nervous. 'Lord Mauger will whip me.'

Julitta gripped Benedict's sleeve. 'It does not matter now that I've found you. I'll willingly return to our lodgings.' She smiled through her tears. 'I will even bow to my husband and admit that I was wrong to fear for your safety.'

'You weren't wrong,' he contradicted. 'If I am here now, it is because of a Moorish physician named Faisal ibn Mansour.' Abruptly he turned to the groom. 'I will escort Lady Julitta back to her lodgings. You can go and find Lord Mauger and tell him I am here and that I take full responsibility.'

Austin deliberated, saw that it was the best that could be salvaged from the situation, and departed in haste to find his master.

Together, Julitta and Benedict began to walk. 'Are you staying in the city?' she asked.

Benedict shook his head. 'No. We sailed up from Corunna on a horse transport galley, and we sleep there.'

His use of 'we' caused Julitta to make a wrong assumption. 'Is Gisele there now?'

'No,' he said quietly. 'Gisele is . . . is dead.' He lengthened his stride as if to outpace the thought and Julitta had almost to run to keep up.

'Dead? What happened?'

'Let it wait until Mauger comes. It's not something I want to relive more than I must.' He swallowed and glanced at her sidelong. 'It has been a hard road, Julitta.'

'I'm sorry.' It sounded inadequate, but she could think of nothing else to say.

Benedict shrugged and said nothing. They walked on in uncomfortable silence until they came to the wharves and the ships riding at anchor. He showed her his transport galley, the *Constantine*. It was one of the larger ships in dock, with two decks, and the forward hull doors. 'We load the horses in there for the journey, and then seal them in with pitch,' he explained. 'It means there is more room, and more animals can be loaded at a given time. Once we're underway, we get down to them by hatches and ladders from the top deck.' He went into a detailed explanation of the techniques involved, drawing away from the rip-tide words *Gisele is dead*. And Julitta followed his lead, nodding sensibly, asking questions whose replies she was not later to recall.

Then Benedict suddenly paused in mid-explanation and shaded his eyes against the sun as a figure emerged from the depths of the vessel and came walking down the gangplank on bandy legs. His tunic was tattered at cuff and hem; he wore a battered felt pilgrim hat on his head, and his face was browner than the oak boards of the vessel's deck. His lower jaw was working busily, folding into his upper as he chewed some black concoction from one side of his mouth to the other. Julitta recognised him from her walk the previous day, and after a momentary recoil, held her ground.

Beside her, Benedict had relaxed, and there was even a smile on his lips.

The old man reached them and leered at Julitta through his horrible, milky eyes.

'Hah!' he said to Benedict in a harsh voice. 'Been doing some trading on the sly, have you?' He looked Julitta up and down as if assessing the points of a horse. 'Something to keep you warm on the journey to Rouen, eh?'

Benedict went red beneath his tan. 'Sancho, I want you to meet Julitta. Do you remember, I spoke of her to you when I told you about my home?'

Sancho appraised Julitta more thoroughly, chewing with

great vigour on his liquorice root. 'Rare,' he approved, nodding his head. The leer narrowed. He spat out of the side of his mouth. 'Where's the husband?'

'Being fetched.' Benedict turned to Julitta, sensing her barely contained anger at being thus treated. 'Julitta, this is Sancho, the best stud overseer in all of Castile – for all that he looks like a brigand and he hasn't any manners,' he added pointedly.

'Waste of time,' Sancho growled. 'Say what you mean and be done with it.'

Julitta exchanged glances with Benedict. He saw irritation in her eyes, and a sparkle of amusement. 'What have you told him about me?'

'Everything that I should know,' Sancho interjected. 'And as private as the confessional. I may be a mannerless oaf, but I know when to stitch my lips.'

Which meant that he knew everything. This time it was Julitta who blushed.

Sancho cocked his head to one side. 'So how come you to be in Bordeaux, my lady?'

'My husband is here to buy warhorses at the market for Robert of Normandy, and he desired to bring me with him on this occasion.'

'Ah,' said Sancho. 'Keeping his treasure chest where he can see it.' His eyes glimmered like moonstones, and he grinned wolfishly at Benedict. 'Trouble is, he left it unlocked, didn't he?'

Benedict pulled a warning face at the old man. 'I thought you knew when to stitch your lips,' he said.

'I do,' Sancho retorted. 'Most of the time.'

Sancho insisted on accompanying Benedict and Julitta to the lodging house. He would be a chaperone, he said. Nothing unseemly could possibly happen with him in attendance. Benedict was not certain that he agreed. Sancho's tongue was a razor, and as a matter of bad habit he used it to cut. But at least Julitta would arrive home under the escort of two men instead of just himself. He decided that Mauger would judge the little overseer's presence the lesser of the two evils.

Mauger was already at Madame Clothilde's, his face like thunder, his fist clamped around a goblet of wine which he was just draining as Benedict walked in. The groom stood a little to one side, a fresh red graze on his cheek, his eyes afraid.

The presence of others held Mauger's temper in check, although every muscle was corded and tense. 'I told you to stay,' he said to Julitta, his voice hoarse with the effort of control.

'I was right about Benedict,' she defied him, her chin raised, her body quivering, 'but you chose not to listen.'

'He looks remarkably hale and hearty to me,' Mauger said coldly.

'Late spring he wasn't,' Sancho said, and removing his battered felt hat, sat down on a bench near the window embrasure.

Mauger eyed him with disfavour. 'Who are you?'

'I'm head overseer of the stud belonging to Rodrigo Diaz of Bivar, although that will mean nothing to a barbarian such as you.' Sancho spat his wad of chewed liquorice root onto the floor.

Disgust flared Mauger's nostrils. 'You call me a barbarian?' His gaze swept over the haphazard assembly of rags before him.

'He knows more than either of us,' Benedict defended swiftly, 'and probably more than Rolf, since he's been alive that much longer.'

'I don't believe you,' Mauger said through compressed lips.

'Believe what you want, it's the truth.'

Madame Clothilde appeared then, bearing more wine and two large baskets of bread and fresh fruit. She too looked at Sancho as if she considered him a barbarian whom she would rather not entertain beneath her roof.

She deposited the food and departed to her cooking pot, wiping her hands on her apron and muttering.

Mauger replenished his wine cup and took another long drink. 'Where is Gisele?' he asked.

Benedict hesitated. When he spoke, his voice was devoid of expression. 'She lies in a small chapel on the pilgrim road to Compostella.' His hand shook slightly as he took a drink of his own wine. It was still difficult to talk about. He could feel the weight of Mauger's stare, studying his reactions, judging them. 'We were attacked by Basque brigands in the mountains and she was killed – an arrow through the heart. All of our pilgrim group were slaughtered except me. I . . .' He broke off with a shuddering breath. It was impossible to continue.

Mauger cleared his throat. His gaze slid away from Benedict, and he tilted his cup to his mouth. 'I am sorry,' he said gruffly.

The sound of Benedict's ragged breathing was loud in the silence. Julitta chewed her lip. Her eyes flickered once to her husband, and then, with sudden decision, she went to Benedict and put her arms around him. 'I am sorry too,' she said. 'She was my sister; she deserved better of life, and of death.'

Benedict made a strangled sound and put his face in his hands. His body was wracked by dry sobs as behind his eyes he saw again the look on Gisele's face as the arrow pierced her heart and brought her down like a doe. Mauger looked on, his expression appalled and embarrassed. Julitta said nothing, just held Benedict, trying to convey sympathy and grief by touch. She could understand why he had shied from the subject on the wharf.

'It is good that he weeps,' said Sancho, the least perturbed of anyone in the room. 'It cleans the wound of poison, makes it easier to heal. I have been concerned about him.'

Julitta raised her eyes to Sancho's. Behind the prickly facade lay compassion and care. 'What happened to him?' she asked.

Briefly Sancho told her the entire story as he had heard it from Faisal, not once glancing at Mauger, as if he felt the other man should not be present.

'I would have gladly died too,' Benedict muttered through the bars of his fingers.

'Not gladly, son,' Sancho reproached. 'If you had truly desired to yield up your soul to God, you would not have fought so hard to live when Faisal was tending you. It is the self-pity in you speaking, not the man.'

Benedict raised his head and stared at Sancho with narrowed eyes. Sancho returned the look, unperturbed. Benedict wiped his eyes on the heel of his hand and pushing himself out of Julitta's embrace, rose and walked to the window embrasure to stare out on Clothilde's sun-filled vegetable garden.

'So what are you doing in Bordeaux?' Mauger demanded, an edge of resentment and suspicion in his voice.

Benedict's left shoulder rose and fell. 'Returning to Brize with my burden of tidings and a cargo of Spanish horses.' His tone was weary now, uncaring. 'I hear that you are seeking a war stallion for Duke Robert.'

Mauger drank off his wine and refilled his cup. 'What of it?'

Julitta glanced at her husband. It occurred to her that with Gisele dead, Benedict was no longer the automatic heir to Brize-sur-Risle, that Mauger was the one with the better claim through herself. She wondered if Mauger had realised it too.

Benedict shrugged again and did not look round. 'Nothing,' he said dully. 'Congratulations.'

'Lord Robert specifically requested that I be sent,' Mauger added defensively.

'I am sure you are capable of selecting the kind of horse the Duke requires.'

'I am,' Mauger said tightly. 'And I have. So don't you go parading your own fancy Spanish wares beneath his nose when we return.'

'Christ, Mauger, do you think I care at the moment?' Benedict demanded in a voice that still cracked with the raw emotion of grief. 'I don't give a split rivet for your petty schemes!' He made an abrupt throwing gesture with his clenched fist. 'I think we have nothing more to say to each other that will not end in a fight.' He strode from the room without looking at its other occupants, not even Julitta.

Mauger drank down the wine. 'Don't look at me,' he growled. 'It's not my fault.'

Julitta gave him a disgusted glare. 'I know that you would

prefer him to have died,' she said, and rising to her feet, followed Benedict out.

Sancho stepped into the breach as Mauger made to stride in pursuit of his wife. 'Stay,' he commanded, his cracked voice suddenly imperative. 'You will only goad him into a corner, or he will goad you, and there will be bloodshed. Let the woman handle him.'

Mauger glowered, but Sancho glowered back far more effectively, and held his ground. 'You say you are capable of selecting bloodstock for your Duke? Come then, tell me what you know, and see if your talent matches up to mine.' He gestured to the bench that Julitta had vacated. 'Sit, cease drinking and eat some of that bread to soak up all the wine you've consumed. I don't suffer fools gladly.'

'Why should I listen to you?'

'Because mine is the voice of reason.' The little overseer drew a fresh liquorice twig from his pouch, poked it in the side of his mouth where two teeth still opposed each other in the gum, and started to chew.

Mauger continued to scowl, but he made no attempt to thrust Sancho out of the way, and in a moment, he sat down and reached to the bread basket. 'I've been in this trade since the cradle. I don't need lessons from you.'

Sancho sat down beside him and stretched out his legs, easing their stiffness. 'I too was taught from the cradle and this year I will see out seventy winters. And still I find much to learn. A man who says he knows everything, knows nothing.'

Once out of the house, Julitta hitched her skirts to her shins and ran to catch up with Benedict who was striding out as if the devil were at his heels.

'Wait!' she gasped out. 'Ben, please wait!'

'Leave me alone!' he snarled raggedly over his shoulder.

Julitta redoubled her efforts to reach him, and catching him by the arm, swung him round to face her. 'I won't impose on you beyond a moment,' she panted, 'but there is something that you must see. I know that you don't want my company or

Mauger's – we're only salt in your wound, but . . .' Her voice trembled and she broke off.

His eyes had been opaque, a little mad, but now they cleared and he focused on her, breathing hard. 'I should have known that I could not run from you,' he said and squared his shoulders. 'What is it you want of me?'

What I cannot have, she thought. 'I want to give you something. Come.' She tugged at his sleeve, drawing him back toward the house and the stable shed beyond the courtyard. 'Here.' She drew him into the first stall.

He stared at the two horses, the grey gelding and the small chestnut mare. The grey swung his intelligent head and absorbed the scent and sight of the man. A sound, somewhere between a nicker and a grunt, rippled from the gelding's nostrils, and he tugged at his halter, eager to reach Benedict. The mare, too, pricked up her ears and whickered softly.

'Cylu?' Benedict whispered. He went to the grey and laid his hand against the glossy, muscular neck. Cylu nudged him lovingly with his nose. Benedict inspected the horse, turning disbelief into reality as he felt the solidity of bone and muscle, the satin hide, the warm, sweet breath. 'Where did you find them?' His attention flickered briefly to the mare, to Julitta, then back to grey gelding. A part of him was restored, and although it was only a small part, by its very presence it assumed great importance. A straw upon which to cling, a foundation on which to rebuild.

We bought them from a coper here in Bordeaux,' Julitta said, watching him with a mingling of love and pain. 'He said that he obtained them from a Basque trader.'

Benedict laughed harshly. 'A Basque cut-throat more likely. I wonder how many other pilgrims' horses have been sold that way?' He pressed his palm against Cylu's warm, dappled neck. 'I saw her die,' he muttered. 'Mercifully it was quick, she knew nothing beyond the first moment, but her eyes were on me as she fell. There was nothing I could do . . . nothing.' His voice quivered and his fingers tightened in Cylu's mane. If they had not, he would have turned round and engulfed Julitta in his grief and anger, and he knew that he dared not. A step too far on the crumbling edge of a precipice. Behind him, she was silent, as if she too sensed the danger of the moment. Then he heard the straw rustle. When he dared to look round, he discovered that he was alone.

He took time to compose himself, washed his hands and face in the water pail and went outside. She was sitting on a bench in the shade of the stable wall, her skirts tucked beneath her. He went to her and sat down, keeping a body's distance between them.

'I am sorry,' he said wryly.

'You needed a moment to be alone – and so did I.' She looked at him, and then down at her hands.

Benedict watched her toy with her gold wedding ring. 'Was Mauger so jealous of you that he had to bring you all the way to Bordeaux?'

'In a way. Robert of Normandy decided that I was the perfect dish to refresh his jaded palate. He wanted Mauger out of the way, so sent him down here to buy an Iberian warhorse. Mauger saw straight through his ploy and made me accompany him – not that I was unwilling. Robert of Normandy is no safe harbour for a runaway wife, and besides, I enjoy the freedom of travelling. Of course,' she added to the gold ring, 'instead of Robert of Normandy, Mauger now has you to contend with.'

Benedict sighed. 'You and he, I thought you had found contentment?' he said, remembering that time he had walked in on them making love on the solar floor.

'Resignation,' she murmured and darted him a glance. 'I have tried to adapt to Mauger's ways, he tries to compromise, but the road is strewn with thorns.'

Benedict thought about Sancho, about the tale the old man had told him of his youthful elopement. '*It was hard for her,*' he had said. '*We never really had any peace.*' He leaned his head against the stable wall and looked at her. 'When I have spoken to your father and delivered the horses, I am returning to Castile.'

'For always?' Dismay widened her eyes and she caught her full underlip in her teeth, a mannerism that had always maddened and enchanted him.

'For the next few years at least. Sancho will more than welcome me. If I return to England, it will only be to face the persecution of William Rufus. I know between him, Robert of Normandy, and Rodrigo Diaz of Bivar, which lord I would rather serve.'

'But what of my father?' Julitta protested with indignation. 'I can understand that you feel no loyalty to Rufus and Robert, neither of them are worth a spit in the wind, but surely you owe my father more than that?'

Benedict met her gaze which was fierce-blue with anger. 'I owe your father more than I can ever repay, most of it in regrets and apologies,' he said bleakly. 'I will do my best to make reparations in Spanish horse stock and silver. You do not need to tell me that it is not enough.'

She said nothing, just continued to stare at him, and he plunged on, further justifying his decision in the face of her silence. 'You are now your father's heir, and through you, Mauger. You may say that I am cutting off my nose to spite my face, but I could not bear to take orders from him at Brize and Ulverton. I have made friends in Castile and the beginnings of a new life. The threads of my old one are too tangled and broken to be mended.'

Julitta reddened, and compressing her lips looked the other way for a moment.

'Julitta?' He leaned toward her.

She shook her head and swallowed valiantly. 'You are right,' she said. 'A life in Castile will suit you, and my father too, since he will have a source of fine-bred Iberian horses at the flick of his finger. He can always find another overseer for Ulverton. It is just that I...' She broke off and angrily wiped her eyes. 'It is foolish.' Her voice quivered. 'I have loved you since I was five years old. You would think I would know better by now.' She sprang to her feet before he could close the gap between them. 'No, let me be,' she warned. 'I am overjoyed to know you are alive, let that be enough.'

Benedict rose too, not knowing what he was going to do or say, only aware that they could not part like this. There had to be a better balance. 'Julitta, listen,' he pleaded, but whatever he would have said went unspoken as two grooms entered Clothilde's courtyard, leading a plunging black stallion, its eyes white-rimmed and its upper lip wrinkled back to show vicious yellow teeth. Its mane and tail in contrast to its coat, were a bright silver.

Open-mouthed, Benedict stared. 'Christ on the Cross,' he said softly. 'Don't tell me that Mauger's gone and bought that brute.'

'What do you mean?' Julitta demanded sharply, a note of fear in her voice.

'Sancho and I saw that black earlier. He'd just kicked one of his handlers in the thigh and nigh on cracked the bone. Fine colour, fine looks, but I doubt that any man will come close enough to mount him, let alone stay in the saddle. He's not just wild, he's savage.'

Julitta shook her head. 'Mauger would never buy an animal like that. You know how cautious he is.'

'Cautious or not, it's been brought here, and it's certainly neither for me, nor Sancho.' He started forward to help the grooms, but Mauger and Sancho emerged from the house, and Benedict halted.

'Where shall we put him, lord?' enquired one of the attendants between grunts for breath as he strove to hold the horse.

Mauger indicated Clothilde's small stable. 'Bring out the chestnut and the grey, and put him in their place,' he commanded.

'He'll kick the place to bits,' Benedict said, appalled.

Mauger strode up to his grooms. 'Mind your own business, I know what I'm buying.'

'An early grave by the looks of things,' Sancho declared with a curl to his upper lip. He watched the black stallion rear and buck, plunge and kick. 'Still, you do not need lessons from me,' he gave an exaggerated shrug, 'or so you say.'

'Mauger,' Benedict entreated, his hand outstretched. 'Don't be a fool. Swallow your pride.'

'Pride has nothing to do with it,' Mauger said through his teeth. It was obvious that rather than swallow he would choke. 'Take your horses and go!'

Benedict contained his anger, although it flashed in his eyes, and tightened his mouth corners. 'And so I will,' he said quietly, accepting the lead reins of Cylu and the mare from a groom. 'We have nothing more to say to each other, at least not without bloodshed.' He looked at Julitta. 'Go with God,' he murmured. 'You will be in my thoughts.'

'And you in mine.' Her lower lip quivered.

'Leave Julitta alone,' Mauger hissed. 'She is my wife, you lost yours.'

Benedict flinched from the fury in Mauger's bright grey eyes. He seemed almost as mad as the black stallion. 'Yes, she is your wife,' he answered. 'You ram it down my throat at every opportunity.'

'Lest you forget!' Mauger snarled.

It was too much. Benedict's resolve broke. 'How could I?' he attacked. 'We both know why she was married to you in the first place!'

The air between them was drenched with more than just the heat of the day. Mauger's right hand eased towards the hilt of his sword. Benedict was not wearing a blade, had only his meat knife at his belt. He wanted to seize it and plunge it into Mauger's arrogant body, but by a supreme effort of will, he clenched his fists and kept them down at his sides. 'This is foolish,' he said impatiently. 'There can be no winner from this.'

He mounted Cylu, held out the chestnut's rope for Sancho, and rode out of the courtyard. Although he did not look round, he could feel the stares striking his spine – Mauger's hatred, Julitta's love and anguish.

The sides of the horse shelter shook as the black stallion kicked and kicked again, the hollow drumming filling the world.

'He thinks he is better than everyone when he is nothing,' Sancho said contemptuously. And then he grinned, revealing the interior of his juice-blackened mouth. 'Your woman, she is very beautiful. Never have I seen such pretty hair.'

Benedict thought about murdering the little overseer. 'She is not my woman.'

'You think because I am old and I squint that I have no eyes?' Sancho snapped his fingers in front of Benedict's face.

'I think that because you are old and you squint, you should mind your own business.'

Sancho snorted. 'You are my business, lad.'

'Then leave me alone.' Benedict kicked his heels against Cylu's flanks and urged him to a trot, putting distance between himself and Sancho's gargoyle grin. But the overseer's words followed him, and so did the eyes, with their knowing squint.

CHAPTER 59

The September sea was a calm green-blue with the gentlest of swells as the *Constantine* sailed up the tidal estuary of the Garonne and entered the wide bite of the Bay of Biscay. White caps rolled shorewards and gulls soared above the slow wake of the galley, their cries piercing in the clear air.

Benedict descended the crude stairway from the hatch on the main deck, and entered the caulked-up hold where the horses he was bringing to Rolf were stabled. As an extra precaution, in case they met with rough weather, each animal was supported in a canvas sling so that it would not lose its footing and be cast over on its back. The animals had access to food and water, and there were two grooms with them at all times to deal with difficulties, should they arise.

The *Constantine* was ploughing her way north on the swell and they were making good time. Benedict anticipated that by evening they would enter the port of Royan, there to take on fresh fodder for the animals and give them a day's respite from the slings. From Royan, it was only three more days of sailing to the Normandy coast. The route was shorter than the overland one, less sapping of the horses' strength. Many traders did not trust the vagaries of the open sea, and no-one would have attempted the passage in winter, but here, at summer's end, the weather was still benevolent enough for Benedict to have few qualms. The overland route held too many memories, none of them pleasant.

He went among the horses, checking that their slings were

secure and that the animals were comfortable. He spoke gently to each one, and laid his hands upon them, stroking, scratching, soothing. In his imagination, he saw Sancho sitting in the corner watching him with a mocking twist to his mouth and an approving look in his eyes. The feeling was so strong that he even flashed a wry smile into the lantern-lit darkness.

Even as Benedict had turned his eyes to the north, so Sancho had turned south, heading home to his duties at the stud of Bivar. They had parted on the wharfside at Bordeaux, the tide running high, slapping against the sides of the *Constantine*, a north-easterly evening wind ruffling Benedict's black hair and the catskin trim on Sancho's short cloak.

'God speed your path and look favourably on your dealings,' Sancho had said soberly, without the customary leer or salty remark. There had been affection in his eyes, and concern.

Benedict embraced the wiry old man heartily. 'Look for me in the spring,' he answered, affirming his intention of returning.

But spring lay on the other side of winter, a winter Benedict had to endure in Normandy and England. He had tragic tidings to bear to Rolf, and the wound-salt of the presence of Mauger and Julitta for some of that time. He did not think he would stay long at Brize. There was always his father's house in Rouen in which he could over-winter.

He finished making a fuss of Kumbi and went back on deck. The wind billowed the canvas sail and ropes creaked. The *Constantine* rode forward on the gentle swell, the steersman making occasional adjustments to the tiller. Out on the sea beyond them were the masts of other vessels taking advantage of the tide – galleys bearing salt from the pans stretched along the sandy coast, Spanish iron, and tun upon tun of Gascon wine for England and Normandy.

Benedict stared across the water at the other vessels. The *Draca* was out there among them, but he could not detect her sail. Beltran, its master, had come visiting as he and Sancho prepared the *Constantine* to embark, and there had been a troubled look in his eyes. Over a meal of bread and saffron fish soup, he had confided that he was not entirely happy about the cargo he was expected to bear back to Normandy.'

'Lord Mauger says that he wants me to transport that stallion he bought. I am a wine trader, I know little of animals. Yes, I have carried sheep before, and even once a cow, but it is not the same. I suggested to him that he should take the overland route, but he became angry. I think that he wants to arrive in Rouen before you.'

Benedict grimaced and laid down his spoon. 'And you think right,' he said. 'But there is nothing I can do. There is no foundation for reason between myself and Mauger. We parted on a quarrel, and whatever I say will only make him the more determined to go his own way.'

Beltran nodded. 'I do not expect you to talk to him. I know how it is between you. But if I have to take this horse, then I want you to tell me the best way of making him safe.'

'Knock him on the head,' Sancho advised. 'And every time he wakes up, knock him on the head again.'

Benedict darted him an amused glance, then turned back to Beltran. 'Make sure he is securely tied and hobbled, that he cannot break loose. And don't let him see that you are afraid, it will only increase his aggression.'

Beltran had rolled his eyes at Benedict. 'I don't intend going anywhere near that beast,' he said. 'Let Lord Mauger load him, let Lord Mauger tend to his needs. My only concern is sailing the *Draca* whole into Rouen. Say a prayer for me.'

And now, gazing out to sea, Benedict did say a prayer, and asked God to keep Julitta from harm.

Beltran paced the single deck of the *Draca* and glanced sky-wards with a worried frown. Storm clouds were building, one on top of the other, piling to fill the sky. Dirty grey, rimmed with heavy charcoal, expanding and contracting like the chest of a breathing giant. The sea was a choppy green-grey, the crests of the waves licked with white curlicues of spume. The *Draca* was holding a steady course at the moment, and running well before the wind, but Beltran did not really like the idea of rounding the tip of Brittany in the teeth of a storm. It might yet blow over, but his experience and instinct told him that it was unlikely. He turned to give instructions to one of the crew, and caught sight of Mauger leaning over the wash-strake, retching dryly into the waves. His garments were drenched from the splash of the spray against the *Draca*'s sides, his blond hair plastered to his skull, his eyes sunken in cadaver hollows. The grooms were sick too. Only Lady Julitta went unaffected, possessed of Rolf's natural sea legs. She stood beside the steersman, talking cheerfully, her cheeks whipped to startling rosiness by the sting of the salt wind.

Beltran walked down the ship towards her, picking his way over a coil of rope, a water barrel, and past the open hold. On one side of the mast, his cargo of wine barrels was protected from the elements by a covering of oiled canvas secured with hempen ropes. On the other, hobbled, muzzled, immobilised, was Mauger's black Spanish stallion. His back was covered with a blanket to keep him from catching a chill, and he was fairly well protected from the worst of the spray, but Beltran won-dered if the beast would be approachable, let alone rideable by the time they reached dry land.

He had been blindfolded at the outset of their journey while he was hobbled and tied, but that had been removed once he was secure and they were underway. The stallion's eyes showed a permanent white rim, and there were tension grooves run-ning from nostril to orbit. The grooms had to untie his head to permit him to eat and drink, but as they were now, Beltran doubted them capable of controlling the beast should there be an accident.

Skirting the stallion, never taking his eyes from him, he continued on to Julitta.

'Storm rising,' he said, pointing at the clouds. 'Best to find a harbour soon and ride it out.'

Julitta nodded, and although concern filled her eyes, there was no serious anxiety. She knew that Beltran was more than competent which was more than could be said for Mauger. His face was almost the same shade of green as his tunic and he had retched so much that he could barely stand straight for the pain in his abused stomach muscles. Despite herself, she felt sympathy for him.

After his behaviour in Bordeaux, she had hated him, but it had been impossible to maintain such intensity of emotion for long. He was jealous of her because he was uncertain of himself, and when she saw the bewilderment in his eyes, the incomprehension of his own actions, her rage diminished. She would never cease loving Benedict, but she knew that if she continued to live on dreams, they would destroy her.

The clouds continued to scud and darken, and needles of rain prickled Julitta's face. The wind whipped the cloak that she drew around her body, and tried to tear it away. A freak gust swirled off her wimple. Her braids, dark and bright, tumbled down over her breasts. The *Draca* responded gallantly to the increasing surge of the sea beneath her keel. Her prow rose and dipped, rose and dipped, still knifing the waves with a keen edge. Spray shattered over her bows and spattered the crew, the passengers, and the covered cargo. Mauger's black stallion tugged on his securing ropes and neighed in protest and fear as time and again stinging drops of cold, salt water peppered his hide.

Mauger and the least incapacitated groom strove to erect another canvas cover over the stallion for protection, but the wind was too stiff and their bodies too weak, and all they succeeded in doing was wrapping the canvas around themselves and hampering the frantically working crew. Julitta hurried to help them out of their dilemma. Her hair whipped around her face, her gait was a drunken weave as she strove to walk on the heaving deck. Reaching Mauger and the groom, she untangled them from the clogging canvas, the fabric heavy and rough in her hands. All too close, the stallion threshed and struggled against the ropes confining him. Mauger reached his feet by sheer determination of will.

'Give me the end.' He beckoned, and swallowed hard.

With some difficulty, Julitta did so. Between them, she and Mauger, and the groggy groom, managed to erect an awning over the stallion, but it was scant cover from the incoming rain and wind.

Task finished, Mauger collapsed, retching weakly. 'Why should you be gifted with sea legs?' he gasped at Julitta, his voice husky and strained.

'My father's never sick either, I get it from him,' she answered. 'Beltran says he's taking shelter. It won't be long.'

'I never want to leave dry land again,' Mauger gulped. 'Never!'

Julitta returned to Beltran. The captain's eyes were narrowed against the worsening weather, and he constantly snapped out orders to his crew. 'We're off the Breton coast,' he told her. 'There's a bay beyond the next headland. We'll ride this out close to shore. It's going to be a rough night, my lady.'

Julitta gathered her wet, dishevelled braids in her hands and squeezed out the water. She gave Beltran a rueful smile. 'I think that sailors are very hardy, very brave, and utterly foolish,' she said.

'Not so foolish as to lose their lives; my crew are the best.'

'Knowing you, and knowing Aubert de Remy, I would not argue,' she said, and went to sit in the lee of the wine cargo, out of his and the sailors' way. She said a quiet prayer, both for the safety of the *Draca* and for those on board the *Constantine*, wherever she was on this wild and stormy passage.

The *Constantine* also took shelter from the bad weather by hugging the Breton shoreline. Breakers drove in towards the beach – a long strip of fawn sand and shingle giving way to dark forest through the driving rain. Gulls screamed and wheeled; the air was salty with spindrift and the wind was raw.

Benedict checked on the horses in the hold, and found them uneasy and uncomfortable, but not given to outright panic. He went among them, soothing and stroking, making sure that all had sufficient feed and water. The chestnut mare was the most nervous of all of them, and he remained with her longest, talking to her, coaxing. She and Gisele had suited each other, their temperaments a match. He thought of his wife, of her simple grave in the mountains, and of the road he had travelled since then. It seemed as close as yesterday, and as distant as the end of the world.

He gave the mare a final, affectionate pat, and went back on deck. The wind howled through the lateen rigging, sounding notes like an off-key bladder pipe. The canvas sail snapped and billowed. A rope clattered against the mast.

Benedict lunged his way to the cabin and galley in the vessel's stern, where a sailor was stirring a cauldron of soup over a hearth of glazed tiles. Just before he ducked into the shelter, Benedict cast his eyes across the murky horizon. Other ships were seeking shelter inshore. There were two wine traders heading north like themselves, a smaller, southbound Scandinavian Nef, and a fleet of local fishing boats. The farthest sail was a square one, striped in yellow and red-orange, the same colours as those of the *Draca*. Benedict narrowed his eyes, trying to focus on the ship, but the wind gusted and the rain suddenly began to pelt down, obliterating all vision beyond a few yards. Sighing, Benedict entered the galley, to fortify himself with a bowl of the hot soup. If the weather worsened further, there would be no time for taking sustenance, and besides, the galley fire would have to be doused so that it was not a hazard.

The full force of the squall struck as evening darkened the sky and the wind rose beyond a whine to a scream. The *Draca* was sent writhing out of control, bucking and kicking on the waves like a runaway colt. The steersman cursed and fought the tiller, striving to bring her round. Bellowing orders, Beltran ran to help him.

Lightning ripped the sky apart, giving the struggling sailors a fleeting vision of heaven's brilliance. In the darkness as the *Draca* plunged into a trough, they saw the gates of hell and the black mouth of eternity rising up to devour them.

The rain slashed down in a million lances of black light. Sea water broke over the deck and waterlogged the bilges. Sailors frantically pumped and scooped. The *Draca* wallowed, trembled, and fought back at the sea. Like the Viking ships from which she was descended, she snarled defiance at the silver-clawed waves, her prow dripping trails of crystal and obsidian water.

Soaked to the bone, Julitta huddled against the wine casks and endured the fury of the storm. In its early stages it had been exhilarating, but now she was becoming frightened by its fury. As far as the eye could see, there was nothing but a wild darkness, and it roared so loudly that it left no room for any other sound. It filled the world to bursting and threatened to rend its very fabric. Even the terrified screams of the black stallion were overridden by the bellowing of the storm.

Julitta searched her mind for the best saint to invoke for protection, but it was impossible to think. Gisele would have known, or Arlette, but both were dead. Perhaps she was going to join them.

Julitta sternly curtailed her over-active imagination. Beltran said that it was an ordinary storm, that the *Draca* had weathered worse, and would doubtless do so again, and when he spoke, his eyes had been calm.

Beside Julitta, Mauger lay doubled up and groaning, oblivious to anything but his own suffering. His stomach was empty and produced nothing but a watery bile. Julitta had begun to feel queasy too, but she knew that a part of it was fear. She could swim – her father had insisted she learn after she had strayed near the dew ponds as a child, but it was a long time ago, and she had been taught in shallow water where her feet touched the bottom, not in a rough, black sea. Her imagination ran riot again. She squeezed her lids tightly shut and prayed. And the name she sobbed was Benedict's. For he was the only rescuer she had ever known.

The *Draca* rode out the storm and with the coming of dawn, battered and bruised, but still intact, rolled at anchor on the swell of an iron-hued, sullen sea. Over their heads the clouds still churned, driven like the gulls by the directionless, boisterous wind. Feeling as stiff as an old woman, Julitta clambered in ungainly fashion to her feet and went in search of a cup of water and a crust of bread to calm her quailing stomach. Beltran was sitting on a rowing bench near the steersman and chewing on bread and smoked herring. His eyes were pouched with weariness and there was a troubled frown between his brows.

'Good morrow, my lady,' he greeted Julitta and offered her a share of his breakfast. She declined the herring, but accepted the bread and a cup of watered wine.

'Have we seen out the worst of it now?' she asked as she made to return to Mauger.

'I hope so, my lady. We took a fair battering last night. Sail's stretched beyond good use. It'll be slower progress from now on.' He sucked his teeth and shook his head. 'I'm sorry it could not have been a smoother passage.'

Julitta managed a weak smile. 'So am I.'

Mauger sat up groggily and with a groan, took the cup that Julitta handed to him, having sipped her share. He drank thirstily, his body in desperate need of moisture after the terrible purging of yesterday. Red-eyed, rumpled, stained, he looked at Julitta over the rim of the cup. She had bound up her hair in a tightly knotted kerchief, her cheeks were scarlet, her lips salt-dried. Her shoes and the hem of her gown were sea-stained too. She looked like a fishwife. It was in her blood, a product of her tough, Norse heritage. Thus the women of her forefathers who had crossed the seas in open boats must have looked. Mauger acknowledged to himself that he would have been one of the farmers who stayed at home and never went a-viking.

Cynwulf was a sea-raider, a pirate, whose home for the past twenty years had been the deck of a longship and the high seas between Dublin and Ushant. He was an English exile, a huscarl who had survived to flee the battle of Hastings, and found sanctuary in the Norse pirate port of Dublin. Robbed of his homeland, he now robbed the Normans who had stolen it from him, exacting his revenge on their traders and merchant vessels.

His ship, the *Fenrir*, had seen better days, so had its crew, and the recent storm had done little to make them any more presentable. They had sailed out from Dublin on a promising wind together with three other raiders, but the squalls of the last two days had scattered the longships and each had now to make his own way. Cynwulf was irritated. Prey was easier when hunting in a pack. One to one could be dangerous, and although he had never shrunk from peril, he was aware of his encroaching years and the slowing of his body.

Cynwulf scanned the horizon with weather-creased eyes. The jagged coastline of Brittany rose out of the mist on the *Fenrir's* larboard bow. A sailor dropped a knotted sounding line and drawing it back up, shouted the depth to the steersman. Gulls screamed overhead and a watery sun pierced the clouds. Cynwulf had contemplated putting about and returning to Dublin, but now he squared his shoulders and took the decision to remain at sea. Storm-battered they might be, but there would be other vessels in similar case, probably up from Biscay, and if he chose carefully, the *Fenrir* could yet earn her keep with a hold full of booty to replace her ballast of common rock.

It was midday when the sail was sighted on the horizon. The muscles stood rigid in Cynwulf's jaw. He strode to the raised deck on the prow and followed the sailor's pointing finger to the tiny red and yellow patch off the starboard gunwale. It was almost beyond vision, but in the fullness of time, unless it altered direction and sailed out to sea, it would cross their path . . . or they would cross its path.

'Break out the oars,' Cynwulf commanded. 'Let's take a closer look.'

'Sail to port!' bellowed the *Draca's* lookout. 'Coming up fast!'

Beltran cupped his eyes and squinted across the glittering heave of the sea. He saw a rig similar to the *Draca's* own, the sail a plain, cream-coloured canvas. She was using both wind and oar power. He counted the number of rowing ports – a dozen either side, dipping and rising in smooth, powerful motion. Beltran cursed under his breath and began shouting rapid commands.

'What's wrong, what's happening?' Mauger came to Beltran's side and narrowed his lids in the direction of the captain's scrutiny.

Beltran shook his head. 'I may be wrong, but I'm not about to wait around and find out. Yonder vessel, she's bearing down on us too fast to be friendly.'

'You mean she's a raider?' Mauger looked appalled. His recovering complexion turned green again.

'We're in the right waters. They usually hunt in packs, but there are always lone wolves out on their own.' He glanced at Mauger from beneath his brows as he went to help trim the sail. 'Best look to that beast of yours; make sure he's well tied. There's some spears stacked at the side of the rowing benches. Arm yourself . . . and Lady Julitta too.'

'We can outrun them, surely,' Mauger said, a swallow in his voice.

'I hope so. Depends how much ballast she's carrying against the weight of our cargo.'

Mauger took two spears and retreated to the hold. Julitta was leaning over the painted gunwale, staring at the oncoming vessel. Red strands of hair had escaped her kerchief and were whipping against her face. 'Beltran says they could be raiders. You've to arm yourself,' he said.

She turned round. Her eyes had widened at his words, but she nodded sensibly, and took the weapon from him as if it was something that she did every day. 'What will they do if they are raiders and they catch us?'

Mauger thought of all the tales he had heard about the viciousness of Dublin pirates. 'I don't know,' he answered. 'Ransom us, I hope.'

Julitta hefted the spear the way she had seen the soldiers do at battle practices. She wondered whether it should be thrown, used as a stabbing weapon, or as a stave to keep the other vessel from grinding up sufficiently close for a boarding party. Like Beltran, she had counted twenty-four oars. Their own crew numbered a dozen, plus themselves. Odds of two to one at least.

It quickly became clear that the pursuing vessel had far from friendly intentions. As she approached, tacking to meet the *Draca*, Julitta saw the glint of sunlight on spear tips and shield bosses. She was a low-slung dragon-ship, built for speed, otter-sleek in pursuit.

Beltran ran the *Draca* as close to the wind as he dared, her sail trimmed as best could be managed after the stretching of the storm, and the heaviest members of the crew leaning out on her windward gunwale. She cut through the ocean swell with a smooth, hissing force, the waves parting beneath her knife-blade hull. But despite her surging progress, the sea-raider closed in, grapnels and spears at the ready.

Julitta could see the men on the longship now – salt-bearded warriors, some in armour, some in plain tunics, all of them bearing weapons. She could hear their shouts too. In a mingling of Anglo–Saxon and Irish–Norse, they bellowed their intentions across the diminishing gap of sea between themselves and the *Draca*, none of them remotely honourable.

A spear curved through the air. Its sharp iron tip ripped its way down the *Draca*'s sail and rested, embedded in the cloth. Another flew, shaving past Beltran and thrumming into a wine barrel in the hold. Red liquid spouted like a slashed artery. Mauger's stallion struggled against his restraints, and whinnied. Despite the cold sea breeze, sweat creamed his dark hide.

A grapnel struck the *Draca*'s straking and splashed back into the sea. A second and third were thrown, both clawing fast in the gunwale. Crew members strove to free their ship of the barbs. Spear-silver flashed and a sailor staggered backwards and collapsed. his task incomplete, his chest pierced. Mauger stepped over him to take his place, but it was already too late. The two hulls ground together, and a helmeted warrior hauled himself aboard the *Draca*.

Mauger thrust with the spear and the man died. He wrenched the shaft from the body with a snarl and leaped to tackle the next raider. But although Mauger held his own ground, he could not hold the entire length of the ship, and the pirates swarmed aboard.

The *Draca* lost her momentum and began to pitch and roll beneath the onslaught of violent activity and an untended sail. Julitta staggered and fell against the wine casks, losing the spear with which she had been keeping an amused raider at bay. He straddled her, and hauled her to her feet by a fistful of her gown.

'What have we here?' he said in Saxon, and dragged off her head covering. Her bright hair blazed free, and he whistled in admiration. 'Irish red,' he said.

'Take your hands off me!' she spat, using her mother's native tongue to reply rather than the Norman French of her daily usage.

For a moment, surprise blinked in the hard eyes. 'English,' he said. 'You should not be on a Norman trader.' The gaze narrowed. 'I will put my hands where I want upon my captives.'

She kicked him in his unprotected shins and swooped to bite his hand. He yelled and snatched it away, cursing; his sword came up. A spear thrust from behind gouged his side. Impaled he staggered on the pointed tip, swivelled, tried to beat it away, but Mauger leaned into the shaft and pushed the point in deeper. The raider screamed and swung his sword in a wild arc, catching the black stallion's halter rope and severing it in two. Mauger wrenched out the spear with a grunt of effort, and as the raider fell across the wine casks, clambered across him to secure the horse.

Her belly a vast, empty pit, Julitta swooped upon the dead man's sword. The weight hurt the tendons in her wrist and it felt unwieldy in her hand, but she braced it, holding it across her body in defence.

Mauger had reached the stallion, but he could not grasp the shorter, loose end of the halter rope attached to the headstall. The black whipped his head from side to side and snapped and fought. Such were his struggles that the rope hobbling his forelegs broke, and suddenly he was free to rear. Mauger dived to one side, but was not fast enough, and a red gash opened along the line of his temple. Julitta screamed her husband's name and leaped onto the wine casks to try and help him. He sat up, blood pouring from the wound.

'No, stay back!' he roared. 'Julitta, in Christ's name . . . ' His words were never completed, for a gust of wind slammed into the untended sail, sending it hard aback and, with the same slow grace as a diving whale, the *Draca* curved over into the water.

Julitta was thrown backwards onto the canvas-covered wine barrels. The raider Mauger had downed was still alive. She heard the air rattling and sucking in his lungs, before the rush of cold, green sea took away every other sound. Too dazed to scream, she was rolled under with the ship. The water was as icy as the fingers of death and it invaded her clothing, weighting her down. She kicked violently for the surface and broke through the heaving barrier to draw the pain of air into her starving lungs. Sea water slapped into her mouth, making her choke and gulp. Her garments dragged at her legs. Death smiled, biding its time.

Other heads bobbed in the water, shouting and choking, members of both crews now victim to the sea. She could not see Mauger and screamed his name. Wine barrels, sea chests, oars floated past her. Before her eyes a raider gave up the struggle to swim in his armour and sank. 'Mauger!' Julitta shrieked, casting desperately around. Sea water filled her open mouth and she choked violently. A wave slapped over her head, and when she broke surface again, struggling for air, scarcely able to draw it in for coughing, she knew that she was going to drown. Waves pushed at her in rapid succession. Her eyes were so salt-stung that she could not keep them open. Nor did it matter. The forces of wind and tide carried her away from the *Draca* and the raiding vessel. Death opened its arms and said Welcome.

She was drifting towards oblivion when a hairy tentacle slapped against her arm, and she heard a shout. For a moment, disoriented, she thought she was being dragged down to hell, and thrust out her arms, trying to beat the beast away, only to realise that far from being a sea-monster or a denizen of the underworld, it was a hemp rope. To have hit her so strongly and from such an angle, it could not possibly be a part of the capsized *Draca*. She seized upon it, clinging to a last hope of rescue upon death's open threshold, and felt the line go taut.

Squinting, almost blind, through the heave of the sea she saw the hull of another vessel, and spidering out from her gunwales, a dozen such ropes, with crew members leaning to pull survivors in to the spread of fishing net against her sides.

Julitta turned her back on death's door, but it did not close behind her. She was weak, more than half-drowned, and the insidious cold of the water was chilling her body beyond functioning. Although she reached the side of the rescue vessel, she had not the strength to let go of the rope and set her hand to the netting. And the climb was so far, the vessel much deeper in draught than the *Draca*. It was a mountain, and it was a mile too high.

'Julitta, don't let go!' an anguished voice yelled. 'In the name of Christ, hold tight! I'm coming down to you!'

'Ben?' The word croaked out of her, and brought on a paroxysm of coughing. For a moment the world spun into darkness and her fingers loosened on the rope. Then she tightened them with a convulsive jerk, obeying a command that was stronger than death itself.

He seemed to take an age, but it could not have been more than a matter of minutes before she felt his weight on the net above her. Then he was in the sea beside her. She shook her head, she dared not speak lest she begin coughing again.

'Christ, Julitta, don't fail me, don't let go!' he commanded again. 'Not until I tell you. Look, I'm going to put this around you to stop these other ropes cutting in. It's a spare horse sling. We're going to pull you up. Just nod if you understand.'

Julitta nodded and compressed her lips. There was so much she wanted to say, and all of it jailed inside her head. Nor were her thoughts coherent, for she was barely conscious.

Aware that he had very little time, Benedict worked rapidly, passing the sling around her body, tossing the loop to another crew member halfway up the netting, who then threw it to another man on deck. He could tell that Julitta was almost spent. Her face was ice-white, her lips bloodless, and there were blue shadows beneath her closed eyes. It was God's mercy that the *Constantine* had been close to the *Draca*. Whether it was God's mercy too that the *Draca* had been attacked instead of the *Constantine*, Benedict did not want to explore. God's will, perhaps. A shout floated down from the deck. Benedict acknowledged it with a wave. 'You can let go of the rope now,' he said to her, and laid his hand over hers, where her fingers were clutched in spasm on the dark hemp. She did not respond, and he had to prise away her grip gently.

Carefully, they lifted her from the water, and laid her down upon the deck. A strand of hair lay over her face like a ribbon of dark-red kelp, and emphasised the white coldness of her skin. Her eyelids fluttered.

'Ben?' she whispered.

'I'm here, Julitta, you're safe, you're safe. Nothing can touch you. The raiders haven't the strength to take us on too. In a moment you'll be warm and dry.'

'Mauger, he . . .' With the last of her strength she rolled over and vomited sea water. The deck came up to meet her, heaving and tilting on the swell of the waves. 'Mauger . . .' she croaked again, trying to stay conscious.

'Hush, Julitta, it's all right.' A warm, coarse blanket was wrapped around her and she felt herself being raised and carried. The daylight behind her lids darkened and a heavy stable scent filled her nostrils, removing the deadly sea-tang. She was deposited on a pile of hay and a flask was pressed to her lips.

'Drink,' Benedict commanded. 'It's strong mead.'

Obediently she took a swallow and felt the fiery sweetness slip down her throat and burn in her hollow stomach. She opened her eyes and saw that she was in the *Constantine*'s port hold among Benedict's horses. The only light was provided by a single horn-sided lantern suspended from a hook – it was too dangerous to have more. She took another sip of the mead and returned the flask to Benedict. 'Mauger . . . he – I lost him when we went over. He was wounded. The horse; it broke free and struck his head.' She looked up at him with haunted eyes. 'I fear for him.'

Benedict uttered neither platitude nor reassurance. There was no use in either. Given the speed at which the *Draca* had capsized, Mauger was not likely to be the only victim. 'I'll go back on deck and help look out for survivors,' he said, and hesitated, awkward before her now that the immediate crisis of her rescue was over. 'That blanket's soaking now, and so are your clothes. If you want to take them off, I'll lend you my spare clothes.'

Julitta nodded her thanks, wary of using her voice. The urge to retch was still strong. Behind her eyes, there was a hot, swollen ache, as if the sea had poured in there too, and was now seeking to flood out.

Benedict handed her a fresh blanket, disappeared into the gloom among the horses, and returned with a pile of garments. 'Here. Are you strong enough to put them on?'

Again she nodded.

Benedict hesitated, stooped to stroke her cold cheek, and went to the hatch ladder.

Julitta listened to his footsteps recede on deck and realised that he had not changed his own wet tunic, probably because he had given his only dry clothes to her. She clutched them for a moment, buried her face in their familiar smell and fought the scalding tide behind her lids. Her spirit struggled against the wave of self-pity and exhaustion engulfing her. She wiped the heel of her hand across her eyes, and set about exchanging her saturated garments for Benedict's dry ones. It seemed to take forever to remove her gown and shift, her clammy hose and loin cloth. Chills shuddered through her body, and her fingers were clumsy. Trying to attach Benedict's hose to the dry loin cloth seemed impossible, and by the time she finally succeeded, she was sobbing with frustration and fury at her own impotence. Once started, she could not stop, and the more she tried to hold back, the harder she cried. She lay on her stomach in the pile of straw, her face buried in her arms, and wept herself dry. From there, she drifted into an exhausted doze, her limbs twitching and jerking in the aftermath of hard, physical effort. But although her body was exhausted, her mind would not rest. A vision of Mauger's drowned, bloated face swam across her mind. And then she saw him astride the black stallion, swimming through the depths beneath the *Constantine*, seeking a way in through the pitched-caulked hull doors.

Her entire body jerked with the shock of the vision and her eyes flew open, a scream stifled behind her lips.

She heard voices and the clump of footsteps on the hatchway stairs, and sat up. Her heart thumped against her ribs in rapid strokes and her cheeks were damp, not only from her hair. Even in sleep she had been weeping.

By the hazy light of the single lantern, she saw Benedict and a sailor carrying Mauger between them. His blond head sagged, his mouth lolled open.

'Mauger . . . Oh Jesu, is he dead?' Julitta was unable to move, could only watch with widening eyes as they brought him over to her.

'No,' Benedict said, his voice constricted by the effort of setting Mauger carefully down on the hay, 'but he's barely breathing, and this gash on his head is still bleeding.'

Julitta stared at her husband, at the shallow rise and fall of his chest, the blue tinge to his flesh, the red trickle from the deep gash in his forehead. She reached out her hand and took hold of one of his. The fingers were as cold as effigy-marble.

Benedict studied her for a moment with brooding eyes. 'I'll go and fetch Sampson,' he said. 'He's one of the crew members, but he once trained for the church. It is the nearest Mauger will get to a priest.'

Julitta silently nodded, and did not look up as he turned and left.

Mauger was shriven by Sampson, who, despite having given up the church more than ten years ago, was still comfortingly familiar with its rituals. Certainly Mauger did not seem to notice the difference as he weakly made confession and was absolved of sin.

For the rest of the day, watched over by an exhausted Julitta, Mauger drifted in and out of consciousness, but never regained coherence. His grey eyes were opaque and unfocused, his breathing rapid and shallow. Just before midnight, in the presence of herself and Benedict, it stopped altogether.

Julitta composed Mauger's hands upon his breast and drew the blanket up to his chin. His eyes were closed and he looked as if he fallen from utter weariness into sound sleep. She bowed her head, unable to weep, for she had wept herself dry before he was found.

'He tried to be good to me in his way,' she said. 'Only I never wanted to wed him; never gave him a chance.'

'It isn't your fault,' Benedict said sharply, alarmed at her response even while he understood it.

'But it is. He was always trying to prove himself to me. I made him lose his judgement. He would never have bought that horse of his own accord.'

Benedict looked at her with pain in his eyes. He well understood her attitude. After Gisele's death, he had felt the scourge of guilt, still did on occasion if he had the time to brood. 'Grief heals,' he said, laying his hand upon hers. 'Guilt destroys.'

'Playing the priest again?' she bit out, and flashed him a glance full of anger. But there was misery there too, and need.

'No, just a man who lost the wife he had wronged before he could make atonement,' he said.

She flinched as his pain pierced hers. 'I'm sorry,' she said in a small voice with a break at its edge. 'I didn't think.'

'Ah, Julitta.' He folded her in his arms, and she accepted the embrace, her body stiff and hesitant. 'I don't want to lose you too. All our lives we have been coming together and breaking apart.' He swallowed, then raised one of his hands to touch her gaunt, hollow face. 'I want you, Julitta, not your guilt, not mine, just the two of us, and a new start. No,' he added, as she opened her mouth to speak. 'Now is not the time. We still have Mauger to honour and lay to rest, and there is grieving to be done. Let the time turn under heaven. Just think on what I have said.' Gently he released her, and went up on deck to fetch such things as would be needed for the washing and laying out of a corpse.

Dry-eyed, Julitta gazed upon the body of her husband and wished that she could weep.

CHAPTER 60

BRIZE-SUR-RISLE, SPRING 1088

Julitta knelt at the feet of the statue of the Magdalene Mary in Brize's convent. The flagged floor was cold beneath her knees, and the breath of her prayers broke from her lips in puffs of white vapour. This was Arlette's domain. Even in death, her father's wife dominated the place. Not content with the small chapel dedicated to her beyond the high altar, her presence pervaded the rest of the church. The wood and ivory statue of the Magdalene was clad in a green robe, a neat white wimple framing a vacant, half-smiling face, its complexion made luminous by the glow of the sanctuary lamp.

A thick wax candle burned on a spike. Beside it, in a specially cut niche, a pyramid of votive tapers flickered, each one a prayer for the souls of Arlette de Brize, her daughter Gisele, and now for Mauger of Fauville. Julitta crossed herself, rose from her knees, and lit another taper to add to those already burning. Since her return, she had made it her daily ritual to visit the church and pray for the soul of her dead husband.

Coming to terms with his death had been difficult, because it had meant coming to terms with herself and the guilt which Benedict had warned against. She could well recall the bitterness and rage of her childhood on discovering that the world did not revolve around herself alone, and that a hitherto unknown half-sister had laid claim to all that Julitta held dear – her standing in the world, her father's love, Benedict. She had hated Gisele even without knowing her. There had been a dark triumph in lying with Benedict, in taking him from her sister. A fleeting victory, paid for a hundred times over by her marriage to Mauger – and Mauger had done much of the paying.

Outside, a February dusk was gathering strength, the light a pale grey-blue. With a sigh, Julitta adjusted her cloak and walked towards the open doorway. Before she could reach it, she heard the snort of a horse and the ring of hoof on stone. Freya whinnied and was answered by a low, stallion nicker. Julitta's heart began to thump. But it was her father who stepped inside the church and made the sign of the Cross on his breast, and she was aware of a pang of disappointment.

He was nine and forty now and still handsome, although he wore the lines of his years and the brilliance of his hair had faded to a dusty ginger. During her absence, he had begun negotiating to marry a widow twelve years younger than himself, a merry, handsome woman with three children to her credit and a dowry as magnificent as her bosom. Julitta approved of the Lady Amicia. At least she need not worry about her father. There was a twinkle in his eye and a bounce to his stride.

'Daughter,' he acknowledged. 'I knew I would find you here.'

'I was about to leave.'

He nodded. 'It'll be dark soon.'

His way of saying that she had stayed too long. She knew that he had come to fetch her. Praying at his wife's tomb in the winter dusk was not one of her father's habits.

'Wait but a moment and I'll accompany you back,' he added, and went to bow his head at the altar and light four candles to add to the pyramid – one each for his wife and daughter, one for Mauger, and one for Ailith. A nun appeared from a recessed doorway, respected the altar, then Rolf, and went to trim the sanctuary lamp and attend to the candles. He crossed himself, left the woman at her task and returned to Julitta.

She eyed the nun wistfully. 'I wish that I possessed such tranquillity,' she murmured.

Rolf took her arm and led her out to the horses. The air was dank and raw, the trees bare and black. 'It will come,' he said. 'You are too impatient with yourself.'

Julitta gave him a bleak smile. 'Whose trait is that?'

'Assuredly your mother's.' He cupped his hand to boost her into the golden mare's saddle.

'Not yours?'

'I am merely impatient with others.'

'Then it seems I have both failings.' She settled herself in the saddle and took up the reins.

'And a stubborn will, too,' he said.

They rode in silence for a while, until the stone keep of Brize rose from the landscape, its high windows flickering with torchlight. Smoke wisped from the cooking fires in the bailey, promising food and comfort.

Rolf said softly, 'You are younger than your mother when I first knew her. You have all your life before you.'

'As she had hers?' She was shocked at the bitter note in her own voice.

Rolf winced. 'There was a time when we had great happiness,' he said. 'I know that what happened later was my fault. If I could undo it, I would.' He eyed Julitta's wooden expression. 'I still think of her, I still miss her. The regrets are carved so deep they are always with me, but I have learned to live with them. What use is there in looking back except to gain the experience of hindsight?' His hand rose to touch his cloak fastening – a brooch in the shape of Odin's six-legged horse, Sleipnir.

'So, what would you have me do?' She dismounted rapidly, a sure sign that she was agitated. 'Return to my old, hoyden ways?'

'That is not what I meant and you know it.' Rolf swung himself out of his saddle. His knee joints ached, and he had to flex his legs several times before the stiffness eased. 'All I am saying is that if you are going to drag a cross around with you, there is no need to carry it so high that you can't even see where you're going . . . or who walks beside you. In God's name, daughter, go with Benedict now and make your life with him. You have my blessing. Indeed, if you weren't so contrary, I'd order you to it.' He looked her up and down, exasperation and humour in his eyes. Then he said calmly, 'He would have come to the chapel himself, but I wanted to see you first.'

She caught her breath and her eyes widened. 'Benedict is here?'

Her father rubbed his jaw, feigning nonchalance before her surprise, but secretly delighted. 'He rode in from Rouen about the hour of nones. At the end of the week he sails for Corunna on board his father's new salandrium galley – but then he'll probably tell you himself. It is the reason he is here.'

Julitta's fingers tightened in the folds of her gown. 'Where is he, Papa?'

Rolf shrugged. 'I left him in the solar, but that was a while ago. Best find him. The dinner horn will be sounding soon.' He cocked his head on one side. 'Well, what are you waiting for? Go on!' He made a shooing gesture.

Julitta dithered a moment longer, then gathered her skirts, turned from her father, and hurried away in the direction of the keep. He stared after her, a smile on his lips, poignance in his eyes.

'I am leaving in the morning, and I want her to be with me.' Benedict laid his hand against the dormant bee skep. Sleeping. There was scarcely a vibration, but he knew that the insects were still alive. Rain misted down, cobweb-fine, dewing his hair and his dark woollen cloak. The heavy scent of soil filled his nostrils, of spring renewal, and the turned earth of graves, both awarenesses strong within him.

September it was when the *Constantine* had docked in Honfleur. Now in mid-February the spring bulbs were poking through the soil and milder days interspersed winter's cold. He had given Julitta her period of mourning, keeping his distance, letting the season mature and turn, but he did not know if she had turned with it, or whether her world remained frozen at the moment of Mauger's death. He had watched her pray, even joined her on occasion, but whether prayer had healed her wounds or kept them open, he could not be sure. But now he was about to find out.

With or without her, he would leave on the morrow. From Rouen he was bound for Castile with three brood mares for Rodrigo Diaz as a gift from Rolf. It would be good to feel the wind in his hair again and the call of the sea birds, the peppery Iberian heat, the scent of lemons. He would be subjected to Sancho's acerbic tongue, and fed until he burst by Faisal's dark-eyed wife and pig-tailed daughter. The thought warmed him, even brought a smile to his face.

The wicket gate creaked and he heard a whistle, then Julitta's voice in stern rebuke. The sound of paws pitter-pattered along the path, there was a gruff bark of greeting, and suddenly he was assaulted by Rolf's slot-hound Grif, its jaws slobbering and its huge, dirty pads staining his breeches as the dog jumped up at him. An exuberant tail swished like a whip against his thighs.

'Down!' he commanded sternly. 'Down, Grif.'

The dog yodelled at him and trotted away to the wall where a mount of fresh earth had been dug. The sound of copious urination filled the evening.

Julitta appeared, a flambeau in her hand. Smoke eddied from its pitched tip, and filled the air with the smell of resin. 'I've been looking for you,' she said. 'You weren't in the solar.'

'I was too restless.' He gave her a pained smile.

The torch flared and spat in the garden silence. He could see that she was gnawing her lip. 'My father said that you had come to make your farewells,' she said. Her hand shook slightly on the torch, her wrist quivering with the prolonged holding.

'Yes, I have. The *Doro* sails with the evening's tide tomorrow, bound for Corunna. We've a cargo of horses and wool on board. She'll return with more horses and wine.' His tone was conversational. It was also forced. The things that he really wanted to say hovered like the smoke from the flambeau, tangible but out of his grasp.

'Your father is pleased with the *Doro*?' She followed his

wooden lead, as if they were two strangers, but recently introduced. And perhaps they were, he thought, so much had
happened to change them.

'It has taken his mind from the loss of the *Draca*. Yes, he is
well pleased. She is higher-sided than his other vessels, better
freeboard and handling, if not quite so fast.'

She nodded. Chew, chew, went her lower lip, until it was all
he could do not to lean forward and cup her mouth, preventing
the motion.

In the distance, a horn sounded, the note long and sustained, summoning the castle folk to eat in the great hall.
They gazed at each other in the twilit darkness. Beyond them,
Grif snuffled among the borders, his keen bloodhound's nose
intoxicated by the powerful, damp scents.

'There was another reason I came here, to the garden,
besides my restlessness,' Benedict said. 'I came to talk to the
bees.' He pointed over his shoulder at the skep. 'You used to
tell them everything. I thought it was only common courtesy if
I told them too.'

'Told them what?'

'That depends on you.'

There was a long silence. Two strangers who had run out of
things to say. Then, the flambeau Julitta was holding wavered
and dipped. 'I am afraid,' she whispered, and it was not just her
wrist that trembled, but her entire body.

'Of what?'

'Of having wanted too fiercely and for too long. Of having
my heart's desire offered on a platter.'

Benedict grimaced. 'Hardly on a platter,' he said. 'The pain
has been too fierce and endured far too long.' A considering
frown lined his brow. 'Ah Christ, let there be an end to this, let
me tell the bees the truth as I feel it.' Taking a pace forward, he
removed the torch from her hand and thrust it into the dug
earth beside the skep. Then he drew her into his arms, gently
lowered her chin with his thumb so that she was no longer
chewing her lip, and kissed her.

It was fierce and tender, swift and slow, subtle and raw. She felt the pattern of the dance in her veins as she had felt it on that long ago May evening, and again in the garden at this very place when she was a married woman on the verge of adultery. Her loins were suddenly liquid. She pressed against him and the anguish of his voice in her ear melted her bones.

'I swear I will go mad if I cannot have you – tonight and for a lifetime,' he muttered. 'Julitta, say yes.'

Julitta laid her head against his breast and felt the swift thump of his heart. Lower down, against her belly, she could also feel the hard proof of his need. 'I choose the future,' she said, and gripped him, clenching her fists to grasp her decision so that it could not be taken from her as so much else had been.

He gripped her in return, speaking her name over and again, kissing her, and being kissed.

Their embrace was curtailed by the hound. He pushed his moist muzzle at them and stood on his hind legs, pressing muddy, wet forepaws against their joined bodies. Gasping for breath, laughing, they broke apart. Benedict snapped at Grif to get down. The dog whined and sat back on his haunches, his wrinkled face reproachful. Then he yodelled at them.

Dizzy with emotion, Benedict looked at Julitta. Her wimple was unpinned, her braids an unwinding dark tumble over her breasts. His Julitta, his lovely, brave, Maytime Julitta. 'Come,' he said. 'Grif is right. It is time to go in.' He held out his hand, and she linked her fingers through his.

Handfasted, like a bride and groom, they entered the keep.

AUTHOR'S NOTE

I wrote my first novel at the age of fifteen in response to falling in love with a knight in the BBC children's television programme *Desert Crusader*. It was for my own personal satisfaction, but it led me to the discovery that I wanted to write historical novels for a living, and that I had an awful lot of research to do to make the backgrounds of my novels convincing. Almost twenty-five years later, I am still learning and revising what I know; the process never ends.

I have always been fascinated by the medieval warhorse and the many fallacies surrounding its origins. There is a commonly held belief that the warrior of the middle ages thundered around on an enormous cart-horse. Nothing could be further from the truth.

The heavy horses that we know today, breeds such as the shire and the Clydesdale, were bred from the industrial revolution onwards when weight was required to pull weight at the haulage industry expanded. Such animals would have been disastrous as the mount of a medieval warrior. A knight would have been unable to sit astride such a horse with any degree of comfort, and to have endured a battle charge thus ensconced would have been nigh on impossible, not to say disastrous to the begetting of future generations.

The medieval warhorse had to be easy to mount at a moment's notice, i.e. not too high off the ground. It had to have a strong back, powerful quarters, and be capable of fast manoeuvre. In constitution, an ideal horse would have resembled a modern heavy hunter or small showjumper, and would have stood no more than fifteen and a half hands in height.

Horses with infusions of Spanish or Middle-Eastern blood were much prized by the warriors of Western Europe, and huge sums of money were paid for ideal mounts. It is recorded that William the Conqueror was given a Spanish stallion by the King of Spain, obviously a gift of prestige from one ruler to another. There is a description of the young Geoffrey of Anjou, on the eve of his marriage to the Conqueror's granddaughter, Matilda, which says: 'The Angevin led a wonderfully ornamented Spanish horse, whose speed was said to be so great that birds in flight were slower.'

Throughout the Medieval period, Spanish and Arabian horses were used to polish up the characteristics of native European animals. 'Top of the range' horses were viewed in much the same way as Rolls Royces, Lamborghinis, and Sherman tanks are viewed today.

Another point I want to mention, is brought about by an interview I did on local radio a while ago, when the comment was made that I use modern names for towns and cities instead of the old English. I prefer to do this because I feel it gives my readers a point of reference in a landscape a thousand years from our own. Thus I use London instead of Lundunwic or Lundenburg, and Hastings instead of Haestingceaster. The same is true of Ailith's name which is the slightly later medieval rendition of the Anglo-Saxon Aethelgyth, which was, I decided, too much of a mouthful!

BIBLIOGRAPHY

Barlow, Frank. *The Feudal Kingdom of England 1042–1216*. Longman, 1992.

Bautier, Robert-Henri. *The Economic Development of Medieval Europe*. Thames and Hudson, 1971.

Bernstein, David J. *The Mystery of the Bayeux Tapestry*. Weidenfeld & Nicholson, 1986.

Brown, Allen R. *The Normans*. Boydell, 1994.

Brown, Allen R. *Castles, Conquests and Charters*. Boydell, 1989.

Cassady, Richard F. *The Norman Achievement*. Sidgwick & Jackson, 1986.

Douglas, David C. *William The Conqueror*. Methuen, 1990.

Gies, Frances & Gies, Joseph. *Cathedral, Forge and Water Wheel – Technology and Invention in the Middle Ages*. HarperCollins, 1994.

Hagen, Ann. *A Handbook of Anglo-Saxon Food – Processing and Consumption*. Anglo-Saxon Books, 1992.

Hayes, Andrew. *Archaeology of the British Isles*. Batsford, 1993.

Hinde, Thomas (Ed). *The Domesday Book*. Phoebe Phillips Editions.

Hyland, Ann. *The Medieval Warhorse from Byzantium to the Crusades*. Alan Sutton, 1994.

Loyn, H.R. *The Making of the English Nation from the Anglo-Saxons to Edward I*. Thames and Hudson, 1991.

Morgan, Gwyneth. *Life in a Medieval Village*. Cambridge University Press, 1989.

Muir, Richard. *Portraits of the Past – The British Landscape Through the Ages*. Michael Joseph, 1989.

Pollington, Stephen. *Wordcraft: Concise Dictionary & Thesaurus Modern English/Old English*. Anglo-Saxon Books, 1993.

Savage, Anne. *The Anglo-Saxon Chronicles*. Heinemann, 1982.

Sorrel, Alan. *Reconstructing the Past*. Batsford, 1981.

Stenton, Sir Frank. *Anglo-Saxon England*. Oxford University Press, 1988.

Triggs, Tony D. *Norman Britain*. Wayland, 1990.

Triggs, Tony D. *Saxon Britain*. Wayland, 1989.

Walker, Barbara. *The Women's Dictionary of Symbols and Sacred Objects*. Harper & Row, 1988.

Whitelock, Dorothy & Douglas, David C. *The Norman Conquest, Its Setting and Impact*. Eyre and Spottiswood, 1966.

Wise, Terence & Embleton, G.A. *Saxon, Viking and Norman*. Osprey Men-at-Arms Series Number 85, 1993.

	Fire and Shadow	David Hillier	£5.99
☐	Storm Within	David Hillier	£5.99
☐	Trevanion	David Hillier	£5.99
☐	Half Hidden	Emma Blair	£5.99
☐	Nellie Wildchild	Emma Blair	£5.99
☐	Hester Dark	Emma Blair	£5.99
☐	Another Day	Evelyn Hood	£5.99
☐	Pebbles on the Beach	Evelyn Hood	£5.99
☐	McAdam's Women	Evelyn Hood	£5.99

Warner Books now offers an exciting range of quality titles by both established and new authors. All of the books in this series are available from:

Little, Brown and Company (UK),
P.O. Box 11,
Falmouth,
Cornwall TR10 9EN.
Telephone No: 01326 372400
Fax No: 01326 317444
E-mail: books@barni.avel.co.uk

Payments can be made as follows: cheque, postal order (payable to Little, Brown and Company) or by credit cards, Visa/Access. Do not send cash or currency. UK customers and B.F.P.O. please allow £1.00 for postage and packing for the first book, plus 50p for the second book, plus 30p for each additional book up to a maximum charge of £3.00 (7 books plus).

Overseas customers including Ireland, please allow £2.00 for the first book plus £1.00 for the second book, plus 50p for each additional book.

NAME (Block Letters) ....

....

ADDRESS ....

....

....

☐ I enclose my remittance for ....
☐ I wish to pay by Access/Visa Card

Number ☐☐☐☐☐☐☐☐☐☐☐☐☐☐☐☐

Card Expiry Date ☐☐☐☐